LANCELOT

www.penguin.co.uk

For more information on Giles Kristian and his books,
see his website at www.gileskristian.com

LANCELOT

GILES KRISTIAN

BANTAM PRESS

LONDON · NEW YORK · TORONTO · SYDNEY · AUCKLAND

TRANSWORLD PUBLISHERS

61–63 Uxbridge Road, London W5 5SA
www.penguin.co.uk

Transworld is part of the Penguin Random House group of companies
whose addresses can be found at global.penguinrandomhouse.com

First published in Great Britain in 2018 by Bantam Press
an imprint of Transworld Publishers

A CIP catalogue record for this book
is available from the British Library.

ISBNs 9780593078556 (cased)
9780593078563 (tpb)

Typeset in 11.5/14 pt Adobe Caslon Pro by Jouve (UK), Milton Keynes
Printed and bound in Great Britain by Clays Ltd, Bungay, Suffolk

Penguin Random House is committed to a sustainable
future for our business, our readers and our planet. This book
is made from Forest Stewardship Council® certified paper.

1 3 5 7 9 10 8 6 4 2

For my father, Alan James Upton (1946–2016)
who, in his last weeks, taught me what courage is.

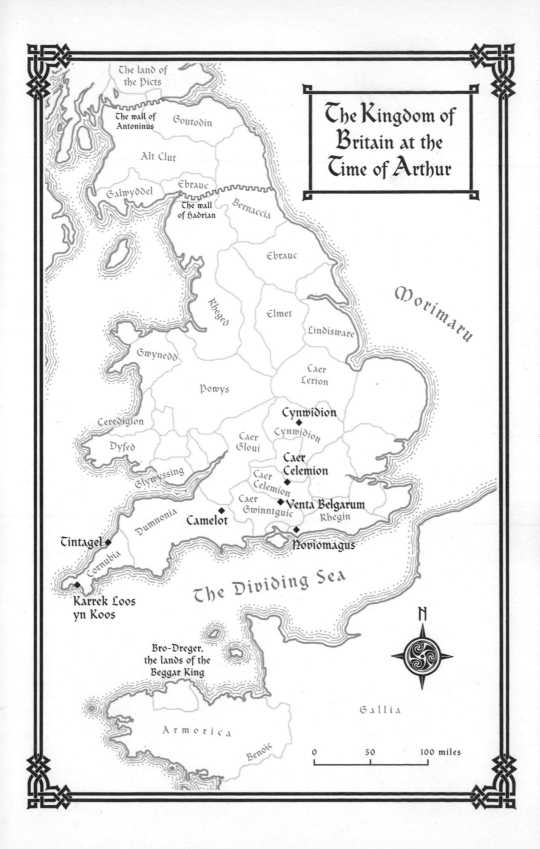

The land of
the Picts

The wall of
Antoninus   Goutodin

Alt Clut

Galwyddel   Ebrauc
                 The wall of
                 Hadrian   Bernaccia

                              Ebrauc

                    Rheged   Elmet

                                        Lindisware
         Gwynedd

                     Powys   Caer
                                        Lerion

Ceredigion   **Cynwidion**
                          Cynwidion
     Dyfed   Caer
                    Gloui
         Glywyssing   **Caer
                    Caer   Celemion**
                    Celemion
                    Caer   **Venta Belgarum**
     Dumnonia   Gwinntguic
              Camelot   Rhegin
Tintagel
                                 Noviomagus
    Cornubia

**Karrek Loos
 yn Koos**

Morimaru

The Kingdom of
Britain at the
Time of Arthur

The Dividing Sea

N

Bro-Dreger,
the lands of the
Beggar King

                              Gallia

   Armorica

              Benoic

     0   50   100 miles

Prologue

I PURSUE. RELENTLESS. THROUGH *every twist and turn, through the bitter smoke rising from countless steadings. Over the swell of burial mound and the glitter of stream. Between corn stacks and ancient oaks and standing stones, the woodlark an undulating streak of brown a talon's length ahead. Now the white flash of his neck. Now the black and white on the leading edge of his wing. His song forgotten, his terror a taste on the wind.*

I cannot catch him. Roll. Turn. Rising to the gods and swooping to the land. Stitching earth to sky. I revel in the chase but more so in the sight. All the bounty of the world crammed into my fierce eye.

I swerve, breaking from the lark's wake. Drawn to the hum rising not from the nearby ocean but from men. I alight atop the branchless tree. The tooled tree, around whose waist hangs a belt of iron chain. I smell the rising fog of the crowd's breath. It warms my feathers against the thin dawn air and I watch. I feel, too. More than a bird should feel. The sorrow which lies over the assembly like a shroud. The fear. The uncertainty and the regret.

The hum rises, rolls across the gathered like a wave, and subsides again. Spearmen come, parting the congregation, clumsy with fear and duty. Among them a woman. Her back as straight as their spears but far nobler. Hair black as a crow's wing. Blue as a beetle's shell. The burnished copper of beech leaves at the season's turn. And she still owns such beauty that the air of the day is at once drawn into three hundred chests, like smoke and sparks sucked up the forge hood.

Arms snake out, hands clutching, grasping at her russet gown. Men and women coalesce, hungry to touch her as she passes. They crave a portion of her tragedy. Thirst for a sliver of her power. Fear her craft.

My hunger fades with the memory of the woodlark. A mean-spirited boy sees me and throws a stone and I rise from the stake, my broad, pointed wings beating faster than thought, and I hover in the gathering breeze, still watching the woman as she is led, pulled now and then like an unwilling mare to the stallion.

The tonsured man is talking now, but my ears are not my eyes and his words are as the honking of a goose. Up they pull her, ungraceful onto the faggots of sticks and wicker, and bring the cold chain round her waist, marrying her to the stake. She fights only with her eyes now and her carriage. Pride and shame are her only magic, whatever the tonsured man says, his arms stretched up, hands grasping at the sky.

Hanging there above them all, I am a quivering ball of energy, pent up with the tension of a drawn bow. I hope I do not spy another lark or a stonechat, a finch or a pipit, for my mastery over this creature's instinct is thin as smoke; I may cut off west, chasing some quarry to the ends of the earth.

Fire now. Bright enough to hurt my eye. Blooming from a stave with the stench of pitch. The man holding this torch comes forward, his eyes cast down, as if he fears to meet the woman's gaze. And well he might fear it. Might dread those blue-green eyes which have seen men's souls as the hawk's eyes see the world: in infinite, immaculate detail.

He is frozen, this fire-bearing man. Still and stiff as the stake which he dare not approach. Perhaps he is afraid of the woman. Perhaps he fears the crowd, which holds itself like a stuck breath. Wanting fire and yet not wanting it.

Now the golden man comes, his scales glittering in spite of the day. Folk shrink back from him in contrast to the way they had swarmed to the woman. They avert their eyes but I do not avert mine and I watch him snatch the firebrand from the other, his face the pallor of cold hearth ash.

He calls to the crowd in a voice like pain, and with long strides across the mud he carries the flame forward, an offering of fire to that which can be nothing without it.

But then he stops. He stands alone in a sea of souls. Not afraid to look at her as the other man had been. Their eyes are in each other now. Talons snarled in talons. Roots entwined in roots.

Somewhere a woman shrieks. More cries rise on hate-filled breath and the golden man lifts the wind-whipped firebrand, limbs steeled, purpose renewed, and takes the last three steps.

The woman's tears fall to the dry wood. She turns her face away, looking above them all. Looking beyond them all, through the veil which separates one life from the next. The flame catches amongst the dry straw thrust between the wicker. A crackle of fire. A gasp from those who have come to bear witness. The first foul tendril of sickly yellow smoke curls up and a gust washes me in its charred stink. Too much for a creature of the clean sky. I careen up, away from the devouring hatred and fear, and I let the wind slice me away down the valley.

Fire in the Night

I STILL REMEMBER MY father's smell: leather and steel. The wool grease which was in his cloak and on his trews and on his blades, keeping the water out but stinking of sheep. The sweet hay scent of the stable and the old sweat of the saddle pads. His own sweat, too, and a man's muskiness. And the sometimes terrifying taint of breath made sour by ale and wine.

Mostly I cannot conjure his face any more. Perhaps I do not want to. But I remember his smell. I only have to think of it to be a boy again.

I remember his touch, too, but because of its rareness, its unfamiliarity. The big hand scrubbing my head, leaving my hair standing in tufts. The granite of his chest against my back as he helped me draw my first bow. The pungent softness of his beard when he whispered to me one evening by the hearth that my mother was the most beautiful woman in all of Benoic.

And less rare, the sharp stones of his knuckles across my cheek which would leave me deaf and hot in one ear for a day. The bite of his belt when I had displeased him. Or someone else had. The iron grip of big hands on my arms and the shaking which rattled my brain in its skull and the raging, rain-flecked gale of his fury in my face.

Strangely, amongst all the swirling chaos of that night, I vividly recall the feel of my father's hand. The coarseness of his skin wrapping mine. The thick, callused vice of it as he pulled me through the churning smoke and the flame-licked dark because our enemies had come.

I had been in the stables, brushing Malo, my father's stallion, because he was in such a foul mood that no one else, not even Govran, would go near him. The snow lay thick that winter and lingered into spring. A white pelt on Benoic which had kept folk by their hearth fires, kept cattle in the byre and the horses in their stalls. For you did not risk a prince of beasts and beloved of the horse goddess Rhiannon by riding him in the snow without good reason. But try telling Malo that. Fifteen hands high and of Spanish stock, so Govran said, Malo was strong and fast, contemptuous and dangerous. Hot blood in a cold land. And he was bored. Frustrated by stillness. Blamed the world and the gods and man for it, but did not blame me.

And like all stallions, Malo reckoned the next best thing to a run was a fight. 'Damned devil near bit my arm off when I took the brush to him,' Govran had come in saying, stamping from his boots great clumps of snow, which melted in the floor reeds.

My father's groom, Govran knew horses and loved them more than he loved people, including Klervi his wife, so she said often enough and got no argument from Govran.

'Put Erwan on his arse when he tried to lift his hoof to check for rot,' Govran spat, huffing into cold hands. 'Ought to let that black devil loose and watch him run across the roof of the world, spitting fury an' trailing fire.' He looked first at my mother, then my father. He did not look at me. 'You want the devil groomed you'll have to send the boy.'

Not many could speak that way to my father. But Govran could. They had been sword-brothers long before my father was king.

'Doesn't say much for you, Govran,' my father told him. And it didn't, for I was not yet nine years old. 'Should I be sending out for a new groom?'

'Or a new horse,' my mother hissed.

Govran muttered something which, fortunately for him, was not heard because the pine logs in the hearth popped and cracked over him. We had long used up the properly seasoned wood by then.

Outside, the wind was getting up and I knew that would not help the mood in the stables. 'He won't bite me, Father,' I said. Almost certain of it.

A frown from my mother, heavy as snow-laden thatch. 'That beast could bite off the boy's head and swallow it in a gulp,' she said.

'He bites me because now and then he forgets what's what,' Govran said, rubbing some warmth into fingers and palms. 'Goes back to thinking he's the master and I'm the underling and tries to put me in my place. Bastard.' He lifted his chin in my direction. 'He's not threatened by the boy.'

'Boys don't become men tied to their mothers' skirts,' my father rumbled, lifting the jar to his lips and drinking deeply.

'Boys don't become men by having their heads bitten off by bad-tempered beasts,' my mother said.

No smiles. Just fire and lamp flame, smoke and stale air. We were all aching for the season's turn.

A mutter and flick of the hand from my father. Enough. I was out the door, not even a horn lantern to light my way, tramping through the brittle snow and into Malo's lamplit stall. Inside, it was warm with his musky scent and sweet with his breath, which plumed with the rhythm of forge bellows, fanning the ire which had driven all other humans away.

'I am here,' I said. 'I am here.' Spoken as softly as snow on snow. At first he snorted with derision, knowing full well that the men had retreated and sent in a boy. Ashamed of them for it. But I let him sniff my hands awhile, whispering that he could bite me if it would make him feel better. And when he didn't bite me, I stood up on the farrier's stool, buried my nose in his thick mane and inhaled him, then whispered that we two were friends and be damned the rest of them. Then we set to work: I on his raven black coat, ridding it of straw dust and dirt, he on the task of letting go his hatred.

The mares and colts and other stallions in the stables were fidgeting. A horse fears the wind's hiss because he fears snakes. It is in him, deep down, passed from sire to foal. So a foreigner had told Govran, who told me. 'If you ask me, it is more likely they fear the sounds they cannot hear for the wind, such as a prowling wolf pack,' Govran said, which seemed more likely to a young boy who thought a prince like Malo could not mistake the currents and tides of the sky for a creature which slides on its belly.

I would get to three or four of the other horses after, if I could. But I loved Malo best, and when I was in his stall the world outside was as smoke dissipating on the draughts. It was Malo and me and the pig-bristle brush. Head to neck, chest, withers, then foreleg, all the way down to the knee and even the hoof. Now and then rubbing the bristles through the stag-horn comb to rid them of debris.

Then his long back, side, belly, croup, and, finally, his hind legs all the way to the hoof. Each stroke teasing his skin's oil to the surface until he gleamed like polished ebony. Then to his mane and tail with the comb, gentle as thought, yet careless of the half-moon's passage across the sky, until they were as silk rippling in the gusts which squeezed their way between the stall timbers.

Even Malo could not hold a grudge for long. Not with me. By the time I had finished, the glint in his eyes which had been indignation before was pride now. And there he stood, snorting and arrogant, living up to his name, which meant shining hostage, for he had belonged to my father's enemy before. When I was still at the breast, he was taken in a raid along with other treasures, though in the end my father had liked him too much to sell him back.

'A horse can be as vain as any warrior,' Govran had said. Malo was vainer than any of my father's men. But I liked him and he liked me. And he never once bit me. Not once.

And the first I knew of the attack that night which would change my life for ever, was the scream.

Grooming cloth in hand, I was almost done, stroking away the last of the dust left behind by the soft brush, wiping around Malo's eyes and ears where he would not tolerate bristles. I was immersed in the task, relishing the gleam in his black coat just as my father's hearth warriors indulged themselves when they worked a lustre into helmets and blades and scabbards and the leather of their sword belts. So that at first I had not caught the shrill note of a horn in the wind's wild keening beyond the fragrant haven of the stables. It was Malo who told me. He snorted and lifted his head, ears flicking, sifting screams and a braying horn from the wind's own lament.

I smelled smoke in that same heartbeat and I knew our enemies had come. The horn sounded again and I ran out into the night, which was copper and bronze now because they had fired the grain store and the smithy. The cows in the byre lowed in fear and I saw shapes running through the snow. Saw fire in blades and helmets and was frozen beneath the spell of it.

'Boy! Run, boy! To your father!' It was Gwenhael, plunging through the mantle, sword in hand, his eyes wild with ale and his breath fogging as he yelled. 'Go, boy!' he bellowed at me, then turned his fur-clad mass towards a warrior who jabbed a spear at him. Gwenhael parried the strike before sheathing his sword in the man's belly, but there were three more closing in on him, like wolves on a bear, and Gwenhael raised his steaming sword and roared his challenge. I watched him go down under a deluge of blades and insults and then I ran.

Though not towards the hall and my father. I ran alongside the stables, as terrified by the whinnying and squealing of the horses as by Gwenhael's killing, then I cut across the open ground in front of the barn, fleet as a hare over the fire-bronzed snow. The old smokehouse had been home to Hoel and his hawks since King Peredur's backside warmed the oak throne of Benoic and I had never known the door to be locked. It was not locked now and it flew wide with a clump that had the birds screeching and flapping in their mews, straining at their leashes in mad excitement.

'Who has come, boy?' Hoel croaked, his curiosity the only thing staying his hand and the leather lure it gripped, which would otherwise have stung me for scaring the hawks. Though what the old falconer thought he would do with that lure against the men who were killing my father's warriors, who could say? 'Well, out with it, lad! Who is killing who?'

'They are Claudas's men,' I said, knowing it without needing the proof of the King of the Wasteland's stag banner or sight of Claudas himself in the flame-licked night. 'I saw them kill Gwenhael,' I admitted, ashamed for some reason.

Hoel made a sound in his throat which I heard even with the hawks shrieking all around us. Behind him my father's gyrfalcon was a fury of white trying to escape his perch, his shrill *kee-errk, kee-errk* piercing the musty gloom and his great wings causing the candles to gutter.

'Well, what in the name of Taranis are you doing here, boy?' Hoel asked, his head tilted in mimicry of one of his hawks so that he could pin me with his one eye. The other was a clot of cream amongst a mass of wrinkle and scar, thanks long ago to some fierce creature's talons. A horrifying wound for a boy my age to behold, more horrifying still for the boy he had been to endure. Even so, the one-eyed apprentice had become master, and I was used to the horror of it.

I watched Hoel's back as the gusts from the half-open door where he stood peering out swathed me in the familiar scent of his sweat. In truth I liked the old falconer better than I liked my father and Hoel knew it and felt guilty for it. He also knew that my fondness for him and his birds might get me killed.

He turned back and glared at me and his good eye told me it had seen something terrible in the flame-chased dark outside.

'Your mother will be in torment, boy. Off with you! Before all is lost.'

'We'll go together,' I said and heard a scream in the night which could have been a vixen though I knew it was not.

'Don't be a fool,' Hoel said, lurching towards me as if to strike me with the rope and leather bird which he still clutched in his claw-like hand. 'I'll not run with the rest. Couldn't if I wanted to.' I knew it was true. It was impossible to imagine Hoel's whip-lean old legs carrying him at pace through the snow. I had not even seen him ride for as long as I could remember and neither did he accompany the men on the hunt these days, trusting that my father was good enough with the falcons not to ruin them.

'Go! Now!' he yelled, and he did strike me with the lure. Twice, though I stood and took it. Hoel should have had an apprentice but he had refused all suitors – not that there had been many – and I believed he was saving the position for me, though it would be a few years yet before I was ready. I spent half my life in that dark, pungent place and whilst the master falconer's knowledge was vast, his work all but incomprehensible to me, I was fascinated by the birds. I admired them. Loved them even. And though the world would have me be more, being a prince, I would gladly have become Hoel's apprentice. Hector my brother would have Benoic's high seat and I would have the hawks and the falcons.

But it would never be so, and I knew it then as surely as I knew that dead white eye of Hoel's would never see the peregrine dive fast as thought to snatch a grouse in mid-flight. Still I stood there, wanting more from the old man. Needing something.

'They will not kill me,' he said. 'King Claudas is not a barbarian. He must love the hunt as your father does and will not kill me.' His mouth was not practised at lies, for his birds did not need to be lied to, but he swept an arm back towards the mews and their inhabitants, some of which were still bating because they could smell fire and blood. 'His own master falconer does not know these birds. He will keep me on.' That one eye of his could pierce like a thin blade. 'But they will kill you. Or worse.' He waved his arms, shooing me. 'Now go. And quickly!'

He was too old and stiff to flee and we both knew it. Nor would he leave his hawks to the care of strangers, so I resigned myself to abandon him. To leave the mute-scented sanctuary in which I had been happiest. I turned and went to the door beyond which chaos reigned.

'Wait, boy!'

I spun back, hoping past hope that the old man had changed his mind and would fly with me into the night.

'Here, come here. Quick now.' He was fumbling at the latch of the sparhawk's mews, his fingers clumsy with age and perhaps fear. King Claudas was as cruel as winter. Crueller even than my father, I had heard men say. No doubt Hoel had heard it too. He reached in and took the bird in gentle hands. 'Take her,' he said. 'She's yours now.'

I was confused. The sparhawk was a juvenile, her plumage all mottled browns and her eyes still yellow, though even then she had that angry look all sparhawks have. I had been with Hoel when he found her before the snows came, in the forest near Gourin. We were drawn by the noticeable absence of other nests; a sure sign, said the master, that a female sparhawk was in residence thereabouts. He was never wrong about such things.

'The sparhawk?' I said now, not understanding.

'Yes, the sparhawk,' Hoel said, bringing the bird up to his face to study her, as if fixing the memory in his mind. 'Keep her safe. Rear her justly. Learn from each other.'

I was just a boy and I looked over my right shoulder to where my father's snow-white gyrfalcon sat his perch, glaring at me like Hoel had. '*Ee-ack, ee-ack!*' he said. I felt his wrath and understood it. If I was to take a bird and save it from this terrible night and our enemies, then surely it must be the king of them all, and he was the gyrfalcon. The tercel was trained in the art of the hunt, worth more than his weight in gold. Many times had I seen him high against the roof of the world, cutting across the sky like a shooting star. I had revelled in that moment when he tucked his wings and started his dive, his silhouette growing until at last he was seen or sensed by his prey but too late. The tercel was a killer. But the sparhawk? She was untrained. A fledgling, not long since all untidy fluff and gaping beak, shrieking to be fed.

She was shrieking now and Hoel had the kindness to whisper love to her even on a night like that. 'I'm sorry, Princess, be good now,' he soothed, with one hand taking a wicker basket from beneath the table and plunging the bird into its unfamiliar darkness. 'She'll need feeding as soon as you can,' he told me, making his offering. I nodded, accepting the basket and its furious occupant, though I had one eye still on the gyrfalcon. Hoel picked up his own falconer's gauntlet, the leather worn and stained by blood, sweat and rain, but clean. It was a magical thing, that glove, cut and stitched from a tracing of Hoel's own left hand and, but for the birds themselves, which anyway belonged to my father by rights, was the old falconer's most treasured possession. Yet now, without a second glance at it, he moved closer and tucked the glove into my belt.

'Now go. To your mother and father. They will be looking for you.'

So I went.

Flame, my almost tame fox, was waiting for me by the wood pile under the smokehouse eaves, his rich coat a reflection of the fire which flapped from the roof of the barn like a great sail, spewing innumerable sparks into the black sky. He must have followed me first to the stables, then to Hoel's place, silent and with almost feline caution and stealth. Now he could smell the sparhawk in my basket and he held his body low against the snow, looking up at me with his amber eyes as he did when begging for whatever meat I had pilfered from the table for him.

'Come, boy,' I said, retreading my own tracks, though there were others in the icy snow now. There were bodies too. Six or seven of them. Warriors I had known all my life, lying there like animal carcasses. Bravely, dutifully, they had stumbled from their beds out into the night to face our enemies and had died for it, returning to a sleep from which they would never wake. And when I passed Gwenhael where he lay torn and staining the snow, I did not look because I knew he would be ashamed to be seen thus. But I had seen neither Tewdr, my father's champion, nor my brother nor my father, and so I dared hope they still lived. Then my heart kicked in my chest at a sudden terrible thought. Perhaps they had fled already.

I stopped and Flame did too, because a knot of King Claudas's warriors had come round the corner of the byre, all pluming breath and laden with the treasures they had stolen from the shrine: silver statuettes and gold dishes and candle holders and even the silks from behind which the priests spoke the words of the gods. And even as I stood there, too afraid to move in case I drew their eyes, I was disgusted that men would seek riches for themselves before they had won the fight. Before they had even fought, from the look of them. Like a pack of dogs after scraps they were, and I hated them. Yet the ringing of steel on steel from inside the great hall told me the King of the Wasteland had worthier men serving him, too. Men who would fight first and steal later.

A hand clamped over my mouth and I was hauled back against a mountain of muscle and cold ring mail all wreathed in ale breath.

'Easy, lad,' Tewdr growled in my ear. I stopped thrashing and let Tewdr all but drag me backwards, my heels ploughing furrows through the snow until we were hidden in the shadow of the cooper's workshop. Though not in time.

One of King Claudas's men had seen us and alerted his company of thieves. For a moment they seemed reluctant to set aside their treasures, but then they did so, dropping them and drawing swords and raising spears, their insults whipped away by an icy gust. Tewdr growled a curse.

'He's here! Thank the gods!' I turned to see my mother and brother and several of my father's household warriors, many of them bloodied, their eyes shining with the battle lust. Behind them stood half a dozen of the servants and some slaves, all crushed by the weight of the belongings which my mother would salvage from this night's ruin. 'Here, boy,' my mother hissed. 'Where in Cernunnos's name have you been?'

My uncle Balsant was there too, gripping the thick ash shaft mounted with the silver boar. My father's standard. I could tell Balsant had had to fight for it. Even so he winked at me before handing the standard to Hector and coming to join Tewdr, pointing his big sword and threatening our enemies who were coming, joined now by others fresh from killing.

'Go to them, lad,' Tewdr gnarred, pushing me towards my family, and then my father was there too, looming in the flame-chased shadows, his face set like a granite cliff but his eyes betraying his horror at what was happening. I saw that his sword glistened with blood. With him were Govran, Budig, Salaun and three other warriors, their hot breath clouding round their beards as they readied themselves to fight or flee, half-watching their wives and children who were escaping towards the eastern woods, bundled in pelts, bent by sacks and a few of them leading pack horses.

'Go, my king,' Tewdr said over his shoulder. 'Go now.'

'Aye, we'll catch up,' my uncle told my father, though he was look-ing at my mother and she at him. Then he put a stride between himself and Tewdr so that each would have the space for sword-work. Three of the other warriors tramped over to join them but my father ordered Govran and the remaining men to stay with my mother, whose keen-ing demands washed over me like water off a gull's wing. I stood there adrift, a boy clutching a basket with a frightened bird in it, wishing I held a sword and owned a man's strength to use it.

'Come, then, you sons of Balor!' Tewdr roared at King Claudas's men, striding forward to meet them. Tewdr bear-slayer. Champion of Benoic.

My uncle and the others went with him. No chants or war songs. Just brave men who knew they must die.

'Come, boy!' I almost dropped the basket because a hand grabbed mine and wrapped it tight. Rough, hard skin. A vice grip. One which had never dropped a sword. Or a drinking horn. 'You got the gyrfal-con,' my father said. 'Good. Now come.' He pulled and I went. Quickly through the snow. Following the others towards the distant tree line. Fugitives beneath the stars and the swirling copper embers of our ruin and the gods who scorned us.

Behind me I heard the clash of blades. And screams.

Peregrination

W E MADE A PITIFUL caravan. A procession of the dispossessed. Pilgrims devoted only to survival, stripped of all else but the will to endure. Many of the women and children were weeping because their husbands and fathers had not come and so never would. Most were freezing and weary with grief. Some of the men were wounded and dripped blood on the snow, and one of them, a big man called Alor, who had taken a spear in his belly, walked off into the trees to die alone and in peace. No one stopped him. We could not rest and warm our flesh beside fires for fear of our enemies catching up and finishing what they had begun. For they must have known by then that Ban, King of Benoic, still lived.

If you could call it living. I would have preferred the raging, wrath-filled king I better knew than the man in his place now. I would have my father cursing the gods and swearing vengeance. I would have fury, his knuckles across my cheek. Anything but what he was then: a shrunken man, bent by a burden of shame, the fire gone from his eyes, doused by the disgrace of his fall. I could see that even by the light of the stars and with my child's eyes and I feared it terribly. And so I avoided him, my mother too, for she had greater concerns now, such as making sure we sank no further than the depths to which we had come.

Smoke rising, stars falling. All in that one foul, ill-fated night.

Hector had shared some bread and cheese with me and I had saved a hunk of the bread for Flame, who I knew was tracking me from the safety of the trees. I was looking for the fox when I saw my mother ambush Hector. She and Govran had been talking out of my father's sight and now she all but dragged my brother into the darker shadow of a snow-laden pine while Govran waited nearby, huffing into cold hands. Mother hissed at Hector to stand tall, to square his shoulders and be a man while our father drowned in self-pity.

'Uncle Balsant is dead and the kingdom is lost,' Hector protested, still gripping my family's standard, the silver boar gleaming dully in the nearly-dark.

My mother seemed to miss a breath then. Somewhere in the canopy above, a bird flapped and a trickle of snow fell, and my mother's eyes hardened, becoming as sharp as her cheekbones which pressed like blades beneath her pale skin.

'Balsant did his duty and we will honour him, if we survive,' she said, then she grabbed hold of Hector's shoulders and he flinched at her touch. 'But if you do not act the man now, they will turn wolf on us,' she rasped, lifting her breath-wreathed chin towards a knot of three warriors who trudged past, shields slung across their backs and using their spears as staffs. 'They will smell our weakness and turn on us. They will rob us and abandon us. They may already conspire to sell us to our enemies. Do you understand me, my son? Would you see your mother raped? Your brother's skull staved in?'

I thought of Gwenhael lying far behind us torn and dead.

Hector set his jaw. Shook his head. 'Never,' he said.

My mother nodded and stroked his cheek and I felt it from where I stood. 'That's my Hector. Your father has cost us much. We will not let his failings murder us.'

I was close enough, standing there amongst the pines, to taste my mother's venom on the night air. My father the tyrant fed her own ambition. Lifted her far above her birth. But the king without a kingdom? That man dragged her towards ruin and she could not allow it. She resented him already, even with the smoke of his defeat still on the breeze.

'We will survive, my son. And rise again,' she told Hector. 'But you must shed the spoilt prince and become the man and you must do it this very night. Govran will support you if any give us trouble.'

Hector glanced over to where my father's groom waited. 'Mother,' he said with a nod, then looked up at the silver boar, trying to draw courage from that totem which had stood above many battles, witness and shining spur to our father's victories. Then my brother strode out of the shadow and across the starlit snow, the standard in his grip and my mother's hopes on his shoulders.

He ordered five men to stop and take their ease while the rest passed, for those five were to make a rearguard in case King Claudas's men even now tracked us through the forest. They were not happy about it, those five, and muttered and moaned, but my father's glowering presence and long shadow were close enough to dissuade them from questioning the boy who could not yet grow a man's beard. Then Hector ordered Derrien and Olier, who both led horses, to ride ahead to ensure that we did not spring an ambush, and to warn the folk of any farmsteads hereabouts that we would expect provisions: food and drink and even clothing for those of us who had fled ill-prepared for the rigours of an exodus through the snow.

And I should have been proud of Hector then, to see him commanding grown men and experienced killers. Trying to steer us through the wreckage of that night so that we might survive. But I was a boy with a boy's small view of the world and I had my own troubles. The sparhawk would need fresh meat in the morning and I had none to give her. Added to this, Hoel had begun the bird's manning, which must progress daily or else the creature would return to her wild state, and so this responsibility was now mine, for all that I did not want it.

I would have gladly taken the gyrfalcon. Of course I would. That magnificent tercel would catch us much-needed food, take pigeons, waterfowl or rabbits and return to my father's arm. But were I to open the wicker basket and slip her jesses, the sparhawk was more likely to fly like a dream into the dawn and never return. And so I must feed her and man her and keep her alive even though I had not a belonging in the world other than the clothes I wore, a cloak not thick enough to keep out the cold and an old man's hawking glove.

I could never hate Hoel for it though. I believed he was dead, slain in his musty hovel amongst the mews and their shrieking inhabitants. Cut down by unthinking men who neither respected his white beard nor considered the lustreless value of his knowledge. But the sparhawk, with her fierce, haughty eye and her hunter's instinct, which was as yet useless to man, was an encumbrance. An unwanted charge. And so I hated her.

We trudged on, more than one hundred of us, a procession of refugees through the forest, like lost souls wandering the spirit world in hope of being called back to the flesh. With the dawn we came to

Calangor, where we rested. No one had given the order to lay down burdens, collect dead-fall for fires and tend wounds now that there was enough light to see by. Neither my father, nor Hector, nor even my mother had called the halt. Rather there was a collective weariness, an overwhelming need to stop, as much to give proper thought to what had happened as to rest, perhaps. For dawn brings light to the mind as well as the world, and can vanquish the devils and spirits which seek to confuse and deceive and would see us lost in the dark.

Women and children took men's helmets and used them to carry water from the stream. Fires were lit and fir boughs were cut and laid on the ground for folk to sit on. People melted snow to slake their thirst and shared what food they had managed to stuff into knapsacks before fleeing their homes. They shared stories, too, those who could summon the words. Tales of the night before, of courage, catastrophe and escape, and with the words came realization, if not acceptance, and tears. Tears to make the ambling stream envious.

Many found loved ones by the light of the new day: husbands or wives, fathers or daughters they had feared lost. Friends greeted friends, embracing, weeping, comforting the bereft and the broken as best they could. The fighting men boasted of kills, swore vengeance on our enemies, even clamoured about going back that very day. They talked of taking King Claudas's ale- and blood-drunk war band by surprise, killing as many as they could and bringing back those of our people who were otherwise destined for new lives as slaves in another kingdom. But their boasts were no more than hot air on a cold day.

Including the rearguard, there were thirty-three warriors amongst us, along with another twelve men, young and old, who could be called upon to fight if necessary. Not enough to beat King Claudas. Not without my father and Uncle Balsant and our champion Tewdr leading them. We all knew it. But warriors need their boasts like kings need wine, and that dawn the men's threats and promises were as a salve to their wounded pride. Because while friends had lain dead in the snow, picked at by Claudas's men, while spear-brothers had raised their shields and stood their ground and fought to the last breath, these men had fled into the night.

So had my father and my brother. So had I.

I could see them in my mind now, my uncle and Tewdr, Budig and Salaun and the others, as I gathered wood for the fire which my father's

steward, Meven, had summoned to life with feathered sticks and dry
tinder. Like heroes from one of the old tales they had made their stand,
those brave men, so that we who now lay about by that stream, dazed
and drained and beaten, could live. We would sing of them one day. I
was certain of it. When my father came back to himself and raised a
war host and paid our enemies back in steel and blood.

Steel and blood. That was how it would be, I swore to myself as I
tramped shivering back to Meven, my arms full of sticks. Then over
the bundle I saw a boy some four or five years older than I holding the
sparhawk's wicker basket which I had set down against a silver birch
tree. He was carrying it towards another fire beside which three men
crouched, blowing the flames and feeding them a morsel at a time.

I dropped the sticks and ran.

'This will burn better than—' the boy called to those gathered
round the fire, but he did not finish what he was saying because I
threw myself at him, hitting him in his side so that the two of us were
flying for a heartbeat, then we were in the snow, flailing. Fists whirring, his larger than mine, and he was yelling wildly. A man's curses
from a boy's mouth. Until hands bigger than either of ours grabbed
his cloak and hauled him up and he was flying again, this time landing in a hole all his own.

'Are you mad, boy?' the man bellowed at him. It was Reunan the
potter, and his son, who had thought to burn my basket, was called
Tudi. 'This is the king's boy!' Reunan cried. 'You'll get us hanged or
worse. Beg his pardon for the love of all the gods!'

'I didn't know it was his basket, Father!' Tudi protested, the colour
gone from his face except for a raw graze on his forehead above his
right eye where one of my blind punches had caught him. 'He just
came at me. Like a little boar. What was I to do?'

The only reason I knew Tudi was because he had put himself forward to be Hoel's apprentice, for which I could not blame him, hawks
being infinitely more exciting than the pots his father made. Not that
Reunan saw it that way and in all likelihood would never have allowed
his boy to learn the falconer's art even had Hoel accepted him. Which
of course he had not.

The potter grabbed his boy with one hand and with the other struck
him across the cheek. 'Beg his pardon, lad, or I shall beat you halfway
past death.'

'Reunan!' His wife Briaca was standing behind him, her chafed red hands to her mouth. But Reunan hit Tudi again and this time blood flew from his lip onto the snow.

'I'm sorry,' Tudi spat towards me as I gathered the upended basket and wiped the snow off it, fearing that some damage might have been done to the little creature inside.

'This is mine,' I said.

'Cry your pardon, I did not know. It was so light,' Tudi protested. 'I was just looking for dry fuel for the fire.'

'He's a fool, my prince. I know it. But he meant you no harm,' Reunan said, wincing at the hurt he had done some fingers in hitting Tudi. Bad for business, that. Not that he had a workshop now, or customers clamouring for his wares.

'Well, this is mine,' I said again, lifting the basket so that I could peer in through a small gap in the weave.

'No, boy. It's mine.' I turned to see my father, sitting by Meven's fire on an oak chest which one of the slaves had carried through the night. Most of the slaves had taken their chances and fled in the chaos and the dark, but this one, having to bear my father's own chest, had been watched closely. 'Bring him to me, boy,' my father said, his head lifted slightly from the fur-clad mass of his body.

They were the first words he had spoken since we had turned our backs on Balsant and Tewdr, and all eyes were on him. Every tongue around those half-dozen fires was still. My mother nodded and hissed at me to obey and quickly, for she could see the king emerging from his dark languor and would have me draw him out further.

The basket pulsed in my hands. I could feel the life in it, beating like a zealous heart. I nodded and walked towards my father.

'Even as those rancid swines were burning and slaughtering, the boy here had the courage to save my bird,' he told them all, beckoning me to him with a flap of his big hand. 'A shame he could not carry old Hoel off too, hey.' His voice was flat as a pond and folk did not know if they should find humour in the words, so wisely kept their faces straight.

I should have said something then, before it was too late. I should have explained what had happened. Told him I had only done what Hoel asked of me. But the weight of all those eyes, like ring mail pressing me down into the snow. And it was already too late.

'Father,' I said, stopping five feet from him in the space his retainers had made for me.

'Take him out. Let me see him,' the king said. He sat a little straighter in anticipation. Everyone knew how he loved the gyrfalcon. His people hoped the sight of it now would restore him to his nobility.

I put the basket down and pulled Hoel's gauntlet from my belt, thrusting my left hand into the soft, cavernous space which reeked of sweat and sheep grease, feeling that I was betraying Hoel by doing it. Then with my other hand I reached for the latch, my fingers fumbling at the peg fastener as Hoel's had done at the mews, until the little door was open.

'That son of a sow Claudas did not rob me of everything,' my father mumbled into his black beard, and I peered inside the basket, as if by sheer will I could change the sparhawk into the tercel. She shrieked at me for a coward. In my peripheral vision I saw my father sit a little straighter, his dark brows knitted. I shushed the sparhawk, easing my gloved hand into her mute-spattered prison, hoping she would not savage me when I lifted her out, for she did not know me well. Then I brought her out of the basket into the crimson-hued dawn and the gasps made her bate wildly but she could not fly because I gripped her jesses and held on.

I turned my face, wary of her beating wing, knowing she hated all those eyes on her as much as I did. She was confused too, by the familiar glove but the strange hand within, which did not come close to filling it.

'What is this?' my mother asked. Some others were whispering or murmuring but most were watching my father again now, fearing his reaction.

'She's broken her tail feathers, see?' Derrien told the gathering, and to my horror I saw he was right. It must have happened when I made Tudi drop the basket. But breaking the sparhawk's feathers was the least of my crimes and everyone knew it.

'Boy?' That was all my father said. His eyes said more. He stood and came over to me and I turned slightly, pulling my left arm behind me because I thought he would take the sparhawk off the glove and snap its neck. Or else he would hit me.

He did neither. But loomed over me, the stench of his bear fur in my nose, and glared at the bird, which glared at the king. In truth the bird met my father's challenge with such a look of mad defiance that he surely must have admired her. Or envied her.

But she was not the snow-white gyrfalcon and would never be.

My father's eyes came back to my own and I shivered. His hands clenched and unclenched at his sides. His teeth dragged across his lip and then he turned his back on me. On the hawk. And trudged back through the snow to the fire.

And then, as men and women found their voices again and went back to feeding the flames and warming themselves, my uncle Balsant came back from the dead.

Folk cheered when they recognized who had come. They clambered to tired feet and called Balsant's name and lifted their cups of melt-water as if raising cups of mead at a wedding feast. And Balsant knew they needed this moment, this small victory in the midst of defeat, so he sat tall in the saddle, like a conquering hero, though stopped short of drawing his sword and pointing it at the sky.

My own heart leapt in my chest, for my uncle and for the stallion which carried him. Malo. Still shining from his grooming, his muscles bunching and smoothing in beautiful rhythm, the warrior swaying gently upon him. My father's greatest and best horse. Polished ebony. Night made flesh, emerging from the woods into the dawn, as aware of the stage he trod as was the man on his back who should have been dead but was not.

They had tried to kill my uncle by the looks. A bloodstained strip of cloth bound his right thigh and another wrapped his right forearm, ill-tied and soaked through. There was dried blood in his beard and on his neck and the flesh around his left eye was blue and so swollen he could not have seen much out of it. I tried to imagine the fight from which he had come, the only Benoic man still standing. I spun the picture in my mind, of Balsant hacking our enemies down with his great sword. Defying them until all was lost and he chose, almost reluctantly, to escape so that he might fight another day.

'It is good to see you, Balsant,' Govran greeted him, patting Malo's neck where the jagged veins bulged beneath the skin.

'This all of us?' Balsant asked, looking over the gathering whose breath rose to him in a cloud. He had expected more than this. Was disappointed perhaps that Tewdr, Budig, Salaun and the others had given their lives for so few. He expected greater than the debris he now saw floating on the dawn tide. It was true we had left too many behind.

'This is it,' Govran admitted, ashamed. My uncle made a deep sound in the back of his throat and Malo lifted his head towards the fire and nickered. I knew the proud beast was wondering why his lord and master had not come over to fuss him. My father would pay for that next time he climbed onto the stallion's back.

'Meven, fetch Balsant a drink,' my mother called over her shoulder, her eyes on my uncle's back as he dismounted. Govran took Malo's reins. My mother went over and took Balsant's hand. I saw his big fingers curl round hers. A stab of hatred twisted in my guts. 'Come. Warm yourself,' my mother said, leading him to the fire where my father sat, one of the only sons or daughters of Benoic who had not risen to greet Balsant. His eyes were on his brother, though, and he must have been relieved to see him alive, even if he would not show it. Even if I had finally broken him by bringing the sparhawk instead of his gyrfalcon. Even though I had brought him such disappointment.

'Tewdr?' Derrien asked. We all knew Tewdr was dead of course, but even as low as we were, men were not beyond morbid curiosity. Derrien was not alone in wanting to know how our champion had spent his last moments in this life.

'He fought. He died,' Balsant said and would be drawn no further. He was no bard, my uncle.

'You saw King Claudas?' Hector asked. It was a good question if the nods at his asking were anything to go by. More important I suppose than the gory telling of Tewdr's last moments.

'I saw him,' Balsant said, wincing as he raised his hands to the fire to warm them. That wound in his upper arm would need cleaning and stitching. But he'd had worse. 'Would've liked to give him a proper welcome,' he said through a grimace, 'but I'd just put two men down when I saw one of the whoresons fighting with Malo.' A grin came to his lips then. 'Trying to pull the beast by his halter he was, the damned fool, and o'course Malo was having none of it. So I bid my farewells to those I was killing, ran over to the beast, killed the idiot who was trying to steal him, and mounted while I had the chance. Once we cleared that mess, there was not a bastard among them who was going to catch us.' He shrugged. 'Here I am.'

Hector glanced at my father but it was clear the king, all furs and glower, had nothing to say. He was staring into the fire, listening to the whispering tongues of the flames rather than looking at his brother. 'Well, we will thank the gods for your deliverance, Uncle,' Hector said, gaining an approving nod from my mother.

'Don't thank the gods, lad. Thank this,' Balsant said, gripping the silver-chased hilt of the sword at his right hip. 'And thank those other men who stood with me, shoulder to shoulder.' It was not meant as an insult to those warriors who had not stayed, but some of them could not help but take it as such. Not that Balsant cared what they thought. He had said it for those women amongst the gathering who were swaddled in grief and swallowing their tears. Tewdr's wife Annaig. Budig's wife Madenn. Salaun's woman Enora, and others besides.

'So where will we go?' my uncle asked, looking from the king to my mother and even at Hector. But Hector was still more boy than man and he could only squirm under the weight of a question like that.

'West,' my mother said. 'To King Ronan's land. He is no friend of Claudas and will help us. For a price.'

'And we have the silver to buy his help?' my uncle asked. Mutterings at that.

My mother frowned. We did not have the silver. Or if we did, she did not want everyone round her knowing about it. Even with Balsant returned to us, she feared my father's own men turning on him. She believed they might rob us and kill us and seek service with another king, perhaps Claudas himself.

'No, we continue north,' my uncle said, seeming to look through the pines ahead, beyond to the white heath and oak woods and further still. The dawn sunlight cast the right side of his face in a sickly hue and in the shadow on the other side I saw liquid oozing from his swollen left eye. 'North, to Bro-Dreger,' he said.

'To the Beggar King?' The king's voice was a low rumble, like rocks tumbling down a hillside.

'He will help us, brother,' Balsant said, nodding at my father. 'As well you know, he will help you just to have you in his debt.'

'We would not put ourselves in that man's debt,' my mother said through a twist of lips. The very idea put a bad taste in her mouth.

'What choice do we have?' Balsant asked her. Then he shrugged. He looked exhausted. Too tired almost to talk. 'He won't call in the debt until my brother sits on the throne again. By then we will be stronger. And when we are stronger . . .' He shrugged again.

'We repay in favour, silver or blood. However my husband sees fit,' my mother answered for him, coming round to my uncle's way of thinking.

They both looked at my father, who nodded then turned his gaze back to the fire. And so it was decided we would continue north. To the lands of the Beggar King.

3

The Beggar King

W E MOVED SLOWLY THROUGH that white, sleeping world. Fur-clad like beasts. Trudging and sluggish, weak with hunger but relentless. To the soaring eagle and the swan we must have looked like a trickle of old blood working itself across clean linen.

We were too many and too well-armed to prove a temptation to brig-ands. And we always maintained a rearguard, in case King Claudas's men had taken up the scent, so we did not fear man or wolves. But we did fear the unnatural winter, which still reigned long after it should have given way. It was cruel and spiteful. Murder to some of the old and the wounded, and hard even on the young and strong, because they were not accustomed to it. We had shut our doors on the world these last months. Smoked ourselves like mutton joints by the hearth and half drowned in hot spiced wine. We had shared the bestial warmth of hounds and sheep, cocooned ourselves in pelt and fleece and crawled with lice.

Now our greatest enemies were starvation and the cold, and by the time we came beneath the Beggar King's sky we had left another six corpses for the wolf and the carrion crow. No tools to dig a grave in the frozen earth. No strength to anyway, nor to gather wood for pyres. The dead were abandoned by the living, some with their dignity stripped along with their wools and linens. Left there naked; blue-skinned offerings to Arawn, lord of the dead. I saw two given a shroud of brittle ferns and snow for their kinfolks' need for some ritual, and it struck me that come the thaw those corpses would emerge as grisly gifts among the wood anemone and lady's smock. The dead seeming to rise with the sap.

I saw no further sign of Flame and was sad for it. Either the fox was wary of coming near such a caravan of hungry people, or else he knew

I had no food to share with him. It was possible he had even been caught in one of the snares which the men set every night away from the camp, but I heard of no one catching or eating a fox and so I hoped my little friend was alive and well and wished him good luck nightly as I lay looking up at the stars.

Each day before the dawn I would climb out of my nest of skins and pelts, melt the snow with the steaming contents of my bladder, and go shivering with Govran into the woods to check his traps. The groom thought I went to be away from my father and admitted he did not blame me, what with the king mired in his dark mood, and I let him think that. But really it was because I wanted to make sure he had not caught Flame, and because I needed whatever scraps of flesh he would give me for the sparhawk.

One morning, he gave me the head and both forelegs of a hare. Another day, he let me take the ribs, hips and neck of a squirrel, but nothing more because he knew it was for the bird and he would not see folk starve on her account. In truth I still begrudged the bird for not being the gyrfalcon and for having to carry her basket every step of the way. Added to this, my own stomach ached with hunger such that it took a great determination not to eat those meagre morsels myself. But I was all the more determined to keep the sparhawk alive because my father had so readily dismissed her. Had, with quiet contempt, dismissed us both.

And I was angry. It was not the sparhawk's fault that she alone of the creatures had been plucked from the mews, pulled from that night's ruin. If anyone was to blame it was her master the falconer. Poor old Hoel, who I was sure must be dead, his soul borne to the hereafter on the gusts made by the beating wings of his bating, shrieking hawks.

I was angry and I was confused. Was my father delirious? Had the events of that bloody night unbalanced his mind? What was the loss of the gyrfalcon compared with the loss of his kingdom? Of course I was too young to know that the sight of the sparhawk was to my father the final confirmation of his own destruction. In that bundle of mottled feathers, beak, talons and wrath was his downfall. It was the loss of hope, while his precious gyrfalcon now belonged to another man. That magnificent bird would sit on Claudas's arm, and Claudas would sit on Benoic's throne.

Yet I would not abandon the sparhawk. If I could keep her alive, if

I could train her to fly to my arm, to stoop to the kill and come to my voice, then my father would see. He would know he had been wrong to give up on us all. He would take up his shield and spear and be the warlord again, and our enemies would pay in blood.

The seemingly boundless, rich alluvial fields had at last given way to marshland, through which we had toiled all but to the ends of endurance. Soaking. Sinking with every step through the reeds and wind-stirred grass. Not knowing whether the ground beneath the white mantle would hold us or try to claim us for itself and the spirits who dwelt below. Only eight of the twenty-three horses survived. The others were sucked into the liquid earth and struggled until exhaustion claimed them or the blade ended their misery.

I did not know which was worse, the sight of the horses in their rolling-eyed terror, fighting in vain against this unfamiliar but inexorable enemy, or the sound of their terrified whinnying, which cut through me like a cold wind. Balsant rumbled and cursed the greed which had inspired folk to take the horses into a marsh because they neither would abandon nor could carry on their own backs the belongings loaded on the animals.

'Should have eaten the beasts before now, when we still walked on honest ground,' Balsant told anyone who would listen. 'Could've kept our strength up. I didn't turn my back on a good steel death to drown in a cursed fen.' It was dusk and he knew we must gain solid ground before night came and with it who knew what?

My mother asked him if he would have our people cast their last possessions into the marsh and take on the existence of beggars and cut-throats, no better than the creatures that lived only to eat, breed and die. She said this as Govran, up to his thighs in freezing water, cut the throat of a small bay pony which was squealing because it belonged to the marsh now. I watched my mother turn to the servants and household warriors who were pulling and pushing her two mares on and promise each of them one of her silver siliquae which were minted long ago in the days of the usurper Magnus Maximus and stamped with the emperor's face. They redoubled their efforts. The mares struggled on.

'Silver shines even in a darkling swamp like this,' Govran muttered to me, filling raw hands with warm breath before patting Malo's withers and whispering encouragement in his ear. The stallion was one of the eight horses that lived. Govran laboured tirelessly with him, used all his lore and experience and sometimes even the whip to incite Malo's ire so that he would toss his head and snarl and plunge on, his hooves breaking the snow crust and churning the cold water beneath.

My father, though he seemed no longer king, yet had enough of the man in him to help the groom and do what he could for his horse, getting himself sodden to the bone, shivering and blowing for the beast's sake and even getting a kick for his trouble, which Govran murmured had broken a rib, though my father did not admit it.

And the stallion himself was too proud and stubborn to die in that marsh anyway, to be drawn down into cold oblivion in full sight of men he thought of as his inferiors. So he survived and in his exhaustion I told him I was proud of him. Admitted in his ear I had wanted his survival more than I had wanted that of some of our two-legged travelling companions, a sentiment he seemed to understand, replying with a derisive snort.

Then, as the sun slipped behind the horizon leaving only a wake of pale light in the sky, we came to a more substantial world.

We did not so much make camp as collapse where we could, and spent the night trembling with cold and racked with misery, and I being threatened with the murder of the sparhawk by Derrien because of her constant *hi-aa, hi-aa* shriek from the basket. So I picked up the basket and the sodden nest of my cloak and moved away from Derrien and the others, finding a rock against which I placed the bird in her wicker cage. Then I lay on the sparhawk's other side so I could protect her should her clamour rouse any of the others to murder.

Who could blame her for shrieking in fury? Shut in the cramped darkness, barely able to spread her wings and starving so that she would surely have gone for my eyes given the chance.

Up with the sun we trudged on, heartened a little by the feel of good solid earth beneath our feet, and some of the warriors even sang the songs of their fathers' fathers, which lifted spirits further.

At last the snow was melting. The day was clear and there was no rain and just enough wind to help dry our clothes and the cloaks on our backs. We camped before dusk that day so that some of the men could go hunting and return before nightfall. Derrien and Olier, who had lost their horses in the marsh, went off with bows and returned with four ducks, a hare and a pigeon. Govran strode back to the fires with a small deer across his shoulders and we cheered him, and others came in with waterfowl and rabbit and whatever creatures they had managed to shoot or spear. But Balsant, the only warrior on horseback now, because he took Malo out to the woods on the eastern horizon came with a boar slumped behind him. It was a fearsome-looking beast even in death and gutted, all bristle, tusk and blood. How my uncle had caught and speared that boar alone, he and Malo bone-weary as they were, was a wonder, but he made sure every mouth tasted its flesh that night.

Two days later we came to the Beggar King. I knew we were near the coast because of the gulls wheeling in and out of the mist and because I could smell the sea in the air, the brine and the dark green wrack spewed upon the shore. I fancied I could even make out the scent of wet rocks and wave-licked pebbles and shells, and the metallic tang of the sea creatures themselves. No snow here, the last fall eaten away by the salty wind if it had settled at all. Just dunes and thick grass, gorse and heather.

I asked Govran why the Beggar King was so named and he could not tell me. He did say that even if the lord of this land, situated between the estuaries of two great rivers, was master of only the sea terns and the wild wind, he would still be a wealthier man than my father was now. Though the groom made sure no ears but mine heard him say it.

It was Olier who saw them first. Then a murmur rose behind us as others all along the column saw warriors on the high ridge to the west. Sentinels watching us. Some on foot, others sitting sturdy ponies built for life among the wind-scoured dunes and weather-beaten rocks of the fretted coast. Spear blades prodding the low-slung belly of the sky. Iron helmets, grey as rain cloud. Faces we could not read from an arrow's flight away, but eyes which we felt across the distance boring into us.

We knew they were the Beggar King's men. Not that he was a real king. At least not in the eyes of the other kings and lords of Armorica. But whatever, whoever he was, he had warriors and he had land and now he had us, too, for we had come to him for sanctuary. And we must have made a sorry sight, for all that the warriors amongst us straightened, and my father, who now sat Malo, seemed to own his great size again as he had before King Claudas came to Benoic with fire and sword.

And yet Malo told our tale to anyone who had eyes to see. The dull black hide stretched taut over his ribs. His head carried low and his ears pinned. Of course, we all looked like Malo, beaten and forlorn. Withered like grape vines after the blight. But to me, seeing the stallion like that was the most shocking thing.

Those of our warriors who still owned shields, who had not abandoned them in the marsh, held them above their heads to tell those watching we came in peace. Not that we could be mistaken for a war band, having more women, children and old folk than fighting men. And we followed the track round to the west, past the edge of the ridge, and there before us, with the sea at its back, was the town. All we could see was the palisade of sharpened stakes which enclosed it and the pall of smoke which sat above it, brown against grey. Rust and iron.

A party of the Beggar King's men were waiting to greet us, their leader and a score of others on horseback holding long spears, another thirty or so on foot. Few had helmets. Fewer still swords. Leather armour, thick wool, furs. Spears, long knives, bows and small shields. No blades of the quality of my father's sword or my uncle's or those at some of our other men's hips. No, they were not impressive to look at, but then neither were we. The warriors of Benoic were not exactly awe-inspiring. Not even Balsant or my father gleamed in their war glory now.

Behind the Beggar King's unremarkable warriors were gathered pedlars and merchants, wild-looking children and wanton-looking women, all come to cure us of need and unburden us of our coin or whatever else we could trade. They bustled with arms full of loaves and wine skins and smoked fish strung through the gills. They carried baskets brimming with who knew what? And buckets of steaming broth which I could smell on the breeze and which had our mouths watering. Which was of course their intention.

'Now is the time to look like men,' Balsant growled over his shoulder and I saw Hector lift his head as though he were on the other end of a string tugged by a god. 'This place might be our salvation. Might put food and wine in our bellies and a roof over our heads, but we are Benoic men.' My uncle's stomach must have been growling with the delicious smell of the broth, same as everyone's, but he did not want us falling on those vendors like savages out of the hills.

'Listen to Balsant,' my mother called. 'Have your pride. The gods know we don't have much else.'

My father raised his hand and we came to a shuffling halt. He walked Malo forward to meet the helmeted, lean-faced leader of the welcome party, and Balsant went with him. My mother hissed at Hector and shoved him forward and he fidgeted with his sword and cloak, then hurried to catch up with the men.

I could not hear what was said but it cannot have been much for we were soon moving again, I clutching the sparhawk's basket, feeling her own trepidation through the weave, the folk around me squeezing out their last dregs of strength and the will to walk a little further. To deliverance.

The Beggar King's warriors did not help us with our burdens but they did fall in beside us, forming a corridor of blades and muscle so that the sellers who had come from the town could not get to us if we did not want them to.

'At least wait until we are inside the wall before you fall to it like slobbering hounds,' Balsant called, his voice carrying the length of the column and giving rise to groans and curses from those who were halfway to tasting that freshly baked bread and the wine and the other wondrous delights. If only in their minds. 'Once inside, buy if you have coin. Trade if you can. If you have nothing, fear not. You will not starve, for we have made arrangements with our hosts. Your king will see you fed.'

The men cheered their king and the women called on the gods to protect my father and favour him, but I saw my mother grimace. So did Govran, who walked beside me holding his wife Klervi's hand.

'Your mother knows this Beggar King's game,' he said. 'He means to be generous when he knows we have neither the heart nor will to refuse. He'll stack up the debt your father owes, stack it right up till it touches the straw of his roof.' The groom shook his head. 'But I would not turn my nose up at a meal and a fire and a skin of good wine.' He grinned at Klervi. 'Even bad wine.'

I was barely listening, my eyes full of the strange kingdom in which we found ourselves when we passed through the open gates. This kingdom on the edge of the ocean. There were only a few solid dwellings I could see, smoke seeping through roofs thatched with coarse grass, so that they might have been giant dogs steaming by the fire. There was a smithy from which a black serpent coiled smokily upwards until vanquished by the sea's breath. There were several wood-framed workshops in which craftsmen toiled, though their hammers and planes, pole-lathes and adzes went still when they saw us. We exiles. Vagabonds drifting into that place like feathers from a fox's kill.

The other dwellings, lying thick as gorse on the ground, wreathed in the fog from countless peat fires, were tents, goat and calf skin, greased to keep out wind and rain, protected from the sea weather by each other and the encircling palisade. And yet all of it so insubstantial, a town of skins and smoke that looked as if it might be swept into the sea by a staunch southerly gale. And it reeked. Tent leather. Human waste. Rotten fish. Peat smoke and dried sea wrack. And people. So many people. Clinging to the place like mussels to a rock, folk packed so tightly the lice could crawl from one to another.

'Doesn't look like much, eh, lad?' Govran said as we followed my father on Malo, along with my uncle and my brother. We passed through the main thoroughfare, trying to keep our footing on the slippery reed mats which made narrow walkways across the mud. Many of the others had broken away to buy food, but most stayed with their king, nervous in a strange place amongst strange people.

'It is more than we have now, Govran,' my mother said, cursing under her breath and lifting her dress, whose hem was already sodden with filth. And when we came at last, slipping and sliding, to the king's hall, I could feel my mother's shame coming off her like heat. She glowered as we were made to wait in the squelching, freezing sludge. She a queen, by the gods, and her husband a warrior king. A real king. Lord of Benoic and master of hawks and stallions. Now come as a supplicant to the hall of a prince of the gulls and the strand and the weed upon it which farmers inland buy to enrich the soil beneath their crops.

We waited long enough that I could no longer feel my feet and had given up trying to crunch up my toes inside my shoes to keep some life in them. A steward had told us the reason for the waiting was so that they could make ready within the hall to receive us. But my mother was convinced it was done to further humiliate her and my father, and she stood there refusing to shiver like the rest of us. My father said not a word, perhaps thinking his presence was enough, his physical presence and the authority of his kingship. Or perhaps he had nothing to say. Whatever, he left the talking to my uncle, who at least had the nerve to growl at the wolf-faced leader of our escort that the women and children were hungry and cold and could not be expected to wait much longer before their menfolk took it upon themselves to seek food and shelter where they could.

'I will see if they are ready for you, lord,' the man said with a nod, for he knew a warrior when he saw one and had just enough respect in him. But before he got to the door, the steward appeared again and announced that King Ban, his family and a small retinue were welcome to go inside.

'Out of the cold and into their debt,' my mother said, as Balsant told the other warriors and the rest of our people to wait patiently while he and the king spoke on their behalf and arranged for them to spend the night under a roof, even if just a roof of leather. They nodded obediently, rubbing hands and hugging children close for warmth.

'And may our cousins from Benoic enjoy all the hospitality it is the Beggar King's pleasure to provide,' the steward said, with a smile like grease on a plate.

The sparhawk shrieked with hunger. My father dismounted, leaving Malo with a servant, and took my mother's arm in his, she straightening her back and lifting her chin. My brother turned to me and winked and I lifted the basket so that I could all but hide behind it, and thus we entered the hall.

It was wonderful coming under a roof. The floor was thick with dried grass and reeds which sweetened air that was otherwise made foul by the fish oil burning in the myriad lamps and the peat fire smouldering in the long hearth. Made foul by us, too, for we were filthy and reeking and I had not realized how reeking till we bustled into that place. But it was dry and warm and every restless flame lifted a Benoic soul, vanquished our misery just as they chased the darkness off to linger in pools of shadow among the rafters and corners and beneath the long tables where hunting hounds would lie were the man sitting before us a real king.

But the lord of this hall was not like my father, did not fit any kingly mould that I knew of. Indeed, standing there silhouetted by the hearth flames he looked like something which the sea had cast onto the shore. A slick of the green weed which entangled the legs of the geese and sandpipers scavenging on the mudflats and rocky reefs at low tide. He was reed-thin. No shoulders to speak of. No brawn from sword and shield work. No tree trunk legs to root into the earth in defiance of some enemy. Skin too pale for a coast-dweller, as Govran observed later, sunken cheeks, a long nose and a tangle of sandy hair that mocked the shears. Not handsome or fierce-looking like Balsant. Not haughty or noble like the sparhawk in my basket, nor meek like the Christian monks who had come to Benoic from Britannia proclaiming their god's great power with restless tongues. But he did look clever, this lord of tents. I did not see it at first – I just saw a man who did not look like a king – but Govran saw it. The groom could read a horse and believed he could read a man too, and whispered to those around him that our host had more slyness in him than a fox, which of course had my stomach aching for the loss of Flame.

'Welcome, brother!' our host called, his arms outstretched as if he would embrace my father, who did not so much as stir the dried grass beneath his feet but stood there, the dulled spearhead of his people. 'We can see how our cousins from Benoic have suffered,' the Beggar King announced. 'You have been tested.' He frowned. 'Driven out by your enemies, your people butchered.' His eyes fastened on my father's once more. 'And how you must burn to reclaim what you have lost, my lord king.' The eyes in that too-pale face glimmered like embers in the ashes.

'King Claudas came in the night, like a wolf into the fold,' my mother said, which roused a sneer from my father, who did not care for the inferred comparison of his people to sheep. His champion, Tewdr, and those other brave men who had fought and fallen deserved better than that.

'Claudas will die,' my father rumbled, which raised some half-hearted murmurs of agreement from the warriors of Benoic around me.

'None of us can escape death, great king,' the Beggar King said. 'But let us not dwell on such dark matters now. You have sought my protection and shall have it until such time as you are ready to leave us. All are welcome here.' He smiled at my mother. 'We have few laws and I am no tyrant.' He clapped his hands twice and from the back of the hall, where darkness still ruled, came forward a score of servants carrying jugs and cups. 'Take your ease. Regain your strength. Drink and eat. Whatever I have is yours.'

'Not while my people stand out there shivering in the mud,' my father said.

Balsant turned and nodded at our men, who nodded back in agreement though they must have been eager to wash away the sour taste of defeat with the Beggar King's wine and ale.

'As you say, lord king,' the Beggar King said, then clapped his hands again and gestured at his servants to carry drink to those waiting outside. 'All will be provided for. Now allow me to feed your family and loyal warriors,' he said, gesturing at Balsant and the others. 'And these two fine-looking young men who must be your sons, yes? The older one has your noble features, King Ban, and looks every inch a king-in-waiting.' The Beggar King smiled and turned his gaze on me. 'But this young prince has his mother's fearsome beauty.' He raised an eyebrow at my mother. 'He has your piercing eyes, Queen Elaine. Your fire. There is no mistaking it.'

My mother thanked our host for the compliment but I did not know what to make of his words and so frowned at him. A warrior like Derrien or Olier would surely take being called beautiful as an insult. And neither did I like hearing that I looked like my mother, while Hector apparently looked like a king. My brother was happy enough with it though, standing there in his frayed cloak and filthy trews, trying to look taller than he was.

Servants wove amongst us with brass bowls of warm water and even dried our hands with linens after we had washed off the worst of the filth. Then they brought out boards of bread and cheese and honey and dried fruits, which we fell on like wolves to flesh. Not even Balsant or my father resisted. Decorum and pride all but abandoned now, they chewed and scoffed, shoving the food into their mouths as they moved off to one of the tables to talk privately with the Beggar King, leaving the rest of us to savour that simple bounty.

'Well, we made it, lad,' Govran said, grinning at me through a mouthful of ripe cheese.

Olier came over and slapped Govran's back. 'We'll get our strength back, buy horses from this king and ride back to Benoic. And if King Claudas is there drinking our wine from our cups, we'll slaughter him like a hog. What do you say, Govran?'

Govran washed the cheese down with ale then dragged an arm across his lips. 'Let's just enjoy being alive for a day or two, lad,' he told the warrior and shook his head at me. 'Young bloods. Always so eager to die, boy. Remember, there are plenty of ways to come across death, without going looking for it.'

Olier shrugged and went off in search of someone who would swear oaths of vengeance over ale with him. I knew he would find a willing accomplice in Derrien.

I admired Olier and in truth I enjoyed hearing him talk of paying back King Claudas in blood. That was the way it should be. I knew it. I even wondered if Govran had perhaps lost the courage he must have owned when he had fought shoulder to shoulder with my father.

The world seems so simple to a boy.

We ate and we drank and when my father had finished talking with the Beggar King we were shown to an area against the palisade on the east side of the town, where tents had been erected or emptied for my father's people. We made ourselves as comfortable as we could, my mother and Balsant singing our host's praises whilst inside they simmered at the indignity of it all.

Tents and mud and fish. That would be my life for the foreseeable future. Tents, mud and fish. And Celice.

I first saw her at the market on the north side of the town, two days after coming to the place. Revived by salty fish stew and eager to be away from my mother and father and the others, I had taken to exploring, which no one minded, if they even noticed when I left the cramped tent I shared with the dispossessed King, Queen and Prince of Benoic.

'You will not venture outside the walls,' my mother had said. 'Promise me.' I had sealed that promise with a kiss and that was that, I was free.

Traders had set up simple stalls or spread their wares across skins laid out on ground which sloped gently up towards the dunes beyond the palisade and so was less muddy than the rest of the town. There were the usual leather goods – belts, shoes, horse harnesses and saddle gear – and wool in bales, bone-hilted knives and jars of oil and coloured glass beads and brass and copper brooches and iron spear heads, axe heads, bows and sheaves of arrows. There were folk selling horses and others selling goats or pigs, cattle, hens, or women for men's pleasure, or a combination of any of these. It was such a confusion of goods that it was almost impossible to tell what a man or woman's trade was. And yet compared with the markets I had visited before, there was not much of any quality on show.

'Stolen, the lot of it,' Govran told me later that night. 'Poached and robbed and brought here to the land's edge where this Beggar King has built a nest for thieves. The best of it, the olive oil and the good horse stock, gets shipped across the sea to Britannia. What's left passes from one bandit's hand to another and this so-called king takes a slice from every deal.'

'Are men afraid of him?' I asked. 'Is that why they share with him?'

'Afraid? No, lad. He doesn't need men to fear him. Not when he's got a ship. Two ships, as it turns out. And those ships carry the loot to Britannia. His wealth is his power, lad.'

I didn't know any of this that first time I saw Celice. I heard her before I laid eyes on her. I was watching a man mistreating a piebald mare, lashing her flank with the bridle she would not let him put on because he had not won her trust. She refused to keep still, and who could blame her?

I had been about to offer to help, for I was sure I could get the bridle on her if I could find something to stand on, when I heard a song on the breeze. A song which my mother used to sing to me when she wanted me to go to sleep, about a hero from the forgotten times who fought and beat Balor, god of death, thus bringing his wife back to life. But even my mother had never sung it as I heard it being sung now, and I left the man and his mare and followed the voice, wriggling through a knot of men and women until I popped out of the throng like a bung from a flask.

And there she was, sitting on a barrel in a long tunic of white linen, hugging her knees to her chest as she sang. Much older than I. Fourteen, perhaps. Fair-haired and pale-skinned and so pretty that just looking at her was almost painful. It seemed that my insides were rising on beating wings. Fire burned in my cheeks and scalp and I wanted more than anything for the girl to look my way, to see me amongst the crowd. At the same time there was an unexplained dread that I might catch her eye.

'Have you ever heard a voice like what my Celice has got?' a man, whom I took to be the girl's father, challenged the gathering. 'The only thing sweeter in all Armorica is this here cider, which is on its way to some great king in Britannia.' He grinned and patted one of the barrels which were stacked beside him and guarded by a big-bellied man with a long-hafted axe, who looked bored, not seeming in the least affected by the girl's singing. 'Well, apart from these barrels here. They're damaged, see?'

The big man beside him smiled and tapped the cheek of his axe head, implying that the damage was no accident.

'Can't send damaged barrels to a king, can we?' the trader said. 'Which means I'll have to sell them to you lot at a price that'll see me and my girl starve, but what can I do?'

Celice was singing still and I was staring still and her father was proclaiming the quality of the cider to the crowd, who were all but licking their lips, when all of a sudden that fair head turned and those blue eyes were looking at me. And that voice, far sweeter than cider could ever be, was singing to me. If I were the sparhawk I would have bated and been snarled by the jesses. But I was a boy and I did the only thing a boy could do.

I ran.

4

Pelleas

I LEFT IT A DAY, that my shame might subside, before returning to
look for Celice again. And again she was singing, a livelier tune
now, though her voice was even sweeter than I remembered, undulating like a finch in flight, melodious and bewitching. Again drawing a
crowd to her father's stall, though today he was selling tall clay jars
full of olive oil from some far-off land. This time nothing was 'as
much like silk, as rich and healing as my fair daughter's voice'. Nothing, that was, apart from the oil in those tall jars, which he had bought
from a trader on his way to somewhere called Pyro's Isle off the coast
of Cambria in Britain. The Christian monks who dwelt on that craggy
rock lived on prayers, more prayers and olive oil from the Greeks,
apparently. But their next shipment would be a score of jars short.

I stared and fidgeted and willed those blue eyes to look at me again
and at one point I thought they did, but too fleetingly to be sure. And
when her father was done with his business and Celice stopped singing, the dispersing crowd left me feeling so like a crab caught in a pool
at low tide that I scuttled off again, cursing myself for a coward.

For two days I stayed away from the market. I fed the sparhawk
what meat I could bring her, now and then taking her out of the basket to get her used to me. I groomed Malo and I helped Govran clean
and polish his saddle and tackle. I sat with Hector and watched him
sharpen our father's sword, and I accompanied old Meven the steward
when he went to collect two skins of wine from the Beggar King's
own store, a small token of his esteem for my parents.

But Celice's voice was still in my ears. Her face still in my mind. So
dawn of the third day saw me sliding in the mud and soaked by a thin
drizzle as I set off to see Celice again.

The market was busier than I had ever seen it. There seemed to be twice as many traders hawking their wares, inviting folk to examine their stock, or bartering with one another. An old man exchanging a pair of boots for a brace of dead hares and a small knife. A woman trading a necklace of amber beads to a dark-skinned man for two wine skins and a small copper coin. There were half a dozen of the Beggar King's warriors threading the crowds this morning and some guarding a man who was weighing tin ingots on a set of brass scales. As I understood it, a ship had come in on the dawn tide, returning from Ireland, land of the Gaels, and the tin was part of her cargo.

'He'll be a proper king before long,' I had heard my mother saying of the Beggar King to Hector, who had asked when we would return to Benoic to take back what was ours. 'And when he is a proper king, we will persuade him to help us beat King Claudas.'

I knew that tin was worth a great deal but even so I was shocked by how folk crowded round it now in the rain, so that the Beggar King's men had to push them back with their spear shafts, yelling at them to keep their distance so that the business could be done.

But I was not interested in tin. To me it was worthless compared with one glimpse of Celice. This time I would smile at her, I told myself. Perhaps I would even tell her that her singing was wondrous. The best I had heard in all my life.

There was her father, still trying to sell his Greek oil and also a fine-looking helmet with a steel crest and cheek pieces. His bodyguard was a different man today, and there were three or four people admiring the helmet but I could not see Celice. Where was she? Surely her father should be peddling his lies, declaring that the only thing that shone more than his daughter was that helmet, which was of the Roman type, so said one of the men admiring it. Why was Celice not singing to draw customers in as she normally did?

Did I have the courage to ask her father where she was? He would surely laugh at me. He would ask how I knew his daughter, and the truth was I did not know her. Had never spoken to her, nor knew if she would even recognize me, for I could not be sure our eyes had met. Not really.

No, I would not ask after her. I would wander the market, the whole town if necessary, until I found her. And then I would tell her that I was a prince of Benoic and ask her to sing for me.

Feeling brave and resolute, I turned away from the lying man and his Roman helmet, and that was when I saw the big guard with the axe, who usually stood watch over Celice's father and the merchandise. He was standing by a large tent made of thick leather, which I presumed to be where Celice and her father lived. No doubt the man was guarding his master's stock.

Or . . . else . . . what if Celice was inside the tent? I was struck with a vision of her lying ill, which would explain why she was not helping her father this morning. I was walking towards the tent, my bare feet squelching in the cold mud and the big man staring at me.

'Where is Celice?' I asked him.

'Who wants to know, boy?' he said.

'I do,' I said.

He spat into the mud. 'And who are you, little man?'

I thought about telling him the truth. Surely he would not look at me with such disdain when he learnt I was a prince. But Govran had warned me against telling anyone who I was, for we could not be sure who our friends were in this strange town.

'I am . . .' I began, then stopped. I could not say I was her friend, when it was not true. I thought hard. 'Celice has a beautiful voice,' I said.

He grunted at that, which made my blood hot.

'Your master will have to wait. She's not to be disturbed,' he said. 'Now piss off, little man.'

I stood there. Hating him. Not knowing what to do.

'I said piss off,' he growled, lurching at me with that big axe before straightening again at his post.

Your master will have to wait. What did he mean by that?

I walked off a little way, until screened by people and tents, then I doubled back, approaching the big tent from behind, where that big-bellied man could not see me. I had to know if Celice was in there. My biggest fear became the most likely explanation for Celice's absence: that she was ill, perhaps even dying from some disease, but that maybe there was something I could do for her. Fetch her some of the wine which the Beggar King had given to my mother and father. Show her the sparhawk to cheer her. Something.

There was a rent in the leather at the back of the tent, small enough that it might not have been noticed, yet big enough to put my eye to. I waited for two men laden with baskets to walk by, on their way to the shore to gather seaweed, most likely. I did not want to be seen peering into someone else's tent. Not that anyone would take notice of me. The day was grey and a light rain was still falling and wasn't everyone in this town a thief anyway? So Govran said.

I heard a chime of laughter that could only have come from Celice and for some reason it hit me like a blow. Clearly she was not ill and so I crouched and closed one eye, putting the other to the tear, breathing in the smell of leather and pine resin.

And I saw her. Her long hair and her left shoulder and the round swell of her breast, white in the gloom. White against the darker skin of the hand upon it, fingers splayed and pressing until the whole breast was covered and the man to whom the hand belonged grunted with satisfaction.

'It'll cost you another coin to touch the other one,' Celice told him. 'Two if you want to touch down there.'

I pulled away from the tent, a churn in my stomach like protests against meat gone bad, and spun round. I saw a bent old crone watching me and she grinned and cackled through toothless gums. I ran away, slipping and sliding through the mud, burning with shame, the rain in my eyes and the memory of what I had seen filling my mind. How could she let that man touch her like that? Why would she do it? Celice had betrayed me and so I ran, back past the men weighing the tin ingots, squeezing through a crowd which had gathered to watch a huge man performing feats of strength with a pair of anvils. And then I saw something which stopped me in my muddy tracks.

Flame! I knew it was him. The black patch of fur on the white bib of his throat. The black sock which was longer on his right foreleg than his left. He recognized me too, was sitting there watching me even though he was drawing the attention of several men and women who no doubt saw a lustrous red pelt to be had. Then the fox turned and ran and so I ran after him.

Weaving between stalls and tents. Jumping a selection of buckles and brooches spread across a cow hide. Round a stack of barrels and a rack upon which a deerskin was stretched for scraping. Between a man and woman who were yelling at each other. Past a gaggle of lewd, ill-dressed women who called out to me, laughing. The fox never slowed but was a fleeting dart of fire, the brush of his tail leading me like a burning brand.

'Watch it!' a man growled, because I had made him drop some firewood he was carrying.

'What you been thieving, boy?' a pockmarked warrior bellowed in my wake. Then another man made a grab for me but he would have had more luck catching smoke and I ran on, weaving in and out. Jumping guy ropes and pegs and slipping in the mud but not falling, then round the rumps of two tethered mares, just in time to see Flame flatten himself to slink under a tent's hem.

I slid to a stop, breathing hard. The tent was bigger than most of those around it. I came round to the entrance and saw that the flap was not fastened. There was a gap and beyond it the flicker of lamplight. I smelled the sweet pungency of smouldering herbs. Saw a faint wisp of smoke curling out into the grey day. I could not simply walk in. But neither could I do nothing, knowing that Flame was inside. Alive when I had thought I would never see him again.

Carefully, slowly, I pushed the flap aside. And, filling my chest as though breathing in courage, stepped into the tent.

Within, the smoke was thick and I coughed, wafting it away, my eyes adjusting to the darkness at the centre of which a lamp flame burned tall and steady. Not enough to light the interior but enough to reveal her face.

'Hello, Lancelot,' she said. This golden-haired woman. This Lady who looked like we imagine the goddesses Epona and Macha to look, serene and wise and beautiful.

'Hello,' I said, not even thinking to ask how she knew my name.

There were dried plants hanging from the roof beam as well as strange objects: little horses and birds and people, too, made of braided reeds and grass. They swayed gently in the small draughts which snuck through the gap I had left in the door flap.

'What can I do for you, son of Ban?' she asked, leaning forward on her stool so that even more of her face was revealed.

I looked down at Flame. The fox sat beside her stool, looking at me with those amber eyes. Watching me.

'He's my fox,' I said.

The golden Lady raised an eyebrow, the curl of a smile touching her lips. 'Is he now?' she said.

I wondered why the creature had not come to me but still sat beside this stranger. Had he forgotten all the times I had fed him from my own plate?

'His name is Flame,' I said.

'It is a good name,' the Lady said. 'Now tell me, how fares your sparhawk? You're not overfeeding her, are you? Thinking to make up for her starving before?' She lifted her chin towards the entrance flap. 'When you were out there in the wilds together.'

'How do you know I have a sparhawk, Lady?' I asked her.

She almost shrugged. 'I hear her crying in that basket. I know a sparhawk's voice when I hear it.' She smiled and there was warmth in it. 'And I share your affection for such remarkable creatures, Lancelot,' she said.

'Her tail feathers are bent,' I said. I felt the need to confess it, for it was my fault. 'From being in the basket.'

The Lady nodded. 'You must dip them in hot water,' she said. 'Hot, not boiling. And not too long. Say . . . the time it would take you to put on your shoes.' She looked down at my bare feet. 'If you had any.'

She was teasing me.

'She'll hate me,' I said, imagining the bird's furious shrieks and glaring eyes as I immersed her tail in scalding water.

'Have you manned her?' the Lady asked.

'No,' I admitted.

She nodded. 'Then what have you to lose? Sooner done the better. When she flies true again she will know it is because of you. Not that she will thank you, of course. Sparhawks are never our friends. But she'll know it.'

I did not know what to say. I looked at Flame. The fox looked up at the golden Lady and made a guttural chattering sound, at which the Lady produced a dead vole from an earthen jar and dropped it into Flame's open jaws. The fox chewed and crunched, the sound filling the smoky, herb-scented tent.

'So you will do it? With the hot water?'

'Yes, Lady,' I said.

'Good.' She sat back on the stool, her face retreating into shadow. 'So, for how long will Benoic's king reside in this stinking place?'

I shrugged. 'King Claudas attacked our home. We have nowhere else to go.'

'Perhaps,' she said. I thought that a strange thing for her to say and suspicion gnawed at me. What if this golden Lady was our enemy? I supposed she might have gained Flame's trust with tidbits. Voles and rabbits and such. But she had not earned my trust and I knew I should leave. Knew I should not have entered her tent in the first place.

Then the entrance flap was pulled aside and light flooded the interior and I turned to see a huge man standing there, swathed in a damp fur, his face all beard and frown.

'This him?' he said.

And I did not wait to find out who he was but ran for the gap, slipping past him before those big hands could grab hold of me.

Then I was out in the day and running again. Back through the mud and the rain. Back to my people.

We had been guests of the Beggar King for nine nights and this night we were to be feasted. Every one of us who had fled our home and survived the march north had been promised a banquet at our host's expense.

'His expense now but ours later,' my mother had pointed out, but even thoughts of the debt we would owe the Beggar King could not dampen the excitement which seemed to have the dispossessed of Benoic buzzing like bees in a hive. Men and women scrubbed their clothes and combed their hair and wore whatever finery – necklaces, rings, buckles and brooches – they had not yet exchanged for food or wine or anything else which could make their new lives more comfortable.

'Welcome to my table,' the Beggar King announced as our dispossessed flooded into his hall, pushing down the sides and into every space between the tables. Warming hands above lamp flames. Burning with shame, resentful of those who had not suffered as they had, yet expectant of alms all the same and ravenous. 'Tonight, you will all sleep soundly and with full bellies,' our host said. 'This is my gift to you in honour of our friendship.' He spread his arms and smiled. 'Sit, good people of Benoic. Take your ease. Smile and laugh and put your trials from your minds.'

There was not much laughing, yet a murmur did fill the hall as we crammed into the benches, the warriors of Benoic sitting together near their king, their wives and children and the rest sitting where they could. I squeezed between Govran and Derrien, opposite my father and mother and Hector and Balsant. I was near crushed between those men but I managed to put the sparhawk's basket under the table with the latch door facing me so that I might feed her some meat should we get some.

She screeched at the clatter and flurry as men put their spears, axes and swords on the rushes nearby, along with whatever belongings they had not trusted to leave in their tents. *You are screeching now but wait until I dip your tail in scalding water,* I thought, remembering the golden Lady's advice. I had not seen the Lady again nor told anyone about her. Nor had I mentioned Celice, of course, but then who would I tell? I would rather forget about her. And especially what I had seen through the hole in her father's tent.

Ki-ki-ki-ki! cried the sparhawk in her dark nest. I wondered if the golden Lady could hear her now, wherever she might be. And I wondered if Flame was by her side still, or if he had vanished again, leaving her as he had left me.

'Keep an eye on the bird, lad,' Derrien said, leaning on me because he was already into his third cup. He was the one who had first noticed the sparhawk's broken tail feathers and it crossed my mind that if Derrien knew about hawks he might help me with her tail and with her manning in the days to come. For surely old Hoel's work was undone now and she would have gone back to her wild self. 'This whole town, if you can call it a town, is teeming with outlaws and cut-throats,' he said. 'The swill of a dozen other places. The leavings of the civilized world.' His words slewed one into another. 'Mark me, boy. Any one of them would kill for a bird like her and the silver she'd fetch, even with her gnarled tail feathers.'

'I would not let anyone take her,' I said. He nodded and scrubbed my head with a hand even as I pressed my legs against the wicker basket beneath the table, fearing that some seaweed harvester or one of the lewd and salacious women I had seen about the place might be crawling unseen on hands and knees to take the sparhawk from me.

She was still shrieking in the cramped dark. Needful of meat. We could all smell the pottage warming over the hearth and after the lean pickings of the last days our stomachs clenched for whatever steamed in those cauldrons. But the hawk's wailing might have been fear too, because a din rose in the hall now as folk sailed on rivers of wine. I was allowed ale and had emptied one cup and now Govran half filled my cup from his own, and I felt like a man. Truly I was no longer an eight-year-old boy but a warrior of Benoic.

Ale makes fools of us all, young and old and everyone in between. I felt the flush it had brought to my cheeks and perhaps it made me brave, as well as foolish, because I was thinking of talking to my father and telling him about the golden Lady. She had known me. Had known I was King Ban's son. So perhaps my father knew her, too. Certainly anyone who had met her would remember it, of that I was sure.

But before I summoned the voice to call across the table, aiming as I was for a gap in my parents' conversation, the Beggar King commanded our attention. He jumped nimbly up onto a bench between Reunan the potter and his wife Briaca and called for his servants to bring out some sea-smelling dish which was his particular favourite and would take the edge off our hunger in order that we might fully savour the forthcoming meal.

'My lord king. Men of Benoic,' the Beggar King said, gesturing at his servants to attend to the menfolk first, 'if my wine has revived you, if my ale has lifted you from despair, wait till you taste the moules and you will see why we live here on the land's edge!' His own warriors cheered this, raising cups to their lord and to us too, as the twenty servants, each holding a steaming, cloth-bound clay bowl, spaced themselves evenly between the warriors who sat at our table salivating into their dirty beards.

Govran looked over at his wife Klervi on the next table, and she gave him such a tender smile as made my chest tighten, and I looked at my mother, who was filling my uncle's cup with wine. 'Ever had mussels, lad?' Govran asked me. I shook my head and Govran grinned, eager to see what I would make of the juicy-looking flesh inside those gaping, blue-black shells. The aroma itself had my head spinning. Butter and wine. Parsley and onion. I wondered if the sparhawk would eat this strange bounty from the sea. Hunger would broaden her tastes, I thought. Or else she would have to wait for whatever meat was in that bubbling pottage over the hearth. Though I knew what she really needed was raw meat.

No sooner had the servants placed the first clay pots on the table than our warriors were raiding them, grabbing the steaming mussels, digging them out with filthy fingers or using the shells themselves as pincers to grip them before shoving them into their mouths, all slurping and hooming with pleasure and blowing on hot fingers. Juices running through beards. Grins. Laughter. A frenzy of eating, and even my father fell to the food with savage relish, in that moment looking like himself again.

I reached for the pot in front of Derrien and something hot whipped across the bare skin of my arm. Blood. I looked up and saw the blade tear free of Derrien's throat. Saw the servant's gritted teeth as he turned and stuck the blade in the man beside Derrien.

Death was in the hall.

Our warriors could not get out from the table fast enough, could not grab their weapons from the floor. Most had their throats cut while they fiddled with the moules, bled out with the food still in their mouths, for every servant had brought steel to the table.

'No! No!' my father roared, throwing one of the Beggar King's men back with a sweep of his arm, heedless of the knife jutting from his shoulder. Then he drew his sword and climbed out from the bench.

'Run, boy,' Govran croaked, his throat half ripped out and spraying gore. Then a warrior thrust his spear into the groom's back, driving him forward onto the table.

'No!' I heard my uncle bellow and I looked back across that table and saw them cut my mother's throat.

She clawed at the gash as though she could close that horrible wound, her eyes wide with terror.

Reunan the potter, his wife Briaca and their son Tudi were slumped on their bench. Govran's wife Klervi was screaming, clutching the hilt of the knife in her chest, and Meven, my father's old steward, was looking up at the roof, a savage grin sliced into the gristle beneath his chin. All around me men, women and children were being slaughtered and amongst that horror I saw the Beggar King standing there, picking moules from a pot and popping them into his mouth.

'Balsant! Balsant!' my father bellowed as he held three warriors at bay, scything his great sword at men who knew they were unworthy to be killed by it. Olier was behind him and cut a man down, and two of my father's best men were with them, still fighting hard. 'Here, boy! To me!' my father yelled, beckoning me with a hand even as he put a man down in the rushes.

A hand gripped my neck, the fingers burrowing into the tendons and flesh so that I was caught like a fish in an eagle's talons. I saw the knife coming. Saw flames reflected in the steel. *I will walk to the afterlife holding my mother's hand*, I thought.

The man grunted and staggered forward and Hector chopped at him again, his face a vision of terror. 'To Father,' he shouted, and we scrambled up onto the bench and across the table, as everyone we knew died around us and the air took up the startling, iron stink of fresh blood.

'My sons!' said the King of Benoic, thrusting his sword into an open mouth and hauling it back. 'Don't be afraid, boys,' he growled. 'It is only death.'

Olier went down, skewered by three spears. The others were dying too.

'Balsant!' my father roared, spittle lacing his dark beard, his fury ruling him. He was a lord of war and did not know how else to be.

Then my uncle came.

'Brother!' the king said.

Balsant barrelled Hector and me aside and thrust his sword into his brother's stomach. Enough muscle behind it so that the blade burst from the king's back. From my father's back.

Hector shrieked and flew at our uncle but one of the Beggar King's men speared him and he fell to the floor, clutching the shaft that was in him, mewling like a child.

Balsant stepped back, all grimace and tears as one of the treacherous servants came for me with a knife, but my father stumbled over and cut him down before dropping to his knees before me, his wounds spilling blood, his paling face level with mine. I looked into his eyes. Right into his eyes. The first and last time.

Thuds and grunts all around us and now the Beggar King's men were falling. Arrows streaking through the smoke which was being drawn towards the open door. Warriors coming into the hall, loosing bows and hurling spears, and one of them coming at my father. No. At me! He loomed in the flamelight, his mail shirt and helmet shining.

'King Ban's boy,' this warrior said, glancing from my father to me, holding his iron-rimmed shield between me and the melee of fighting men. It was the same man I had seen at the entrance of the golden Lady's tent. The one who had tried to grab me. He glanced at the Beggar King's men, who had either thrown themselves at his companions or closed around their lord to protect him. 'You're coming with me, boy,' he said.

I looked at my father, who was dead though his eyes were open and he knelt still.

'Bring him, Pelleas.' A woman's voice. I looked round to see her standing in the doorway. Golden hair tied back. A green gown and a wolf pelt about her shoulders. 'Bring him,' the Lady told the shining warrior. He went to grab me but I slipped his grasp for the second time and dived under the table, crawling through the cut grass and reeds to the sparhawk. I sat in the dark, my arms wrapped round the wicker basket, my cheek pressed against it as steel sang and men screamed.

'Come, Lancelot. You're safe with me.' The golden Lady was peering under the table at me while the big warrior growled at her that they must go and go now.

I did not move.

'If you do not come with me they will kill you,' she said. 'Like they killed your mother and father.'

And my brother, I thought.

Still I did not move but clung to that basket like a shipwrecked boy holding fast to a floating timber. Then the golden Lady gestured at the big warrior, who nodded and dragged the bench back and bent to peer at me under the table. All beard and growl.

'Bring him, Pelleas,' the Lady said.

And so Pelleas did.

It was my second time fleeing into the night, running from death. Not that I was doing the running myself. Pelleas had slung me over his shoulder like a sack of grain and was plunging through the mud. Long strides in the dark. Tents and workshops, men and women and their wind-whipped flames all a blur as I struggled for the breath which Pelleas's shoulder drove from me with every stride. I clung on to the wicker basket and its fierce-eyed occupant as if holding on to life itself.

There were fewer than twenty warriors running with us, not enough to fight the Beggar King's men who pursued. And yet I knew that the man carrying me, and his companions, would fight to the death for the golden Lady. Two already had and even now lay in that bloody hall with my slaughtered family and all those sons and daughters of Benoic.

Mother! The terror of it filled me. Swamped me like a black tide and I slipped away into some dark place inside myself.

The coolness of ring mail on my skin. The iron smell of it and the stench of the grease which had been rubbed into it, and the old leather stink of the baldric which I grabbed with one hand now, suddenly back in the savage world. I could see but little, knowing only that we ran down to the sea.

We clumped onto a wooden boardwalk that was treacherous with slime, and I saw two of Pelleas's companions slip and fall, cursing, but Pelleas kept his feet. Then thick mud again, spattering my face and the basket which I somehow clung to still and which was banging against the warrior's backside. Then we passed through the north gate, the sentries' challenges loud in my ears, and Pelleas's boots were no longer sinking, because we were running across rock. A sea mist had rolled in and was rising up towards the palisade and the men chasing us, and I was certain that the golden Lady had summoned that sea fog with some powerful magic.

Up a grassy hill, down a sandy path. Splashing through a pool brimming with slick weed. Now uneven rock which looked pink in the moonlight, Pelleas never losing his footing. Never coming close to falling or dropping me. Now thick bristling grass. Now shingle. The bark of a cormorant disturbed into flight. The breath of the waves reaching up the shore. The sparhawk screeching in fury and sandpipers scattering up from their scrapes on either side.

And my parents' killers almost upon us.

'Not far now, boy,' Pelleas said, breathing hard. Encumbered by muscle and war gear and the boy he had stolen from death.

I looked left and right and saw water and did not understand how that could be. Then I realized that we were running out into the sea along a narrow sand and pebble path. Just three spear-lengths from sea to sea, the water breaking white in the darkness along the causeway's western edge and all of it cloaked in thick mist. The Lady's magic.

'Little further,' the warrior carrying me said. The Beggar King's men were on the pebble path now too. I heard their curses and threats above the jangle and clump of the Lady's warriors' mail and sword scabbards.

Then the sea's sighing loud in my ears and I lifted my head to look back at the mainland we had left behind, thinking that we were going to give ourselves to the water. We would come to the end of this narrow, fragile causeway and let the sea swallow us whole, and that would be that.

'There! I see the flame,' one of Pelleas's companions said.

I fought for every breath and thought my ribs must have snapped like twigs against the shining warrior's bulk, and then he stopped and lifted me off his shoulder and put me on the wet stones. 'Get in,' he said, catching his breath, nodding at the nearest boat. There were three of them, bobbing on the calmer side of the causeway, each guarded by a spearman.

My legs would not work and so the shining warrior picked me up and put me in the boat and the golden Lady got in behind me, sat at the bow and pulled me onto the bench beside her as Pelleas and the others piled into the three craft, the hulls grinding and scraping against the stones. The men took up oars and bent to the task and a spear plunged into the slack water beside us. Another streaked from the mist to hit our stern. Then stones clacking and warriors emerging from the sea fog, pointing spears and brandishing blades and yelling at us with impotent rage.

Pelleas and the others pulled the oars, dragging the dark water past our hulls and taking us out. The night air was cold on the back of my neck and rushing in my ears as I stared back at that fog-wreathed finger of land that dared accuse the vast grey, shifting world beyond.

I saw my uncle. The traitor. A man I had admired. Hated too, in my secret heart. But now feared. He pushed his way through the clamorous crowd until he stood on the edge of the causeway, on the slippery wet stones, and I was certain he would wade into the sea and swim after me and kill me.

But Balsant did not stride into the water or dive head first. He just stood there, his boots in the brine and his sword in his hand. The sword which was dark with my father's blood. Cursed iron. Tainted by fraternal murder. His stare clung to me and would not let go, even as we slid beyond range of their spears. Soon beyond the range of their insults and threats, though my uncle had said not a word nor flailed. The betrayer. The king killer. His eyes in me like hooks and mine in his, until at last the mist rose as a living wall between us, and all of them and the path too were hidden from sight as if none of it had ever really existed.

If I'd had the words I would have asked the Lady where we were going. Even though I thought I knew. We were rowing to the next world. These silent, broad-shouldered men would keep pulling the oars, the rhythm of the blades hitting the water and biting as strong and regular as my heart thumping in my chest. They would row and row and we would glide further from all that had been, deeper into the dark unknown. And then we would pass through some watery gate into the next world where my father and mother and brother waited for me.

'You are safe now, child,' the Lady said, taking off her wolf pelt and wrapping me in it, pressing it to my trembling flesh. Pelleas told the others to ship their oars and I twisted on the bench, eager to see this entrance to the world beyond, but all I saw was a wall of wood. Nail-studded oak planks which stank of pitch.

'You'll have to climb now, boy. I'll not carry you up,' Pelleas said, as a net thumped against the hull and faces appeared above us. His legs braced in the thwarts, the warrior reached towards me, nodding that I should give him the basket. I shook my head. He took it from me easily, then tossed it up to one of the ship's crew who caught it, thank the gods.

'Don't be afraid,' the Lady said. I stood, looking into her eyes, one hand clutching old Hoel's hawking glove which was still tucked in my belt, the other grabbing hold of the net. One hand on the past. One on the future.

'No harm will come to you now, Lancelot. I give you my word,' the Lady said. I had never before heard a woman give her word but in that moment I trusted the golden Lady. I knew that her word was a bond that she would never, could never break. Besides which, the sparhawk was aboard that ship now and where she went I must follow.

I stood up onto the bench and took hold of the coarse ropes in both hands, glancing once more at the man who had carried me from that death-filled hall. He nodded and gestured at the net.

I climbed.

5

The Island

I SPLIT THE RABBIT'S head to get to the brain, but the movement startled the bird and she bated, attempting to leap from the glove in a bid for freedom. It ended badly, as it had a hundred times since we had come to the island, I holding the jesses tight and she hanging upside down, revolving, flapping and shrieking in the flickering light of the lamp on the table.

I put the knife down and slowly, gently, lifted her back onto my fist but she bated again. And again. And again.

'Better to wring its damned neck, lad, and save you both the trouble,' Pelleas said, sitting on the edge of his bed to lace his boots.

I had cried out in the night again. In my dreams I had seen them cutting my mother's throat. I had seen Hector lying there in the rushes and, as is the way of dreams, it had all come with fresh terror and I had thought I might prevent it by crying out. Pelleas had said nothing. But we both knew it.

He shrugged now. 'Or else let her go.'

He knew how to be big, did Pelleas. Knew how to use a sword and spear and growl filthy curses under his breath which had the other boys sniggering. But the man knew nothing of hawks. Even less than an eight-year-old boy, which was saying something.

'If I let her go she'll die,' I said, 'because she does not know how to hunt and kill. They learn it from their parents. Or the hawk-master, if they are taken from the nest.' I thought of old Hoel then and resented him for not having trained the bird before that night when King Claudas wreaked havoc in Benoic.

Pelleas shrugged again. 'As I said, wring its neck then. Be done with it.' He thrust a foot into the other boot and laced it. 'For you do not seem to be getting very far with it. That bird hates you.'

'She hates everyone,' I said, looking into the sparhawk's yellow eye, which glared back at me with suspicion. Her talons, like little scimitars, gripped the gauntlet upon which I placed the rabbit's head, away from the fist so that she could see the brains inside the skull.

So many times she had ignored this invitation when we first came to the island, having grown used to me dropping food into the basket for her to eat unobserved. But I knew she must get used to life outside that false nest and learn to feed properly or else die of starvation. And so I would stroke her talons with the meat, caress her chest and the edge of her wings with it until she would peck at what annoyed her, and thus might get the smallest taste of the brains and know it was food. Know too that I was not her enemy but her friend.

Sometimes she bated at me, furious at my presumption in touching her, enraged by the intrusion. Other times, perhaps lulled by the same gentle words I had often spoken to soothe Malo, she would, scowling, stab at the offending gobbet. If I kept still as a corpse, she would even step to the glove. Then one day, hunger, or curiosity perhaps, had overcome her hawkish pride and she had pecked at the rabbit, smearing her curved beak with blood. Then had fed with ravenous abandon as she did now. Devouring the brains. Filling me with hope that she would survive in spite of everything.

That I would fix her. In spite of everything.

'You're a determined little lad, I'll give you that,' Pelleas said, gathering his spear from the corner of the room and stopping for a moment to watch the sparhawk feed. I said nothing, trying to keep my arm still so as not to scare the bird and set her bating again. 'Still, I s'pose it gives you something to do,' the warrior said. 'And takes your mind off . . .' He cleared his throat. 'You know,' he said, picking up his shield, 'the past.'

Then he was gone and we were left in the flame-lit gloom. Just us two. The hawk and the boy.

Once called Ictis by the Romans, the island was now known as Karrek Loos yn Koos, meaning hoar rock in woodland, and perhaps that harkened back to a time before the sea had flooded the bay. We called it Karrek, or simply the Mount. It was a small tidal island nestled in a bay off the south-western coast of Cornubia, which was a sub kingdom of great Dumnonia, in Britannia. A lofty mass of rock, trees and gorse cut off from the mainland by some five hundred yards of sea. The Lady's island. My new home.

The Dark Isles. That's what we in Benoic had called Britannia, though many of our people's ancestors had come from there during the harder times of Roman rule, and folk were still sailing south across the Dividing Sea to escape the Saxons who spilled from their boats into Britain to burn and kill and take the fertile land for their own. Britain. A place at the edge of the world, so said the Romans. A harsh land of wild peoples and bogs and wind-scoured heaths. An island rearing out of the northern seas and infested with outlaws and barbarians and would-be kings, so that you had to wonder why the Saxons wanted it so badly.

The place of my ancestors too, before they had taken ship to Armorica. Before they had carved out a kingdom with the sword and become lords of Benoic. And now I lived on this rock which was a place between worlds, not Armorica and not quite Britain. But I lived. Perhaps the last of my people. Except for my uncle.

I thought of the traitor now and the sparhawk screeched as though she had seen him in my mind and so I hummed that tune which my mother used to sing, and which a girl who had betrayed me had sung, and the bird went back to her meal and I put Balsant from my thoughts, thinking instead of that night when I had come to Karrek. The shaven-headed warriors who had burst into the Beggar King's hall and spirited me away from that butchery were sullen and quiet when we came ashore on the ebb tide, climbing up the slick rocks with the sea's murmur in our ears. They had left two of their sword-brothers behind as corpses and I think they blamed me for their loss. As for me, I was still not certain that we had not passed to the other world. I had never been aboard a ship before, and sailing through the mist, the hull and rigging creaking, the men silent in the dark and the sound of the sea kissing the bows, had woven some spell around me.

I had found a coil of rope into which I placed the basket to safeguard it against the ship's roll, and had fallen asleep neither knowing nor caring if I should ever wake. So deep and death-like had that slumber been that I missed much of the next day and only awoke when the sun was sinking to the western horizon and the Mount loomed black and ominous against a molten copper sky.

I admit that as I stood at the rail I searched for my mother and father and Hector on the shore. I imagined they might somehow be standing there looking out to sea. Waiting for me.

Now I knew I would never see them again in this life.

'This is your home now, child,' the Lady had said as her warriors, but for Pelleas, strode off towards the dwellings snugged at the foot of the towering rock, their spear blades threatening the sky, their voices like the low rumble of distant thunder. 'Pelleas has a bed for you.'

The warrior had spat. 'What am I supposed to do with a wet-behind-the-ears boy?' he grumbled, but the Lady paid no heed and I looked up to see a group of older boys running across the rocks to greet the warriors, chattering like gulls. Eager for stories but getting only growls, curses or flailing arms as though they were buzzing flies that needed shooing.

'Well? You coming, boy?' Pelleas said, walking off. I looked at the Lady. She nodded that I should go. 'That bird of yours keeps me awake, I'll eat it,' the warrior added, his mailed back broad as a closed door.

Inside the basket the sparhawk shrieked and I heard the frustrated flutter and flap of wings.

'Go with him,' the Lady said, her voice as soft as the murmur of the sea from which her island arose as if summoned by some god.

And then I had followed Pelleas, my ribs still aching from being carried over his shoulder, my mind's eye still full of blood and the sight of men cutting my mother's throat. *At least you were in your basket and did not have to see it,* I thought to the bird as we walked across the dark rock.

That had been two moons ago. Just two. And yet I felt I had been on the island for a year. Partly that was because by now I knew every rock and stand of gorse, every pool left behind at low tide and each twisting, rocky path through the hazel wood which the Mount wore like a cloak. But it was also, perhaps, because the hawk and I spent our days alone. Days unmarked by the duties and tasks which had filled my previous existence. Here on Karrek I was as free as the bladder wrack drifting in the bay. As lordless as the gulls wheeling above the Lady's windswept fortress crowning the Mount.

Yet even with the days all my own I still had not fully manned the hawk or taught her to kill for herself. I would lie on my bed and torture myself with the memory of the blood feast. I would imagine myself jumping in front of my mother and thrusting my eating knife into the heart of the man who came to kill her. I saw myself take up my brother's sword and hack my uncle down, cursing him as he died, telling him that this was his punishment for betraying my father. Betraying him long before that awful night.

Or I would stand on the beach looking south across the sea, sending promises of vengeance on the breeze. The Beggar King and his people would see me again. My uncle would see me too. And they would suffer the worst pains I could inflict on them. I had time and imagination enough to conjure all sorts of tortures and contemplate which would be the most painful and vile for a man to endure. One thing I knew: I would take my uncle's hand, the one I had often seen brush my mother's hand when he thought no one was watching. I would chop off that hand and make my uncle watch as I fed it to the pigs.

And so, with all this revenge to plot, the sparhawk was neglected and still unable to hunt for herself. 'Today will be the day,' I told her, stepping out of Pelleas's simple dwelling and blinking against the glare.

It was a warm, still day and the tide was rising, reclaiming the last weed-slick humps of the mainland foreshore. Beyond that, impenetrable forest. A green mass which filled my eyes and whispered to me on breezy days. But not today, and I turned my back on it, the sparhawk sitting on my left arm, the seabirds wheeling above, the day stretching before us.

'There he goes, the little lord,' a boy called Melwas shouted. Armed with a wooden practice sword and a man's shield he stood with the other boys on the flatter ground between the shore and the rising mound, waiting for the men who would train them this morning.

'And the bird that flies like a broken arrow,' Agga called, pointing a spear whose blade was sheathed in leather so that it might bruise but not kill. Both boys were some three or four years older than I and begrudged me the freedom I enjoyed while they and the other eleven boys living on Karrek spent their days learning the arts of war. Sword, spear and shield work. Running up and down the Mount for endurance and speed. Holding rocks above their heads for strength. And Agga was right about the bird but I said nothing, ignoring them as I always did.

During her rages and struggles inside the basket the sparhawk had snapped off the tips of her primary wing feathers as well as mangling her tail feathers. I had tried dipping them in hot water, as the Lady had suggested that first time we had spoken, and the tail feathers were undoubtedly straighter than they had been, but I could do nothing about her wing tips, and so she flew poorly. She knew it, too, and landing on the ground or alighting on a perch would flap and shriek with rage and frustration, cursing her incompetence, the clumsiness which was so contrary to her nature.

We emerged from the shadow of the trees into a sunlit clearing and she flapped, the nervous creature she was, her *eekipip, eekipip* filling the glade in which I had set up a perch, putting two almost straight branches in the ground as the uprights and securing a thin, bowed hazel branch between them. I had tied a long leather leash to the perch and by now the bird was used to the routine. Used to not doing what I asked of her, too. But we could work in peace here, out of sight of those with whom I shared the island, and even if the others knew where we were, they left us alone.

Now, I slipped the leash through the loop of the jesses on the hawk's leg and she stepped willingly from my arm onto the perch. Then I tied a length of twine to the leash using the falconer's knot old Hoel had taught me, hoping the twine was not too heavy for her to carry in flight. I laid the creance in a double line out from the perch into the glade and back to the bird, and while I did this she pecked at the leash. Pecked the twine. Fidgeted. Lifted her head and watched me.

Slowly, so slowly, I walked away from her across the clearing, feeling her yellow eyes on me, that mistrustful stare of hers searing into my back. Even after I had carried her on the glove every day since I set foot on the Mount.

I counted twenty paces and stopped. The twine creance was twenty-five paces in length, giving her a surplus of slack to avoid her snapping it with a jerk and flying off, never to be seen again.

Barely breathing now, I turned as slowly as a flower turns towards the sun. She sat there, twenty paces away, her scimitar-armed feet clutching the hazel branch, her head cocked. She was a haughty princess sitting before a line of would-be suitors. She was a queen of Persia waiting to be flattered with gifts of gold and jewels and silks.

I eased my right hand into the pouch on my belt and brought out the rabbit's leg and a piece of its liver and laid them on the glove, then gently lifted my left arm up away from my body. My heart beat its own wings in my chest. Today is the day. She would fly to the glove and finish under sun and sky the meal she had begun by candlelight.

Pursing my lips, I gave the sing-song whistle that she knew so well. The cuckoo call that told her I had food for her. There would come a time, I hoped, when I flew her at game and she would be lost from sight, and I would need to know that the call would bring her back to the glove.

She shrugged herself. Gripped the perch. Eyed me with apprehension and bitterness. But would not come.

I whistled again, making sure to keep my arm still. Several times over the last days she had flown, but always to the ground halfway between the perch and the glove with its glistening, blood-scented offerings. Today she would fly to my arm. She would wing her crooked way to me and savage the liver and the leg with that wicked curved beak.

I stood there. Above us, the sun moved across the glade. In the distance, the whisper of the sea and the shrieks of gulls. All around us the flutter and soft rattle of leaves in a breath of sea breeze. The sparhawk watched me but did not move. I whistled again. Waited. Whistled again. Lifted my aching arm a little higher. Whistled again.

Time passed. I lowered my arm because it ached. Took a breath and raised it again. Whistled.

She did not come.

My throat tightened. I was no hawk-master. I did not know how to do this. Not any of it. The creature was wild and hate-filled and who was I to think I could teach her anything? I clamped my teeth together. I had not cried for my mother and father. Nor for Hector. I would not cry because of this hawk.

I wanted to whistle again but could not. I should let the bird starve. Why had I carried her in that basket from the ruin of Benoic, all the way to this rock off the shore of the Dark Isles?

Better to wring its damned neck, lad, and save you both the trouble. Pelleas's words ran through my head. My arm ached and my mouth tasted the bitterness of tears. Perhaps she could not fathom that, although she was still tied, she was free to come to me. Or was she simply too stubborn and proud to obey?

The sparhawk shook herself. Blew out her feathers to their full extent and strode up and down the hazel perch, looking this way and that.

I gave the call, the worst I had ever done it because my heart wasn't in it now.

The hawk cried back, opened her wings, dropped from the perch and came. With three flaps of those imperfect wings she gulped up the space between us, but then a guttural clamour and two crows dived at her, one a wing's length from striking. The sparhawk shrieked and swerved ungracefully and landed flapping amongst the grass as the crows mobbed her, up and down like a pair of little smith's hammers, calling in their gruff voices *a hawk, a hawk*, incensed at the intrusion, thrumming with an eternal and innate hatred.

I ran forward and scattered the crows, which flew like shadows before a flame, and the sparhawk screamed at me in a voice that was almost human.

Your fault! I should never have trusted you! she cried.

'We should never trust anyone,' I said, and threw the rabbit's liver and leg at her, pulled off Hoel's leather gauntlet and cast it onto the ground. Then I sat down in the grass and glared at the bird, understanding why my father had looked so defeated when he saw this spiteful creature instead of his snow-white gyrfalcon. I understood why Pelleas said I should wring her neck and be done with it. What did it matter now anyway? My father would never see her hunt. He would never be king again and lead his people. I should cut the jesses and let the bird fly off and be damned.

She fluffed her feathers, strode then skipped over to the liver and impaled it with those scimitar claws. She cocked her head and glared at me with that hateful yellow eye. Then she stabbed down with her beak and began to eat.

Shearwaters, razorbills, guillemots and kittiwakes shrieked and called from the island's south side, furiously building nests on the ledges and crags. The cormorants and shags which roosted near the foot of the cliffs now perched on rocks by the sea's edge, their wings spread, hanging out to dry. Gulls wheeled, keening above the bay, diving to plunder the votive treasures left by the ebb tide, whilst black and white oystercatchers waded in the shallows, stabbing at mussels and crabs with their spear-like bills.

An arrow's flight from the shore, the Lady's ship, *Alargh*, 'Swan', rocked at her mooring, a gull resting atop her bare mast. Further out, too far to see men's faces, four currachs bobbed like nutshells. I imagined their thwarts brimmed with flapping silver. Herring, mackerel, whiting and perhaps even a haddock or two would crowd the feast table that night, with the surplus carted off to the smokehouse whose sweet oakwood breath was already on the morning breeze.

That dawn before swimming I had watched dolphins against the distant skyline, more of them than I could count, arching and diving, sewing the horizon. Then, squinting against the sun's glare off the water, I had seen an osprey, higher up than the quarrelling gulls, a darker shape against the endless blue firmament, proclaiming all he had witnessed on his travels. I knew from what old Hoel had taught me that the bird had begun its journey in far-off Africa and would fly further still, to some part of the northern Dark Isles, to spar and mate and claim a kingdom of sky and water. Awed by that sea-hawk and his perseverance, I wished him well as I picked a way across the rocks and shingle and eased myself into the shallows, gasping as I kicked out and gave myself to the colder depths.

I swam most days, when the other boys began their weapons training and the forge anvil began to knell, and the few girls who lived on Karrek Loos yn Koos occupied themselves with their mysteries under the Lady's watchful eye. But for the last nine or ten mornings I had swum all the way round the island, taking an age to do it but emerging eventually, exhausted, shivering and ravenous.

'Seems to me you'd rather be an otter than a boy,' Pelleas had observed the first time I stumbled ashore having circled the island.

The truth was there was something about the water that drew me to it again and again. It was part fear, part defiance that enticed me, compelled me to immerse myself and, always with a blood-shivering thrill, wade out to the uncertain deep. I would think of death. I would wonder what my mother and father and Hector had thought at the very moment of theirs. I would lift my feet. Fill my lungs with air. Yield for a moment to the course and current, then kick and pull and fight. The waves could not bury me like a creature under the plough-turned earth. No unseen, underwater tide could catch me in its net and drag me out too far to claw my way back. No lake or ocean or sky could overwhelm me. I would defy it all. I would swim.

Now, having filled the hollowness that came after a swim with half a loaf of bread and a wedge of cheese, I sat on a rock overlooking the grassy slope below the Lady's keep, chewing samphire and relishing the saltiness on my tongue and the warm light on my face. Watching.

The thirteen boys stretched their limbs and sinews, rolled their freshly shaven heads round their shoulders and pulled their heels to their backsides. They took no note of me, nor of Pelleas and the other warriors who were taking their ease in the sunshine, all thought and ambition turned towards the coming race. Nor did the boys make a show of noticing the girls who had come chattering from the Lady's keep to watch the sport, though they were as aware of them as they were of the sky above their heads and the rock beneath their feet.

On the Lady's word they would set off from the keep like hounds after the hart, down the steep track through the trees and around the Mount, keeping to the fringes where grass met bare granite, over the crags and bluffs, then back up to the keep. They would complete this circuit three times in honour of three gods: Morrigán, Queen of Demons, goddess of war; Cernunnos, the horned one; and Arawn, lord of the underworld. For these gods were the three which the Lady most venerated.

For the winner, a gift from the Lady herself. Traditionally, a knife or a belt buckle or an elm bow. A fine woollen cloak or a pair of boots. But really the winning itself was the prize. It was all for the honour of it. For the victory at the end of the hard-run race.

'Goes back years. Long before you came mewling into the world, lad,' Pelleas told me. Agga was the current champion, having won the race a year ago to the day and by a good distance too. The bone hilt of the knife sheathed on his belt still gleamed like fresh milk.

He and Melwas stood apart now, their friendship put in the shade by something deeper: rivalry. They being the biggest and strongest and knowing it.

Jowan looked fast, I thought, with those long, lean legs, big hare's feet and not so much in the way of heavy muscle as some of the others. In contrast, Peran was short and stocky but there was strength in those legs of his and he did not lack for stamina, which would play an important part. I had watched him training with Madern, hammering his sword against the grown man's shield long after all the other boys, but for Melwas and Agga, had given in to exhaustion and sat cradling aching arms and bruised pride.

Melwas, Agga, Jowan or Peran. One of these would be the winner, I was sure. Florien could throw a spear as far as any of them but he was no runner. Branok was almost as good as Goron with a bow and could split an apple with a knife thrown from ten paces, but he was a slow and steady boy and I doubted he would even try in the coming race. Similarly, Geldrin seemed to me to lack the fire in his belly to win. He was the smallest boy on the island, smaller than me though he was at least a year older, and he might have been as fleet as Malo, my father's stallion, but he would not want to challenge the others for fear of provoking them to revenge.

'Agga will have it again,' I heard Madern say to Benesek, the two of them scratching their chins or pulling their moustaches as they eyed the racing stock. I had seen Benesek fight like a mad fiend that night in the Beggar King's hall. Now, he grinned and shook his head whilst taking something from inside the neck of his tunic, threaded on a leather thong.

'This says Melwas will win,' he said, showing Madern a bronze coin, green with age now, minted in the time when the Roman legions marched in Britannia. His teeth were white against his long, dark moustaches. 'For he has sulked a year now and will not let Agga beat him again.'

Madern's eyes flicked from the coin back to Agga, who was bent forward, hands clutching his muscular calves. Limber and strong and confident was Agga.

'Well?' Benesek said.

Madern nodded. 'A carafe of that Syrian wine I brought back from Durocornovium says Agga will win.'

Benesek spat on the coin and rubbed it against his tunic. 'Two carafes,' he said, turning the coin to make it catch the light so that a little of the original bronze colour gleamed. It worked.

'Agreed,' Madern said.

Just then the Lady came over the bluff and all the boys ceased their preparations that they might look at her. Her warriors and the girls looked up too, for her presence alone cast an ensnaring spell.

I spat out the samphire and straightened, wanting the Lady to see me, though I knew she had more important things to do than notice a boy sitting in the sunshine while the others puffed up their chests in readiness for the great race in her honour.

An overdress of fine green wool was cinched at her waist by a gold-studded belt, and her arms were bare but for several silver wire bracelets on her wrists. She wore a twisted silver torc at her neck and her golden hair was coiled and fixed behind her head with two long copper pins. She wore sandals on her feet but bent and took these off and handed them to one of her girls before picking her way effortlessly down between the rocks towards the waiting athletes.

She looked like a queen and I supposed she was a queen here on this little island.

A pretty, freckly-faced girl called Wenna ran up to the Lady and gave her a circlet of red campion, beaming with pride. The Lady accepted the gift and placed it on her head, which had Wenna blushing as red as the flowers that she must have spent all morning picking and weaving.

Then the Lady went and stood in front of the boys, giving each of them a moment under her gaze. Some fidgeted. Others tried to look taller or broader than they were. Melwas, I saw, gave Wenna a champion's grin before he had even run a dozen paces.

'Who is going to win the day?' the Lady asked the boys. I could not see her face properly now but I knew she was not smiling. It was a serious question and everyone knew it. Such a weighty question that no one, it seemed, dared answer her. They just stood there, sweat-sheened skin taut over eager flesh and muscle. But tongues as still as the rock upon which I sat.

'Well?' the Lady said. 'Can none of you tell me? Is it beyond any of you to know?' She glanced across at Pelleas, who stifled a grin, then she turned those green eyes back onto the boys. 'Who is going to win?' she asked again.

A gull shrieked overhead, flying out to sea, laughing as he went. Near silence fell again, the only sound that of the surf stroking the shore. Until the spell was broken by two words.

'I am,' I said.

I took off my shoes and dropped them in the grass, knowing that my own feet would grip the rocks of the shore better than those hobnailed soles. Agga, Jowan and a couple of the other boys were barefooted too, but the rest wore shoes or boots and as I walked over to join them Melwas nodded at my feet and smirked.

'You'll rip them bloody,' he said.

'Does a wolf cut his feet chasing down prey?' I asked him. He laughed.

'We're not all flat-footed like you, Melwas,' Agga said, hoping to provoke his rival before the race.

But Melwas did not take the bait. 'So little boys are given the honour of competing now?' he said, not to the Lady directly but loud enough for her to hear.

I looked up at her, hoping she would not forbid me to run.

'Melwas has a point,' Pelleas said, 'about Lancelot being just a boy. He's too young for it. You know what they're like when they get going, my Lady. Lad's only half the size of some of 'em.'

I held the Lady's green-eyed gaze, my lifted chin and braced chest and shoulders an echo of my earlier claim that I would win the race. When I had said it the girls had giggled and some of the warriors had laughed. Twirling the coin on the end of its leather thong Benesek had jokingly called to Madern that all bets were off now that there was a new contender to consider. As for the boys, a few grinned and some even whooped, relieved that I had broken the spell which the Lady's challenge had laid upon them, binding every tongue.

But the commotion was short-lived and subsided as, one by one, every person standing beneath the Lady's keep realized that I was serious.

And I was serious. The Lady saw it in me.

'Lancelot will race,' she said with the slightest nod of her flower-crowned head, our eyes still locked. 'And he will be treated no differently. Come what may.'

I did not take the time to look at Pelleas or Melwas to see their reaction. I was forcing my way amongst the other boys who were already lining up, leaning into the sea breeze.

'So be it, lad. But if you end up drowned, or get your head smashed in on the rocks, don't expect me to look after that bloody bird of yours,' Pelleas growled at me.

I ignored him.

'Are you ready?' the Lady asked us, and received a chorus of *yes*

Lady as we jostled and elbowed each other for all the difference a foot or two's lead would make in the overall scheme. Then a stillness descended over Karrck. My heart was thumping. My mouth was dry, my palms were wet, and deep in my ears there was a rhythmic whooshing which flooded all other sound, so that the cry of a seagull somewhere above might as well have come all the way from beyond the veil that separates this life from the next.

For some reason I thought of Hector then. I imagined him standing amongst us, bent forward over his leading leg, face clenched, eyes narrowed, determined to prove himself as he always was. He would beat us all now were he here, I thought, for Hector was fast and strong and had been born to be a king. Desire and blood combined, woven together like silken threads in the richest of tapestries, shining brighter than all around it.

Hope of our people. My brother, who had inside him my father's courage and vigour but none of his cruelty. And yet all of it, Hector's promise, his ambition, our people's prospects, all had been snuffed out in one foul night. A blazing flame doused in blood.

Blood. My mind turned against me then, conjuring another vision of my brother, of him throwing himself at our uncle the traitor and being speared by another man. Hector's gore-slick hands grasping at the shaft sticking from his flesh. A crimson bloom on the tunic which our mother had adorned with whorls of bright blue yarn.

'Go!'

Born to be king and killed for it.

'Lancelot!' Pelleas bellowed. 'Run, lad!'

That voice hauled me back to myself and the sight of the other boys' heels as they hared off down the hill.

So I ran.

I tripped on a tussock of long grass, almost falling on my face, but somehow kept my feet, the girls' squeals and the men's roars in my ears, and then I was already past one. Clemo. Fat and slow was Clemo, though when he did score a hit with the sword in training, boys ended up on their backsides. He was out of this race now though and I doubted he would even finish it.

Over the bluff. Down the worn track between the granite ledges and across the sun-browned grass. Leaping shelves of bare rock. Not thinking, just trusting my eyes and my feet to find their way. Onto steeper ground, my legs all but overtaking themselves as I hurtled headlong, towards the birch and hazel, slipping in between Enyon and Kitto, getting an elbow in my shoulder and hearing curses billowing in my wake.

Then we were amongst the trees where the path narrowed and there was no choice but to keep in single file, the boys' breathing loud beneath that leafy canopy, their shoes scuffing against the ground.

Quick feet. Arms spread like wings for balance. Reckless.

'You may as well give up now,' Melwas called from somewhere up in front. 'This is my race.' His words came stuttering like cart wheels over cobbles. All heard. None replied.

In front of me was Branok and in front of him a gap was opening, though there was no way to pass without taking off into the trees and getting snarled in the blackthorn brambles and gorse thickets.

Down and down. Cascading. Coursing down the track like a mountain stream. Eyeing the ground for roots and stones. Kitto was on my heels now that we had been forced to slow, but I would leave him behind, and Branok too, as soon as the path widened.

Boys slipped and slid on the loose, dry ground. Growled curses. Invoked gods. Then the trees thinned and more paths opened up and I tore off to the right of a big elm and did not slow but leaped off the edge of a hillock, landing and rolling and was on my feet again racing towards the sea.

'Little shit!' one of the boys yelled as I looked over my shoulder and saw that I had overtaken Branok, Florien and Hedrek, because those three had chosen a safer route. But I was flying across the goat-cropped grass, fleet and silent as the shadow of my hawk stooping from the soar.

Another jump, this time down onto the stones of the shore, which clacked and moved underfoot, though my feet barely touched them. Agga led the pack now, with Melwas close behind, those two far out in front, leaping from boulder to sea-kissed boulder. Confident and unyielding both.

Time enough to catch them, I knew, but first to pass those who were less than an arrow-shot ahead. Not that I needed to push for the lead yet, so early in the race and with more than two circuits still to run. But I was not one for tactics. There were boys to beat and so I would beat them.

I saw Geldrin by his fair hair and was surprised at how far ahead of me he had got. He was fast and running well and I had been wrong to think he did not have it in him to compete with the others.

Good for Geldrin, I thought, but then having leapt onto a large, flat rock he stopped. I saw why. Jago, who had been five spear-lengths ahead on that same rock, had turned back and now came at Geldrin, who seemed stuck there like a limpet. Jago gripped him by the shoulders and the next thing I saw, Jago was running again while Geldrin was thrashing in the surf.

I did not stop to help Geldrin. The sea there thrashed itself white but Geldrin could swim well enough, and in no time I had caught up with Jago. He swerved towards me and swung a fist, but I ducked and he stumbled and then I was past him too and gaining on Goron.

Up the bank and onto the grass again, and Goron knew I had the beating of him even if his pride had him fighting hard for a while, matching me for pace until I unleashed a burst of speed to put him out of his misery.

'Win it, lad,' he called after me, still running hard to stay ahead of Jago and the others.

Up the feet-worn, dusty path and back into the woods, my eyes half blind in the dark after the golden day and the silver glare of the sea, so that I was not sure which boy was my next opponent. Whoever it was, he was blowing hard, not liking the uphill slog. Perhaps his chest burned with the effort. Perhaps the muscles in his thighs were fire and he wondered how he would keep up this pace for another two circuits of the Mount.

I was only getting started. My breathing was smooth and measured and if anything my legs were warming to the task. My eyes were adjusting too and I saw that the puffing but dogged boy digging his way up through the trees ahead was Peran. Short legs and thick arms pumping. His hot, used-up breath in my nose now that I was on his heels.

Sensing me, he veered into my path but I anticipated it and cut across his wake and overtook him on his left and after twenty paces I could no longer hear his incessant panting.

It took me the whole of the next circuit to catch up with Agga, Jowan and Melwas. Those three were making light work of it still, biding their time, saving themselves for the third and final lap. At least, they were until Agga glanced over his shoulder and saw me. He must have told the others that I was upon them, because they all speeded up, their legs devouring the sloping ground on the Mount's east side, goaded by the unthinkable: that they might be beaten by the youngest boy on the island. And by an outsider, too, for I did not train with them or eat with them or sleep in the round hut with them. They had not minded me racing, because they never imagined I might actually compete. My being on their heels now shocked them. It angered them. And the only thing they could do about it was run.

And now we four were on the south side. To my right, trees. Thick and verdant, leaves flickering in the sea breeze; a wide green belt above which the steep, craggy rock face rose up to the Lady's keep, that tower of worked stone and aged timbers sitting like a crown upon Karrek Loos yn Koos.

The others too will be surprised to see me still in the race, I thought, imagining the faces of those waiting by the keep, idling in the sunshine while we sweated and toiled. They had cheered before, seeing me in fourth place out of fourteen with only one circuit to go. As I had turned back to them, having pressed my palm against the ancient oak of the keep's door as we all must each time we reached the top, I had seen Pelleas's teeth flash against his brown face.

'Go on, lad, give 'em a run of it,' he growled and two or three of the girls had chanted my name and that had put little wings on my heels like those on the sandals of a statue of the Roman god Mercury I had seen in a temple in eastern Benoic.

Now my ears were full of the wind's rush, the breaking of white water amongst the sea-carved rocks, and the plaintive calls of wheeling gulls, as my feet slapped on the granite of the foreshore, the sudden firmness announcing itself in my ankles, knees and hips. But I was young and supple as a new beech leaf and swift as an arrow off the string.

Fifty paces. That was all that separated me from Agga in third place. If I did not take him now I would take him across the grazing meadow before the trees. Maybe I would take Jowan there too, I thought, gaining on them all the while, leaping from rock to rock, never stopping nor even slowing to pick my route across.

Forty paces. Breathing easily. Jump. Run. Three strides and jump again. Smooth as dawn sunlight spilling across the isle. With a surge of effort, Agga gained on Jowan and threw out a leg and Jowan flew.

He hit the rock with a scream and a flail of limbs, and I saw blood bright in the day as I leapt over the tangle of him.

Just Agga and Melwas to beat now and less than half a circuit to do it. Up the slope, easy as thinking it. Fleet as a hare. The stink of Agga's sweat lingering on the air. He was worried, was Agga. Pricked by the tines of two fears: losing to Melwas and being beaten by me. So now those big, powerful legs of his moved as fast as he could make them.

Not fast enough.

Ten paces. Like a hawk sweeping down to the kill I was on him, then past him and into the trees.

'Damn you!' he roared. 'I'll have you, you shit!'

And I laughed. Couldn't help myself. Laughing as I flew up the track. Laughing as I jumped a fallen birch. Laughing as the stick cracked against my face and I reeled and stumbled and fell headlong onto the stony path. How had I not seen him? For there he was. Melwas. Standing there grinning as I bled.

I looked up at him and at the branch in his hand which he had swung at me like a club, knocking the wits from my skull. He raised that branch towards me, as though saluting me with it, then tossed it aside.

I thought he would gloat but he didn't. Just turned and ran up the path. Towards the victory which he knew must now be his. And I watched him go.

Blood in my mouth. Blood spilling from my nose. Blood on my hands, forearms and knees. But no pain. Just fury. Hot as forge flame. And Agga's footfalls and ragged breath in my ears getting louder.

I was up and running, even though I could not see properly for blood and snot and the tears which flood the eyes after a clout to the nose. Up and up. No thoughts of anything cramming my head, for even thoughts cannot dwell in fire.

And there he was, the blur of him, which was all I needed. I ran without grace and rhythm now, but with more than enough rage to make up for it, my feet pummelling the ground. Gaining a spearlength with every thirty strides. Through the last of the trees and out onto the craggy outcrops beneath the Lady's keep, the sea's breath filling my chest. The crowd chanting, 'Lancelot! Lancelot!'

I was above it all, the Mount, the keep, the shimmering sea, soaring like a feathered shaft, then with a jolt I struck the oak door with both hands and I spun round and there was Melwas pounding up the hill, red-faced and furious.

'Lancelot! Lancelot!' they called, the warriors and the girls alike, not two or three but twenty or more, their voices creating a strange harmony which wreathed Karrek Loos yn Koos and rose to the heavens.

I had won.

6

Lady of Karrek

'WHO HIT YOU?' the Lady asked as she poured the red liquid into a long-stemmed cup which gleamed in the flamelight. It might have been bronze made with good tin from the mines of Cornubia, burnished until it shone, but by the lamplight the cup looked like gold or silver.

I felt Melwas's eyes on me. Heavy. Hot as coals.

'An elbow, Lady,' I said, touching the swollen mess of my nose. 'An accident as I pushed between two boys to get ahead of them.'

She lifted an eyebrow as she handed me the cup, then filled another, giving it to Melwas.

'There is always a drop or two of blood in the race. Did you know poor Jowan's arm is broken?' She held her own right arm, long fingers caressing the pale skin of her elbow, knowing that Agga was responsible for Jowan's injury. Knowing also that Melwas was behind my swollen nose. I knew I looked a sight, having caught a glimpse of my face reflected in the water barrel outside. Besides which, Pelleas had laughed so hard when he saw me that his sun hat had fallen off and he had trodden it flat when trying to gather it up again.

Two blackened eyes and a nose twice its normal size. That was what I saw in the water and what had Pelleas laughing his hat off. Hardly the handsome hero from the stories. Not quite the proud Achilles or noble Hector whose tales had held my brother and me spellbound as children. Still, I had won their foot race. As I said I would.

'Well, do you like it?' the Lady asked. I had put the shining cup to my lips and let the wine seep into my mouth. But I could taste nothing. It was cool and wet and nothing more. 'Vino rubeo Melfie,' she said, 'all the way from a place far to the south of Rome. Just think of the journey it has made to reach us here.'

In Benoic my father had used to near drown himself in wine but I had never thought anything about how far it had travelled from the vine to his mouth. Nor did I know now how far away Rome was, but I looked into the cup and raised my eyebrows and went along with it.

'As sweet as ripe blackberries, my Lady,' Melwas said, drinking again. The Lady smiled.

'Lancelot?' she said, nodding at the cup in my hand.

I frowned. 'I cannot taste it,' I said, shrugging my shoulders. My nostrils were plugged with dried blood and, just as when the nose is blocked with snot and it makes food tasteless, so this expensive Roman wine seemed no more special than water on my tongue. Albeit water that warmed my belly and was already beginning to make my head feel light.

'I see,' the Lady said, taking a sip from her own cup which matched the ones Melwas and I gripped. I looked at Melwas and he looked at me, and for a few heartbeats neither of us tried to hide the hatred between us. 'So you would lie for your enemy's sake but not to please me?'

I did not know what to say to that and so I shrugged again and looked about the Lady's bedchamber, then took another sip of the wine which I could not taste.

'He should never have been allowed to run, Lady,' Melwas blurted into the silence.

'Why? Because he is faster than you, Melwas?' she asked. 'Because he is not afraid to beat you and Agga?'

Melwas's face turned a similar colour to the Vino rubeo in our cups.

'Because he had not been training with sword and shield as we had and came to the race fresh.' It was a desperate grab and Melwas knew it and so he tried again. 'And because he has not earned the right to run,' he said. And I could not disagree with that. For while the others trained for war, sweating through the days under the men's tuition, I hunted with my bird or swam in the sea or cleaned Pelleas's war gear for him or sharpened his blades.

'Perhaps you are right, Melwas,' the Lady said, her green eyes fixing on my own. 'Lancelot runs wild on this island, free as the fox and the hare. He has received none of the instruction which you and the others have. He neither hones his body nor learns the arts of war. Lancelot does not know those with whom he shares this place. Does not know what they would do to win the foot race.' *I know now*, I thought, a throb of pain in my nose bringing water to my eyes. 'And yet despite all this, he won anyway,' she said.

There was a shout outside, where the men were putting the boys through their paces with spears and shields. I looked to the window, framed in thin red brick and through which the sea breeze came now. I had sometimes seen the Lady looking out that window, watching the boys at their war games.

'He won't win next year,' Melwas murmured into his cup as the Lady set her own cup on the table and went over to an oak chest which sat at the foot of her bed. It was swathed in green and purple silks, that bed, and I considered that there were benefits to receiving traders from as far away as the lands of the Byzantine Greeks and beyond. Wine and silks to name but two.

'You ran well, Melwas, and you deserved the wine,' the Lady said, bringing something towards me which was wrapped in oiled leather. 'But you may go now,' she told him with a smile and a nod of her golden head.

Melwas thanked her for the wine, shot me a hate-filled glare and walked out through the open bedchamber door. I heard his feet scuffing down the worn stone staircase followed by the creak and slam of the oak door. So now the Lady and I were alone in the flickering light of the oil lamps whose smoke I could not smell because of the blood clogging my nose. I threw the rest of the wine down my throat and placed the empty cup beside the others. Perhaps it was the drink that was making my stomach roll over itself. More likely it was because I had not been alone with the Lady since that day, so long ago now, it seemed, when I followed Flame into her tent and she had known me.

'Pelleas said I should give you your gift in front of them all. Make a thing of it.' She held out the leather-bound mystery and I took it, surprised by how light it was. 'He thinks it would make the other boys respect you, seeing me present your prize and with a little ceremony woven in.' She shook her head. 'I think Pelleas is wrong. I think it would make the others resent you more.'

'I do not care if they hate me,' I said.

'You should care, Lancelot,' she said. 'You may be faster but you are not stronger. Not yet.'

This was true enough, for all that I did not like hearing it. I looked at the bundle in my hands.

'May I?' I asked. She nodded. Carefully, I unwrapped the prize, already having an idea what it was by the size and shape. But even when my eyes confirmed it, I was not prepared for the beauty of it.

A hawking glove. Not ancient and sweat-stained and stinking like old Hoel's which I used daily. And not too big like that one, either. But new and tightly stitched and gleaming with oils and perfect. I placed the wrapping on the table and slipped my left hand into the gauntlet, relishing the way my fingertips reached the ends if I pulled the glove along my wrist. Almost a perfect fit, yet enough spare room for my hand to grow into it.

'It is deerskin,' the Lady said.

'I've never seen one like it,' I said, turning my gloved hand over and tracing with the fingers of my right hand the hawk, wings out-stretched, that someone skilled with a needle and thread had stitched into the leather.

'It should fit perfectly by the time your bird is fully manned,' she said. 'It was made in Cambria, across the Hafren, by a man named Dywel.' She nodded. 'Dywel once made a saddle for King Uther.'

I had heard the men talk of Uther, or Uturius as those who liked to pretend they could speak Latin – though they could barely muster six or seven words of the Roman tongue – called him. The Pendragon. The High King of Britain and by all accounts a fearsome giant of a man. A warlord who spat lightning and farted thunder and the only man who could save the Sacred Isles from the Saxon hordes that were spilling ashore with each spring.

'How did this Dywel get the size right?' I asked. 'I have never met him, have I?'

'No, you have never met Dywel. He is old and crooked these days, I hear, and has no need to go far from his workshop. His skill and reputation travel for him.'

Another shout from outside, a booming tirade of curses aimed at Branok and Geldrin. The Lady tilted her head towards the window.

'Goalien brought the glove back with him,' she said.

Goalien was one of the Lady's warriors, one of the Guardians of the Mount, and several weeks previously he had crossed the Hafren with a merchant who traded tin for Cambrian wool. For as well as serving the Lady, the warriors of Karrek served as bodyguards to mer-chants wishing to venture even beyond Tintagel, deeper into the Dark Isles. These merchants were often far-travelled foreigners from the

Mediterranean, who paid the Lady in silver for the use of her men as guides, protectors and translators.

'When he came to Dywel's village, Goalien pointed out a boy who was your age and size, so far as he could say. Dywel took the measurements from that boy.'

But Goalien had returned to the Mount three days prior to the foot race. The Lady saw my frown. 'I had already decided to have Dywel make you a glove,' she said. 'Of course, I could not have known you would race with the others, let alone win.' She shrugged. 'But you did win. And so what better opportunity to give you a gift?' She smiled. 'You have done well with the bird. In truth I never thought you and she would come to an accord. And yet now she answers your call and flies neatly to your arm. Even to that old glove which is too big for you.'

'She took a dove the day before last,' I said. 'As well as any goshawk could.'

The Lady half smiled. 'On the cliffs overlooking the old wreck,' she said. 'I saw it.'

'I was going to give it to Pelleas for his pot,' I said, embarrassed to know that she had been watching. I talked to the sparhawk more than I should, when I thought we were alone. Talked about my brother and father. About the traitor Balsant and about my mother. 'But she took the dove up onto a branch and ate her in front of me,' I said.

The Lady laughed. 'I know,' she said, and I frowned again and she raised a hand by way of an apology.

My cheeks flooded with heat. 'I have never seen its equal, Lady,' I said, taking our conversation back to the glove and lifting it to my tortured nose, fancying that I caught the faintest scent of the leather hide and the oils which had been worked into it to keep it supple.

'I am pleased,' she said, and seemed contented to see my appreciation of the workmanship. I had thought old Hoel's glove was wonderful, but this one was fit for a prince. Fit for a prince of birds, too, and it made me wish, as I had not done for some time, that I had brought the white gyrfalcon from Benoic rather than the sparhawk.

'Thank you,' I said. 'And for the wine.'

'Which you could not taste,' she replied, one eyebrow arched.

I smiled.

'Beware Melwas,' she said. 'He will be a formidable warrior one day. One of our best.'

'I do not fear Melwas or any of them,' I said, though my reflection in the water barrel should have told me that perhaps I ought to.

'I know you don't,' she said, and those green eyes were so knowing that I suspected she could see my thoughts as clearly as the swollen nose on my face.

She nodded at my gloved hand. 'She will not like the new glove at first but she will grow used to it soon enough if you put her food on it. And once it smells of you.'

I wanted to ask her things then. Questions that had been simmering away in my mind for weeks, ever since I had grown used to living on the Mount. Such as why had she saved my life that night in the Beggar King's hall? And why had her men not helped my father in the midst of that bloody betrayal? Why just me?

I had asked my bird these questions many times, but all I got from her by way of reply was silent defiance or, when she was in fair mood, grudging respect. Neither of which was much use to a young boy with unanswered questions.

But standing here in the keep on the heights of Karrek, that deerskin hawking glove warming to my skin, I could ask the Lady herself. What better time than now, when we were alone and my victory in the foot race was still fresh enough that she might indulge me further.

'Thank you,' was all I said. For whilst I did not believe that I feared Melwas or Agga or any of the older boys on the island, I could not tell myself that I did not fear the Lady. This golden woman who ruled an island of boys and girls and battle-scarred warriors.

More boots clumped in the stone stairwell then, followed by three thumps on the oak door.

'Come in, Madern,' the Lady said, and the door opened to reveal the warrior who, seeming not in the least surprised that the Lady had known it would be him, announced that a boat from the mainland had beached.

'Lord Cynfelin's men, Lady. Come to fetch Wenna,' he said.

The Lady frowned, still looking at me. 'Sooner than I expected,' she said to herself, turning to Madern. 'The girl shows ability, Madern. I would have had her stay with us longer.'

The warrior shrugged broad shoulders in a gesture which said it was none of his concern.

'So be it,' the Lady said.

Wenna was promised in marriage to this Lord Cynfelin, so Pelleas had told me, and she had been sent to Karrek by her father to protect her from other would-be suitors and the temptations of the world, as Pelleas put it, until a deal could be struck between her father and Lord Cynfelin. It seemed that two powerful men had come to an agreement and Lord Cynfelin had sent for his prize.

'Is Wenna to marry?' I asked. I thought her too young and this news of a lord's men coming to take her away came as a surprise.

'She is the same age as you,' the Lady told me, heavy-browed. 'Off you go now,' she said, taking a small pot from the table and with a slender finger painting her lips with red ochre. 'And do not antagonize the other boys,' she added in a stern tone while rubbing a little of the powder into her cheeks too, as I had seen my mother do times beyond counting.

'No, Lady,' I said, thanking her again, then took my new hawking glove, squeezed past Madern and ran down the stone steps which were cold on my bare feet. And, my victory prize still on my hand, so snug, so perfect compared with Hoel's old glove, I stepped out into the day.

For the next six days I barely took the new glove off and even slept in it, in order that my scent would seep into the deerskin and the sparhawk would become accustomed to it the sooner. In that time she caught another dove and also a small herring gull, and on both occasions I got to her before she could carry her kills up into a tree and humiliate me.

I held her jesses and had her eat gobbets of flesh from the glove, a little at a time each day, until I was confident that she was happy enough with the change. And nor did I scrub the blood out of the leather, because I wanted her to associate the glove with filling her belly. It pained me to see that new deerskin blemished already and I knew that I would have to clean it soon or the leather would stiffen, but for now it was more important to earn the bird's trust.

'Never thought I'd say it but it would seem you've made a hunter of her,' Pelleas said, appearing at my shoulder one dawn as I stood on the Mount's south side looking west across the sea. 'So I've heard.'

I felt awkward, unaccustomed as I was to company when the hawk and I roamed the island. A light rain hung like mist in the air and the day was as grey as the sea which surged landward in furrows of shattering foam and spray.

'She does it for herself, not me,' I said.

'Aye, then she's found the thrill in it,' Pelleas said, as if that was something he understood intimately.

Like me the sparhawk was staring out to sea, perhaps wondering what lay beyond that dull horizon where cloud met ocean, where it was impossible to tell which was which. The bird seemed almost as comfortable in Pelleas's company as in my own, which was perhaps not surprising seeing as we three still shared a hut. For her part, perhaps, the hawk was earning the warrior's respect.

'One day we'll take her over to the mainland so she can have a proper go at the hares,' he said. 'I think she's big enough and brave enough to take a young'un.'

'Would the Lady let me go across?' I asked, intoxicated by the idea of escaping Karrek and its isolation. I also relished the thought of seeing how the bird would fare against this new prey which she was unused to. She had learnt to fly well after those ungraceful early days with her broken wingtips, mangled tail feathers and suspicious hatred, so that I was sure that together we could learn to catch a rabbit or hare early in the season. If the Lady allowed us to try.

'I think I could persuade her,' Pelleas said, almost smiling. 'If you can prove your bird is worth the effort.'

The sparhawk would not take that bait but just glared into the west.

'Well then?' Pelleas said. 'Did I come up here to look for the faces of old lovers in the waves?' He had been staring out to sea but now he turned in time to see the flush in my cheeks. 'Or are you going to show me what she can do?'

I looked at the hawk's yellow eye. 'She prefers hunting with the sun behind her,' I said. I didn't want to fail in front of Pelleas. Not now that he had come out of his way to find us and watch us take a blackbird or starling or some other prey. Not for any reason.

'We don't always get to choose the battlefield, lad,' he said.

I frowned, knowing we must try even if it ended in disaster.

Pelleas had almost given up complaining about the bird's shrieks and occasional bating in the night when he was trying to sleep. Now, if he was prepared to entreat the Lady on our behalf about going over to the mainland, it was the least we could do to show him what we spent day after day learning while he and the others were training in the arts of war.

I turned my back on the grey sea and sunless dawn and walked towards the flickering green of elm and elder, at which the bird on my glove stretched her wings in readiness, knowing it was time. For like all sparhawks she hunted from cover, coming at her prey unseen until the very last when it was too late to escape her.

No talking now. Soft footfalls and slow movements, me slipping the leash off the sparhawk's jesses and she keeping almost still, eyeing the wood. Waiting.

We went a little further but stopped short of going where the trees and thickets were more tightly packed, for whilst she was supremely adept at negotiating more open woodland, as a large female she did not often risk flying amongst dense undergrowth.

Then, by a stunted solitary ash we waited. I wondered if Pelleas the warrior had the patience for this. Often the sparhawk and I would stand this way for what seemed an age, me barely breathing, moving only my eyes, the bird even stiller. Tense. Bunched like a muscle before a fight. Pelleas was a shield cleaver. A spear breaker. A man who never seemed more content than when he was swinging a sword at an opponent or an axe at a log, or wrestling the other men into submission to the joy of the boys and girls of Karrek. But what we were doing now required restraint. If there was not a good chance of catching the prey, the sparhawk and I both knew it was better not to fly. In truth I was not yet sure that *I* was suited to it, for there had been times when I had cast her at some uncatchable bird, which was a waste of her strength and an unnecessary risk. Even so I had manned the hawk and was still flush with the triumph of that, and my heart was beating fast now.

'The art of hunting with birds is not much known in the Dark Isles,' Pelleas had said that first night the sparhawk and I shared his hut. The Sarmatians taught it to the Gothic tribes, he explained, who in turn gave it to the Romans. 'But you won't see it much in Britain now. And I'd wager never a hawk on the arm of a lad young as you.'

How a man like Pelleas knew such things was a mystery and I nevertheless expected him to ruin things now with some gruff curse and a flap of his arm as I eyed the wood, waiting for a tree sparrow or a bullfinch or some other bird to break cover.

Waiting. The sparhawk forgetting her ill temper, setting aside her mistrust of me, her mind on the task at hand. I just keeping the perch of my arm still and my eyes scouring the trees in the unlikely event that I should spot some prey before she did.

Had Pelleas gone, I wondered after a while, for I could not hear him breathing behind me. *He has snuck away so as not to ruin our hunt,* I thought. A pity. Surprised as I was to see him, I had now grown excited by the prospect of showing him what my bird could do. Not the white gyrfalcon but an imperfect sparhawk, a creature which barely tolerated me and which defied me whenever she could. But my bird nevertheless.

A rock dove clattered amongst the leafy branches of an elm, its wing-beats like the clapping of hands as it found a new perch. My bird had seen it. Her yellow eye was fixed on it, fixed in it like a hook, and her body thrummed like a heart about to burst. She knew she could not catch a rock dove if it got a head start. But the dove had not seen her yet. Had not noticed us half hidden by the trunk of that stunted ash.

Unsatisfied still, the rock dove flapped its grey wings and dropped from the branch, landing in the grass a short spear-throw to my front and right and already pecking about. Looking up incessantly, as creatures will that know they are some other animal's prey.

Now! I had barely thought it when the sparhawk ghosted off the glove, quick and low against the ground, so low that she almost scythed the grass. And for a half-breath I lost sight of her amongst the trees, but then there she was, rising, wings spread, tail open, the dark striped bars of her underside vivid in the grey dawn.

'Gods,' Pelleas said. Behind me still. There all along. My sparhawk had the dove in her talons as she banked round and came back towards where we stood. She climbed above the ash and dropped the kill, which landed at my feet, and I saw that the rock dove's neck was snapped. There was also a deep bloody gash along its breast.

'Fierce little fiend, isn't she?' Pelleas said, turning his admiring eyes up to the canopy of the ash where the sparhawk sat preening herself, making sure each of her tail feathers was aligned perfectly after the excitement of the hunt. And while she feigned indifference to the kill, perched in that branch tidying herself like that, what I saw in her was pride.

'Seems you've not been idling the days away after all, lad,' Pelleas said. 'Benesek and the others won't believe it.' He bent and picked up the torn rock dove. 'So let's show them this, hey. Forget beating

Melwas and Agga in a foot race. Some more of these for the pot and you'll be a proper hero around here.'

I nodded. Not that I cared what the other boys thought of me. But I did want to earn Pelleas's respect and so I looked up at the sparhawk and gave her my whistle, which more often than not she ignored as if she were deaf. This time though, perhaps because she was not done showing off, she swooped from the branch, lighted on my outstretched arm and settled on the deerskin glove.

There has not been such a storm for years. Nor one so out of nowhere, the day having dawned fair and calm. Now, roiling clouds, bruised and black, pushing each other eastward across the low sky like an armada of black ships bearing tragic news of death and defeat. Difficult to fly in this.

Below me, the sea as black as the cloud but for the white gashes here and there where the storm sheers off a wave's crest and scatters it to the wind like an offering.

Before the world was full of wrath, I had spread my wings and shrieked with joy to ride the salty air. Thinking only, let the boy's sparhawk not be untethered and hunting, for she is a savage, blood-thirsting creature. The boy has made her so. A herring gull is neither small nor meek, yet that sparhawk would go for me if she saw me. But she will not be on the wing today. Not in this.

I test my voice. A mad laughing shriek as if in defiance of the storm. Oh the joy of it! And now, as I near land, that green island besieged by white-plumed furrows, I smell the mussels and the crabs and the sea urchins far below, where the ocean throws itself onto the rocks, trying to break but being broken. Over and over again. But I fight the need to plunge into the breakers for shallow prey. To forage amongst the stones and pools. For now at least. I have come for something else. Someone else.

There. There he is. Surely that is him and I shriek again, spiralling down and down, my outstretched wings buffeted by the winds, my feathers trembling with the thrill.

Yes, that is the boy, though he has grown since last I saw him. A handsome thing he is. Dark and lean-faced. Noble-looking yet somehow wild too, like the sea-battered coast of these Dark Isles.

What is that he clutches in his hand? I shriek as though to ask the question but the boy cannot hear me amongst the storm's baleful roar and the ocean's self-sacrifice upon the ragged shore. A glove. An austringer's glove and beautiful too. Even my herring gull's eyes can see the craftsmanship in it. I shriek again, this time to warn the boy to stay back from the cliff edge lest he be blown off to smash his bones on the rocks far below. Like a mussel dropped to crack open its shell.

Closer to the edge he goes and now my scream is one of terror because I fear he will jump to his death, and would that be so strange given all he has suffered?

He stops and I let the storm toss me closer until I see that beneath that tangle of dark hair his face is ashen. Tight as his sparhawk's claw on a kill.

He pulls back his arm and . . . there. He throws the leather gauntlet and it turns over itself twice, three times. Falling. Falling into the suck and plunge of the white water at the cliff's foot.

I am too close to the rock and my wings open, catching a gust which lifts me up and turns me and I beat into the wind, gaining the rain-flayed sky, my plaintive mewing call lost in the tempest. Keow! Keow! Keow! Up through the grey. Up and up towards the grim, shifting black.

For a moment I thought I saw the glove amongst the breaking water, small and lost and doomed, being drawn back out with the retreating sea. Being claimed. But then it was gone and I was glad of it. Damn that glove and damn this island. Damn the gods too, who sought to punish me. And yet had I not brought their judgement upon myself? By accepting the Lady's gift and forgetting who I really was? When I had shut Hoel's old glove in a chest and put on that new deerskin one I had cast off Benoic. I had betrayed the past and all but forgotten my father's face. What was I doing here? Swimming with the rising tide each dawn and running laps of the island to prove myself, when I should have been raging against those who killed my family. Or perhaps I should have been with my brother Hector in the grave.

Dark thoughts. Raging and storm-tossed like the water below, though perhaps not as fully formed at the time as I saw them after. Still, I was bitter and self-loathing. I was cursed.

I had been sitting on a milking stool in the thin dawn light, scouring the rust from an old mail shirt of Pelleas's, when Geldrin came running across the sand and grass, his fair hair sticking up in sweaty tufts from being under the leather helmet he now gripped by the chin thongs. With breathless excitement he asked me to come back with him to the practice field to judge a fight between Agga and Peran.

'Come, Lancelot!' he said, pointing off to the smokehouse beyond which some of the boys were fighting, their occasional shouts and the *clack clack* of their wooden swords now and then carrying to me on the breeze. 'They want you to decide it.'

I looked at the mail shirt across my knee then glanced up and down the strand for sign of Pelleas. He had told me that he wanted every spot of rust gone and the iron rings greased against sea air and salt spray by the time he returned from wherever he had gone before first light.

'You can finish it after. He won't beat you,' Geldrin said, sweeping his helmet through the air. 'You're his favourite. Everyone says it.'

'Everyone can say what they like but it doesn't mean anything,' I said, eyeing the dark interior of the hut, then turning my ear towards it. I could just hear the soft tearing sound of the sparhawk eating, ripping flesh from a duck's neck which I had saved for her.

'Come on!' Geldrin pleaded. 'Before Madern gets back with the others. They'll take it out on me if you don't come.'

Geldrin believed that, I could tell. I believed it too, for though he was older than I, Geldrin was no bigger and I often saw him running errands for one of the others. But in truth, part of me was flattered that the other boys should want me to judge a practice bout. I had thought they all hated me for winning the island foot race. Perhaps it would do me good to spend some time with others my own age, or near enough, rather than roaming Karrek with a hawk as my sole companion. That was my mother's voice in my head. Still, I stood, laying Pelleas's mail shirt on the stool, and nodded at Geldrin who grinned and nodded back.

The practice bout was over soon enough. Agga won and they hardly needed me to say it, for by the end Peran was limping and swiping blood from his lip while Agga was busy challenging Kitto, Clemo and Florien to a fight. I congratulated Agga and tried to catch Peran's eye to acknowledge his courage, but he would not look at me. Then I left them to it and ran back to my work, hoping to be scrubbing those rusty iron rings before Pelleas returned.

I was a spear-throw away from the hut when I heard it. The sparhawk's incessant *kew-kew-kew-kew* which pierced the gathering wind and made my blood run cold. For I was familiar enough with her voice by then to know that something was the matter, and that she was suffering.

I found her dangling upside down from her perch, twisting round and round and bating, and in a heartaching moment I saw the reason for her panicked shrieking. Her left wing flapped madly but the right was only twitching, because the leash was wrapped around it. There were feathers on the floor and spots of blood and I stood there as bound by the horror of it as was the hawk held by her own leash, and did not know what to do.

'Hold still,' I said, reluctant to touch her for fear of making things worse. 'I can't help you if you don't keep still,' I hissed, and maybe she understood me then, or perhaps she was exhausted from fighting, but she ceased her bating and just hung there, twisting slowly on the leash which had snapped her wing. Panting for breath. Her yellow eyes sharp not with arrogance or enmity now but with fear and confusion and pain.

'There we go,' I said, fingers more gentle than they had ever been, unwinding the leather leash, her hot body filling my left hand with vibrant life, her little heart thumping against her breastbone. She flapped and *kew*ed in vain and I tried to soothe her, stroking her neck with my thumb and whispering that she would be all right though I knew she would not. Then she was free of that damned leash and I saw the full horror of her broken wing and it sickened me.

'I'm sorry, bird,' I said, knowing I was to blame for her ruin. 'I'm sorry I left you.' And now her fear turned to anger and she stabbed my arm with her beak, breaking the skin so that blood welled. She raked me with her talons. Scoured my face with her blazing eye. Accused me.

'I'm sorry,' I said. If I hadn't gone with Geldrin I would have heard her call the moment she became entangled. But she had bated, tried to fly, and the leash had snagged her and she had swung down, somehow getting snarled in the leash so that through continued attempts to escape she had snapped her right wing. And all the while I had been away from her as no proper austringer would have been so soon after manning his bird.

In my mind I heard old Hoel scolding me for my stupidity. I saw the disappointment in my father's eyes and I saw my brother standing up for me, telling them all that I was only young and that I would learn, and that hurt like a cold hand squeezing my heart because I wanted to see Hector again but I never would.

'You should never have come with me,' I told the sparhawk. 'Hoel should have kept you. It is his fault,' I said, but I knew the fault was mine and only mine. She looked at me and gave a pitiful little shriek and I would rather she yelled and clawed and stabbed me but she had neither strength nor heart for that now.

I carried her outside and took the polishing cloth from the ground beside the stool with the mail laid upon it, then wrapped the bird in that cloth, keeping her wings against her body, as a mother would swaddle her infant. I remembered Hoel doing something similar with an injured kestrel, though he had killed the bird soon after.

'We will fix you,' I told my sparhawk, who shrieked and glared as I placed her back in the basket which had been her home and her prison from the night we had fled from my own home across the sea until we came together to Karrek Loos yn Koos. But I hoped that the familiarity of that confinement, as well as the dark, would calm her now. At least she could do herself no further harm in there, I told myself, fighting the temptation to close the lid on the basket so that I would no longer have to see her. So that her eye could no longer burn into mine. And in that yellow eye I saw my own condemnation. In that thin little cry I heard my crime.

I snatched up the fine deerskin hawking glove and I turned my back on the bird and when I went back out into the day I found it changed. The sky in the west was black and low and swollen. The fingers of the storm were already clutching at Karrek, flinging waves upon the rock and flicking white spume up onto the strand.

I ran. Across the pasture beside the ragged western shore, leaping white rocks and tufts of long grass. Then climbing. Up through the trees. Scrambling over ledges and boulders. Skirting to the west of the Lady's keep and gaining the higher ground. Racing only against myself, the wind hissing past my ears and through the long grass and rattling the leaves on the trees.

I ran because I wanted to escape that baleful, accusing yellow eye. Wanted to escape the island itself and throw myself into the rushing sea and swim back to Benoic. Back to the time before, when I had a mother and a father and a brother.

I watched the deerskin hawking glove being swallowed by the thrashing, slathering waves. The wind as fierce as a god's breath in my face, dragging the water from my eyes and pushing it into my whipping hair. A herring gull, riding the storm, wound up and up into the blackening sky, shrieking, passing judgement on me on behalf of all the winged creatures. The only bird out there in this. Alone. Lost perhaps.

Then I saw something else. Something further out. A darker shape beyond the veil of rain lashing the sea. I narrowed my eyes against the gusts, thinking my ears must be falling for some trick of the gale, hearing screams in the wind's keening. Hearing the crack and splintering of timbers, fragile as twigs in the maw of this storm which had come from nothing, as though summoned by some dark and powerful magic.

There it was again. A ship. A ship storm-driven onto the rocks and foundering, its oaken belly ripped open. Its ravenous hull drinking the sea. I could see it more clearly now. The bow lifted, part of it fully clear of the white water. The stern heeling so that I could see the deck and, crammed against the nearside rails, those of her crew trying to cling on as the ship died beneath them.

I was already moving. Down over the rocks, light on my bare feet, fingers brushing the cold granite. Leaping from ledge to ledge. Sliding on my backside. Down to the boulders that were wet with sea spray, then racing across the smooth stones and plunging in amongst the rocks that bristled with mussels, those black shells always flooding my mind with a memory of the bloody feast in the Beggar King's hall.

Then the gush of water in my ears and the briny taste in my mouth and I was swimming. Arms plunging over and over, dragging myself deeper. Legs kicking, churning the water in my wake, my torso twisting slightly, screwing through the surging swell.

I swallowed some and retched and kept swimming, burrowing beneath the waves which wanted to hurl me back onto the shore, feeling the water grow colder the further from land I went. Now and then between the rolling furrows I heard the screams of the drowning and I swam towards those screams. Not thinking, just moving, as the rain thrashed the racing sea and the world dissolved: cold, grey, insubstantial.

I swam beyond the place where I thought I had seen the ship and for a moment stopped to catch my breath, rising and falling on the swells as I listened, turning this way and that, eyes scouring the soaking, leaden shroud for a glimpse of the doomed vessel. *It has sunk,* my mind said. *The sea has claimed the ship and her poor crew. And days from now, having gorged on the fruits of the storm, it will puke white corpses upon the shore.*

Another scream. Close. I twisted, blinking away the water that slapped my face. Then I saw her. Black hair, black as a crow's wing, and pale skin. The only living thing in the teeth of this wailing storm. Clinging to a spread of canvas that was still attached to a splintered spar. But the canvas was sinking, its edges descending into the depths, and as more of it was swamped so more of it vanished beneath the surface. If the girl did not let go it would pull her down to the seabed with it.

'Here!' I yelled, kicking hard to raise myself above the waves. 'Here!' But the wind moaned and the sea breathed and the girl could not hear me and so I swam to her. It was further than it had looked and I knew the sea wanted me then, hungered to pull me down with the others from the doomed ship. But it would not have me. Nor would it have the girl.

I was swallowing too much seawater now because I was exhausted and open-mouthed, breathing hard, and the sea was spilling down my throat, burning it. Choking me.

'Here!' I gurgled and spat, 'over here.' Arms flailing, the stroke ruined now and my legs feeling so very heavy, I reached out for the girl and missed. Choked. Rose on a swell and kicked through it. Stretched again and missed again. Kicked and fought through the surge as the wind whipped stinging spray into my eyes. Then I had her. My hand clutched her arm, her flesh warmer than the sea. 'Let go of it,' I spluttered. 'It will pull you down.' There was not much of the white canvas left on the surface but the girl's fists were still full of it. 'Let go,' I spat, and pulled her around and saw her eyes which were round with terror and her lips which were blue and trembling. 'Please!'

She nodded and let go of the sailcloth and I put one of her arms around my neck and told her to hold on, already kicking for the shore. But then we were lifted by a swell and when we fell she was gone and I twisted but could not see her. I plunged under and I saw those eyes glaring at me from a face which was sinking, pale as a moon in the darkness. Then a flash of silver on her reaching fingers.

I dived down through the streaming bubbles of her silent scream, kicking through the murk, my ears full of pain and my hands clawing at the sea. And I made a desperate grab at the pale glow of her skin, clutching the floating tendrils of her black hair. That was enough and so I writhed back around until I could see the black sky beyond the surface and, holding tight, kicked again. Lungs screaming. Searing.

We broke from the sea together, gasping and coughing, and this time I screamed at her to not let go, knowing that if we went under again we would sink to the depths together. 'Kick!' I told her. 'Kick or we'll die!'

She kicked and clawed at the sea with her free hand and we fought for the wave-beaten shore. Behind us, the broken ship was being pummelled upon the rock and would soon be given to the sea. Her cargo was sunk. Her crew and passengers were lost: corpses floating on the waves or sinking down and down to lie for ever amongst the slick weed of the seabed. All of them but for the girl, whose warm body and beating heart and thrashing legs were fierce with life. The sea could have it all and the storm could rejoice in its savagery but neither would claim us so long as we had breath.

Not far. Keep kicking. Keep breathing. The thunderous crash of the waves upon the shore was louder than the wind's keening. Nearly there. Then my foot brushed against slippery weed and struck a rock and I tried to stand, pulling the girl upright with me, but we stumbled together and fell forward into the surf. Then she pulled me up and we were surrounded by voices and men wading into the breaking water.

'Here, lad, I've got you.' Pelleas.

'I've got the girl,' another man said, resentment flooding me as he prised the girl from me and took her off in a cradle of arms.

'Anyone else alive out there?' someone asked. Madern, perhaps.

I could not answer. I was coughing, spitting bitter-tasting strings which flew off on the wind, but I heard a big warrior named Edern say that the sea had given back all it was going to. 'Nothing else alive out there. Not in this.'

Nor was there.

'We'll get you inside by the fire,' Pelleas said, and then my feet were no longer on the sand and stones because the warrior had scooped me up, so that his hot breath was against my cheek and his big chest engulfed me. And it was the second time that Pelleas had carried me.

'Peran, fetch the Lady!' he called. I heard the chatter of boys amongst the storm's din. 'Clemo, I want dry blankets and hot broth.'

Somewhere above me a herring gull shrieked against the squall, flying great circles through the grey and watching us all with its keen eye. And I watched that gull for a while, shivering in Pelleas's arms as he carried me up the foreshore.

7

The Freedom of Birds

THAT NIGHT OF THE STORM I lay outside the small room in the Lady's keep where the girl slept. We had sat shivering together by Pelleas's hearth, watching the flapping flames and slurping steaming broth as the Lady fussed around us. Around the girl really, making her drink herb-infused potions and frequently checking the strength of the blood beating in her neck or wrist. And when the Lady had been sure that the girl was not going to drown in the sea that had already swamped her lungs, she said they would go up to the keep where she could rest more comfortably. But the girl had looked at me then as though I were a floating timber out there in the storm, her eyes brim full of the horror of that splintering ship and her ears ringing with the screams of the drowned.

'Lancelot will come too,' the Lady said, and so I had, though I was not allowed into the chamber itself and had been given a blanket to soften the hard boards outside, as you might give to a puppy on its first night in a new place. I was so tired I could have slept in the saddle of a galloping horse, but sleep did not come straight away because I could hear the girl crying. I could tell she was sobbing into her bed furs to muffle the sound and I wished that the oak door was thicker.

'She has lost much,' the Lady whispered, on her way to her own bed but stopping to crouch beside me, shielding her lamp flame against the breeze sweeping through the keep. 'Her uncle was one of those who drowned. And her chaperone, who had nursed her since birth.' She looked at the closed door through which the sobbing seeped like blood through gauze. 'I daresay she knew the other men of her escort and maybe even the crew.'

The captain of that ship, who had been tasked by the girl's father with delivering her safely to Karrek and the Lady's keeping, had lost his bearings in the storm. Having been blown past the harbour he had tried to turn and had not reefed his sail in time, so Madern, who had long experience of the sea, said after, when the men talked about the sinking and raised a cup to those who had perished.

'The shock is as a wound in her,' the Lady said. Those green eyes burned into my own. 'But she will heal in time. She will live and have a full life. Because of you, Lancelot.'

She stood then and I felt the urge to confess that I had thrown the deerskin hawking glove into the sea. She should know that I planned to leave Karrek and seek passage back to Benoic before I forgot the faces of my mother and father and brother. I would tell her that I meant to plot my revenge against my uncle Balsant and the Beggar King. That the gods were angry with me for hiding away on this island and had shown their anger by urging the sparhawk to bate so madly that she snarled herself in her own leash and broke her wing.

'You are an extraordinary boy,' she said.

I am a traitor to their memory, I thought, cringing under her scrutiny. Old Hoel's glove and a suspicious, hate-filled bird. My only possessions from before. One discarded, damp and mildewed, the other now a ruined, pitiful creature who would never fly again. Because I had fled. I had survived.

And yet I knew that I would not leave. Not now.

She glanced once more at the iron-studded door. 'Sleep now, Lancelot.'

And so I did.

The girl's name was Guinevere and I did not see her again for many days. She stayed up in the keep with the Lady while I remained down on the shore with my bird and with Pelleas, who said I was a fool if I did not break the sparhawk's neck and be done with it.

But I was defiant. 'I have bound the wing,' I said. 'And look. She eats what I give her. The wing may heal. She may fly again.'

He was busy packing his sea chest and would sail with the tide, escorting a Greek olive-oil trader called Paulus to Tintagel. He shook his head and sighed, pressing a folded cloak down onto the other contents and checking that the lid would still close.

'You are a strange one, lad,' he said. 'You'd jump into the mouth of a ship-killing storm and somehow survive what would have drowned most fish, yet you are too timid to put a useless bird out of its misery.'

'She might fly again,' I protested, feeding the hawk a gobbet of beef heart which I had got from Yann the cook, who did not know that the sparhawk was injured. Had he known, he wouldn't have wasted good food on a ruined bird.

'And I might travel back east with Paulus and kick the Emperor of Constantinople off his throne and reign in his place,' he said, fastening the chest. 'But somehow I don't think I will get around to it.'

I said nothing and went back to feeding the bird, though I could feel Pelleas watching me.

'You want me to do it?' he said. 'One twist and it's done.'

'No,' I said, and he shrugged those big shoulders of his.

'I'll be back before the new moon. Don't go challenging the other boys to a race or swimming out to wrecks while I'm gone.' The sparhawk gave a weak, plaintive cry. The first few days after the accident she had glared at me, accusing and bristling with enmity. But now I saw only fear and confusion in those yellow eyes. 'And stay away from that girl,' Pelleas said. 'Girls are nothing but trouble, even for a lad your age.'

'We are not allowed to mix with them,' I said.

'I know that, lad. I also know that Agga and Erwana meet in the woods by that old ash when there's no moon and they think they're as cunning as can be. Agga won't spoil the girl though. He's stupid but not that stupid.' I looked at him, surprised. 'Yes, I know the tree. The one the boys carve up.'

In the bark of that tree I had read the nicknames the boys had for Pelleas, Madern, Benesek and the rest, and felt guilty then.

'And I pulled Jowan out of the girls' quarters by his curls one night when the Samhain fires were burning and everyone was up to their eyeballs in wine. Pulled him out just in time, too, for his own sake,' he said, tapping the hilt of the sword scabbarded at his hip. 'That was before you came.'

He grabbed his spear from where it leant against the wall and hefted the chest onto his shoulder. Then he paused at the threshold. 'Kill the bird and stay away from the girl,' he said, and then he was gone, though his parting words seemed to linger in the room. *Kill the bird and stay away from the girl.*

I did neither.

Some days the sparhawk and I watched the boys training for war, the bird sitting on Old Hoel's glove as she used to; but now both wings were bound tight against her body so that she could not try to fly even if some instinct fired her sinews. The boys taunted us when they had the breath for it, when they were not fending off each other's sword blows or being made to hold rocks above their heads until they staggered and fell.

'You should give that feathered rag to Jowan,' Melwas said one day. 'They would be perfect for each other.' Jowan was always there, watching the others train, his broken arm splinted and his face pinched with envy and bitterness. Pelleas had told me he doubted Jowan's arm would ever be right again, and that if it did not set straight and true he would in all likelihood have to leave Karrek, such an impairment being unacceptable in a Guardian of the Mount.

'Look at him,' Jago called, stepping back from his opponent and pointing his wooden sword at me. 'A prince without a kingdom and a hawk that can't fly. The bards could weave a sad tale there.'

We watched, the sparhawk and I, and we tried to pay their insults no heed. And while those boys trained with shield, sword and spear, I learnt each one's strengths and weaknesses. I studied them and in my mind I fought them.

Other days we wandered together, hiding in the thickets, waiting for rock doves to break free of the woods as we had done before, the hawk aware of every snapping twig and fluttering leaf. If nothing else I did not want her to forget herself. I thought that if she saw her prey living unthreatened and carefree she would burn to heal herself and punish them. Her wing would set neatly, neater than Jowan's arm, and she would fly again.

And the only times I saw Guinevere were fleeting and from a distance. A glimpse now and again when she and the other girls were about the island with the Lady collecting plants, roots and leaves for their herb lore.

Then one day the Lady appeared at the door of our hut, dressed in a gown of green wool with a wolf pelt draped around her shoulders against the early morning chill. The first leaves were starting to turn, flecks of copper shimmering amongst the green forest which blanketed the mainland across the water.

'I would like you to do something for me, Lancelot,' she said. She was watching me feed the sparhawk. Rather, trying to feed her. The bird was uninterested in the squirrel flesh I offered her. I was stroking her beak with the bloody scrap, hoping to rouse her appetite, which had ebbed day by day. 'Will you help me?' the Lady asked. She could plainly see what I was trying, and failing, to do, but she said nothing about it. Perhaps she too thought I should have killed the hawk by now. That I was weak for not snapping the bird's neck. Weak for hoping. Or perhaps she believed I might actually have the hawk flying again in time. Whatever she thought, standing there watching me stroke the bird's beak with the meat, she said nothing about it. 'So?' she asked.

I nodded. Of course I would do whatever she asked of me. Unless it was to kill the sparhawk.

'Good,' she said. 'It's Guinevere. I've tried, Lancelot, but I have failed to draw her out of herself.' I was still looking at the bird but I was listening hard now. 'I have failed to lift the girl's spirits and fear her sour mood is beginning to taint the other girls.' She came closer and I could smell the pungent sweetness of burnt herbs on her. It made me shiver inside my own skin. 'Guinevere misses her home. You understand that, I'm sure. And yet I wonder what she misses so. They could not see her promise.' She frowned. 'Or perhaps they could and that was the problem,' she said with a weary resignation, 'why Lord Leodegan sent her to me. For Guinevere's own good. Do you understand, Lancelot?'

I didn't but nodded anyway.

'What can I do, my Lady?' I asked.

'Be her friend, Lancelot.' She put a hand on my shoulder and I trembled under her touch. 'Be her friend.'

The sparhawk turned her beak away from the raw flesh and I gave up trying to feed her. I would try again later, when we were alone.

'You'll do this for me?' she asked.

I nodded.

'Good,' she said, then studied the sparhawk, who looked a sorry sight swaddled like an infant. 'So, what will you do about her?' she asked.

'I won't kill her,' I snapped.

She seemed taken aback and I feared I had offended her.

'I know you won't,' she said, reaching out and running her thumb down the back of the sparhawk's neck.

Old Hoel would never have allowed anyone to stroke one of his hawks save my father, and neither should I have allowed it. But I could not forbid the Lady. Besides which, the bird seemed comforted by her touch. *Perhaps you would also let the Lady feed you, just to spite me,* I thought.

'Tomorrow then,' the Lady said. 'Come to the keep at dawn. Guinevere will be ready.'

I nodded again, already wishing the night away.

'I don't need looking after,' she said. She stood facing me, hands on her hips, feet planted wide in the doorway of the keep. You would have thought I had come to steal and burn, to slaughter all those whose sanctuary lay within those Roman-built stone walls. 'I am older than you,' she said. 'I am eleven.'

'Then we are almost the same age,' I said. She was older by a year. She had seemed two years older to me, though I did not say as much. I just watched her watching me, her lips pursed and her black hair lit by a copper sheen in the dawn sun.

'I am taller than you,' she said.

I shrugged.

'You are not even big enough to learn how to fight like the others.'

'I already know how to fight,' I said, standing a little straighter. I wished I was wearing shoes, to be taller even by the thickness of a leather sole.

'Do you?' she asked, cocking her head slightly.

'I have seen men killed in battle,' I said. 'Seen them lying in pools of blood.' I don't know why I said that but there was a flash of surprise in her face and I liked seeing it.

'I have seen men drown,' she said. 'My own nurse too.' She seemed to shudder at the memory. 'Drowning is worse than being killed by a blade. Being burnt alive is the worst of all.'

I did not know what to say to that. I thought of that night when I had slept outside her door listening to her crying into her pillow. She must know I had heard her.

'I don't need you to look after me,' she said.

I shrugged again. 'The Lady told me to come.'

She glanced over her shoulder to make sure we were alone. 'Lady Nimue thinks I am the bad apple that will ruin the others,' she said. *Lady Nimue.* I had heard her name spoken only twice in the time I had lived on Karrek and yet this girl, who had been on the Mount only days, was comfortable saying it aloud. 'She thinks that if I'm prowling around this island with you I won't be ruining the other girls. Though I must still learn the herb lore and . . . other secrets.'

'The Lady thinks you are sad because of the ship. Because of all those who drowned.'

Her eyes narrowed. They were green and blue. 'Do I look sad?' she asked.

'I don't know,' I said.

'Why did you save me?'

I frowned. 'I don't know.'

'You don't know much, do you, Lancelot?'

'I know how to swim,' I said.

Her pale cheeks flushed red with that.

'I can show you the island,' I said.

'I can explore by myself. I'm not afraid. And I have a knife,' she said, touching the bone-hilted knife sheathed on the belt which drew her long tunic of undyed wool in at her waist.

'I can teach you how to swim. Properly. So that if a ship sinks under you again you will be able to save yourself.'

Her eyes widened at that and I thought she would spit some insult at me but she did not. She just looked at me and folded her arms over her chest, which I noticed was flat, unlike some of the girls on Karrek.

'What happened to your bird?' she asked. 'Why can't it fly?'

I knew she had seen me and the sparhawk walking the island but was surprised to know she had taken an interest.

'She bated and got tangled in her leash. Broke her wing,' I said, lifting my right arm and holding it crooked.

She raised an eyebrow. 'Then she will die,' she said.

'Not if I can keep her alive until the wing heals,' I said, resenting her doubt. Did no one think it was possible? 'She will fly again. You'll see.'

Her lips twitched up at the corners and my stomach rolled over itself.

'You really don't know anything,' she said. Then she undid a leather thong on her wrist, swept her loose hair back and tied it with fast, nimble fingers. 'Well then, let's fly this keep before I get tangled in my own leash.'

I nodded, trying to make sense of this strange girl who seemed to despise me one moment and yet agreed to explore the island with me the next.

'I'll show you the old ash where the other boys make fun of the men,' I said. 'You can read the tree like one of those books which the Christians revere so much.' I grinned. 'I don't think you will find the same words in one of their books.' No sooner had the words left my mouth than I feared I had embarrassed her. 'You can read?'

'Of course I can read,' she said. 'But I don't care to look at some old tree.' She pointed out to sea, where the furrows were breaking white here and there though it was calm enough. Gulls wheeled and clamoured in a sky that was mostly blue but for some thin shreds of white cloud. 'I want to swim.'

This caught me off balance, albeit swimming had been my suggestion in the first place. 'Even after what happened?' I said, thinking that being out there again so soon would bring memories of the shipwreck flooding into her mind. I was supposed to be making her happy, not reminding her of that.

'We will swim all the way round the island,' she said. 'That is what you would be doing now, isn't it? If Lady Nimue hadn't told you to come up here and keep me away from the other girls.'

I nodded. 'You promise not to sink like a stone this time?' I said. 'The Lady will be angry with me if you drown.'

'You mean you would not swim down and pull me up by my hair again?' she said, turning her head sharply so that her long black mane flicked onto her shoulder.

Now I thought about it, that must have hurt her.

'I'm surprised I have any hair left,' she said, running fingers through the tresses, teasing out a knot or two.

Three girls came giggling round the corner of the keep, clutching baskets full of the woodland mast – beechnuts, acorns and chestnuts – and looked surprised to see me standing there with Guinevere.

'Does the Lady know he's up here?' Erwana asked Guinevere, spite making slits of her big eyes.

The other girls were Alana and Jenifry and they grinned at the thought of me getting into trouble with the Lady for being up at the keep without one of the men, or the Lady herself, being present.

'I wouldn't get too close to him,' Jenifry said, putting her basket on the ground and standing straight to show off her height and the bumps under her tunic. 'You've seen what happened to his bird.'

'Never mind his bird, what about his family! Ask Lancelot what happened to them,' Erwana said, still holding her basket brimming with such fruits of the forest as had not been plundered by the pigs that roamed Karrek's woods. 'Go on, ask him.' She put her basket down next to the other two and swept her golden hair off her forehead. 'I would be careful around Lancelot if I were you.'

Guinevere glanced at me but would not indulge Erwana, though I could see that she was curious. Perhaps she recalled my talk of pools of blood and fighting men. 'Tell the Lady that Lancelot and I have taken a boat over the water,' Guinevere said, pointing to the mainland. 'And that we shall be back in a day or so. If we have not been eaten by wolves or slain by Saxons.'

The three girls looked at each other wide-eyed and perhaps I had a similar expression on my face because I thought that Guinevere was serious. That we were going to take a boat across to the mainland, which of course was forbidden.

'Come on then,' she said, striding past me.

And so I went.

That first day we did not escape Karrek and cross to the mainland. That had just been Guinevere's way of trying to shock the other girls, and it had worked. We did swim halfway around the island though, on the landward side, from the old upturned skiff amongst the rocks on the west side to the pebble beach on the east. It was far enough for Guinevere to show me that she could swim well enough and needed no lessons from me, though she was red-faced and puffing by the time we waded ashore.

It must have been fear or the cold water which had all but paralysed her that day of the storm, I thought, though said nothing.

'Do you imagine that it hurts? Drowning?' she asked. We sat shivering on the rocks, watching the gulls wheel high above the furrowed sea, waiting for our clothes to dry. She had swum in her under-tunic and I in my braies which came down to my knees, so we would have to walk back for the rest of our clothes. 'When you take that last desperate breath and your lungs fill up with water. Do you think it hurts?'

I had never given it any thought but I did then. 'No,' I said after a time. 'And even if it did hurt, it wouldn't for long. You would sink fast as an anchor.'

Guinevere considered this for a while, though I could not tell whether she agreed with me. 'Just think of all the creatures you would see as you sank. If it didn't hurt too much to notice.' She picked up a small smooth pebble and threw it and it plopped into a breaking wave. 'Down and down into the deep,' she said. 'With the fishes and the eels and far stranger creatures for which we have no names.' She frowned, rubbing the pale skin of her arms upon which the breeze had raised goose flesh. 'I suppose it's very quiet down there on the seabed.'

'I have never heard a crab talk,' I teased, but she did not smile. People she had known were down there now. Their flesh even now being picked at by fish. Her old nursemaid's hair swaying with the seaweed in the currents and tides.

After that, we picked our way across the rocks, looking for sea creatures left behind by the ebb tide, Guinevere's tunic still dripping; and the whole east side of the Mount was cast in shadow by the time we went up to the flat ground to watch the boys practising with bows. They were shooting at straw targets forty paces away, under the watchful eyes of Edern and Benesek, who now and then put an arrow in the centre of a target with their own bows to show the boys – and each other – how it was done.

'That one is strong,' Guinevere said, gesturing at Melwas, who of all the boys was repeatedly drawing the bow string back to his chest and holding it there without trembling with the effort, patiently awaiting Edern's command to loose.

'He's strong,' I agreed, 'but Agga has the better eye.' As if to prove me right, Agga's next arrow struck the target where, if it were a man, his heart would be, whilst Melwas's shaft struck the right shoulder. 'Though neither is as good as Goron,' I said, pointing. 'He will put ten arrows into the kill spot, one after the other. He's even better than some of the men.' I liked Goron. He was the one who had yelled at me to go on and win the foot race when I had passed him. There was no spite in

Goron, though you would not want to upset him if he was holding an elm bow and a straight arrow fletched with eagle's feathers.

'No doubt you are even better than Goron,' Guinevere said, challenging me with a dark eyebrow.

I shrugged. 'I don't know,' I said. 'I have not done much shooting. None since I came here. Anyway, when I kill my enemies I will do it close up so that I can look into their eyes as they die.' Geldrin now loosed before he was ready and the arrow flew high, arcing and diving twenty paces short and ten wide of the intended target. 'Doesn't seem very noble, killing people who might not even know you have come for them.'

'You are young to think about such things,' she said.

'My father was a king,' I said. As though that explained it.

We collected our clothes from the other side of the island and I walked with Guinevere back up to the keep as the sun plunged towards the horizon and the first stars glowed in the endless sky.

The door opened and a broad-shouldered girl named Senara beckoned Guinevere with a flutter of her hand. 'Hurry! The Lady is about to show us how to mix a potion.' Senara shot me a look which told me that I was not permitted to know any more than that, then grinned and disappeared.

Guinevere slipped through the gap and I did not think she was even going to say goodbye but then she stopped, half cloaked in darkness, and pulled at her finger. She held a fist out to me and nodded, so I reached out and our hands met and she put something in mine. Something cool.

I turned my hand over and opened it and there was a simple silver ring. I remembered having seen it flash like fish scales underwater when Guinevere had reached for me, trying to claw her way back from the dark depths which hungered to swallow her.

'Tomorrow you can show me that silly tree,' she said.

I nodded but she had already gone.

For three days after that, Guinevere and I roamed the island together from sunrise to sunset, the sparhawk perched on my arm for much of the time because I did not want to undo all the hard work of manning her by letting her forget me. But I knew she was dying. Guinevere knew it too.

'It is crueller to let her suffer,' Guinevere said, gently stroking the bound and broken wing. It was a grey, damp morning and we were sitting on the rocks outside the keep. There was little point taking the hawk to wait for prey in the woods. She was no longer interested. Would barely turn her head when a rock dove broke from the trees and clapped into the sky.

'She does not want to die,' I said, gently running my finger over the dark bars of her chest plumage. I could feel her little bones sharp beneath the feathers.

Guinevere frowned at me and I frowned back.

'Maybe tomorrow,' I said. She nodded, understanding.

For days now the bird's mutes had been small and dry and hard where once she had flung them across the room, streaking the floor rushes to Pelleas's dismay. Now, she hardly ate and was half her healthy weight and did not even care who touched her, which was as good a sign as any that she was dying. Her spite and her mistrust, that fire that used to light her amber eye, was gone. I knew it, but I carried her on my arm anyway, hoping beyond hope that her fierce nature would overcome her sorry condition. That somehow, some day, I would unbind her and slip the jesses and she would spread those broad, blunt wings and streak after some prey, fast and low and nimble as the breeze.

But the next day I did not go up to the keep to fetch Guinevere, because my sparhawk was dead. Before I went to bed the previous night I had managed to get her to eat a sliver of beef heart and had foolishly thought it a sign that she was recovering. In truth like a condemned man she was taking her last meal and I woke to find her lying lifeless in her basket, her spindly yellow legs sticking straight up and her body stiff and cold beneath my fingers.

I cried. Though she was just a hawk, I cried until no more tears would come and a hollow weariness swirled in me like sickness.

I sat holding her a long time and eventually I carefully unwound the linen binding, because I wanted her to at least look like a hawk again before I placed her back in that basket which I had carried all the way from Benoic, and fastened the latch on the little door. I was glad Pelleas was not back from his travels yet.

Told you this would happen, I heard him say even in his absence. *Should've killed the hawk yourself rather than watch her endure all that. What good is a bird with one wing? Tell me that, Lancelot.*

'What will you do with it?' a real voice said and I turned to see Guinevere. I had not gone up to the keep and so she had come down to the shore.

I shrugged. 'I don't know. Bury her in the basket,' I said.

'You could set the basket adrift,' she said. 'It will be as if she is going on one last journey. We could go up to the cliff to watch until her basket vanishes beyond sight.' She was serious and solemn and beautiful.

I nodded. It was as good an idea as any and so we walked down the rocks, both holding the basket, and waded into the retreating tide together, the gulls shrieking above us because they thought we were setting a crab trap. When the water was up to our waists we looked at each other and Guinevere nodded and we let the basket go.

'Goodbye, hawk,' I whispered, sorry for having wished she were my father's white gyrfalcon instead of what she was: a crooked-tailed, furious she-hawk who had been manned by an inept boy.

'Come on,' Guinevere said, already climbing out of the surf onto the rocks while I still stood there watching the basket bob amongst the small waves, wondering where the sea would take my hawk. Thinking that perhaps she would drift all the way across the Dividing Sea back to Armorica. And that she might return there, to the land of my people, long before I ever did.

By the time we got up to the cliff top the rain was sweeping across the sea like a black veil and we soon realized that it would not be quite as we had imagined it. The basket looked so small from that height, and the sea was grey and the day was grey and the wicker itself was old and dirty, so that after no time at all we could not be sure if what we saw was the basket or just a trick of the currents.

Still, Guinevere sat there with me, the rain blowing into our faces, until long after either of us had claimed to catch a glimpse of the basket on its journey across the rain-dappled sea.

'Hear that?' Guinevere said, then stood and walked closer to the edge. Unafraid of the wind-buffeted heights and the precipitous drop, she leant over the edge to find the source of the sound she had heard. Bleating. Terror-inspired bleating. 'A sheep,' she said, as I joined her on the ledge, swiping rain from my eyes. 'A lamb not long ago by the looks. Poor thing must have fallen from there,' she said, pointing to a grass ledge off to the right.

'It was lucky to survive the drop,' I said.

'It will die if we don't help it.' She looked at me. 'It will starve, Lancelot.'

'You want to break your neck for a sheep?' I said.

'We'll go back. Find one of the men. Edern will come, or that big one with the long moustaches.'

'Benesek,' I said, then shook my head. 'We don't need them.' I looked back down at the pitiful creature and wondered how long it had stood there facing the cliff face, its rump towards the sea which spilled over its hooves now the tide was in. 'Wait here,' I said and was already running across the rain-slick rock which was warm beneath my feet, then up the steep grassy slope and down towards the north side of the island and the hut I shared with Pelleas.

I was slower on the way back to Guinevere because the rope which I had wound round my waist and looped over my shoulder was heavy and long. It was old too, and green with ancient dried seaweed because it had long been used as an anchor rope, and I did not know how strong it was but was sure it would take the sheep's weight. My weight, too.

'If you fall you'll break your legs or your back. Or your neck. You might even die,' Guinevere said.

'I won't fall,' I said. Halfway down, fingers and toes seeking what purchase they could in the rock face, I looked up at the wide, blue-green eyes peering down at me. Guinevere lay on her tummy so that just her head stuck out over the ledge, rain dripping from the end of her nose and from her black hair which hung loose around her pale face.

'Or you may end up stuck down there with that sheep,' she called. Was she smiling? I could not tell for sure. 'At least you won't starve.'

Lose a hawk and gain a sheep. That was some bad bargain.

Down I went. Faster than Edern or Benesek ever could. Faster than the rainwater which coursed down the rock in little rivulets, the sheep bleating as if I did not already know it was there and afraid, its new fleece lank with salty sea spray and fear sweat. She was a ewe, less than two years old, and when I set foot on the ledge she backed away until her right hind shank was waving above the breaking surface of the sea. She scuttled back onto solid ground, baaing at me as though it were my fault that she was in this situation.

'Rope!' I called up, and a moment later the rope whipped down, snaking against the cliff because Guinevere was holding on to the other end. For all her fear the ewe stood while I passed the rope under her belly, tying it over her crops.

'Keep still,' I told her, hoping that Guinevere would let go of the rope quickly enough should the ewe bolt and leap off that ledge into the sea. Then I was climbing, hands and feet finding the same familiar crevices again, up against the falling rain, ascending without thinking.

'You climb like a cat,' Guinevere said as I pulled myself over the ledge and stood straight, blowing onto my fingers which were chafed and aching from gripping the slippery rock. 'Stop idling, then.' She nodded at the rope which stretched from around her waist down over the cliff's edge to the ewe, and so I stood in front of her and took hold of it and together we hauled back. Perhaps that little sheep was water-logged but she was heavier than I had expected and took some heaving. Yet up she came, dangling on that old ship's rope, striking the rock now and then and bleating and doubtless more confused than she had ever been.

'Told you we did not need help,' I said, untying the ewe. But then she tried to bolt before I had got the knot undone and I fell forward after her and her hind foot struck my head.

'Lancelot!' Guinevere yelled as the ewe fled off across the rocks, trailing the rope behind her.

'It's nothing,' I said, though my vision was blurry as I got up on my feet and brushed the muck off my tunic.

Then Guinevere laughed, which was quite something given that in the short time I had known her I had never seen her smile. But that laugh! Strong and wild and dauntless. Even my own embarrassment was carried off on it like a leaf in the wind, so that I felt myself grin-ning dumbly.

Her face straightened and she gasped. 'Oh,' she said, walking towards me, 'you poor thing.'

I put a hand to my head and taking it away saw the blood on it. The ewe's hoof had gouged the skin above my left eye.

'It doesn't hurt,' I said, wiping the blood on my trews.

Guinevere raised one dark eyebrow. 'You may be a good climber, but you're a bad liar,' she said, then she leant towards me and kissed me on the lips. It was over almost before I could be sure it had hap-pened, and we stood there facing each other, Guinevere with her head tilted to one side, as if waiting for me to say something.

My tongue could find no words.

'Thank you,' she said. 'For saving that poor animal.'

'And look what I got for my trouble,' I said, touching the cut above my eye, but my stomach was looping over itself, tying itself into a knot.

Guinevere took her long hair in both hands and squeezed the rainwater out of it. 'That was not all you got,' she said.

'No,' I admitted, wishing the day was colder so that the breeze might chase the heat from my cheeks. 'Thank you,' I said.

Guinevere laughed again though this time she covered her mouth with a hand, trying to stifle the sound, and I felt like a fool though I did not know why.

'Oh, Lancelot! You mustn't thank someone for kissing you,' she said.

I shrugged, frowning. I could still feel the kiss. More so than the gash in my head. I wanted to take a step and kiss her back, to experience that unfamiliar taste again. But my feet had somehow grown roots, sent them deep down into the rock itself, and I had no courage.

'A ship,' she said, looking past me. 'See there!'

I turned and looked west across the sea, sifting the murk until I saw, far away, the red sail and black hull.

'He's here,' she said. 'I was beginning to think he would never come.'

'Who?' I asked, knowing it could not be Pelleas, for the ship he had gone west in with the Greeks had two white sails and a more rounded hull. This red-sailed ship hugging the coast was low and sleek in the water.

'My father,' Guinevere said, walking back to the cliff edge. 'That is the *Dobhran*. It means Otter in Irish. The High King himself gave it to my father.'

'King Uther gave your father a ship?' I asked in awe, blinking away rainwater and keeping my eyes on that red sail.

There were some two hundred men who called themselves kings in Britannia. Some were powerful men with retinues of warriors and great halls and swathes of land rich in cattle and wheat and silver and tin. Others were men who could barely call on a dozen spears and owned little more than a pot to piss in, so Pelleas had told me, yet these sat at the top of some hill and crowed louder than they ought. But Uther, the High King of Britain, the Pendragon, was above them all. He was the power in the land. Had won that power with his own courage and the sword's edge, and had raised himself above all the other so-called kings who bent the knee to him, accepting Uther's hegemony.

'The Pendragon is the only reason why Britannia is not overrun with Saxons, like a corpse buried under maggots,' Pelleas had said, touching the iron of his blade to avert the evil of that image of a dying Britain. 'But even Uther cannot live for ever.'

'Your father knows the High King?' I asked, watching Guinevere.

'Of course,' she said. 'They sometimes hunt boar together. My father can throw a spear further than any man.' She cast her own imaginary spear and watched it soar high over the cliff edge and down to the white water. 'Though he always lets King Uther cast his spear first, of course,' she said, turning back to me.

I imagined a famous warrior like the Pendragon could throw his spear further than Lord Leodegan, whom I had never heard of before I met Guinevere, but I kept that thought to myself.

'We should tell Lady Nimue that my father is here,' Guinevere said. 'She will want to prepare a welcome.'

I nodded and together we ran through the rain.

8

Songs of Britain

'WHICH ONE IS LORD Leodegan?' I asked Benesek, who, in Pelleas's absence, commanded those fifteen Guardians of the Mount currently not off on some escort duty or carrying messages from their Lady to the lords of Britain and the parents of the children in her care.

'Lord Leodegan?' Benesek said. We were watching those coming ashore on tenders from the red-sailed ship anchored in the bay where it was deep enough for her hull. 'None of 'em is Leodegan,' he said. Like the other warriors he was dressed in his war gear. A breastplate of leather boiled in urine to harden it, leather greaves to protect his shins, and a steel helmet. He carried his round limewood shield, its bleached leather cover emblazoned with the Lady's symbol, Karrek's high keep perched on the round metal boss which represented the island itself. He wore his long sword on his back and carried a thick-shafted war spear whose blade was keen enough to cut the air. The men always dressed for battle when any sizeable ship came to the island, even if they recognized the vessel and knew it to be no threat, and I admit that I longed to own such war gear myself one day. I lusted after it.

'Leodegan, ha!' Benesek said, his long moustaches quivering with amusement. 'High and mighty lords such as Leodegan don't bother themselves by coming here, lad. They give us their brats and bastards and we turn them into fighters or,' he said, nodding in the direction of Alana, 'protect their virtue. Then, when cleverer people than me decide the time is right, we give 'em back.' He shook his head. 'No reason for lords such as Leodegan to come all the way down here to the arse end of Britain.'

A big-bearded, leathery-skinned sailor approached the Lady on bandy legs long used to a ship's roll. Sweeping the rain from his face, he inclined his head.

'Lady,' he said.

'Welcome, Baralis,' the Lady said, arms wide, her girls huddled behind her, hooded like she against the rain, though I was looking at Guinevere, whose straight face and tight lips spoke louder of her disappointment than tears could have done. I felt her avoiding my eye because she was embarrassed to have shared her joy at the prospect of her father coming, when it was clear Leodegan was still in his hall at Carmelide in northern Dumnonia.

It was obvious that Baralis, the captain of Leodegan's ship, was in awe of the woman standing before him, for he could barely look Lady Nimue in the eye as he paid the respects of his lord and master. The Lady returned the compliments and then, the formalities out of the way, made a thing of looking over the captain's shoulder towards the activity going on behind him.

The ship's cargo was being unloaded from the tenders by six or seven sun-browned sailors. Barrels and amphorae and baskets and sacks and even a terrified, rolling-eyed bull, which, being led by its nose ring, was surrounded by four sword-armed warriors whose shields, slung on their backs, bore a red dragon.

We had watched amazed as that beast, almost the same size as the boat itself, had been rowed across the bay, like a king borne to some newly conquered realm.

'Gifts from Lords Leodegan and Gwalather,' Baralis said, sweeping an arm back towards the cargo.

'And the bull?' the Lady asked. It was a fine-looking beast and much needed on Karrek, because the one currently living on the island was a good few years older than me, by Pelleas's reckoning, and had long since lost interest in the cows.

'From the High King himself,' Baralis said, standing a little taller with that declaration, which had a similar effect on the Lady's warriors, for they were always eager for any news from the mainland, whether from Dumnonia or the kingdoms beyond such as Powys, Gwent and Gwynedd. That Baralis had come from Dumnonia's northern coast meant he must have some tales to tell of happenings in Britain, and that was one thing, but talk of the High King was quite another.

'The King is generous,' the Lady said.

'He is that, my lady,' Baralis said, inclining his head again.

Benesek, beside me, grunted. 'The King should be generous,' he said, the words escaping from the side of his mouth. 'Needs us holding the hands of all these bloody Greeks who come to Tintagel to buy his tin.'

That was true enough, for Uther needed silver to pay his warriors and buy the loyalty of other powerful kings. And merchants, be they Syrians or Franks or men from Armorica across the Dividing Sea, made Uther richer when they did not get themselves murdered and robbed by Dumnonians or Silurians or anybody else. That was if they had not already been killed by the Saxon pirates who thronged on Ynys Weith thick as gorse on the moor.

Still, a gift from the High King of Britain was no small thing. Benesek might not have been impressed but I was. I had not realized the Lady was held in such esteem. Why then did she live on a windswept island which hung off Britannia's coast like a thread off a cloak's hem, and not in some great hall? Or even one of the old Roman palaces which I had heard were still to be found in the land, some of them boasting wall paintings and deep baths which filled with hot water gushing from the ground.

'Truth to tell, Lady, I'll be glad to be rid of him,' Baralis admitted, scowling at the bull. 'I've had easier passengers, I can tell you. Damned beast shitting all over my deck.'

The Lady smiled. 'Thank you, Baralis. And how is King Uther?' she asked, at which Benesek, Edern, Madern and the other men's ears pricked up. The boys crowded close, too. Melwas and Agga at the forefront, hoping to be noticed even by a sailor such as Baralis because of his association with lords of Britain and the High King himself.

Baralis smiled and there was a blood-lust in that smile which did not become the sailor. 'The old dragon still breathes fire, thank the gods,' he said. 'Just three moons ago he killed a Saxon king in single combat. Took his head off with one blow. Clean off.' Baralis frowned and coughed into his hand. 'So men say,' he said, uneasy now about talking of such things in front of his host, and after that he spoke no more of it, much to my disappointment. I would have listened to such tales all the day and night, even from Baralis, who was hardly one of Britannia's famous bards.

'A fine beast,' the ship's captain said, coming back to the gift, which was lowing now, pulling against its handler so that I feared the ring would be torn from its suffering nose. Head down, the bull lurched forward and slammed into the man holding the rope, throwing him several feet to land hard on the rock.

The Dumnonian warriors surrounding the animal panicked, not knowing how to calm the bull and doubtless horrified by the prospect of having to slaughter a gift barely given. Quite aside from the insult, the omen in that would be bad and everyone knew it.

The Lady pushed her hood back, and her pale face shone and her braided hair was bright as spun gold in the grey day. She approached the furious creature and one of Uther's men told her to go no closer, putting himself between her and the snorting, raging gift. I did not see the face which the Lady showed that man but it made him step aside with a clatter of shield and spear and a palm raised in apology.

'Hush now, my proud, strong friend,' the Lady told the bull, whose breath shot from his tortured nose in long plumes amongst the sheeting rain. 'You will have a good life here with us,' she said, then whispered other things and pressed herself against the bull's flank and stroked its neck and poll between the sharp horns. And if I had not seen what she did with my own eyes I would have thought one of her warriors had stepped up and slammed his sword hilt down on the bull's head, as we sometimes did to daze cattle before cutting their throats, so still and calm had the creature become. Yet she had done it with mere words and touch and it raised a hum from those gathered on the shore, particularly from the sailors and Uther's men, and even her own men and the boys, who all saw witchcraft in it. It would have been near enough impossible not to. Nor did it help that her girls stood there grinning and proud where the rest of us were uneasy.

'I will make an offering to the gods and ask that they continue to favour King Uther. To give him the strength to continue leading his people against those who threaten his land,' the Lady said, still standing beside the placid bull and stroking its back. 'And I shall send a gift back with you for the king.'

'It will be my honour, Lady,' Baralis said.

But the Lady was not looking at the *Dobhran's* captain now. She took her hand from the bull and stood tall, for some reason pulling her cowl back onto her head even though her golden hair was soaked through. And at that same moment a murmur rose from the warriors of Karrek because they too had seen something. Or someone.

'What's he doing here?' Benesek muttered to himself, sliding his hand up his spear's shaft until thumb and forefinger touched the wet iron of the socket.

The girls were whispering amongst themselves and Melwas, Agga and some of the other boys were wide-eyed and slack-jawed as they stared at the man whom no one had seen until that moment, though he must have come ashore on one of the tenders with the *Dobhran*'s cargo. Behind him stood a skinny, fair-haired boy who was bent beneath a sack on his back, which he gripped in raw-looking hands.

Seeing that he was no longer the centre of anyone's attention, not least the Lady's, Baralis mumbled something about needing to make sure his men had unloaded an amphora of honey, a gift to the girls of Karrek from Lord Gwalather's wife, and strode away, growling at a grey-bearded sailor to have care with the barrel he was rolling to the store hut.

The Lady and the newcomer, whose sudden appearance had men fingering the charms hanging at their necks or touching iron blades, now stood face to face. Not that any of us could see much of the Lady's face now she was hooded again. And perhaps that was the idea.

'It has been a long time,' she said. The rain hissed and the sea breathed and the gulls cried far above in the wan sky.

'Perhaps it seems so,' the newcomer said.

He was not a tall man. Neither was he broad nor built like a warrior used to sword and shield work, as were the men of Karrek Loos yn Koos. Yet he did not look a weak man, for his bare arms, covered in strange symbols which had been etched into the skin with blue dye, were knotty with sinew and muscle, and I suspected he could cause even a big man harm with that gnarled ash staff he held in his left hand. His dark-skinned face was set with quick eyes and his moustaches reached down to the point of the black beard which wisped from his chin like a goat's. But the hair on his head receded so far that it looked like it had been shaved from ear to ear in the style of the tonsures worn by the Christian monks who had sometimes visited my father's hall in Benoic. His remaining hair was dark and stood in tufts despite the rain.

'Why are you here?' This from Benesek who had stepped forward and thrown that question into the heavy silence. It was what Pelleas would have done were he here, for there was something about this man that troubled the Lady, and her warriors did not like this. Madern's granite face was all scowl and I noticed that Edern's knuckles were white as bone on his spear shaft.

The tonsured man, who was barefooted and dressed in black trews, a sleeveless tunic of black wool and nothing more, leant his ash staff towards Benesek but kept those lively eyes of his on the Lady. 'Do not concern yourself, Benesek. Does a woodlouse burden itself with matters of the moon and stars?' The warrior reddened but held his tongue as the man stared at the Lady, awaiting her words and hers alone.

After what seemed an age she nodded and rain spilled from the oiled hood. 'You may stay,' she said, 'but you will leave with the *Dobhran.*'

The man accepted this with a bow, then lifted his staff for the benefit of his fair-haired slave, who swung the sack off his shoulder onto the rock and stood straight with a grimace, pushing those chafed hands into the small of his back.

'Madern, show our guests where they will sleep tonight,' the Lady said, asking him to do it because Benesek was still smouldering at the insult he had borne in front of everyone.

'Shall I not stay in the keep?' the dark-skinned man asked. He glanced over at me and there was a flash of something like recognition in his eyes. Then he looked back at the Lady.

'You shall not,' she told him.

The man shrugged. 'It is cold up there anyway,' he said. 'No life in Roman stone.' He gestured with his staff up at the tower which crowned the mount. 'You might be closer to the gods up there, but give me a fish-stinking driftwood hut and the company of killers,' he said, flicking a hand towards Benesek, who muttered something filthy under his breath. 'Oh but there was a time,' the man said wistfully.

'When you have told me what you came here to say, you will leave with Baralis,' the Lady confirmed. 'And you will sleep down here on the land's edge.' The man nodded in resignation and with that the Lady looked over at me. 'I am sorry about your hawk, Lancelot,' she said. I just nodded, wondering how she had known. Perhaps one of the girls had seen Guinevere and me set the wicker basket adrift and told the Lady, who now turned her back on us all and ushered her girls up the path to the keep.

Agga took the job of showing Uther's men and the bull to the grassy slope which was the closest Karrek had to pasture, while Baralis and those of his crew who would not be sleeping aboard the *Dobhran* followed Madern to the hut where they would spend the night. Better than sleeping on the *Otter*'s open deck in the rain.

'Are you coming?' Madern called back to the man with the ash staff who was still standing on the rain-glistened rocks, looking at me. As though waiting for me to do or say something. As though we knew each other. As though we were old friends.

I said nothing and did nothing but just returned the man's stare.

'Your Lady says I must sleep down here,' he said, looking at me but talking to Madern, 'but any fool can see it is not night yet. At the very least I deserve a wine skin, having spent the better part of a day aboard that leaking pail with that witless Baralis. Come, Oswine,' he said and set off after the Lady, and his yellow-haired slave swung the sack onto his back without hesitation, as sure as his master that none of the spear- and sword-armed men standing there in the rain would move to stop them. And neither did they.

'Who is that man?' I asked Benesek, watching him go and watching his slave Oswine, too, because I had never seen a real Saxon before and this one was not the hulking, blood-drinking, pelt-wearing fiend of bard song.

'You don't know?' Benesek said, pulling in his chin. 'Still, why would you? Though I'll wager you'll wish you never did know him by the time he's back on board the *Otter*.' He hawked and spat a wad of phlegm onto the wet rock where his spear butt rested. 'That, lad,' he said, nodding after the man who was now squawking at poor Oswine to hurry up with the sack, which was not much smaller than he was, 'that is the only man in Britain who Uther listens to. And some say that's only because Uther fears the bastard shrivelling his cock to the size of a maggot if he doesn't.' He shook his head. 'Uther fears no man. Not Saxon, not Irish. If you ask me, he keeps that fiend around because he was the one who somehow got Igraine to let Uther into her bed.'

'But who is he?' I asked, frustrated at being the only person on Karrek who did not know.

'That mad-eyed bastard is a druid, lad,' Benesek said, 'one of the last who can still speak with the gods. His name is Merlin.'

*

The next night was the first time I had been allowed into the main chamber of Karrek's keep. Outside it was still raining, endless veils which swept across the island in gusts, one after another like waves. While not cold enough for furs and gloves, it was a blustery, pitch-dark autumn night which had Baralis's *Dobhran* rocking violently at her mooring so that the poor sailors who had been left aboard to guard the ship, if they were not throwing their guts over the side, must have been sick with envy of their fellows who enjoyed the hospitality of the Lady of Karrek.

The keep had been built by the Romans long ago at the western extremity of the Saxon shore fortifications, and no doubt it had been used as a vantage point from which to look out across the Dividing Sea. And though the neat Roman stone and brickwork had crumbled and fallen away here and there and the repairs had been made with crudely shaped stones, timber and wattle, the rain only spat through in a few places, which was a testament to the skill of those long-dead Roman builders. And now the main chamber of the keep was warm and golden with flame-glow and stinking of men's wet woollen cloaks and sodden leather boots and smoke from the hearth which billowed up to the rafters, questing out into the night where it could, and the dried herbs – sage, basil and mint – which hung from those smoke-blackened beams. It stank of bodies too, because it was crammed with them, for Pelleas and the Greek merchant Paulus had returned from their travels just as the light leached from the sky above the western sea.

'You must have smelled the mead!' Madern had called to Pelleas as the warrior came ashore, handing his shield, spear and helmet to me because it would be my job to polish and grease them against sea air and salt spray, though I could see he had already scraped the new rust off his gear. It did seem an unlikely coincidence that Pelleas had followed so soon in the *Dobhran*'s wake.

'You think I'd let you gluttons feast on Lord Leodegan's pork and rinse your beards with his wine without me?' Pelleas growled back, and all the warriors of Karrek greeted him with good-humoured insults and a deal of back-slapping, because men did not always return from such trips. It turned out Pelleas's return was indeed no coincidence, for he and Paulus had been moored in Tintagel bay awaiting a favourable wind when the *Dobhran* slid past and Pelleas had recognized Lord Leodegan's ship.

'I told the Greeks that there was a good chance that the *Otter* would be putting in here,' he said to me as I set to work rubbing unspun sheep's wool along the blade of his long sword, 'what with Leodegan's daughter living here now. And truth be told they liked the sound of a feast as much as any men would.' He had hung up his cloak, which dripped onto the rushes, and was busy pulling off his filthy tunic to change into a better one for the feast. His muscled torso was crosshatched with scars which shone white by the candlelight and I wondered how many fights Pelleas had been in. 'You took my advice, then,' he said, glancing round the room.

He had told me to kill the sparhawk because a ruined hawk was no use to anyone, least of all itself. 'She died before I could do it,' I said. Not a lie exactly.

'And my advice about the girl? Guinevere. I hope you've been steering well clear of her, Lancelot.'

The way he had dismissed the hawk made me want to defy him now. 'I have spent every day with her. We are friends,' I said, which made the warrior sigh as he examined his new tunic to make sure it was clean enough.

'You're a fool, boy,' he said.

And maybe I was. Still, it felt good having Pelleas back. I missed my hawk, and other than Guinevere, Pelleas was my only friend on the island, even if he did think me a fool. So, we walked through the rain up to the Lady's keep together, towards the sound of laughter and song and the smell of woodsmoke, and I hoped that Guinevere would be there.

But she was not there. None of the girls were. The first person I saw was Benesek, who, wine jug in hand, was threatening the boys with a beating that would rouse the gods from their sleep should any of them embarrass the Lady in front of her guests.

'Chin up, Lancelot,' Pelleas said. 'You think the Lady would risk one of these Greeks taking a fancy to young Jenifry or Erwana?'

I had not realized my disappointment was so obvious.

'Worse,' he said, waving his empty horn cup which he had brought with him, 'imagine we caught one of King Uther's men in some dark corner with one of them.' His brows lifted. 'I'd have to kill the man and then we'd be in a tangle.'

'I know,' I said, trying to shrug it off as if it meant nothing to me who was there and who was not.

Having pushed his way through the crowd to us, Benesek now filled Pelleas's cup with wine the deep red of heart blood. To my surprise, instead of drinking it himself, Pelleas offered the cup to me. 'To help you get over the heartache, lad,' he said, 'which you won't escape, being handsome and young and stubborn and a bloody fool.'

He had barely settled into his land legs and yet he was letting me drink from his cup before he had slaked his own thirst. The generosity of the gesture was not lost on me, and I remembered seeing my father do something similar after a hunt, offering his own silver-chased cup to a man who had just come of age to join his retinue and fight in his war band. And so now I said the words that that young man had said before wetting his lips with my father's wine.

'Thank you, lord.'

Pelleas and Benesek looked at each other and burst into laughter, which had other men in the press turning to see what was so amusing. Pelleas leant towards me. 'I'm not your lord, lad,' he said, lowering his voice to spare me more embarrassment. 'One day you'll find yourself serving a lord, I've no doubt. A proper lord if you're lucky. One who knows how to win a fight. Or better still avoid one.'

'And one who rewards his men,' Benesek said into his cup.

'Aye, that too,' Pelleas said with a hard eye and a firm nod. He gestured at me to drink. 'And even if I was a lord, I'd be needing fighters, not swimmers.'

Benesek grinned and tipped his own cup towards me. 'If he fights as well as he swims and runs, he'll be serving King Uther himself and we'll be the meat in his shieldwall,' he said.

They laughed again and I felt like a dolt. Of course Pelleas was no lord. And even if he were, or even a chief in his own right, what service could I offer other than scrubbing the rust off his ringmail and blades? And yet I wanted to be useful. Not just useful, I wanted to become a warrior. I wanted to learn how to fight. The gods know I was never going to make a falconer.

Benesek's dark eyebrows lifted. 'Shouldn't we be calling him lord?' He grinned at me. 'Aren't you a prince of Benoic, lad? My father was a tanner.'

'Let's not have any of that talk,' Pelleas growled at his sword-brother. 'Lancelot already takes little enough notice of my advice.

About hawks or women or the best way to get rust off a blade. I don't need you putting ideas in his head.'

Benesek winked at me. 'Still, it's time the lad started his training, if you ask me.' Beads of sweat were bursting from his shaven head. 'Or would the Lady have him run wild until he's a grown man?'

Pelleas shrugged. 'All I know is that I came up here to drink, which I can't do while you're still holding my cup, boy,' he said, gesturing at me to drink.

I breathed in the wine's perfume: oak and stewed fruit and some far-away land and also, somehow, my father. I drank, thinking how different this experience was from that day after the race when the Lady had given me a long-stemmed cup of her own wine, which had tasted of nothing, my nostrils being clogged with blood. But this wine was like some intoxicating nectar and I craved another sip and so drank again, this time keeping some of the wine in my mouth, swishing my tongue through it. Ripe berries. Worn leather. Wood and earth.

'Good, isn't it?' Benesek said through a grin and I nodded as I handed the cup back to Pelleas. 'But don't let the others see you drinking it,' he said, and I looked over at Melwas and Agga and the rest, who were too deep in ale to be worried what I was doing. It was a rare day when they were allowed to partake in a feast at the keep with the men. Perhaps the Lady was in generous mood, feasting King Uther's men because of her relief at having her own man, Pelleas, back safely, for he had been gone longer than normal. Or else maybe she thought we ought not miss the opportunity to see the great Merlin with our own eyes and perhaps even hear what he or Uther's warriors had to say about affairs in the kingdoms of Britain.

Benesek turned back to Pelleas. 'So. Any excitement?' I assumed he was talking about Pelleas's journey as guide and bodyguard to the Greek, Paulus, whom I could see telling the Lady all about his time at Tintagel, describing the famous high cliffs from the look of his reaching arms and wondrous expression. The Lady had of course been there many times, yet she seemed to be listening to the small, brown-skinned merchant with patience and interest.

'Nothing worth getting Boar's Tusk dirty for,' Pelleas said, sipping the wine. Boar's Tusk was the name of his sword, which was shorter than most swords I had seen, because he favoured stabbing rather than slashing 'like a man cutting barley', as he put it when teaching the other boys sword work. Neither Boar's Tusk nor its scabbard were at Pelleas's hip now though, having been left with the other men's weapons in the shelter of the lean-to outside in accordance with the custom of the feasting hall when we had important guests. 'But we may be called upon to fight before winter,' Pelleas added in a low voice. 'King Gruffyd ap Gwrgan has been sending war bands across the Hafren to test Dumnonia's spears. As for the Saxons,' he added – and at this he frowned and I could see he would have spat but for the press of bodies around him – 'the Saxons push deeper into Caer Gwinntguic.'

'The truce is broken?' Benesek asked. Clearly this was worrying news, but all I could think about was that wine and how I wanted to taste it again.

'King Deroch preserved the truce as best he could and longer than anyone thought possible,' Pelleas said. 'But with boatloads of land-hungry Jutes sailing up the Solent . . .' He lifted his shoulders in a shrug and drank.

'Who are the Jutes?' I asked, resigning myself to the sad truth that I had drunk all the rich red wine I was going to that night.

'Just another type of Saxon,' Benesek rumbled.

'But unlike those Saxons who have grown soft farming the land which King Deroch has allowed them to keep,' Pelleas said, 'these new men still have war in their veins. So now the Saxons who were at peace with Deroch are breaking the terms of their truce and threatening Caer Gwinntguic. And blood will follow. Sure as a bad head follows good wine.'

Benesek grunted. 'I wouldn't mind some proper fighting for once,' he said, pulling the forks of his long moustaches through a big fist. 'A chance to earn war silver again.' He lifted his own horn cup. 'Instead of being paid in Greek wine and Sicilian oil for guarding merchants and teaching beardless boys how to use a blade without cutting off bits of themselves.'

Pelleas must have sensed my eagerness to hear more about the wars in Britain and the peoples who threatened her kingdoms. 'Don't get all giddy over his talk of fighting, Lancelot,' he said, nodding towards the other warrior. 'Benesek wouldn't trade this soft life. The shield-wall is for young men who have yet to learn how dangerous it is to be in one.' He swept his cup through the smoky air. 'Let some snot-nosed farmer's son take a Saxon spear in the belly. Let the men of

Dumnonia blunt their swords against Dyfed and Gwent.' He shrugged those big shoulders of his. 'We did our bit even before Uther reigned, when Ambrosius was king and Hengist's hordes needed killing. And if the day comes when we have to make a shieldwall again, then so be it. But until that day, I'll guard this island and keep merchants alive long enough to sell their wares beyond the Iron Gate. But most importantly,' he said, lifting the cup, 'I'll drink their wine.'

The two warriors banged their horn cups together and drank again.

'So,' Pelleas said, swiping wine from his moustaches with the back of his hand. 'What's Merlin doing here?'

Benesek grimaced. 'Damned if I know,' he said. 'But I don't like it.'

'Nor do I,' Pelleas said, looking into his cup as if Merlin's presence had soured its contents, as the tide of bodies around us shifted and the boys ushered the Greeks and Uther's men closer to the herb-fringed dais, to give our guests the best view. Though as yet the only thing to see on the dais was a lonely stool.

The murmur of men's voices retreated and in its place flowed the bright sound of a lyre being plucked, its strings singing like the first spring meltwater questing over pebbles. The melody was tentative, seeking its way through the press of those who now turned towards the dais. Rising with the hearth smoke to taunt the rain-filled night beyond those Roman bricks and tiles.

'We didn't come to a death vigil! Faster!' one of King Uther's big-bearded men roared, perhaps drunk on mead or wine, but our warriors barked at him to hold his tongue and the man shrank into himself, flushing beneath his beard.

But anyway, the player would not be rushed. I went up onto my toes, stretching to get a look at whoever was teasing those strings. For a moment, just a brief moment, I did not recognize her for she looked so different from the girl I knew. Then my breath caught. It was Guinevere. She sat upon a stool of dark polished oak, the lyre fashioned from lighter wood – sycamore perhaps – standing on her lap as she plucked the gut strings.

Her dark hair was braided and coiled and pinned at the back of her head. Her lips were red, stained with a salve of alkanet root and ochre. Her eyebrows had been darkened with a mixture of soot and galena, but the most striking thing about her was her eyes. Blue pools in a green wood, painted with the powder of ground malachite stone.

Ordinarily, without these dyes to accentuate them, her features were striking. Now her appearance staggered me, and though the melody which she drew from the lyre was slow and wistful, my heart was galloping in my chest.

Guinevere. That night, standing there in the company of warriors, merchants, the Lady herself and the most famous druid in Britain, I realized that I was in love with Guinevere. I was not yet eleven years old.

'A rare tune, this,' Pelleas said, caught in the music's spell, as were many of the warriors in that chamber. Their women too. Guinevere played the Lament of Adaryn, a tune we all knew, though it seemed, judging by the scarred and bearded faces around me, that the story never got any less sad the more men heard it. The Lament told of a young warrior called Kavan, who was called to war by King Gudavan's drums just two days before he was to marry Adaryn, his childhood sweetheart. Kavan marched under Gudavan's banners and stood his ground in the shieldwall against the king's enemies. And there, in the heart of the blood fray and knowing what he stood to lose, Kavan fought like a demon, cutting men down by the score that he might return to Adaryn.

The hack and hew. The ringing of Kavan's sword in the death-filled day. The screams and moans of the wounded. The clamour of battle. Guinevere's fingers told it all, dancing across those six strings now, nimble as the flames in the hearth. And as the music eddied and grew, she rocked her body back and forth in time with it, like a boat riding the waves.

King Gudavan saw how well and bravely Kavan fought and how deadly was the young man's sword and, the battle won, he invited Kavan to his feast table. An honour most men would crave. Yet Kavan declined the invitation, wanting only to return to his village and marry his love. To sheathe his battered sword and raise crops and children and grow old with Adaryn. King Gudavan told Kavan to go in peace and with the kingdom's thanks, but in his chest the king's heart burned with anger at the offence. So that no sooner had the young warrior turned his back than King Gudavan was plotting his revenge.

'Trouble, lad, that's what women are,' Pelleas growled under his breath as I stood there savouring the music as I had savoured Pelleas's Greek wine.

'It never stopped you,' Benesek said.

'That's how I know,' Pelleas said, earning a hiss or two from folk who did not want gruff talk breaking the lyre's nectarous spell.

Pelleas raised a hand by way of an apology, because Guinevere's fingers were weaving the sad part of the tale now and we did not need a bard to sing the words to know it. Bone-tired from battle, his wounds barely clotted and King Gudavan's victory feast far behind him, the young warrior Kavan was walking the drover's path back to his village, the sun on his face and his heart light with joy. He sang as he walked, his voice as charming as a thrush's, rehearsing the song he would sing to Adaryn that night at their wedding feast, and, nearly home now, he stopped to pick a handful of stitchwort, that Adaryn might weave those white flowers into her hair on this their wedding day.

That was when the king's men sprang from their concealment, knife blades flashing in the day, and murdered brave Kavan, cutting the young hero down beside the hedgerow flowers for his offence to King Gudavan.

'I've never heard it played better,' Pelleas admitted to me under his breath. The men and women in that chamber were enthralled. Tears glistened in warriors' beards. Men had taken hold of their wives' hands and held them tight as ships' knots. But Guinevere, Guinevere held us all in her spell.

The Lady stood to the side of the dais, dressed in a long gown of pale green linen cinched at her waist by a delicate gold chain. Her golden hair was glossed by flamelight whilst at her neck she wore a torc of twisted gold, its deer-head terminals meeting at her pale throat. Her face was painted in such a similar way to Guinevere's – the red lips, the dyed eyes – that she must have applied the red ochre and crushed green malachite to Guinevere herself. And the Lady was beautiful. No one in that keep could have thought otherwise. And yet every eye was on Guinevere. Every ear drank in each honey-sweet note.

We allowed Guinevere to bind us with the strings of that lyre, and then to pull us down into the sad depths. And thus she came to the end of the unhappy tale, her fingers slowing, her own eyes shining with tears, as Adaryn in her bridal dress searched the woods and heath beyond the village for sign of her true love.

'Kavan will come,' she tells one and all, the shepherd and the woodsman, the hare and the fox. 'He promised to marry me. Swore neither spear nor sword could keep him from me. And we shall be wed.'

Adaryn searches all the long day, never doubting she will meet her young man on his way home to her. Then, as dusk falls, she follows the mournful song of a thrush, whose music is usually as bright as summer wheat, and there by a hedgerow she finds her love. He is pale-skinned and cold to touch, looking up to the sky with those eyes which once looked at her with burning adoration. And in his hand he still clutches the stitchwort meant for her hair, holding the delicate white flowers tight even in death. A promise, perhaps, that they will still wed, though not in this life.

'No sword nor spear kept him from you,' sings the thrush who sits amongst the bramble, 'but that knife, which pierces your young warrior's heart. That knife which I have seen in the king's own hand.'

The king's no more. Now the hateful blade is mine, Adaryn thinks, as she draws the knife from her young man's still heart and sheathes its cold steel in her own warm breast.

A collective catch of breath in the Lady's keep then. Such a gasp as might draw a flame. Guinevere's fingers slowing now. Is it finished? No. A few more gentle tugs of the strings. A few notes, sad as feast leavings, given now to us who were still hungry for more.

When it was over, when the last note of that song had vanished with the smoke through the cracks in the roof, a heavy silence lay across the gathering. But for the flapping of the hearth flames you could have heard a mouse scrabbling in the floor rushes. Guinevere herself kept her head bowed, looking at the lyre on her lap as though making sure that none of those six strings yet had more to add to the tale.

I just stared. I was not the only one. It seemed to me that half the men in that keep had just lost their hearts to Guinevere, never mind that she was only a child. She did not look like a child though. And in that stifling silence I resented all those eyes being on her. The Greek, Paulus, was wet-lipped with lust, or so it seemed to me. Uther's men were like hounds with the scent of prey in their noses and Melwas and Agga and the other boys were wide-eyed and stupid-looking with infatuation. And I hated it.

But what angered me most was Merlin. The druid's eyes were in Guinevere like fish hooks. He stood in the shadowed alcove near a stout door beyond which stone steps led up to the Lady's chamber, so that in his black clothes one might not have known he was there. But I knew and so did the Lady, who was watching him watching Guinevere.

Not that Guinevere seemed aware of anyone as she stood and turned, those sad strings still and quiet now, and laid the lyre on the chair. At the edge of the dais she looked out across the gathering, catching my eye for two heartbeats, then stepped down from the platform and went to the Lady, disappearing from my sight.

'Aye, she'll be trouble, that one,' Benesek said, then shouted to Geldrin to fetch him another jug of wine, while Pelleas was looking at me with sympathetic eyes.

'Go on, then,' he said. 'You don't want to stand here listening to us all night.'

The smell of roast meat and of fish and chive broth was in the room now. We would be eating soon. If I threaded my way to Guinevere, we might sit and eat together as we so often did on the rocks overlooking the Western Sea, sharing an apple or some bread and cheese we had saved from breakfast. But Melwas and the others were already crowding round her, so that I knew I would run their gauntlet of jibes. Bad enough that Guinevere should witness my humiliation, but I would answer insults with fists and my inevitable beating would prove more embarrassing still.

Pelleas and Benesek were discussing Uther's gift and when would be the right time to slaughter and salt the old bull, that would be eating grain better saved for the other animals were it not given to the butcher's knife. So I went, squeezing between the men and women of Karrek and past Uther's big men, who stank of their damp woollen cloaks, and then I wriggled between Baralis and Edern, who were so deep in talk of tin prices that they paid me no mind. But then I saw dirty bare feet in the floor rushes and above those feet black trews, and I looked up into a brown-skinned face that made me start.

'Hello, boy,' said Merlin.

It was a most striking face. Fierce. Intelligent. Cruel.

'Lord,' I said, wondering if there was some particular way to address a druid. I had never met one before. There were only a handful of druids left in all of Britain and Ireland, though there had once been many. Long ago, the druids kept the secrets of the Dark Isles. They communed with the gods, interpreted dreams, read the future and advised kings. But when the Romans came to these lands they strove to stamp out the order by trapping and killing the last surviving druids in a great slaughter on the island of Mona. That slaughter had been done four hundred years since, and yet here I was standing before the druid who men said whispered into the ear of the High King himself.

'Do you miss your home, boy?' Merlin asked. His thick dark brows angled back from his eyes like eagles' wings and his sunken cheeks were pools of shadow in the flame-lit room. His beard, which had been wisped and frayed by the sea wind before, was oiled and jutted from his chin like a spear blade now.

'Do you cry for your mother and poor Hector? Do you whine into your pillow while Pelleas snores like a hog?'

'No,' I said, wondering how he knew that Pelleas snored loud enough to make the thatch quiver above our heads. I did miss my home of course. I missed the hawks and falcons and Malo my father's proud black stallion, but I was not going to give this stranger the satisfaction.

'Then do you pine for the power that might have been yours one day, had your family not been murdered?'

A stranger he might be, yet there was something familiar about his eyes. 'You know my brother's name?' I said. I had not liked hearing him speak it.

'Of course,' he said. 'I knew your mother and father. Queen Elaine was mean-spirited and greedy, while Ban was a drunkard and a cuckold.' One of those eagle-wing eyebrows stretched itself. 'We do not choose our parents, boy.'

It was as if he had struck me. Hard. Then seeing anger in me he raised a placating hand, the palm of which was etched with a triskele, the three conjoined spirals drawn in green ink. 'None of all that is your fault, boy,' he said, 'before you fly at me like some savage hawk.' His eyes flashed. 'That is to say a hawk that can fly.'

Another insult? On top of the last? And what did he know of my sparhawk? Why this man was goading me, or how he knew the things he did, I could not say, but I did know that the best thing would be to walk away from him.

'Wait, boy,' he said before I had taken a step.

I waited. Wondering if my legs would obey me if I did try to walk away. There was something about this man, something familiar and yet something which sent a chill up my arms and to the back of my neck, and I wondered if he were working some spell on me right there and then, some magic which bound me to that spot on the keep's rush-strewn floor when I so wanted to be anywhere else.

'You are the boy who saved Guinevere, aren't you?' he said.

I neither nodded nor spoke, just looked into his dark eyes. Outside, the rain was flaying the night. Now and then a keening gust found its way in through the old stonework, flaring the hearth flames and spitting rain into the keep.

'You swam out to the wreck and saved her. Pulled her from the cold depths.' His eyes narrowed. 'Did you not, boy? Am I mistaken?' He pointed a long finger towards Melwas who, to my distress, was talking to Guinevere. 'Was it in fact that ruddy-faced boy who saved her? He has a hero's looks, don't you think?'

'I saved her,' I said.

He nodded. 'I thought so. Mind you, your father never lacked courage. Just sense.' Edern's woman Avenie was playing the lyre now, and more skilfully even than Guinevere had, though no one seemed to be paying attention to the music. The Lady's servants were passing through the room handing out bowls of steaming broth, starting with Uther's men, whilst other folk sat down amongst the rushes ready to eat.

A thin servant offered Merlin a bowl of fragrant-smelling broth and a spoon but he waved the woman away, pulling me into the dark alcove off to the side of the dais. His Saxon slave, Oswine, appeared from nowhere, snatched the unwanted bowl and spoon and began slurping at the fish broth like a starving man.

'But you don't understand what you did that day, boy,' Merlin hissed at me, giving a flash of white teeth. He was not an old man, nor was he young, yet he still had all his teeth so far as I could see. 'For when you pulled the girl up from the depths you also prised her from Manannán's clutches.' Behind us a gust of wind fanned the hearth flames which I saw flash bright in Merlin's eyes. 'You cheated the sea god of the rich haul which he had promised to Arawn. He is angry, boy.'

A spit of rain hit my face, having gusted through a gap high up in the keep's west wall, and I shuddered because I knew that Manannán mac Lir also had some power of the weather and could raise a storm if he so wished. Perhaps it was the god who rocked the *Dobhran* at her mooring now and hurled water against Karrek to shatter in foaming spray. Merlin looked past me and I turned to see that his eyes were fastened to Guinevere again. 'The lord of the underworld was meant to have that girl,' he said, then plucked something invisible from the smoky air, 'but you took her from him.'

'I could not let her drown,' I said. My blood ran cold.

'Ah, but that is precisely what you could have done, boy,' the druid said, swinging his glare back to me. 'But you did not. And so now your soul is in danger. Guinevere's too,' he added, his eyes not leaving mine this time. 'Even now, Manannán and Arawn conspire against you, boy. The lord of the dead would have your soul for his plaything and heap untold torments upon you for your theft of what was rightfully his.'

I was dazed and could find no words. I had no answers to any of this. Here was a druid, a man wise in lore and the magic arts, a man who advised the Pendragon of Britain no less, telling me that I had offended the gods by saving Guinevere. That those gods had wanted Guinevere dead and now wanted me dead too.

I tore my eyes from Merlin's and twisted to look for the Lady or for Pelleas, needing an ally. Needing someone who could tell me that the druid was wrong. I saw Oswine licking the last drops from his bowl, oblivious to any of the things his master was telling me. I looked for Guinevere but she was obscured from my sight by Melwas and the other boys, who were still standing because they had not been served their food yet.

'So it is just as well that I can help you, Lancelot,' Merlin said. 'You don't mind if I call you Lancelot? You haven't taken a different name to escape the sad fate which befell your kin?'

I shook my head. I nodded. My tongue was stuck to the roof of my mouth and my gums were dry as dust. I wondered if Manannán or Arawn had broken my sparhawk's wing to spite me. No. Gods have more important things to do than torment hawks.

'I can intercede on your behalf, Lancelot,' Merlin said, 'and perhaps I can convince the gods that they would be better served by letting you live.'

'Thank you, lord,' I said.

'Thought I told you to fetch me a jug of mead,' said a voice and I looked round just as Pelleas cuffed me around the ears. The warrior shook his head at Merlin. 'Lives inside his own damned head does this one,' he told the druid. 'Needs telling three times to do one thing.'

Merlin smiled despite the interruption. 'Then you are not hard enough on him, Pelleas,' he said. 'Some boys must be beaten. Beat the foolishness out to make room for knowledge. Or sword craft, if you must,' he admitted. He raised an eyebrow at me. 'One doesn't need brains to be a warrior, Lancelot, but there is still a modicum of learn-ing involved.'

'We can't all speak with gods and kings, Merlin,' Pelleas said, grab-bing my shoulder and steering me away from the druid.

'Be glad of it, Pelleas,' Merlin said, gesturing me away with a flutter of long fingers. 'The knowledge I glean is more of a burden than you could know.'

'You're better off keeping your distance from that one,' Pelleas growled as we picked our way amongst the guests, who were sitting on the floor eating while Avenie plucked the lyre and the hearth wood cracked and popped and laughter and conversation filled the keep in defiance of the wind's howl in the night beyond those old walls.

'Am I to stay away from everyone, Pelleas?' I asked. He knew I was referring to Guinevere.

A deep rumble came from his throat. 'I think I preferred it when the only friend you had was that hateful bird,' he said, taking a jug of mead from the table and filling his cup to make good the pretence in case Merlin was watching. 'You can't trust a druid,' he said. 'What did he want?'

'He says the gods are angry with me because I did not let Guinev-ere drown,' I said, still feeling the cold of the druid's words in my bones.

Pelleas pulled his head back and looked confused. 'Which gods?' he asked.

'Manannán mac Lir and Arawn,' I said, then explained how the sea god had promised the lord of the underworld every soul on Lord Leodegan's ship and thus I had as good as stolen Guinevere from him.

Pelleas considered this for a long moment, drinking deeply to water his thoughts. 'I cannot pretend to know the will of the gods, or the mind of a druid,' he said, shaking his head, 'but I do know that what you did, swimming out there into the maw of a storm, was brave. As brave a thing as a man can do, and that includes standing toe to toe with men who want to kill you in the shieldwall.' He picked up an empty cup, half filled it with mead and gave it to me. 'And I know that the gods love courage.' He shook his shaven head again. 'Never heard of a man being punished by the gods for having courage.' I knew that Pelleas was no expert on such matters, and yet his words comforted me.

'Besides which,' he said, smiling, 'you're just a young'un. You've not lived long enough or done enough in your life to get on the wrong side of gods.' He banged his cup against mine and some of his mead was flung over the lip of his cup to splash on my bare feet. 'You might one day, of course, but we'll worry about that then. Bear the druid no mind, lad. Men like him will stick their heads into a cauldron and then fret when they find a spot of rust at the bottom.' He beckoned a servant over who was carrying two plates of roasted meat. 'Let's eat,' he said.

And so we ate.

9

Journeying

T HE MEAD AND THE WINE flowed that night, and by the time the festivities were over, there were plenty of folk snoring on cloaks and furs amongst the floor rushes, passed out or unwilling to walk all the way back down the Mount in the rain to their homes on the shore. A knot of King Uther's men were awake still, huddled round the hearth, drinking and talking in low voices. Melwas and Agga, Peran and Jago were awake too, giggling and farting and sharing a jug of wine which I guessed they had stashed earlier in the evening. And if Pelleas or any of the other Karrek warriors knew the boys were getting drunk on the Lady's wine, they did nothing about it. Edern and the others would make them pay during training next day, I thought.

Everywhere else, men and women slept where they had found space and now snored and grunted, moaned and dreamed, their bellies full and their heads spinning with drink. Benesek and Madern were slumped asleep against the curved wall on my right, Benesek still holding his horn cup. Caelan, the Lady's deerhound, lay as near to the hearth as she could get, her legs twitching as she dreamt of chasing a hare. I must have slept a little too, for the last thing I remembered was telling Pelleas that I would rescue Guinevere from Melwas, as she must be tired of his boorish conversation. Now, most of the lamps had burnt out so that the chamber was gloomy and smoky, those flames that yet flickered guttering feebly in the thin gusts which ghosted through the place. And it was cold even with all those bodies crammed in there, because the stone walls did not hold the heat as well as mud, wattle and thatch, and I wondered how the Romans who built the keep so long ago did not freeze to death in the winter.

I did not wonder it for long, however, for my stomach was churning and my vision swam and I feared I might see that roast venison again. The mead was far stronger than the ale we boys were usually given, I realized, pushing myself upright against the wall, trying not to disturb Edern and Avenie beside me. Snoring louder than Edern, Avenie was wrapped up in the warrior's brawny arms, the two of them looking as peaceful as the dead. Then I almost tripped over something else and saw, by the shifting copper glow of the hearth flames, another sleeping, fur-shrouded figure at my feet. Only when stepping over this dormant soul did I see the shock of yellow, straw-like hair sticking out from the pelt, which told me it was Oswine, Merlin's slave. There was an empty wine jug beside him and it struck me that whatever had befallen the Saxon for him to be with Merlin rather than his own people, life could not be that bad with a master who allowed him to eat and drink like any other guest in the Lady's keep.

Where was Pelleas? Gone outside to relieve himself, I guessed, thinking I would go outside too, so as not to puke in the Lady's keep in front of the other boys. They would enjoy seeing that and I would suffer long after my head cleared.

'Ah, Lancelot.' I looked to the door and saw Merlin standing there, his gaunt face all bone and shadow by the failing light of a nearby fish-oil lamp. 'Have you seen that waste of good skin Saxon?' he asked, stepping amongst the sleeping bodies, his head twitching this way and that like a crow scouring the wheat stubble for grain. With the butt of his staff he prodded a man, one of the *Dobhran*'s crew, who jerked and half spat a curse, swallowing the rest of it when he realized who had woken him. He mumbled some apology but Merlin ignored him, moving on.

'He's here, lord,' I said.

'Enough with the lord, boy,' he said, changing direction and stretching his leg over Edern and Avenie. 'Look at him, the lazy toad.' He glared down at Oswine who was sound asleep. 'I knew I should have bought that pretty young thing with the limp. I daresay she would have been twice as useful as this lump of Saxon turd.' With that he jabbed the staff down hard onto the fur and Oswine groaned awake.

Merlin bent down and sniffed the young man, then hit him again.

'You're drunk, you piss-reeking son of a Saxon sow.' This time the druid brought the staff down onto the empty wine jug which shattered into a dozen shards.

'I was thirsty, master,' Oswine said, sitting up and rubbing bleary eyes. 'The broth was salty.'

'And where was my broth? Next I'll find you crawling into my ear to steal the very thoughts from my head, you greedy maggot.'

Those of Uther's men who had looked over turned back to the fire, perhaps well used to Merlin and his temper. But Mclwas, Agga and the other boys were watching, half in awe of the druid and half in surprise that he had addressed me by name when he entered the hall.

'Get up, maggot,' Merlin hissed at Oswine, at last lowering his voice because several fur-wrapped bundles around us were stirring now.

Oswine dutifully obeyed, though when he was up he stumbled and fell upon Edern and Avenie, who woke with a start, the warrior grabbing Oswine and throwing him off as he might cast aside a bolster, threatening to pull the Saxon's guts out of his backside and throw them to the fish if he came near him or his woman again.

Oswine slurred his apology and climbed once more to his feet, but suddenly threw both hands up to clamp them over his mouth and Merlin and I both stepped back, thinking he was going to spew his stomach's contents across the rushes.

'Outside with you, you Saxon devil. Quickly now,' Merlin said, sweeping his staff towards the door, and off Oswine stumbled, leaving a wake of curses and insults hanging in the smoke from those he disturbed as he passed. 'And that is why we must rid Britain of the Saxon,' Merlin said, swinging his staff, 'why King Uther must sweep them back into the sea.' He put a hand on my shoulder and squeezed hard enough to hurt. 'Lancelot, you must take his place. Just until sunrise,' he said, bending to put his face close to mine. 'You must, do you hear?' I could smell the herb-scented oil which he had used to tame his moustaches and beard. His dark eyes glistened like wet pitch. 'Will you help me?' he asked, then gestured with his beard towards the chamber door. 'I cannot trust that worthless Saxon with the simplest task.'

All I could think of was Pelleas warning me to stay away from Merlin.

'I don't—'

'Think before you flap your tongue, boy,' the druid hissed. 'Remember what I told you, Lancelot,' he said, looking at me from beneath his bushy eyebrows. 'I am the one who can smooth things over between you and the gods, whom you have offended.' He had whispered this, as though him being my ally in this cause should be a very great secret. 'You would be wise to prove yourself useful, boy,' he said.

I thought of Guinevere and what Merlin had told me about how she was supposed to have drowned with her maid and her father's warriors and all those aboard that ill-fated ship. I remembered the look in her eyes as she had slipped beneath the wind-shredded surface of the sea.

'What would you have me do?' I asked.

And Merlin grinned.

In the event I felt disappointed, cheated even by Merlin for making me agree to help with such a dull task. And yet part of me was thankful that it was at least easy enough, if made miserable by the rain. He had told me to go down to his hut on the shore and fetch his belongings, which Oswine had stored earlier that evening.

'Don't go snooping,' the druid warned me, 'do not even look inside the sack. Just bring it to me. And be quick,' he said.

When I found the bulging sack, having rummaged around in the hut's dark interior, I slung it over my shoulder as I had seen Oswine do, and lugged it all the way back up the Mount, trudging through the muddy little streams that coursed down the paths. Something sharp inside that sack dug into my back no matter how I shifted its position. My feet were cold and for the first time I wondered if my old shoes would still fit me, for I had not worn them since coming to the Mount, but at least the fresh air and the rain cleared my head, so that I no longer thought I would vomit.

I found Merlin waiting in the lean-to against the keep's wall where the men's weapons lay on a table beneath oiled skins. He snatched the sack from me and pulled out what I first took to be a lustrous black pelt, but then realized was not fur but feathers. Raven or crows' feathers woven into a cloak. Hundreds upon hundreds of them. Iridescent in the white moonlight spilling through a sudden rent in the fast-moving clouds. For just a heartbeat that otherworldly cloak shone blue and purple and green, but a cloud cast the night into darkness again and the feathers were black. Black as soot from Gofannon the smith-god's forge. Black as Malo, my father's stallion.

I asked Merlin what it was for. He had thrown the feathered cloak around his shoulders and I could see the weight in it as he shrugged himself deeper into the thing. It fell almost to the ground.

'It is for the journey, boy,' he said, fastening the cloak over his chest with a silver ring brooch which glowed dully in the dark. The ring was a snake chasing its own tail, its baleful little eye a piece of red enamel no bigger than a louse.

'Where are you going?' I asked. The rain seethed and it would soon be the deepest part of the night, and I wondered where Merlin was bound at such a time and in such a cloak.

He bent and thrust his hand into the sack and pulled out a necklace made of bird skulls, all shapes and sizes, some dark with age and ancient looking, others still pale. All with large empty eye sockets and curving beaks. He held this strange necklace up towards the veiled moon and muttered in a language I did not understand, then with great reverence he put it over his head, the skulls rattling softly on their leather cord. The next object that he pulled out was very delicate, judging by the care with which he removed it from a skin pouch, though when I saw it I was struck with revulsion. It appeared to be another necklace, only this one looked too small to fit over the druid's head, and I had never imagined such a thing. It was made of birds' feet: gnarled and clawed, some complete with scaly flesh and others worn to the bone and all somehow threaded together to make a grim chain. Merlin lifted it to the moon, made the same utterances as before, then placed it upon his head so that it made a grisly wreath which for some reason made me think of the circlet of red campion which Wenna had woven for the Lady's hair on the day of the race. I was not cold standing there in my thick cloak, the mead glow still warm in my belly, and yet I shivered in my skin to see the druid like that. He no longer looked like a man, but like some half-bird, half-god creature, his eyes seeming to catch fire now as he looked at me with the rain hammering on the lean-to and gushing over the edge in streams.

'Bring it with you,' he said, gesturing at the sack on the ground between us and taking up his staff from where it leant against the shelter's upright.

I could not help but peer inside the sack as I lifted it and saw that there were still things in there, though most were wrapped in leather or cloth. But I did spot what had been digging into my back as I had carried the sack up the Mount. A pair of cream-coloured antlers gleamed even in the dark and I could only wonder why the druid needed those.

'When you have pulled your nose out of things which are none of your business, follow me,' Merlin said, stepping back into the rain. I hurried after him.

Into the keep, the smoke stinging my eyes after the cold night air. Up the worn stone steps which I had last climbed after winning the island foot race. Only this time I was even more nervous than I had been then, because I knew I had somehow been drawn into things I neither understood nor thought I should understand. And yet the dread gnawing at me as I followed this bird creature up the winding passage was as nothing compared with the horror that filled me when, Merlin having rapped on the door with his staff, we entered the Lady's chamber.

Smoke drawn by the open door engulfed me and I tried to swallow the cough which snagged in my throat, but spluttered and choked instead, swiping at the sage- and cedar-scented fog as I peered into the room. It was dark. As dark as the night outside, being lit only by three small pottery lamps which must have been filled with expensive olive oil, for they did not give off the fish stink like the lamps in the main chamber downstairs. By this frail light I saw the girls of Karrek, eight of them sitting cross-legged on pelts spread across the floor boards, their hands clutched in their laps and the whites of their eyes glowing in the dark.

Guinevere was there but she, like the others, was looking at Merlin, and then Merlin's slave Oswine loomed in front of me and his eyes were hard and cold and he did not look befuddled by drink now as he snatched the sack out of my hand and walked off with it.

'Lancelot, what are you doing here?' It was the Lady. She was standing opposite us though I had not seen her until now.

'I brought the boy,' Merlin answered before I could summon a reply. I just stood there, my long hair soaked through and water dripping from my cloak's hem onto the floor with a rhythmic tap.

The Lady did not look happy about it but she said nothing, and perhaps she too was awed by the druid in his coat of crow and raven feathers, his necklace of beaked, empty-eyed skulls and his wreath of rotten bird's feet. He was not a big man and yet he seemed so in that smoke-hazed dark, and the girls sitting in a tight knot on the floor instinctively drew together, seeking safety within the group.

'Shut the door,' Merlin told me and so I did, and the moan of those old iron hinges might as well have been my own lament, for at that moment I would have rather been outside in the pouring rain and up to my ankles in mud than in that room with unseen magic eddying around me.

'Is she ready?' Merlin asked the Lady.

The Lady nodded.

'Did she drink it all?' the druid asked and again the Lady nodded.

'Keep her safe, Merlin,' she warned him, but the druid dismissed her concerns with a flutter of fingers and walked over to the girls, planting the butt of his staff on the floor with a thud. He stood perfectly still, looking down at them, his feather-cloaked back to me, and I did not know what I was expected to do and so edged backwards until I felt the stone wall of the lady's chamber through the damp wool of my cloak and tunic.

'Stand, Guinevere,' Merlin said. 'I have come to see if you really do have the gift.'

Guinevere looked to the Lady, who nodded that she should do what the druid asked, and so Guinevere stood and the other girls shuffled apart to let her through. Merlin nodded over to Oswine, who had taken a skin drum from Merlin's sack and now sat with his back against the Lady's bed with the drum held vertically on his thigh. In his right hand he gripped some animal's leg bone, perhaps from a fox or small dog. And with that bone Oswine began to beat the drum.

Merlin pulled the pin from his snake brooch and swung the cloak of feathers off his shoulders while kicking aside the floor skins. He bent and placed his gnarled ash staff on the floor, then took Guinevere's hand and pulled her towards him, holding her against his chest as he threw the cloak of feathers around them both.

The room was smoky and dark and I was two spear-lengths from Guinevere and yet I thought I saw that same look in her eyes that I had seen on the day of the shipwreck, when she must have felt Arawn's claws in her, dragging her down, the god trying to claim her for the underworld. But if I saw it at all it was gone one breath later as she and Merlin closed their eyes.

The drum beat was fast and even, a relentless rhythm that Oswine beat out with that leg-bone tipper, so that I knew that the Saxon was not drunk at all now and wondered if Merlin had used some magic to cure him of the effects of the mead. Either that or Oswine had only been pretending to be out of his tree earlier, which begged the question, why?

Wrapped in black feathers and in the ceaseless beat of the hide drum, Merlin and Guinevere swayed now, like a ship's mast in a wind-driven sea. The Lady took a bundle of smouldering herbs from a brass dish and went about the room with it, sweeping it this way and that before her. When she came to me she held the tightly bound herbs in front of my face so that the smoke thickened and curled towards me and I found myself breathing deeply of that white smoke as I had seen the girls do. After a while the smoke thinned slightly and curled upwards and the Lady said nothing but moved on, bending to do the same to Oswine, though he seemed not to even see her, so lost was he in the beating of his drum.

Smoke from a hearth fire will usually rise into the thatch, but this herb smoke quested around the Lady's chamber in wispy white tendrils, as though seeking something, and I wondered if this was magic too. Some spell of Merlin's or the Lady's. Or even if that smoke was the spirit of some god moving amongst us, called to this place by a druid who men said carried within him the lost knowledge of Britain. And yet when I looked at that feather-shrouded man what I felt more than awe, more than fear or reverence, was hatred. I did not know what he was doing with Guinevere under that druid cloak but I knew nothing good could come of it. I even hoped that some war band of far-venturing Saxons would come ashore that very moment, and that the clash of steel would break this spell. I wished that Oswine would be overcome with drunkenness again and spew his guts over that drum and end its relentless beating. I hoped that Guinevere would resist whatever enchantment the druid wove.

But no enemies attacked Karrek. And Oswine did not puke but kept drumming. And Guinevere journeyed.

I fly above wood and meadow, east towards the far-off pale glow which makes a dark and ominous horizon of hill and forest, a black realm where gods could roam unseen by men.

East towards the light which rises like a slow but inexorable tide, seeping into the night. Too little moonlight to see by. No snow on the ground to brighten the world, and so I fly on towards the dawn.

The hoot of an owl follows in my wake. A vixen's screech cuts blade-like through the breeze. Some unseen creature snaps a twig in the oak wood below me but I fly on, beating into the current, the stroke of each downbeat moving my wing tips forward and downward. I feel I am an old raven, full of knowledge and craft and sorrow too, for my lost soul mate, whose absence is a dull ache in my beating breast.

Two bats flit away, tumbling down to a hedgerow. There are no other creatures on the wing and I fly on, thinking that she will not come. That she cannot. I could not journey at her age. Or, perhaps I could. It was long ago and thought is fogged now by the needs of the bird.

Above me, the cloud rips itself apart and in the sudden flooding moonlight I see something on the hillside below. I fly down and land beside the skeletal remains of a sheep carcass. I flap and sidle and hop closer, my head twitching this way and that, looking for danger in the silver glow, then peck between two gleaming ribs for a scrap of tough flesh. But there is nothing here for me and I voice my irritation then crouch low and spring into the air, beating my black wings, climbing back into the night sky.

Then some ancient instinct strikes and I swerve and beat hard. I roll with the breeze as a black shape bursts up at me, its wings brushing mine as I veer away, its voice a rasping 'karh-karh-karh'. Up I climb, my old heart thumping, and this crow climbs with me, young and wild and unafraid.

It is she. I know it. Up and up we climb, jostling in the cold night, she cawing with the thrill of it as we circle, owning the sky. Black feathers against the black night, while our brothers and sisters huddle in their cosy roosts. We cavort, unburdened of the laws of men. Unbound and untamed.

Free as gods.

They were no longer swaying with the beat of the drum. The feather cloak had fallen away and now lay on the floor beside them, and Merlin clutched Guinevere by her shoulders, his hands like claws digging into her flesh. The druid's eyes were closed but Guinevere's were half open, though they were rolled up into her head so that only the whites showed, and I shuddered to see this because I knew that wherever Guinevere was, she was no longer here in the Lady's chamber with me. Her mouth was opening and closing, yet she made no sound, and Oswine kept beating his drum, and the girls sitting on the floor stared with wonder and horror and perhaps even jealousy.

Behind me, the door creaked open and I turned to see Pelleas come quietly into the room, his shaven head glistening with rain and beads of water shining in his beard. He moved up to my shoulder and leant down so that his wine-sour breath was hot against my cheek. 'Been looking high and low for you,' he hissed. 'What are you doing up here?' He looked up at Merlin and Guinevere and touched the iron of his belt buckle for protection against whatever magic was taking place in that gloomy, smoke-filled chamber. 'Thought I told you to stay away,' he growled. He did not say whether he meant from Merlin or Guinevere but I supposed in that moment it amounted to the same thing.

Now it was the Lady's turn to hiss at Pelleas, who frowned and straightened, his eyes, like mine, fastening on the druid and the girl whose flesh-and-blood-made bodies were before us though their souls might be soaring with the gods for all I knew.

I realized that this was what Merlin had meant when he said he was going on a journey. Wherever he was roaming now, it seemed that Guinevere was his travelling companion, and that soured my guts.

The Lady muttered something under her breath and I looked over at her, wondering what part, if any, she played in the strange sorcery. Her eyes were not on Merlin but on Guinevere and only Guinevere, and there was something in the Lady's face that had my heart racing, pounding almost in time with Oswine's drum. She was afraid for Guinevere. She was afraid and that meant that wherever Merlin had taken Guinevere, it was not a safe place – for a druid perhaps, but not for a girl who was not yet twelve years old.

I wanted to call out, to tell Merlin to stop. And if he would not, to beg the Lady to beckon them back from wherever they wandered. I looked round at Pelleas, who must have read my thoughts for his eyes hardened and he gave a slight shake of his head. I swung my gaze back just as Guinevere threw back her head and her bare throat gleamed white and her eyes shone white and her whole body was shaking now, her flat chest heaving, her hands flapping at her sides like fish pulled into the bilge. There were bubbles and spume on her red lips and there were tears on her cheeks, glistening in the lamplight.

I could not bear it any longer.

'No,' Pelleas growled, his big hand fastening on my shoulder, and just then there came a roaring, hissing, clacking din, which had us looking at the walls and the roof above us. The girls fingered hare's foot charms, knot amulets or sprigs of dried hawthorn, seeking the protection of these talismans against whatever indignant spirits whirled in the night beyond those stone walls. To me it sounded as if some angry god was hurling handfuls of stones against the Lady's keep, but neither Merlin nor Guinevere seemed to notice the commotion, so bound up were they in their spell.

'It'll be over soon,' Pelleas gnarred under his breath.

But I wanted it to be over now. My blood, which had earlier run cold in my veins, now gushed hot. It flooded my limbs, demanding movement, keening for action even as Pelleas's strong arm held me to the spot.

Guinevere made a whimpering, moaning sound and her legs almost buckled but Merlin's hands still gripped her shoulders and I saw the strain in his arms as he held her upright. And I could watch no more.

I broke free of Pelleas and threw myself at Merlin, my shoulder striking his side, knocking the breath from his body and sending him staggering so that he hit the wall and crumpled to the floor.

'No!' the Lady screeched, stepping towards the druid, but then she stopped, her hands over her own red lips and her eyes blazing.

I went to take hold of Guinevere but Pelleas took hold of me instead and this time there would be no escape.

'You damned fool,' the warrior growled into my ear. His shield arm was around my neck, clamped so tightly that I could barely breathe and I thought he meant to strangle the life out of me.

Released from the spell, Guinevere looked this way and that, her hands clenched at her sides, knuckles glowing white. She seemed not to know where she was or who we were, and I tried to call out to her, to tell her that she was safe, but I could get no words past Pelleas's chokehold.

'What have you done, Lancelot?' the Lady said. She took Guinevere's hands in her own and whispered to her, and Guinevere nodded, coming back to herself. Oswine was helping Merlin to his feet.

Satisfied that Guinevere was safe, the Lady turned her attentions to the druid, who was bent over, one hand pressed flat against the Roman stonework as he caught his breath and gathered his wits.

'Don't you know how dangerous it is to interrupt such a journey?' the Lady asked me, staring at Merlin. 'A soul may become disembodied. It may remain trapped in the other world,' she said, her eyes round with the horror of that thought.

'Want me to beat some manners into the lad?' Pelleas asked her, spinning me round to face him and raising his right hand to strike. I sucked smoke-thickened air into my lungs and braced for the blow.

'Hold!' Merlin said, shrugging Oswine off and stooping to pick up his staff, which lay abandoned on the rushes. 'Do not touch him, Pelleas,' the druid warned, coming to stand before me. His face was hard with shadow and flame-glow. His head twitched now and then and it seemed that some part of him was still wherever it was that his soul had wandered before I knocked him down. 'How is the girl?' Merlin asked over his shoulder.

'Returned,' the Lady said. 'She is returned.'

His eyes glowing like hot embers, Merlin lifted his staff and pointed its gnarly end towards me. 'You would dare to attack a druid, boy?' he asked, pressing the staff against my chest. I flinched at its touch, feeling the power within it. 'I could make your young heart wither in your chest like an old apple,' he said. 'I could fill your pure lungs with writhing maggots.' His head twitched again. 'I could make your soul burst into flame. I could promise you eternal pain or make it your fate to never find your kin in the afterlife. To wander lost and tormented unto wild madness.'

With that the druid pressed the staff hard against my breast bone, then raised it until the warm wood rested beneath my chin. He lifted my head and narrowed his eyes. 'I could do any of this, boy, and yet you dare to attack me?' He half turned, swinging the staff to point it at Guinevere, who stood there, shoulders slumped, her face drawn and ashen. 'You would risk your soul for her?'

I looked into Guinevere's eyes but she seemed not to see me, and I knew that the journey, the soul flight she had just undertaken with Merlin, had taken a dreadful toll on her.

'Well, boy?' Merlin spat.

'Best answer him, Lancelot,' Pelleas said in a low voice.

I straightened. Oswine, standing behind Merlin now, stared at me with his light blue eyes and gave an almost imperceptible shake of his fair head.

'Yes,' I told Merlin. 'I would.'

There was a collective gasp from the girls, who had sat watching the whole episode in silence and must have thought they were about to witness a druid's terrible revenge.

'I'll give him a thrashing,' Pelleas said, and I knew he hoped that

Merlin and the Lady would agree to that, thus the worst I would suffer would be bruises and wounded pride, rather than whatever soul's torment Merlin would conjure for me.

But Merlin's face changed then. One heartbeat he had seethed with ire and threat and malevolence. The next he looked as light and content and cheerful as a man at his daughter's wedding feast.

'There is no need for that, Pelleas,' he said, holding my eye for a long moment before turning back to the Lady. 'No need. The boy is as the boy should be.'

I did not know what Merlin meant by that. I just stood there, my body still tensed in readiness for pain.

The Lady was watching the druid with suspicious eyes. 'You do not want him punished?' she said.

'Punished?' Merlin said. 'And what would that achieve?' He looked back to me and raised a finger in the air, a thick golden ring on it burnished by the lamplight. 'I want him trained,' he said. 'Like the others. I want him to learn every sword stroke, every spear thrust. I want him worked each and every day until he can barely walk back to his bed. Pelleas, you will take this boy as a smith takes good iron and you will hammer and forge and polish and hone him, do you hear? You will make him rouse the envy of Belatucadrus himself.' Merlin locked eyes with me. 'Or even the Roman god, Mars,' he said almost begrudgingly, 'for one cannot deny that for all their avarice and vainglory the Romans were so very good at war.' He pointed that ringed finger at Pelleas. 'You will hone him, Pelleas. For as long as it takes. Until he is ready.'

Pelleas glowered. 'Ready for what?' he asked.

'To do what must be done, of course,' Merlin said, and with that it was clear that the druid was finished with me, for he waved me away with an ink-etched hand and turned to Guinevere. 'So, young Guinevere. I think we know now why your father sent you here.'

I could not guess what was in Guinevere's mind then. Her eyes were cast down at the floor rushes and I wondered if she felt ashamed, for it seemed her father had sent her here because of the talent which she had just demonstrated. For her own good, was how the Lady had put it. Some could not see her promise, she had told me. Well, Merlin could see it. He was twisting the end of his dark, oiled beard between finger and thumb as he considered the girl in front of him.

'You have done that before, haven't you?' he asked. 'No lies, girl. Your father and his Christian priests are not here now. Do not be afraid, Guinevere.'

Guinevere shivered and her teeth worried at her bottom lip. Even with her face painted she looked no more than her eleven summers then, and the anger which had seethed in me earlier, at the way Uther's men looked at Guinevere as she had played the harp, welled in my chest again.

'No one could have such control as you did,' Merlin told her. 'Not on their first journeying. Nor their second or third.' He removed the garland of bird's feet from his head and held it out to Oswine, who stepped up and took hold of it as one might handle a poisonous snake or a razor-sharp knife.

'Have you done it before, girl?' Merlin asked again, snapping the words with growing impatience.

Guinevere glanced up at me and our eyes met, just for a moment, then she looked at Merlin and nodded.

The druid dipped his head at the confirmation of his suspicions, then lifted an eyebrow at the Lady. 'It would seem you might raise a decent crop for once, Lady,' he said with a wry smile. 'After years of famine and blight, at last some young people who may be of use.' He shrugged at Pelleas. 'Then again, a youth's promise is like the froth on water, hey Pelleas?' Pelleas did not reply and Merlin turned back to Guinevere. 'We shall see, girl,' he said. 'We shall see.'

'This is why you came to the Mount?' the Lady said with a knowing look. 'To test our young men? To test my girls? What have you seen, Merlin?'

'Too much, Lady. I have seen too much, as well you know.' Merlin showed the Lady a palm as he handed the bird-skull necklace to Oswine. 'But are we not old friends, Nimue?' He smiled and his dark face was at once both handsome and wicked-looking. 'I heard that Lord Leodegan was sending another ship,' he gave a sour grin, 'one with a better captain than the last ship, I hoped,' he said, 'and it seemed a good opportunity to pay you all a visit. Balor curse me if I lie.'

The Lady pressed her red lips into a fine line as she considered this. 'We will talk tomorrow,' she said, then turned to her girls and clapped her hands. 'To bed now. In the morning, Guinevere will tell us of her journey, but now we will sleep.' She clapped her hands again. 'Hurry, all of you. To bed.'

As they filed out, Erwana stared at me with her pretty eyes and tall Jenifry whispered something to Senara which made her giggle.

'I trust you will be comfortable in your lodgings, Merlin,' the Lady said, herding the girls, who were chattering with excitement now that the magic and its grave mystery had dissipated like the smoke from the Lady's smouldering sage.

The druid looked at me and sighed. 'You see how I am treated, boy?' he said. 'Sent out into the rain like a dog.' He looked up at the smoke-hung beams. The rain still beat on the thatch; a soft hiss now, not the god's fury of before. 'There was a time I was welcome under this roof. But the past is the past. Tell me, Lancelot,' he said, his eyes glinting, 'whatever happened to your fox? Flame, wasn't it?'

My mouth fell open. How could Merlin know about Flame? But then, he was a druid and his powers were beyond my understanding. Or perhaps the Lady had told him about Flame, for she had met the fox when I had chased him into her tent. So long ago now, it seemed.

'I last saw him in Armorica,' I said. 'But never knew when he would come. He was not tame.'

Merlin laughed at that. 'No,' he said, 'many things but never tame.'

'Pelleas will escort you back down the Mount,' the Lady said, far less impressed than I with Merlin and his insights.

'Ah, to be as free as a fox and come and go as one pleases,' the druid said to me, then turned to his slave. 'Well then, Oswine, into the cold and rain with us. We do not linger where we are not wanted.'

Pelleas rolled his eyes at the Lady and I watched Guinevere, hoping she would look at me before she left the room, but she did not, and a heartbeat later she was gone.

'You can carry it back down to my master's dwelling, boy,' Oswine said in his harsh accent, gesturing to the sack on the floor into which he had placed Merlin's folded feathered cloak along with his master's other accoutrements.

'You can carry it yourself, Saxon,' I said, certain that Oswine had feigned being out of his skull on mead earlier. He had tricked me and I disliked him for it.

'You heard him, Saxon,' Pelleas said, nodding at the sack.

Oswine grinned at me and shrugged, then bent, grabbed hold of the sack and slung it over his shoulder. Thus we four set off into the windswept night, down to the sea which churned white on the rocks, the breaking water glowing in the dark.

Pelleas was snoring like a hog when I eased myself out of bed and flung my cloak around my shoulders. I fumbled my way through the dark hut towards the door, barely helped by the feeble flames losing their fight for life in the hearth. Pelleas was too deep in sleep to know that the fire needed feeding, or else he had too much wine in his belly to feel the cold. Besides which, he would have expected me to keep the flames dancing on a night as damp and cold as this. Instead I had lain shivering beneath the furs. Waiting. Because I wanted darkness.

Now I crept through that darkness, light-footed and holding my breath as the warrior snored in his pelts and the weak flames writhed in their death throes. Pelleas stirred neither at the latch nor the creak of the door, and I turned, taking one last look at the snorting, snuffling lump before stepping into the night.

The rain had stopped at last, though the wind had not yet blown itself out and the surf still hurled itself upon the rocks, hissing as it flooded back down the strand to regroup for the next assault. An arrow-shot off shore, the *Dobhran* rocked at her mooring amongst low, fast-running, white-crested furrows, and in a gust of wind I heard the faint murmuring voices of the men keeping watch from her stern.

I looked over to Merlin's hut and saw that it was all quiet. Smoke curled up from the roof in silver wisps and I reflected that Oswine, a Saxon and enemy of our people, was doing a better job with his master's fire than I had done with Pelleas's. Most of the other huts were cold and empty because few of the island's inhabitants had wanted to face that wrathful night and now slept where they could in the Lady's keep.

Everyone but for me and those poor men on the *Dobhran* was asleep or happily swathed in pelts, and I shivered again at the touch of the sea air on my neck.

Then I ran. My cloak flying behind me like a broken wing, I ran. Not to warm myself against the damp, blustery chill but because some need compelled me. Across the rocks and the bristling grass. Sliding on ground churned to a muddy, glutinous mess by booted feet, then onto the stony trail which snaked amongst the trees that cloaked much of the Mount. Up the track which my feet knew so well, my clothes still pungent with the strange smoke that had hung in drifting veils in the Lady's chamber.

Running. Not needing the moonlight which now and then flooded the night to reveal glistening drops falling from branches around me. Running as fast as I had run to win the island race. Perhaps even faster, for the need to gain the summit was like bellows to the forge burning hot in my chest.

Through the last soaking, wind-flayed trees and across the grassy bluff from which, up ahead, the granite burst in cold outcrops, dark, jagged shapes against the sky. And then I stopped.

What now? I had not thought about that, lying awake listening to Pelleas snoring, waiting for the fire to die. I would go back up to the keep. That was all I knew, and now I stood feeling like a clod, sucking in the night air and staring up at that Roman tower.

I looked east over the water, across the forests of Dumnonia, beyond which the far horizon was a white ribbon on night's hem, and I knew there was not much time. Perhaps folk would rouse themselves late this morning, because of the night's festivities, but Pelleas always woke with the dawn no matter how much wine or ale he had drunk. And so I steeled myself and walked up to the keep and just then the door opened. I froze. The man who stumbled out was one of King Uther's men. Fumbling at his trews, he growled something to me about needing to piss, and I had to twist aside or else he would have knocked me down in his hurry. Then I slipped through the half-open door and crept up the winding stone steps, hardly breathing at all now, until I was in the narrow corridor above the main hall where men and women were sleeping, courtesy of the Lady of the Mount.

I walked past the first and second doors and stood in front of the third, the sight of that simple oak plank door flooding my memory with storm fury and wild eyes and waves which tried to bury us. It was the same door against which I had slept on a blanket that night when she had come to Karrek. When I had cheated Manannán mac Lir of his full haul of souls. Guinevere's door.

The look in Guinevere's eyes that day she had so nearly drowned was the same look I had seen in her eyes earlier this night, when she had clawed her way back to the surface of her conscious mind. I did not care what Merlin wanted or what the Lady wanted, or what they hoped to achieve by forcing Guinevere to take part in their magic. I had seen the dread in her eyes and I would do whatever I must to protect her.

And so I was here in the Lady's keep when I should have been asleep in my own bed in Pelleas's hut on the shore.

It was possible, I thought, that the Lady had moved Guinevere up to the next level of the keep, where her own chamber was and where there was another room in which half the girls slept. Then again, Guinevere had not mentioned moving to another room and surely she would have said, for she found it amusing that she had been kept apart from the other girls because her dark moods frightened them.

'Really it is because the Lady does not want me to share my gift with the others. They are not ready yet,' she had told me one morning as we waded in the shallows gathering oar weed for Yann the cook who wanted it to thicken his fish broth. Though at the time I had not known what she meant by her gift. Not really. 'I am used to it,' she had said with a shrug, bringing up a handful of slick green weed.

Guinevere was on the other side of the oak door in front of me. I knew it and I would protect her. Merlin would not draw her into his spells again and the Lady would not test her and Uther's spearmen would not stare at her. I took off my cloak and rolled it up, then lay down with my head upon it, peering up through the darkness at the cobweb-draped timbers and wondering whether they were from the Roman times, or if some Briton had long ago replaced the old beams. Then my thoughts turned to Flame and I wondered again how Merlin knew about the fox. I was still wondering when the door by my feet opened, just the width of a spear shaft, so that a small wash of golden light lit some of the dressed stones around the door frame.

The light retreated and all was dark again. But the door remained open. Somewhere nearby, a mouse scrabbled in the wall. The low rumble of a man snoring in the chamber below seeped through the boards but otherwise all was so quiet that I could hear the soft spate of my own blood flooding in my head.

I stood, wincing as a board creaked beneath my feet, holding my breath. Remembering, I bent and retrieved my cloak, then gently, slowly, pushed the door just wide enough that I could squeeze through.

Guinevere sat on her bed, upon coarse, dun-coloured blankets which were still neatly stretched over the wool-filled mattress. In her lap she held a rushlight in its iron stand and by that pure light I saw her.

Unpinned now, her hair fell in dark tangled tresses down to her chest. Her eyebrows were still strikingly dark with sooty dye, but the green around her eyes was smudged and had been dragged into her hairline above her ears. The paint which had made a rosebud of her lips had fled across her left cheek in a blood-red smear and her dress of pale blue linen was stained with colour and tears. She looked like a girl who had raided her mother's cultus cabinet and felt the hazel switch across her legs because of it.

I shut the door behind me and sat on the bed beside her, aware more than ever that Guinevere was taller than me. Sometimes she teased me about this. Not now.

The room smelled of the rushlight's burning tallow and the sage and cedar smoke which had wicked into the weave of our clothes. But there was another scent too and it came from Guinevere, from the pale skin of her neck which had been laced with sandalwood-infused olive oil.

'Are you hurt?' I asked. A stupid question. I knew she was not, not in her body, anyway, but I had not known what else to say.

'No,' she said, no louder than a breath.

A silence drew out between us, spooling into the dark like a ship's anchor rope into the depths. I was thankful at least for the rushlight's gentle hiss.

'Sometimes I don't want to come back, Lancelot,' Guinevere said. 'When I am journeying,' she clarified.

'Where do you go?' I asked.

She shrugged. 'Anywhere,' she said, her voice soft and somehow distant. She turned her face to me then and her tear-glistened eyes were wide and fierce. 'If you could only see what it is like,' she said, then put a hand on mine. 'You could come with me.' Her hand squeezed mine tight. 'I could teach you.'

I felt the scowl tighten my face.

'I don't like magic,' I said, and immediately regretted saying it because she took her hand away, the spark in her eyes already gone.

We sat there in uncomfortable silence a while longer and then Guinevere leant over and placed the rushlight on the table beside her bed. She lay down on her side facing the cold stone wall, her back curved, head tucked, legs pulled up to her abdomen.

I sat watching the rushlight and the sooty tendrils that snaked up to the roof beams, thinking I should go back to my place on the hard boards in the corridor, when Guinevere shifted on the bed so that her knees were touching the wall.

'Stay,' she said. So quietly that I could not be sure I had heard it. I sat a while longer, hoping she would say it again so that I would not upset her by doing something wrong. But she said nothing more and so I held my rolled-up cloak behind my head and lay down next to her, watching the flamelight shivering in draughts I could not feel, until I fell asleep.

A hand on my shoulder. I gasped and scrambled upright against the wall, blinking foggy eyes, my heart thumping in my chest as I remembered where I was. Pelleas loomed over me and my nose filled with the sheep stink of the grease which he had rubbed into his leather breastplate so that it shone now. He gripped a spear in his right hand.

'Time to go, lad,' he said.

I did not know how long I had slept but it could not have been very long. The dawn light bleeding into the room through the Roman glass of the small window was pale and thin and it seemed to me no time at all had passed since Guinevere had told me to stay.

'Up you get,' Pelleas said, then he nodded his freshly shaven head at Guinevere, who was now sitting with her back against the wall, cradling her legs against her chest. 'Sorry to intrude like this, Lady Guinevere,' he said, 'but if my Lady catches Lancelot in here you'll both be in trouble.'

I rubbed my eyes and looked over to the window.

'They're stirring downstairs,' Pelleas said, 'but if we go now they'll just think we've been about our business early.'

I nodded, gathering up my cloak. How had Pelleas known where to find me?

'And say goodbye, Lancelot. You won't be seeing much of each other from now on,' he said, then frowned. 'Your days blowing about like a leaf in the wind are over, lad. It's the warrior's way for you. And not before time,' he added, glancing at Guinevere. Then his eyes widened at me as he nodded towards her. 'Well, lad, say goodbye.'

I turned to Guinevere. Her face was still daubed in the Lady's paints and her dark hair hung in tangles or loose coils either side of her pale face.

'Goodbye,' I said, sure that I would see her again soon. Unless Pelleas meant that I should leave Karrek?

Her ochre-smeared lips made a thin smile that did not reach her blue-green eyes. 'Thank you, Lancelot,' she said.

'It would be better, Lady Guinevere,' Pelleas said, gesturing to Guinevere's bed with his spear shaft, 'if we kept this between us.' He raised his left hand. 'I know, I know, it's all innocent. But still. Not a word to anyone, understand?'

Guinevere and I both nodded and Pelleas bowed his head just once in response, affirming that this was near enough a solemn oath between the three of us, then he went to the door and pulled it open just enough that he could peer out to make sure no one was walking the corridor. He beckoned me with a big hand and I moved up behind him, close enough to smell the fresh sea air on his cloak.

'No fuss now, lad. We're just fetching my sword which I left here last night after too much wine,' he said, and I noticed that the scabbard at his hip was empty. He must have put Boar's Tusk in the lean-to before coming up to find me.

I looked back at Guinevere one last time, and she gave a slight nod of her head as if to tell me it was all right to go. That she would be all right. Then I followed Pelleas out into the corridor and down the stone steps, and at the bottom we met Edern and Avenie who were coming blinking and yawning from the main chamber where they had slept with the rest.

'A good night, hey, Pelleas?' Edern said, stretching his arms wide and wincing at some ache or pain as Pelleas collected Boar's Tusk and Edern's sword too, which lay in a pile of other weapons covered in skins.

'Tell that to my poor skull,' Pelleas replied, handing Edern's sword to him. 'Still, no one can say that we don't know how to treat our guests, hey, Lancelot?' he said, cuffing me around the head. I tried to smile but I was thinking of Guinevere and what Pelleas had said about us not seeing much of each other from now on.

It was a chill, damp dawn. The gulls were already shrieking high above a bleak-looking sea, riding the thin westerly breeze which ruffled the grey-green tufts of marram grass that bristled on Karrek Loos yn Koos like the fur on a bear's back. In front of us, further down the slope, other head-sore men and women wrapped in pelts and cloaks traipsed back to their dwellings on the shore.

'You'd best not be too tired to work today,' Pelleas said, as we over-took Edern and Avenie who seemed still half asleep and fragile in the brisk dawn. 'Though I won't put you with the others. Not yet.' I looked at him. 'They would enjoy it too much and I'd be setting bones by the last light of the day. No, you'll train with me and you'll train hard. And we'll see if your hands are as fast as your feet.'

Why Merlin had demanded that I should begin my training in weapon craft I could not say, nor did Pelleas comment further on the druid's instructions. But I did not care about the why. All I knew was that I was going to learn my weapons like the other boys on the Mount, and that thought flooded my blood and had my limbs thrum-ming. I would make Belatucadrus, the Fair Shining One, the lover of battle, take notice. Mars, the Roman god of war, would wake from his slumber and hear an echo of the ancient heroes in my sword's song. And one day I would avenge myself on my uncle and those men who had taken everything from me.

'And another thing, lad,' Pelleas said, interrupting my reverie, 'the next time you feel the need to creep around in the night like a little mouse, at least have the decency to put another log on the fire on your way out.'

10

Young Bloods

I MOVED MY SWORD across to my left, dipping my shield and turning its edge towards my neck so as not to obstruct my sword, which I slashed diagonally into Jago's left shoulder before he got his own shield across. He went down to one knee and I spun, catching Florien's sword on my shield and deflecting that heavy blow down towards Florien's left side, which exposed his right, and I thrust my sword into his shoulder and he roared with pain.

'I'll take him,' Peran growled, scything his sword in a cut that would have knocked my teeth out had I not thrown my head back in time, so that I felt the severed air against my neck before I dropped to one knee and thrust my sword upward into Peran's belly. He doubled with a grunt and I spun to take Branok's sword on my own before it could crack against my skull, then sprang upwards, driving my shield into his shield and sending him reeling. But he came again, lunging this time, and our swords met, kissing along each other's length as I let Branok's momentum carry him forward, twisting my body so that his sword's point passed my left side. And then I was behind him and he cursed as I struck him between his shoulder blades. His leather armour did its job but Branok knew he was beaten and he cursed again.

On came Melwas, grinning and thumping his sword's hilt against the inside of his limewood shield. 'You're mine now, Lancelot,' he said, then made two practice cuts through the air.

In contrast I remained still. Balanced. Centred. Breathing evenly as I raised my sword and shield towards him.

'Put him down, Melwas!' Clemo said.

'Make it quick, Lancelot,' Jowan said.

Melwas's first attack was all power: a series of blows which I took on my shield and which jarred my arm with their ferocity, for Melwas wanted to remind me that he was bigger and stronger. Again he hammered my shield and my arm bones rattled under the impact as I led him in a wide circle, always keeping him on my left so that my shield was between us. Another thunderous blow. And another, yet I knew Melwas possessed skill as well as brute strength, and so I would not let him force me into making a rash move but instead ceded ground and kept my shield high.

Sure enough, his next attack had more craft than brawn, a mid-level strike to my right leg delivered from a semi-crouch, which I parried. Then his broad chest loomed and his sword struck down. I pulled my right leg back in time and as his sword struck the dry ground I brought my own sword down onto his exposed arm and might have broken the bone had he not bound that arm in thick felt. Nevertheless, he yelled and swung his shield into mine with enough force to send me flying.

I let go of my shield and rolled out of the path of a sword thrust which pierced the earth, then I was up on my feet and Melwas was on me, because he did not consider my hit a debilitating one even though he would likely have lost an arm had we been fighting with iron swords rather than short lengths of sharpened ash. And I ducked and twisted, parried and struck, and sweat flew from us both as the other boys cheered and bellowed.

Melwas scythed his sword at my head and, having no shield now, I brought my sword up to block. But Melwas's attack was a feint and he reversed the blow, crouching low under his shield and scything across to take my legs below the knees. Except that my legs weren't there. I leapt forward, striding so that the ball of my left foot hit his shield just above the iron boss and I pushed off, high enough to catch a glimpse of the sun-dappled sea before my bare feet struck the grass. I turned on landing, ducking Melwas's desperate swipe as he spun on his haunches and came up only to find my sword at his throat.

'You're dead,' I said, feeling the ire come off him like heat.

He knocked my ash sword aside with his own and spat into the grass. 'I'd like to see you try something like that when you're a grown man,' he said, for at seventeen Melwas was three years older than I and nearly full grown himself. He had always been big-boned and strong but the years on the Mount had put muscle on his bulk so that of all the young men of Karrek only Agga could match him in strength.

And he might have been right; the move had worked because I was smaller and lighter and could leap a crouching man and his shield as easily as think of it. But what did that matter? I had won.

'A rematch then?' I proposed, and Melwas nodded and banged his sword against his shield while the others clamoured, all of them eager for the chance to fight again and survive longer this time.

'Not today!' Pelleas said, striding into our midst and putting himself between me and Melwas. 'As entertaining as it was watching you ladies tickle each other beyond all decency, Benesek wants to see if any of you can throw like a man.' He gestured across the gentle slope to where Benesek stood gripping a long spear and circling his right arm to loosen the joint.

'A cup of mead to the one who gets his spear nearest mine,' Benesek called, a grin stretching beneath his drooping moustaches, and so we gathered our own spears, some of the boys moving gingerly or checking bruises already blooming in their flesh, and went to join him. And for some reason I looked up past the green swathe of trees and the grey rock to the Lady's keep which overlooked all. Gulls wheeled and cried around its heights.

'You think she's watching?' Bors asked, falling into step beside me. His question took me by surprise and it was only his asking it which made me realize why I had looked up at the keep.

'I doubt she even remembers me,' I said, which was as good as an admission. I remembered that night long ago when Merlin had visited and I had run up to the keep and lain with Guinevere until the dawn. I had been a child with a child's simple view of the world, but Guinevere had seemed wise beyond her years, as if she could see things that others could not. A gift which both intrigued and terrified her.

Four winters had come and gone since then and yet even now, to think of Guinevere was to tie a great ship's knot in my chest. A knot which was only undone when I had a sword or spear in my hand and an opponent before me, for at those times I thought of nothing else but the contest.

'Some days I cannot see my mother's face in my mind,' Bors said, testing the fit of his spear blade on the shaft and finding that it was a little loose. 'Other days it's so clear I have to stop myself reaching out to touch her.' He shrugged as if to say that was how the mind worked when it came to such things.

Like all the boys on Karrek, Bors was otherwise alone in the world, his parents having died when he was a boy. The Lady had brought him to Karrek the summer after I had begun to learn my weapons. He had been raised in the court of King Claudas, my father's enemy whose men had attacked that snow-filled night and brought death to my father's people. I had expected to despise Bors on sight, but I had found that I could not. He had a broad, open, honest face and an easy smile which made it impossible to dislike him. And then to our surprise we had learnt that he and I were related, for his father, King Bors of Gannes, had married my mother's sister Evaine, and so Bors and I were cousins, though neither of us remembered ever having met as children.

'King Claudas attacked us the summer after his victories in Benoic. My uncle died fighting. My parents were imprisoned,' he told me some days after coming to live on the Mount, and explained how we had suffered such similar fates. Now we were firm friends and Bors was the only person on the island, other than Pelleas, who knew that I was such a fool that I still thought every day about a girl to whom I had not spoken for four years.

'Perhaps in another four years I will have forgotten about her, too,' I said, wanting that to be true and yet dreading the very idea of it.

'Or you could humiliate Melwas so much that one day he'll knock all thoughts of her out of your skull and I'll find you much more cheerful company,' Bors said. He had stooped to pick up a smooth rock and was now hammering it against the spearhead to make it fit more snugly on the shaft.

'I didn't bring it up,' I said, loosening my own shoulder ahead of the throwing contest.

'You didn't have to,' Bors said with a grin, thrusting the spear three times to make sure the head was on properly. 'You wear it like a cloak.' He nodded, satisfied with the repair, and tossed the rock away.

'You haven't met her,' I said.

'Maybe I should. She sounds worth the beating,' he said, for a beating was what we could expect for trying to mix with the girls these days. 'So long as you don't take offence when she falls in love with me because I'm handsome, brave, cheerful and can throw a spear further than you.'

I punched him hard on the shoulder and he laughed, even though the blow was hard enough to affect his first cast. Maybe even his second.

'When you two have finished, perhaps you would do us the honour of joining us,' Benesek called, mocking us with a deep bow. Bors and I shared a grin and took our spears to where the other boys stood taunting each other, boasting about their own legendary past throws or announcing that the competition was as good as won, even before any of us had shown our spear blades to the sky.

In the event I did not further humiliate Melwas, who won the contest, with Agga coming second, Peran third and Bors fourth. My throw was one of my best, but I would have to put some more bulk on my shoulders before I could challenge the older boys.

At least I would not have to wait another four years to know whether or not Guinevere had forgotten about me. It turned out I would learn the answer to that the very next day.

'Well? What do you call that?' Pelleas asked. He was standing by the cook fire, ladling steaming pottage into his bowl. The other warriors and most of the boys were sitting cross-legged on the hay-strewn floor of the hut where we gathered each night, but I knew Pelleas was talking to me.

'It just happened,' I said, blowing into my bowl.

'I never taught you that nonsense,' Pelleas rumbled. 'Leaping about like a salmon.' The boys shifted to clear a path so Pelleas could sit in his usual place with his back against the wattle wall.

'I'd have knocked your balls off if you'd tried jumping over me like that,' Edern said, then swept a hand through the smoky air. 'A swooping gull would have taken them on the wing.'

'Not much of a meal though,' Madern said, slurping from his spoon. That had the boys grinning.

'So,' Pelleas said, loud enough to get everyone's attention. 'Tomorrow one of the young ladies will leave the Mount.' A murmur rose as the boys speculated as to which girl was leaving. My stomach sank. It had been two years since anyone had left Karrek for good and that had been a girl called Clarette, who had spent less than a year with the Lady before her father had taken her back because her mother had fallen sick and Clarette was needed to take on her mother's responsibilities. 'I'll put you out of your misery,' Pelleas said, then sipped from his spoon and winced. 'It's Senara.'

I remembered Senara as a broad-shouldered, brown-haired, smiling girl who had been popular with her companions. A young lady now, I thought, wondering how Guinevere must have changed too over the years.

'Lord Evalach will come to The Edge tomorrow at midday,' Pelleas said. 'Evalach is a Dumnonian lord, but King Menadoc has permitted him and his small retinue to cross Cornubia.' He waved a hand to show that none of this was important. 'As from tomorrow, Senara will begin her new life as Lord Evalach's betrothed, his last wife having died two winters past.' He sipped from a cup and winced again, as though the ale was sour. 'They'll be married by summer's end.'

'And the old goat will have put a child in her belly by the time the sand martins fly south,' Benesek said with just a touch of bitterness as he refilled his own cup.

None of this meant anything to us. We barely knew the girls these days. The glimpses we caught of them now and again were enough to fire our imaginations and fill the meal hut with crude talk for a short while, but then we would fall back to talk of weapon craft and famous battles and warriors who had won renown so that their names echoed through the years long after they had crossed to the otherworld. And because it was Senara and not Guinevere who was leaving Karrek, I fell back to my food and would have thought no more about it had I not heard my name spoken.

'Lancelot?' Melwas blurted. 'Why Lancelot?'

I looked up.

'Because I say so, that's why,' Pelleas told Melwas, then put his bowl down beside him and nodded to Edern, who had stood to help himself to more food. 'Lancelot and Edern will escort the girl and I am sure I can rely on you to show Lord Evalach the proper respect, Lancelot,' he said, eyeing me.

I nodded. I was stunned. The Edge was our name for the beach across the water, the sea-lapped fringe of the island of Britain and the south-westernmost coast of the kingdom of Cornubia. It was little more than a good arrow-flight from our own island's northern shore. Indeed, a person could wade through the shallows at low tide, from Karrek to the mainland, with little risk of drowning, and yet I had never been to The Edge. I had never left the Mount, unless you could call swimming around it leaving, since the Lady and Pelleas had brought me here one dusk years before, when everything I had known lay in ashes or blood behind me back in Armorica beyond the Dividing Sea.

'It's time you lot learnt something other than how to gut a man with a spear or take his head with a dull blade and a flourish. You need to learn respect.' Pelleas glowered at us all. 'Responsibility. Duty.' He tensed a moment, seeming to hold his breath. 'Lancelot was last man standing today . . .' he hoisted an eyebrow and shook his head, 'despite hopping about like one of the painted fools in King Uther's court.' For a fleeting moment that pained expression darkened his face again. 'So Lancelot's earned the honour of escorting Senara to The Edge.'

'But I won the spear-throwing,' Melwas said.

Pelleas nodded. 'And I don't see any of your friends drinking mead tonight, Melwas,' he said.

'A cup of mead is a poor reward compared with escorting a lady to The Edge,' Melwas dared, holding Pelleas's eye.

'And yet it seems to have loosened your tongue, lad,' Madern said.

'It was a good throw,' Benesek, sitting beside Pelleas, admitted, putting his empty bowl down in the hay beside him. He had been drinking steadily all evening. 'Stuck in the ground not three spear-lengths behind my throw,' he said, which had Edern and Madern's eyebrows raised, for it was said in jest that Benesek could throw a spear all the way to the otherworld if he wanted to. If you ever needed a man killing twice, just ask Benesek, they said.

Pelleas began to speak but stopped as his body seemed to tighten. He pressed a hand to his stomach and cursed under his breath.

'Perhaps you can go next time,' Edern told Melwas, taking up the thread which Pelleas had left hanging. 'Sooner or later another girl will—'

'Melwas can go tomorrow,' Pelleas interrupted. Edern and the other men looked at each other, not even trying to hide their surprise. Melwas himself was wide-eyed at the pronouncement.

'But I will still escort Senara,' Edern said.

Pelleas shook his head. 'Lancelot and Melwas will do it. It's time they earned their food and the roof over their heads. We won't be here to hold their hands for ever, Edern.' He looked at me with question-ing eyes and that was the first time I noticed the white hairs amongst his big black beard. I had never thought of Pelleas getting older. With his bulk and his beard and his shaved head, he always seemed as much a part of Karrek as the rock itself, but I supposed the years that had seen my strength grow were the same years that saw his begin to wane. Not that he couldn't have still beaten us all with sword, spear or his bare hands even then.

'If Lancelot and Melwas can escort Senara to The Edge, and do it in such a way as not to offend Lord Evalach, then they will prove that they are not the quarrelsome, petulant young men they would have us believe.'

Bors, grinning, elbowed me in the ribs, but I was looking at Melwas and Melwas was looking at me.

'You think you can do it?' Pelleas asked us. 'Without trying to kill each other or embarrassing either Senara or the Lady, or me for that matter?'

I was going to The Edge, which meant I would set foot on ground that was not Karrek Loos yn Koos. I would accompany the hounds of Annwn themselves for such an opportunity, never mind Melwas, but then I touched my iron belt buckle to ward off the evil of that thought. Perhaps Melwas thought the same, that he could put aside his hatred for me if it meant being given a man's task and the honour of escorting Senara to a lord of Dumnonia.

'Well?' Pelleas said, looking at the floor and cupping a hand to his ear.

'We can do it,' I said.

'We can do it,' Melwas said.

'Perhaps there should be three,' Bors suggested. 'Someone to stop these two trying to out-row each other and tipping the poor girl overboard while her lord watches from the beach.'

'Don't push it, Bors,' Pelleas said. Bors shrugged as if to say it had been worth a try.

'I would imagine that Senara could out-row both of them,' Agga said, which had even Melwas and me laughing, for no one could deny that Senara had an impressive set of shoulders on her.

Then talk turned to that day's mock battle, with boys claiming that those who had beaten them had been lucky, and others saying how things would turn out differently next time, while Benesek, Madern and Edern talked amongst themselves.

I just ate my broth, thinking of the task I had been given and wondering what the next day would bring, and I was perhaps the only one in that hut who noticed Pelleas leave his food uneaten and quietly stalk out into the night.

*

The next morning dawned bright and warm enough that I woke drenched in sweat and thirsty. The sea was blinding to look at, a dazzling reflection of a blue sky in which a few wisps of cloud hung as if they had nowhere to go. The white flowers of the sea kale growing in large clumps above the high tide line buzzed with black and yellow flies. Scattered tufts of pink thrift, lilac-coloured sea lavender and white sea campion shivered in the breeze on the cliffs and amongst the boulders on the shore. Guillemots and razorbills cried from their nests on Karrek's high ledges, while cormorants and shags set out to fish in the shallows, or else perched in their nests lower down the cliffs, wings stretched out to dry in the warm sun. And Melwas and I set off up the Mount to fetch Senara and take her to Lord Evalach.

We were both dressed in our best or cleanest clothes. I wore a tunic of green linen, dun-coloured trews and a pair of soft leather shoes which had known previous owners but had been newly stitched and rubbed with beeswax. Melwas wore his Roman leather breastplate. I did not yet possess such armour, so Bors, who had brought his own armour with him from Gannes, lent me his, which I was proud to wear. Nor did I own a sword yet. We practised with a variety of blades, most of them poor quality swords which Pelleas and the other warriors of Karrek had taken as plunder over the years, the idea being that we would not become too familiar with and thus reliant on any particular length, weight and style of blade before we were fully trained.

'Better to be able to beat your enemy with whatever is in your hand at the time, be it a farmer's scythe or a Saxon long knife,' Pelleas told us.

Or perhaps we had not been given our own swords because Pelleas believed such a thing must be earned. For now, though, because it had been his idea that I should escort Senara in his stead, Pelleas had lent me Boar's Tusk and his sword belt, so that I thought I was Mars or some other god of war striding up the Mount with that sword at my hip.

'Can't do anything about that beardless face of yours, lad,' Pelleas had said that dawn, taking the belt and scabbarded sword from his own waist and handing them to me, 'but we can at least make you look the part from the neck down.' He had stood back to appraise me while I got used to the feeling of the borrowed accoutrements and the smell of Bors's sweat, which stained the leather breastplate. 'A good sword like that might at least discourage Lord Evalach's men from insulting you for your age.' He grinned. 'A beardless lad carrying a blade like that. It'd make me think twice.'

'But I haven't earned it,' I said, feeling as embarrassed as I did invincible.

'All in good time, Lancelot,' he said. 'And so long as you don't try that shield-jumping lunacy in your first real fight.'

Melwas wore Benesek's long sword: a beautiful and deadly weapon with a silver-gilt hilt of gleaming ivory and a pommel set with red garnets. It was sheathed in black leather wound with silver wire, while the scabbard mount itself bore some Saxon script which Benesek called runes. He had killed the sword's previous owner, a Saxon chieftain, in some long-ago battle, and High King Uther himself had told Benesek that he had fought well enough to earn that magnificent sword and more. 'Before most of you were born, that was,' the warrior had told us, 'in the days when we still believed we would throw the Saxons back into the sea.'

Benesek had never named the sword because he believed such a fine blade must already have a name and would resent being renamed and bring him bad luck. And years ago, when Merlin had come to Karrek with his slave Oswine, and Pelleas had told the Saxon to read the inscription on the scabbard, Benesek had growled at Oswine to keep the runes to himself in case he did not like the name.

'What if the sword is called Slayer of Britons?' Benesek had asked. 'Or what if there is some curse in the runes?' After considering this, Pelleas agreed they were better off not knowing. But that sword looked well at Melwas's hip now as we walked in silence up the track, already sweating in the heat of the risen sun. We did not wear our leather helmets. For one thing it would be a blazing hot day come noon, and for another, we would be escorting Senara across a few hundred yards of water to a friend and ally, not going into a fight. And so I had tied my hair back with a strip of leather, as I alone of the boys did not shave my head. It was Merlin who had said that I must not take the shears and razor to my hair but should let it grow. He did not say why and I did not ask, but today was one of those days when I would have gladly cut it all off to feel the sea's breeze on my scalp.

'I will do the talking when we meet Lord Evalach,' Melwas said now, the first words either of us had spoken since meeting on the shore.

'Fine by me,' I said.

And when we crested the grassy rise that was yellow with buttercups and bird's-foot trefoil and thick with butterflies and humming with bees, we found the Lady and her girls waiting for us. Having expected Pelleas and Edern, they were shocked to see Melwas and me, so that Jenifry and Erwana, who were sobbing and lamenting over Senara, now cuffed at their tears and lifted their chins as we strode towards them.

And then I saw her. She had been standing behind the Lady's left shoulder but now she stepped out into the bright day and in that moment there was nothing and no one else on the crown of that hill. Her dress, the blue of a song thrush's eggs, was drawn in at her waist by a narrow leather belt whose brass buckle glinted in the sunlight. Her long hair, dark and glossy as a raven's wing, was loose and tousled by the sea breeze, and her eyes gleamed like the swirls of iron and steel in the best swords forged by a master smith.

Guinevere.

I couldn't breathe. My stomach lurched like a barrel from a wrecked ship, having risen fast to the surface, now rolling and bucking amongst the waves. In the years since I had last been so close to her, I had tried to see her in the eye of my mind, but now I realized that my imagination was a blunt and useless tool compared with the gut-wrenching reality of seeing her in the flesh.

'Keep up,' Melwas growled over his shoulder, for I had fallen behind. My stride had faltered at the sight of Guinevere. My courage had flown with the sudden, almost crippling burden of that long-awaited, often dreamt-of moment.

'Do not row too fast or seem too eager,' the Lady told us, 'but keep a steady pace and remain dignified until your duty is discharged.'

'Yes, Lady,' I heard Melwas say.

'Lancelot?'

I tore my eyes from Guinevere. 'Yes, Lady,' I echoed.

'Give my compliments to Lord Evalach and his son, Saret, if he has accompanied his father. Pelleas told you the words?'

'Yes, Lady,' Melwas said again.

She nodded. 'Do not rush them. Do not mumble.'

'No, Lady,' Melwas said, for it was he who would repeat the words Pelleas had shared with us that dawn. The warrior had eyed us suspiciously, as if, having woken to a fresh day, he'd regretted giving us the task of delivering Senara to her would-be husband.

'Do not embarrass me,' he had said again, in case we had not heard the previous three or four warnings. 'The Lady wanted me to send Edern with you but I convinced her you two were ready. So you had better be.'

Melwas and I had looked at each other and made a silent agreement to keep the truce between us, for Pelleas's sake. For our own sakes too. I don't think either of us considered poor Senara in all of it.

Now, at a gesture from the Lady, I walked forward and picked up two plump satchels which were stuffed with Senara's belongings, and slung them over my shoulder, then stepped back so that Guinevere would once again be in my line of sight. Our eyes met and my chest tightened and it was almost like pain. But then Guinevere broke the moment by shifting her gaze to Senara, smiling as she and the other girls bade their final farewells, wishing Senara a long and happy life and calling on the goddess Epona to bless her with all the earth's abundance.

The Lady embraced Senara, inhaled the scent of the white flowers bound in her brown hair and then kissed her cheek. Melwas, doing his best impression of an implacable Guardian of the Mount, had turned his back on them all and faced down the slope, which was the signal to Senara that it was time to go. I looked at Guinevere, hoping to meet her eyes once more before I turned, but she was watching Senara and I could stare no longer without making a fool of myself.

The three of us set off down the hill, butterflies scattering before us, Melwas and I pretending we could not hear Senara softly sobbing, for neither of us had any words of comfort for a young woman being given to an old man. She was still sobbing when she and Melwas climbed into the currach and I waded into the shallows, pushing them out before jumping into the boat. I was still thinking of Guinevere as I set my oars and took up the stroke in time with Melwas behind me, but he had tired of Senara's weeping now and told her to stop for her own sake.

'Your eyes are puffy and red,' he said, his oars and mine striking the water together. 'You look like you've been sitting by a smoky fire all night. It doesn't make you prettier.' Up came the oars, dripping water beads which shone in the golden day. 'Lord Evalach will not be expecting a miserable, puffy-faced, red-eyed girl,' he said.

There was no malice in the way he said it, and it was true that Lord

Evalach might be offended if he thought that his future bride had been crying at the prospect of going back to Dumnonia with him, so Senara wiped her tears and her snotty nose on the sleeve of her dress and sat straighter on her bench, looking beyond us both towards the shore.

I looked over my shoulder and saw no sign of the Dumnonians either on the strand or amongst the trees beyond the shore, and as much as Senara must have thrilled at the thought of becoming a rich and powerful Lady as Lord Evalach's new wife, perhaps part of her hoped that Evalach would not come at all, that she might return to her friends and her simple life on Karrek. Who could say what thoughts wove and knotted behind those eyes? Those eyes which were on me now, so that I saw them properly for the first time. Lively, hazel eyes, made not ugly by the tears, as Melwas had suggested, but alluring, even pretty, in a sad way.

Lean, plunge, pull, lift. We worked the oars as neatly as we could, keeping the rhythm even and unhurried, driving that skin-hulled boat across the bay, and all the while Senara stared at me. Anyone would have thought I had three horns and eyes of fire from the way she stared, and even Melwas noticed it.

'Any sign of your soon-to-be husband?' he asked her. I could tell by the sourness in his tone that his intention was to divert Senara from whatever thoughts occupied her mind as she sat there watching me row.

Her eyes flicked to the shore. 'No,' she said, then swung those hazel eyes back to me, so that I could feel the hot flush in my cheeks and knew my face must be as red as the garnets set in the pommel of the sword at Melwas's hip.

'They say Lord Evalach had his last wife poisoned,' Melwas said, 'because she grew so fat that he could not stand to share his bed with her.'

If there were such whispers I hadn't heard them, and I wondered if Melwas had made it up from some spiteful wish to unnerve Senara. If he had, then he must have been disappointed when she dismissed the rumour simply by checking that the coil of brown hair pinned at the back of her head was still firmly in place. 'I heard that Lady Seva died from the flux,' she said, 'and that her doting husband mourned her for a year.' She shrugged, her eyes still on me. 'And besides, didn't the

Lady ask you to give Lord Evalach's son, Saret, her compliments?' she said, not waiting for Melwas to answer. 'I rather doubt Saret would accompany his father to collect me had Lord Evalach murdered his mother.' She gave me a wry half-smile, then looked out across the water to where a gull bobbed on the gentle tide. 'And they say we girls are the wellsprings of rumour.'

Melwas's oar blade bit the water ahead of mine, ruining the rhythm for the next few strokes. 'All I am saying is that I would not let myself get fat if I were you,' he said, and I thought Senara's gasp was in response to that, until I realized she was looking at something, or someone, on the shore.

'They're here,' she said, her teeth worrying at her bottom lip and all of a sudden looking like the girl I remembered from my first summer on Karrek rather than the young lady she was now. Her hands were clenched in her lap so tight that her knuckles were as white as the flower petals in her hair.

I looked over my shoulder at the shore and saw that Lord Evalach had come to The Edge.

If I had not pitied Senara before, or thought much about her at all, my mind being full of Guinevere, I pitied her now I had seen Lord Evalach. I had known he was not a young man but I had not known he was white-haired and warped with age and almost toothless. And yet for all that he looked a withered old thing, particularly standing beside his handsome young son, he seemed to tremble with lust when he laid eyes on Senara, who was so much taller than him. With his bent spine and bowed legs he would need to stand on a stool to look her in the eye, but then I recalled what Benesek had said about him putting a child in her belly before this summer's end, and thought the difference in height would not matter in the marital bed. At least he would be hard pressed to beat her, I thought, imagining that Senara could throw her new lord over her shoulder and walk off with him should she wish to.

'On my honour she is a maiden,' Melwas said, 'a daughter of the Mount and sister of Britannia, respectful of the gods, versed in the healing arts and—'

'On your honour?' Lord Evalach blurted, glancing at the grizzled-looking warrior beside him, who hitched his top lip to bare his teeth.

'Your honour?' Lord Evalach said again, tearing his rheumy eyes from Senara to glare at Melwas. Spittle seeped from the corner of his mouth but if he knew it he did not care. 'And what have you done in your short life that your honour should mean anything to me?' he asked, the word 'honour' dripping with scorn.

Melwas bristled but held his tongue, either out of respect for this Dumnonian lord or else because he had no answer to Evalach's question. There were twenty spearmen standing sweat-drenched amongst the humps and hollows of the grassy dunes, their shields painted with their lord's symbol of a bull's head. Flies buzzed around them. Nearby, a colony of shrieking silvery-grey terns flapped and dived amongst the dunes, angry at the invaders who threatened their nests. Even with the sea breeze blowing towards them I could smell the Dumnonians' stink and sense their hostility.

'Are there no grown men left on Karrek Loos yn Koos?' Lord Evalach asked. 'Or perhaps Lady Nimue amuses herself at my expense?' He gazed at Senara, the spittle having slid amongst the grey bristles of his ill-shaven chin, and I pitied the girl. I did not even want to look at her for fear of seeing the horror in her eyes at what her future held. 'She resents losing one of her precious girls,' Lord Evalach went on, 'and is sickened by the thought of young Senara being rutted by an old man. So she sends boys by way of insulting me.'

'I am no boy, lord,' Melwas said, and neither did he look like a boy, being tall and broad and in his leather armour with Benesek's long sword at his hip.

'You're a boy until you prove otherwise,' the scarred warrior beside Lord Evalach said, trying to provoke Melwas. It worked. Melwas stepped forward, drawing Benesek's sword. I pulled Boar's Tusk from its scabbard and moved up to his left shoulder.

'Enough,' said the young man on Lord Evalach's right. I had assumed he was Evalach's son, Saret, the bad start having spoiled the formal introductions and the exchanging of compliments. 'Let them be, Father,' he said, confirming my assumption. Saret was neither tall nor broad but his face was open and honest-looking and as clear-skinned and handsome as his father's was sallow and time-ravaged. 'These young men are Guardians of the Mount and deserve our respect,' he said, looking me in the eye. I held his gaze, Boar's Tusk still raised before me. 'You have tested them and they have shown that they are no cowards.'

'See this, dear Senara?' Lord Evalach said, sweeping an arm towards Saret. 'My son already speaks as though he commands. He cannot wait until I am dead.' He gave a toothless grin. 'Do you really think I want to make an enemy of Lady Nimue, boy?' he asked Saret. 'You think I would spill blood in King Menadoc's land?'

'I think these young men have discharged their duty,' Saret replied. 'I think we should thank them and be on our way.' He nodded at me and I nodded my thanks to him for intervening. The other men of Lord Evalach's party were watching us with a mixture of disdain and amusement, and no doubt some of them hoped to see blades flash and blood fly, as bored warriors will. But there would be no crimson this golden day.

'We have been told,' Lord Evalach said to his champion, whilst beckoning Senara to him. She looked at me and I nodded, sheathing Boar's Tusk.

'Good luck, Senara,' I said and with that she walked towards Lord Evalach and I picked up her two satchels and gave them to a Dumnonian spearman who had stepped forward to take them from me.

While his lord took Senara's hand in the claw of his own, Evalach's champion grinned at Melwas. 'Off you run, little boys,' the warrior said, fluttering ringed fingers at us, and Melwas stood there for a moment, stiff with anger and embarrassment, then plunged Benesek's sword into its scabbard, turned his back on the Dumnonians and strode across the sand past the pile of dry wood which would be lit to warn Karrek in times of danger, towards the boat which rested above the high tide line.

And I followed him.

Neither of us spoke as we took up the oars and rowed, watching the Dumnonians disappear over the dunes with their prize, who, to her credit, did not look back at us or at Karrek beyond our bow. Not once did she look back, and then she was gone, and we rowed in silence and shame, neither of us wanting to acknowledge the insults we had borne.

Instead, I lost myself in the rhythm of the stroke and thoughts of

Britannia, having just set foot on the mainland for the first time in my life. Our sweat dripped onto the skin hull and the oars clumped in the tholes and I wondered at the kingdoms and lords and peoples that lay beyond those dunes and forests.

When we were halfway across, Melwas broke the silence. 'I saw you,' he said as we both leant back in the stroke, pulling our oars through the calm, sun-dappled water. 'Giving Senara the eye. You were worse than that slobbering old toad back there. I know what was going on.'

'Nothing was going on,' I said. 'And anyway, how could you see my eyes? You're behind me.'

'Don't get clever with me,' he said. 'It's because of you that we were humiliated back there by that old goat and that other big pile of dung. If I'd had Agga or Branok with me they wouldn't have dared. They would have seen proper warriors.' The oars bit and the currach scudded across the bay like a cloud before a gale, and my blood pounded in my ears. 'But they saw you and thought the Lady mocked them by sending a boy,' Melwas said. 'Lord Evalach looked at you and was reminded of the little bastards he's whelped on his slaves over the years.'

The muscles in my thighs thrummed and my hands tingled on the ash oar handles and I reminded myself of Pelleas's warning not to embarrass him.

'You are not one of us and you'll never be a Guardian of the Mount,' Melwas said. 'You should leave Karrek. Go back to Armorica.' He laughed. 'Do you remember that sparhawk of yours? Of course you do, that bird was your only friend. And what kind of a hawk was she? Couldn't even fly straight. Even before I snapped her wing.'

It took me the next oar stroke to unravel that confession. A black veil fell across my vision. I twisted on the bench and flew at him, fists flying. I struck his cheek with my left and slammed the knuckles of my right against his temple, my weight on top of him, pushing him down into the currach's bow. But somehow he got his knee up between us, then worked his foot into my stomach and launched me backwards and my calves hit the aft thwart. I fell heavily against the craft's hazel ribs.

'I broke her wing and she squawked like a mad thing,' Melwas said, crouching and holding on to the currach's sides because the boat was rocking dangerously. 'Clawed and pecked at me, savage as a Pict,' he said, then I was up and launched myself at him but this time he was ready and threw an arm round my neck and we fell together against the stern, and I could not breathe because Melwas was strangling me. He was the stronger but I was rage itself for what he had done to my hawk; I broke his chokehold and then it was just a flurry of fists, some landing true, most missing, scuffing off heads or striking shoulders.

'We were all in on it,' Melwas managed to say as we struggled and grappled and the currach rolled from side to side, water spilling into the hull. 'We all heard you cry yourself to sleep over that useless bird.'

I wanted to kill him. I drove a fist into his stomach and he twisted out from under me and threw himself back, then he pulled Benesek's long sword from the silver-bound scabbard and pointed it at me.

'I'll kill you,' he snarled through bloody teeth. And perhaps some part of me knew that this fight was not worthy of Pelleas's sword, or else I forgot I was wearing it. Either way I left Boar's Tusk in its scabbard and bent to snatch up one of the discarded oars and held it across my body, legs bent, feet braced against the currach's skeleton.

'You're not good enough,' I said, knowing Melwas and what he would do next. He came fast, sure-footed even on that rocking boat, but I swung the oar blade at his head. He got the long sword up with enough muscle behind it to check the oar's flight, and in doing so fell for the feint. I threw my left foot and left arm forward, bringing the oar's grip across and twisting at the waist to slam the handle into his unguarded left temple. The blow spun him and he fell. I heard a crack as his face hit the top edge of the currach's side and saw a flash of silver and gleaming ivory as Benesek's sword flew. Barely a splash and it was gone.

The loss of that sword stunned me in a way none of Melwas's blows had. Gripping the hide hull I peered over the side, drops of blood from my nose spilling like red garnets onto the sun-shimmered water. I could see dark patches of weed and lighter swathes of sand and clouds of small fish darting this way and that like flocks of silver starlings. But I could not see Benesek's sword and I knew the current had already carried us away from it. I turned and looked at Melwas lying face down in the bilge. He was not moving. Blood swirled with the water that had come over the sides and his shaved head was smeared with blood and I looked towards Karrek, aware that Pelleas or Benesek or any of the other boys might have seen the whole thing.

I had lost Benesek's sword, that beautiful, deadly, precious sword which he had won in battle against a Saxon chieftain. And I had killed Melwas. In truth I only regretted one of those things.

11

For Friendship

'HE'S NOT DEAD,' Pelleas growled, lifting his ear off Melwas's chest. 'Not yet anyway. But when Benesek finds out his sword is on the seabed you'll both be dead. And you'll be glad to be dead because it'll mean the pain has stopped.'

I looked at Bors, who grimaced on my behalf.

'I'll find it,' I said. 'When the tide is out you can see the bottom. I'll go back out. I'll find it.'

'You'd better,' Pelleas said. 'And soon, before it rusts. You can find the oars while you're at it,' he said. Because three of the currach's oars had fallen overboard when I flew at Melwas, I had been left to half paddle, half punt the boat back across the bay, so that I was exhausted as well as bleeding by the time I dragged Melwas onto the strand. Pelleas did not say whether or not he had watched my ungainly, undignified crossing from the shore; I hoped he had not.

'But first you and Bors are going to take Melwas to his bed and hope that he doesn't stop breathing before Geldrin gets back with the Lady. She'll know what to do with him.'

Melwas was already groaning by the time Bors and I left him, and as much as I wanted my face to be the first thing that Melwas saw when he woke, I knew I had to face Benesek and explain how we had lost his sword.

'If I were you I'd be swimming back to Armorica now,' Bors said as we walked barefoot back across the shingle bank along which purple sea pea flowers crept and golden-yellow horned poppies shivered in the gentle, warm wind. The other boys had come from spear training with Madern and Edern and were gathered on the rocks looking out across the water as if they might see that ivory-hilted Saxon sword standing proud of the burnished sea. Benesek glared at me and I could not look him in the eye as I went to my fate. 'His moustaches are quivering, he's so angry,' Bors said, which did nothing to comfort me.

'He won't kill me,' I said, sounding more confident than I felt. 'I'm the only one who knows where the sword went in.' I glanced across the bay. 'Look, the tide is on the way out. Benesek will have his sword back before dusk. Maybe even before he's finished his first jug of wine.'

I did not need to look at Bors to know that he did not share my confidence. I fancied I heard his eyebrows rise towards the stubble on his sun-browned scalp, and yet he said he would help me look for the sword seeing as Melwas wasn't going to be much use, today at least.

And then Benesek raged. It could have been worse. Much worse. I suspected that Pelleas had said enough to dissuade his friend from wringing my neck there and then. But Benesek did rage. He bellowed and flailed his arms, red-faced, eyes bulging, his spittle wetting my face as I stood there thinking how lucky Melwas was to be getting away with it, just because he had not been quick enough to stop my oar from knocking the wits out of him.

And then, just like that, the squall of Benesek's wrath was gone, though he still glared at me with eyes like boiled duck eggs.

I glanced at Pelleas beside him but he said nothing and so I looked back to Benesek, waiting for him to catch his breath and begin yelling again. From the corner of my eye I could see Agga and Peran smirking, and no doubt all the boys, apart from Bors perhaps, were enjoying watching me being upbraided.

'Well, lad?' Benesek said. 'You're not going to find my sword, standing there like a pissing post!' he bawled, pointing out across the bay towards the mainland foreshore which glistened, dark and slick with green weed abandoned by the falling tide.

And so Bors and I undressed there on the rocks and waded out until the water was up to our chests, at which point we kicked off and swam, as I had used to do each morning, in the days before I had begun to learn my weapons. We swam to the place where I thought the currach had been when Melwas and I had fought. We dived under times beyond counting, raking fingers through the sand and tangles of weed, salt water stinging our eyes as we looked for the glint of steel or red garnets through the billowing clouds of silt which our hands or feet had stirred up. We were still out there when the sun slipped behind the horizon and the tide rose by six feet in the time it takes to put an edge on a blunt knife.

And we did not find the sword.

I went back out at dawn the next day and every day after that, and Bors came too when he could. But more often than not, Pelleas or Edern or one of the other men yelled at my cousin to get out of the water and join the others at their weapons.

'Don't stay too long and freeze,' Bors would say, reluctant to leave me searching alone, for the men never called me in. They knew it was a serious matter, losing another man's sword, and perhaps they also knew that I would not give up until I found it, and so they let me be, and I spent more time in the sea than on land. I would only stumble ashore when I got so cold that my limbs would not do what I asked of them and I could no longer make fists with my hands because of the numbness. Even though the days were clement and the sea was not too cold, after so much time in the water I could not seem to get myself warm. After four or five days, sores opened in my skin, until eventually my body was covered in them. It was agony when the salt water got in to these lesions but I did not care, and often I saw Pelleas or Benesek himself, watching me from the shore, though they never spoke of the sword or my search for it when they saw me in the communal hut. Not that I went in there much, not wanting to face Benesek until I could return his sword.

Melwas was out of his bed the day after our fight, and smashing Agga's shield to splinters on the training field the day after that. And yet he never helped me look for the sword. Not once. Which was fine by me, for had we to spend any time together out there in the bay I might have tried to kill him properly for breaking my sparhawk's wing, never mind that it had been four years since he had committed that heinous crime.

One day, Bors came and crouched beside me in the hut, handing me a bowl of pottage which he had managed to almost fill with the dregs from the pot suspended above the greying embers. I had just come ashore and was still wet and shivering and almost too tired to eat, even though I was ravenous. 'You know, Lancelot, the blade will be ruined by now,' he said.

I spooned the food between numb lips, surprised to find it was still warm, and fell to eating like a starving man.

'Perhaps not,' I said, scraping the bowl. 'Not if it is buried.'

He shrugged, then reached into the scrip on his belt and took out a clay pot, not much bigger than a hen's egg. The pot's cream-coloured contents were set hard like tallow.

'For the sores,' he said, then frowned. 'You're to use it sparingly.'

'From the Lady?' I asked. I had not seen the Lady since she had come down the Mount to tend to Melwas and I wondered how she knew about the weeping wounds in my skin.

Bors shook his head. 'From Guinevere,' he said, nodding over to Pelleas, who sat asleep by the far wall, his untouched meal beside him. 'He must have told her,' Bors said. 'Must have asked her to make something to help the sores.'

I looked at Pelleas, and perhaps I should have noticed how thin he was then, but all I could think of was Guinevere. In the years since we had roamed the island together as children, Guinevere had become somehow ethereal to me. The time we had spent in each other's company, exploring the woods, climbing the granite cliffs and leaping like salmon in and out of the shallows, had in those intervening years seemed more like a conjuring of my own imagination than real memories. She was no more real than that, no more tangible than smoke or morning mist, and so I had taken to my weapons training in earnest.

After my first season, Pelleas admitted that he had never known someone to whom weapon craft came so easily.

'You're gifted, Lancelot,' he said after I had parried a dozen of his thrusts and strikes, not that he had been trying his best. 'Perhaps the gods put this talent in you. Or maybe you just learn things as quickly as a fish learns to swim or a dog to bark. It's not for me to say.' He lifted his shield and practice sword. 'But being a warrior is more than this,' he said. 'None of us are born knowing that. We have to learn it. And you will.'

Four years of sword, spear and shield. Of triumphs and defeats. Pain, bone-tiredness and the occasional joy of mastering one of Edern's sword techniques or Benesek's spear strike combinations. Four years of learning to be a Guardian of the Mount so that we could serve the Lady when Pelleas and the others were too old to escort Greek merchants to Tintagel or train boys how to fight. Four years since I had been close enough to Guinevere to look into her eyes, and in that time she had shimmered just beneath the surface of my thoughts, as elusive as Benesek's sword as I swam face down in the shallows or dived deep enough to hurt my ears when the tide was in.

But now she was real again. I had seen her and she had seen me, and as much as I wanted – as much as I needed – to retrieve that sword for Benesek, in a strange way I would do it for Guinevere too. She would know that once I had set my course I was steadfast in it. I wanted her to know that.

I held the little pot as a man might clutch an ingot of silver or tin, because it belonged to Guinevere and she must have been familiar with its rough texture and the chip in its lip which was sharp to the touch. I put it to my nose and inhaled the herbaceous scent of yellow meadow bright and rosemary and the sweetness of honey.

'The sword is lost, Lancelot,' Bors said. 'There is no point killing yourself trying to find what cannot be found.'

Beneath the pungent sweetness now came the aroma of comfrey root and with it a memory of my mother smearing green ointment onto Hector's arm, which he had broken falling from Malo, my father's stallion. I inhaled that scent and told myself I would not use Guinevere's salve. There were too many sores anyway, on my feet and legs, back and chest, and rather than emptying that little clay pot I would keep it and in keeping it be in some small way closer to Guinevere.

'Thank him for me, Bors,' I said, nodding towards Pelleas.

'Thank him yourself,' he said.

I nodded. Tomorrow, I thought. When I had given Benesek his Saxon sword.

The next dawn brought stinging rain on an unseasonably chill wind. This wind came from the west, bringing great veils of rain which surged across the open sea like the ill will of angry gods, darkening a day which had barely begun. It raised the water around Karrek into furrows which raced across the bay to crash and shatter upon the mainland, hurling white spume onto the rocks. It was a miserable, menacing day and perhaps I should not have been choking amongst those racing black breakers, not least because it was almost impossible to search in any one area since I kept getting carried off. It was dangerous to be out there, too, for there were rocks on the seabed and more than once I was hurled onto them and had to fight the current to get clear or else risk being thrown against them again and again until I was pummelled to death.

But I was out there and I hoped that the violence of the wind-whipped water might have disturbed the seabed and perhaps uncovered Benesek's sword, which had so far remained hidden from me. After what Bors had said the previous night, I had visions of finding a rust-eaten blade that was a mockery of that dazzling Saxon-forged weapon.

Five times that day I had climbed ashore, thrown a cloak over my shoulders and sat shivering on the shingle, dry-retching from the sea water I had swallowed and muttering prayers to Manannán mac Lir that he might return the sword, for it was not Benesek's fault that it had sunk to the seabed and nor had I meant it as an offering to the god. Then, exhausted and cold, I had given myself to the sea once more and continued my search, the sores on my skin weeping into the water and half blinding me with pain.

Yet there was a serenity beneath the surface, the rain's hiss and the sea's onslaught upon the rocks reduced to a distant, dull roar, as I clawed and raked the sand, certain that at any moment I would grasp that ivory hilt.

It was following one such strangely alluring moment of calm, when I had broken the surface to draw a breath of dusk air, that I saw a figure on Karrek's shore. Even at that distance the figure loomed in the darkening day, and then something else caught my eye. High above the Mount, above the Lady's keep, a crane beat its wings westward into the rain-filled skies, its neck outstretched and its stilt-like legs trailing behind, and I felt that bad omen like a shiver as I looked back at the man waiting on the shore.

His hands were raised to his mouth and I could just about hear my name in the teeth of the wind, so I swam towards him, against the tide, kicking with what little strength I had left, and as I came closer I realized that the man calling to me was Benesek.

He had not spoken to me since the day I had lost his sword. He had raged that day and I wondered if the omen of that crane was a warning that Benesek had come to kill me. Yet, I swam to the shore anyway and had to crawl from the sand onto the shingle because I had no strength to stand and walk through the shifting shallows.

I coughed and spat sea-tainted saliva and climbed to my feet, racked with shivering and so tired that I could barely lift my head. 'I will find it,' I told Benesek.

Rain ran down his face and dripped from the ends of his long, drooping moustaches. 'Forget about the damn sword, Lancelot,' he said, unpinning his thick felt cloak. He was heavy-browed and solemn and I knew then that he had not come to kill me, because he stepped forward and put that big cloak around my shoulders. I tried to grip it at my neck but my hands were clumsy and numb and so Benesek fastened it with his own brooch. 'It's Pelleas,' he said, those two words like a kick in my guts. 'He's dying.'

I found the Lady at Pelleas's bedside when I entered the hut which I had shared with him during my first years on Karrek. She leant close to the warrior and whispered to him that I had come, but I stayed at the door, dripping onto the floor rushes, unable to move as Pelleas pushed himself up against the bolsters. He grimaced with the effort.

'There you are, lad,' he said, forcing a smile onto his wan face. He looked exhausted. His bed had been turned north-south to confuse malevolent spirits and there was a bunch of mint tied around his wrist. Remedy for a bad stomach.

'Come, Lancelot,' the Lady said, beckoning me closer.

I told myself that Pelleas would not want me to see him in this frail condition, when in truth it was I who was terrified to see him like this. I just stood there, hands knotted at my sides, teeth clenched to stop them chattering with cold.

'Closer, lad,' Pelleas rasped. 'Dark in here.'

The hearth had been well fed and the flames were tall and hungry, their copper light filling that wattle hut. I walked to the bed and the Lady stepped back so that I had no choice but to fill the space she had ceded to me.

'Gods, Lancelot, you look worse than me,' Pelleas said and this time the smile reached his eyes.

Someone had tied bunches of rosemary and mint to the roof poles above Pelleas's bed, though their fragrance could not smother the sharp stench of fresh faeces and Pelleas knew it.

'My guts,' he said through his teeth. 'They're rotting inside me, lad.'

'I can only smell the mint,' I lied. Pelleas nodded, then closed his eyes and kept them closed.

'The pain is back,' the Lady told me. 'Stay with him, Lancelot. I will fetch something stronger to help him. Something that will make him sleep at least.' With that she drifted out into the rain-scoured twilight and only when the door clumped shut behind her did Pelleas open his eyes again.

'I haven't found it yet,' I said, not knowing what else to say.

'You never will,' he said. 'Wasn't you dropped it.' Melwas had let go of the sword. It was his fault as much as mine. Perhaps more so. 'Benesek knows it,' Pelleas said, 'so whatever you're trying to prove out there with the fish—' He stopped to shift position beneath the bed pelts. 'Pride. Honour. Whatever damn reason. Not worth dying for, lad.' He grimaced with pain. 'Not at your age anyway.'

'Benesek might never find another like it,' I said.

'Benesek has enough silver squirrelled away to have some Frankish blacksmith make him a better sword. Not as pretty, perhaps, but a Frankish blade that'll cut stone and keep its edge. Don't worry about Benesek.'

Talking hurt him and so I was reluctant to encourage further conversation. Not that words would otherwise pour out of me.

'Watch Melwas,' he said. 'He hates you more now than before.'

'He killed my bird,' I said. As if such a thing was important to a man on his deathbed. I felt a fool for saying it.

He nodded. 'I heard some talk, those years ago,' he said.

'You said nothing,' I said. The old anguish and sorrow of that first year on the island stirred in me like a dull pain. I wondered who else had known that my sparhawk's broken wing was no accident.

'I knew you'd try to kill him,' Pelleas said, shifting again. The stench became worse. 'I was right,' he said.

'Is that why you asked for me?' I said. 'To warn me about Melwas?'

The whites of his eyes were yellowish. His cheeks were sunken pools of shadow and I realized for the first time how much thinner he was. Whatever foul disease was killing him had been in him a while, only I had not seen it because I had been thinking of nothing but Benesek's sword. And Guinevere.

He looked to the door and his face tightened, then he curled a hand to usher me closer. I bent, holding my breath for the smell.

'Need you to do something for me, lad,' he said.

'Anything,' I said, remembering the formidable warrior who had slung me over his shoulder and carried me from that death feast at the Beggar King's hall. 'Anything. Just name it.' I wanted to turn and fly to the door. To flee into the night and fill my lungs with clean air. To pretend that Pelleas, that brave and noble warrior, was anywhere but lying in that hut in his own filth and misery.

'I want you to kill me, Lancelot,' he said.

For a heartbeat I thought I had misheard. And yet his eyes held my own, so that with a shudder of horror I realized I had heard well enough.

'You must do it, lad,' he said, 'before this gut rot makes a mewling beast of me.'

'No,' I said, shaking my head; then his hand took mine and squeezed it hard. There was still strength in him. The savage strength of a desperate man.

'You think I want to die like this, boy?' he growled, spittle flecking at his lips. 'Lying in my own reeking filth?' There was fear in his eyes and for a moment he did not look like the man I knew. Then he let go my hand and seemed to sag back into the pelts.

'The Lady will give you something,' I said, 'some infusion to help the pain. Something stronger perhaps. There are plants.'

He shook his head, from which grey stubble sprouted because he had not shaved it in days. 'Long ago I resigned myself to a blade death. A warrior's death,' he said. 'Rather a quick blade than drifting away on some potion without knowing about it.' He tensed with pain as I had seen him do before and it took him a while to find his breath and the composure to speak again. 'I will face death, Lancelot, not hide from it, oblivious in some stupor.'

My heart was thumping. The spitting hearth fire had begun to thaw my flesh and I ached all over now. Every sore and lesion announced itself like a candle flame against my skin. My salt-stung throat was so tight that I could not swallow. I thirsted for water, but I could not move to take up the jug on the table by Pelleas's head.

'Ask Benesek,' I said. 'Or Madern.'

'They would not do it,' he said. Then he grunted. 'Perhaps they would. But after what we have been through together over the years . . .' He shook his head. 'I would not put that on them.'

'But you would put it on me?' I said.

'What am I to you, lad?' he asked. 'An old man.'

Pelleas was in his late middle years and I had never thought of him as old, though those years showed hard on him now.

'You are my friend,' I said.

He exhaled through his cracked lips and closed his eyes. When he opened them again they were flat with sorrow. 'Then do it as my friend,' he said.

My blood itself had soured. My vision was blurry and my legs threatened to give way.

'Lancelot, you are unwell,' the Lady said, not looking at me as she came into the room, pushing back her rain-soaked hood. I caught sight of Geldrin outside. He was bent double and panting, his breath fogging in the rain, and I knew that the Lady had sent him up to the keep to fetch the wooden cup which she now lifted to her nose to smell its contents. 'You will forget about the sword and you will eat and drink what I send, do you understand, Lancelot?' she said, moving to the other side of Pelleas's bed and taking hold of the water jug.

'Yes, Lady,' I said, at which she nodded, pouring a thin trickle of water into the cup.

'What's in it?' Pelleas muttered, suspicious eyes going from the Lady to the cup and then back to the Lady.

She stirred the mixture with an eating knife, then smelled it again. 'Cramp bark and white willow bark,' she said, 'and feverfew herb. I would have liked to add some valerian root but it seems we have none.'

'Just for the pain?' Pelleas asked.

'Just for the pain,' the Lady assured him, holding the cup to his lips. 'You will sleep long and deep but you will wake again,' she said.

Pelleas grunted and drank, then cursed into the cup and dragged a trembling hand across his lips. 'Tastes like rat piss. Next time mix it with wine,' he said, shooting me a grin which contorted, becoming a sneer as the foul-tasting medicine hit his stomach.

'You've seen the boy, Pelleas, now let him go,' the Lady said. 'He needs to rest.'

'Away with you, then,' Pelleas told me, nodding at the Lady that he was ready to finish what was left in the cup. 'But you come and see me soon, Lancelot, do you hear me?'

I said that I would and then I left them, the dying warrior's voice still in my skull as I walked through the seething rain towards the hut which I shared with the other boys of Karrek.

I want you to kill me, Lancelot.

Geldrin ran up to me to ask how Pelleas was, his small face tight with worry as he chewed his thumbnail. But I could not answer him because Pelleas's words flooded my mind like water gushing in through a crack in a boat's hull. And the next thing I knew, Geldrin was yelling. He was calling for help and I wondered what could have happened to him seeing as he had been fine a moment ago.

'Somebody! Help me!' he shrieked and so I asked him what all the fuss was about. Well, I tried to ask him, but I could not form the words and all that came out of my mouth was a low burble of unintelligible nonsense, because I was lying face down on the mud-slick grass. And then the darkness swallowed me.

I woke in the Lady's keep with no knowledge of how I had come to be there. Neither had I ever been in the room in which I now found myself, though I knew it must be at the top of the keep because all I could see from the window slit was endless blue sky and the white gulls that laid claim to it, shrieking madly as though mocking all other creatures for being shackled to land or sea. I was sweat-soaked. Unbearably hot. My mouth so dry that my lips were fastened together and I could not open them.

The surge of the sea sounded more distant than usual and I was struck with the need to escape the blankets and furs which held me captive. To go to the window and peer out, so the cool breeze upon which those gulls caroused could scour the stupor from me and I would be restored.

But then, perhaps I was not in the Lady's keep at all. Perhaps I was in a dream and in reality still lying in the mud outside Pelleas's hut. Because my eyes were seeing, albeit through a haze which distorted everything, that which I knew could not be real. And yet if it were a dream it was more real than any dream I had ever had, which made me suspect I had not spun it alone. Had the Lady poured some herbal draught down my throat as I lay where I had fallen, so that now my mind was no longer fully my own?

'The Lady asked me to look after you,' Guinevere said, handing me a cup of water. I spilt a good deal of that cool water on the furs but at least the moisture broke the seal of my parched lips. Yet still I could not speak. 'You've been asleep since yesterday,' she said, pressing the back of her hand against my forehead and holding it there a moment. 'But now you are awake you must eat to keep up your strength.'

'I'm hot,' I said.

She touched her own head for comparison and frowned. 'The fever is still in you.' She went over to a chest beneath the window and took out another blanket, then came and laid it on the mound of pelts which already swamped me. 'We shall sweat this fever out,' she said. 'But you must drink every cup of water that I give you.' She wore her hair loose and with the light of the day behind her it took on a reddish hue and I remembered her saying when we were children that it was the fire in her.

'You know, Lancelot,' she said, giving me a sidelong glance and showing me the small clay pot of untouched salve that she had made for the raw sores on my skin, 'it works much better when you put it on the bits that hurt.' She shook her head, touching a gentle finger to the salve.

I pushed back the covers and tried to sit up to better get a sense of where I was.

'Bors and Branok carried you on a litter,' Guinevere said, knowing the question before I asked it, then proceeded with exquisite care to dab the ointment onto the sores on my neck and shoulders. I breathed in the aroma of meadow bright, rosemary and comfrey root and I shivered at her touch.

'Back under the furs with you,' she said when she had finished.

I slid back down into the bed, dizziness swimming in me from the effort of moving.

'The Lady wants you close to her. Close to the gods, too,' Guinevere added, gesturing at the small chamber around us, which must have been the lookout back in Roman times, for there were several window slits affording views to the north, south, east and west. Guinevere nodded at the simple bed upon which I lay. 'The Lady comes up here when she hopes to receive dreams from the gods,' she said, filling the cup with water again. 'You are honoured to be here, Lancelot.'

She did not trust me not to spill the water and so held the cup to my lips, and as I drank I remembered lying face down in the grass. Then I remembered more and my stomach rolled over itself. 'Pelleas,' I said.

Guinevere leant over the bed, her ear turned towards me, and I realized that I had barely spoken aloud. 'Pelleas,' I muttered again, coughing into the pelts as Guinevere straightened.

'He lives,' she said, 'though Madern and Agga had to force him back into his bed.' She shook her head in wonder. 'He was on his way up here to see how you were. Not that he'd have got far, poor man. The Lady says there is nothing we can do for him now.'

I laid my head back onto the sweat-sodden pillow, my eyelids feeling impossibly heavy. And I went away again.

The next days passed in a fevered fog. I was either freezing cold or scorching hot and time after time besieged by waves of bone-rattling shivers against which I was helpless.

'Don't fight, Lancelot. Just let it take you, as we used to lie on our backs and let the currents carry us,' Guinevere said during one such episode, holding my hands in hers as she would whenever these tremors took hold. And sometimes I was able to escape the fever for a while and be ten years old again, floating like bladderwrack in the shallows off Karrek's eastern shore, the sun warming my face and Guinevere beside me.

Other times, I was aware of her fingers raking through my hair or her cool breath on my forehead, and more than once I thought I heard her singing or humming in a voice that drifted in and out of my head like a gentle tide.

At some point in my delirium, I later learnt, they had carried me down to the sandy shore when the tide was coming in, and the Lady had asked the retreating waves to carry away the disease and leave me well. Perhaps it had some good effect, or perhaps it did nothing but tire out those who bore me, but the fever had me still.

Whenever I was in my right mind I would know that Guinevere was with me, dousing the fire in my skin with wet cloths, dabbing my lips with cool water and spilling foul-tasting potions into my mouth.

Much of the time, though, I was confined in darkness, held captive by the sickness which, in Guinevere's words, I had brought upon myself with stubbornness and pride.

'You would kill yourself for a sword?' she asked one night, the scorn in her voice sharp enough to cut through the fever's bonds and wound me.

Not just a sword. For honour, I thought, but lacked the strength to say. Whenever I could summon my voice I'd ask after Pelleas, fearing to hear that he had died. And perhaps fearing to hear that he still lived.

The days and nights passed in this way until one night I woke to find that I was alone in that chamber at the top of the Lady's keep. I had been dreaming of my sparhawk and in that dream she and I were in the woods of Benoic where I had roamed as a child. My father was in the dream, too, as the man he had once been, rather than the man he became, and the white gyrfalcon was perched on his fist just as the sparhawk was perched on mine.

'Show me, Lancelot,' he said, stroking the proud falcon, and I grinned at him and we walked together, my chest brimming with elation at the prospect of proving myself, my bird's arrogant yellow eyes fixed on the woods and her body tensed in readiness should some prey reveal itself.

Soon enough, a quail clattered up from a patch of long grass and I extended my arm towards it and let go my sparhawk's jesses and she leapt from the glove, beating hard. But then something was wrong. In a flail of wings she tumbled from the air, spiralling like an arrow, and struck the ground. Shrieking in terror. Flapping madly. Writhing in vain amongst a flurry of shed feathers, she cursed gods and men. She cursed me too, for she could not fly. She was an abomination to her kind. A ruined creature, in my dream and in life, and I was not brave enough to end her misery.

This dream's claws still in me, I was out of the bed and stumbling down the stairwell, feeling the stones' coldness on the skin of my shoulders, arms and hands as I scuffed against the wall to steady myself. I was neither fully awake, nor well. Not even close to being free of the sickness which had weakened my body and clouded my mind, but I opened the keep's door and careened into the night, gulping at the cool sea air and lumbering down the moonlit slope.

My legs gave way and I sprawled headlong onto the dewy grass. Clambered to my bare feet and stumbled on and fell again, feeble and unsteady as a newborn foal. Up again, staggering on, looking up at the iron-grey clouds which raced through the silver black sky and dizzied me so that I had to stop for several heartbeats or else fall again. I looked behind me up the slope. No one following. I ran on, reaching the woods without falling, and wove between the trees whose branches grasped at me but could not catch me. The breeze whispered through those woods but I did not stop to listen to what it said, nor did I look for omens or stand a while upon the shore to watch the white-haired waves roll across the submerged rocks.

Instead, I skirted the communal hut and Edern and Avenie's place and fell against the wattle fence of the pig pen, earning a contemptuous snort from one of the beasts as I stood looking up at the fast-sailing clouds, the stench of manure tainting every ragged breath. The incessant, drawn-out sighs of the ebb tide sounded distant and dull. The full moon above me was not a searingly bright and cloud-beset disc, but a smear of silver, dull as a dirty blade, and for a moment I was not sure where I was. An ear-piercing ringing had me pressing my hands against my ears, though some part of me knew the sound was inside my own head.

I prayed to Taranis, master of war, to whom my father used to pray, that the god would give me strength now. Strength to do what must be done, before my body failed me and the black void swallowed me again. That come the dawn, I would not be found by Benesek or Edern or one of the others, naked but for my loincloth, face down in the grass.

I was moving again, faltering, almost falling yet somehow keeping my feet, towards the hut from whose thatch grey smoke rose like steam into the chill night.

What if someone was with him? What then? I shook my head, trying to rid it of that accursed ringing, then pushed open the door and stepped inside. And there he was, sitting up in his bed, the lines of his haggard face etched by the bronze glow of the hearth fire. Boar's Tusk lay in its scabbard beside him and he had one hand on its hilt as if he had been waiting for an enemy.

Or waiting for me.

'Took you long enough,' he said.

I looked to make sure that we were alone, then went over to him and this time I lifted the jug from the table by his bed and drank from it. When I put the jug back I saw him notice my trembling hands.

'Knew you'd come,' he said. 'I knew it.' He yet had enough life in him to look amused by my standing there in the dead of night, thin and pallid and wearing only enough cloth to preserve my modesty.

He frowned. 'You will do it, lad?' he said.

I nodded. 'How?' I asked.

He closed his eyes and exhaled, then smiled and told me how.

There were tears in my eyes as I drew Boar's Tusk from its scabbard. The blade was polished and honed to a razor's edge and beautiful.

'You'll need strength,' he warned me, 'to do it right.'

'I know,' I said. The swirls along the sword's length reminded me of blood eddies on water.

'And you'll have to help me out of this damned bed,' he said, lifting a hand and offering it to me as he grimaced with the effort of shifting himself to the edge of the bed.

I laid Boar's Tusk on the table and told him to hang on round my neck as I put my arms around him, under his arms, and eased him off the bed. The strain of it flooded my vision with blackness and the ringing in my ears was deafening, but Pelleas's legs buckled and I lowered him until he was kneeling on the rushes.

We were both gasping so that neither of us could talk for a while, but then Pelleas straightened his back and sat tall, his backside resting on his heels, and so I took Boar's Tusk from the table whilst arming sweat from my forehead and eyes.

'You're a good lad,' he said with a nod, smoothing his tunic of undyed wool.

'I can't do it,' I said. The sword grip was slick in my hand. I felt the need to void my bowels and the muscles in my thighs quivered incessantly.

'Yes, you can, Lancelot,' Pelleas said, lifting his head, though he could not see me because I stood behind him. 'You have it in you. I should know.'

I shook my head. 'No,' I said.

'Come here, lad,' he said, and so I moved to stand in front of him, then fell to my knees so that our faces were no more than a foot apart. I could smell the disease on his creaking breath but could not hold his eye and so looked at the floor rushes instead. Pelleas took hold of my chin and pushed my head back up so that our eyes met. 'You can do it, Lancelot. And you must do it.' His hand fell away but I held his gaze now.

'Ask Benesek,' I said, hoping beyond hope to escape this dreadful responsibility. Even then.

Pelleas shook his head. 'It must be you,' he said. 'It will be you.' There was a gut-wrenching sadness in his eyes but no tears. He smiled thinly. 'Besides, Benesek hasn't got a decent sword,' he said.

Silence. A log spat an ember into the rushes where I watched it die.

'You didn't come down here to tell me you won't do it,' he said.

'No,' I said, looking down at the sword in my hand.

'Lancelot, look at me,' he said, and so I did. 'You are my friend,' he said. 'What you do for me now takes more courage than a man might see in his life. I know it. And I thank you for it. And if our shadow bodies meet in the hereafter, I will thank you again and we shall be friends again.'

I said nothing because I could not speak. But I did look into his eyes and in that look I tried to tell him that I loved him.

'Now, lad,' he said, nodding and straightening again as he steeled himself. 'Do it.'

I let out the breath I had been holding and climbed to my feet, moving around him so that I stood looking down at his head, which I could see by the flame-glow was newly shaved. Then, with two hands on the grip, I lifted Boar's Tusk and placed its point gently on the skin of the hollow between his neck and his left collarbone. Pelleas did not so much as flinch at the blade's cold touch. He knew the sword was as sharp as it could be, and that one massive thrust would drive that blade down to tear open his beating heart. And so he knelt there, straight-backed, his hands on his thighs and his eyes closed.

'Goodbye, my friend,' I said, and whispered to Taranis to make me strong enough.

Then I plunged the sword down.

I escaped the horror I had made and stood for a while outside the hut, drawing long breaths and looking up at the night sky. A bat wheeled in its erratic and graceless flight and then was gone, and I wondered if it had in fact been Pelleas's soul fleeing his mortal body. I did not know how long it took a man's soul to reach Annwn's shores far beyond the Western Sea, but I hoped that Pelleas would soon be hunting the boar and the stag in that realm where disease held no sway and pain was unknown.

High above me the clouds raced on as before, charging past the moon which shimmered through my tears. Around me, the inhabitants of Karrek Loos yn Koos slept on, and around us all the sea murmured as it ever did, its breathy cadence unaffected by what had just taken place. One heartbeat Pelleas was here with us, like the rocks and the trees, like the surf rolling up onto the shingle and the fish swimming in the bay. Then, he was gone. Just like that, Pelleas was nothing more than my memory of him.

I then did the second hardest thing I had ever done. I went back inside that hut. For a moment I just looked at him and I was struck by how much his face had changed since his life had fled, so that if someone had walked in then who had not known Pelleas well, they might not even recognize him. His face was impossibly gaunt and had turned a greyish yellow that not even the fire glow could warm.

Thankfully there was little blood. There was a neat crimson cleft against his collarbone and the tunic around it was stained dark, but the blood from his ripped-open heart had filled his chest instead of spilling all over him. Carefully, or as carefully as my own fevered and frail body would let me, I lifted him, taking pains to keep his torso upright so as not to spill any blood as I moved him back to his bed. Then I positioned the bolsters behind him until he looked almost as he had when I had come, but for his face which was hollow and sallow by the flamelight and so barren without the spark of his soul.

When this was done, I cleaned Boar's Tusk and polished the blade until it gleamed, then I put it back in its scabbard and laid it on the furs over his thighs. I looked at him sitting there, even though it tortured my own heart to do it, and then I said goodbye to my friend for the last time, before heading into the night.

12

Conceived in Blood

I SAT SHIVERING IN A SMALL clearing amongst the blackthorn, oak and hazel, where the breeze blowing in off the sea could do nothing to help dry my tunic and trews. It was one of those warm, late summer days, when the air itself is sluggish and thick with the scent of honeysuckle, and the woodland clearings and thickets are glutted with the drowsy buzzing of flies. When bees and butterflies throng at the flowers and caterpillars plague the oaks and beetles scuttle through the litter and, now and then, you hear the distant hammering of a woodpecker chiselling out grubs from their tunnels in old timber.

Above me the sky was the blue of cornflowers, and I watched the martins and swallows joining together to celebrate the seemingly endless summer and the infinite bounty of insects to be plundered. They chased and swerved and plummeted, imitating each other in flight, and then as one flock they veered and cut away, vanishing as quickly as they had appeared.

Black bryony and bindweed twisted and twined in the thickets around me. Thorny dog roses and brambles grappled and grasped, and goosegrass scrambled its way along the forest floor. It was just one small clearing amongst the profusion of life beyond the place which we called The Edge, on the mainland shore. And yet whenever I came here, no sooner had I dried from the swim across the bay than would my palms become slick with sweat. Having barely slowed after the exertion of the swim, my heart would beat faster again, urgent as a hawkmoth's wingbeats as it hangs above a cluster of honeysuckle. I would feel the blood thrumming in my veins as it did before a fight or contest against one of the other boys. And none of this was because I had broken the Lady's rules by coming here to the mainland.

A twig snapped somewhere behind me and I stood from my log

seat, turning towards the sound. Nothing. A deer perhaps, which had not smelled me, with there being no breeze to carry my scent. I had swum from Karrck's north-east shore as I always did on a sunny day. The seabed from there to the mainland was rocky and weed-covered, making the sea look dark, so that anyone looking out would be less likely to see me. Elsewhere, the seabed was sandy and the sea clear, meaning I would stand out against it on a day so bright as this, and I did not relish the thought of having to explain to the Lady why I had broken her rules. Nor would I escape Benesek, who would wonder why I was deemed still too weak to train fully but not too weak to swim from shore to shore.

But I had made it across unseen and now I waited in that small glade, watching a tribe of wood ants carrying their prey – a butterfly with reddish-yellow and black wings – across the woodland floor. I could hear the rustle of their vigorous, inexorable progress, but then another sound made me look up in the direction of the shore.

'One day they will catch us,' Guinevere said, dripping in a shaft of sunlight beside an old blackthorn which had been raided for firewood in the recent past. Yann the cook said that faggots of thorn bush baked the sweetest bread and regularly sent one of us to cut some for the store.

'And what would they do?' I asked with a shrug.

'Cast us out?' Guinevere suggested, bending to squeeze the water out of her sodden dress. 'It has happened before, to a girl and boy who were found together in the smokehouse.' The cream-coloured linen clung to her lithe body in such wonderful ways.

The first time we had met beyond The Edge I had done my best not to stare, though my best efforts had been feeble. Not that Guinevere ever seemed embarrassed or told me not to look. Now though, as she stood there drenched and breathing hard after the swim, I let my eyes wander to the swell of her breasts. Even down to the small dark patch which showed faintly through the dress at her crotch.

'The smokehouse?' I said.

Guinevere smiled, amused by the thought. Somewhere in the branches nearby a raven gave that strange call that sounds like the *glug, glug* of wine being poured from a bottle. 'They must have thought that was the last place anyone would look.'

I grinned. 'At least their love was preserved,' I said, impressed with my own joke. Guinevere rolled her eyes. 'They wouldn't cast us out,' I said, standing and walking to her. 'You are the Lady's most gifted student. And I am the best sword on the island.' I grinned again. That boast was unearned, for while none of the other boys could beat me with the practice swords, both Benesek and Edern could. But being with Guinevere brought out my arrogance. When I was with her I feared nothing. I thought myself capable of anything.

'How do you know I am the Lady's best student?' she challenged me, watching me from the corner of her eye as she turned her head and grasped her long dark hair so that water ran from her fists.

'Aren't you?' I said.

She answered that with just a look and I kept my eyes on hers now, even though they were being drawn to the swell of her breasts in that sodden linen dress like a bee to a teasel flower.

'So what shall we do, Lancelot? Creep around like mice afraid of the cat? Stealing a moment here, a moment there?'

I shrugged. 'For now,' I said. 'But one day, you will take the Lady's place and I will be as Pelleas was, a Guardian of the Mount and the Lady's champion.'

'Poor Pelleas,' she said. 'You must miss him.'

I half nodded and looked away, regretting having brought Pelleas into it. No onc had been accused of killing the warrior, nor had there been any talk of it openly, for everyone on the island knew that whoever had sheathed a blade in Pelleas's heart had done it out of love or comradeship. To end his suffering. But the memory of that night, of looking into his living eyes before sending his soul to the afterlife, was sharp still. Painful still.

Guinevere took my hands in hers. We were standing so close that I could smell the sage which she had chewed to sweeten her breath. She gave a sad smile. 'You think life will be so simple?' she asked.

'I think we will always be together,' I said.

She arched her brows. 'And the vengeance you have sworn on your uncle? On those others who did those unspeakable things? You would forget all that and live here to grow old with me?'

I frowned. 'At some time I will have to leave for a while,' I admitted. 'But will return as soon as I have avenged my family. Then we will grow old here together. We will swim all the days of summer and in the winter we will tell stories to our children by the fire.'

I kept my face as straight as I could while Guinevere's eyes widened in feigned shock at my presumption. 'So how many children shall we have?' she asked.

I pretended to give the question some thought. 'Two boys,' I said after a while, 'and perhaps a girl also. Who will be headstrong and troublesome like her mother.'

She pursed her lips. 'And there was me thinking you only thought of fighting and running and hurling your spears and trying to be better than Melwas,' she said, 'but it seems you have planned our future.'

Neither of us could keep up the pretence any longer and we both laughed, and of the half a dozen times we had met here across the water, this was the longest Guinevere had let me hold her hands before breaking the grip.

'Where are you supposed to be?' I asked.

Her lips, as full and pink as the corncockles which throng among the summer rye, curled up at the corners.

'I should be gathering ingredients.'

'What ingredients?' I asked.

She frowned, trying to remember. 'Ash leaves, cowslip root, eyebright, lavender, mugwort, thyme and yarrow,' she said. 'But Alana will give me half of whatever she finds.'

'Alana knows you are here?' I said.

'Of course she does,' Guinevere said. 'But she won't say anything to anyone. So long as I tell her what we get up to.' She almost smiled. 'Some of it, anyway.'

I tried to hide my alarm at that thought. 'What potions are you girls making?' I asked.

Guinevere narrowed her eyes at me. 'You know I can't talk about the craft,' she said.

'I tell you when I have learnt a new spear block or sword strike,' I said.

'Whether I want to see it or not,' she said.

For the first time it was I who broke our hand hold, my brow tightening like a belt cinched at the waist.

'Oh, Lancelot, for such a formidable young warrior you are easily harmed,' she said, and I did not know if she was still teasing me but she took hold of my hands again.

'You know some herbal lore?' she said. 'Thyme for courage. Basil for wealth. Rosemary keeps a woman young. Sage wards off evil.'

I gave a half-hearted nod and wondered what her sage-chewing said about me, as she gestured to a clump of tall plants which looked to my eyes like any other thorny furze. 'Some of what we are supposed to gather today is to help us to journey,' she said. I wished then that I had not asked, remembering that night years ago, when Merlin had come to Karrek and he and Guinevere had journeyed together.

'Perhaps it is for the best if I do not know,' I said gloomily.

She nodded and to my surprise leant forward and kissed me on the lips, then pulled back, a mischievous smile playing at the corners of her mouth. 'So long as you do keep showing me the sword tricks you have learnt,' she said, 'for I am interested. I swear it.'

'They are not tricks,' I said, then smiled. 'I could teach you how to knock a sword out of a man's hand and cut a flying arrow in two. If you like.'

'I am sure such skills will come in useful growing old here with the gulls and the fish,' she said, and with that she leant in again and this time I was ready. I shivered with the forbidden thrill of that kiss, the blood gushing in my ears and in my groin like an echo of the surf rolling up the shore beyond the trees.

Then we pulled back and for several heartbeats just looked into each other's eyes, Guinevere's white teeth dragging at her bottom lip. Not, I think, because of some nervousness or fear of getting caught with me, but rather because she feared revealing so much of herself, of her secret thoughts, to anyone. Especially me, perhaps.

'You are the most beautiful thing I have ever seen,' I said. It was true, for all that I feared how trite it must have sounded to her, though she did not say so. I wondered how Guinevere's father could have sent her away. Surely she was a light in his life. This radiant, fearless girl.

She pouted and it was all I could do not to kiss her again. 'You have lived in the forests of Benoic and on this island and this is the furthest you have ever been into Britain,' she said. 'When you have actually seen something of the world I will ask you again if you still think I am the most beautiful thing in the world.'

'And I will say the same again,' I said.

She frowned and shook her head and some strands of her dark hair fell over her left eye. She did not sweep the hair away but left it there, as if half hiding behind it. As if my gaze frightened as much as intrigued her.

'So what will you tell Alana?' I asked.

She gave that half-smile which hinted at mischief. 'I will tell her that we kissed,' she said.

'Just that?' I asked.

She lifted her chin. 'There is nothing more to tell,' she said. 'Though she will not believe that and will try to wring me like a sponge for every last detail.'

The horror of that thought must have shown on my face.

'Don't worry,' she said. 'I shall tell her that we kissed and I shall say no more than that. She will of course spin her own version of it in her mind, but that can only help us. The more our meetings feed Alana's own imagination, the more likely she is to keep our secret.'

'I suppose so,' I said, still feeling uneasy about anyone else knowing. But then Guinevere kissed me again and I did not care about anything else in the world.

They were happy days on Karrek. That summer seemed to stretch on and on, like the blue skies beneath which we trained with our weapons until the sweat poured down our bare torsos and the breath rasped in our throats. And still we fought and competed against each other in foot races, and lifted rocks and swam circuits of the island, each of us eager to prove himself and earn the praise of our betters.

In spite of the fever that had laid me low after my fruitless search for Benesek's sword, as that summer slowly slipped away I grew strong. By the time the nights drew in and our shadows lengthened on the shingle shore, and the prevailing breeze from the Western Sea raised bumps on bare arms, my shoulders had filled out. The leather thong around my neck upon which I had hung the silver ring Guinevere had given me was tight now. My stomach was ridged with bands of muscle, while the muscles in my arms were hard and taut as ship's knots. Yet even with this new muscle I was still fast and with the wooden swords landed blows even on Benesek and Edern almost as often as they hit me.

I was good with the bow, too, and could hit the target almost as often as Agga, and though I could still not throw a spear as far as Melwas, Agga or Bors, I could cast with more accuracy than they, which even Benesek admitted was more advantageous in a real fight. 'Unless your enemies are running away,' the warrior had joked, 'and you don't care which one you kill but just want to stick one of them before you go home to your wine and your woman.'

I was strong and fast and confident. And I was in love.

Bors knew my secret of course. For one thing, shortly after he had come to Karrek and we had become friends, he had asked whose ring I wore around my neck and I had told him. For another, he had seen my face when he gave me the salve which Guinevere made for me back when I had been covered in sores.

'You may as well chase the tide, Lancelot,' he had said with pity in his smiling eyes as we sat one warm summer night on the shore, watching the black water break white on the rocks.

'You've seen how fast I am,' I replied, smiling. I did not want his pity. 'And besides, her father Lord Leodegan is a Christian,' I said. 'His hall is glutted with Christians, which is why Guinevere is here on Karrek.'

Bors flinched his head back a little, which was his way of saying that he still did not understand.

'The Christians fear Guinevere's abilities,' I said. 'They do not understand her talents and feel threatened by the old ways.'

Bors grunted. 'That doesn't surprise me,' he said. 'Their god seems weak next to Cernunnos or Balor or Taranis.'

He knew about Guinevere's journeying. Thanks to the girls who had been there, the whole island knew what I had done to Merlin that night in the keep.

'He may seem weak but look how he gathers men,' I said. 'Merlin says that one day our gods will be gone from Britain and the Christian god will rule here.'

'Christians are strange,' Bors said, his only comment on the druid's grim prediction.

'So Guinevere will stay here on the Mount,' I said, 'and of all the girls, she has the greatest ability. And one day the Lady will be old.'

'Guinevere will inherit the Lady's power and position,' Bors said, understanding now, 'and you will be a Guardian of the Mount and the two of you will rule this little island like Uther and Igraine.'

He shook his head, looking up at the moon. 'Then I hope you are not just fast but patient too, cousin,' he said.

I touched the ring at my neck and turned to look up at the keep on top of the hill. I had once manned a hawk. I had taken a spiteful, starved and broken-winged sparhawk and taught her to tolerate me, as her keeper at first, then as her companion in the hunt. I could be patient, I thought.

With Bors's help and Alana's too, Guinevere and I met in secret whenever we could. Sometimes we swam across to The Edge and waited for one another in the thorny glade. Other times, I saw her when the Lady sent her down to the shore with medicine or ointment when one of us boys had been cut in training, or if one of the men suffered a toothache or sore back. More often than not, Guinevere and I came no closer than a shared smile or furtive glance: morsels to the starving, and yet delicious. There were times, though they were too few, when we managed to contrive it that I took the remedies from her. For a heartbeat, no more, our fingers would touch and the thrill of that illicit moment would thrum in my blood like a bow string when the arrow flies.

Eventually, the summer faded. We slaughtered and salted some of the pigs and raided Cornubia's woods for their mast of beech and hazel nuts, acorns and chestnuts. We unburdened the orchards of apples, pears and plums, pillaged the brambles of their blackberries, rosehips and sloes, and dived down to the oyster beds for their rich harvest.

After the Lady or one of her girls had spoken the calming charms, we smoked the bees from their hives and stole their sweet honey for our mead, their reddish resin for its healing properties and their wax to make candles to light when the Lady hosted important guests, for they burned with a bright and steady flame and did not stink like the mutton-fat candles. We slaughtered two old ponies and smoked their flesh and one blustery afternoon Melwas, Agga and Edern, who had taken the currach across to the mainland, returned in boastful triumph with a full-grown boar which they had speared to the north-east, not a day's walk from King Menadoc's hall.

'And what would you have done had a king's man found you hunting Menadoc's beasts in Menadoc's woods?' Benesek challenged them as they hefted the carcass from the boat, but the only answers he got were grins. The boys were not punished. Even Benesek was impressed with the prize and we gutted and skinned the beast and hung it to smoke.

The skies seemed either to be heavy and grey and thronged with cloud, or else bright blue and clear and so cold that the mornings greeted us with the hoar frost crunching underfoot. Dunlins and turnstones and other wading birds wore their winter plumage of dull browns and greys, and now and then a throbbing noise would have one of us looking up to see a pair of swans in flight, their great wings beating into the south.

If I saw a stoat bounding across the leaf-littered hill, its coat was completely white, and in its looping run I always heard old Hoel in my head. 'He'd rather turn and let the gyrfalcon rip into him than flee through the mire and get that pretty coat filthy,' he had told me one winter when Benoic lay under a quilt of snow and we were out hunting other creatures that would be easily seen against the white. 'An ermine would die for his pride,' the falconer said.

Snow fell on the Lady's keep that winter. As fine as flour on the threshing-room floor, yet it lay on the grass of the Mount and on the strand above the lapping tide, and before long that thin mantle was stitched with the tracks of hare and badger, pigeon and gull. And with the snow came a ship.

The *Elsam* came from Tintagel and her arrival prompted a celebration on Karrek because we knew it was likely the last ship we would see before the spring. It brought grain, ale and wine and it also brought Edern and Madern back, which was another reason for lighting the beeswax candles to chase away the dark, and for bringing a joint of venison down from the hooks to add its salted flesh to the broth. The men had escorted a party of Greek merchants first to Tintagel, where they unloaded their amphorae of olive oil, and then across the Irish Sea to the slave markets on the Liffey, where the Greeks were hosted by the high king of Ireland himself, Lugaid mac Lóegairi. Then, having bought a number of slaves, the Greeks had returned to Tintagel, where High King Uther feasted them.

'King Uther treated them like kings,' Edern told us, shaking his head, 'gave them wolf pelts and women, to loosen their tongues about all they had seen in Ireland and all they'd heard from Lugaid mac Lóegairi's own mouth.'

'Even offered to buy their Irish slaves for three times what the Greeks paid for them,' Madern said, 'but they claimed their Emperor would pay ten times that and so wouldn't sell. Still, they accepted Uther's invitation to stay the winter rather than risk a return so late in the season.'

Their duty discharged and their purses full, Edern and Madern had bought grain, ale and wine and paid the skipper of a small coaster to convey them and their cargo to Karrek, and the day after their return, we gathered to the harp's song and fed the fires until the flames leapt high as though revelling in their coming reign over the winter nights.

I was fifteen and I raised my cup of strong ale to Pelleas's memory with the rest of them, although I did not have the thirst for ale that Melwas, Agga, Bors and some of the others had. They drank until they staggered outside to heave the contents of their stomachs onto the snow in steaming streams. Then they would continue drinking.

'He can't take his ale,' Melwas would say, gesturing at me with his cup, even if he was still wiping the vomit off his tunic. Maybe he was right. But wine and ale had ruined my father and I would not let it ruin me. Yet I drank enough to warm my insides and flush my cheeks. And make me want to declare to every living thing under that roof, under the stars themselves if it came to it, that I loved the girl who sat cross-legged on the dais plucking the lyre's strings. Which might have been already obvious to anyone with eyes, had they not been fixed on Guinevere too.

For if she had been able to hold a room full of people spellbound when she was a girl of eleven summers, at sixteen she could steal their souls.

'Erwana is prettier,' I had heard Peran tell Branok and Florien one day when we were putting arrow after arrow into the straw targets.

And Erwana was pretty. She was golden-haired like the Lady and long-limbed and her clear-skinned face had a luminous quality which made it easy to imagine Erwana as a queen in a silken gown, dripping with silver and gold. Her eyes were large and blue and she knew how to use them. Jenifry too, with her almond eyes, full lips and fuller breasts, was considered a beauty, and the boys would curse the name-less lord of Britain who would one day marry her.

But none of these girls had what Guinevere had. Her beauty was elemental. She was fire and she was ocean. She was air and she was earth, and you just had to be in the same room as her to sense that wild spirit and be enchanted by it.

And I drank in the very sight of her as I sipped my ale.

'She will meet you in the Lady's dream chamber,' someone whispered in my ear. I turned and Alana gave me a knowing look as she lifted a jug of ale towards the cup in my hand. I glanced around to see if anyone might have heard, then nodded at the short, copper-haired girl as she filled my cup, and how she managed not to spill any I could not say, for she did not take her eyes off me. Not even after she had finished pouring, until Benesek called her over to replenish his own cup. And even as she walked off through the crowd, she kept glancing back at me, the pale skin of her neck reddening.

I looked at Guinevere, wanting to acknowledge the message Alana had delivered, but her eyes seemed not to see anything in that round chamber. She was far away now, borne on the wings of that harp's song to another time, another place, and we who stood in that flame-lit dark were as the mice in the rushes or the bricks in the wall or the distant murmur of the sea.

Perhaps Guinevere's mysterious quality, that ability she had to enchant those around her, was god-given. Perhaps when she had escaped Manannán's clutches that day she first came to Karrek, the sea god had left his mark on her. Or perhaps it had always been in her. Maybe the midwives had seen it when they first looked into Guinevere's eyes the day she came into the world. The Lady saw it, Merlin had seen it, I saw it. And we were not the only ones, as she played the battle hymn of Belatucadrus and the men hummed along in their deep, sonorous voices, like echoes of times past when they had sung that hymn before battle.

I should have taken more note of the sailors of the *Elsam* staring at Guinevere like hungry men, but I was halfway drunk and humming with the rest and the Lady's keep was crammed with bodies and I was building up to declaring my love for Guinevere to anyone who would listen.

'Pelleas!' Benesek called out, lifting his cup to me as the last notes from Guinevere's lyre faded against a chorus of appreciative grunts and the thumping of hands against roof posts and table tops. It was the third time I had drunk to Pelleas that night, but we all missed him, none more than Benesek, who had been Pelleas's friend and sword-brother for more years than I had been alive.

'To Pelleas,' I said, the pain of his loss still enough to rob me of breath like a blow to the stomach. More painful still when I could see the grief in his friend's eyes. I drank deeply. Benesek nodded, dragging a hand across his long moustaches. 'To Pelleas and the man who put Boar's Tusk into his heart.'

The breath caught in my throat. My blood ran cold and I looked into Benesek's dark eyes and he looked into mine.

'Whoever did that, not in a fight, mind, but in cold blood . . .' he grimaced, 'went in there in the dead of night. Looked him in the eye.' He dipped his head slightly and then looked into the hearth flames which were leaping to cast copper light on the cobweb-slung beams and ancient roof timbers. 'He's a brave man who did that. I could not have done it.'

He knew very well who had done it, and his knowing it hung in the air between us like smoke. But I said nothing, hoping that Benesek would not force my admission for I did not want to speak it aloud.

His eyes bored into mine. He raised his cup again and we drank together. Then he turned his gaze towards the dais and for a while neither of us spoke as we watched Madern giving Hedrek some last advice before Hedrek's sword demonstration.

'Who'll wager against him cutting off his own foot?' Bors asked, coming to stand beside me, feeling that he had walked into something but saying nothing of it.

'Why do you think Madern chose Hedrek?' Benesek asked, finding a louse or some dirt in his moustaches and flicking it into the hearth. 'If he'd wanted limbs flying and blood everywhere he'd have chosen you for the demonstration, Bors.'

We grinned at that, even Bors, who never seemed to take offence at anything or anyone. And anyway, Benesek had a point, for whilst Hedrek was easy enough to beat in a proper fight with the practice swords, of all of us he had the best memory for the positions and looked the neatest when performing them. Bors, drunk as he was, could have walked up onto the dais, picked up one of those blunt swords and beaten Hedrek to the rushes with it. But it would not have made for a pretty display.

'Talking of swords, Lancelot,' Benesek said, turning to me. I cringed, expecting him to bring up the Saxon sword. 'Pelleas wanted you to have Boar's Tusk,' he said.

Just like that.

I stood there dumb as a roof post, still taking in Benesek's words even as the bones in my shoulder and arm rattled under Bors's congratulatory blow. 'Are you sure?' I asked the warrior. He handed his cup to Bors so that he could lift the baldrick over his shaven head.

Then he wound the belt around Boar's Tusk and held it towards me and I just looked at it for a moment, wondering why he was only telling me now, so many weeks after the smoke from Pelleas's balefire had drifted eastward on the breeze.

'Take it,' Bors hissed at me.

I took it.

'You're sure?' I asked again.

Benesek turned to Bors and rolled his eyes. Then he fixed me with his gaze once more. 'Course I'm sure, lad,' he said, an edge of irritation to his voice. His wine-stained lips parted, revealing his teeth. 'I thought about keeping it myself, what with you and Melwas having thrown my sword into the sea,' he said. 'Couldn't see why you should have a sword like Boar's Tusk while I should be left nothing but my good looks.' He shrugged, nodding at the sword in my hand. 'But that's what the fool wanted.'

What would the others say? I wondered, glancing back to the dais, where Hedrek and Madern, having loosened their limbs and made their practice cuts through the smoky air, now stood facing each other awaiting the Lady's word to begin the demonstration.

'Why do you care what they'll think?' Benesek asked, tipping a wash of ale down his throat. 'Nothing to do with them what Pelleas wants—' He stopped and hoomed in the back of his throat. 'What Pelleas wanted. Wasn't any of them he coaxed from under a table and carried over his shoulder back from Benoic chased by a rabble of cut-throats.' He shook his head. 'He loved you, lad. Even took an interest in that broken-feathered hawk of yours. Was always going on to Edern and me about how you refused to give up on that bird. Said your stubbornness was a thing to behold. He admired you for it.'

Holding the scabbard in my left hand I gripped Boar's Tusk by its leather and silver-wire-bound hilt and drew just enough steel to catch the fire's molten copper glow as it had done the last time I had seen it, when I cleaned it of the dark blood which had made patterns on the wool grease coating the blade.

'Thank you,' I said.

'Don't thank me, lad,' Benesek said, retrieving his cup from Bors. 'I just told you I nearly kept it.' He pursed his lips as though considering this. 'Might have done had I not been drunk tonight.'

'Then thank you for not being sober,' I said, wondering if it really had been Pelleas's wish that I should have Boar's Tusk, or if this was just Benesek's way of acknowledging what I had done for our friend with that very sword.

The ring, hiss and scrape of steel on steel announced that Madern and Hedrek had begun their demonstration of sword craft. I knew every lunge and retreat, every cut, thrust and parry, and no doubt the handful of sailors from the *Elsam* would be impressed by Hedrek's speed, skill and grace. And yet I knew they would almost certainly have preferred to be watching Guinevere still. I looked for her myself but could not see her amongst the knot of girls who clustered around the Lady beside the raised platform at the far end of the room. Those girls looked less interested in the swordplay than they did in Melwas, Agga, Kitto and Florien who edged the dais, and that was not perhaps surprising, this being one of those rare nights when all of us – the maidens of the Mount and we future Guardians – were gathered together under the same roof. The boys on the other hand, for all their brave talk on the training field and in the communal hut of pretty girls and future conquests, seemed more beguiled by the flashing blades than by the girls' flashing eyes.

She will meet you in the Lady's dream chamber. Alana's voice whispered in my head.

Bors slapped my shoulder again. 'You're the first of us, cousin,' he said, looking at Boar's Tusk as though it were one of the lost treasures of Britain, 'to win your own sword.'

'I didn't win it,' I said, feeling unworthy, nagged by the thought of Benesek's beautiful sword rusting on the seabed while I, who had never fought for a king, a lord or a lady, now owned such a weapon.

'You won it, Lancelot,' Benesek said, and he did not need to take his eyes off the demonstration for me to know what he meant by that.

Hedrek was a flurry of movement as he attacked Madern, their swords weaving through the smoke.

'Whether or not you can hold on to it, well that's another matter,' Benesek said, though he knew full well it had been Melwas who had dropped his sword over the side of the currach.

'I'll look after it,' I said.

Benesek nodded and for a moment I stood and watched Hedrek's sword dance, admiring his mastery of the techniques. He was good and could be better still if he learnt not to fear pain. But I had seen it

all before and had other things on my mind. Ale for one thing. Guinevere for another. And perhaps the gift of Pelleas's sword, given to me
by Benesek, whose respect it seemed I had earned, emboldened me to
daring action.

With the folk of Karrek Loos yn Koos deep in their cups now and
cheering Hedrek's every sweep and stroke, I went to find Guinevere.

The stairwell was dark and empty and as I climbed it seemed that every
sound – my leather shoes on the worn stone, my breathing, the blood
pulsing in my ears and, somewhere, the drip, drip of water which had
found its way in through the old Roman tower – was abnormally loud.
And though none of the rushlights in the wall mounts were lit, my eyes
penetrated the darkness so that I saw every tool mark in the dressed
stone, every rust-like patch of lichen and each crevice where the old
mortar had crumbled away.

I heard the latch and creak of a door behind me and pressed myself
against the wall, holding my breath to listen for the sound of feet
ascending, my heart thumping in my chest. But whoever had left the
girls' chamber was heading down and so after a moment waiting in
the dark, I continued up towards the Lady's dream chamber.

I stopped by a window slit and put my face to it, breathing in the
cool air to clear my head of the smoke which had hung like a gauze in
the chamber below. A breeze blew a few fine drops of rain onto my
cheeks and lips. My mouth was dry. Somewhere in the night a screech
owl cried and for some reason I shuddered at the sound and looked up
into the darkness. Then I climbed the last few steps and stood outside
the oak door, my hand on the cool ring handle of twisted iron as I
steadied my nerves and remembered those fevered days I had spent in
this room. Dark, flesh-shattering days during which my soul would
surely have fled had it not been for the sound of Guinevere's voice
calling it back, commanding it to stay, coaxing the sickness out of me.

I took one last full breath. No one downstairs would hear me open
that door. Even so, I turned the handle slowly and pushed, wincing at
the creak of the hinges. That's when I heard Guinevere's muffled scream.

I threw the door back and stepped into the chamber and by the
sooty flickering light of the bedside candle I saw a man on top of
Guinevere, one hand pushing his trews down, the other on the back
of Guinevere's head, thrusting her face into the bed furs. Faster than

a stooping hawk I flew, throwing my arms around the man's neck, trying to haul him off. But he was big and heavy and he twisted in my grip and drove his left elbow into my temple, sending me staggering.

He turned, slurring curses at me as he found his feet, and I put my head down and launched myself at him and Guinevere leapt from the bed onto his back and for a moment he withstood us both, strong legs planted wide as I tried to drive him back while Guinevere clawed his face and eyes. He reeked of wine but he was not too drunk to ignore the threat to his eyes and he reached behind and took hold of Guinevere. Grunting with the effort, he threw her across the room and I hammered a fist into his groin and another into his belly and he doubled over, then I threw my fist against his bearded cheek as if I were launching a spear. I heard the crack of some bone in his skull, yet he swung a brawny arm and his knuckles caught me below my right eye and spun me round.

'This how you treat guests?' he said, for he was one of the *Elsam*'s crew, and I turned back just in time to see the fist as it slammed into my left eye, knocking me down to the rush-covered boards. I tried to rise, throwing my arms up to shield myself and blinking furiously, desperate to see past the flashing spots which filled my vision.

'I'll kill you,' the sailor growled. His hands were around my neck and darkness was flooding the dream chamber, swallowing me.

I heard Guinevere's shriek as she smashed a clay jug against the man's head and he should have fallen but he was too drunk or too hard-headed, or perhaps it was his seaman's balance, but he kept his feet and backhanded Guinevere, who spun away. But in that same moment I knocked his other hand away from my neck, grabbed hold of his thick beard and pulled down with all my strength and now he lost his balance. I drove his face down into the floor and there was a splintering sound, like a walnut shell being cracked.

A blade flashed and I leapt away from it as his bloodied face came up and he swept the knife out again, coming onto his knees now, growling and choking on blood from his ruined nose. I pulled Boar's Tusk from its scabbard but before I could thrust the blade down Guinevere flew at him, snarling like some fierce creature. She took hold of his head from behind and forced her fingers into his eyes, her blood-smeared face a terrible sight as she hauled him backwards onto herself, still clawing and gouging and wreaking her savage vengeance.

And though the sailor must have feared for his eyes, he knew the greater threat came from the sword in my hand and he blindly flailed his arms towards me even as I thrust the sword down.

Boar's Tusk was a wickedly sharp sword. Its point burst through the wool tunic and the skin and muscle beneath, sinking deep into the cavity between his ribs. He knew well enough where my sword was then and he clutched it, trying to pull it from his chest as that double-edged blade bit deep into his hands. He spat blood at me, muttering some curse through the bloody bubbles and gore which frothed his mouth and dribbled into his salt-crusted beard. I was horrified then, because it seemed this man would not die, that he would pull Boar's Tusk from his body and hack Guinevere and me to death with it.

'Kill him, Lancelot,' Guinevere hissed, blood spilling from her split lip in ruby drops. The sailor's bulk was crushing her yet she would not let go and I saw that her fingers were deep in his eye sockets and so I gritted my teeth, gripped Boar's Tusk's hilt in two hands and threw myself down onto the man, driving the sword deeper still, and for a moment something held it, but then gave way and I felt the point break through more muscle and viscera before sticking fast.

I was half lying on top of the man, still gripping the sword's hilt as he let go the blade and grasped my face in his hot, slick hands. The reek of fresh blood was overwhelming, though now cut with the rotten stench of the mess in his trews, but I held on and Guinevere held on and the man's legs kicked and thrashed amongst the reeds and a warm dark pool spread beneath us. Then, like a bird finding its way out of a house by the smoke hole, his strength just vanished. His big arms fell with a thump onto the boards but we held on for several heartbeats more, gasping for breath and staring at each other across the sailor's body.

At last, I nodded at Guinevere and together we let go. I grabbed fistfuls of the man's tunic and pulled so that Guinevere could wriggle out from under him, then I let his head hit the floor with a thud.

I left Boar's Tusk sticking from the dead man's chest and scrambled over to Guinevere, who sat pale and wide-eyed in the candle-lit gloom.

'You're hurt,' I said, holding her face in my hands.

She shook her head. 'No,' she said.

We were both slathered in blood. Both trembling.

'He's dead,' she said, looking deep into my eyes.

'He should be,' I said.

She lifted her hand and laid a bent finger on my cheek beneath my left eye and held it there. For a moment I wondered what she was doing, then I realized she was letting the blood from a cut well against her knuckle. Her eyes still fixed on mine, she drew the finger to her lips and kissed the trickle of blood which ran down it towards her pale wrist. And with that I pulled her face to mine and she winced with pain as we kissed. I tasted the salt and iron tang of her blood and a shiver ran through my flesh and then we were pulling at our clothes, fumbling and snatching and casting them aside until there was nothing between her skin and mine, and still we were not close enough.

'You are mine,' she whispered, hot breath in my ear.

I pulled my head back so that our eyes could meet once more. I could not read her face, though for a moment I thought she seemed full of sorrow. Then she smiled and nodded and all the tension left her body.

The candle on the far side of the bed crackled and Guinevere gasped, and now we could not have been closer than we were. Not in body or spirit.

'And you are mine,' I said, speaking the words into her mouth, our gore-smeared bodies moving together, writhing like some insatiable beast in the blood of the kill.

Afterwards, we sat against the foot of the bed, holding hands in the dark, staring at a corpse lying in a pool of blood.

'What will happen to us?' Guinevere asked.

For a while I did not reply. I wanted to hold on to what we had just shared. I wanted to savour it, even in the presence of the dead, rather than try to untangle the mess of that night. In truth, the dark but heady enchantment which had gripped me was fading fast. The stench of blood was repugnant now. The corpse on the floor beside us sickening.

'Lancelot.' Guinevere's voice was anxious. Impatient.

I prodded the dead sailor with my foot. He had clung to life, that Dumnonian. Dead meat now.

'He followed you up here. He tried to—'

'I know what he tried to do,' Guinevere said.

She said nothing more and neither did I want to drop more clumsy words into the silence. 'The Lady will ask what I was doing up here,' she said, following the thread of her thoughts, 'and when she learns that you were here too, it will all be clear. Everyone will know. My father will hear of it.'

'What is the worst they can do to us?' I asked. Perhaps I was a fool but I felt neither fear nor regret. The sailor from the *Elsam* had got what he deserved and as for Guinevere, I loved her and she loved me, and perhaps my blood was still running hot in my veins but I believed that was enough.

'The Lady will make one of us leave the island,' Guinevere said. 'That will be our punishment for what we have done.' She lifted her chin towards the corpse. 'Not for what we did to him, but what we did together,' she said.

'We'll tell her I saw that big ox go up and I thought he intended to steal from her. So I followed him.'

'She will know, Lancelot,' Guinevere said. 'Believe me, she will know.'

'So we go on as before?' I said, wanting her to look at me instead of at the body which still had Pelleas's sword sticking out of it. 'Stealing a moment here and there? Hiding in the woods like outlaws?' Yet even as I said it I knew that was how it must be. So did Guinevere.

'We must get rid of the body,' she said, still looking at the corpse. 'We can sink it.' She got to her feet, tying back her dark hair. 'Most of the blood will have soaked into the reeds. We can replace them. Wipe the blood off the boards before it stains. The Lady doesn't come up here often.'

Guinevere might have been staring at the sailor but I was staring at her. I could hardly believe what I was hearing. 'And how will we carry that great lump down and get him out without being seen?' I asked her.

She looked over to the part of the chamber which was beyond the candle's glow and at first I did not know what she was looking at but then I saw it. Another door. I had taken no notice of it before, but now I recalled having on occasion seen the Lady standing on a ledge at the top of the keep looking to the south-west. For the Roman soldiers garrisoned on Karrek long ago, it would have been the highest lookout from which to watch the Saxon Shore. Now that ledge would have another use.

I pulled Boar's Tusk from the dead sailor and cleaned it on his tunic, reflecting as I pushed it back into the scabbard that I had worn my own sword for less than a day and had already killed a man with it. Then we dragged him out onto the ledge and together lifted him so that he sat slumped on the low wall, a cold, reeking, blood-soaked corpse, and Guinevere held him there while I left the dream chamber and made my way back down the spiral stairwell, past the main chamber in which the celebrations were in full flow, then out into the night.

I was drinking in the clean fresh air when the door opened behind me and I spun round, my heart jumping in my chest. To my relief it was Bors. Drunk as he was, he knew something was wrong as he came over to me, frowning and untying the rope belt which held up his trews.

He did not even bother to go to the rocks but just began to urinate onto a clump of gorse. 'You're playing a dangerous game, cousin,' he said in a low voice, then glanced up at me and his mouth fell open. He jerked his head back. 'What in Balor's name happened to you?' he asked.

'You hit me,' I said. 'We argued about which of us is the better spearman. We fought. You won.'

He frowned. 'Are you drunk?' he asked, shuddering as the steaming liquid left his body.

'We fought, cousin, that is what you will say.' The sound of raucous song came as if in waves.

He considered this as he tucked himself away and tied his belt. 'I'm happy to say I beat you, and doubtless the others will believe you deserved it,' he said. 'But what really happened?' He grinned. 'Not Guinevere, surely?' The grin disappeared when he saw the look on my face.

'Come with me,' I said, thinking of Guinevere still holding on to the dead sailor up there in the dark, and we walked around the keep until we stood below the high ledge and I looked up, though my left eye was so swollen now that it was almost closed. Still, I could make out Guinevere as a dark shape against the star glow of the night sky. She waved to me.

'Back,' I hissed to Bors, moving away from the great tower, then I gave the *hoo hoo* call of a tawny owl and a moment later a shape plummeted from the heights and thumped onto the ground.

Bors cursed, the whites of his eyes flashing in the shadows.

'He attacked Guinevere. I killed him,' I said.

'Let me guess how you did it,' Bors said with a sour grin. Even in the dark you couldn't miss the hole in the sailor's chest or the blood-dyed wool around it. 'He's big,' he said, going closer to get a better look.

'I know,' I said, wincing. I had the aches and pains to prove it. I bent and took hold of the sailor's wrists. They were cold. 'Grab his legs,' I told Bors. 'We've got a long way to carry him.'

Bors did not move but just stood there staring down at the corpse.

'What is it?' I asked.

'His eyes,' Bors said through the downward curl of his lips, then spat to ward off the evil of those little wells of dark blood and gore where the sailor's eyes had been.

'Take his legs, Bors,' I said.

Bors grimaced and bent to grab hold of the sailor's ankles. They were perhaps the only parts of him not daubed in blood or wet with urine. 'I'm beginning to wish I hadn't come outside,' he said, then we lifted the corpse and moved away down the hill as fast as we could, avoiding the main track in case we should be seen by anyone on their way up to the keep or down to the shore.

But it was hard going through the trees and before long we stopped and looked at one another, both thinking the same thing, then took a foot each and proceeded to drag the sailor down the woodland track, his head bumping over rocks and divots and his ruined eyes staring up at the branches above and the night sky beyond.

We had not got far when a figure stepped out of the trees ahead, stopping us both in our tracks until we realized it was Guinevere. She wore a black cloak over her green linen dress and her hair was tied back from her face, making her high cheekbones even more striking.

'I thought you would have got further by now,' she said when we reached her and stopped to catch our breath. Even in the dark I could see that her lip was swollen. I suspected there would be bruises beneath the drying bloody crusts on her face.

'You could have killed a thinner one,' Bors answered, looking at Guinevere with a combination of astonishment and awe. She did look beautiful, even blood-smeared like that, and I could not blame Bors if he found himself struck by that beauty. Her eyes were still wide and glinted like a blade's edge in the dark because of the horror which they had witnessed. And perhaps because of what had come after, too.

'Let's move,' I said, and so we did. And by the time we got down to the shore, Bors and I were puffing and spent. Bors fetched some rope while I found some rocks and then we carried the currach down the shingle and heaved the corpse into it.

When Bors moved to get in the boat, Guinevere put a hand on his shoulder. 'No, Bors,' she said, and for a heartbeat I saw again the ferocious creature who had stooped like a hawk and clawed the sailor's eyes to pools of red ruin. 'I'll go,' she said. 'I will do it.'

Bors looked at me and I nodded. The truth was that I had not killed the sailor alone. Guinevere had helped me do it. His death was on both of us and if Guinevere felt that we should send his corpse to the seabed together then that was what we would do.

'Wait for me,' I told Bors and pointed to my swollen eye, which Bors had said was starting to look like a ripe plum. 'You and I need to walk back into the keep together so you can tell everyone how you gave me this,' I said.

He lifted his chin. 'And you don't think they'll wonder there's not a mark on me?' he said, but I was already pushing the currach out into the calm water, which lapped around her skin hull as if eager to swallow the offering which lay at our feet.

We rowed to the east side of the Mount where the water was deepest and there I ran Boar's Tusk into the dead sailor's stomach and chest several more times to make sure he would not swell and float to the surface when he began to rot. Then, just to make sure that the current would not bring him up, we put the rocks inside his tunic and trews, tying the leg ends closed and the tunic's hem tight against his body to keep the rocks in place. When it was done we pitched him over the side and he slipped into the water with barely a splash and vanished.

Guinevere looked at me and I nodded, then we leant over the currach's sides and washed our hands and faces in the cold water, so that we were shivering when we came ashore and I put my hand against her face, looking into her eyes which were brimmed with tears.

'I'm fine,' she said. 'You?'

Other than her swollen lip, there were no bruises that could not be disguised by a little crushed lead and chalk and a touch of the rouge which the girls made from crushed mulberries.

I nodded. Who could put into words the strangeness of that night? Its horror and its wonder. Then we lifted the currach from the lapping tide and found Bors standing where we had left him.

'Not the nose,' he said when we had turned the boat over on the shingle. He grinned. 'I wouldn't want to ruin these good looks. A black eye to match yours. That should do it.' He pointed a finger at me. 'Don't miss, cousin.'

'I won't miss,' I said. And then I hit him.

13

The Edge

THE OTHER BOYS LAUGHED at my eye, which was the colour of a ripe olive, and they laughed even more when they saw Bors's matching one. We made a show of pouring each other a cup of ale and slapping each other's back, friends again after our disagreement, and the next time I saw Guinevere through the roistering throng she was whispering into Alana's ear. I did not breathe until I saw Alana's eyes, which were round as coins, and her teeth half buried in her chubby bottom lip, so that I knew Guinevere's confession was vivid enough to slake the girl's appetite, yet short of the whole truth.

At one point Alana looked up at me and her cheeks coloured, so I looked away and feigned interest in a grinning *Elsam* man who, drunk as he was, juggled a cup, an eating knife and an apple, keeping all three chasing each other through the smoky air to the cheers of those gathering around him.

Another two sailors sang the song of Manannán mac Lir, god of the sea, and the voices which poured from those leather-skinned, wind-blasted men blended like milk and honey. By the time they came to the part about Manannán's seaborne chariot and his horse Enbarr of the flowing mane, the Lady herself had taken up the harp to accompany them. An honour, that, and little surprise that the *Elsam*'s crew were all puffed up with pride and raising cup after cup of ale.

The next day, there were many sore heads on Karrek. To my surprise mine was not one of them and I woke early, my blood simmering still after all that had happened the night before. And yet there was a heaviness in my stomach too, as though I was weighed down by one of those stones which we had put in the dead sailor's trews to take him to the seabed. It was not guilt for having killed him – I would have done the same again and more to keep Guinevere safe – but rather the dread at what might happen to Guinevere should the Lady or Benesek find out what we had done.

By noon we were sweating out the previous night's ale, training with spear and shield out on Karrek's gusty southern slope. Thrust and parry. Counter-strike and back to high guard. Strike and low guard, our arm bones rattling beneath the shield.

I had soon taken two new bruises to add to those earned the night before, because my mind was drifting and Agga was quick to punish my mistakes. Yet even this new, bright pain could not raise me to my usual standard.

Agga's leather-sheathed spear blade struck my shoulder and I wondered what Guinevere felt about what we had done together naked in the blood-soaked rushes. Agga's low thrust took me on the outside right thigh, deadening the muscle so that I could barely stand, and I feared that Guinevere regretted giving herself to me.

'You're a sorry heap today, Lancelot,' Agga said.

I glanced up at the keep. Did she feel ashamed?

The leather helmet did nothing to stop Agga's next blow from rattling my brain around my skull. He was grinning, enjoying himself. 'Too much ale last night?' he said.

'Three cups too much,' I said. Which might have been true. Perhaps if I had been sober I might not have needed Guinevere to stop that big sailor strangling me.

'Lucky for you you've got me and not Melwas,' Agga said, jabbing with his spear again, though this time I met it with my shield and turned the blow aside before ramming my spear into his shield hard enough to force a small split between two of the limewood planks. 'He would've knocked your head off your shoulders by now.'

I glanced over at Melwas. He was all teeth and snarl as he battered poor Geldrin, whose only recourse was to keep moving backwards under that deluge of blows.

Melwas and I had barely spoken since our fight out on the currach, which was fine by me, for I had nothing to say to him now I knew it was he who had broken my sparhawk's wing, and I daresay he had nothing but bile for me because I had knocked him senseless with an oar and made him drop Benesek's sword into the sea. We avoided each other on the practice field and our mentors rarely paired us up, knowing it would only end in blood and malice.

'What's that about?' Clemo said, pointing his spear towards a knot of men at the foot of the hill. They were moving along the strand and across the rocks, peering over the edges and into the gullies and little channels where the water churned and leapt. They were sailors from the *Elsam* and for a moment we all stopped, breathing hard, and watched their progress along the shore. It was not long before one of them trudged up the hillside towards us and I recognized him as the juggler from the night before. Now, though, his face was taut and his brow heavy.

'We can't find Briac, our carpenter,' the man said. 'None of us has seen him since last night.'

He addressed Madern, who stood there with his arms slung over the spear which lay across his shoulders. 'What's he look like, this Briac?' he asked.

'He's big, bearded and ugly,' the *Elsam* man said, then frowned. 'Big as you, I'd say, but his beard has never seen a comb. Scars on his hands—'

'Saw him last night,' Madern interrupted, 'not since.' He twisted at the waist to look at the rest of us. 'Any of you seen the man?' he asked. We shook our heads and Madern turned back to the sailor and shrugged, then nodded down to the rocks further along the shore where Briac's companions were still searching. 'You think he got drunk out of his skull and rolled all the way down to the sea?' he asked. No hint of a smile. 'Or perhaps he was hungry. Came down in the night and put out in the currach to catch a mackerel or two.' He winked at Agga. 'Fell overboard and drowned.' Some of the boys sniggered at that.

The *Elsam* man was not amused. But he was wary enough of Madern not to admit taking offence at the warrior's unhelpful suggestions. He thanked him before turning to walk back down the hill to join the others searching for Briac.

'Back to it, you lazy swines,' Madern barked. The clack of spear staves and the clump of leather-sheathed blades striking shields rose once more on the breeze. And under my breath I prayed to Manannán mac Lir that he would keep Briac's sword-ripped corpse under the sea until the fish and crabs had feasted on it and there was nothing left.

The men of the *Elsam* looked for their carpenter until dusk. They scoured the shoreline and the woods and every crevice at the foot of the rocks on Karrek's western side. The Lady had the keep searched and we heard that she even wove a revealing spell with some of Briac's belongings, such as a chisel, adze and gouge, which his friends brought ashore from the *Elsam*. Though if she gleaned anything from that magic she kept it to herself, for no one took a currach out to the deeper water east of the Mount with ropes and hooks to fish Briac from the swaying sea grass. And the next morning, under a low and leaden sky, we watched the *Elsam* slip her mooring and drift off across the grey, her square sail beaten by rain and wind.

There were whispers that the gods must have had a hand in it, for men did not simply vanish like smoke seeping into the thatch, as Benesek put it that night when we gathered in the men's hut to eat. This made some touch the iron of their eating knives or sword hilts, though not Madern, who made a gruff sound in the back of his throat as he sat amongst us on the floor, spooning broth into his mouth. 'What business would the gods have with a nobody like him?' he asked. No one could say and so Madern continued, 'More likely that one of his crewmates hated his guts and saw the opportunity to do something about it. When Briac stepped outside to piss, this man followed him, cut his throat, dragged him down to the shore and sank him. Weighed him down with stones as you would a crab pot.' He shrugged and slurped from his spoon as though to suggest there was nothing mysterious at all about the carpenter's disappearance.

'If that's true, whoever did it must have really hated him to drag that big bastard all the way down,' Edern suggested, so that all of a sudden it seemed everyone agreed that Briac must have deserved such an end and from then on no one said any more about it.

That night I went to my bed furs thinking of Guinevere. But I dreamt of Pelleas. In my dream he was not the ailing, thinning man he had become in his last days, but the formidable warrior he had been when I first laid eyes on him in the Beggar King's hall. In my dream he was teaching me sword craft, explaining how the Romans, who had conquered Britain four hundred years in our past, had used short swords, while the Britons had used longer swords more like that Saxon blade of Benesek's which now rusted on the seabed. Safe behind their shieldwalls and fighting shoulder to shoulder, the Roman soldiers stabbed up into the bellies of the Britons, who fought not as one solid body of warriors like the Romans but as individuals. And because the Britons' swords were long, cutting weapons, they were unwieldy in the press of bodies and so those brave Britons died with their guts spilling onto the soil and earth and bones of their ancestors.

Pelleas thrust Boar's Tusk again and again, teaching me how it was done. And then my father and mother and Hector were there in my dream too and we were back in our hall in Benoic, searching in the spear racks and amongst the floor rushes and even in the thatch for swords, for any weapon we could find, because old Hoel's shrieking birds had warned us that King Claudas's war band was coming.

'They will be here before the dawn,' my father said, grim-faced, gripping his great boar spear and bristling with violence. But I could not find a blade anywhere. I scoured the dark corners and even searched beneath a great table that had in life never been in my father's hall, but I could find no weapon and dread lay upon me like a sodden fur.

'Your hawk told us,' my mother said, and even she held a long knife in readiness to fight what was coming. Then in my dream I looked up and saw the sparhawk dangling on her leash from a roof beam, spinning and screeching and flapping.

'They're coming,' Hector said, and even in the dream my blood ran cold because I feared someone must have found Briac of the *Elsam*. Such confusions dreams are, that the past and the present, and even sometimes the future, will weave together with other happenings and leave you grasping at something as elusive as the gods themselves. And in my dream they had surely found Briac's corpse washed up on the tide and somehow they knew that I had killed him.

'Fire. There's fire,' my brother said in the dream.

'The beacon is lit,' Pelleas said, pointing Boar's Tusk at me. 'Come, Lancelot.'

'Wake up! Wake up, cousin!'

I opened my eyes to see Bors. He was pulling on his leather armour and I saw that his spear leant against the wall beside him. Around us the other boys were waking, scrubbing sleep from their eyes and throwing off bed skins. 'The beacon is lit,' Bors said and I knew that it was Bors and not my brother that I had heard in my dream. My cousin's eyes flashed with excitement, for the beacon on the mainland shore would only be lit if we were in danger. It was forbidden for anyone to come onto our island unannounced and uninvited, might well be suicidal for someone who did so in the middle of the night. For this reason the Lady had an arrangement with King Menadoc of Cornubia that in the event of an invasion of his kingdom, or some other threat to Karrek or the Lady and her people, King Menadoc would light the pile of wood above the high tide, that we might arm and ready ourselves.

That warning beacon had not blazed in all the years I had lived on Karrek, and both Bors and I were intoxicated by the prospect of standing in a shieldwall with Benesek and Edern and the other Guardians of the Mount against whoever threatened us. What had we trained all these years for if not to safeguard our Lady and protect the young women in her care?

'Shields!' Madern yelled in the open doorway. 'No one comes to the shore without a shield.'

I had put on my thickest winter tunic for its added protection against blades, pulled on my boots and slung the sword belt over my left shoulder so that Boar's Tusk hung in front of my left hip. Then, side by side, Bors and I strode through the night to join those who were already forming a wall of shields on the island's northern shore facing the mainland.

The beacon flames leapt high into the night sky, the crack and pop of the fire-ravaged wood carrying across the water which was dark but for the copper gloss which those flames cast a spear-throw's distance out into the bay. And beside that ember-spewing fire, illuminated so that their spear blades and helmets and shield bosses glinted, stood a line of warriors.

'How many?' Benesek asked. A tear appeared in the veil of dark cloud above us and through that rent the silver light of a waxing moon shone, so that Benesek's helmet with its silver-chased cheek pieces and white horsehair crest, and his tunic of riveted iron rings, all glowed silver. He did not look old or ale-ravaged or afraid. He looked like a god of war sent down in that shaft of silver light to defend our little island and lead us to victory.

'Forty,' Geldrin replied before I had even counted fifteen.

'There'll be more of them behind the dunes,' Edern said.

There were nineteen of us armed and ready on the strand above the gentle waves that spilled one after another, seething and bubbling into the shingle. No one spoke. We gripped our spears and our shields and we watched those men who had come to The Edge, and we kept our thoughts to ourselves, knowing that Benesek would tell us what to do and when to do it.

I looked over my shoulder and saw that the beacon fire had brought the Lady down from the keep. She wore a white dress which seemed to glow. Her golden hair, braided and coiled, was pinned at the back of her head. At her neck she wore a torc of twisted silver which glinted dully against her pale skin, kissed by that same moonlight which illuminated Benesek. I felt Bors beside me stand a little taller and straighter knowing that the Lady was with us. Doubtless I stood straighter, too, for there was not a man amongst us who did not crave to be noticed planted there on our island's shore, his shield rim kissing his neighbour's, his spear blade pointing at the iron-grey cloud which slid inexorably into the south-east. The gash in those clouds had healed now so that the moon's presence was marked only by a wan glow which leached into that veil but could not penetrate it.

And yet even in the nearly dark I could see that not all the girls had accompanied the Lady down to the water's edge. Erwana and Jenifry were there and Jenifry was crying by the looks. But Alana was not with them. Nor was Guinevere.

'You can all stop dreaming up your own glorious death songs,' Benesek said, his helmet's long horsehair plume stirring in the sea breeze. 'The bards will have to wait a little longer. That lot aren't here to fight.'

'How do you know?' Melwas asked him. It was more than disappointment in his voice. It was defiance. As though he was not ready to accept that there would not be a fight.

'Anybody want to answer him?' Benesek offered, his gaze still fixed on those warriors spread along the far shore.

'Because they have no boats,' I said, but rather than feeling relieved that there would be no clash of swords in the night, no blood swirling in the slackening surf, I sensed a creeping unease come over me.

If not to fight, why had these men come to The Edge? I looked behind me. Why was Jenifry crying? And where was Guinevere?

'Because they have no boats,' Benesek repeated. 'And because it was them that lit the fire.' Melwas and Agga looked at each other in surprise. 'So I suppose I'd better go and see what they want,' Benesek went on, then he ordered Peran and Jago to fetch the currach so that he could row across to those warriors and learn the reason for their coming.

'Wait, Benesek,' the Lady called. I was not the only one who turned to look at her, even though we were supposed to be keeping our eyes on the far shore and on the water between us and the mainland, in case there were boats stealing through the dark, or even men in the water sent to crawl ashore and surprise us in a welter of blood and savagery.

'I know why they are here,' the Lady said. 'And Benesek is right. They are no enemies. They are Dumnonians. Still, we will let them wait a while longer, I think.'

I looked back across the water and saw no banners by which the spearmen could be identified. Then I saw the look which passed between Benesek and Madern, which told me that even they wondered how the Lady knew so much, though neither warrior saw fit to ask their mistress.

'Why would a Dumnonian war band come to The Edge in the middle of the night?' Jowan muttered.

'Because they don't want King Menadoc to know they're in Cornubia?' Agga suggested with a shrug, though he knew as well as any of us that even had they lain low, moving only at night, a war band that size was unlikely to go unnoticed.

'Whatever they're doing here, it's important, else why not wait until morning?' Peran said.

'Perhaps their lord just likes a good fire,' Bors said, amusing himself.

'We should throw the bastard into it,' Melwas said in a sullen voice. He was still disappointed that there would be no chance to show us all what a great warrior he was. 'Watch him burn for dragging us out here without good reason.'

'You think Lord Leodegan would come here without good reason, Melwas?' the Lady asked.

'Leodegan? What's he doing here?' Benesek growled, running a thumb across his spear blade, instinctively testing the sharpness of its edges. But my stomach knotted itself. The hairs on my arms and the back of my neck tingled and my mouth tasted sour.

I knew why Lord Leodegan had come.

When Guinevere came to the shore she looked so lovely that I could hardly breathe. She wore a green dress hemmed with gold and a red cloak edged with ermine and fastened with a silver pin brooch. Her hair was loose, which suggested that she had not had the time to braid and coil and pin it, as the Lady had done with her own. And so that untamed hair, as dark as Malo my father's stallion's mane, fell in waves past her shoulders, and a few wind-stirred strands drifted across her eye, across her lips, and I was helpless.

'She's leaving?' Bors asked, as if I should know. Like all the others he was staring at Guinevere. Just staring. I gave no reply. My mind reeled as if I had taken a blow to the head. I stood there with my back to the flames on the far shore, still gripping my spear and shield and watching Guinevere and hoping against hope that Bors's assumption was wrong. That perhaps Lord Leodegan had come to see and speak with his daughter. No more than that. Just to talk, because they had not seen each other for several years.

And yet I knew this Dumnonian lord had not marched his war band through the night and lit the warning beacon just so that he could pass some hours with Guinevere.

'Do nothing rash, cousin,' Bors warned me. It was as if his voice came from far away. As if I were underwater and he was speaking to me from the shore. Alana was fussing around Guinevere, trying to pull a comb through her hair, and the Lady was talking to Guinevere in a low voice. But Guinevere was looking at me.

'Here he comes,' Bors said, meaning that Benesek was on his way back in the currach. Presumably because she did not like that Lord Leodegan had come unannounced and in the dark, or perhaps because she had not expected to be saying her farewells to Guinevere this night, the Lady had made Lord Leodegan wait on the far shore. She had kept us in our shieldwall and the Dumnonians waiting until the ferocity of the beacon fire had subsided, and only then had she sent Benesek across the water to greet Guinevere's father.

Now the warrior was coming ashore and I knew he was coming to fetch Guinevere, and I also knew I could not stand there like a storm-struck tree and do nothing.

'Have a care, cousin,' Bors said, because I was walking towards Guinevere as Bors knew I must, and his advice warned me against saying too much. Against revealing the depth of my feelings for Guinevere or the truth of our secret intimacies. 'Did you hear me, Lancelot?' he called after me, and likewise Guinevere, seeing what I was doing, warned me with her eyes, which were wide and bright in the darkness because she was as surprised as any of us by what was happening.

But the Lady stepped into my path and raised a pale hand. 'It would be better if you just let her go, Lancelot,' she said.

I looked at the Lady and what I saw in her eyes was pity; something I neither needed nor wanted.

'Go where?' I said.

'Home, Lancelot.'

I threw my spear and shield out wide. 'This is her home.'

'No, Lancelot,' she said. 'Carmelide in the north of Dumnonia is her home.'

Guinevere shrugged Alana off and stepped around the Lady so that we were facing one another. 'We always knew this day might come, Lancelot,' she said.

'I didn't,' I said, knowing I sounded petulant. I looked from Guinevere to the Lady. 'Did you know Lord Leodegan was coming for her?' I asked. I saw Jenifry and Erwana look at each other aghast, shocked that I would speak thus to the Lady. I knew I was overstepping my boundaries but my blood was up and my world was falling apart. 'Did you know?' I asked again.

The Lady frowned and I thought she would put me in my place but instead she gave a slight nod. 'I could not know with certainty,' she said. 'Leodegan did not send word. But I dreamt it this very night. The gods told me.'

I imagined the Lady waking in her dream chamber at the top of the keep, swinging her legs off the bed and setting her feet on the blood-stained floor boards over which Guinevere had laid new reeds.

'Why now?' I asked. 'Why has Lord Leodegan come now?'

The Lady shrugged. 'I cannot say, for I do not know,' she said. 'That is between Leodegan and Guinevere.'

I turned away from her. 'Stay,' I said to Guinevere. 'Tell your father that you must stay.'

'My lady,' Benesek called. 'I think we have kept Lord Leodegan waiting long enough.'

'Tell him you have more to learn here,' I said. 'Tell him that you will not renounce our gods in favour of the Christian god,' I blurted. 'So that he will not want you in his hall. Tell him anything.' I was desperate. Horrified at the prospect of Guinevere leaving, I revealed too much but I did not care. I only cared about Guinevere and I could not stand to lose her now.

'I cannot,' she said. There were tears in her eyes as she shook her head. 'If my father has come to take me back, nothing will stop him. He would send his men to carry me off this island if need be.'

'Lady Guinevere,' Benesek said. He was standing at my shoulder now. 'You must come with me.'

'She is staying here, Benesek,' I said. This took Benesek aback. He looked from me to the Lady, expecting some explanation.

'I am ready, Benesek,' Guinevere said, sweeping a wisp of hair from her eyes and cuffing a tear from her cheek. Benesek gave a curt nod and I stared at Guinevere, not wanting to believe what was happening.

'Go back to the others, Lancelot,' the Lady said.

I did not move.

'Something wrong with your ears, lad?' Benesek asked me.

I ignored him, still looking at Guinevere. 'Guinevere?' I said, trying to hold her to the rock with my eyes alone.

'Don't make me embarrass you, Lancelot,' Benesek growled under his breath. 'Let the girl go to her father.'

'She doesn't want to go,' I said. 'I'll tell Lord Leodegan that myself.'

Guinevere stepped forward, reached out her hand and touched my own which gripped the spear. 'I have to go,' she said, squeezing my hand in hers. At that moment I knew there was nothing I could do. She was leaving. She would step into that currach and, just like Clarette and Senara before her, she would cross the water to The Edge, never to return to Karrek Loos yn Koos.

Yet, knowing it was not the same as accepting it.

'Take her,' the Lady told Benesek, who nodded, reaching out to take Guinevere's other hand. I threw my shield up to deflect it but Benesek anticipated my move and his left arm was around my neck and his right hand grabbed his left hand and locked tight so that my throat was being squeezed between the clamp of his arms. I dropped my shield and spear and tried to pull Benesek's arms apart.

'Hold still, lad,' he said, but I bucked and writhed, desperate to break his grip before I passed out, and then there were other arms holding me and I knew it was Melwas. And then Madern was there too and I was screaming my fury which was nothing more than a pathetic, strangled gurgling.

'You got him?' Benesek asked the other two, kicking my spear aside as Melwas's arm replaced his around my neck.

'He's not going anywhere,' Melwas snarled in my ear. And nor was I. Benesek let go his grip on me and stepped away. Guinevere looked at me one last time, tears on her cheeks, before she too turned away and walked beside Benesek down to the shore and the currach which two of the Lady's servants held steady in the gentle surf.

Edern was already in the boat and when Guinevere and Benesek were aboard and settled on the benches, the two Guardians of the Mount took up the oars and began to row the hide boat out into the dark water.

'Peace, cousin,' Bors said. He had come to help me but I did not want help. I wanted to break free of the arms holding me and run down to the sea. To wade into the cold water and take hold of the currach so that it could not carry Guinevere away from me. 'It's done, Lancelot. We can't stop it now,' Bors said, then he growled at Melwas to let me go. Madern had already lessened his hold in preparation to release me, but Melwas was enjoying choking me and it took a command from the Lady for him to finally slacken his muscle and sinew so that I fell to my knees on the rock, gulping at the sea air. Watching the currach bearing Guinevere across the bay to the Dumnonian warriors who still lined the far shore, cast in the glow of the beacon fire.

For a while I thought Guinevere was looking back at me. I could see the pale shape of her face and her hands gripping the sides of the boat, but then she half stood and turned and when she sat down again on the bench her back was to Karrek and her dark hair was just a part of the night. Still I knelt on the cool rock staring after her. There were tears in my own eyes. Tears of anger and frustration. And self-pity.

'She has gone, cousin,' Bors said, placing a hand on my shoulder. 'She has gone.'

And she had.

14

The Death of a King

A S WE ROUNDED THE HEADLAND I looked up at the towering grey granite cliffs, as I did every time I sailed round that great peninsula on Dumnonia's west coast, awed by the looming rock walls and my neck aching from peering up at the grass-crowned heights. I saw folk up on those heights. Tiny figures who risked being blown over the edge and dashed on the sea-blasted rocks in their eagerness to watch our slow and careful progress. There was but little wind, at least at the level of the sea. Even so, at the foot of the cliffs the water hurled itself against the rocks to churn and plunge and scatter in leaping white gouts. Away from that ever-seething sea, all was peaceful. Calm and blue as the cloudless sky.

It was a warm summer's day. So warm that several of the *Swan*'s crew were bare-chested and sweat-sheened as they worked, responding to the helmsman's barks to set and trim the white woollen sail. We turned into the warm wind so that the sail filled from the wrong side and we were pushed backwards a good spear's throw, until the crewmen took the sail's lower corner and hauled it across to the starboard side where they secured it again. They worked well, those men from Cornubia whom the Lady employed at need to sail her ship, so that the rest of us, so long as we kept out of their way, had nothing to do but enjoy the journey. And enjoy it we did. Bors and I loved escaping Karrek. We revelled in being at sea, just as the shrieking gulls overhead revelled in their dominion of the coastal sky, and that day we stood either side of the *Swan*'s prow, grinning like madmen as we came on a rising tide into Tintagel bay.

There we saw a broad trading vessel and two smaller currachs sitting on the beach above the tide line. Beyond them, a knot of sailors thronged around the women and children who always gathered to sell hungry sailors their smoked fish, loaves, wedges of cheese and small pots of olive oil. Now, these travellers and hawkers turned to watch the *Swan* make her entrance into the bay, some with casual interest, others with the knowing study of experienced seamen.

The sea was almost always rough in the cove, and as we came in, several weed-slick rocks which had loomed when we rounded the headland were already sinking below the tide, so that a skipper hoping to run his boat up Tintagel beach needed to know his business. Fortunately for us, Cledwyn, the captain, knew his and he lowered the sail just at the right time so that the *Swan* rode into the shallows on the rolling waves which carried her gently up onto the sand in a flood of foaming white spume.

The crew jumped over the sides with ropes to pull the *Swan*'s light hull a little further up the strand. Bors and I did not wait to see if they needed help. We were already running up the beach, past the yawning black cave into which the flood tide quested, boots in our hands, bare feet sinking in the sand, ignoring Benesek who, encumbered by his fine war gear – the long mail tunic and the iron and silver helmet with its white horsehair plume – yelled after us to wait for him. I beat my cousin to the foot of the carved stone stairway, where I was stopped by four Dumnonian spearmen who stood guard there.

'You had a head start,' Bors complained when he caught up, though he was grinning as much as I. His cheeks were flushed but neither of us was out of breath, for we were strong and young, eighteen years old, and we believed we could outrun a horse, outswim a salmon, outfight a boar and outdrink Benesek. And perhaps three of those four beliefs were justified.

'It's not my fault you had trouble dragging those tree-trunk legs over the *Swan*'s side,' I said, standing on a rock to brush the sand off the soles of my feet. In truth Bors was fast even with all his muscle, but he took the insult with his usual good humour and assured me that next time he would beat me because he would jump overboard and swim in on the breakers before Cledwyn even lowered the yard.

'You two could at least try not to look so happy,' one of the spearmen said. He knew us from our previous visits to Tintagel and ushered his companions aside so that we could ascend the steps which led up the mainland cliffs. 'King Uther's on his deathbed, the Saxons are raping and burning their way across Britain and you two look as though your only worries are whether there'll be girls and ale at the top,' he said, pointing his spear up the steps ahead of us.

One of the other spearmen muttered something about young men having no respect these days, and perhaps we tried to force our faces to look serious then, if only for a moment, because for all our excitement at returning to Tintagel, the reasons for our coming were indeed dire.

It had been four days since an envoy had come to Karrek with the news that King Uther, High King of Britain, was dying. Merlin, who had been at the king's bedside these last weeks, had sent word throughout Britain that the High King would announce his heir four days hence and that at the next full moon all the other kings and the greatest lords of Britain would be expected to come to Tintagel, there to swear fresh oaths of loyalty to the new king. Einion ap Mor of Ebrauc and King Cynfelyn ap Arthwys of Cynwidion. King Cyngen of Powys, King Meirchion Gul of Rheged far to the north and King Menadoc of little Cornubia, and a half-dozen other rulers and warlords besides would, all being well, set aside their right to challenge Uther's heir and bend the knee to Dumnonia's ruler.

But none of this took away from the hard truth that the man who had by strength of will and arms forged an alliance, albeit an uneasy one, between the kings of the Britons, so that they might at least stem the Saxon tide which had been spreading inexorably westward across Britain, had at last come to the end of his long life.

The great king had fallen sick in the depths of the previous winter and had been coughing blood ever since. Merlin's spells and potions had worked for a while, and there were days, the envoy said, when the Pendragon was his fierce, raging self. He had even faced the Saxon kings Octa and Eosa in battle just twelve days ago, having ordered his men to carry him to Cynwidion in a litter so that his presence might inspire the Britons. But there were still more days when he was sullen and bitter and hawking blood into a bowl, and he must have known that his victory against the Saxons at Verulamium would be his last.

'Go to Tintagel,' the Lady had told Benesek when the royal envoy had boarded his fast little ship on the rising tide and turned her prow into the south-west, bound with his bad news for the land of Lyonesse. 'I need you to be there when Uther names his heir.'

'Surely he will name Lord Constantine,' Edern said, as if suggesting that Benesek need not travel to Tintagel to learn what we already knew.

'There is no one else,' Madern agreed.

Lord Constantine, named after his grandfather whose men had elected him Emperor of the Romans though he had never been to Rome, was the son of Ambrosius Aurelius, who had been High King of Britain for ten years before he was assassinated and Uther assumed the throne in his brother's place. By all accounts Constantine was a brave and steadfast man and no one could deny his claim or that he had been Uther's sword these last years.

'You won't come?' Benesek asked the Lady.

She shook her head. 'There is nothing I could do for Uther that Merlin cannot do. But we must know who is to be the High King's successor. We must know if he has recalled Arthur, for my dreams tell me that he has. So, go to Tintagel and learn what you can.'

'I'll ask Merlin what he knows,' Benesek said, 'and if he's not forthcoming I'll wring him like a wet cloth. And . . . thank you,' Benesek had said, and had even kissed the Lady's hand, because not only was she doing him a great honour by sending him to King Uther in her stead, but she had known that Benesek would want to pay his respects to the man with whom he had fought many battles in the years before Benesek had become a Guardian of the Mount.

Bors and I took the stony path which led to the narrow land bridge, then climbed the hill that was bright with milkwort, thrift, kidney vetch and yellow irises starting to bloom, up towards the gate in the wooden palisade. That fence of sharpened, fire-hardened timbers was set atop an earthen mound and ran from the northern edge of the peninsula across the uneven hummocks and dips to where the ground fell away so steeply on the southern side that it was no longer necessary. Yet even without that palisade, the peninsular fort of Tintagel was surely the most unassailable in Britain.

'My father said the gods carved this fortress from the earth with their own hands,' Benesek told me the first time we climbed that narrow shoulder of land onto the great promontory where a lord called Gorlois had once ruled, before King Uther killed him and married Gorlois's wife. 'Fifty good spearmen could hold this land bridge until the sky fell on their heads. Fifty spearmen in a tight shieldwall,' he had said, looking up at the birds wheeling and crying through the sky above, 'and if you wanted to take this rock, your only hope would be for Manannán mac Lir to turn your spearmen into gulls.'

'Merlin did it,' Edern had said, which had Benesek frowning in thought.

For it was said that it was through some magic of Merlin's that Uther breached Tintagel's defences all those years ago and took it from Lord Gorlois. Some said the druid summoned a thick sea mist which hid Uther's warriors until they were over the palisade. Others claimed that Merlin wove a spell of concealment on Uther himself, who slipped through the main gate beside a wool merchant's wagon and opened the gate for his warriors, who poured across the land bridge in a killing wave of steel and fury. And still others believed that Merlin's magic had made Uther resemble Gorlois so that Gorlois's warriors had opened the gates for him themselves. So perfect was the illusion that even the Lord of Tintagel's wife, Igraine, was fooled and, believing her husband had returned from hunting, she took Uther to her bed.

'Then it's just as well that Merlin is on our side, hey?' Benesek had said, at which I had merely grunted, for I could not like the man.

Tintagel was an impressive place. Not in the way that the Roman ruins of palaces and temples are impressive, but in a wild, intimidating, breathtaking way. More than three dozen houses, halls, barns and workshops perched on the grassy summit of a wind-blasted rock. A rock which loomed two hundred and fifty feet above a sea that hurled itself in eternal rage against the foot of the cliffs. It was an impregnable bastion and royal court whose sheltered, sea-carved cove welcomed merchant ships from the far reaches of what had once been the great empire of the Romans. But more importantly as far as I was concerned, it was not Karrek Loos yn Koos.

I did not recognize the men guarding the gate and they did not know us, so we were made to wait for Benesek, who was doing a much better job of looking solemn as befitted the occasion. Or else he was feeling the climb in his legs, for Benesek was in his late middle years and had long since given up trying to compete with us on the training field.

'Don't need to prove myself to untried boys who have never stood in the shieldwall,' he would say when one of us challenged him to hold the stones aloft or run up to the Lady's keep in full war gear of leather tunic, mail shirt, helmet, and laden with shield and spear.

And yet he could still throw a spear further than any man on Karrek. Maybe any man in Britain.

'Now remember,' he said, when the guards, who knew Benesek well enough, had let us through and we began to trudge up the steep path which led to the main part of the settlement, 'we're not here to hold some Greek wine merchant's hand or buy wool or arrowheads.' He sidestepped a pile of wet horse dung and raised a hand in greeting to the bull-like figure of Tinas the smith, who was working in his forge to our right. Tinas lifted the tongs and the blade they gripped in salute to Benesek. Then he plunged them into the quenching trough and for a moment the big man disappeared in a cloud of steam as the waters hissed and seethed. 'Nor are we here so that you two young heroes can strut around trying to impress Tintagel's young ladies.'

Bors and I shared a grin which Benesek chose to ignore.

'We're here to pay our Lady's respects to a dying man,' he said, stepping over more horse dung, 'and not just any man but the Pendragon himself.' And that straightened our faces yet again. Uther had been High King for so many years that men feared what would become of us all when he was gone. Talk of his imminent death was accompanied by reports of terrible portents. A lamb born with two heads. An ancient oak which had burst into flame. A pike which, when gutted, had produced a human hand. All signs, folk said, that whispered of the doom of Britain.

Not that the end of Britain would stop Bors and me from enjoying a few days at Tintagel, even if it meant we would have to slip Benesek's leash later. And as if to prove that our ambitions in this regard were worthy, three girls who were carrying jugs of water, or more likely mead, down the path to the sentries at the wall smiled coquettishly and giggled as they came towards us, and as we stood aside to let them pass, one flicked her fair hair for Bors's benefit while another looked at me from beneath eyelashes which fluttered like butterfly wings. And we, eager to show that we were friendly and happy to be there on that sun-blessed day, gave them our best smiles.

'The gods help me,' Benesek muttered, swiping sweat from his forehead and using the moisture to smooth the forks of his long moustaches. We continued along the well-worn, gorse-lined path which snaked southwards and up towards the ridge of rock that crowned the flat summit like an inner rampart and within which sat the majority of dwellings, including the king's court. And it was only once we had climbed up the slope and over this craggy ring of earth and rock that I realized just how desperate things were in Britain and how dark were the clouds that were gathering beyond that blue, gull-chased sky.

Tintagel swarmed with soldiers. There were always spearmen at Tintagel because although the High King was itinerant, moving between his lys, feasting at each until his retinue had stripped bare his host's food stores, Dumnonia's chief court, or penlys, had been here on this near-island fort since the legions sailed away. It was at Tintagel that King Uther spent the winter months but it was here that he would die, too, and so all the greatest warlords of Britain had come. I had never seen such a gathering.

'That accounts for all the dung,' Bors said, as we stood for a moment by a thicket of yellow gorse on the crest of the bluff, taking in the sight. For as well as the groups of spearmen clustered in the open spaces and around the thatched buildings, there were scores of horses picketed in the longer grass.

'Getting an audience with the king won't be easy,' Benesek said, frowning at the view. There were hundreds of men gathered on those wind-buffeted heights, playing games, drinking, wrestling, sitting around cook fires, idling amongst the white sea campion and yellow crowfoot or sleeping under the clement sky.

'Even getting into Uther's hall won't be easy,' Bors said, and neither would it judging by the crowds; the makeshift shelters and canvas tents clustered thickest around the largest of all the buildings. Smoke sifted through the thatch of that hall even on such a warm day, and I remembered my own sickness three years since, when I had shivered so hard that my bones had rattled though I lay beneath piles of furs.

We made our way through the camps of spearmen and I saw that each group of men had a different device painted on their shields. Some had a bull's head in black on a red field. Some had a red eagle on white and some had two white wolves pawing at each other above the shield's iron boss. One group of spearmen had yellow shields painted with widening stripes emanating from the central boss so that those shields resembled little suns, and another war band's shields were painted with what appeared to be stag antlers. And as we pointed out each new device Benesek told us which lord those spearmen belonged to.

'They are King Menadoc's men, of course,' he said of the sun shields. 'That lot are King Cyngen Glodrydd's men of Powys,' he said, pointing at the shields painted with the stag antlers, 'and those scarred bastards are Einion ap Mor's men,' he said of a band of spearmen who were taking their ease in the sunshine. I looked long and hard at those men because Einion ap Mor was King of Northern Britain and thus a ruler almost as powerful as High King Uther. A large contingent of men even had big, curved, oval shields and iron helmets with stiff crests of red horsehair and these, Benesek told us, were Lord Constantine's men.

Yet amongst these war bands of the kings and lords of Britain, there was one group who stood out more than any other, even more than King Uther's own men who carried shields that bore his symbol of the red dragon, and Lord Constantine's soldiers in their Roman armour with their long shields. These others had the look of strangers amongst strangers. They were big men all and had the self-assured look of those experienced in war. Some had sun-darkened skin, darker even than that of the Greek traders whom we escorted to Tintagel now and again, and their shields were covered in bleached white leather and painted with a black bear standing on all fours upon the iron boss. But it was not their shields, their skin or their seasoned confidence which commanded our attention. It was their horses.

'What beasts are they?' Bors asked, as if we were not looking at horses at all but some other creatures from the legends we'd heard as children. We had threaded our way through the soldiers and the hawkers, servants and slaves who attended them, and come to the king's hall, outside which thirty tethered horses cropped the grass and summer flowers.

'They're war horses,' Benesek said, watching us, for Bors and I had chosen a horse each and stood stroking their muscled necks and shining flanks. 'Bred for size, strength and speed and trained for battle.'

Draped over a makeshift rail were great sets of scale armour, enormous ringmail coats, leather shaffrons to protect a horse's head, and hardened leather breastplates, and I tried to imagine what so many big, armoured horses must look like together at the gallop.

'Even in Armorica we did not have such as these,' Bors said in wonder. The mare whose withers I patted gave a gentle whinny of pleasure.

'My father's horse was a hot blood,' I said, remembering Malo and wondering if he'd had a good life serving my uncle the traitor. With any luck that proud black beast had thrown Balsant, either to avenge my father or more likely because he was ever a malevolent horse. 'But I have not seen or heard of such as these in Britain,' I said.

'That's because there aren't any others like these in Britain,' Benesek said. 'Least there haven't been since long before you two came mewling into the world.' Not liking the idea of strangers interfering with the horses, one of the big bear shields came over, scowling at us, but Benesek told the man that we were with him and, seeing Benesek in his war glory, the man muttered a greeting then turned and went back to his patch of flattened grass.

'They're beautiful,' I said, putting my face against the mare's muzzle and inhaling her sweet scent. She nickered softly. I could smell new grass and comfrey on her breath and I knew from the brightness of her eyes and the lustre of her coat that it was unlikely that any horses in Britain were fed so well as these.

'Beautiful they may be to us, Lancelot, but I doubt the Franks think them so when they're thundering at them with mailed, spear-armed men on their backs.'

Casting a glance at the men taking their ease in the grass, I tried to imagine what it must be like to face twenty or even more of these big men and horses on a battlefield and I looked again at the bear-painted shields which lay on the ground beside the warriors.

'Whose men and horses are they?' I asked Benesek.

When he did not answer, I turned and saw that he was looking off towards the granary and smokehouse and the knot of warriors walking past those buildings towards the king's hall.

'They're his,' Benesek said, and even though there were five men walking towards us there could be no doubting which one of them was the lord of these horse warriors.

'Who is he?' Bors asked. We were not the only ones staring. In fact, the only folk not ogling the approaching warlord were those men whose shield bore his symbol of the bear.

'He's Arthur,' Benesek said. 'Arthur ap Uther ap Constantine ap Tahalais. And if it were up to me, the next High King of Britain.'

And he was a warlord. In his early thirties, I guessed, he was tall, broad-chested and handsome, and he walked with the assurance of a man who knows that the men around him would draw their swords against the gods themselves if he commanded them to.

If I had thought Benesek looked impressive in his armour and his silver-chased helmet, he paled in comparison to the spectacle which this man made. If Taranis, god of war, had taken human form and come down to walk the same ground as us, he would have looked like this lord of horse warriors. His armour was made of thousands of small overlapping bronze plates which resembled fish scales and which had been burnished so that they glinted in the midday sun. His helmet, which he carried under his arm, was polished iron and adorned with heavy golden eyebrows, gold-chased cheekpieces and mounted with a blood-red plume as long as a horse's tail. His sword belt was studded with silver scales and his lower legs were protected by strips of iron, and it was the first time that I had seen such splinted armour. His cloak, billowing in the breeze as he walked, was as red as his helmet's plume and fastened with a silver gilt and red enamel ring brooch whose pin could have been a weapon itself, so large was it.

He was magnificent.

'Lord Arthur,' I said under my breath, watching as Arthur seemed to see something which made him veer from the track towards a group of King Uther's men, who were sitting around a cooking fire whose smoke was being strewn eastward by the salty sea breeze. One of those men had lost his sword arm up to the elbow, and recently by the look of the bloodstained linen which bound the stump, so that he struggled to get to his feet until Arthur helped him up.

Of the men who accompanied Arthur, one wore the black gown of a druid and carried nothing but a staff. It was Merlin. He and the other three stood talking amongst themselves, as if it was not the first time that they had been made to wait while their lord conversed with the wounded.

'He's always at the centre of the web, that one,' Benesek said, meaning the druid, but I was more interested in Arthur. I watched him reach inside his cloak and bring out a coin, which he gave to the one-armed veteran before rejoining his small retinue and continuing on.

'You know Lord Arthur?' I asked Benesek.

'Not the man,' he said. 'I know him by reputation, though I have seen him before, when he was just a boy. He has been fighting for some king in Gaul these ten years or so. But if he's back . . .' He left the words hanging, then shrugged as if to say we would have to wait and see.

I wanted to ask more about Lord Arthur's reputation then and there but I did not get the chance, because the red-cloaked, scale-armoured warlord was just two spear lengths away now and in truth I was awestruck.

I hoped I would catch his eye but he swept past me, his men in his wake, and then came a voice I had not heard for many years.

'Benesek, where is Lady Nimue?'

I turned to see Merlin standing there. He had not followed Lord Arthur into King Uther's hall and now leant the gnarled end of his ash staff towards Benesek. Almost threateningly.

'It's good to see you too, Merlin,' Benesek said.

Merlin ignored the sarcasm. 'She is not here?' he asked.

'I am here,' Benesek said. It was clear that their feelings for one another were less than warm. I remembered that Pelleas had not liked Merlin either.

The druid turned and looked at me. 'At least you have brought Lancelot as I asked,' he said.

That came as a shock. I had not known why Benesek had chosen Bors and me to accompany him to Tintagel. If I had thought about it at all, I might have supposed it was a reward, a prize of sorts, for we had been the last two standing in the recent melee of swords, when we all fought as pairs until only one pair remained. And the Lady, who had been watching that day, stared at me with those knowing green eyes as I stood panting and sweat-soaked.

'Haven't you sprung up like a mushroom after the rain?' the druid said now, looking me up and down. He grinned and I saw that he still had all his teeth. 'If you pushed me to the floor again I might never get up.'

My face flushed with heat as I recalled that night some seven years ago now, when I had thrown myself at the druid to break his spell on Guinevere. To bring Guinevere back from whither her soul had flown.

'I would like to see the king,' Benesek told Merlin and gestured to the door overhung with golden thatch through which Lord Arthur and his men had gone.

'And yet my Lord Uther has no mind to see you, Benesek,' Merlin said. Then he grinned at me. 'I never heard the High King say, "Fetch Benesek from the Mount, Merlin. I cannot die until I have spoken with him."'

'I would pay my respects, druid,' Benesek growled. 'The Lady's too.'

'You think my lord Uther cares about any of that now?' Merlin asked him. He looked just the same as I remembered him, as if he had not aged a day. 'You folk of the Mount have high opinions of yourselves for people who turned their backs on the affairs of Britain years ago.'

'We play our part in the affairs of Britain,' Benesek said, pouring scorn on the last three words. 'And we would know who the High King names as his heir.'

'Whoever will be king, let us hope that he can swing a sword, hey Lancelot?' the druid said, narrowing his eyes at me. 'For the gods are turning their backs on us and we are beset by enemies. The way things are going, sword-swinging and spear-thrusting will be the only course of action left to us, so let's hope the next king is even better at it than Uther was.' He pulled his pointed beard through a fist. 'Not that blades and brawn will be enough. Not in the end.'

'Merlin,' Benesek growled, his patience ebbing now.

Merlin raised a hand towards the warrior. 'Lancelot will accompany me into the king's hall,' he said, turning to Benesek. 'You and this young ox—' He stopped and regarded Bors for a moment. 'What's your name, young man?' he asked.

'Bors, lord,' my cousin said.

'Well, Bors, close your mouth before the flies get in,' Merlin said, for Bors was staring at the druid as one would gape at a long-dead ancestor found eating the pottage left out for the ghosts on Samhain eve. Merlin turned back to Benesek. 'Whatever message you have from Lady Nimue for Uther, tell it to Lancelot.'

Benesek's long moustaches were quivering, such was his anger now. But Merlin was Uther's adviser and so long as the High King himself was unable to make decisions about who should and who should not be given a royal audience, Merlin's word was the power in Tintagel, perhaps in all Dumnonia.

'I am the Lady's emissary, not Lancelot,' Benesek said.

I knew I should echo Benesek's words and beseech Merlin that Benesek, and not I, should accompany him unto King Uther's deathbed, not least because I knew if not I would suffer Benesek's ill mood for the rest of our time at Tintagel. And yet I said nothing.

'You may be a lord on your little hill, Benesek ap Berluse,' Merlin said, 'but here in the world you are chaff on the wind.'

'And him?' Benesek said, pointing at me. 'Who is he to have earned such an honour? Is the lad not a Guardian of the Mount like me?'

'He is,' Merlin agreed, his quick eyes flicking back to me, 'but he is young enough to be much more than that.' He pulled again at his billy goat's beard. 'Are you ready?' he asked me.

I swallowed and looked at the hall's door above which the words 'A fronte praecipitium a tergo lupi' were painted in the Roman script. I had learnt enough Latin in Armorica to read it: 'A precipice in front, wolves behind'. That was Britain then, though I didn't know it at the time.

I nodded but Merlin had already turned his back and was walking towards the door beside which Uther's stewards waited to collect the swords, spears and long knives from those who had not already left these behind.

'Wait,' Benesek told him. 'I need to tell the lad our Lady's words should he get the opportunity.'

'Be quick,' Merlin said.

But Benesek took his time, even making me repeat the Lady's message for Uther word for word so that I would not embarrass myself or the Guardians of the Mount. Then, frowning, he dismissed me with a flick of his hand and I went with Merlin to meet Uther Pendragon, High King of the Britons.

I had never stood under a roof as large as that which covered King Uther's hall. Its timbers were old and gnarled and spattered with bird droppings, and above them the ancient black thatch made a stark contrast to the new thatch outside. The earthen floor, hard as rock under my feet, was strewn with sweet-smelling, newly scythed grass and, above the three round fire pits which ran the length of the hall, joints of cured meat hung on chains, suffused by the ever-rising smoke.

'Come, Lancelot,' Merlin said, for I had stopped to look up at the great swathe of wool which hung from a cross beam below that old rotting thatch. Once white, the wool was grey now, besmirched by smoke and time and perhaps even the filth of ancient battlefields. But the dragon on it was still blood red and vibrant looking; a terrible sharp-clawed and winged beast from whose gaping mouth curled a long-barbed tongue. Or perhaps this arrow-like protrusion was meant to be fire. Either way it was a magnificent banner and I wondered how many enemies in Britain had felt their guts sour with fear at the sight of that red dragon and the warlord who flaunted it as his symbol.

Then I came to the press of men who had gathered at the hall's far end. They had their backs to me and yet their finely woven cloaks, neck torcs, sword belts, mail armour and the embroidered hems of their tunics announced them as the warlords of Britain, as did their bearing. Still, Merlin's hissing had them shuffle one way or the other, splitting the throng so that the druid and I could get to the front.

I followed him, stepping around a sleeping wolfhound, feeling men's and women's eyes on me as we threaded our way through. My shoulder brushed a cloak which was more purple than red and I knew I had just passed Lord Constantine, nephew of King Uther and son of Ambrosius, named for his grandfather who had been King of Britain and, some said, Emperor of the Romans.

And then I stopped, because there in front of me, so close that I could have reached out and touched the bear skin covering him, close enough that I could smell him – the sour wine on each frayed breath, the sweet, fetid tang of old fever sweat and, faintly beneath these other scents, the odour of sickness and impending death – was Uther the Pendragon, King of Britain, sword of the true gods and scourge of Saxons.

And he looked nothing more than an old, feeble, dying man.

He lay in his bed, which had been set up in front of the dais upon which his dragon-carved, oaken throne sat conspicuously empty, and for a while I just stared at him. At his sallow-skinned, hollow-cheeked face. At his unhinged mouth and the worn, black teeth in it, and the straggly white hair which was so fine that I could see the brown age spots on his flaking scalp. Here was the great warrior of Britain. The strongest of her kings. The man whose reputation and victories filled as many songs as there were bards to sing them. No wonder the other lords of the Dark Isles had flocked to Tintagel like wolves to a stag's carcass.

Five big spearmen lined the dais overlooking the assembly, their leader a thin, grim-faced, grey-bearded man called Gwydre who commanded King Uther's bodyguard. Now, Gwydre stepped down from the dais and forbade me to take another step until he had lifted my cloak and patted the sleeves of my tunic to ensure that I had not concealed a blade. Satisfied, he nodded and stepped back, allowing me to approach the king's bed. And someone somewhere hissed. I looked round and saw a woman baring her teeth at me. Her eyes shone amongst dark charcoal shadows. Her copper hair tumbled in a mass of fiery curls, her cheeks were high and sharp, and she was both beguiling and yet somehow terrifying.

'Bear her no mind, boy,' Merlin said, shooting the woman a look which would wither a briar but only had her hissing at him too. Clearly she did not care for me, though the gods alone knew what I had done to cause her offence. Or perhaps she was mad, I thought, and so pulled my gaze away from her and followed the druid.

'Lord king,' Merlin said. He had been trying without success to wake his lord but now he gripped Uther's emaciated shoulder and gave it a vigorous shake. For a moment the king's ragged breathing stopped, his mouth hanging open, and the other kings and lords around me looked at each other and I knew I was not alone in thinking that Merlin's touch alone had been enough to kill Uther. But then Uther opened his eyes and there rose a low murmur in the smoky hall, most men relieved, a few perhaps disappointed, that the High King was still with us.

'Closer. Come closer,' Merlin rasped at me.

Stiff and self-conscious, I glanced over my shoulder. Of all the faces in that room, the authoritative and magisterial, those lined with worry or pinched with suspicion or scarred by battle, the one which my eyes met was Lord Arthur's. The expression on his lean and handsome face, in contrast to most of those around him, was something between curiosity and mild amusement. He gave the merest nod of his head, and so I turned back to the king's bed and took two steps forward, then stopped, my knees touching the bear skin whose fur was stained and matted in places and here and there slick with some or other bodily fluid.

White smoke curled up from several iron dishes placed around the king's bed. Herbs smouldered and blackened in these dishes and I guessed that they, along with the newly cut summer grass on the floor, were intended to sweeten the foul air.

Merlin leant over the king, close enough that his lips brushed Uther's ear. 'I have brought you the young man we spoke of,' he said, jutting his neat beard at me. The High King's eyes were cloudy, as though he were peering through Roman glass like that which filled the small window of the dream chamber in the Lady's keep. But slowly, painfully slowly, his gaze sharpened until I knew that he saw me.

'Lancelot,' he said. So quiet, little more than an outward breath. As insubstantial as the smoke which meandered up to the thatch. And yet my name. From the Pendragon's own mouth.

'Lord king,' I said, my own voice barely louder than his had been, for I was aware of all the eyes in that hall. I felt them on me like the lice I saw crawling in Uther's scant white beard. Lord Constantine glared at me, his bare arms, criss-crossed with white scars, folded across his Roman breastplate. As if to remind us all that his grandfather had been declared Emperor of Rome, if only by his own troops, Lord Constantine grew no beard or moustaches but shaved his face to look like the statues of the old Roman generals which could still be found in parts of Britain. And yet there was nothing soft in that face, nor any obscuring the curiosity in it as he watched me now.

'Lord king,' I said again, louder this time. 'The Lady Nimue of Karrek Loos yn Koos sends you greeting. My Lady thanks you for—'

I would have gone on with the message I had memorized had Uther's grimace not stilled my tongue faster than a bard kills a note with a hand against the lyre's string.

'No time,' he hissed.

He lifted an arm and beckoned me closer, the effort making the limb tremble. I glanced at Merlin, who nodded, and then I went closer and Merlin straightened and took a backward step that I might lean over the king as he had done.

What was Lord Arthur thinking now? Or King Cyngen Glodrydd of Powys or even Menadoc, King of Cornubia? Knowing now that I was a Guardian of the Mount, these men must have wondered what the High King of Britain could possibly have to say to the likes of me.

Uther put two fingers to his lips and whispered something into my ear and at first I thought he had said 'He Merlin' and I nodded to show that I knew Merlin well enough. But then I realized that the High King had not said 'he' but 'heed'. He had told me to heed Merlin.

'Yes, lord king,' I said, my eyes flicking to Merlin. The druid gave me a knowing look and nodded to show that he had heard me assent to Uther's command.

Uther's eyes widened. 'He sees you,' he hissed. 'In his dreams.'

I did not look up at Merlin then, because we both remembered what had happened that time on the island when I had interrupted his spirit journey by throwing myself at him and knocking him down.

I was hunched awkwardly over the dying king when, without warning, Uther's hand took hold of my tunic and he pulled me even closer and his reeking breath brought bile to my throat. His moustaches tickled my cheek and I knew I would leave that hall with some of the High King's lice in my own long hair.

'Protect your king, Lancelot,' he said, his fetid breath hot in my ear. 'Be loyal.' He tensed and instinctively I tried to pull away but his hand gripped my tunic still and he yanked me close again. 'Protect . . . your . . . king,' he hissed.

'I will, lord,' I said. Of course, I knew it must all be nonsense, the ramblings of a confused, dying man, for I was a Guardian of the Mount. This was my eighteenth summer and come Samhain I would swear an oath to the Lady, to serve her. To fight for her. And that oath, sworn at the Winter Solstice, would supersede all others, for such was the Lady's standing in the Dark Isles. How then could I serve the new king of Dumnonia, whoever he might be, even if he kept Tintagel as his chief court as Uther had?

Even so, I told the doomed king that I would protect his heir. What harm in words?

'Protect him,' Uther croaked at me. His eyes were fierce and I caught a glimpse of the old Uther, the warrior king of the bards' songs who haunted the dreams of Saxons all across eastern Britain from Rhegin in the south to Lindisware in the north. 'Swear it!' he rasped into my ear.

'I swear it, lord king,' I said, his greasy beard tickling my cheek, his stench in my nose as I lifted just my eyes to glance at the kings and chieftains of Britain who, I realized, had edged forward, hoping to hear the king's words. But they were barely words at all. More like rasping sighs, and even Lord Arthur seemed to be leaning forward, his head cocked to one side and his ear turned towards us.

Uther's eyes dulled again and a drawn-out wheeze escaped his throat, making me pull away and step back because I thought this long creaking sound would end in a death rattle. But instead of dying, the High King growled that he was thirsty and Queen Igraine herself took a cup from a slave and held it to her husband's lips. Most of the wine dribbled into Uther's beard, dark red streaming through white.

Yet he seemed for a moment revived and managed to grunt thanks to his queen, who stayed by the bed, her hand resting upon his.

Merlin dismissed me as a man might flap his hand to waft away a stench and so I stepped back still further into the press of folk who stood in sombre silence between the head of the High King's bed and the dais with its spearmen and empty, dragon-carved throne.

Though not all of those around me were kings or chieftains, lords and ladies. 'What was all that about?' Benesek growled in my ear. Somehow he and Bors had got past the spearmen who guarded the hall door and worked their way to the front of the crowd. Bors nodded and half smiled at me, clearly proud of their accomplishment.

'I don't know,' I told Benesek, which was the truth, and yet I was ashamed to think that Benesek and Bors might have heard me swear an oath to the High King just months before I was to swear myself to the Lady's service. No wonder Merlin had not wanted Benesek in the hall, not that Benesek had contested Uther's demands of me even if he had heard them.

'Well?' One of the kings across from us called out, throwing that word into the silence like a challenge. 'Who is the heir?' He was a short man with copper-coloured hair, a narrow face and hard eyes, and I guessed from his looks, and his brazenness, that he was Einion ap Mor, ruler of Ebrauc and King of Northern Britain. 'Who is the heir?' he demanded again, ignoring those Dumnonians who were hissing and growling their disapproval of his behaviour. 'That is what we came here to find out.'

Whilst many harangued this king for his outburst, some others murmured their support.

'For once I agree with King Einion,' a big man with a thick black beard said, drawing every eye in the hall. I surmised this was Cyngen Glodrydd of Powys, which currently enjoyed an uneasy truce with Ebrauc. 'We did not come all this way to watch Uther die. We came to witness who will be king in Dumnonia when Uther burns on his balefire.'

'You mean who will be High King of Britain?' Merlin said, raising an eyebrow at Cyngen.

Cyngen spat onto the grass-strewn floor to show what he thought of that. 'Uther earned that title,' he said. 'It cannot be passed along like a horn of mead.'

More appreciative muttering, but it was stopped abruptly by Gwydre thumping the butt of his spear on the boards of the dais. 'Respect for the High King!' Gwydre bellowed. 'Remember your place, King Cyngen.'

'Remember yours, Gwydre ap no one,' Cyngen spat.

Gwydre bristled at that. One of his men levelled his spear.

'Stay where you are!' Merlin snapped at Uther's men, raising his staff to add weight to his command, then he walked across the hall towards Cyngen, barely stirring the scythed grass on the floor, and stopped two paces from the King of Powys.

Cyngen was a bear of a man, a broad, hulking, black-bearded beast with a warped nose, a savagely scarred face and eyes as hard and dark as wet granite. And yet he flinched when Merlin lifted the ash staff.

'We are all friends here, lord king,' the druid said. 'But I warn you, if you interrupt proceedings again I shall weave a spell that will turn your guts to foul stinking water and have you squatting in your own filth for seven days. And after seven days of this affliction you will be weaker than a day-old lamb. You will struggle in vain, flapping like a fish, but no one will want to wade into your slime and so you will die and be remembered by your people as the king who drowned in his own dung.'

Cyngen grimaced at this threat and Merlin pointed the staff at the King of Ebrauc, though his eyes were still on Cyngen's. 'That goes for you too, King Einion,' he said, 'only, you will drown after just four days seeing as you are a head and a half shorter than Cyngen here.'

This last prediction had enough humour in it to raise a few laughs and so break the ice of the moment, which may have been Merlin's intention, for it was no small thing to threaten kings, even for a druid.

'We just want to know who is to be king,' King Cyngen rumbled, 'and from the looks of it, if Uther does not tell us soon he never will.'

'It is not as though we do not know who will be named,' a man behind me said and I saw Benesek and some others look over at Lord Constantine, whose breastplate of hammered bronze, cast to mimic a well-muscled torso, glinted with reflected flame in the smoke-hazed gloom. As Uther's warlord, he was permitted to wear his sword in the king's hall and I saw that its ivory hilt was carved into the shape of an eagle's head. He was a tall, broad-shouldered, bull-necked man who wore his lineage as proudly as he wore that plum-coloured cloak and Roman armour, and now he lifted his smooth chin a little higher still as he anticipated the words that would put him on that oaken throne with his uncle's last breath still hanging in the smoky fug.

Merlin turned and looked up at the gable wall of the hall's western end. There was a hole up there to let light in and smoke out, and Merlin stared at it, stroking his beard. 'I had thought to wait until sunset,' he said, 'to give every lord of Britain time to get here and witness the High King's decision. But I suppose it won't matter now and I hardly expected King Cadwallon to be here when he could be running through the hills waving his sword around after the Irish.' And with that he went back to the king's bedside and spoke softly in Uther's ear.

I looked at Lord Arthur. His lean, handsome face lit by the nearest hearth flames, his full lips almost pursed in his neat golden beard as though he were weighing up the possible outcomes of the day. Then I glanced at Lord Constantine and saw him and Arthur share a look of hawkish suspicion before they both turned their eyes back to the king's deathbed.

Igraine was helping Merlin pull Uther up onto a rich bolster of bright yellow silk which I could not help but think was at great odds with the stained bear fur and the grave solemnity of the occasion. And now some men touched iron armour or scabbard mounts for luck as a hum rose amongst the audience because folk knew that the long-awaited announcement was almost on the royal tongue.

Uther cursed at the effort and strain of moving up onto the bolster, then closed his eyes and caught his breath: a rasping wheeze that was too weak even to stir the smoke which lingered around his bed. Then he growled for wine and this time drank without spilling a drop.

'Lord High King Uther ap Constantine ap Tahalais, supreme ruler of Britain,' Merlin said in a clear and commanding voice, 'speak the name of the man who will rule in Dumnonia and, if the gods will it, inherit the mantle of High King of Albion after your death.'

No hum in the hall now. Just the crackle of fuel in the hearths, the soft snoring of a hound and, somewhere in a dark corner, the scrabbling of a mouse after grain amongst the cut grass.

All eyes on the dying king. All ears waiting, hearts barely daring to thump for fear of missing the words we had come to hear. Who amongst the lords and leaders gathered beneath that rotting thatch would strive to unite the kingdoms of Britain and continue King Uther's long fight against the invaders? Who would esteem the old ways and entice the favour of the gods so that even they might help us throw the Saxons back into the sea from whence they came?

'My heir,' Uther said, his voice stronger than it had been before, 'is the man who will do more than stem the rising Saxon tide . . . the way a linen dressing soaks up blood.' Some glanced at Constantine then, who I saw was frowning, but most eyes were on the dying king, whose gaunt and cadaverous body was heaving for breath as he gathered his strength for the next words. 'He will take up my sword against our enemies and scour them from the land with the fury of Beltane's cleansing fire.' The effort of making that proclamation in a voice all could hear had been prodigious and it left Uther blown, his eyes closed as he summoned the last of his famous strength.

No one said a word. The fires cracked and spat, Uther's wolfhound snored contentedly and we waited.

And eventually the High King opened his eyes again.

'My heir,' he said, pressing both hands onto his straw-filled mattress to steady himself, 'is my son. Arthur.' He almost shouted that name so that there could be no mistaking it, and then he slumped back against the silken bolster, his eyes closed once more.

For several heartbeats there was silence. Men and women looked at Lord Arthur, who looked at his cousin Lord Constantine, who was glaring at Uther.

'No!' Lord Constantine roared, the horror clear on his clean-shaven face even in the shadow-played hall. 'No,' he said again, quieter this time, but it seemed he could say no more. Could not summon the words.

The murmur of voices rolled in like the surf upon the shore but receded again as King Einion of Ebrauc stepped forward, the gold torc at his neck reflecting the flame from a nearby oil lamp. 'It cannot be Lord Arthur,' he declared, throwing out an arm in Arthur's direction. 'What does Arthur know about Britain? He has been in Gaul these last ten years.'

'And what do you think my lord has been doing there, King Einion?' the man on Lord Arthur's right asked, having stepped forward as if to challenge the King of the North. 'He's been fighting the Franks. He's been winning battles.'

'Impudent dog,' one of the Ebrauc men snarled.

'And who are you?' King Einion demanded of Arthur's man.

'I am Gawain, son of King Lot of Lyonesse,' Gawain said.

'Lord Arthur's nephew,' Benesek muttered in my ear.

Like Arthur, the warrior wore a neatly trimmed beard, though Gawain's hair was walnut to Arthur's pine. Unlike his lord, Gawain's face was scarred and his nose broken. It was a brawler's face and it made him look at least Arthur's age though he must have been some years younger.

'Ah, Lyonesse,' King Einion said, scratching his beard. 'I heard this very morning that King Lot could not be here with us because he is fearful of a Saxon attack. Even now he guards his shores.' Then he turned towards the other kings and lords. 'And yet his son, like Uther's son, instead of standing at his father's shoulder against our enemies, chose to fight for another king across the sea.'

Gawain tensed, his hands becoming fists, but Arthur breathed a word to him and he gave an almost imperceptible nod, his hands softening even if his face did not.

'We are here now, King Einion,' Lord Arthur said.

'Aye, like a dog slinking into the feast, you have come for the king's leavings,' King Einion said, and the man beside him, a hulking, muscle-bound, flat-faced man whose black beard reached down to his belt, grinned provocatively while a collective gasp drew the flickering lamp flames. It was a vile insult, even had Lord Arthur not just been named as Uther's successor. But before Arthur could answer that insult, Lord Constantine took two steps forward, having at last found some words.

'Lord Arthur turned his back on Britain many years ago,' he told the assembly. 'He serves King Syagrius in Gaul and now we are expected to welcome him like a conquering Caesar home from the wars?'

'Arthur,' Uther growled from his bed.

'But he has not fought beside us,' Lord Constantine protested.

'Arthur,' the High King snarled again, then was seized by coughing so that both Merlin and Igraine tried to comfort him, the druid with mumbled charms and the queen with more wine.

'The bards will not sing it like this,' Bors said under his breath, and he was right, I thought. I saw four men amongst the crowd who I guessed were bards, here to gather the strands that they would later weave into verse, but the way this day was going it was hard to imagine even a half-decent song coming out of it. Unless of course the bards substituted their own inventions for the truth, which was the usual way of it after all.

'It is true I have not fought beside you, cousin,' Arthur said, squaring his shoulders to Constantine. 'But when I am king I will fight in front of you.'

This was well said and I saw King Menadoc and a few others nod in appreciation.

'You will not lead the men of Ebrauc,' King Einion said. 'Lord Constantine's claim is the stronger. He is Ambrosius Aurelius's son.'

Arthur seemed to consider this for a moment, while Constantine, who seemed surprised by the vehemence of King Einion's support, nodded in gratitude to the King of Ebrauc.

Einion nodded back. 'The king is not in his right mind,' he said. 'Perhaps he has forgotten the years that his son has been absent.'

'Judgement and good sense often flee the dying,' King Cyngen of Powys rumbled, his dark brows knitting. 'In his last days my father did not recognize my mother or me, nor could he remember what he had eaten that morning. And yet he remembered a song from his boyhood days. Every word of it.'

'Enough!' Merlin called, lifting his ash staff, but Arthur raised a hand towards him and the druid frowned but lowered the staff.

'Lord king, you are not so deep in the wild lands that you have not heard my reputation,' Arthur told King Einion, 'and you must know that I have never lost a battle. And that my horsemen are feared from Noviomagus to Argentoratum.' He pursed his lips and absently brushed at a speck of dirt on the shoulder of his red cloak. 'So, I am beginning to wonder if the reason you do not want me to be king is because you would rather have a lesser soldier on Dumnonia's throne.'

Arthur avoided Lord Constantine's eyes then, for he knew that was an affront to the man who had guarded the eastern border lands against the Saxons these last years. And Constantine was offended. His hand fell to the eagle-head sword hilt at his waist, though he did not pull the blade from its scabbard. He knew that to draw his sword against Uther's son – Uther's unarmed son – in the High King's own hall was to invite bloodshed, for there could be no going back from such a thing.

And yet of Arthur's two offences, both given in calm and measured voice, the insult to King Einion was the gravest.

'You go too far, Lord Arthur!' King Einion roared, and many men in that hall voiced their agreement, a clamour rising to the old thatch as men spoke for or against the rival claimants. For in suggesting that the King of Ebrauc would prefer a weaker king in Dumnonia, Arthur was questioning Einion's loyalty to the alliance which bound Britain against the Saxons. Perhaps he was even insinuating that the King of Northern Britain planned a war against Dumnonia.

I saw Merlin shake his head at Lord Arthur, eyes wide as if pleading with Uther's son to change course before it was too late. But Arthur looked composed and untroubled and even spread his arms out before him as though inviting the King of Ebrauc to seek whatever redress he considered appropriate.

'Perhaps I will challenge you on the day of your acclamation, before Merlin gives you King Uther's sword,' Einion said. The huge, mail-clad warrior beside him grinned again, confirming that he was King Einion's champion, which made him the foremost warrior in all of northern Britain.

Arthur turned his palms to face the roof. 'Why wait, lord king?' he asked.

'He's a confident bastard,' Benesek beside me growled into his long grey moustaches, for he had worked out Arthur's strategy even if I had not. 'Clever bastard too,' he said. 'Or stupid,' he added after a moment's consideration.

King Einion jutted his copper beard towards the deathbed and its grim human cargo. 'Your father,' he said, almost spitting the words. He gestured to his surroundings. 'It would be unseemly.'

Lord Arthur did not take his eyes from the King of Ebrauc. 'The High King is dead,' he said. Just like that he said it, and we all looked at Uther and some of the women in the hall gasped while a low rumble rolled amongst the men. For Arthur was right. Uther the Pendragon, High King of Britain and scourge of Saxons, was dead.

Only Merlin did not seem surprised and perhaps he had already known, but Queen Igraine had not and now she fell to her knees and buried her face in the stained bear skin, her hands clutching Uther's dead hands.

'So?' Lord Arthur said, repeating his gesture inviting King Einion to do what he must.

The King of Ebrauc glanced about him at the other kings and lords of Britain, then pointed a finger at Lord Arthur, which was itself insult enough.

'So, I challenge you,' he said. 'My champion against yours. Today. Here. Before the sun sets.' The enormous warrior beside him rolled his shoulders and stroked his long beard as he glared at Gawain. I saw that there was a silver ring tied into the end of that long beard. A lover's ring perhaps. Or else taken from the finger of some warrior he had killed.

'If anyone should challenge him, it should be Lord Constantine?' King Cynfelyn of Cynwidion said, at which Constantine nodded, though not convincingly.

'There is no need for blood to be spilled,' King Menadoc said. 'Would we tear Britain apart before King Uther is cold?'

Some men agreed with the King of Cornubia, but not enough. Menadoc was a small king of a small kingdom at the far end of southern Britain and he only ruled at Dumnonia's pleasure, and so his was not a voice which could stop what was happening.

'Merlin,' Lord Arthur said, ignoring King Menadoc and two or three other men who were protesting that this behaviour was abhorrent in light of King Uther's passing, 'is King Einion's challenge lawful before the gods and according to the ancient laws?'

Merlin thought about it. 'Any challenge to the named heir should be made on the day of acclamation,' he said, nodding to King Einion and to Lord Constantine too.

'Then let us acclaim Lord Arthur today,' King Cyngen of Powys said, throwing his arms wide. 'We are all here. Those of us who matter, anyway. Let us get it done now so that we do not have to come back to this wind-blasted rock again for another few years.'

'Three days, lord king,' Merlin told the King of Powys. He pointed his staff up at the hole in the gable wall. 'The moon is waxing gibbous but in three days it will be full,' he said. 'That is when we shall acclaim the new king.'

'But I can answer King Einion's insults today,' Arthur said.

Merlin sighed. 'If you must, lord,' he said. 'But *we* must await the moon.'

'And who is your champion, Lord Arthur?' King Einion asked. 'Gawain of Lyonesse? Or perhaps one of your dark-skinned horsemen? A soot-black fiend from some gods-forsaken land across the sea.'

'I am not yet a king,' Arthur said, his face grim, 'and prefer to do my own fighting than ask other men to fight on my behalf.'

'You see, lads?' Benesek murmured in my ear. 'You see what's happening?'

And all of a sudden I did see.

The truce between the kingdoms of Britain was ever a fragile thing and Arthur knew it. Whether or not he had known that his father would name him as his successor, Arthur had chosen to meet the challenge of dissenting voices head on. King Einion might as well have been a hawk held by the jesses for the way he had been brought to this. For Arthur knew that it was better to deal with any opposition now, before it could grow like a boil and burst later. Furthermore, if in doing so he could prove his own courage and worthiness to lead, if he could inspire loyalty in the other rulers, or even fear, then so much the better for his acclamation and accession to the dragon-carved throne of Dumnonia.

He had wanted this fight. He had needed it.

But he still had to win it.

'What is your name, champion of Ebrauc?' Arthur asked the huge warrior beside King Einion.

'Odgar, lord,' the big man said.

'I have watched Odgar kill twelve men in single combat, Lord Arthur,' King Einion said.

'Twelve men,' Arthur repeated. He seemed impressed. 'Well then, Odgar, I shall be waiting for you outside.'

A hum rose in the hall. Queen Igraine still knelt by her husband's bed, holding his hands, her old face, which still hinted at the famous beauty she once possessed, glistening with snot and tears. But everyone else, the lords and ladies, kings' champions, bards, servants and slaves, jostled their way to the main doors and spilled out of the hall.

'Let us hope the fool lives long enough for you to keep your oath,' Merlin gnarred at me as we pushed along the stream of babbling folk and came into the golden glow of that late afternoon. And off he went, clearing a path through the crowd with his staff and leaving me to collect Boar's Tusk from a steward, who must have remembered me for he was holding the scabbarded sword and belt ready. And as I strapped the sword belt on and waited for Benesek and Bors to retrieve their own swords, folk looking at me because I had no name that anyone knew and yet the High King had spoken to me, I thought how strange it was that I shared Merlin's hope.

I had come to Tintagel for no other reason than to accompany Benesek and, selfishly, to enjoy two or three sun-blessed days at the peninsular fort before sailing back to Karrek. And yet somehow, and for reasons I could not fathom, Merlin had shaped events so that I had stood at the dying king's bedside and sworn an oath to protect the next king of Dumnonia. All being well, Arthur ap Uther would be that king and it did not matter to me that I had never spoken to Lord Arthur nor seen him before that day. Nor did I know what sort of man he was or whether he would make a good king or turn out to be a tyrant.

In spite of all this I, like Merlin, wanted Arthur to survive. As I walked across grass smudged with purple dog violets and yellow kidney vetch, all trodden flat beneath soldiers' feet, I wanted more than anything for Lord Arthur to kill that big champion of Ebrauc and be acclaimed king with the coming of the full moon.

So that I could keep my oath.

15

Arthur

IT SEEMED TO ME THAT every spearman in Britain was on Tintagel's heights. Word of King Einion's challenge carried on the sea-whipped breeze until each lord's retinue of warriors had gathered beside the High King's hall like crows swooping in dark clouds to the scent of blood.

King Menadoc's Sun Shields were there. Cyngen's men with their stag-antler-painted shields and Cynfelyn's spearmen and the soldiers of King Meirchion Gul of Rheged stood shoulder to shoulder with Lord Constantine's Roman-armoured troops and the warriors of several other rulers and minor kings. Arthur's horse soldiers pushed their way to the front of the thronging, spear-armed mass to watch their lord, and opposite them, on the other side of this temporary arena made of flesh and iron, stood King Einion's men of Ebrauc, along with Einion himself.

'He looks confident,' Bors said of Ebrauc's king, for there was almost a smile on Einion's thin lips and in his pale blue eyes as he watched his champion scything his great sword through the air to loosen shoulders that could have borne an ox's yoke.

'Why wouldn't he be?' Benesek asked. 'He's seen the man slaughter twelve enemies in fights such as this.'

'You think he'll beat Lord Arthur?' I asked.

Benesek raised an eyebrow. 'Didn't say that,' he said. 'Lord Arthur wouldn't have survived in Gaul if he were not a fighter. And he's good reason to win. Better reason than just to live, for if he beats that big bastard he's as good as won Uther's high seat.' He nodded at the spearmen all around us. 'This lot will have seen a little blood fly on a summer's day and will be content. They'll go back to their lands knowing that Dumnonia's new king is a warrior like his father before him.'

I watched Arthur as he walked along the line of spearmen who formed the arena's far boundary. From end to end he stalked, gripping sword and shield and ignoring all those who growled encouragement as he passed. He had removed his cloak and given it to Gawain but he still looked magnificent in his bronze armour, its countless burnished scales reflecting the setting sun's light so that as he moved he seemed cloaked in fire.

His helmet's red plume swished as though in tribute to his fine war horses and the hinged, gold-chased cheekpieces were down, obscuring much of his face and making him look even more intimidating, and whatever good looks could still be glimpsed were marred now by a grimace and wild eyes; a savage mask that made him seem a different person from the man I had seen in King Uther's hall. It was a transformation which chilled my blood.

'Back in Gannes, when I was a child, some hunters caught a wolf,' Bors said. 'Not just any wolf but the pack leader, so my father said. They put it in a cage for the whole village to come and see. Bigger than me it was, snarling at us all and hungry. Pacing up and down in that cage and wanting to rip our throats out.' He lifted his chin towards Arthur and did not need to say more.

King Meirchion of Rheged, whom men called Meirchion the Lean, had taken it upon himself to be the arbiter of the fight. The epithet was a good one, for Meirchion was without a doubt the fattest man I had ever seen. He was a bald, sweating, stout-limbed man with florid cheeks and narrow eyes. But Rheged was a large and powerful kingdom and so when Meirchion addressed the lords of Britain there was not a man who did not hold his tongue and show him respect.

'This fight can only be stopped by a crippling wound or by death,' he said, puffing for breath so that I wondered how he had managed the climb up to the plateau, and how his horse had survived the long journey south from Rheged. Then he lifted a hand upon whose fat fingers rings of silver and gold shone. 'Or if one of the combatants yields, in which case the other may spare the man's life,' he said, wiping sweat from his bald head. He squinted at Merlin. 'Tell us all what this fight is about, druid,' he said, then gestured to the spearmen around him who had not been in the king's hall. 'Just so that we are all clear.'

Merlin sighed. 'King Einion does not believe that Lord Arthur should be king,' he said in a tired voice. Then fluttered a hand towards no one in particular. 'There were some clumsy insults cast about, none worth repeating, and here we are like halfwits at a cock fight, about to watch two men who should be fighting the Saxons go at each other until one of them is dead.' He looked up at the sky. Dusk gathered in the wake of the sun's descent towards the western horizon. Not so long ago the day had been golden and the Pendragon had still been with us. It seemed much had changed already. 'It is no wonder that the gods are deserting us,' Merlin said.

Meirchion the Lean nodded. 'That'll do.' He looked at Odgar. 'You ready?' he asked.

The champion lifted the end of his long beard to his lips and kissed the silver ring that was knotted there. Then he picked up his shield, which was painted with jagged black lightning, thrust his left arm through the rope loops to grip the handle and nodded.

'Are you ready, Arthur ap Uther?' the King of Rheged asked, his mention of Arthur's lineage deliberate, it seemed to me. Rheged and Ebrauc had not always been friends and Meirchion was wise enough to know that Arthur and his famed horse soldiers could make for useful allies if ever his kingdom found itself at war with its eastern neighbour.

'Ready, lord king,' Arthur said, and beat his sword pommel twice against the inside of his shield. 'Odgar of Ebrauc fights me today because his lord dares not,' Arthur said in a clear voice, then pointed his sword at King Einion's champion, 'but no one can say that this man is a coward. Behold him now and hereafter remember him as a brave son of Ebrauc.'

Arthur was a tall man but Odgar was a head taller and far broader. He was Ebrauc's champion and, as such, a warrior of reputation. He was a towering cliff face of a man, enormously strong and an experienced killer too. And yet the way Arthur spoke made it seem as though Odgar was some untested spearman out to kill his first man.

The expression on Odgar's flat face was one of confusion. It was normal for men to trade insults before a fight and so he did not know what to make of his opponent's behaviour. He glanced at his king but Einion just nodded at him to get on with the killing. So Odgar came forward and the spearmen from seven kingdoms took up the cheering for whichever man they wanted to win.

'Lord Arthur can fight on four legs but can he fight on two?' a man shouted.

'He'll need his horse to reach that big bastard!' another called.

'Come then, Odgar,' Arthur said. 'Let the gods decide it.' He swept his sword through the air, his top lip hitched back from white teeth. 'The gods and iron,' he said.

Then Odgar attacked.

Arthur caught the first blow on his shield, reeling under the impact, then leapt forward, his counter strike just as ferocious and sending a shiver through the limewood boards of Odgar's lightning-painted shield, such that men cheered to see that this might be a good fight. Then Odgar came on, scything his sword down again and again, from left to right, right to left, but he hit nothing because Arthur was fleet of foot and would not let any of those mighty blows land. He side-stepped and twisted and led Odgar on, the champion of Ebrauc snarling and slashing about him like a man hacking a path through brambles, and any one of those cuts might have smashed Arthur's shield or lopped off a limb had Arthur's feet not danced across the grass.

The combatants broke off, breathing hard. Already sweating.

Each having taken the other's measure, both men thumped sword against shield and strode forward.

'Lord Arthur plays a dangerous game,' Benesek said, as Arthur seemed to open himself up, inviting the strike and then wrenching himself aside as Odgar's blade flashed down. 'One of these times he'll guess wrong, or else Odgar will reverse the cut at the last,' Benesek said.

As if he had heard Benesek, Arthur thrust his sword at Odgar's face and the big man checked his advance and raised his shield. But Arthur's thrust was a feint and now he swept his sword down across his body then up towards the champion's right thigh. Somehow Odgar got his sword there to parry and the blades sang, then Odgar threw a foot forward and swept his shield across, slamming it into Arthur's right shoulder to rattle the bronze scales and send Arthur staggering.

Cheers for King Einion's man then. Perhaps for Arthur, too, for he had kept his feet after a blow that could have felled a stallion.

'He's quick for such a big man,' Bors said admiringly.

'The big ones tire easily,' I said and Bors thrust his shoulder into mine, because he knew I was teasing him. 'Lord Arthur will tire him,' I said.

'He might if he lives long enough,' Benesek said, for Odgar was on Arthur again and this time it was all Arthur could do to get his shield between himself and the champion of Ebrauc's sword. Splinters flew from Arthur's bear shield and he was driven back, his arm bones surely rattling under the onslaught.

This was a desperate contest. Each move and counter-move a fear- and sweat-soaked thread to be woven later into fireside verse by those who had the gift. For now, though, they made just a dreadful, dis- cordant song. The clank of blade on shield boss. The dull thud of sword on limewood boards and, now and then, the scrape of a blade's edge across iron ringmail or down bronze scales. And always the breathing, ragged and urgent. A man's lungs pumping in his chest like forge bellows, feeding the fire of hate and the blood lust. These sounds told the true story. They were the lyre strings before they are tuned to melodious accord, before the bard's fingers caress them to lift our hearts and our ideals.

No glory now. Just two men hacking at each other with sharp steel. Each craving the other's death. Both desperate to live.

I wondered what King Uther would have thought had he known that men would fight over his throne with the echo of his last heart- beat still reverberating around Tintagel's heights.

'Put him down, lord!' one of Arthur's red-cloaked horsemen barked.

'Gut him, Odgar!' someone else yelled. 'For Ebrauc!' And as if in answer, Einion's champion swung his sword backhanded with such strength that it sliced off the bottom third of Lord Arthur's shield and I saw a glitter of scales in the air.

A cheer went up from the men of the north. Einion smiled and nodded, as if at last his champion was doing what he should have done the moment the fight began, for Arthur was bleeding. Odgar's sword had cut through his shield and scale armour and even through the heavy leather jerkin beneath and gouged into the flesh above Arthur's left hip.

Odgar himself grinned, scenting the blood, and such a wound, though not fatal, might have shaken some men's confidence. Not Arthur. He looked down at the gash, at the fish-scale armour which was slick with blood, then he roared at Odgar, calling him the reeking dung of a spavined mare. He threw what was left of his shield at the big man, who lifted his own shield to bat it aside, but then Arthur was on him. Arthur ap Uther thrust high to keep Odgar's shield high, then dropped to his knees and scythed his sword backhanded into Odgar's right leg below the knee. The champion of Ebrauc bellowed in pain and hammered his sword down but Arthur spun away on the balls of his feet and came up still spinning to slash his sword into Odgar's left shoulder where it crunched against the rings of Odgar's mail, splitting some so that they flew like water glittering in the late sun.

The champion swept his shield wide and Arthur leapt back out of his blade's reach, then sprang forward, quick as thought, and thrust his sword into Odgar's open, braying mouth. For a heartbeat the big man's skull checked Arthur's momentum but then Arthur rammed the sword forward and there was a crack of bone, a gush of blood and a low groan from spearmen who knew that Odgar was dead, even though he still stood.

But Arthur had not finished with him yet. He bent his sword arm and reached out with his left hand to grab hold of Odgar's long beard, that beard of which the champion was so proud and which had the silver ring knotted in it, and when the end of it was in his fist Lord Arthur pulled hard. He hauled the big champion forward with such violence, at the same time thrusting his sword deeper still, that with the sound of metal scraping metal the sword blade burst through the back of Odgar's helmet, gleaming red in the red twilight.

Now Odgar's big legs gave out and he collapsed, spewing gore, and Arthur let the great weight of his opponent's armoured body pull him off the long blade. Then Arthur, his golden beard spittle-laced and blood-spattered, lifted that glistening red sword and pointed it straight at King Einion.

'This man died for nothing,' he yelled at the king. His eyes were wild with terror and the savage joy of battle. The veins in his neck strained against the skin. He might have been speaking to a king, but that fact did not blunt his rage. 'Odgar of Ebrauc would have been a good man to stand shoulder to shoulder with against the Saxons,' he roared. 'Instead he lies here and will never know the glory of throwing the invaders back into the sea.' He jabbed the bloody blade towards King Einion. 'That is your doing, lord king. Not mine.'

The King of the North was all scowl and knitted copper brows but he did not refute the accusation, as his men came forward to gather up their champion's body.

'Wait,' Arthur told them and strode back to where Odgar lay face down in the grass, his blood pooling on the sunbaked earth, drowning a clump of buttercups. The spearmen stepped back, affording the victor his right to the spoils, and I expected Lord Arthur to take the helmet, even split as it was, and Odgar's mail coat, as well as his sword and his studded belt. But he took none of these trophies, telling Ebrauc's spearmen that they should keep it all for they would need good war gear in the coming struggle against the Saxons. But he did use his own sword to saw through the end of Odgar's beard until the silver ring came free.

He stood and turned until he found me in the crowd and there was a cold hardness in his blood-splashed face. 'Lancelot, isn't it?' he asked, rubbing the ring on his trouser leg then holding it up to examine it by the fading light.

'Yes, lord,' I said.

'Merlin must know something which I do not,' he said, 'to have brought you to my father's deathbed today.' Then he tossed the ring to me and I caught it. 'So, remember, Lancelot, the waste you saw here.' He almost spat the words. 'The misuse of a brave man.' I nodded and made a fist around the ring which was warm in my hand.

Then Arthur turned and walked back to Gawain and the rest of his men, and they slapped his back, praising his victory as much as chiding his mistakes in the fight, and he took it all in good humour, his teeth flashing white in his beard. In that instant I could have sworn I saw the battle wrath fly out of him, like a crow flapping up from the barley.

Uther the Pendragon, High King of Britain, lay dead and stiffening in his bed. Odgar, the champion of Ebrauc, was being hauled off by his arms through the summer flowers, streaking the grass red as he went. But Lord Arthur's soldiers, those big, battle-scarred men who were short in Britain but long in war, laughed and cheered, and it seemed to me they were as happy as children allowed to stay up to hear the bards.

The day after Uther died, grey cloud rolled in from the ocean to cloak Tintagel in a dark pall and the sound of women's wailing hung in the air like the threat of rain. I'd heard some women saying that Britain was gods-cursed, which was why the Saxons were getting stronger while our own great warlord lay stiff and cold. Bors heard a druid called Senorix telling a group of King Menadoc's Sun Shields that the Christians were to blame, and that even now they gathered in their churches to work their spells against us pagans.

'You think a man like Uther would suffer such a miserable lingering death had not some foul magic been worked against him?' Bors screeched in imitation of the druid.

But Benesek warned us both against listening to druids. 'Men like Senorix and Merlin stir up trouble wherever they can,' he told us, filling a cup from a wine jug he had bought from one of Uther's stewards. We were settling down for the night in a round hut on the exposed, wind-blasted north-east side of the peninsula, having eaten a meal of bread and smoked mutton from the supplies we'd brought from Karrek in the *Swan*. Gwydre, commander of Uther's bodyguard, had put us in there with King Menadoc and his men, saying we Cornubians ought to get along fine, and in truth we did not envy Gwydre, having to keep the peace in Tintagel between all those men from different kingdoms.

'Druids stir trouble. That's what they do,' Benesek said, swirling the wine round in his cup before downing half of it. 'Because they thrive on chaos. They feed on it.'

I did not know enough about druids to disagree with him. I knew Merlin was cunning. When I was a boy, he and his slave, Oswine, had tricked me into witnessing his rites with Guinevere in the Lady's keep. It had been some sort of test. And now, years later, he had tricked me again, this time into swearing an oath to serve – to protect was how he put it – the next king of Dumnonia, who must surely be Lord Arthur. And I knew that Pelleas had not liked Merlin, just as Benesek mistrusted him still, though I did not know if their reasons went beyond a warrior's natural mistrust of magic.

'So don't you concern yourself with any of Merlin's nonsense, Lancelot,' Benesek said, meaning the oath I had muttered in the High King's hall. 'I'll straighten it out with him before we leave. As for Uther, he was past knowing what he was saying.' He drained his cup, dragged a hand across his long moustaches and reached for the wine jug. 'Steer clear of druids. That's my advice to you.'

'So you don't believe Senorix that the Christians killed King Uther with the help of their god?' I said, guiding the conversation away from Merlin, for I was not yet ready to forget my promise to Uther. Not before I had at least seen Lord Arthur acclaimed. Not before I had found out why Merlin had put me in the position to be making such a promise to the High King of Britain.

'No, I do not,' Benesek said, clenching and unclenching his right hand. 'That old goat would have me believe these swollen knuckles are the Christians' fault. That every time my guts are loose it's because some Christ-follower prayed to his god to sour my belly.' He shrugged. 'Druids,' he said, then drank again.

Even so, the High King was dead and women wailed and the blue summer sky had been usurped by grey, swollen cloud which weighed above our heads like a low roof. For a full day and night that cloud threatened rain, which did not fall until at last, on the day of Uther's funeral rites, the gloom above our heads released its burden. That rain fell all day, hissing down upon Dumnonia's peninsular fortress to flatten the grass and summer flowers, even finding its way through old thatch to puddle on earthen floors. To the south we could see patches of clear sky between thin gauzes of distant rain, but Tintagel and the seas breaking on its ragged shore were flayed by the downpour, so that we all feared that King Uther's balefire would not burn. And if Uther did not burn, then how would his spirit body make the journey to the afterlife? If there was no fire because the gods did not believe Uther, scourge of the Saxons, was worthy of the hereafter, what would that say about Britain's future?

I saw Merlin standing out in that seething torrent, a black shape in the hissing gloom, his staff raised to the cloud as he chanted words that were lost, drowned by the rain's sibilance. Spearmen sheltered where they could or walked about with their shields held above their heads. Servants journeyed back and forth across the land bridge to the mainland granaries and storehouses, bringing smoked legs of mutton, fish, bread, cheese, olive oil, wine and ale across for the funerary feast to be held in the glow of Uther's balefire.

From the doorway of the roundhouse I watched twelve slaves lead three of the High King's bulls to the great mound of sodden firewood, the beasts' fearful lows steaming in the air as the slaves slaughtered them under Merlin's watchful eye and set about butchering them. And the only living things who did not look utterly miserable were Lord Arthur's proud horses, which were still picketed along the length of the king's hall. They cropped the wet grass and did not seem to notice the rain which glistened on their flanks and I knew, from having known Malo my father's stallion, that they enjoyed the respite from the summer flies which usually plagued their eyes, mouths and noses.

And then, as the gloom darkened from iron to charcoal, betraying the dusk, the rain fell with less anger. The grey veil thinned. The downpour slowed and then stopped altogether. The pall above Tintagel shredded to reveal the waxing moon, near full now, wearing a silver torc whose lustre lit the blackening sky. The scattering cloud was borne off on a warm briny breeze which came from the west to dry our cloaks and the roof thatch and bristle the tall grass at the settlement's fringes. One by one the stars revealed themselves and men and women ventured out of smoky buildings which stank of wet wool and damp straw.

Benesek had been snoring by the hearth, adrift on a sea of wine, and so Bors and I prodded him awake and the three of us went to join the crowds which were gathering around the timber mound. Closely watched by Merlin, Gwydre and three of his soldiers carried the Pendragon in his litter up the pile of wood, stumbling and struggling and more than once nearly dropping the whole thing. Perhaps encouraged by Merlin's threats that he would shrivel their manhoods to the size of maggots if they let go the litter, they got Uther to the top and set him as straight as they could, wedging the litter amongst deadfall branches, gnarled driftwood and worked timbers which must have come from an old building on the mainland.

'No easy task,' Bors said admiringly, and neither was it, though it seemed to me that Gwydre was a good and reliable man who did not need Merlin's threats to do his best for his dead lord. Merlin himself, wearing a dappled cloak over his black robes to signify that he could move between the realms of the living and the dead, conducted the rites, calling on Arawn King of the Otherworld to welcome King Uther to Annwn with feasting and hunting and the honour befitting a man who had ever respected our gods and protected his people. And we hundreds watched spellbound as Gwydre and his men carried Uther's war gear up the mound: a golden helmet and a golden shield etched with a silver dragon. A coat of scale armour similar to Lord Arthur's. A great spear with a broad leaf-shaped blade that glinted in the moonlight, and a sword whose bejewelled hilt glittered like some nocturnal creature's eyes. All these were placed on the litter beside the pale-skinned corpse, for above all things Uther had been a lord of war and would need those accoutrements in the afterlife. Added to all this was Uther's favourite silver drinking cup, an amphora of olive oil, two skins of his finest wine – one for himself and the other a gift for Arawn – and several joints of meat from the slaughtered bulls, also for Arawn, to propitiate the King of Annwn.

Then Merlin carried the burning brand to the pyre and we held our breath, fearing that the rain-soaked wood would not catch and wondering what would happen then. For what seemed an age, the druid worked his torch into the gaps which had been stuffed with dry straw. The kindling smouldered before bursting into flame without igniting the wood around it. Then Lord Arthur himself took his spear and thrust it into the pile, levering branches up so that Gawain could stuff more tallow-soaked straw and cloth rags deeper amongst the fuel and when Merlin put the burning brand to one of these bundles it flared bright and hungry. The exposed wood was too sodden to hold a flame but the timber in the heart of the pile was still bone dry and when that first flame caught, we breathed again because we knew that Uther's balefire would burn.

And how it burned.

The breeze whipped great flapping flames high, stretching them until they ripped apart into tongues of fire that lashed the night sky and warned the otherworld of the coming of a great king. The wood cracked and spat loud enough to wake the fish sleeping in their weed beds and the glow from the fire lit up the plateau an arrow-shot in all directions. It illuminated the buildings, giving the illusion of new golden thatch on their roofs, and it cast everyone gathered upon Tintagel's heights in a bronze hue, like metal glowing in the forge ready for the smith's hammer. And, in a way, weren't we all there to be forged by Merlin and the gods and by a new king in the glorious death glow of the last? The kingdoms of Britain reforged into one blade to be wielded against those who came across the sea with other gods to take our land and make us slaves?

Having dried the exposed wood and scorched the grass black in a ring all around the pyre, the flames now sought the reason for their existence. With a sound like Arawn's own breathing they ravaged everything in their path and even though we were some forty feet from that fire we had to turn our faces from its savagery.

'Watch your moustaches, old man,' Bors told Benesek, who was transfixed by the wrathful flames. My cousin raised his hand as a shield against the heat. 'If they catch fire we shall all burn alive.'

'Might be worth it to join the feast he's going to,' Benesek said, staring dry-eyed at the litter and war panoply atop the pyre, his face cast in the golden light.

'Now,' Bors muttered a little while later, 'there.' A gasp rose from the congregation and I saw a bright flare as Uther's cloak and hair caught. I thought I even heard the hiss of burning fluid among the fire's roar. And then King Uther was gone, swallowed in flame, devoured by it. Transformed by it.

Uther Pendragon's balefire lit the world. It turned the night sky to molten copper, spewing more glowing sparks than I could think there were blades of grass in all Dumnonia. Up and up those cinders swirled on the fire's hot breath, as if each was the soul of an ancestor of the living gathered around the burning king. And each ascending spark followed its own forebear up and up, back until the very beginning. Back to the first kings and further still to Cernunnos the horned god, and even as far as the white mare Eiocha, who had been born of sea-foam. For such a lineage had the High King claimed and there had been few men brave enough to dispute it.

But all mortal men must die, even those descended from gods and horses spawned from the sea, and, knowing that their king's life was ebbing, Uther's people had prepared for this night. For weeks they had gathered firewood, bringing it across from the mainland in carts and dragging it behind oxen, so that it made such a pile as dwarfed any Beltane fires I had seen built to celebrate the sun's return.

'Lord Arthur has big boots to fill,' Benesek said, brushing a still-glowing cinder off his shoulder before it could scorch his cloak.

'He's still young enough,' I said. 'And he can fight.' Which were two things that the great Uther Pendragon had not been able to claim these last few years even if he were descended from gods.

'And he has shown everyone here that he is brave,' Bors said. 'And honourable,' he added, recalling Arthur's treatment of Odgar and the words he spoke in victory.

'So, you think King Einion will forgive the humiliation he suffered yesterday? That he'll acclaim Lord Arthur in two days and ride back to his northern fortress having forgotten all about it?' Benesek asked, his eyes still full of the fire.

I looked at Bors, who shrugged.

'Maybe he will,' Benesek went on. 'He's hot-headed but he won't risk ripping Britain apart.' He turned his face away and nodded. 'What about Lord Constantine?'

I looked across the flame-lit space, through the steam which rose like fog from the wet grass beyond the charred black ring, and saw Lord Constantine, warlord of Dumnonia. His beardless face all sharp lines. His Roman breastplate gleaming.

'If he was so hungry for the throne he could have had it before now,' I said. For Uther had been a long time dying and Constantine could have helped him on his way easily enough. It would not have needed a blade whispering against the collarbone, seeking the ailing heart, I thought, seeing my old friend Pelleas in my mind's eye. A hand pressed to the old king's mouth would have done it. As warlord of Dumnonia, and with Arthur still fighting in Gaul, Constantine would have been acclaimed in the absence of a rival and in the interests of the kingdom's stability.

Benesek hoomed in the back of his throat, perhaps agreeing with me, perhaps not. And yet as I looked at Lord Constantine I wondered what he was thinking as he stared up at the balefire. The litter and most of the war gear was gone now, consumed by the raging flames, though I could still make out the armour, its scales glowing bright red like the skin of some malevolent serpent from one of the old stories. I could see King Uther's helmet too. It had fallen several feet amongst the disintegrating timbers and caught in the crook of a thick tree limb where it glowed and pulsed a deep red, looking like the fire's beating heart. As for the High King himself, his flesh was gone, ascending even now on the smoke which smudged the black sky and the stars, but it seemed to me that his bones were still visible as thin, dark shadows within the flames.

Was Lord Constantine cursing those smouldering bones? Was he himself burning with rage that the Pendragon had not named him the heir of Dumnonia, despite his defending the kingdom and Uther's throne since he came to manhood? And he being the son of Ambrosius Aurelius, who might have ruled still had the assassin's blade not cut short his life. Or was Lord Constantine secretly glad that the keeping of the throne, and perhaps the saving of all Britain, would not rest on his shoulders? That this burden would fall on his cousin Arthur, who had already fought and killed for it?

'That's that,' Benesek said and coughed into his fist. 'I need to rinse the smoke out of my gullet.' All around us men and women were drifting away from the fire, heading back to the king's hall or one of the many small fires which burned on Tintagel's heights and around which the spearmen of the kingdoms of Britain gathered. The sound of a bard singing drifted eastward with the smoke. Off to my left, a woman played the flute while another danced for the crowd's pleasure, her bare shoulders and dark hair glossed by the light from Uther's pyre. Somewhere else, someone was playing a harp and all across the peninsular fortress there rose a hum as folk proceeded to indulge in the festivities, their relief almost palpable. The rain had stopped and the Pendragon's balefire had burned as well as any fire ever did.

And so perhaps the gods still loved Britain, we thought, as we went to find wine and food and the pleasures of the funerary feast.

Queen Igraine was as generous a host as any spearman in Britain had ever known. The royal stores were plundered of ale, wine and mead. As well as the remaining meat from the three bulls which roasted in great troughs over the fires, spitted pigs, legs of mutton, haunches of venison and countless platters of succulent boar had our mouths watering long before we got to taste their flesh.

The evening still clung to the balefire's heat. Even the sweet smoke and herb-scented breeze wafting across that sea-fretted promontory was as warm as breath, so that nobody wanted to be under any roof but the sky, which was the colour of woad-dyed wool but streaked with rust and blood at the hem above the western edge of the world.

It was a night to sleep beneath the stars. And so an army of servants carried the food from fire to fire, because Queen Igraine was determined that every man who had come to Tintagel, be he from nearby Cornubia or distant Caer Lerion, would have a full belly when he wrapped himself in his cloak and lay down in the grass to sleep.

But sleep was a long way off yet. For now, bards held audiences enthralled with songs of heroes and ancient treasures. Spearmen from the different kingdoms challenged each other in contests of strength or drinking or hurling insults. Women danced or played harps or flutes, or beguiled men, no doubt breaking the hearts of some who were far from their own hearths and wives. And surprisingly there was little in the way of trouble. I saw only two fights. The first between one of King Einion's men and a spearman from Powys who claimed Einion's man had stolen his cloak brooch, and the second between three of King Menadoc's Sun Shields and several of King Cynfelyn's Cynwidions. One group had challenged the other to an eating contest, which just showed how much food there was on offer, but an argument had broken out when one man was accused of cheating by spewing his guts into the gorse so that he could fit more in his stomach.

There was little blood spilt, though perhaps a broken bone or two, but Gwydre was vigilant and his men for the most part were able to keep the peace and those who had come to bear witness to the High King's deathbed behest now honoured the Pendragon's memory by drinking enough wine and mead that they might even forget their own names.

'We leave in three days,' Benesek said to Bors, pulling a fork of his moustaches through a fist to smooth it while pointing his cup in the direction of three young women who were trying to get Bors's and my attention by conspicuously ignoring us. 'Are you going to go and talk to them? Or will you wait until the *Swan* is into the breakers before deciding you need to know their names?'

They were the same three we had passed on the steep path the day we came to Tintagel, and whenever we looked over at them from where we sat by a fire they swung their faces away, grinning and conspiring until one would glance back to see if we were still looking.

The one with the fair hair began to plait another's hair and as she gathered the three tresses she looked our way and seemed to let her gaze rest on Bors a little longer now that she knew her friends could not see her eyes. Bors looked at me, one of his eyebrows cocked as if he thought Benesek had made a good point.

I grinned.

'Lancelot's the second wave of the assault,' Benesek told Bors. 'First he's coming with me. Won't keep him long.'

'Where are we going?' I asked, but I already knew.

'We're going to find Merlin,' he said, tilting his cup towards me, so that wine sloshed over the lip, 'and I'm going to remind him of your duty to Lady Nimue.' He put a knuckle to his mouth and sucked the red liquid from it. 'I'll make him release you from that damned oath he tricked you into when he thought I wasn't looking.'

Benesek mistook my frown for frustration at seeing Bors go off to meet the girls without me. 'It won't take long, Lancelot,' he said. 'Believe me, better to rid yourself of this oath before it settles.'

But I was not sure I wanted to be free of the oath.

Bors grinned. 'I'll tell them you're a famous warrior,' he said, drinking deeply for courage.

'Second in prowess only to you of course,' I said.

'Of course,' he said with a flash of teeth, then he relieved a passing servant of a heavy wine jug and strode towards the three girls, who looked surprised and excited and yet defiant.

Benesek and I watched Bors for a moment as he all but ploughed through the crowd, his broad shoulders set as square as the sail of a boat running with the wind.

'He's a brave lad, I'll say that for him,' Benesek said.

'Nothing frightens him,' I said, remembering my own unease when Merlin had taken me to the king's bedside. 'When Uther lay dying,' I said, 'there was a red-haired woman standing with the others. Across from Lord Arthur.'

Benesek smoothed his moustaches as he cast his mind back. 'Good-looking woman?' he asked. 'Enough hair to braid into a ship's rope and cheekbones you could cut your hand on?'

I nodded.

'Morgana,' he said, his lip curling a little at the name. 'Queen Igraine's daughter and Lord Arthur's half-sister. Her father was Gorlois, who was lord of all this,' he said, gesturing at the buildings around us, 'before he made the mistake of flaunting his pretty wife in front of Uther.' He gave a knowing smile. 'A strong man, Uther, until it came to a pretty girl. Then his lust ruled him. Had to have Igraine so he went to war with Lord Gorlois. Once he set his mind on something . . .' Benesek shook his head. 'I reckon Lord Arthur gets that from his father. That fight the other day? Odgar of Ebrauc was a dead man from the start. Arthur would have fought any champion in

Britain for Dumnonia's high seat. He'd have won, too.' He nodded again. 'Aye, he's got plenty of Uther in him. But Morgana? They say she's more mad than sane.' He thought about that for a moment. 'Put yourself in her place. You're a young girl with a golden future, bound to marry well and all the rest of it. Then some vicious warlord kills your father, takes your mother to his bed and claims your home as his own.' He shrugged and drank. 'Or maybe Morgana was mad before all that.'

'Are she and Lord Arthur friends?' I asked.

He scowled in a way that was almost a warning. 'It's none of my concern,' he said. 'None of yours, either. We'll be away from all this and back on Karrek in a day or two.' I nodded. 'Right,' he said, then groaned as he got to his feet. 'Let's get this over with.'

I found Arthur ap Uther dancing with two women to a tune being played on flutes and a skin drum. It was a lively melody and had attracted a large crowd of boisterous men and women, who laughed and drank and made merry by the light of the High King's dwindling balefire. All across Tintagel's plateau, folk congregated around cook fires; rings of men and women carousing around flames. Here, though, they encircled Lord Arthur. He was the heart of their revelry and, like the flames, Lord Arthur danced and leapt and lit the faces of those around him.

He laughed as he danced, and the two women, whose eyes were shadowed with soot and galena and whose lips were painted red, laughed with him in between sharp cries and shrieks in time with the music. And many of the spearmen who just two days before had stood shoulder to shoulder around their lord as he fought the champion of Ebrauc now stood around him again, only this time they clapped their hands and thumped knife hilts against their shields along with the beat of the drum.

Benesek had not made it as far as Lord Arthur's camp. We had been a spear-throw from King Uther's balefire when one of Lord Constantine's warriors had recognized Benesek even in the flame-shivered gloom and the two had greeted each other with the jovial familiarity of old friends.

'This man and I fought King Hengist when we were your age,' Ben-esek told me, his arm round the spearman's shoulder. 'His name is

Cunittus and if you can believe it he's even older than me,' he said, almost smiling.

I could believe it. Cunittus's long hair and beard were completely grey, his face was a mass of creases and scars and I had seen that he walked with a limp.

'But even now I'd pity any Saxon who faced this old dog in a shield-wall,' Benesek said. 'I've seen him scatter his enemies like a man winnowing grain.'

'Ah, there was a time,' Cunittus said wistfully. He held out his empty cup and in a heartbeat it was full and Benesek was filling his own. 'We broke a shieldwall together once,' he told Benesek. 'You, me and Pelleas, remember?' His eyes gleamed with that glorious memory. 'Is he here?'

Benesek frowned. 'I wish he were,' he said. 'He's been dead three years.'

Cunittus growled under his breath and drank deeply. 'A blade death?' he asked.

I looked at Benesek and he looked at me.

'A good sword pierced his heart,' Benesek said, and Cunittus nodded, content to know that, and then the two old warriors fell to reminiscing about other old friends and fellow spear-brothers who were even now waiting for them in the otherworld, perhaps on just such a night as this, with a warm breeze and flames and a feast. And so I had left them to it and now I stood watching Lord Arthur, the next king of Dumnonia and perhaps High King of Britain, dancing and laughing and spinning those two women round in the fire's golden glow.

'I've told him he's going to rip the stitches and reopen the wound,' someone beside me said, his voice raised above the flutes and the drums and the singing. 'But he takes no notice.' The man held out a hand and I shook it, realizing it was Lord Arthur's nephew Gawain even before he introduced himself and asked who I was.

'I'm Lancelot,' I said, and was about to say that King Ban of Benoic had been my father but the words got trapped behind my teeth.

Gawain's scarred face and broken nose made him look fearsome in the flamelight, yet his eyes were friendly.

'Well, Lancelot, that is a fine-looking sword,' he said, nodding at Boar's Tusk. 'And the man I saw you with looks as though he might have been formidable once.'

'His name is Benesek. He's a famous warrior,' I said, thinking Gawain should be more respectful.

'Famous, is he?' he said, his eyes smiling. 'Perhaps when the Pendragon's roar was still enough to make the Saxons foul their trews.'

One of the red-lipped women cried out and we looked over to see that she had broken from Lord Arthur's embrace and was pointing down at his left hip where his green tunic was dark and wet with fresh blood. The musicians had stopped playing and men and women's faces were now heavy-browed with concern, but Arthur threw out a hand to cast away their fears. Then he pulled the woman close and kissed her cheek, at which the spearmen cheered, and Arthur yelled at the musicians to play again and so they did. And now others flooded into the circle to dance, as Lord Arthur came over to where Gawain and I stood.

'What did I tell you?' Gawain chided him as Arthur pulled his tunic up to look at the wound. I saw the cut which Odgar had given him and the broken threads which had allowed new blood to spill.

Arthur winced. 'That Odgar was strong as a bull and his sword was wicked sharp,' he said to me. 'A dangerous combination, Lancelot.' The other woman with whom he had been dancing came and gave him a scrap of linen which could have been torn from her undergarments. 'You still have that ring I gave you? Or have you spent it on wine and women?' he asked me.

I lifted the thong round my neck so that he could see Odgar's ring, which now hung beside a smaller one. Guinevere's ring.

Arthur smiled and pressed the cloth to the wound. He pulled his tunic back down and kept the pressure on with his left hand while holding out his bloody fingers to Gawain, who rinsed them with ale from his own cup.

'Merlin tells me you're a good fighter,' he said.

'I can fight,' I said.

He nodded. 'I always need good fighters,' he said. 'How is your horsemanship?'

I considered that question. I had not ridden in years. 'I like horses and they like me,' I said.

Arthur laughed at that and Gawain grinned. 'Well, that is a good start,' he said.

'Lord,' I said, feeling that I was on a horse there and then, a horse which was bolting and needed stopping. 'I serve the Lady of Karrek Loos yn Koos.'

'You did serve the Lady,' he said, stressing the word *did*. 'Merlin assures me that Lady Nimue has given her blessing for you to fight for the next king of Dumnonia.' He fixed me now with eyes that had been the blue of the sky on the day he had fought Odgar, but which were now as dark as pitch and glossy in the fire's amber glow. 'And I will be king, Lancelot,' he said.

Behind him his spearmen and those others who had been drawn to Arthur's camp were celebrating as if the gods themselves had come down to Dumnonia and promised to help us drive the Saxons out of Britain. But Arthur had cast off his mirth and looked hard and imposing as he stood beside his father's pyre, a big hand pressed to the wound in his hip to stem the blood. 'I will be king and I will reclaim Britain from those who would take it from us. From those who even now prepare to yoke their oxen and turn soil which they believe is theirs because they have won it from us. Because they have watered it with their own blood.'

Gawain frowned at him and tilted his head towards me.

Lord Arthur gave his nephew an almost imperceptible nod, then smiled at me and his face transformed once again. 'But there is time for all that another day. Tonight, we celebrate, Lancelot.' As if he had overheard his lord, one of Arthur's tall warriors handed him a cup of wine. 'And if you are worried about that oath you mumbled in the king's hall, don't be.' He swatted the issue away like a fly. 'Merlin is always stirring the broth. His scheming is beyond my understanding.' He shook his head. 'He says you're a good fighter and I need fighters. My soldiers are the best in Britain—'

'Best in Gaul too,' Gawain put in.

Arthur nodded. 'You'll make your name with me, if you're as good as I have heard. You might even rise amongst my companions. Like cream in the pail.' He grinned. 'Or you might just get lucky like Gawain here.' Gawain grunted. 'Luck or talent,' Arthur said, then drank from the cup and swiped a hand across his golden moustaches. 'Or both. That's even better.' His eyes suggested he thought he himself enjoyed those twin blessings. He gestured behind him with the wine cup. 'They look like drunken fools, Lancelot, but they are the bravest and most skilled horse soldiers since the legions left. And they are loyal.'

'They're fond of the silver and the wine with which my uncle rewards them,' Gawain said with a mischievous grin that softened even his battle-scarred face. 'That's why they're loyal.'

Lord Arthur pointed the finger of the hand curled around his cup. 'They are loyal because I never lose, nephew,' he said.

'That too,' Gawain admitted.

'So, young Lancelot, did you seek me out to make good on the oath Merlin tricked you into?' He grinned. 'Or did you come for the ladies?' He looked towards the two women with whom he had been twirling through the flame-licked night. Both were now dancing with other men, though it seemed to me they were not having quite as much fun as before.

'I don't dance, lord,' I said, which was answer enough.

He smiled and put a hand on my shoulder. 'You're sure you wouldn't rather live your life on a rock off the coast of Cornubia, now and again escorting fat merchants to Tintagel?'

I thought of my duty to the Lady and my future as a Guardian of the Mount. Had the Lady really given her blessing for me to leave Karrek and serve this man? This horse lord, this lord of battle who, in two days' time, would be acclaimed King of Dumnonia?

Gawain gestured at Arthur's hand which was still pressed against his left hip. 'Need to get that stitched again,' he said.

Arthur lifted his tunic. 'It's barely bleeding,' he said, but Gawain arched his left eyebrow, through which a white scar ran up to his hairline. 'One more dance and I'll get it stitched,' Arthur said, then handed me his cup which was still over half full. 'Drink up, Lancelot. If I was as handsome as you, I'd have conquered every pretty girl in Dumnonia by now.' With his strong, blue-eyed face, white teeth and neat golden beard, Lord Arthur looked like a hero from a bard's song, yet here he was bringing a flush of heat to my cheeks. 'Enjoy yourself, young Lancelot. We shall speak again.'

'Yes, lord,' I said. He nodded and with that turned and walked back to join those who were spinning and contorting and jumping to the beat of the drum and the trilling notes of the bone pipe. You could hardly tell he was limping.

I did not speak to Arthur again that night. I suspected the wound was worse than he admitted, for I saw him and Merlin and a grey-haired woman with a horn lantern head towards a tent near the horse picket beside the king's hall. I didn't see any of them again before I found a space by one of the fires, wrapped my cloak around me and, my head spinning from too much mead and wine, fell asleep.

And in the morning, death came to Tintagel.

16

Betrayal at Dawn

I WOKE TO A DISCORD of horror. A chorus of shrieks and squeals that seemed to freeze the blood in my veins and still my heart. Dew-soaked and bleary-eyed, I sat up in the grass. All around me in the half-light men were pulling swords from scabbards, hefting spears and yelling, their raw, sleep-drunk voices thickening the confused clamour. I saw the first blood fly in the dawn as a warrior slashed his spear down, ripping open a man's throat before that man was fully awake. Another streak of bright vivid red in a morn of muted greys, and I realized they were amongst us, warriors in mail armour and helmets. Men in iron with spears and blades which shone dully in the new day as they plunged and hacked at Lord Arthur's men, who were still waking to the chaos.

I drew Boar's Tusk and held it before me, looking for Benesek and Bors. Looking for Arthur and Gawain, but I saw no faces that I knew amongst the frightened, panic-gripped masks of those who had been sleeping one moment and were now being slaughtered.

'Who are they?' I shouted to one of Lord Arthur's men, who was pushing his helmet onto his head with the sober resignation of an experienced warrior.

'Lord Constantine's men,' he growled, then hefted his spear and strode into the maelstrom, and I watched him deflect a spearman's thrust and disembowel the man with a savage riposte. Others too were fighting back, throwing themselves at Constantine's men with whatever blades they had, and the enemy, seeing that the easy killing was over, drew together, shoulder to shoulder, preparing to advance through the camp like a killing wave of wood, steel, leather and flesh, their big oval shields held before them.

Beyond this wall of death, in the shadow of the king's hall, I saw the last of Lord Arthur's horses being hamstrung by men with dripping red blades. The beasts' terrible screaming sounded like the torment of a thousand souls, a tumult that tore into the gloomy dawn. Ripped into men's guts too and sowed fear that soured the mouth.

'Shieldwall! Shieldwall!' someone was bellowing and I looked over my shoulder to see that one of Arthur's men, a huge, dark-skinned warrior with a black beard, had set himself with his back to the smouldering timbers and ember-glowing remains of King Uther's balefire. The gods knew what fate Arthur himself had suffered. Perhaps he had been slaughtered while he slept and even now lay paling in the damp grass. The next king of Dumnonia dead before the first voice could be lifted to acclaim him.

'Shieldwall!' the big warrior yelled again, smoke billowing around him so that he and those men flooding to join him looked like wraiths emerging from the otherworld on Samhain eve.

A hand grabbed my shoulder and I spun to see Benesek in his war gear and Bors at his shoulder, his sword drawn and his eyes large as they drank in the horror.

'Easy now, lad,' Benesek said. 'Best get back to that lot.' He gestured with his spear to the shieldwall forming of Arthur's men. His moustaches were frayed and unkempt and his eyes were swollen with sleep, but he and Bors were alive and my heart leapt in my chest to see them.

We walked backwards, facing the wave of Dumnonians who were tramping through the remains of the camp, the clothes and furs, the empty wine skins and the abandoned war gear, thrusting their spears down into the wounded and coming on. Driving on. Many of them wore similar mail or scale armour over russet tunics and all wore an iron helmet with a short red crest, so that I imagined this was a sight our ancestors would recognize, having faced the legions who marched under their eagles those many years ago.

'I thought if any of them it'd be Einion,' Benesek said, 'not Constantine.' He spat with disgust at the man's treachery.

'Look there,' Bors said, pointing his sword to the west.

The breeze blew smoke and ashes from Uther's pyre towards us now. It billowed around us, making men cough and splutter, but even through the smoke and murk I saw King Einion and his men of Ebrauc, their shields painted with jagged bolts of black lightning. More men were flocking to their king but Einion himself stood like a rock at their centre, his face unreadable across the distance separating us.

'And there,' I said, pointing Boar's Tusk at a band of warriors gathered by the cattle byre to the south of the king's hall. 'Men of Powys,' I said, recognizing King Cyngen Glodrydd's stag antlers on their shields.

'I see them,' Benesek growled.

There were other groups of men too, other war bands, other spearmen of Britain mustering around their respective kings and lords between the smoking remains of the fires on Tintagel's heights. And Benesek cursed again, because none of these leaders was bringing his men to help us.

'At least they're not joining Lord Constantine,' Bors said, for he could always see the sun behind the cloud. Then the men of Lord Arthur's shieldwall were shuffling left or right so that we could take our places in that small rampart of warriors. Except that it was not a shieldwall, because at least half the men had not had the chance to fully arm themselves. We were sixty men. Most had helmets, swords and spears, but only twenty or so had any armour, their gear being either with their screaming, hamstrung horses or still amongst the flattened grass where they had slept. Facing us were one hundred and fifty spearmen, all armoured, all carrying large oval shields and bristling with confidence that they could finish what they had started and drown the dawn in a welter of blood.

'Stay together and stay strong!' the man who commanded our line roared. I was on Benesek's right and Bors was on his left, and I thought my heart would hammer right through my breastbone.

'Can we hold?' Bors asked Benesek.

'We can fight, lad, and we can kill,' Benesek said.

I saw Lord Constantine in the centre of his shieldwall. He wore his sculpted armour and a bronze helmet with long ear-and-cheek guards and a stiff bronze crest which added to his already impressive height. In his left hand he carried the curved oval shield and in his right he held his sword raised towards us, its ivory hilt, carved in the shape of an eagle's head, glowing dully in the murky dawn.

'Kill Lord Constantine and they'll break,' our leader called, his breath clouding, and some men roared their defiance at the Dumnonians, but not many. Most said nothing, just waited. They knew death was coming in the dawn, and all they could do was try to kill at least once before that shieldwall ground us to bloody meat.

'Kill them all!' Lord Constantine roared. 'Send them to Arawn!' he yelled. He had found his voice now, I thought, remembering how he had all but choked on his words in the king's hall.

Thirty paces. Men peering over their big oval shields, close enough that I could see a warrior's wide eyes fixed on me. As if he had chosen me as his kill, reducing this mayhem of hordes to one against one.

My own senses seemed to sharpen like a blade kissed by the whetstone. My blood thrummed as if intoxicated. I absorbed it all. Men coughing around me. Smoke surging, thickening the air and stinging my eyes and reaching towards the enemy shieldwall like ghostly fingers. My heartbeat deep in my ears now and a trickle of sweat running down my back, and the muscles in my thighs fluttering.

Twenty paces.

'Hold,' Benesek growled at us. 'Hold, you hear me!'

My teeth clamped together so that my skull ached. That Dumnonian warrior still staring at me as the distance closed between us and I lifted Boar's Tusk, pointing the sword at him to acknowledge our unspoken covenant. To the death.

'Artorius!' a man yelled. 'Artorius! Artorius!' others took up the cry, and I thought they were chanting the Roman form of their lord's name as a battle cry. That they were invoking Arthur the way men invoke gods of battle. Then I heard the low rumble of distant thunder and for a heartbeat I thought the gods were answering these men but then I realized it was not thunder but the sound of horses' hooves hammering the earth.

'Artorius!' the men around me called. 'Artorius!'

Lord Arthur, mounted on an enormous white mare, spearheaded a group of seven riders who galloped across the plateau, their horses' hooves flinging clods of dew-damp earth into the wan day. Arthur wore his scale armour and gripped a long spear in both hands, its shaft crossing the mare's neck so that its iron blade hung two feet in front of the animal's left eye. And how those horses galloped!

'Arthur,' I whispered, the name like magic across my lips.

'Taranis and his thunder, look at that,' Benesek said. 'The man is mad.'

His helmet's long red plume flying behind him, Lord Arthur and his men looked like gods come down to earth with the dawn, summoned perhaps by last night's great balefire whose flames had whispered into the moonlit sky.

The Dumnonians on the right of their shieldwall were turning to face the horsemen and most got their shields up in the press, though fear had bunched them tight and some men sought to put themselves slightly behind their comrades. And yet there was no hiding.

A loud crack filled the day, followed by a scream as Lord Arthur's spear pierced a shield and mail and plunged into a man's chest, and Arthur let go the spear and drew his sword as his mount drove on into the press of bodies. Scything at heads and shoulders, he laid about him with shining blade and men fell under that onslaught, while the other six horsemen ploughed into the gap, their spear blades piercing men where they stood or slashing faces or necks and sowing terror.

The shock of Lord Arthur's impact surged along the whole of the Dumnonian shieldwall and I saw Lord Constantine yelling at his men to hold the line, shoulder to shoulder, shield to shield. To stand firm. Cursing any man who broke formation, while he and his body-guard of ten spearmen left the centre and strode towards the mayhem on the right. Towards the place where men died under blades and horses' hooves and where Lord Arthur drove his mount on, his men on his flanks as he strove to reach Lord Constantine, whose death might end this madness.

'We should attack now,' Benesek called.

'We hold!' our leader bellowed in reply.

'If we don't hit them now, Arthur will die,' I said.

'It's too late,' the spearman on my right said, and perhaps he was right, for in his eagerness to drive through the Dumnonians and kill Constantine, Lord Arthur had led his men deep into the enemy ranks. Now, the momentum of their charge spent, they were vulnerable as some of the Dumnonians gave those slashing swords and stabbing spears a wide berth in order to get behind Arthur's men, whose horses were not clad in their scale or leather armour. The lustre of their flanks was from well-groomed coats, not bronze or steel. The impetus of their stampede into the enemy had been born of muscle and sinew and noble obedience, not from the added weight of armoured shaf-frons and peytrals and the heavy quilted under-garb.

I saw one of Arthur's men arch horribly in the saddle. Saw the spearman pull his weapon free only to plunge it home again and lever the rider off his horse. I saw another horse and rider sink into the press, the horse shrieking as its hamstrings were cut, its master swinging his sword madly this way and that before a spear took him under the arm and another was driven into his side.

'They'll finish Arthur off and then they'll come for us,' Benesek said, because the men with their oval shields facing us had stopped advancing and now stood firm. Waiting.

Arthur and Constantine were almost upon each other now, though they could not close for the press of men between them, and were like war dogs straining at the leash. Behind Arthur I recognized Gawain by his bulk and his grim face as he hewed off a head with his sword then parried a spear and back cut, slashing a man's face in a spray of blood and teeth.

'There's still a chance if we hit them now,' Benesek shouted.

'Hold!' our leader bellowed. I could sense the desperation in the men around me. They wanted to fight now, to meet the Dumnonians in the fray and fight beside their lord. But another of Arthur's horsemen was down, pulled from his saddle and pummelled with spear butts, and if we broke now, with Arthur's charge having faltered, our ragged line would die on the rampart of the Dumnonians' well-made shieldwall.

Still Arthur spurred his big horse on with Gawain close behind off his flank, those two hacking left and right, cleaving heads and knocking aside spear blades and leaving a wake of dead and broken men. But Arthur could not meet every lunge, and some of those blades slid off his armour or gouged into it, sending bronze scales flying like fireflies in the dawn half-light. And then Arthur's fine mare stumbled and screamed, leg-cut, and Arthur split the head of the spearman who had savaged his horse, but another man managed to grab hold of Arthur's red cloak and hauled him from the saddle.

And I ran. Unencumbered by war gear I flew, aware of a spear streaking past my right ear as I sprinted across the ground, leaping a dead man and stooping to gather up a discarded spear. Towards that shrieking, white-eyed, spittle-flinging mare that was mad with pain, and her master who was on his feet again fighting for his life.

A big, black-bearded Dumnonian stepped out of the line into my path and threw his shield and spear out wide as a challenge, then staggered backwards and fell to his knees, a spear having impaled him through the throat. I knew if I looked back I would see Benesek spear-less, but I did not look back. I ran. Fast as a breeze across the trodden grass, Boar's Tusk and the spear light in my hands. Towards Arthur.

I had chosen my man, just like that other Dumnonian had chosen me, and this man lifted his shield to catch my spear thrust but I threw one leg forward, dropped and slid along the dewy grass, coming under his shield and thrusting up with the spear into the man's groin. He screamed, knowing the ruin I had done him, and fell, but I was up again and plunged the spear into another man's open mouth as he shrieked in surprise to see me in front of him, before I hauled it back and used the stave to parry a blade which would have pierced my chest. The blade streaked again and I deflected it again, in that heart-beat recognizing the snarling, scarred face before me. It was Benesek's old friend Cunittus, whom I had met the previous night. But we knew we were enemies now, borne on this blood tide like leaves that have landed on a fast-flowing stream, and I stepped back and swept my spear down. But Cunittus caught the blade on his shield and knocked my spear wide with his sword. I could tell he had once been good, perhaps great, but he was grey-haired and old, and I was young and fast and already knew I had a gift for war.

I feinted with the spear then drew it back, reversing it and bringing the butt end down onto the sword which Cunittus had scythed after my spear. The arm fell away and Cunittus swung his shield, but again my spear wasn't where he thought it was and so there was nothing to slow his shield's momentum and it was wide of his injured sword arm, leaving his face open. Boar's Tusk streaked, opening Cunittus's face from his left temple to his lower right jaw, and I finished him in the next breath. Then a spear blade streaked past me to take another Dumnonian in the shoulder, the strength in that thrust enough to break through the scale armour and embed in bone.

'I thought you'd never come,' I rasped at Bors, who buried his left foot into the man's groin as he twisted and hauled the spear free of bone and gristle.

A Dumnonian lunged at Bors but I knocked the warrior's spear aside with my own then slashed Boar's Tusk across his throat, spatter-ing Bors in crimson gore.

'You had a head start again,' my cousin said, as the roaring, scream-ing mass of Arthur's men enveloped us and crashed into the enemy.

They had followed me, even the big, dark-skinned leader who had tried to hold his shieldwall firm, and now all was chaos. Blades sang, steel on steel, and rasped and thumped against shields and thudded wetly into flesh. Men roared with fear and fury and pain. They shrieked at the injustice of the death which they knew had been given them, and they lay in the grass, trying to stem the flood of their life-blood, their keening reminding me of the women's death wail, so desperately did they long to be amongst loved ones as the light faded and the sound of battle receded and cold crept into the flesh.

The mare was on her side, whinnying, teeth savaging the bit, hooves thrashing at the air, her wild eyes rolling and her white coat spattered with dark red drops. I avoided those hooves to reach Arthur, then speared a man in the back before he could bring his sword down onto Lord Arthur's red-plumed helm. Arthur hauled his sword from the belly of a man doubled over from his blow, then turned on me as if to strike, his features twisted into a vicious, hate-filled, exultant mask.

'Lord Arthur,' I said, my sword raised to parry his blow, but in that instant he recognized me and stayed his hand. He was standing over a wounded warrior, one of his brave horsemen who had charged with him into the enemy but who now lay on his side, curled up like an infant and clutching his stomach.

'Lancelot,' Lord Arthur said. His men had caught up with me and they closed around us to protect their lord, yelling encouragement at each other as they drove the Dumnonians back. Arthur bent to the man by his feet. Touched his face and smoothed his hair. Offered calm words and praised the man's courage. Then he went over to his own white mare and knelt by her writhing, vein-corded neck and for a moment discarded his sword to lay his bloody hands on her. Bereft of her armour, she had been savaged. Raw gashes in her withers, shoulder, left hind gaskin and rump steamed in the dawn and Arthur thanked her for her service then drew a long knife, weighted her head down with his own body, hushed her with secret whispers and cut both of the big arteries in her neck. And for just a few heartbeats those long friends were a boulder around which a river of disarray roiled, engulfing men in pain and despair and pulling them under.

Bors careened into the little clearing, slipping on gore-slick grass, and with him was Benesek, his sword red and some of the rings of his long mail coat clotted with blood, though I could not tell if it was his own.

'You get yourself killed and the Lady will have me thrown from the top of the keep,' he said, bent and breathing hard, and I wondered if he had somehow known about the fate of the seaman Guinevere and I had killed all those years ago.

'You said attack,' I said.

He shook his head and some garbled profanity tumbled out on his panting breath.

'Arthur, we cannot win this,' a man shouted. I turned to see Gawain glaring down at us. Miraculously he was still mounted on his chestnut mare, which seemed not to be wounded, though she was panting like Benesek. The only other man still horsed was some twenty feet away, leaning forward over his mare's neck as he compelled her to stave in a fallen man's skull with her big hooves. 'We must retreat, lord!' Gawain insisted, and by his grimace I could tell how much it pained him to say it.

Standing now, sword in hand, Lord Arthur took in the clamorous chaos around him as if he could barely comprehend how we had gone from High King Uther's funerary feast to this welter of blood. How, just a day before his acclamation as the next king of Dumnonia, his dead father's ablest warlord had betrayed him so that under the shadow of the Saxon threat Britons were killing Britons on this summer's dawn.

He nodded to Gawain, who nodded back, relieved to have his lord's consent, then turned to the other rider and ordered him to sound the retreat, which the man did, blowing three long notes on the horn he wore on a thong around his neck.

A Dumnonian spearman slipped through the ring of Arthur's men and lunged at the prince, but Arthur beat the long blade aside and contemptuously gutted the man with a neat thrust.

'This way, Lord Arthur,' someone at my shoulder called. It was Merlin, and he wore no armour over his black robe nor carried any weapon other than his formidable ash staff, for no one, not even Arthur's enemies, would dare harm a druid. Nevertheless, a few steps behind him was Oswine, his tame Saxon, and he wore an old iron helmet and carried a splintered shield and a hand axe whose blade shone with blood. 'You must come now while the way is open,' Merlin told Arthur, who seemed torn between taking the druid's and Gawain's advice and staying to fight till his last breath.

'Come on, boys, time to get out. This is not our fight,' Benesek growled at Bors and me.

'Lancelot swore an oath, Benesek,' Merlin challenged him.

'Damn the oath!' Benesek said. 'He's a Guardian of the Mount.' Still gasping for breath, he nodded at Bors. 'They both are.'

'Why do you think the Lady sent them with you, you dimwit?' Merlin asked him.

Bors and I looked at each other, bewildered that they were arguing over us in the midst of this desperate struggle with men fighting and dying around us.

'You're coming with me, Lancelot,' Arthur said.

'Then so am I,' Bors put in, stepping forward to impose with his height and broad shoulders.

Benesek's eyes glared and his moustaches quivered with anger.

'Lancelot swore to protect the next king of Dumnonia,' Merlin said, 'and an oath is an oath.'

'Who is to say Lord Constantine will not be the next king of Dumnonia?' Benesek asked, pointing his bloody sword towards where I had last seen that bronze, fin-like crest above the other helmeted heads.

'I say it,' Merlin said, as if those three words alone wove prophecy.

'Shieldwall! Shieldwall!' Gawain roared, and those of Arthur's warriors who were still fighting, some fifty men I guessed, drew together like a clenching fist. Those who could broke off from their individual fights and many who did not have shields snatched them up from the dead or wounded and closed shoulder to shoulder with their companions. 'Hold them!' Gawain yelled, his horse standing tall and imperious and dauntless in the midst of havoc.

'We must go now, Arthur,' Merlin warned, turning away from Benesek. 'If we do not, all is lost.'

'Go, lord,' the big dark-skinned warrior said, looking over his shoulder and blinking sweat from his eyes. 'We will hold them. Go now!'

Arthur's teeth flashed in his neat golden beard and he looked like a wild animal that would rather die than flee.

'For Dumnonia,' Merlin told him. 'And for Britain.'

'Bedwyr!' Arthur called and the big, sun-darkened man who had led us in Arthur's absence raised his shield to the enemy and turned his face to Arthur.

'Lord?' he said.

'Hold them just until we are away,' Arthur said, his left hand going to the wound above his left hip, which had opened again by the looks of the crimson amongst the bronze scales of his armour. 'Then disengage and retreat. Find Cai and wait for me.' He spat the words, hating leaving his men to fight while he slipped away. 'Do not fight this out, hear me! Get to Cai and his horses.'

Bedwyr nodded. 'Lord,' he said, then turned back and yelled at his men to keep their shields kissing and gut any Dumnonian dog foolish enough to come close enough.

Arthur went back to the wounded horseman, who was deathly pale now and blood-slathered, though his lip was still hitched in a snarl which showed his contempt for the wound and his refusal to let the darkness flood over him.

'Leave me,' he growled as Arthur took him under the arm, nodding at me to help him, which I did.

'I won't do that, Herenc,' Arthur said, 'just as you did not leave me to ride into this mess alone.'

Herenc grimaced and nodded as we hauled him onto Arthur's shoulder and Arthur braced his knees and found his balance with the weight. Then he turned eyes the colour of storm clouds on me. 'You're coming with me,' he said.

I nodded at him and glanced at Benesek, who took off his helmet to reveal his sweat-drenched grey stubble, and in that moment he owned all the years on his back. 'Here, take this,' he said, giving me the helmet. I started to protest but he spoke over me. 'What chance have I got of keeping up?' he asked, making no mention of the blood on his mail above his hip. 'You lost my sword once,' he said. 'Don't lose my helmet.'

'We must go now, lord,' Merlin said. Arthur nodded, spat a curse towards the Dumnonians and, with Herenc folded over his shoulder like a rolled bear fur, he turned to follow Merlin and Oswine eastward towards the men of Rheged, who had formed their own shieldwall, their backs to the rising rocky outcrop which encircled the plateau.

Bors was staring at me. 'Well?' he said, his eyes wild in his blood-daubed face.

I looked at Benesek. 'Go,' he said, and pointed his sword in Constantine's direction. 'Those wet-behind-the-ears bastards won't get past me.' He grasped my shoulder and there was a sturdy strength in it that said more than words could have. 'Go, Lancelot,' he said. 'And send word when you can.'

I nodded, putting the helmet on and enclosing my face within its silver-chased cheek guards. Then Benesek turned and strode towards the shieldwall, where Bedwyr moved aside to make room for a warrior who had earned his respect. And Bors and I ran after Lord Arthur.

'We should have stayed,' Bors said when we had caught up with the others, even though the clash of swords on shields told us that behind us the Dumnonians were pressing their assault, trying to break through Bedwyr's line to reach Arthur. For in front of us, dominating the higher ground and thus cutting off our route to the land bridge and the mainland beyond, were sixty spearmen of Rheged. Their shields overlapped and in their centre stood King Meirchion Gul. One could not miss him for his enormous girth, and his florid face glistened with sweat beneath a helmet which was set with amber and red garnets, green peridots and other gleaming precious stones.

'Keep going,' Merlin called over his shoulder and I saw Arthur and Gawain exchange dubious glances, yet they did not stop, and Gawain even dug his heels into his mare's flanks as if warning her that they might have to charge again. It would be the last time they ever did, I thought as we came within spear-throwing range and started up the slope towards that new wall of limewood and steel.

'You had better know what you're doing, druid,' Arthur said, scowling with the weight of his burden. Merlin just lifted his staff by way of reply and marched on. Behind us, the clamour of battle. The clash of blades, the voice of struggle; guttural, animalistic, desperate, pitiful. Above us gulls wheeled, shrieking in the dawn and oblivious of our trials. Ahead of us, in the east, the sky was aflame and just then the sun came into view above Dumnonia's far forests and rolling hills. It half blinded me. It seemed to set fire to the helmets and spear blades of Rheged.

'Lord Arthur!' Bors called. We looked behind us and saw that a handful of Constantine's men had got around Bedwyr's line and were running after us.

'Leave them to me,' Gawain said, hauling on his reins to turn his big mare back to face them. With a kick of heels and yell of encouragement he galloped towards the Dumnonians, his spear couched and his helmet glinting in the golden flood of dawn.

'Keep going,' Merlin called, and through the glare I saw the warriors of Rheged shuffling left or right and a gap appearing in the middle of their shieldwall. I looked over my shoulder and saw that Gawain had killed one of the Dumnonians and scattered the rest, and now he trotted the mare after us up the slope to the ridge of rock, the proud animal snorting and tossing her head as if contemptuous of their enemies.

'I'll not start a war with Dumnonia, but I'll not let them follow you either, Lord Arthur,' King Meirchion the lean called as we tramped through the channel between his war band. 'Not until midday at least.' He lifted a fat hand to sweep the sweat from his forehead. 'I'll block this like a plum stuck in a throat, Lord Arthur. Won't let any but your own men through. But you had better be far away by midday, because I'll not have a war for your sake.'

I heard one of King Meirchion's men mutter that the man Arthur carried was dead or would be before we got across the land bridge. Arthur must have heard, too.

'Thank you, lord king,' he said, as five of Meirchion's men came forward, each leading a horse on a leather shank. They were not magnificent beasts like Lord Arthur's horses, which the Dumnonians had so cruelly hamstrung and whose pitiful whinnies still tainted an already foul dawn, but rather the sturdy packhorses and carthorses native to Britannia and which had no doubt borne Meirchion's provender some four hundred miles from Rheged. Each was saddled and carried a water bottle, rolled-up cloaks and a ration bag.

'You will of course pay me back,' Merlin told Arthur. 'These bow-backed wretches cost me more than a brace of pretty bed slaves and an amphora of Falernian.'

I helped Arthur get Herenc onto his horse behind the saddle horns. I felt how cold was the man's flesh but I said nothing to Arthur and mounted a small but stocky dun pony, which snorted as I leant forward to let her smell my hand.

Arthur took the biggest of these horses, yet given his scale armour and with the extra burden of Herenc the poor animal looked sway-backed and cruelly laden as we started off towards the rising sun. Behind us there was a jangle of metal and clatter and clump of shields as the men of Rheged closed the gap in our wake, forming a solid shieldwall once more.

'If King Meirchion betrays us and sides with Lord Constantine we won't get far,' Gawain said, looking over his shoulder as if he half expected the shieldwall to part again and allow the Dumnonians to pour through like water through a split hull.

'He won't betray us, Gawain,' Merlin said. 'I threatened to fill his belly with serpents if he did, and can you imagine how many serpents could happily writhe inside that fat lump of a man? Still,' he added, lifting his staff and pointing its gnarled end towards the sun which was a huge red and gold burnished disc, like a god's shield hanging above the horizon, 'we should make these sorry creatures work for their keep, just to be sure.' And with that he dug his heels into his pony's sides and it whinnied and broke into a trot, its hooves drumming the ground.

So we kicked our own mounts and followed him.

Nightfall found us camped beside the old Roman coastal road amongst a hazel coppice understorey to woodland of oak, ash and birch. And though we could have built a pyre to rival Uther's just from the deadfall around us, we did not risk a fire in case we were pursued by Arthur's enemies. Instead we pulled our cloaks tight around us and took shelter beneath the bright oval leaves which shivered in the breeze.

Merlin cut a hazel rod and set about etching a circle in the ground inside which we were all to sleep. 'Really the stick should be cut on May morning before sunrise,' he said as he bent to the task, using both hands to score the ground, 'but this will suffice. And being surrounded by hazel we shall be safe from demons, serpents and evil spirits, which is something, I suppose.'

'And which of those is my cousin Constantine?' Arthur asked, wincing at the pain in his own left hip as he laid Herenc carefully down.

'Why, a serpent of course,' Merlin replied, getting no argument from anyone, given how we had awoken that morning to his treachery.

The Roman road was wide enough for a swaying cart and to my eyes impressive, even cracked and burst through here and there with weeds as it was, though this state of disrepair had caused Lord Arthur to spit aspersions after the High King's wind-borne ashes. 'Taxes should have been spent on keeping such roads usable,' he'd moaned from the back of a horse which was similar to his own proud mare in the way that a pigeon is similar to a gyrfalcon. 'To beat the Saxons, the armies of Britain will need to march along such roads,' he had said. 'There must be men somewhere who have the knowledge to restore them. Were the Romans our betters in everything?'

'In building, yes. And in war,' Merlin said, 'and in appropriating and improving the inventions of others. And, of course, in wine and administration and getting water from this place to that place, and a great many other things besides. But then they turned their backs on their gods and took up the Christ. And before long their great city, the beating heart of their once great empire, swarmed with big dull brutes like Gawain here,' he said, pointing at the warrior riding up ahead, who seemed neither dull nor brutish to me, though he was undoubtedly big. 'Let that serve as a lesson to you, Arthur,' Merlin had said, holding his hand as still as the pony under him would allow, in order to observe a wasp which seemed to be following the inked swirls on the back of his hand. 'The gods do not put up with being ignored, let alone abandoned,' the druid said. 'They become spiteful.'

'Tell my cousin, not me, for he holds the reins of Britain now,' Arthur griped. 'And anyway, have not the gods abandoned me?'

Merlin had said nothing to that and we had ridden on along that time-ravaged road and Herenc had bled dry and turned pallid yellow, the colour of pus-stained linens. And it seemed to me that this, not the weeds in the road, nor the capriciousness of the gods, nor even his betrayal at the hands of his cousin Lord Constantine, was the reason for Arthur's gloominess.

The previous night, when he had danced in the glow of Uther's balefire, Arthur had shone brighter than the flames. His presence had illuminated the darkness and the faces around him. Now, his ill mood seemed to darken the day. It dissuaded speech. Made one mile feel like two, and the wellspring of that sourness was poor Herenc, who lay on his cloak amongst the faintly glowing stars of white campion, as nightingale and willow warbler streaked through the gloaming.

The rest of us gave those friends what solitude we could and made ourselves busy with things that did not need doing. I had already checked the ponies' hooves, picking out some small stones with the tip of my knife, and now I used saddle cloths to rub the sweat from their coats. As if it would make a difference without having a brush to see to their skin and bring up a shine and do a proper job of it.

Bors was cleaning our weapons, now and then spitting on the blades and scrubbing the bloody saliva off with handfuls of oak leaves and moss. Oswine was off gathering herbs for Merlin, who lay on his back and might have been asleep for all anyone knew, his eyes hidden in the shadow of his black hood. Gawain was a dark shape a short distance off, in his war gear still, so that amongst the moonlit silver birch he looked like the general of a ghost army, silent sentinels looking back along the Roman road whence we had come.

I watched Gawain as I ran the cloth over his mare's flank – making sure to be gentle because she had taken several blows in the fight – and I thought of something he had told me earlier on the way north.

'They are close,' I had said to him, watching the care with which Arthur rode, Herenc mounted in front of him, his arms reaching around to the reins so that Herenc could not fall from the horse though his strength was failing.

'They are brothers,' Gawain had replied with a shrug. 'In the way that you and Arthur are brothers now, Lancelot.'

'He doesn't know me,' I said, watching Arthur speak words of comfort to Herenc, who was slumped over, head bowed so that if not for Arthur's talking I would have thought the man had slipped from life.

'You ran to his side when he needed you, Lancelot,' Gawain said, without turning to look at me. 'You stood with him in the press. Shed blood with him. In Arthur's eyes that makes you brothers. If it came to it, he'd give his life for you.'

I'd frowned at that, but Gawain had shrugged again. 'That's Arthur,' he'd said.

Now, sitting on the ground beside him, Lord Arthur held Herenc's hand in his own and with his other hand pushed the man's sweat-tangled hair away from his face, speaking in a voice a mother might use to soothe her fevered child.

'All will be well, dear Herenc,' Arthur said, then he glanced at the forest around him. 'We are safe here. Gawain watches the road. Nothing can harm us.' He lifted a hand to his cheek and knuckled away a tear. 'Rest now, my friend. Gather your strength.'

Herenc tried to speak but his lips barely moved and the words, if they were words, had no form. He grimaced with pain and I looked away, putting my face against the muzzle of Gawain's big war horse and hushing her though she had made not a sound since we came into the coppice.

Herenc made another feeble attempt at words then gasped, sudden and loud, like a crab diver up for breath.

'Shhh. There now, the pain will ease,' Arthur said. There was no abashment in him, no fear that his intimacies should be overheard by strangers. The unease belonged to us who trespassed with our eyes and ears, and just then Bors looked up from the blade across his thighs, his face drawn and tired, shadow-pooled in the twilight as our eyes met.

Less than a heartbeat only and we were back at our work.

'Leave the poor man alone, Arthur. For all the gods, let him die in peace.' The voice had come from the black cowl and I cringed that Merlin should answer such care with not a scrap of his own. I saw Arthur glaring at the druid's dark shape, though he held his tongue, perhaps not wanting sharp words to tear the peaceful shroud he was winding around his friend.

'Leave . . . me,' Herenc said. Again, barely speech, though close enough.

'I will not,' Arthur said. He had given up trying to dispel the flies which buzzed excitedly around them both, hungry for the blood which was in Herenc's ringmail and on his hands and which had stiffened his cloak. It was on Arthur too. I could smell its coppery scent from where I stood.

'We have ridden far together, my friend, and shall ride further still. No man has more courage than you. More honour,' he told Herenc. 'Look,' he said, but Herenc was too far gone to look, 'the bleeding has all but stopped. Sleep. Tomorrow, when you have rested, you will feel stronger. Merlin will stir some elixir, some foul-tasting draught that will take away the pain and restore you.'

I wet the saddle cloth and cleaned the horses' eyes and noses. Checked backs for sores from the tack. Combed knots from manes with my fingers.

'He will have left us before the moon climbs above yonder oak,' said the voice from the cowl. 'We would be better served talking about what tomorrow holds for those of us who will still be here to see it.'

'Hold your tongue, druid,' Arthur snarled, unable to swallow the rebuke even for Herenc's sake. I looked away but only after I had seen the whites of Lord Arthur's eyes as he glowered at the shrouded, prostrate figure.

'Then I shall sleep, Lord Arthur,' Merlin said. 'Wake me when Oswine returns. If he has found what I need. If he has not, leave me be.' He lifted an arm and wafted it at a cloud of gnats hovering above his head. 'Unless of course you wish to talk about such small matters as your kingdom. Or perhaps the fate of Britain.'

Arthur did not reply. Somewhere off to my left an owl hooted, welcoming the night. It would hunt soon. Closer, amongst the nearby hazels, a soft commotion of flapping wings, some ground-nesting bird dreaming of flight. And still nearer, the gentle voice of a lord of war comforting a dying man.

Gawain had the right idea, I thought, wishing I had taken the first watch. Still, it would not be long now. It couldn't be. No one could bleed so much and live.

I looked at Bors and saw the relief in his face just as he must have seen it in mine. For Merlin, though he had just a moment ago been flapping at the gnats above him, was asleep, and he snored as loudly as a hog.

Herenc died on the cusp of the new day. We had all slept some hours, even Lord Arthur, though when I woke I saw him sitting once more with Herenc, who did not look to be breathing, though he must have been, if only just. And soon after, as I rubbed the sleep from my eyes and shrugged off a dream of my brother Hector, and as blackbirds, robins and wrens celebrated as though they had never before seen the dawn, Herenc at last stopped fighting.

'He has gone,' Arthur said. To himself as much as to us.

Bors nodded. 'He did not want to burden us,' he said.

Oswine had returned at some point in the night with herbs and wild flowers, and Merlin had crushed and added these to wine, stirring the draught with a hazel twig. Then he and Arthur had trickled the liquid into Herenc's grimacing mouth and Merlin said: 'I kill the evil; I kill the worm in the flesh, the worm in the grass. I put a venomous charm in the murderous pain. The charm that kills the worm in the flesh, in the tooth, in the body.' Three times he spoke the words, his ash staff held aloft and its smooth gnarled head gleaming in the moonlight. Then he had left Arthur cradling Herenc and returned to lie on his bed of leaves.

'What use your potions and charms, druid?' Arthur spat. His eyes glimmered with tears.

Merlin shrugged. 'He had a foot and more in Annwn long before we got my potion into him,' he said, then reached for something invisible, failing to snatch it from the air. 'One might as well try to stop blossom being carried off by the wind. I took his pain away. Be grateful for that.'

Arthur frowned and looked at Oswine, to whom I had still not spoken since that night years ago when he had feigned drunkenness to trick me into helping Merlin with his rites in the Lady's keep. The previous day I had seen the Saxon stalking through the carnage of battle gripping a battered shield and a bloodied axe. Now he was preparing us a breakfast of bread, cheese and wine, though he surely felt Lord Arthur's glare.

'Perhaps Oswine brought back deadly nightshade or hemlock to hasten our brother to Arawn's embrace,' Arthur said to Merlin, who sat on an old stump enjoying the dappled sunlight on his face.

Merlin sighed as one who grows tired of having to explain himself to smaller-minded men, and Oswine, knowing it was not his place to refute Lord Arthur's suggestion, continued cutting the cheese into thumb-sized pieces.

'And perhaps,' Merlin said, 'if you had not ridden into a mass of enemy spearmen, your friend Herenc would still be in this world daydreaming of ale and whores and your next foolhardy adventure.' He threw out his hands. 'We do what we do and what does not disgust the gods makes them laugh or else passes unseen.' He considered this. 'The last of those is the least desirable, I might add.' The druid shuffled round on the tree stump. 'Dear Gawain, did I not get Lord Arthur out of that mess back there?' he asked, tilting his short beard towards the Roman road beyond the trees.

'You did,' Gawain admitted through a mouthful of cheese which he had pilfered from the ash stump which served as Oswine's table.

'And did I not take away your friend's pain?' Merlin asked Arthur. 'If not for me, he would have been writhing like an eel. Mewling like a cat gushing kittens under some bush.'

I had seen Merlin pluck herbs from the grass and crush them into a poultice which he had smeared into Herenc's ruined flesh, and maybe it had eased the man's pain. Or maybe Herenc had been too far gone by then to feel much anyway.

Still, Lord Arthur gave Merlin the benefit of the doubt and

nodded. He laid Herenc down, stood and looked at the dead man as though planting the memory of his face in his own mind, then lifted his chin and set his jaw. 'So, what now?' he said.

'And there was I thinking you wanted to wait for your cousin to catch up with us before we actually got to the nub of it,' Merlin said under his breath, turning to regard me with those keen, dark eyes. I was eating bread and cheese and he watched me for a while. I felt uneasy, though I was too hungry to stop eating. 'Did you know that the hazel is the tree of knowledge, Lancelot?' he asked. I shook my head. 'It has many virtues, the hazel, but knowledge is one of them,' he said. 'And so, given that we are surrounded by hazels, it seems fitting that I should share some scraps of knowledge with you now. With all of you,' he added, turning back to face Arthur, 'but mostly with you, Arthur ap Uther. For you are most in need of it.'

Lord Arthur walked over to Oswine, who handed him a piece of cheese and a hunk of bread and Arthur took it over to some deadfall and sat to eat. He should have been sitting on the throne of Dumnonia, yet he looked comfortable enough.

'Will this knowledge help me avenge myself on my cousin?' he asked. Gone now were the tear-brimmed eyes and the face that was all compassion and anguish. In its place was a visage of cold hatred. I had marvelled almost to the point of disconcertment at the care this warlord had shown for one of his horse soldiers, a man who Gawain had told me was no closer to Arthur than any of his other retained warriors. But now? Now I marvelled as much at this other face. This bone-hard, steely-eyed face which must have been the last sight many of his enemies had seen in this life.

'It will do more than help you revenge yourself on that would-be Roman, Arthur. Much more,' Merlin said, then spat into his palm and pulled his sleep-frayed beard through a fist to smooth it. 'If the gods favour us,' he said, narrowing his eyes, 'and I shall do what I can to make them aware of our . . . ambitions, you will heal the land that poor Uther was on his way to ruining. You will heal Britain, Arthur, and you will rule.' He shrugged. 'The gods wish it.'

Arthur studied the druid, his blue-grey eyes unblinking. I looked at Bors, who shrugged and savaged a handful of hard bread with his teeth.

Just days ago we had jumped ashore at Tintagel full of ebullience at the prospect of some time away from Karrek amongst the summer bustle and the gathering of the lords of Britain. Now we were all but exiles, our swords sworn – in my case at least – to fight for the man who would be king but might more likely be killed. A man whose army was scattered and whose powerful cousin had begun a war against him. Prince Arthur ap Uther, the famous horse warrior and scourge of the Franks, had crossed the sea in his war glory. He had come home to the Dark Isles to hear the High King his father's deathbed behest and assume the role conferred upon him. Now he hid with us in a Dumnonian wood, more outlaw than king, more foreigner than Briton.

We had nothing then. Could expect nothing but talk in the dawn. Talk of gods and Britain with a druid and a king who might never be. In a hazel wood by a weed-strewn road, where a corpse lay stiffening in the dew.

Death amongst the white living starbursts of campion.

And yet Arthur had Merlin. And Merlin had an idea. And so Arthur listened.

17

Excalibur

WHEN THE GREAT WALL had come into sight, huge and undulating through the mist-shrouded hills, we had been almost too weary to be properly awed. And yet no man, were he half mad with hunger or tired to his bones, could fail to be impressed by it.

'They talk of the wall even in far-off Constantinople,' Merlin said, looking like a wraith, robed in black on his black pony, vapour writhing around us like dragon's breath. 'From the beggars and thieves in the streets to the palace eunuchs and the emperor himself, they all know of it. Though their own city is surrounded by a wall whose summit you could not reach even if you climbed up ten Gawains standing one upon the other.'

Gawain raised a dubious eyebrow at me and I shrugged, for what did I know of Constantinople?

'And it stretches across the whole of Britain?' Bors asked.

'From sea to sea,' Merlin replied, and even he, who despised the Romans, admitted that the great defensive fortification was testament to the skill and industry of the legions that built it nearly four hundred years ago.

'To keep the Picts out?' Bors asked.

'That was one of its purposes,' Merlin said, and I could almost hear my cousin's thoughts whirring in his skull.

'But the Picts surely had boats,' Bors said. 'And could have rowed around the wall.'

'They could,' Arthur put in, his exhaustion forgotten now the talk had turned to military matters, 'but the imperial navy built the Pictae ships. They painted them green so as to be almost invisible against the sea, then swooped upon the raiders and sent them down to Manannán mac Lir, who ferried their souls to the afterlife.'

Mention of the sea god, even far from the coast as we were, raised the hairs on my neck. Not that the eddying mist helped, or the lingering threat of painted tribesmen springing from the tall grass to pull us from our mounts. For Manannán had tried to claim Guinevere as a gift for Arawn, lord of the otherworld, but she and I had thwarted the god. And yet in the end Guinevere had been taken from me anyway, and perhaps that was my punishment. Or perhaps the gods had not done with me yet and were biding their time, our own long years being but a hawk's wingbeat to them. Even the great empire of the Romans, which had thrived some five hundred summers, had come and gone under the gods' gaze and now the great wall, named after the Emperor Hadrian and once plastered and lime-washed white beneath the grey northern skies, was deserted and forlorn.

We had ridden past the ghosts of ten thousand legionaries and then out of Ebrauc too, on into the lowlands and the kingdom of Alt Clut.

Another moon had waxed and waned since that day we fled Tintagel, the blood of Lord Arthur's enemies wicked into the weave of our tunics and trews, and in that time I had seen the Britain over which Uther had been High King. The heavily wooded valleys and the palisaded hill-forts reclaimed from the bones of our ancestors since the Romans abandoned what they had won. Dumnonia's cantrefs, each with its own king who might have bent the knee to Arthur by now, but whose people did not even know who we were as we passed their rounds, their turf-walled settlements, in which perhaps two dozen souls lived in oval huts.

We sought hospitality from some, food from others, and shared stalls with cows, never seeking much nor paying much either for fear of inviting questions. Always we were guided by Merlin, for he alone of us knew the land and its people. Not all of them knew him, however. Some, mostly younger folk, mistook him for a Christian priest, those men being seen more and more in Britain, spreading the word of their god. Others, seeing his tonsure, staff and black robes, or else knowing him, begged Merlin to heal a sick child or sow, bless fields of wheat and barley ahead of the bread harvest, expel bees from thatch with a curse, cure a boy who was fairy-struck and banish the malevolent spirit, make a charm for a young woman to place under a young man's pillow to make him love her, mediate a boundary dispute, remove a wart, pull a tooth, divine a future and more.

Often Merlin's talents put a roof over our heads or broth in our bellies and neither did he seem to mind these many trivial and some not so trivial requests, for he mined for news and gleaned gossip while he worked.

'That looks like a proper place,' Gawain or Bors or I would say when, after several days sleeping in damp cloaks under the stars, we spied smudges of hearth smoke in the late summer sky.

'That place there?' Merlin would say, pointing his staff at some such round. 'The one with the wall which has clearly been raised not two summers since, which tells us that its people have a feud running with some other community? You want to escape Lord Constantine only to be murdered in your sleep by some toothless farmer with a mattock?' He would shake his head at our stupidity and we would trudge on, imagining roasted meats and sweet mead, thankful that at least it was not winter.

When we did seek hospitality and were granted it, we said we were escorting Gawain's mare to a buyer in Rheged, for she always got attention, being massive and well bred, and it did not seem so unlikely that such an expensive horse would require an armed escort such as we purported to be. The leaders of these rounds would proudly show us the severed heads of their enemies nailed to some gate, and we would nod with solemn appreciation and say nothing of the implied warning. For myself, I would study these boiled heads, preserved in the moment of death, and wonder who they had been in life and why they had allowed themselves to end up as trophies shown off to strangers.

I received two marriage proposals and Arthur received one, and on each occasion Arthur's purse ended up lighter by a few Gaulish coins when we left the rounds, the money given to soothe the offence or embarrassment we caused by refusing the match.

'If I were you I'd have stayed and married the smith's daughter,' Gawain told me as we left one such place. He flapped a hand in Arthur's direction. 'Arthur's got no choice but to search Britain for a sword that doesn't exist. But you?' I looked over my shoulder at the gateway and the copper-haired girl who stood beneath it still, her gaze like an auger boring into my back. 'You could be snugged up somewhere quiet under the skins with her and I wouldn't blame you,' Gawain said.

I looked back round and met Gawain's smile with my own. 'And my oath to serve the next king of Dumnonia?' I said.

Gawain batted that concern away as if it were a gnat on that late summer evening.

'Lancelot is safer with us,' Arthur said, grinning at me. 'Did you see the way the bee-keeper's daughter was eyeing him?' he asked Bors.

'Like a horn of spiced mead on a cold day,' Bors replied through a broad smile.

Arthur laughed. 'She would have clawed the red-head's eyes out had Lancelot stayed,' he said. 'Before we knew it, we'd have Britons fighting each other over the poor lad and then where would we be?' They were all grinning now. 'No, I think I'll keep you close,' he told me with a wink. 'Safer for all of us.'

But I had still turned one last time to look at the smith's daughter.

Many folk had not yet heard that the High King was dead, and we did not enlighten them, fearing to encourage suspicions that we were fugitives from some dispute of succession, which of course we were. There was every chance that Lord Constantine had sent riders south, east and north searching for us and questioning folk who would be well used to seeing his Roman-armoured soldiers, red cloaks against the green, windswept moors like a warning of blood.

We ate, we slept, Merlin made charms, blessed harvests, frightened children, and we went on our way, never staying two nights in one place.

We had crossed the Hafren with a returning wool merchant whose boat was light in fleeces but heavy with ballast of Dumnonian tin ingots, and we passed through the kingdoms of Glywyssing and Powys, hearing from our hosts there how they alone of the Britons had thrashed the Roman legions. And here in Cambria Arthur spent most of his silver, for otherwise we would not have been welcome, being sword-armed and having come from Dumnonia. But we were treated well enough and Merlin advised us that if any of us wished to die of nothing but old age, there was no better place for it than Cambria.

'No Saxons. Little feuding,' the druid explained. 'Too much rain of course, but the earth is rich in lead and silver. Even gold.' He had grinned at me. 'Yes, Lancelot, one could quite easily die of old age here. Or boredom.' He had examined me with those hawk's eyes of his. 'Would you like that, Lancelot? Is that your fate, do you think? To die a bent old man in your bed?'

'You tell me, druid,' I said.

But he had just smiled and I kicked my pony's flanks to move ahead.

We had passed through the great wall via the gates of one of its long-abandoned milecastles, and I saw Oswine spit at the stones, once lime-washed so that the wall shone like a burnished sword belt across Albion, but now yellow with lichen. The gesture was done on behalf of his ancestors who, long ago, Merlin later explained, had suffered terribly against the legions on the banks of the Elba.

'But then a great hero, perhaps Oswine's own ancestor,' Merlin suggested with a grin, 'slaughtered thousands of Romans in some forest. After that humiliation the invaders retreated back to their Limes Germanicus.'

'A line of frontier fortifications on the banks of the Rhine and Danube rivers,' Lord Arthur said in response to my puzzled expression.

'And now we have the Saxons,' Merlin went on, 'who bring their families to drive out our families and their gods to exile ours.' He looked at Arthur. 'And do you think your cousin has the backbone to stem the Saxon tide? Do you think Lord Constantine can unite and lead the kings and warlords of Britain?' Merlin's lip curled beneath moustaches which reached as far as the end of his pointed beard. 'He was dividing us while King Uther's ashes were still blowing eastward on the wind.' He stared at Lord Arthur, who still looked strange on that little horse beside Gawain on his big war horse. Gawain had offered Arthur his own mount but Arthur would not take her. 'No, you are the only one, Arthur. You will unite the Britons. You will drive out the Saxons, as Arminius – yes, I do know the man's name – drove out the Romans.' He stroked the ash staff which rested across the saddle in front of him. 'You will restore the gods, our gods, to their proper places.'

Since the wall, we had ridden a hundred miles across rolling verdant hills, through fragrant pinewoods and valleys of heather and gorse which shivered below threatening slate-grey cloud. We six men and our mounts, wrapped in one of Merlin's concealment spells, rode on, seeing the occasional shepherd or cattle farmer who, the druid assured us, did not see us. Until, one dawn, after a damp shivering night spent hiding from a small war band which had prowled after us even though we were invisible, we came to the other wall.

The summer was ebbing. The first brown leaves were appearing on tall ash and elm and the bracken trembling in their shade was just beginning to yellow. There had been no frosts yet to kill off the maddening clouds of midges, and the earth did not give off that loamy, musty smell that signals that autumn has come. But summer was behind us, and on this morning our horses' breath was expelled in steaming plumes. Everywhere I looked there were dew-laced spiders' webs slung among the heather, the little droplets on the silk gleaming in the sunrise, and it made for such a captivating vision that I did not see the next wall until Bors, riding beside me, kicked my leg to draw my attention to it.

'Impressive, isn't it?' Merlin said. 'The wall of Antoninus or, as the Romans would say, Vallum Antonini.'

It rose from the landscape, huge and forbidding, but whereas the wall of Hadrian had seemed planted upon the earth, imposed upon it by men who believed they ruled even the ground beneath the feet of those they had conquered, this wall seemed a part of the land.

Constructed from layer upon layer of turf, it was ten feet high, and when we urged our mounts up its steep sides we saw that it was some sixteen feet wide. Still standing here and there were the grey bones of an ancient wooden palisade, and a stone-paved road yet ran along the rampart's course on its southern side, so that the legions could move provisions and men easily across its length.

'We stand upon the northernmost frontier boundary of the Roman Empire which set its heel upon Britain,' Merlin said. The view stole my breath. Standing on the southern edge of a valley formed by two rivers and not yet lit by the sun, the wall overlooked three hills and so would have afforded the legionaries good warning of any sizeable war bands coming down on them from the north. Perhaps just as important, this position made the wall widely visible in the landscape for miles around. In its day it had been an irrefutable symbol of Rome's power. And yet perhaps also visual testimony to the limits of her ambition.

'Now it couldn't stop a lame sheep,' Lord Arthur said.

'King Erbin should rebuild the palisade,' Gawain put in. 'Keep the Picts out.'

'He doesn't have the spearmen to man it,' Arthur said. 'This wall runs from sea to sea. Without the spearmen to stand guard it can never be more than a territory marker.'

'Like a dog's pissing post,' Bors said.

Leading his horse by the reins, Lord Arthur bent and pressed a hand into the mound's wet grass and held it there a while. It was as if he was trying to get a sense of the men who had dug the turf and piled it high under the hateful scrutiny of the unconquered warriors to their north. I did not know what Arthur thought of the Romans' influence on these islands and our gods, but it was clear that he admired their skills in building and war. It bothered him to see such a fortification, which must have taken thousands of men many years to construct, now given to ruin by wind and rain and the sheep whose presence hereabouts was evidenced in the black pebble droppings and close-cropped grass upon the earthen bank.

'King Erbin has bigger problems than sheep or even the painted Picts,' Merlin said, having trouble leading his own pony across the deep ditch on the rampart's northern side. The animal was swishing its tail, its ears were pinned back and its whole body was stiff as it pulled back against Merlin, who was muttering under his breath.

I'd had no problem coaxing my own pony across the gully, and could not help but smile to see the druid struggling. 'Erbin's sons are fighting over his high seat while he yet sits in it,' Merlin said, giving the reins a tug. When the pony still refused to move, the druid raised his palms to the sky, at which moment the stubborn beast decided it was time to seize the moment and barrelled down into the ditch and up the other side, half pulling Merlin off his feet as he clung on. We all laughed then, apart from Merlin himself and the pony, which squealed and tossed its head.

'Wretched beast,' the druid said, steadying himself on the other side. Then he hoisted an eyebrow at Arthur. 'At least you waited for Uther to die before tearing his kingdom down,' he said.

'But now we will simply remake Britain,' Gawain said, riding on, the smirk nestled in his dark brown beard like a cat in a basket.

'If you do not believe in this search, why are you here, Gawain?' Merlin asked him. The far-off *cronk* of a raven carried in the dawn but I could not see the bird.

'Because I am sworn to Arthur, just as Lancelot is,' Gawain replied. 'Besides which, while I am here in the middle of nowhere I am not being butchered as I greet the day, like poor Herenc and so many others.' He shrugged his big shoulders. 'If my uncle wants to ride to the edge of the world after something that doesn't exist . . .' He turned his face to the sky and inhaled deeply of the chill morning air. 'It's not like I have a wife waiting for me or anywhere else to be.'

'Well, we are honoured that the courageous and indomitable Prince Gawain ap Lot of Lyonesse chose to save Britain with us, rather than drink and whore himself to death in some harbourside tavern,' Merlin said, lifting his staff as though Gawain's very presence was a gift from the gods.

I caught glimpse of a smile playing at Arthur's lips but he said nothing. Bors looked at me, grinning.

For all his scepticism when it came to this enterprise which had seen us ride five hundred miles across Britain, I knew Gawain well enough by now to be certain that he would follow Arthur into fire. Still, I could not help but share his doubts about both the wisdom of our endeavour and the very existence of the treasure for which we searched.

'It has many names,' Merlin had said that day in Dumnonian woods by the Roman road two moons ago, with Arthur's tears for his loyal soldier Herenc barely dry on his handsome cheeks. 'I have heard it called Caliburn and Caledfwlch and the gods know what else, but let us call it Excalibur.'

'The sword of Maximus,' I said, recalling stories told by the Lady when I had first come to Karrek, and even before, when I was only up to Malo's elbow.

'Indeed,' Merlin said, encouraged to know that he was not talking into the void. 'And who, young Lancelot, was Maximus?'

I had looked at the others, feeling awkward, for surely everyone in those woods, but for poor Herenc, could have told the story of Maximus.

'Go on, Lancelot,' Arthur said, and his smile was enough to spur me on.

'Flavius Magnus Maximus commanded the Roman army in Britain,' I said. 'One hundred years ago or thereabouts, and proclaimed himself Emperor of Rome.' I stopped.

'Yes, yes, carry on,' Merlin said, twirling a hand at me.

I nodded. 'He was a great warlord,' I said. 'When the first Saxon war bands came to the shores of Britain he drove them back into the sea. He slaughtered the invaders.'

'And how did he do that?' Merlin asked. 'On his own? Was he a god?' He swept his staff through the air. 'Did he scythe the Saxons down like wheat?'

'He united the Britons,' I said.

'Yes!' Merlin said. 'He united the Britons.'

'But then his ambitions got the better of him,' I said. 'He became a tyrant.'

'Show me a king who isn't a tyrant,' Merlin said. 'Go on, go on.' That twirling hand again.

'Yes, but he wanted to be Emperor in Rome,' I went on, 'and took the best of Britain's warriors across the Narrow Sea to fight for him in Gaul. He stripped the kingdoms of their spearmen and left Britain weak. The Picts raided in the north. The Saxon boats returned.'

Arthur frowned then. Perhaps he felt some guilt at having left Britain when he was my age to learn war and the ways of the Roman horse warriors known as cataphracts. High King Uther had been strong then and formidable, and Lord Arthur had forged his own way overseas. But had he returned to Dumnonia some years ago, before Uther started to fade, maybe he would have been accepted as the High King's heir without a word raised against it. Too late now to learn from Maximus's mistakes.

'I did not say the man was perfect,' Merlin said. 'Although by taking his soldiers and governors across the sea he had in effect given Britain back to her rightful lords.'

He dipped his head, conceding the man's faults. 'It's true, Maximus was greedy,' he said. 'These so-called Dark Isles were not enough for him. He wanted the shining jewel of Rome herself.' With that the druid had fished inside his robes and produced a coin. It was gold and Merlin spat on it, rubbed it on his robes and tossed it to me. On one side was an imperious-looking face looking right, under neatly combed hair upon which sat an ornate pearl diadem. The man had a long straight nose and his eye was large, as if trying to fit in the breadth of all he surveyed and coveted. I had seen the face before, on silver siliquae back in Benoic. My mother had had an earthen jar full of them.

I turned this golden coin over. On the other side the same man was walking left, holding a wreath and palm, which seemed strange to me, for if this was the famed warlord then why was he not holding a sword?

'Did he take it? Rome?' Gawain asked.

'He was acknowledged as Augustus in the western Roman Empire but was opposed by the eastern Emperor,' Merlin said.

'He ruled Britain, Gaul, Spain and Africa,' Arthur said.

Merlin acknowledged this with a nod. 'He did. But that is not the point, Arthur.' He frowned. 'Or maybe it is.' He turned back to me. 'But let us get back to Maximus in Britain. How, young Lancelot, did he unite the kingdoms?'

'With the sword. With Caliburn,' I said. In truth I knew nothing about it but since Merlin had started off by talking about the sword, it seemed a reasonable guess.

Merlin raised a finger. 'Excalibur,' he said. Then he went over to Lord Arthur and gestured at the sword at Arthur's hip. Arthur drew the sword and handed it to Merlin. 'And was Excalibur an ordinary sword, like this?' he asked me. Asked all of us. I shrugged and so Merlin looked at Arthur.

'It was said by some to be the sword of Hercules, the hero of ancient times,' the druid said. 'By others that it was forged by the Roman smith god Vulcan. Somehow, do not ask me the ins and outs of it, the sword was passed down and down until it ended up in Maximus's hands.'

'He likely stole it,' Gawain said.

'Perhaps he did,' Merlin admitted, 'but who would not covet such a treasure?'

'Maximus brought the sword to Britain. He was still just a general at the time,' Arthur said, 'and he rode to all the kingdoms and showed the warlords the sword and men recognized its power.' He looked at Gawain and Bors and lastly at me. 'He brought peace to these isles and his armies kept Britain safe.'

So we six, who slept in those woods not knowing what the next day would bring, had listened to Merlin, who told Arthur how he could remake Britain. How he could do as Maximus had done and unite the kingdoms under one warrior king, as Uther had tried but ultimately failed to do. And that warrior king would be Arthur. Arthur would wield the ancient talisman as another warlord had done not so very long ago, and we warriors of Britain would free ourselves of the Saxons and throw them back into the sea.

I doubted that this talisman could still exist, for why did no Pictish warlord wield it now? Why was there no talk of it in Britain, other than as a fragment of stories passed down the generations? Gawain doubted its existence too. Bors did not seem concerned one way or the other; it was all just a great adventure to him. As for Oswine, Merlin's Saxon slave, who knew what he thought? But Merlin believed the thing existed and, more than this, that it could be found. Arthur, perhaps wanting to believe more than actually believing, was prepared to at least try, for he must do something to prove that he was the Pendragon's rightful heir and Britain's best hope.

And so we rode the length of Britain looking for a sword. We rode in search of Excalibur.

Oswine saw them first. Behind us. Twenty spearmen on sturdy, well-built ponies rumbling along the great earthen rampart which we had crossed as dawn broke across the hilltops to the north. Not even trying to hide themselves, which was not a good sign, for it meant they saw no need for the element of surprise. Nor was there. We were only four warriors, five counting Oswine, and Bors and I had only been in one real battle before. I felt a lightness in my chest. Felt the blood coursing through the veins in my forearms and a slight thrumming of the muscles in my thighs, as if they were readying themselves. It was not fear but something else. It was that same quiver in the flesh that I had felt in my sparhawk the moment she eyed prey. It was the quickening of the heart. The throbbing of blood before another's blood is spilt.

We watched them ride in column along the wall as if asserting ownership of it. Then they stopped and turned their mounts to look north after us, their spear blades glinting in the day.

'We'll never outride them,' Lord Arthur said. After five hundred miles our ill-fed horses were weary and it was all they could do to plod on into the unknown. Gawain's big mare suffered worse than our smaller horses, being a heavy beast, bred for power and speed, not mile after mile of rough, hilly ground, and while we gave her the greater portion of the grain we had bought along the way, leaving the others little more than their grazing, it was not as much fodder as she was used to. In contrast, the Picts' mounts were surely fresh and strong and familiar with every footfall from here to wherever their masters called home.

'We can't beat that many,' Gawain said, which was not saying that we should not fight, just that we could not win. 'But we could slow them down. Uncle, you and Merlin might get away. Hide up until they give up searching.'

'Gawain ap Lot, how very touching,' Merlin said, and rolled his eyes. 'You and Arthur really are the most warlike princes I have ever known. Though I think young Lancelot was made in the same mould and is a prince too, let's not forget. So too Bors, son of King Bors of Gannes,' he added. 'How extraordinary, Oswine, to find ourselves in the company of so many princes, and none of them with a kingdom to his name or an ounce of sense.'

Arthur and Gawain shared a look of surprise. 'You did not mention that this was King Bors's son!' Arthur said to Merlin. 'Now you tell me?' It seemed that he did not know whether to be angry or delighted.

Merlin shrugged as if to say what difference does it make?

'Lancelot being King Ban's boy is one thing,' Arthur went on, nodding at me. 'But this is Bors, son of Bors?' He studied Bors as if seeing him properly for the first time. 'I knew your father. A good man. Fought beside him. Hunted with him.'

'Drank with him,' Gawain put in, his scarred face not so grim-looking then.

'He talked of you, lord,' Bors said, then nodded at Gawain. 'Both of you.'

'I should think so,' Arthur said. Then his lips tightened. 'They say he died of grief. For your uncle,' he said.

Bors's brow darkened at the memory. 'They were as close as brothers ever were,' he said.

Arthur nodded and smiled, and for a moment one might have forgotten that we were on another king's land, being followed by three times our number of mounted warriors. 'Well then, are we not brothers?' he asked Bors and me. 'Brothers of the sword.' He laughed, remembering past times with Bors's father. Here, as sudden as when the sun breaks through cloud, was the Arthur I had seen on the night of King Uther's balefire. It was the first glimpse of that Arthur since we had set off on Merlin's quest. 'We are well met, Bors ap Bors. And well met, Lancelot ap Ban.'

I could not help but smile and neither could Bors. Merlin shook his head and Oswine grinned. The Picts could have charged us there and then and I would have ridden into them screaming their deaths, Boar's Tusk flashing in the morning sun.

'Do you think we might save the festivities until we have what we came all this way for?' Merlin asked. 'If you princes don't mind, of course.'

Arthur ceded the point with a raised hand.

'You want me to scatter them?' Gawain asked him, grinning at the thought of what could only amount to suicide.

'Cernunnos and his horned snakes, do you think we rode the length of Britain to fight a handful of sheep-stinking savages?' Merlin asked.

'What else can we do?' Arthur asked him.

'What else? We can talk to them, Arthur. Has it not occurred to you that these painted Picts might be the very people we have been looking for? I will know when I get a good look at them.'

'So we just sit here and wait?' Gawain asked. 'Maybe they surround us and butcher us with those spears while you get a good look at them. Or,' he said, turning a palm up to the sky, 'maybe they listen to what we have to say . . . then butcher us.'

'We keep going,' Arthur said, before Merlin could answer. 'They know we are no threat and they are curious. They'll come closer and when they do, they will see Merlin and won't attack then.'

Merlin nodded. 'Only the mad would attack a druid,' he confirmed. 'Let us hope they are not mad.'

'In the meantime, we look for some advantage of terrain,' Arthur the warlord of many victories said. 'Somewhere they can't surround us. Somewhere defensible so that if they do attack, we can kill enough of them to make the rest lose heart.'

As if they had heard Arthur's words across the distance, the horsemen walked their mounts down the steep bank and disappeared into the ditch, at which point we set off.

The horsemen followed us north, sometimes visible when we looked over our shoulders, sometimes hidden by hawthorn scrub or birch woods or the lie of the land, but always following. Until, as dusk fell across the wild lands in a wash of golden light beneath charcoal clouds, we looked behind and they were gone.

'Maybe they've given up,' Bors suggested.

'They haven't given up,' Arthur said.

Half hidden behind the western hills now, the sun drenched the moor in golden light, as though defying its fall, turning heather crimson and the spindly coarse grass as bright as a newly unfurled beech leaf. We wanted the night and yet did not want it.

'Perhaps we can lose them in the dark,' Gawain said.

'Why would we want to lose them?' Merlin asked him. 'These men who have been following us like flies are almost certainly the Miathi. The very Picts with whom we have come to speak.'

'And if they're not?' I asked. If they were not, then we would probably die, I thought.

'We won't know until we meet them,' Merlin said, 'and that will be soon enough, Lancelot. When they are ready to introduce themselves.'

And as the sun fell out of sight we continued towards a great pinewood which loomed dark upon a hill, like a cloak thrown over a shoulder, our progress between blackthorn and juniper scrub lit by a strange ephemeral light the pale purple of June comfrey.

A little while later, Arthur pointed above the pinewoods where a golden eagle soared, still lit by a sun lost to us, searching for one last morsel of the day. And almost with that eagle's passing from our sight did the strange light leach out of the world and the darkness flood in.

We made camp amongst the pines deep in the wood where the trees were close enough to whisper to one another, hoping the Picts would not bring their horses in there. Hoping that they would spend the night amongst the heather beyond our sanctuary and wait for us to emerge in the dawn, and perhaps then we would see if they were willing to listen to what Merlin had to say.

We took turns to keep watch. Arthur first, then Bors, then Gawain, and when he woke me for my vigil it was so dark in those woods that I could barely see my hand in front of my face. If they are going to come they will come now, I thought, listening to Gawain's snoring and the usual discordant music of the woods at night. The screech or hoot of an owl. The squeak of a bat and the peep of a shrew. The scratch and grunt of a badger shuffling along a woodland path and a hedgehog snuffling on its way. And the occasional snap of a twig which stills blood and breath but is nothing more than some unseen creature on its nightly rounds.

I listened and I watched so far as I could, and the Picts did not come and soon enough it was time to wake Oswine for his watch.

'Already?' he grumbled, blinking bleary eyes at me. I nodded and, leaving him to it, wrapped myself in a cloak which was frayed and holed, and lay down to sleep amongst creeping lady's-tresses and fragrant twinflower.

It seemed I had only just closed my eyes when I was awoken by the cold kiss of a blade at my throat. The whites of the Pict's eyes glowed in the gloom, as did his naked torso, the pale skin luminous against the darker glyphs inked into the skin of his chest, arms and neck. His teeth flashed and he shook his head, lifting my chin with the blade, so I took my hand from Boar's Tusk's hilt as another warrior stooped to gather up the sword and baldrick from the woodland bed.

Too late to fight. The Picts were amongst us. Like wraiths in the darkness, they moved with barely a sound, examining buckles and strap ends and helmets with curious excitement, as if those things were in themselves rare treasures. Gawain was growling and struggling beneath three men who pinned him down with the weight of their own bodies, but like me the others were subdued in their cloaks and forest beds, holding themselves still beneath the deadly edge of knife and spear blade.

'Who was on watch?' Lord Arthur gnarred.

'Merlin, lord,' Bors said, as two men pulled his hands together to bind them.

'So he's dead?' Arthur asked, but none of us could answer that question. Gawain gave the struggle up as hopeless and let them take his blades and tie him. Then, with the Picts having spoken less than a dozen words either to us or to each other, we found ourselves being led east through the pinewoods, trussed and shamefaced like slaves on the way to the block.

I wondered if Merlin had fled or else if the Picts had killed him and left his body lying there to be claimed by the creeping lady's-tresses.

Once out of the trees, we came to where our captors had left their sturdy ponies cropping the grass and now I could see the Picts better by the pale light of the dawn breaking in the east. They were wild-looking men, scarred and painted and sinewy, and it was easy to see why such men as these had struck fear into the Roman legionaries who patrolled both the walls we had crossed on our journey north. Easy to see why they still struck fear into the farmers of Alt Clut and the folk of Goutodin.

Wild-looking though they were, Lord Arthur tried to speak to them. He even introduced himself and all of us by name, but the Picts showed neither understanding nor interest, though I thought I saw a flash of recognition in some of them at Arthur's mention of Uther Pendragon. Yet even the High King's name didn't spare Lord Arthur when one of the Picts, having met his words with a gaping yawn, came to the end of his patience and struck him across the temple with the butt of his spear, knocking Arthur to the ground.

We all winced, for it was a savage blow. But even with his hands bound and his skull still ringing like a bell Lord Arthur climbed to his feet and nodded to me that he was not hurt.

Ignoring us, the Picts argued amongst themselves in a language we could almost understand if we unravelled it, now and then pointing off this way or that, and I dared to hope that they were quarrelling about whether or not to keep looking for Merlin, for they had known we numbered six and were now five. I said as much to Gawain.

'Even if he somehow wriggled off the hook, he can do nothing for us now,' he said, then spat a wad of blood-laced saliva and dragged bound hands across his split lip. 'Damned druid would have been more use had he kept a proper watch,' he said, glaring at Oswine. 'What say you, Saxon? Is your master halfway back to Dumnonia by now? Or should we expect him to ride to our rescue on the back of an eagle and take off some heads with his staff?'

Oswine's fair brows knitted together as he considered the question. 'An eagle perhaps,' he said, 'but more likely a seagull or even a wren, for he says eagles are too proud to be easily governed.' He half smiled. 'We will have to wait and see,' he said, to which Gawain replied by spitting more blood into the heather.

The Picts mounted and on we went, northwards now, our own horses led by the youngest amongst them, who were less decorated in the blue symbols than their elders but no less savage-looking. And those young men made a fuss of Gawain's war horse, which was twice the size of even the largest of their animals.

Lord Arthur tried again, telling the painted men that he was Uther Pendragon's son and that Uther was the High King of Britain, for he saw no point in admitting that the great king was dead and burnt. He told them that we searched for the sword of Maximus, which bore the names Caliburn and Excalibur and others besides, and he asked the Picts if they knew where the sword might be found.

'Might as well be talking to the horses, Arthur,' Gawain said, and after a while even Arthur gave up and resigned himself to trudging along the deer paths whither the painted men would take us, as a watery sun hauled itself into the sky and a thin wind shivered the gorse.

The hill-fort impressed even Arthur, who had fought the Franks in northern Gaul and ridden east as far as Swabia where the Alemanni tribes throng in the shadow of the mighty Frankish warlord Childeric. It was called Dùn Uaine, the green fort, and it was a bastion of turf mounds and wooden ramparts which had been burnt onto slag piles, raising walls which might have been forged of iron, so strong were they. There were deep ditches half full of black water that would suck a man down to a cold dark death, and rows of sharpened stakes pointing at the sky, some crowned with smirking skulls whose wisps of dark hair floated in the breeze.

We had passed larger forts on our way north but few had looked so defensible, and yet we had little opportunity to admire the place, being hauled along the tracks between the dwellings like cattle to the slaughter. Being spat on and grabbed at and molested by women, wild-haired children, old men whose ancient skin patterns were faded and shrunken and misshapen now, and knotty woadless youths who proved their courage by landing blows on us with fists or sticks, despite there being nothing we could do to prevent it.

'Warriors of the sword, hey?' Gawain growled at Arthur, as a beardless youth ran alongside us, pulled his member from his trews, drew back the skin and shot an arcing stream of urine at him. 'I'd keep that worm to myself if I were you, boy,' Gawain told the youth, nearly managing to avoid the spray.

Most of the townsfolk, however, were marvelling at Lord Arthur's armour, which our captors had laid over Gawain's mare so that the effect together of the gleaming bronze scales against her chestnut coat was striking even to me, let alone these Picts, many of whom were more naked than clothed and lacked any iron belongings so far as I could see other than spear blades or axe heads.

'I'm beginning to think we should have stayed in Gallia,' Gawain went on, knuckling blood from his eyebrow. Some of the folk were throwing stones at us now and Gawain was receiving the most attention of all of us because he was the biggest and most intimidating-looking, and so hurting him gave the Picts the most satisfaction.

'I'll not end up skewered on the end of a stake,' Bors said, keeping his back straight and his chin high as a pretty little dark-haired girl spat in his face. Then a skinny boy, no more than fourteen summers old, darted in and sprang like a hare to throw a fist against Bors's cheek.

'When you have decided how we'll get ourselves out of this, cousin, be sure to let me know,' I said, looking up beyond the eastern ramparts to a shoulder of high ground which overlooked the fort. For something had caught my eye. A blur of reddish brown moving against the dark green gorse. A young hind, I realized, running upwind, as such a creature will, even over ridges and unknown ground, knowing it will taste danger as a taint in the air. Nevertheless, this deer played a dangerous game, running along that escarpment against the skyline and so close to the fort that someone with a bow might loose a shaft or two in hope, should they see her. As we were driven at spear-point through the place, painted people chattering around us like birds at dawn song, I watched that hind and I whispered a prayer to Cernunnos, that the horned god might hide her from others' eyes. Off with you, little deer, I said to her in my mind. Do not let them catch you as they have caught me. But instead of bounding off over that ridge, the hind stopped by a clump of purple heather and stood stiff, ears cupped forward, head high, staring down at us. Watching us.

Our hands still bound, we were thrown into a sheep pen in the middle of the fort and found that we were not the Picts' only prisoners. Three men cowered in the near corner. They were filthy, beaten and starved, and yet the sight of us seemed to go some way to restoring them, so that before long we knew their names and how they had come, like us, to be guests in the fort, as Arthur put it with a wry smile.

'We are from Goutodin,' the most talkative of them told him. Even had Arthur not been the first of us to enquire how they fared, he had that quality which marked him as a leader of men, and so it was to Arthur that they told their tale.

'Our lord took a raiding party north to pay these bastards back for all their raiding over the years. Thought he would bring back thirty head of cattle and twice that number of painted heads and that the bards would sing of him come winter,' this Dumnagua said, flashing a cold smile. 'We came across a raiding band,' he said, then glanced at his companions as they shared the memory, 'but the blue bastards wouldn't fight us.' He shook his head. 'We thought they were running scared.

We all thought it, so we followed them. Like hounds chasing down a stag, but in the end we didn't know where in Balor's balls we were, and dusk was falling. Lost fools we were, arguing amongst ourselves. That's when they came.'

'It was as if the heather itself came alive and wanted us dead,' a sallow-skinned man named Caradog said, his eyes not seeing us but rather the memory of that day.

'We fought hard, not realizing they were herding us like bloody sheep,' Dumnagua said. 'Led us into a stinking bog. Men drowned. Others pleaded for their lives and were slaughtered like beasts.' He looked at the third man, who had not said a word, then looked back to Arthur and let out a long breath. 'We're all that's left,' he said.

'Your lord?' Arthur asked.

Dumnagua spat. 'Ran into that bog rather than face the savages,' he said. 'Still there, he is. Best place for him, the spineless shit.'

Hearing all this, Lord Arthur did not tell the Goutodin men who he was for fear of raising their hopes that he might somehow get them out of it. Instead he said we were emissaries from Rheged on a druid's business but had ridden further north than was wise, and the Goutodin men, immersed in their own misfortune, did not question him. Besides which, having been stripped of our war gear and left with only the clothes on our backs, we did not look much. Certainly we would not pass for princes, let alone Arthur's warriors of the sword seeking to remake Britain.

And so we spent a cold night amongst old droppings and wisps of rancid wool, surrounded by young spearmen who for the most part ignored us. At dawn we were all hauled up and marched out of a small gate in the western palisade onto the cold-shadowed moor, the sun yet to rise above the looming hills. Above us a pair of buzzards claimed their territory, soaring in circles, their wings stiffly outstretched and their mewing cries carrying as far as spears cast by a god. I wondered at that omen but could not think it was anything good.

Many of the Picts came in our wake, some on foot, some riding stout ponies, but most of them daubed in fresh woad, so that by the time we had climbed the tallest of three hills and I looked behind me, it was easy to imagine that we were being stalked by some great serpent which slithered relentlessly through the uplands.

By mid-morning we came to the Picts' sacred place. From three good arrow-shots away I heard the voice of the falls, like the hiss of a violent rainstorm on the sea around Karrek. But when we came through the pines, birch, rowan and willow, and crossed the slippery rocks and steep banks, and I caught my first glimpse of the gorge, my chest tightened at the sight. Despite there having been little rain these last days, the brown, peaty water spewed over the smooth lip at the summit, hurling itself in relentless, never-ending fury down the rock face. It plunged into the pool some sixty feet below, frothing and turbulent, the roar of it filling my head. But the rest of the pool was calm and flat and dark. In perfect serenity it received its eternal tribute and we all sensed its magic even as we felt the soft spray of water on our skin.

The Picts led us down a treacherous path and we were made to wait by the mouth of a cave at the pool's edge for a long while as the folk from the fort who had followed us took up positions amongst the trees either side of the gorge and upon rocky ledges, and thronged around the little lake itself. At first I thought our captors were waiting for everyone to arrive, but even when it seemed no more were coming we waited still, so that Gawain was snorting like an angry bull by the time the sun was in the west and dusk was not far away.

'What are you waiting for?' he roared at the Pict who had shown himself to be these people's chieftain. He was a fearsome, battle-scarred warrior who wore long moustaches and hair in two long ponytails which fell down his back. 'Fight us like men!' Gawain challenged him. 'Or do you wait for us to die of boredom?'

The Pict, whose back bore the symbol of a leaping dolphin, regarded Gawain with keen eyes, the green vein throbbing in his neck. It seemed to me that he really wanted to accept Gawain's challenge and fight him, but another painted warrior cautioned him against it and they both glanced up at the cave. Then the chieftain turned back to Gawain and growled something which we could not understand, though we got the sense of it.

'I'll fight your champion, if you've got one,' Gawain challenged him. 'Your champion and you together. I'll rip that painted skin off your back and make you eat it, you reeking son of a rancid sow.'

The Pict snapped his fingers and thumb together to show he thought that Gawain talked too much. Grinning, Dumnagua said that he and his Goutodin countrymen could have used Gawain in their fight in the bog, but Gawain told the man that he and his companions, and we too, were fools for letting ourselves be taken alive.

'We are not dead yet,' Arthur said, then looked at me. 'Lancelot, in your heart do you think this will be the last day that you look upon an early autumn sky?' he asked. Then he lifted his bound hands and pointed at a pale yellow butterfly which careered through the air like a wind-driven petal. 'Do you think you will never see such a beautiful creature again in this life? After this day?' The butterfly alighted amongst the trembling leaves of a young aspen at the water's edge and there spread its wings to bask in the last warmth of the day.

'No, lord,' I said.

'So my uncle has bewitched you, too, Lancelot,' Gawain said with a resigned weariness. 'This is how he does it.'

There rose a murmur around the edge of the small lake and the Picts climbed to their feet and next thing we were being yelled at to stand and face the cave.

'Balor be with us,' Bors muttered, staring like the rest of us at the creature for whom we had evidently all been waiting. She appeared in the cave's dark mouth amongst a billow of white smoke, and for a while did not seem to move at all but just stood and stared down at the water. She was naked and lithe and her black hair fell down to the gentle swell of her buttocks, and like the warriors' her skin was adorned with indelible ink. The swirling symbols coiled up her legs and snaked in between her thighs to the dark bush of hair at her crotch. A wolf's face covered her taut belly. A salmon stretched up her left side and eagle's wings spread across her slender shoulders, and even her breasts were decorated with whorls and circles and symbols which none of us could read.

'They're going to slaughter us,' were the first words we'd heard the third Goutodin man speak.

'Of course they're going to slaughter us,' Gawain said.

The priestess made her way down the small hill, from cave's mouth to water's edge, then walked barefoot across the rocks towards the Picts' leader, who bowed his head, as did every other who had come to the falls.

She was young, this priestess, and pretty, and not at all what any of us would have expected to emerge from a cave into the gloaming.

'I am Arthur ap Uther, whom men call Pendragon,' Lord Arthur called above the roar of the cascading water. The priestess's head snapped up amidst hissing from the Picts at Arthur's impiety. 'King Uther, my father and High King of Britain, is dead,' Arthur announced, 'but with his last breath he named me his heir and King of Dumnonia.' The Pict chieftain strode across the wet rock and back-handed Arthur across the mouth to shut him up. It did not work. Arthur straightened. 'I seek the sword of Maximus,' he called. 'The sword called Excalibur.' The Pict struck him again, harder, but Arthur stood tall and noble. 'I am Arthur ap Uther,' he said, spitting blood.

I was proud of him. Gawain growled that he was wasting his breath. Oswine, if anything, seemed resigned to whatever fate his gods had spun for him. Or else he was just bored. It was hard to tell.

'Arthur,' the priestess said, coming to stand before him. Looking up into his eyes. 'Arthur ap Uther,' she said, her voice like a wind-stirred briar scratching a roof. She put a hand between her legs and held it there a moment, then lifted it and pressed her fingers against Arthur's bleeding lips. He recoiled and she laughed, and still I did not think that we were going to die.

And then the killing started.

At a gesture from their priestess, two big painted warriors took hold of Dumnagua by his arms and dragged him into the dark pool, and the priestess followed them, giving her pale, blue-stained body to the water. I saw a shiver run through her flesh. I could not help but look as the buds on her breasts hardened and stood proud.

'I will see you again in the next world, Arthur ap Uther,' Dumnagua called. 'And we shall drink together.'

Arthur nodded. 'We shall, Dumnagua of Goutodin,' he said, his blue-grey eyes hard as granite now because his fury was rising. For the hundredth time I struggled against my own bonds, thinking that if I could only get my hands free I could go for the chieftain or even the priestess. Anything would be better than submitting to whatever murderous ritual these Picts had in store.

Dumnagua did not fight. Perhaps he was too proud to struggle in vain, and the Picts easily thrust his head down into the water, though they stood braced and ready to use their strength. The priestess placed her hand on the back of Dumnagua's head, which was just visible where it broke the surface, and then there came a splutter of bubbles as Dumnagua let go the breath he had been holding. I realized I had been holding my own breath too, from the moment he went under, and I inhaled sharply, straining against the rope as the priestess chanted and Dumnagua struggled because his body craved air and cared nothing for his pride.

His countrymen looked on with pale dread. Caradog, I saw, was weeping. But it was soon done. Dumnagua went still and the watching Picts murmured a prayer to some god, which might have been Arawn or else some god of their own. Then the warriors dragged Dumnagua's body from the lake and laid it on the rocks, his neck on a pine log, so that their chief could hack off Dumnagua's head with his axe. When this was done, their leader snarled his hand amongst Dumnagua's hair and lifted the dripping head high, like a trophy for all his people to see, at which they cheered from the trees and the rocks, the sound of it lost against the rush of the falls.

Caradog was next and he did not make it easy for them but bucked and bent, twisted and writhed, for all the good it did him. One of the Picts drove a fist into his empty stomach, doubling him over, then they thrust him under, at which the priestess put her own hands into the water to press down upon Caradog's head. He drowned quickly, having little breath left by the time he went in, and his head came off easily to the chieftain's axe.

As they pulled the last of the Goutodin men into the water, his eyes wide and bulging with terror, I looked at Bors. My cousin shook his head, refusing to accept that the same fate awaited us. I saw that his wrists were raw where he had tested his great strength against the ropes. I tried to picture my brother Hector in my mind and I wondered if he were waiting for me in the hereafter. If he would show me the woods and the islands and the secret places under warm blue skies, and the feasting hall where the bounty of the table never diminished. And where the wine flowed like the falls here before me in this life, its mist swirling around a frightened man and a naked young enchantress.

'Whoever your god is, I will spit in his eye,' Gawain snarled at the priestess. 'But before I die I will foul this precious lake of yours. I will defile it in the name of Taranis, god of war. Before your god has me, he or she will have my filth as an offering.'

The last Goutodin warrior went to his death like a man who does not comprehend what is happening to him or why. They drowned him and the priestess chanted and the Picts cheered when, after three strikes, his head came off and the bloody axe glanced off the log and tinked off the rock, throwing sparks which raised a gasp from the congregation, for it was a powerful omen.

'I am Arthur ap Uther,' Lord Arthur called, seizing upon the moment and fixing the priestess with a savage glare, as if he had thrown those sparks himself. 'You will untie us or else my gods, the gods of Britain, will avenge me. My men will ride north on their war horses and they will slaughter you, man, woman and child. They will burn your homes and trample your crops. They will butcher your cattle. The name of your tribe will be lost for ever like smoke carried on the wind.'

Now, for the first time, the Pict chieftain looked unsure. He had not liked his axe sparking with that last strike and he looked from Lord Arthur to the priestess, who was still up to her belly in the water.

'Arthur,' she said, her tongue questing over her lips as though she was tasting his name. Then she turned and looked at me and I shivered under her gaze.

'And he is Lancelot ap Ban,' Arthur told her. 'A favourite of the druid Merlin.'

That was stretching the truth, I thought, for Merlin had never given me the impression that he even liked me, but the priestess, staring at me, tilted her head on one side, her breasts still pert from the cold, their nipples dark and stiff.

'Lancelot,' she said.

'We seek the sword,' Arthur said. 'For when we have it we will unite the Britons and sweep the Saxons from the land.'

'Lancelot,' the priestess said again.

'Give her a smile, lad,' Gawain beside me said under his breath. 'What use is that pretty face of yours if you can't persuade some mad Pict witch not to drown us and hack our damned heads off?'

I did not smile but the priestess did. Then the Picts came for me.

'No!' Arthur yelled. 'Not him. Just me. I will go to your god. I'll go on my knees if you spare him.'

The priestess raised a hand and the Picts let go of me.

'Take me,' Gawain said. 'I'm ready to piss in your sacred pool and spit in your god's eye.'

'Arthur,' the priestess said. Arthur nodded, satisfied, and the two

Picts took hold of him and together they walked into the lake to the waiting woman. She was already chanting in a low voice. The fearsome chieftain was grinning, the earlier incident with the axe forgotten now that his priestess had resolved to continue the rites. And perhaps he was spinning the picture in his mind of himself dressed in Lord Arthur's magnificent bronze scale armour, my helmet with its long white plume and silver-chased cheek guards, and riding Gawain's massive war horse.

'This is not the last day, Arthur,' I said. I don't know why I said it. Arthur was up to his thighs in the dark water, the broad-shouldered Picts were steeling themselves for the task of thrusting him under, and their leader was making practice cuts through the air with that blood-smeared axe of his. And yet Arthur looked back at me and smiled.

'This is not the last day,' he said. Then they pushed him deeper still and the water closed around him, becalming so that he was reflected in its dark mirror. It was as if there were two Arthurs, one of them already in the world beyond, looking back from the cold, still depths of the sacred lake.

A murmur rose from the Picts on the rocks above. Then those folk in the tree line were buzzing like flies on a carcass and I looked up and saw why.

The figure stood at the summit of the falls, right out on the treacherous ledge where he risked being swept over into the raging torrent, which would surely pummel him to bloody splinters against the rock. Yet he stood as still as the rock itself, immovable and defiant against the eternal, ceaseless gushing. Forbidding and portentous, a staff in one hand and swathed in robes as black and purple and green as a raven's wing.

'Took his merry time,' Gawain said, the half-twist of a smile on his lips.

Not the last day, I said in my mind, looking up. Knowing that my lungs would not flood with water, nor would my head be mounted on a sharpened stake come sunset.

Not the last day.

Merlin lifted his staff and I could see that he was hurling proclamations down at us, though his words were drowned by the falls' gushing din. Still, seeing the druid up there, the priestess turned her back on Lord Arthur and swept out of the water, shivering like any normal person would amongst clouds of midges in the dusk. She hurried back up the path to her cave and the Picts looked at one another, none of them seeming to know what was happening. When she re-emerged, she wore a herringbone twill kirtle of undyed wool beneath a yellow-brown bear skin, whose head and snout and sightless eyes sat upon her dark head and whose forepaws were crossed and pinned together over her chest. It had been a big beast in life and I wondered if the cave had once been its lair, and if those claws which now gleamed white against the priestess's dress had once pawed salmon out of the water where men were sacrificed to the gods.

She carried a slender staff topped with a polecat's skull, the wicked-looking teeth as long as a finger, and used the staff to make a slow and dignified descent down the hill to the mist-slick rock. There, she stood. Looking up at Merlin. Waiting.

Neither did the druid rush, but kept us all waiting as he disappeared back into the birch and rowan and made his way from ledge to ledge and across mossy boulders, the Picts backing into briars and brambles, muttering charms and looking away rather than risking to meet the eyes of this fierce-eyed, feathered man. They knew a druid had come amongst them and they feared him. Perhaps they thought their priestess had summoned him in her rites. Or maybe they believed their gods had sent him to them in answer to the three sacrifices whose heads sat side by side in a deepening pool of blood around which flies cavorted.

When Merlin came to the edge of the pool he did not look at any of us but kept his eyes on the priestess, his expression as grim as the grey rock around us, the green and purple-sheened feathers of his raven cloak stirring in the breeze coming off the falls.

He greeted the priestess, nodding in a gesture of respect, but then proceeded to admonish her as a father might scold his wayward child. He told her that the gods had gratefully received the three drowned sacrifices but warned her that she would have brought their wrath down upon her people had she continued with the rites and drowned the four men who stood on the rock – he gestured at us then – and the rightful king of Dumnonia, who even now stood up to his waist in the dark water.

The priestess seemed unsure, but Merlin asked her why she had ignored the sparks which had flown from the axe, for that was Taranis showing his anger at their treatment of Lord Arthur. For Arthur was Britain's great warrior, he said, beloved of Taranis. Arthur was Britain's shield and her sword. Arthur was Britain's hope. And had the priestess been fool enough to drown Arthur in this lake, then she would be the ruin of Britain.

She seemed to accept all this, if grudgingly; she was a death-craving thing. Then she told the two warriors who held Arthur to bring him out of the lake.

'What about the others?' she asked in her raspy, little-used voice, turning from a dripping Arthur to point that polecat skull at us. Merlin and Britain could have Arthur, if he was beloved of the gods, but she would have the rest of us. The lake, she said, was still hungry. And perhaps it was, but it seemed to me that it was she who lusted for more drowned men.

Merlin pointed his ash staff at the water and shook his head. 'Whatever promises you have made to Arawn and the spirits of this pool, I absolve you of them,' he said. 'But these men,' he swept the staff towards us, 'these men are mine and I free their souls now.' With that he lifted a fist to his mouth and coughed into it. Then he raised that fist into the air and opened his hand and to my astonishment a tiny bird, a wren perhaps, whirred off into the sky. The painted people gasped and whispered. The hairs on the back of my neck stood up. Even the severed heads of the Goutodin men seemed to stare at the druid in wonder.

Merlin seemed to shiver inside the raven-feather cloak and then he coughed into his fist again and another little bird appeared in his palm for a heartbeat before flitting into the dusk. The priestess watched it fly, muttering some spell under her breath, then turned back to Merlin in time to see the druid cough a third little wren into his fist and free it on the breeze. The fourth bird came reluctantly amidst much coughing and hawking, but at last appeared in Merlin's open hand and I saw that it was a robin. For a moment it crouched, shivering and timid in the druid's hand, so that I feared it was not well enough to fly, but Merlin whispered to it and then all but cast it into the air and it took wing and streaked off amongst the birch and willow nearby.

'Four souls, I have claimed,' the druid announced. 'But that is not all. I have come for Excalibur too.' The Picts might have ignored Lord Arthur when he spoke of the sword but they did not dare ignore a druid, particularly a druid dressed in a feathered cloak who could breathe birds into the air. Children clung to their mothers in fear. Warriors fingered their blades and some of them edged a little closer, their inquisitiveness overcoming their unease. 'For I know that you, the Kindred of Cináed mac Gabrán, are the guardians of Maximus's sword.'

'How could he know?' Bors said under his breath.

'The wily dog,' Gawain said, shaking his head.

Arthur was smiling, if only with his eyes.

'You,' Merlin said, pointing his staff at the chieftain, who stood protectively by the severed heads as if he feared Merlin might steal them away too. 'You are Uradech mac Maelgwn mac Gartnait,' he said. 'And your battle-fame is known far south of the stone wall.' He turned and named another of the painted warriors by his father's father, and then another. Then he told one of the wide-shouldered men whose job had been to drown men in the lake that his ancestor was Drest the Burner, who had been king of these people when the Romans came to Britain.

'He can read the markings, Lancelot,' Arthur said, trying hard not to grin. I looked at Bors, who nodded, both of us understanding now. Merlin only had to get a look at the snake or the horse head, the bull or the eagle or the fish inked into a warrior's arm or back or chest, to know his lineage. To the rest of us the markings were nothing more than representations of creatures and meaningless swirls, eddying patterns and curious symbols. But to Merlin they were stories. They were bloodlines etched in blue woad and he could read them.

'Bastard planned this whole thing,' Gawain muttered. 'He could've saved those poor sods but he wanted to swoop in like the Morrigán and get everyone's hair standing on end.' He spat onto the rock. 'I'd wager he'd have waited for another head or two to swell that pile if the witch hadn't pulled Arthur into the water when she did.'

That we would never know, and probably just as well, I thought, though Arthur was still trying to keep the smile off his face, and he having been heartbeats away from being plunged head first under the water and held there until dead.

'My Lord Arthur needs the sword,' Merlin told the priestess. 'For with it he will reforge Britain as she was before the Romans sullied her. He will drive the Saxons back into the sea and those gods who have abandoned us will flood back.' He glanced at the lake, then nodded at the priestess, who was so slight and pretty beneath that bear skin that it looked as though the great beast had lumbered up and caught her and intended to never let her go. 'Some gods, of course, have never left us, but others were driven away,' Merlin said. 'We will need all the gods of Britain, all those whom our grandfathers' grandfathers honoured and kept in their hearts, if we are to reclaim the land from the ravenous invader and drive out the Christians' god, who infects men as the black flies infect your cattle and swine.'

'What do we care for your wars?' Uradech challenged Merlin, swinging his axe in Lord Arthur's direction. Perhaps Merlin's talk of Uradech's reputation had emboldened the man, but now Merlin marched up to him as if he might strike the chieftain across the face with his gnarled ash staff.

'You fool, Uradech! Any dog can have courage enough to fight, and have its face ripped off. Your victories in battle come from the gods. There is no druid in all Britain who is closer to the gods than I. They whisper to me.' He fluttered a hand up into the air in imitation of the little birds which he had released. 'I fly up to the gods to hear their messages. They have told me that Britain needs Lord Arthur and Lord Arthur needs Excalibur. These matters are as far beyond you as the tides are to the pig or the stars are to the earthworm.'

The chieftain glowered at this but Merlin stared him down. 'If you interrupt me again I will blow a swarm of maggots into your skull and they will feed on your brain and send you mad.' He pointed down at Uradech's crotch. 'I will put wasps in your member and their stinging will make you scream like a little girl waking from a dream of monsters. I will blow a rat into your bowels, where it will scratch and tear and eat you from the inside out.' He gave a savage grin. 'All this I will do, Uradech mac Maelgwn mac Gartnait, if you bother me again.'

The muscle and sinew of Uradech's naked torso and arms seemed to throb as he imagined Merlin's threats made reality, then he stepped back and put the axe across his shoulders and hung his blue-inked arms over the haft. He looked at his fellow warriors and shrugged, and some of them touched the blue whorls on their arms to ward off the evil of the druid's words.

'Where is the sword?' Merlin asked the priestess, pulling the pointed tuft of his goat's beard through a fist.

She turned her head towards the cave, the bear's face upon it looking sightlessly back towards its old den. 'We have kept it safe since Maximus's time,' she said with a nod, and with that she walked barefoot once more up into the cave.

'Untie my friends, Uradech,' Merlin said. 'And tell your people that we will be joining your feast when we return to Dùn Uaine. And the next day you will provision us to ride south. Your men will escort us to the wall of Antoninus to ensure that we are not attacked by some other tribe of painted head-loppers.' The Pict nodded, no doubt still imagining those maggots in his skull and that rat in his bowels. And when the Picts had cut through our bonds and the priestess came back down to the water's edge, she brought with her Excalibur. There was no jewelled scabbard. No gold- or silver-studded baldrick. The sword was bound and tied in a fleece whose grease would keep the worst of the iron blight from further eating that already ancient blade. The priestess untied the thongs, cast the fleece aside and brought the sword up as though presenting it to the cascading water. Dusk had thrown the lake into cool shadow now, but as I looked up I saw that the heights of the falls still glittered in the last light of the day.

'Excalibur,' Merlin said, his eyes the brightest things down there by the dark water. Brighter than the blade itself, though to my surprise that blade was not pitted and thin with age. I saw that the cutting edge bore several nicks and I imagined the long-ago battles in which Maximus had wielded that sword and scarred her on his enemies' blades, shields and helmets.

'She's beautiful,' Lord Arthur said, studying the sword in the priestess's hands. Hungry to hold it in his own.

It was a long, straight sword, longer than Boar's Tusk. As long as Benesek's Saxon sword which Melwas and I had lost in Karrek's bay years before. The shaped hand grip was gleaming ivory, whilst the guard and spherical pommel were of dark wood.

'Come with me, Arthur ap Uther,' the woman said. She shrugged off the bear skin but left the kirtle on this time. Arthur glanced at

Merlin, who nodded, then the rightful king of Dumnonia waded once more into the small lake, only this time it was not to be drowned. It was not to be given to the god whose realm was somewhere beneath the surface over which the gnats danced, but rather to be given a treasure of Britain.

Those two stopped where they had previously stood, the water making the priestess's kirtle stick to her stomach and breasts. Arthur's muscled and scarred torso gleamed white against the black water.

The Picts who had come to witness the sacrificial rites were silent now, so that the only sound was the incessant out-breath of the falls. Even Merlin was captivated. Beguiled by the young priestess and the lord of war and the sword.

'You will take this memory to your grave, Lancelot,' he said, his eyes never leaving the spectacle, reading the shapes of the woman's lips to know the words she spoke unheard above the clamour of tumbling, rushing water. And I knew the druid was right; that I would see this moment again, a clear and vivid picture in my mind of the day Arthur, my lord and friend, inherited Excalibur and took upon himself the task of remaking Britain.

Holding Excalibur by the grip and the end of the blade, the priestess lowered it into the water and for a short while it was lost from sight as she spoke her sacred words. Arthur stood still, his face solemn, eyes peering into the lake, as expectant and yet patient as an egret in the reed bed waiting to spear a fish or frog with its long beak.

Then the priestess lifted the sword out of the water and held it up high, pointing it to the light at the summit of the falls, her thin arm trembling with cold or the sword's weight. Without another word she gave the sword to Arthur, who took it by the hilt and wrapped his hand round that ivory grip, getting a sense of its balance and perhaps imagining the great general Flavius Magnus Maximus, commander of the legions of Britain, leading his warriors against the first Saxons who drew their boats up onto our shores.

'Excalibur,' Arthur said, claiming the sword, and I thought that even if the priestess asked for the sword back now, if she needed it for some last part of the rites, Arthur would not give it to her. That he would possess that sword utterly, and that perhaps the sword would possess him, too.

Then the priestess took Arthur's free hand in hers and led him out of the lake, the two of them shivering in the shadow and the falls' chill breath.

'What now?' Gawain asked Merlin.

But the druid did not answer and we watched as the priestess took Arthur up the path and into the cave.

By the time Arthur emerged it was night.

18

Camelot

IT WAS AS THOUGH all of Britain thrummed as that summer ceded
to autumn and Arthur rode through the land. Each of the kingdoms was like a colony of bees swarming because it cannot build comb
quickly enough to store all the nectar being brought back to the hive.
Men who were ploughing the fallow fields prior to the sowing of winter crops left their oxen standing idle to witness the spectacle of Lord
Arthur riding his great war horse, Llamrei, in his red-plumed helmet
and glorious scale armour, Excalibur raised for all to see. Swineherds
driving their charges into the woods to forage for beechnuts and acorns
hurried quickly back to catch a glimpse of the procession. Women and
children gathering wheat stubble to mix with hay for winter fodder
stopped their back-breaking work and swarmed around us, calling
Arthur's name that he might look at them. They hoped to share some
morsel of the gods' favour which glowed around Arthur like the halo
around the moon.

We rode through Rheged and were feasted by King Meirchion
Gul, he who had given us horses and allowed us to pass through his
shieldwall to escape from Tintagel.

'When I heard you'd ridden north of the wall, I thought you must
want to die,' the fat king admitted, examining a fleshy bone to decide
how best to attack it. 'Everyone said the painted folk would gut you
for the cloak on your back. That your headless corpse would be left to
feed the crows and that your pretty head would be stuck on some palisade somewhere.' He grinned, partly at that thought, partly because
he was happy to see Arthur alive and well, then set about tearing at
the meat with his teeth. He had helped Arthur when Arthur needed
it, and Meirchion knew that dead men are poor at returning favours.

'I daresay my cousin was hoping for it,' Arthur said, sipping his wine.

Bedwyr and just over half of Arthur's warriors had survived that bloody day on Tintagel's heights. And to our joy Bors and I heard that Benesek lived, too.

'He fought like a champion,' Bedwyr told us and we grinned at each other like halfwits.

'He'll be wanting his helmet back,' I said, nodding at the silver-chased helmet which sat on the floor by my shield and a great hunting dog, which had sniffed at the white horsehair plume before deciding to lie down beside it.

'He won't begrudge you the use of it,' Bors said through a mouthful of cheese. 'And I doubt he'll need it back on Karrek. That wound he took on the hip will see his fighting days behind him.'

'Benesek will fight his way from this world into the hereafter,' I said and we grinned again because we knew it was true.

Having checked the advance of Lord Constantine's shieldwall, Arthur's men had spilled enough blood to blunt the enemy's enthusiasm for the fight, and both sides had given ground, drawing back from one another 'like stags exhausted from the rut', Bedwyr said. At this point, King Einion of Ebrauc, the man who had challenged Arthur as Uther lay dying, marched his lightning shields onto the blood-slick ground, roaring at both sides to stop this madness for the sake of Britain. 'The Saxons grow stronger for every dead Briton,' he called, and even Lord Constantine had known that the king of northern Britain was right about that, and this respite gave Bedwyr the chance to lead Arthur's men through King Meirchion's lines and off Tintagel.

Since his men's horses had been slaughtered, Bedwyr followed Arthur's last command and marched to northern Dumnonia. There he found another of Arthur's commanders, Cai ap Cynyr, along with Arthur's thirty remaining horse warriors and a number of spare mounts awaiting word of their lord's accession to the high seat of Dumnonia. These men on their big, armoured horses would have ridden to Tintagel after Arthur's acclamation; a show of power to reassure the lords of Britain that they had done the right thing by acclaiming Arthur, and a warning to any who did not want him on the throne.

It had not exactly gone to plan. And yet, thanks to Bedwyr, Arthur still commanded a formidable war band, mostly comprising his heavy armoured horsemen, or cataphracts as we called them, and these men were overjoyed to be reunited with their lord. Seventy-five battle-hardened men glittering in the autumn sun, their round shields freshly painted with Arthur's bear, spear blades polished to a shine and the red ribbons tied below those spear blades streaming in the breeze like tendrils of blood in water.

'Your lord knows how to make a spectacle,' King Meirchion told me, wiping greasy fingers on his beard, then draining his cup. 'When you rode through our gates today some of my people said that the legions had returned. That Magnus Maximus himself breathed again and had come to lead us against the Saxons.' He grinned. 'But I am glad that you all returned safely from the wild lands,' he added, glancing at Gawain and Bors. He went still then, leaving a morsel of food dangling from his fat bottom lip, his face florid and glistening. 'They say that some spirit . . . or goddess, appeared in a lake and handed you the sword.' His eyes darted from Arthur to Merlin and back to Arthur.

Arthur had reluctantly allowed the king to hold Excalibur, never taking his eyes off Meirchion, but it had been worth it to see the King of Rheged so in awe, of both the sword and its new owner. For like most men, Meirchion had believed Excalibur's existence to be little more than the stuff of fireside tales. Seeing it for himself, holding it in his own hands, even the fat king had witnessed in the reflection of the polished blade an image of himself as a warlord of Britain, a champion who might safeguard her shores and reclaim land lost to the Saxons. If he saw himself cast thus in Excalibur's ancient blade, in Arthur he now saw the next Uther, a man to whom the other kings of the land might bend the knee.

'It was the gods that gave the sword to Lord Arthur,' Merlin told Meirchion, more or less confirming the rumours which had reached the king's ear. They were probably started by Merlin himself, I thought, as I savoured the bounty of the fat king's hospitality. Arthur, I noted, did not gainsay the druid, but let Excalibur and wind-borne rumour work its spell on Meirchion, knowing that such an ally would be invaluable in the days to come.

'And will you seek an acclamation, Lord Arthur?' King Meirchion had asked, peering from beneath fleshy eyelids as he savaged another meaty bone. 'They say you have an army in Gaul. Surely you can make Uther's high seat your own . . . if you desire it.'

Arthur, sitting on a thick pelt on the reed-strewn floor, shook his head. 'Not until there is peace,' he said. 'I will not risk war between the kingdoms of Britain.' He'd placed Excalibur on one of the low tables scattered about, then had laid both hands upon her blade.

'Let all here bear witness,' he called, stilling every tongue in the King of Rheged's hall, 'that I, Arthur ap Uther, will not sit upon Dumnonia's throne until there is peace in Britain. Let me prove myself against Britain's enemies. Let me drive the Saxons back, and then, with the bards singing of our great victories, I will take up my birthright and rule as my father before me.'

But, of course, the kings of Britain would have to let Arthur lead them in war if he was to be the bringer of victory, and that was Arthur's compromise. That was his scheme. He would not be king, not yet, but he *would* be Britain's lord of war. And when he had the victories and the power, when the warriors of Britain were shouting his name amidst the echo of clashing steel and the cries of the defeated foe, then Arthur could have more than Dumnonia. He could become the next Pendragon. Arthur ap Uther, High King of Britain.

Hearing Arthur's vow and seeing flame-glow reflected from Excalibur onto his earnest and sober face, the warriors of Rheged and Arthur's own men, including Gawain, Bors and myself, clapped hands and hammered fists upon the tables, while in his nest of cushions the fat king, a man who had a sailor's knack for knowing which way the wind blew, lifted his cup towards Arthur and smiled.

And we had ridden on, east into Elmet, because Arthur wanted to pay his respects to King Masgwid the Lame, who had not come to Uther's deathbed because he was, in his own words, busy preventing the death of Britain herself. For Elmet was a bulwark of the defence of lower northern Britain, and King Masgwid's lameness, the result of a Saxon spear-thrust many years previously, had not prevented him from campaigning against the invaders every summer that he had the men and provisions to do so. Now, Arthur promised to bring spearmen to Elmet's aid, to share the burden and the cost of war, and the lame king said he would believe it when he saw it. Yet they parted on good terms and with Masgwid no less impressed by Arthur's possession of Excalibur than King Meirchion had been.

We continued south-east into Powys, which was ruled by King Cyngen Glodrydd, the man whom Merlin had threatened to drown in his own dung if Cyngen interrupted him again as he observed King

Uther's ritual naming of his successor. Big-bearded, broad as a bull and just as foul-tempered, Cyngen had not seemed impressed with Excalibur, had even been sceptical of its provenance, booming that no hundred-year-old sword could be so well preserved, let alone a sword far older than that. And no sword, even a treasure of Britain maintained by some god or lake spirit, could emerge looking so fine after spending any time in water.

Still, he *had* been impressed by Arthur. The first time was that day on Tintagel, when Arthur had fought and killed Odgar, champion of Ebrauc. The second time was when he had watched Arthur ride headlong into the dawn fray and fight for his men with no care for his own safety, even as his horse was killed under him. The third time Arthur impressed Cyngen, so the king told us as the servants passed through the smoky roundhouse with bowls of steaming, herb-scented pottage, was by riding north of the Wall of Antoninus and living to tell of it.

'I leave talk of gods and legendary swords to druids, boys and fools,' Cyngen told Arthur. 'But you're a warrior, Arthur ap Uther, and a brave man. I'll fight beside you, whether or not your arse polishes Uther's high seat.'

'And I would be honoured to fight with you at my shoulder, lord king,' Arthur said, his wording careful but the sentiment sincere. 'And what can you tell me about my cousin?'

Cyngen nodded. 'I'll tell you what I know, which isn't much,' he said.

Hearing of Lord Arthur's return and procession through the kingdoms, of how crowds of fervent men and women were pledging loyalty to Arthur and Excalibur, and fearing being trapped on Tintagel and besieged, Lord Constantine had fled east with one hundred spearmen. It turned out that most of King Uther's own spearmen, who had neither supported Arthur, whom they did not know, nor fought against him that summer morning with the smoke from Uther's balefire still tainting the air, had not in the end supported Constantine enough to pledge their spears to his cause.

'They guard Tintagel and your father's silver and tin,' Cyngen said. 'Gwydre has vowed to protect Uther's wealth until the new king is acclaimed.' I cast my mind back to recall the grey-bearded commander of King Uther's bodyguard standing on the dais in the High King's hall, demanding respect for his dying lord. Later, I had watched Gwydre haul the Pendragon's litter up the side of the pyre, followed by Uther's shining war gear. From what I had seen of him, he seemed a steadfast man and honourable, too, for he had refused to support Lord Constantine's usurpation of Dumnonia's throne, and so Constantine had fled.

Merlin cocked an eyebrow at Arthur. 'The birds tell me that your cousin has scuttled off to seek help from King Deroch of Caer Gwinntguic,' he said.

King Cyngen scowled, not enjoying the druid's company under his roof. 'Constantine offered King Deroch help reclaiming Caer Gwinntguic's lost borderlands,' he said.

'And what does the treacherous swine want in return?' Gawain asked, holding out his cup for a pretty Saxon slave to fill. With the cup brimming, the girl made to walk away but King Cyngen reached up and grabbed her arm, pulling her down onto his lap.

'He wants Deroch to support his claim to Dumnonia's throne,' the king said, then pressed his thick beard and face into the nape of the girl's neck and inhaled deeply. 'They smell different to our women, have you noticed?' he asked me.

I shook my head.

'And will King Deroch raise his banner alongside my cousin's?' Arthur asked, deliberately keeping his gaze above King Cyngen's hands, which were busy exploring. The Saxon girl was looking at me but I looked away.

'Doubt it,' Cyngen said, his voice muffled by the girl's flaxen hair. 'Start a war with you for the sake of Lord Constantine's hundred spears?' There was a grimace of teeth in the black bush of his beard. 'He's been fighting the Saxons a long time, but he's still got the wits he was born with.'

If this was true, with Lord Constantine out of the way, Arthur could continue his progression through the kingdoms, from fort to fort, just as his father the Pendragon had done for many years, before age and, towards the end, sickness had confined him to his hall at Tintagel.

You would have thought we rode behind a conquering hero, such was Excalibur's power and Arthur's allure. Thus did the most powerful lords in Britain witness with their own eyes the sword of Maximus, which the gods had returned to the use of man. Thus did they hear with their own ears Arthur's vow to lead campaigns against the Saxons. And thus did the shadow of King Uther's passing begin to shorten. The people of Britain began to dream of a golden future which echoed the island's long distant past, before the legions came. A Britain in which lost lands were reclaimed. In which men lived without fear of boats brimming with warriors coming to her shores by the score each spring and summer. A Britain which was once again beloved of the gods.

And some of us dared to dream that this would be Arthur's Britain.

Before we could remake Britain, we had to remake the old hill-fort at Camelot. Dominating great swathes of rich farmland, the almost circular hill rose steeply towards the plateau, around which the ancient folk had built an inner defensive wall. Into the slopes of the limestone hill they had carved and raised a complex of four banks and four ditches, and yet even these formidable defences had failed to throw back the Romans, who had stormed the fort and put its people to the sword, drenching the hill with blood in their conquest of Britain. For two hundred years the hill-fort had lain in ruin, while Saxons raided across the border from Gwinntguic whenever King Deroch was unable or unwilling to stop them roaming across his own kingdom. But now it was autumn and the Saxons were unlikely to make raids into Dumnonia, and so Arthur had chosen the ancient fort as his base.

'I'll not sleep in Uther's hall until I am king of Dumnonia, Lancelot,' he had told me when he and I had ridden to the hill-fort one autumn afternoon, our long shadows ranging ahead of us towards the outermost gorse-covered ramparts. You could hardly see the contours of the banks and ditches for the long grass and brambles which had conquered the place since it was abandoned. 'Besides, Tintagel is too far away,' he said, studying the great hill. He could see all that it would be, even overgrown as it was. Before the first pick had been struck into the earth to dig out the briar's roots, or the first stake had been shaped and driven into the uppermost bank enclosing the summit. He could see the stone rubble, interlaced with timber supports, upon which the palisade was raised, and the dry-stone walling of the bank's face. He could see the fortified wooden gatehouse in the south-western corner, which was as yet just a tangle of bramble and nettles. He could even see the granary and livestock pens, the smithy, the woodshop, the smokehouse and the great hall right up there upon the summit, and perhaps he could hear the forge hammer and the clump of blades on shields as men trained for war, and the sing-song voice of children playing in summers to come.

'So, what do you think, Lancelot?' he asked me. 'Will this do?'

He had already chosen this hill, this Camelot, to be his base in Britain, and I couldn't think he really needed my approval. Yet, we were all but inseparable by then. We would drink long into the night, he telling me how together we would sweep the Saxons from the land and restore the gods of Britain, I believing him and, though I did not hold such grand ambitions in my own heart, knowing even so that I would follow Arthur into any fight against any foe, no matter who, where or when.

'It's perfect,' I said, gazing up at the heights.

Arthur nodded. 'I can't do this without you, my friend,' he said. He kept his eyes fastened on me, as though waiting for me to acknowledge that I understood this. Understood that our friendship went beyond the bonds of companionship and shared purpose. That he could be Arthur the warlord, perhaps even Arthur the king to others, but that I would know Arthur the man, his hopes and the fears which pulled and plucked at him come the night. And that our fates were ensnarled now, tangled like briar. For good or bad.

'We'll do it together,' I said, feeling the weight of those words as soon as I'd spoken them. Heavier even than the oath I had muttered to his dying father.

He nodded, seeming relieved, then turned back to the hill.

'Merlin told me that the Britons who lived here long ago fought a desperate battle against the legions,' I said. 'They fought and died on this very hill.'

'They did,' he said. He knew that I meant that it was perfect not just for its defensive capabilities, but because it had been the site of a heroic last stand. And so what better place than this for Arthur to make his stand against the invaders of our own time?

'I'd like to see the view from up there,' I said, rubbing my dun stallion's neck. He was a gift from Arthur for saving his life on Tintagel and I had named him Tormaigh, which meant Thunder Spirit. He had earned that name on two accounts, firstly because he was given to bouts of kicking, biting rage and had thrown me the first three times I tried to mount him. And second because of the iron hooves which all of Arthur's horses wore. When they galloped together they made a sound like thunder rolling across the sky. 'Show me, lord,' I said. We had ridden a long way and I wanted to stretch my legs. And I did want to see what the view would be like from our new fort.

'I'll race you,' Arthur said, his eyes blazing. 'Don't give me that look, Lancelot,' he said, throwing a leg over Llamrei and landing with lithe grace. 'You might have youth on your side but I have experience.' He grinned up at me. 'And I don't like losing.'

'I know you don't,' I said, dismounting Tormaigh who tossed his head with a snort, as though pleased to be rid of me, and began cropping the long grass. I saw something in that grass and picked it up.

'An elf bolt,' I said, spitting on the thing and thumbing the soil off it. 'Just lying there.' I showed the flint arrowhead to Arthur, who examined it with keen interest.

'A good one too,' Arthur said.

'I've never found one before,' I said.

'Brings luck, they say,' Arthur said, returning the elf bolt to me. 'Hold on to it.'

I bent and tucked the elf bolt into my boot.

'Are you ready?' he asked me. 'I'm not going to go easy on you.'

I smiled. 'I'm ready,' I said.

Then, the low autumn sun warming our backs, we raced each other up the steep banks and down the ditches in which Roman soldiers must have died, all the way up the formidable hill which once had been a bastion of hope and which would be once again. We raced to the top of Camelot.

We worked hard and we worked fast, clearing the woodland which our enemies might use to their advantage from around the foot of the hill. We reclaimed the plateau from brambles and rowan, dug the rotten posts of long-vanished dwellings out of the ground and began redigging the ditches and enlarging the ramparts. We sweated and laboured until our hands blistered, our backs ached and our muscles screamed for rest, because we wanted to get as much done as we could before winter frosts hardened the earth and the cold drove our workforce inside to their hearths. For though Arthur's own horse warriors and spearmen toiled as ardently and ably as any legionaries who'd worked on the great walls in the north of Britain, we did not labour alone on that hill. Arthur had sent out word throughout Dumnonia that anyone who came to help him rebuild Camelot would be fed, watered and paid, and they came in their dozens. More than we had expected. Sometimes whole families came, using the timber we had cleared to build makeshift dwellings and working from sunrise to sunset.

'I never dreamed so many would come,' Arthur said one night, looking down from the summit to the village which had sprouted like toadstools after rain. Fires lit the night, their smoke drifting up to us and hazing the stars.

'They came to see Excalibur,' Bors told him.

Arthur shook his head. 'They came because they believe in Camelot. They want to be a part of what we are doing here.'

They were both right, for Arthur's fame and word of Excalibur had spread far and wide, and many folk had come to get a glimpse of the new Maximus, as they called Arthur that autumn. But most who came stayed. They saw what we were doing with that ancient hill-fort and they took up picks, axes and spades, and filled wicker baskets with earth, and there cannot have been as many souls swarming over that limestone hill since that day some four hundred years ago when the legions had fought their way up those ditches and banks and put the defenders to the sword.

Some forty or so men had come to Camelot hoping Arthur would take them into his war band. Like most men laying eyes on Arthur's armoured horse soldiers for the first time, these newcomers were in awe. Arthur was canny enough to have his men give a demonstration whereby they charged across the meadow in a thunderous clamour like the coming of a god, and plunged their spears into straw targets to the cheers and terrified thrill of the watching crowd.

Most were beardless youths who had little or no experience of battle. Some were older men who had earned their scars and had stories to tell but who missed the companionship of a warrior band and saw in Arthur their chance to live their old lives again.

'Look at them. Men *want* to fight the Saxons in the spring,' Bors had said one day as we watched three such experienced spearmen come into the camp at the foot of the hill, their shields above their heads to show that they came in peace.

'No, Bors, men want to fight for Arthur,' I said.

Only a handful were told to come back in a year or so, when they had a little more flesh on their bones. 'There will be many campaigns and I will need you soon enough,' Arthur assured these crestfallen young men, who stayed with us anyway and helped with the building. Of all those that stayed, only the three best riders were taken to be trained as cataphracts, because Arthur did not yet have enough horses. The other men were taken on as spearmen and it was Bors's task and mine, when we were not busy on the ramparts, to train them in the use of sword, shield and spear.

One of the newcomers, a broad-shouldered, flat-nosed warrior named Óengus, who boasted his own sword and iron helmet, had been fool enough to protest at the prospect of having to take instruction from, as he put it, waving his shield towards Bors and me, green shoots who had never stood in the shieldwall before. He liked the sound of his own voice, did Óengus, and he was performing for the others, who watched with keen interest, because some of them shared his opinion.

Óengus might have a big mouth, but he was right that we were young, not yet twenty years old. And it was true that we had never yet fought in the terror-soaked tight press of the shieldwall, although we knew we surely would come the spring. Even so, neither of those truths stopped Bors using the butt end of his spear to disarm Óengus of his sword and shield, before pummelling him until Óengus was bleating like a stuck sheep. As Bors walked off, I gave Óengus back his sword and shield and told him, trying not to smile, that I would teach him a way to counter the sword disarm, and he had enough wits still left in his head to say he looked forward to learning it. If any of the others still doubted our competence to teach them, they kept it to themselves.

Now, with just two moons come and gone since Arthur had first shown me Camelot, the place was beginning to resemble the fortress it had once been. In spite of the weather.

'We'll be like pigs in a wallow if it rains any more,' Arthur said, standing to stretch his back, then leaning on his spade. It had rained without respite for two days and already we were covered in filth, so no one would have ever guessed that the man toiling beside me on the eastern ramparts was Lord Arthur, Prince of Dumnonia and son of Uther Pendragon. We were turning the turf, making the ditches deeper and using the spoil to heighten the banks, and had we gone about this in the spring, in no time the earth would have been blanketed in new grass. But it was autumn now and we would have to get used to mud.

'At least it makes the digging easier,' I said, thrusting my own spade into the wet earth, its thin wooden blade shod with sharp iron.

'Easier? Fighting battles is easier than this,' Arthur said, staring into the south. We were working on the highest rampart and yet the grey, rain-filled day did not afford good views across Dumnonia. But Arthur peered, as though he could see the distant coast and the gulls wheeling above the grey sea. As though he could smell the brine in the damp air and hear the retreating surf hissing and bubbling amongst the shingle.

I dug again. Carried the earth on my spade and lifted it. Slid the glistening dark soil onto the bank behind us, which was already a foot taller than me.

He was in a strange mood this morning. Most days he worked harder than anyone, pushing carts of soil, hefting timbers and rocks, digging with a single-minded resolve that put others to shame but made them toil harder themselves. His strength was not exceptional but his stamina was unmatched. But that morning Arthur's heart was not in it, and it was not the first time I had caught him gazing off at nothing.

'Are you unwell?' I asked him, careful not to be overheard. All along the rampart, men drudged, the sound of their digging like an echo across the years, their sweat washed by the rain onto the earth like an offering.

I looked at Arthur, thinking that he had not heard me. But he shook his head. 'I am perfectly well,' he said, scowling, and thrust his spade down with such force that the shoulder was just visible as a ridge in the ground. With gritted teeth Arthur wrestled with the shaft, trying to lever it and widen the incision so that he could haul the spade back out. The shaft snapped, leaving the blade stuck in the earth and sending Arthur stumbling.

'Gods!' he roared, and others on that bank looked over, their dirt-smeared faces unreadable.

'Then something is on your mind, lord,' I said.

'Don't call me lord, Lancelot,' he said. Or rather growled, stepping aside as I thrust my own spade into the earth to retrieve Arthur's broken blade, for not even a prince of Dumnonia would leave that sheath of good iron in the ground.

'Well, you are not yourself this morning,' I said, breaking the soil around the lost spade.

'And you are more talkative than normal,' he replied.

I handed him my spade and dropped to my knees to pull the wooden blade out with my hands. But it was stuck, as though the earth refused to return what Arthur had given it, and my hands slipped off the wet wood and I fell onto my backside, taking a splinter in a thumb for my trouble.

It was worth it to see Arthur smile.

'I'm afraid, Lancelot,' he said, the smile vanishing as quickly as it had appeared. 'I've fought many men in single combat, I've broken shield-walls and I've had three good horses killed under me.' He made fists of his dirty hands and looked south again. 'And none of those things made my palms sweat as they sweat now. None of them made me lose my appetite nor made my stomach roll and flutter like . . .' He frowned, searching for the right words. 'Like bats trembling and tumbling over each other, trapped and driven increasingly mad.'

I laughed at that and he scowled at me as if I had betrayed him. I climbed to my feet, holding my palm towards him to show my remorse.

'I'm sorry, lord,' I said, trying to look serious. 'What's worrying you?' I asked, pushing my long hair off my face and tying it behind my head.

He glanced this way and that, but the others were bent to their work again, their own hopes no less a part of Camelot's construction than the soil and the timbers and the stones which had stood in forsaken Roman villas before Arthur had oxen haul them here to shore up the ramparts.

'It's my wife,' he said in a low voice. 'And don't call me lord, Lancelot. Especially not here with us both looking like a couple of slaves digging a cesspit.'

I nodded. I had known Arthur had a wife but he had never spoken of her to me and I had assumed that perhaps he did not care much for her. After all, a prince did not marry for love, or even for the joys of the bed, but for alliances.

338

'Is she unwell?' I asked, sensing that was not it, but not wanting Arthur to silt up now.

'Why must everyone be unwell today?' he asked.

I shrugged.

'She's coming here,' he said. 'Gawain is bringing her. They left Soissons five days ago. Should be here tomorrow or the day after. Certainly by Samhain.'

Samhain, which stood at the boundary between two halves of the year, was just four days away. Folk were already gathering the herds of cattle and sheep from open pasture and choosing which animals were to be slaughtered and which were for winter feeding and breeding. But more than this, folk were beginning to thrum with the excitement that always came before the great celebrations, because on Samhain the veil between this world and the unseen world dissolves and spirits walk amongst us.

'She is coming and I am not ready. Look at us,' he said, throwing an arm out towards the earthen bank behind us, which had been rising day by day.

'You think she expects a rich hall like your father's?' I asked, throwing up my arms. 'Great beams draped with banners and a roof so vast that two hundred warriors and their horses could look up at it?'

'Of course not,' he said. 'But I had thought I would give her more than a wind-blown tent and a muddy hill. In Soissons we had a villa. Stables of whitewashed stone. Private chambers adorned with paintings of men and women who seemed alive whenever flamelight moved across them. You should see them, Lancelot,' he said, shaking his head. 'We had rows of vines laden with grapes. We bathed, Lancelot!' he said. 'In hot water! There were fires under the floor which heated the tiles in winter.'

'You have Excalibur,' I said before he could go on, for surely that was worth more than a hall and a high seat, which were things any of a dozen lords within a two-day ride could boast. Worth more than grape vines and hot baths, too.

But Arthur's face was agonized. I had never seen him look so ill at ease, not even when the painted Picts had led him into the pool below the sacred falls.

'You don't know her, Lancelot.' He shook his head. 'I don't know her,' he said. 'Not really. We were married at Beltane. Not the last one but the one before.' Rain dripped from his fair beard and his long hair was soaked and lank, but there was a flash of mischief in his grey eyes then. 'I thought she was the most beautiful creature I had ever laid eyes on. Gods, Lancelot, she is extraordinary. It was an arrangement of course. Her father is wealthy and he thought I would be sitting on Uther's high seat by now. Merlin assured him of it. My father wanted me to marry higher.' His lip curled in his rain-beaded beard. 'Some princess of Gaul or even Swabia, if not one of King Syagrius's daughters, who were pretty enough, truth to tell. He hoped I'd bring an army to Britain and that together we would throw the Saxons back into the sea.'

He looked south, across the meadows and the distant woods of beech and oak which were copper in the grey day. A hawk soared in the south, a lonely speck beneath the cloud.

'But when I saw her . . .' he said, and left those words hanging while his mind soared beneath some far-off, kinder sky. He looked so young then as he talked of his wife. Here is an Arthur whom his enemies would not recognize, I thought, and could not help but smile as he confided how this daughter of some rich lord had beguiled him.

'So she's beautiful,' I said.

'Not just beautiful, Lancelot,' he said. 'I have seen many beautiful women. I have known a handful well,' he added, lifting an eyebrow, 'but there was something more about her. A vitality . . . a spirit.' He shook his head, unhappy with his own powers of description. 'Lancelot,' he said, his forehead creasing, 'you know when you hunt a deer and by the will of the gods you manage to get downwind of it, close enough so that the creature does not even know you are there, and for a moment you take the time to watch the deer as it forages.' I nodded. 'And then,' Arthur went on, 'for reasons you cannot explain, the creature looks up. You know. Right at you.' He put two fingers up to his eyes. 'Eye to eye,' he said, 'and in that heartbeat there's no one else in the world and you see the creature's wild soul. Something at once familiar and yet at the same time indescribable. Like a dream you can still feel clinging to you though you can't quite remember it.'

'I know the feeling,' I said, and I did.

'Merlin warned me she would be trouble. He knew her and her father.' Arthur plunged my spade down and brought up a wedge of earth, then carried it to the bank and piled it on top. 'But when I saw her, I knew I'd marry her. The Beltane fires blazed that night and I barely noticed them,' he said, smacking the earth down with the spade.

'You fell in love with a beautiful woman and married her,' I said. 'And now this rare beauty is on her way here, while we flounder in the mud. You'll be together again,' I said, turning my palms up to meet the rain. 'But to look at you anyone would think the Saxons were coming.'

He was digging again but I had no spade and could only watch.

'I would sooner fight the Saxons,' he said, putting a foot on the lug to force the spade deep. 'I don't know her,' he said, then stopped what he was doing and looked at me. 'I barely know her,' he corrected himself. 'The ashes from the Beltane fires were still warm to the touch when a Frankish war band crossed the Meuse. I rode north to war. When I returned, we spent some days together, but soon enough an envoy brought word that my father was dying and I came to Britain.' He glanced round. A huge man carrying a palisade timber up the hill on his shoulder raised a hand in greeting and Arthur waved back. 'I want Guinevere to be a part of all this,' he said. 'That's why I sent for her. I want her to build Camelot with me.'

It seemed as though a cold hand had grabbed my heart and was squeezing it. I could not breathe. I took an involuntary step backwards, slipping slightly in the sodden earth.

'Guinevere?' I said.

Arthur smiled at me. 'You wait till you meet her, Lancelot. When I tell Guinevere how you saved my life at Tintagel, she'll count you a friend. I know she will.' He plunged the spade down. 'I just hope she has feelings for me. That the fire between us still burns,' he said, wincing at his attempt at the bard's craft. He was still talking but I did not hear him. I was watching that hawk drifting in great circles beneath the charcoal grey cloud.

'Lancelot? What's wrong?' Arthur said.

'I'm thirsty,' I said. 'Who is Guinevere's father?' I asked.

He came over and handed me the spade. I dug. 'Lord Leodegan,' he said. 'I've no doubt he'll come too, when he hears Guinevere is back. He's a good man, I think, though I hear he is a Christian now. He's turning an old Roman temple into a church at Carmelide. Now there is a god who spreads like a dog rose,' he said, as though he could not understand the appeal of the Christians' god. 'Guinevere is not a Christian. At least, I don't think she is. Careful,' he said, 'or we'll have no spades between us and no choice but to dig with our hands.'

I dug. I was sick to my stomach. My hands trembled on the shaft but I dug, and I could not look at Arthur. My lord. My friend.

Because Guinevere was coming to Camelot.

19

Malice of the Gods

A T SAMHAIN WE MOURN the death of the old year. We feast and we drink and we look to the future, towards the new year, but we mourn the old. It is a dangerous time, for we linger on the edge of winter and the world stands still, and the gateway between our earthly world and the realm of the spirits stands open. It is at Samhain, too, that the gods visit men, sometimes prophesying when a warrior will die in battle. It is a time when spirits change shape to prowl among the living, when life and death intertwine. It is a time of not being, when order crumbles like an ancient bone brought out of the soil into the air. At Samhain, chaos rules. And that Samhain, chaos ruled me.

She had arrived on the eve of the rites, Gawain and six of Arthur's warriors bringing her across the Dividing Sea from Arthur's hall in Gaul. And from the moment Arthur had mentioned her, to the moment three days later when I laid eyes on her, I had not eaten a morsel of food nor slept hardly at all.

I found some work at the foot of the hill on the northern side and avoided Arthur as much as I could. I avoided Bors. I avoided everyone. My mind reeled and my stomach churned and my throat clenched tight, so that I doubt I could have swallowed my food even had I tried to eat. She was coming. Guinevere. My Guinevere.

Arthur's Guinevere now.

Samhain. When chaos rules.

I knew when she had arrived because Arthur sent word across the fort that all work should cease so that everyone, from the young to the old, could gather by the newly finished gatehouse to welcome Guinevere. Folk left their spades and their picks, their carts and wicker baskets, their timbers and ropes and made their way to the

343

south-western corner of the hill. It wasn't raining but it was a chill, damp day and a fog hung around Camelot, so that there was already a sense of the dead passing through the shreds of the veil between worlds to walk amongst us.

And if I could have passed from my world then, to escape it all, I would have. But I could not. And so I busied myself labouring in the old path which ran through the embankments into the fort from the north, clearing away the tangled undergrowth which over the years had invaded and sunk deep roots. I worked with a sickle, hacking and cutting and not minding the clawing thorns which gouged my hands and forearms and sometimes my face.

Wanting to go and not wanting to.

I had all but defeated the brambles in the channel between the outer bank and ditch when something made me hold before the next sweep of the sickle. I looked around but saw nothing but the fog which hung like smoke on a still day and gathered thickest in the gullies between the steep earthen banks. I shivered. It was Samhain eve and I wondered if some spirit was nearby, having left its burial mound to wander amongst us who still felt the earth beneath our feet, the rain on our skin and the stinging cuts of thorns. I was about to challenge the spirit, to ask what it wanted of me, even lifted the sickle towards the fog.

'You were not easy to find,' said a voice I knew. I turned to see Bors coming down the last bank, squeezing water from the hem of his red cloak. 'I need to grease this,' he said, almost falling and cursing under his breath. I was glad I had not challenged some spirit aloud, for Bors would have laughed and I wasn't in the mood for it.

'You're bleeding,' he said.

I touched my cheek and looked at the blood on my fingers then wiped it on my trews.

'What do you want?' I asked.

He gazed at the ground I had cleared, at the piles of severed briars, then back to the thick furze which still thrived in the ancient walkway, as though appraising my work, though really he was choosing his next words. 'You can't avoid her, Lancelot,' he said, unsheathing the thing sooner than I had expected. But then Bors was never one to tiptoe around the edge of something.

'There's work to be done,' I said.

'Have you told him?'

I shook my head.

'Then, what will you do?'

'What can I do?' I asked. 'They are married.' Saying it aloud gave it the finality of a death blow.

'They are,' he agreed.

'He is my lord. I'm sworn to him.'

Bors nodded. 'He is your friend,' he said. 'He couldn't have known.'

'He barely knows her,' I said. 'He told me.'

Bors considered this. 'Do *you* know her, cousin? You did once but that was years ago. Guinevere will not be the same girl you used to run around Karrek with like hares in a meadow. She's a woman now. A woman who has married for the sake of an alliance.'

'Not much of an alliance,' I said, tasting my own sourness. 'Lord Leodegan is not even a king. And he's a Christian,' I added.

There was pity in Bors's eyes then and I hated seeing it. 'Then perhaps it is love,' he said. 'Or the beginning of love.'

'Did you come here to make me feel worse, cousin?' I asked.

He smiled. 'I came to make sure you left some of these thorns for the rest of us.' He nodded towards the south-west. 'Gawain will have drunk all the mead if we don't hurry. Come with me, Lancelot, before you cut your leg off with that thing,' he said, gesturing at the sickle in my hand.

'I'll come soon,' I said.

'You'd rather be out here on your own with the dead on Samhain eve?' he asked. 'A sickle won't be much use against the Morrigán.' Since coming to Britain I had heard much of the Morrigna, the shape-shifting battle goddesses who, by their fearful presence, affect the fate of armies and warriors on the battlefield. 'I saw a crow just now and the way it looked at me, I tell you, cousin, it was no ordinary crow.' He sighed. 'Come with me,' he said. 'We can avoid her by hiding in the bottom of our cups.'

Guinevere was here. At Camelot. The woman I had loved from the very moment I pulled her from Manannán mac Lir's greedy clutches that storm-flayed day long ago was here on this hill, and I was standing in wet boots in a thorn-filled ditch with a sickle to scare away the roaming dead. And so, with a sickening sensation of excitement and dread writhing in my hollow stomach, I went with Bors to join the celebrations. Because it was Samhain, the time of chaos, and Arthur's wife had come.

In the years since I had last seen her, there had not been a day when I had not thought of Guinevere. Whether I wielded a sword and shield, learning the arts of war, or swam around the Mount. Whether I was picking mussels off the rocks at low tide, climbing down the ledges in search of gulls' eggs, honing blades, polishing the men's war gear or eating in the communal hut. There was a moment of every day, be it as fleeting as a sparrow darting into a lord's hall then out of the smoke hole, that I thought of Guinevere.

At those most often unexpected times, when I was not on my guard against it, she came on me like a stab wound. A wound which, though hidden from sight, never scabbed over. And even when she did not come with sudden, sharp and unbidden anguish, she was always with me; a dull ache deep in my chest. An ever-present absence. Guinevere.

I had been with others. Mostly during those times I visited Tintagel with Bors and Benesek or Edern, but it had been little more than sport, and each time only reminded me of what I really wanted but could not have. And yet now, seeing Guinevere again after years spent holding her only in my secret heart, I was taken aback. Not merely to be under the same swathe of sky as her, to be breathing in the smoke from the same fires and shivering from the same damp air, but because she was not the same Guinevere I had brought with me through the years. Gone was the raven-haired girl with the knowing eyes and the wicked half-smile. In her place was a queen-in-waiting.

Her hair, which had never used to stay where it was put, was now braided and coiled and set in place with silver pins. Her skin, which though ever pale had used to be flushed from wind and sun, was as white as marble. Her eyes were dark with kohl and green with malachite, and her lips were red. Her chest swelled beneath a dress of green silk and a silver wolf's pelt, and that dress, hemmed with silver thread, reached almost to the ground, so that only a glimpse of her silver-studded tan leather shoes could be seen. At her neck she wore a fine torc of twisted silver and around her upper right arm coiled a silver serpent with a red garnet eye.

And I could not find my breath.

Thus did Guinevere come back to me, her back spear-straight, her chin high and her expression imperious as Arthur led her by the hand along the wooden walkway beside which firebrands burned every ten feet, giving the fog a strange and eerie glow. I had laid my share of those timbers upon which she walked, over which they progressed slowly, so that everyone who had gathered at the gatehouse on the innermost embankment, from Arthur's warriors to the craftsmen and labourers, the old, the young and the slaves, could get an eyeful of their lord and his beautiful, regal wife. The future of Britain.

Arthur's horse warriors had taken the red ribbons from their spears and nailed them to the top of the gateway palisade, where they hung limp and damp. From the guard tower above the open gate they had draped Arthur's war banner, that huge red cloth with its squat black bear on all fours, but the effect of all this red on the hill-fort's newly built defences was, if anything, slightly ominous, not that any-one said so.

Arthur himself was dressed for war in his scale armour, which reflected the torch flames, and his polished helmet with its gold-chased cheek pieces and long red plume. His sword belt was studded with silver scales and, unlike Bors's, Arthur's cloak was dry though there was no wind to billow it for the full effect. Even so, he looked magnificent.

And I was thorn-ripped, mud-spattered, damp and no doubt stink-ing of sweat.

I watched her, saw how she smiled at Arthur's men, at Bedwyr and Cai, who both fell to their knees in the mud and pledged their swords to her protection. And yet, where had *they* been that day of the ship-wreck? Where had they been when some fetid sailor had followed Guinevere up the dark stairwell to the Lady's dream chamber and thrown her down on the bed?

'No, Lancelot,' Bors beside me said, taking hold of my arm for I had taken a step. 'No.'

I looked at him. 'Let go of me, cousin.'

He shook his head. 'She has just come. You cannot put this on her now. Gods, Lancelot,' he hissed, 'imagine the embarrassment to Lord Arthur? No, cousin, say nothing. Do nothing.'

He was right. I knew he was and I looked back to Guinevere, who had bid Bedwyr and Cai rise and now crouched beside a little curly-haired girl who had run up to give her a basket of bread. The girl's parents looked on with pride and Guinevere hugged their daughter close and kissed her cheek and the crowd *aah*ed, and in that moment Guinevere had them. Arthur saw it. Smiling, he offered Guinevere his hand and she stood so that her husband could lead her through the gates of Camelot.

Someone called, 'Lord Arthur and Lady Guinevere!' and others echoed it, and in no time they were shouting this in one voice, loud enough to draw any curious spirits making their way through the shredded veil from their world to ours. 'Lord Arthur and Lady Guinevere,' they called, and I still knew Guinevere's face well enough to know that their affection disconcerted her, for all her efforts to maintain the regal grace akin to indifference. I doubted Arthur knew it, though, and that pleased me in some small, sour way. He grinned like a boy, proud of his wall and its gatehouse which he had devised from his memory of Roman ruins, and proud of his wife, who was the most lovely thing on that hill and in all of Dumnonia, perhaps all Britain, and so, grinning, he drew Guinevere towards the yawning, flame-flickered gateway.

Then, as Arthur made a point of stopping to commend one of his builders on the quality of the timber lattice framework and the facing of dressed stone, Guinevere turned her head and she saw me. My breath snagged and it seemed a weight pressed on my chest, heavy as a quern stone. It lasted no longer than a salmon taking a fly, but in that cruel moment, her face lit by the hissing flames, her eyes in me, she was my Guinevere again.

Then she turned her face away and walked through the gate into Camelot and was gone.

That Samhain eve I took Bors's advice and lost myself in my cups. And the next day, when the feasting began in earnest, I did the same, so that even if all the dead of Arawn's realm had crossed over to skulk amongst us I would not have noticed.

The days passed and the refortification of Camelot continued, and whether Arthur was busy playing the husband or else had other matters to attend to, I did not see much of him in the ditches. Some days, when I worked on the ramparts or carried Roman stones up to the inner bank, or helped drive in the timbers of the smaller, lighter palisades on the outer banks, which would protect archers and javelin men from attackers, I half expected to turn round and see Guinevere standing there with that questioning yet knowing look in her eyes. I imagined her finding me, as she used to on the island, and the two of us running off to some secret place beyond eyes and ears. Perhaps I would tell her how Arthur and I had become the best of friends. How I loved him as a brother. But that I loved her too. She would explain how her father had forced her into marrying Arthur and she would tell me not to look so dismal, that we would conceive of a way to be together without betraying Arthur.

And the sea would flow to the well springs of rivers and the rain would rise from the fields to the sky.

But Guinevere never came. Mordred did.

I did not know who he was at first but I noticed him. We all did. He rode through the gatehouse onto the plateau with the straight-backed assuredness of a lord, though he could have been no more than sixteen years old. The fair hair on his chin looked as insubstantial as the downy heads of the cankerworts which children pluck from the fields to blow. Not that I boasted a beard to talk of, unlike Bors, who was rightly proud of his.

I had been instructing three young men in the proper use of the spear, teaching them how, when attacked from behind, a man might turn in to his assailant, perform a quick block and thrust at the face, when we heard someone haranguing the gate guards to let him in. I could not hear the case which the stranger presented, but his tone was belligerent and I did catch the words *father* and *you stinking weasel turd*. Next thing, the gates were hauled open and in rode this young man with the dawn sunlight flooding at his back.

I told the new recruits to continue practising the spear moves and I watched the newcomer on his sturdy little pony, around which small clouds of flies swarmed, though the young man seemed oblivious to them. The reason for the flies was the four severed human heads tied by their long fair hair to the saddle horns. One of the heads looked many days dead but the others were fresh and the flies were feasting.

Then the young man turned his head stiffly and regarded me with contemptuous eyes.

'You there, take me to Lord Arthur,' he said in a disagreeable, screechy voice halfway between a boy's and a man's. Blood had trickled from the trophies' raw necks to stain the yellow saddle and run in dark, sticky trails down the pony's flanks and belly.

'I'm busy,' I said, turning back to the young spearmen who were more interested in the stranger and the grisly heads swinging from his saddle than in their spearcraft.

'Don't turn your back on me,' he whined.

Ignoring him, I lunged at a spearman who had the sense to keep his mind on the task and parried my sheathed spear blade in a manner which showed that he had been paying attention that morning.

'Are you deaf? I said, don't turn your back on me,' the stranger said again. I nodded at the young spearman, which was all the praise he would get for his parry, then turned back to Mordred, for no other reason than I was intrigued by him.

He reached down and patted one of the pale, dead faces. 'Do you think I got these by dancing around with a practice spear?' he asked. He was sure of himself for a young man whose balls had not long dropped, but I did not know who his father was then.

'I'm guessing you found some dead Saxons and cut off their heads so that people might think you had killed them,' I said, for those grimacing faces were unmistakably Saxon.

He did not like that. Not at all, and it took him several heartbeats to get a rein on the fury which burned in his cheeks and blazed in his grey eyes.

'Who are you?' he asked. 'What is your name?'

I shrugged, seeing no point in not telling him. 'I'm Lancelot,' I said.

His eyes widened at that. Mordred's every emotion moulded and remoulded his face, from one moment to the next. Or so it seemed to me. 'You are one of those who rode north with Lord Arthur to bring back the sword Excalibur,' he said.

I nodded.

He grimaced. 'I was meant to be there. It should have been me riding through Britain beside Lord Arthur and Excalibur,' he said with a tone and expression which suggested there was someone he blamed for missing out on those many, many arse-numbing weeks in search of Maximus's sword.

Still, I *was* intrigued. By the Saxon heads as much as by this young man's brazenness, for despite what I had said to him, I knew full well that he had killed the men to whom those heads had belonged. I wasn't sure how I knew, but I knew.

'And why should you have ridden with us, boy?' I asked, adding the last word because I knew it would sting him and I wanted to see it in his face.

'Because Lord Arthur is my father, you ignorant toad,' he said.

I had not expected that. Arthur had never mentioned that he had a son. But then, he had not talked to me of his wife, either, until that day we were digging together. And of the two surprises, this one paled against the heart-piercing revelation that he had married Guinevere.

'Well?' he challenged me. 'Will you take me to him?'

I was taking in the news that here was Arthur's son. I was looking at him with new eyes and those eyes saw now the resemblance: the lean face, full lips and storm-cloud eyes. The fair down which would in time grow to a full golden beard, and the high forehead and fair hair which, in a few years, would have receded from his temples. This young man had killed the four Saxons and he was Arthur's son.

Even so, I did not have to like him.

'You don't need me to take you,' I said, pointing my spear back into the settlement. 'You'll find him up there, covered in wood shavings and sweating with the rest.'

'And I'll be questioned by a dozen spearmen before I get anywhere near him,' he said. He was right of course. He nodded at me. 'If *you* take me, the sooner my father gets to welcome his son,' he said. 'You being the man who saved my father at Tintagel and helped him bring Maximus's sword back to Dumnonia.'

'I didn't save him,' I said. 'It was a fight. I fought.' Behind me the *clack, clack* of spear staves striking each other as the young spearmen practised what they had learnt.

Mordred shrugged as if to say it meant nothing to him either way. And maybe I wanted to be there when Arthur saw Mordred, if only to witness my friend's embarrassment at not having mentioned to me that he had a son. Or perhaps I wanted to go up to where Arthur laboured on what would be his great hall because I knew that Guinevere would be there and I had not seen her since the day she arrived at Camelot.

'Your father has never mentioned you,' I said. One last barb before I did what he had asked of me. 'What is your name?'

'My father does not know me well,' he said, an admission which clearly hurt him. 'But he will. He will know me and we shall be friends.' He smiled then and there was some of his father's charm in that smile. 'As you and he are friends, Lancelot,' he added. Then he lifted his chin. 'My name is Mordred.'

'Well then, Mordred ap Arthur ap Uther, come with me,' I said, setting off across the open plateau which sloped gently towards the hill's summit, upon which Arthur was building his hall.

'Lancelot,' Arthur called, straightening from the timber he had been smoothing with an adze. 'You've come to do some real work?' The hall seemed to be springing up from the grass, and hardly surprising for there were so many labourers and craftsmen planing and hammering, working pole lathes, shouldering beams here and there and sinking posts into holes cut in the limestone bedrock.

'The young men need to be taught how to fight,' I replied, smiling in spite of myself. I too was a young man and had not known Arthur long, yet it seemed we were old friends and I had missed him. Not that missing him made it any easier being there.

'They do, they do,' Arthur admitted, 'but, Lancelot, there's something about building. About making a thing from nothing.' He gestured with the adze behind him, at the framework of timbers which more than hinted at his ambition. A quarter of it was already walled with wattle and roofed with golden thatch, so that with a little imagination it was possible to see the finished hall in the eye of your mind. Smoke drifted out into the day from that finished section where I knew Arthur and Guinevere spent the nights together. It sickened me to look at it.

'It will be perfect,' Arthur said, laying the adze on the timber and coming over to me. 'Ten feet wide and sixty-three feet in length. Sixty-three!' The same size as King Uther's hall, I guessed. The same but no bigger, for Arthur was clever like that. He would not build a hall larger than King Uther's, not until he had proved himself in the eyes of the other kings of Britain. But nor would this hall be smaller than his father's, and I imagined him pacing out the Pendragon's hall and keeping those calculations to himself. Storing them away until they were needed. Until now.

'A fine place to hold our victory feasts,' I said, catching a whiff of parsnips, onion and garlic. But Arthur was no longer looking at me. He was looking at the young man on the pony behind me. Not just looking. Scowling. And then I saw Guinevere. She stood inside the structure at the divide where the thatched roof gave way to the open sky, holding two cups which steamed in the chill morning air. I wondered how long she had been there, watching me as I spoke with Arthur.

'Lord,' I said, feeling the occasion required that formality which Arthur didn't usually favour, 'Mordred asked me to bring him to you.' I tried to keep my eyes off Guinevere, though I felt hers on me.

'Mordred,' Arthur said quietly, as though feeling the shape of that name on his lips. Samhain was almost a moon behind us but Arthur looked as if he had seen a spirit from beyond the veil.

'Father,' Mordred said, and gestured in such a way as though he sought Arthur's permission to dismount.

Arthur nodded. There were tears in his eyes.

Guinevere walked over and handed a steaming cup to Arthur, who took it without taking his eyes from Mordred. She gave the other to me and I took the moment to look her in the eye. We were so close I could have reached out and touched her arm. Her face. Her raven hair.

A shiver ran through me but I sensed Arthur turn and so snatched my eyes from Guinevere's.

'This is my son,' Arthur told me, extending an arm towards Mordred. Then he looked at Guinevere. 'My son,' he said, raising his voice above the constant hammering and planing and the barking of instructions from Donaut, Arthur's ham-armed chief builder. There it was, given to the day like a confession. But a confession to himself perhaps, or even to Mordred, for I could tell in Guinevere's face, and by the way she nodded, that Mordred's existence had not come as a surprise to her. Unlike me.

'I am pleased to meet you, Mordred,' she said with a smile, though what she really thought about coming face to face with this young man whom her husband had sired when she was just a little girl was hidden even from me.

'None of us can say what the day will bring,' Arthur said, knuckling a tear from his cheek as he watched his wife and son greet one another.

'And this, my dear, is Lancelot. My truest friend.' He smiled at me. 'Who has been far too busy digging ditches and teaching young men how to fight, so that I have been wondering if he is avoiding me.'

'Nonsense,' I said and meant it. It was not Arthur I had been avoiding.

Guinevere smiled at me. 'Then you are my true friend also, Lancelot,' she said. 'My husband speaks of you often. One day you must tell me the real story of how you came by Excalibur. The way Arthur tells it, the painted people saw his helmet and armour and Gawain's big mare and thought Maximus had come back from the dead. That they just fetched Excalibur from some shrine and gave it to him. But I have heard talk of human sacrifice.' She raised an eyebrow. 'And of a pretty priestess.' She looked at Arthur in a way that struck me like a blow beneath the ribs.

Arthur spread his arms wide. 'We found the sword. With Merlin's help,' he added, glancing at me. 'And we brought it back. There is not much else to tell.'

'My husband is many things, Lancelot, but a bard is not one of them,' Guinevere said. Then she turned to Mordred, who was watching me. 'I will fetch you some spiced wine, Mordred,' she said, and walked back over the unfinished threshold of her hall.

'My son,' Arthur said, shaking his head at Mordred as if he could still scarcely believe it. He stretched both arms towards Mordred, who stood for what seemed a long while. Too long, in truth, his face a battleground upon which suspicion and yearning fought. 'Come,' Arthur told him, inviting, his tear-brimmed eyes wide and full of wonder and pain, too. The heart-clenching pain of old grief.

Dropping his pony's halter, Mordred strode across muddied ground blanketed white with sweet-smelling wood shavings, and threw himself into his father's embrace.

'I'm sorry,' Arthur said, the words muffled by Mordred's thick hair. 'Forgive me, my son. I was young. So young.'

'The gods spared me, Father,' Mordred said, allowing Arthur to all but crush him against his shoulder and chest. When he broke his father's clinch and pulled back so that their eyes could meet, Arthur nodded. It was strange seeing Arthur, whom I did not think of as so much older than me, looking at a younger reflection of himself. 'They wanted us to find each other again,' Mordred said. 'To remake Britain together.'

Arthur glanced towards the thatched part of the hall, then frowned at Mordred. 'And your mother? How is she?' he asked in a low voice.

Their words were not meant for my ears, so I walked over to Donaut and tried to take an interest in his work. I asked him why there was a neat trench running from what would be Arthur and Guinevere's private chambers, along the building by the far wall. It was a stupid question but the only one that came to me in the moment. Donaut was kind, considering. 'No wonder you're down there showing men how not to cut off their own damned legs, Lancelot,' he said, revealing a smile that boasted all of four teeth. 'That'll be a passageway,' he said, 'along which Lord Arthur will stumble to his bed after his wine. Nothing makes a man so thirsty as killing Saxons.' He looked over to where Guinevere stood ladling hot wine into a cup. 'The lucky swine, eh?' he added with a wink but only got a glower from me, at which the big man flushed then excused himself, cuffing a lad round the head for bringing him the wrong sized chisel and gouge.

So, I went to Guinevere.

I could hear the mumble of Arthur and Mordred talking in quiet voices beyond the wattle wall. In front of me, Guinevere was crouched by the hearth, feeding new sticks to the flames above which a cauldron hung. The vegetable-smelling steam rose to seep into the new reed thatch above our heads.

'It will be magnificent,' I said, meaning the finished hall. My first words to her after so long. After countless reunions in my dreams. After so many imagined declarations, the first words I poured into the pain-filled void were about the home she would share with Arthur.

Guinevere stood, turning to me. 'It will be, so long as my husband does not attempt anything more demanding than planing or digging holes,' she said, her own first words innocuous to anyone else's ears. Agony to mine for the 'my husband' in them.

The new fuel spat and popped as the flames worked into it. 'Every time he tries his hand at some work which requires skill and patience, Donaut has to fix or replace it after, though he waits until Arthur's back is turned.' She smiled. I wondered how she could.

I let out a breath and just stood there, dumb as the roof post beside me, from which Guinevere had hung a bunch of dried lavender tied with a red ribbon. She saw me notice it.

'Lancelot,' Arthur called. I was looking at Guinevere, waiting for her to say something more. Wanting to speak myself but not finding the words. Her eyes flicked to the world beyond the new wattle wall, towards where Arthur waited, and so I stepped back out into the morning.

'See how busy Mordred has been, Lancelot,' Arthur said. He stood by Mordred's blood-streaked pony, examining the heads tied to the saddle. 'If anyone needed proof that Uther's blood flows in the lad's veins.' He batted a hand at the flies then retreated away from them.

'Even a blind man could see he is your son, Arthur,' I said. Mordred was more like Arthur than Arthur was like Uther.

'Lancelot suggested I had taken the heads from dead men,' Mordred said, looking at me with a spite that I had never seen in Arthur's eyes. Not when those other lords of Britain had disputed his right to rule in Dumnonia. Not even when the Picts had led him into the pool to drown him for their gods.

Arthur frowned and I shrugged.

'Lancelot meant no offence,' Arthur assured Mordred. I had meant plenty of offence but said nothing. 'Which lord have you been serving?' Arthur asked his son. 'Who have you been fighting for?'

'I've fought in Caer Celemion and Caer Went,' Mordred said, thanking Guinevere for the cup of wine. The sword which he wore on his back was a rich man's weapon, its iron pommel and guard encrusted in silver and the wooden grip boasting three bands of iron inlaid with silver. Even the polished wooden scabbard was fitted with bronze, at its mouth and at its end, in a chape cast from bronze to resemble a raven or crow's head. He shrugged. 'But for no lord. I fight for myself, Father. As I have always done.'

Arthur glanced at me and I saw his discomfort at Mordred's intimation that he had grown up fatherless, but also because of what the young man had said before that. For warriors swear themselves to lords and serve them, and we have an instinctive distrust of a man who goes from lord to lord selling his sword for silver. Even the Guardians of the Mount, who protected traders for silver, were ultimately sworn to the Lady.

'You are still very young, Mordred,' Arthur said, as if this excused his son for having prowled Britain like a wolf driven from its pack. 'And did the men you fought with know that you are my son?' he asked.

Mordred shook his head. 'I learnt how to kill in the thick of the fray, Father, with the Saxons' reeking breath in my nose and their rancid guts beneath my feet.' He thought nothing of speaking thus in front of a lady, not that Guinevere seemed to mind. 'My sword sings and the crows leave their roosts on beating wing,' he said, that little poesy meant for Guinevere, judging by the flush of his cheeks.

Still, more a bard than his father, I thought sourly.

'And you thought if men knew you were my son and Uther's grand-son, they would shield you from the worst?' Arthur asked.

Mordred shrugged.

In truth there was something admirable about that. And the dead faces on Mordred's saddle were the faces of grown men, so that if he had killed them as he claimed, he did not lack for courage or skill. Certainly he had not found that sword just lying about. Besides which, he was Arthur's son and if he intended to stay here at Camelot, then it would be better if I liked him. Easier for all of us.

'If you will have me, I will fight with you, Father,' Mordred said. 'I'll fight beside you and Gawain and Bedwyr.' He glanced at me. 'And Lancelot,' he added, giving me a conciliatory nod.

'If I will have you?' Arthur said, shaking his head as he walked over to place his hands on Mordred's shoulders. 'If you will forgive me,' he said. 'I was so young.' His fingers were white, so tightly did they grip Mordred. 'The gods know how often I have thought of you, Mordred. How often I have wondered what might have been.'

I did not know what had happened between them or why Arthur expressed such guilt, but I would find out. Guinevere knew, though. I was sure of that.

Mordred's lip quivered a little then, but he did not weep as his father had done. 'I forgive you, Father,' he said.

'Then all will be well,' Arthur said, pulling Mordred close again. 'My boy,' he said and laughed. 'None of us can say what the day will bring, hey, Lancelot?' he called above the dull beating of hammers and the rasp of saws.

None of us, I thought, saying nothing for fear my voice would crack. I just looked at Guinevere. It was as though I had been holding my breath in the years since I had last seen her, and now, when I should have been breathing in the very sight of her, there was no air.

She would not even look at me.

'The soup will burn,' she said. 'Excuse me.' With that she turned and walked back across the narrow trench where a wall soon would be.

20

Spear Song

WE FEASTED TO CELEBRATE Mordred's return. There was music and wine, mead and flesh and fire to defy the dark winter nights. Some cautioned Arthur against the extravagance. They said that come the spring, when the Saxons renewed their raids, we would need all the grain and smoked meats, honey and flour that we had stored at the last summer's end. But Arthur shrugged off their warnings. 'After Beltane we will take the fight to the Saxons,' he said, 'and will be eating their grain, slaughtering their cattle.' He knew how to dispel men's fears, did Arthur, and so we ate and drank because the son whom Arthur had thought lost to him was found.

It was from Merlin that I learnt what had happened between them and why Arthur had sought Mordred's forgiveness that day when Mordred rode into Camelot like the young man in the story which the Christians like to tell, where a lovesick father welcomes home the son who wasted his fortune. Except in Mordred's case I soon realized he had every right to hate Arthur.

'Arthur has a weakness for women,' Merlin said, snapping off a large growth of bracket fungus from a birch trunk. He had needed to go into the woods to gather ingredients and asked me to help him, which I did not mind doing. Anything to take me away from Camelot and Arthur's shining new hall. 'I don't suppose you have any idea how useful this is?' the druid asked, examining the whitish brown fungus which was the size of his outstretched hand. 'Although the tree slugs have been gorging on this,' he said, poking a little finger into a burrow hole.

'It'll carry an ember a good while,' I said. I had taken little notice of the herbal lore which the girls practised on Karrek, but everyone knew how useful such fungus was as tinder.

'Yes, yes,' Merlin said, 'but it is so much more, Lancelot.' He put the fungus to his nose and inhaled. 'Applied to a bandage it will stop bleeding. It can prevent a wound going bad and lessen the scarring. It will numb pain, reduce swelling and even cleanse your guts of worms.' He turned the fungus over to display more holes on its underside. 'Though they are better taken when they are young and tender,' he said, 'before they spoil.'

I was more interested in what he had been saying before he stopped to pilfer from that old birch. 'You were talking about Arthur,' I reminded him.

'I'm still talking about Arthur, more or less,' he said with a wry smile. 'You see, there was a girl. Young and tender.' He reached up and snapped off another white fungus, this one the size of a hen's egg. 'Just right for the plucking, she was. Clear skin. Bright eyes. Tits you could hang your helmet and shield on.' Satisfied with the specimen, he put it in his linen bag. 'Arthur was the age Mordred is now. Younger perhaps, but broad and handsome. As kings' sons are in songs and tales, not as they so often are in reality, snivelling little turds or bullies bloated with self-importance.' He slapped the birch trunk. 'The sap was rising in Arthur, as it will in young men.' He lifted his staff and knocked another small white fungus off the tree, cursing when he couldn't find where it had landed. 'I thought you were here to help me, Lancelot,' he said, leaning his staff against another tree so that he might search for the lost prize. I poked around half-heartedly in the leaf litter with my spear. 'The girl's name was Morgaine and Arthur had his way with her,' he said. 'More than once.'

'He was a prince,' I said with a shrug, yet to see Arthur's crime.

'Spoken like a prince, Lancelot son of King Ban,' Merlin observed, on his hands and knees in the dirt now. I had seen a flash of white beneath an exposed root but did not tell Merlin. I was enjoying seeing him scrabble around like a pig in the mast. 'Poor young Arthur could not have known. He was never the brightest young man, but still.' He glared up at me. 'You are supposed to be helping me.'

Where was his Saxon slave, Oswine, anyway? I wondered.

'Could not have known what?' I asked, with my spear point knocking the little fungus ball out from under the root.

'Ah, there you are,' Merlin said, gathering it up and blowing the dirt off it. 'That a girl was in Igraine's belly when Uther slaughtered her husband, Lord Gorlois,' he said. 'No bigger than this fungus, yet she was in there. After she was born, Uther feared the girl's curse and well he might, having killed her father, but he loved Igraine too much to kill the child and so the girl was sent away to be raised in Caer Gwinntguic. Except she wasn't, because Igraine kept her close without Uther knowing. You see, Lancelot, you cannot blame Arthur for his blindness. He gets it from Uther,' he said, giving me a knowing look.

'Morgana,' I blurted, feeling a fool for not having realized sooner. 'Morgana is Lord Arthur's sister,' I said.

'Half-sister,' Merlin corrected, climbing to his feet and brushing the damp leaves off his robes. 'If that makes it any more palatable.'

'Did Morgana know? When she and Arthur lay together?'

'Queen Igraine saw the girl now and again. In secret. I daresay the girl knew who her mother was.'

'So Morgana must have known who Arthur was,' I said.

'Perhaps,' the druid said, 'but of course Igraine did not know that the two of them were rolling in the straw.'

So Morgana was Mordred's mother. I thought back to the day Uther died, when I had seen Morgana amongst those gathered around the High King's bed. She had hissed at me that day, though I still did not know why. Benesek had said she was mad, and perhaps it was not surprising after what had happened to her.

Merlin put the fungus in the bag with the other things he had collected.

'Arthur found out and sent the baby away,' I said, 'just as Uther had sent Morgana away.'

'Worse than that,' Merlin said, snatching up his staff and walking off. 'A fisherman was paid to row him out, poor little Mordred tied up in a sack with only a heavy rock to play with.' He lifted a hand and spread his fingers. 'Plop.'

'Arthur did this?' I asked, not believing that Arthur could have done such a thing.

'Uther's doing really,' Merlin said, 'to spare his son from the disgrace of incest. But Arthur knew. And when it was done . . . or when they all thought it was done, Arthur was ashamed.'

He gave a little gasp of excitement and pointed his staff at a large puffball which sat like an old white skull amongst the wet, brown leaf litter. 'My favourite,' he said, and prodded the mushroom, at which a cloud of smoke rose into the air. 'Why do you think he ran off to

Gaul?' Merlin said. 'To learn how to fight? He could have done that here. Uther was always fighting someone.'

On we went, ever deeper into the wood. 'No, poor Arthur was ashamed,' Merlin said. 'He went across the sea and learnt his trade. He *is* good at war,' he said, examining branches and trunks as he went. 'The best I've ever known.'

'How did Mordred survive?' I asked.

'How should I know?' the druid said. 'The fisherman Uther had paid to drown the boy like a rat in a barrel was soft-hearted? Or perhaps an otter carried the sack with Mordred inside it on its back and deposited it on the shore? Or maybe Manannán mac Lir sent a wave to carry him to some safe haven.'

'Did you know that he lived?' I asked.

'I heard whispers,' he admitted. 'In the breeze of a swan's wing. In the sigh of a salmon breaking the surface. And now Mordred has forgiven his father for trying to drown him. And Arthur has forgiven the boy for being the issue of a poisonous act. All is well. All is well.'

He was ahead of me, so that I couldn't see his face, but his tone betrayed his words.

'You think it strange?' I asked, 'that Mordred should forgive Arthur?'

'I think the gods love chaos, Lancelot,' he said. 'If they did not, there would be a little pile of bones on the seabed this very day, instead of a young man who collects heads and yet forgives those who wanted him dead.' He bent and picked something up, smelled it, then showed it to me. It was a bird's pellet. 'What bird coughed this up, Lancelot?'

I glanced up at the trees around us. 'A kestrel,' I guessed.

He rolled his eyes and broke apart the little mass of hair and feathers. 'With all these bones? Don't be a fool. It belonged to a brown owl, which I will take as a bad omen, Lancelot. Prophetic of mischief, mark my words.'

I hadn't noticed the bones but nor was I interested in being tested. I was thinking about Mordred and Arthur and wondering why Mordred had chosen to come back to Arthur now after all those years.

'And talking of mischief,' he said, picking out the small bones to examine them one by one before casting them aside. He waved the half-dismembered pellet at me. 'What are you going to do about your own little mess?' he asked.

I frowned at him.

'Don't play the innocent, Lancelot. It's a bit late for that, don't you think?'

I knew then why he had asked me to accompany him. It was not for my spear, for no man, not even an outlaw, would attack a druid.

'You think I don't know about you and Lady Guinevere, your friend's devoted wife?' he asked. 'I knew it long before that night when you—' He tilted his head on one side and pulled his beard, which had grown since I had last seen him, through a dirty hand. 'When you interrupted us,' he said.

Interrupted? That was one way of saying it. I had thrown him into a wall to separate him and Guinevere and ruin the spirit flight in which they had been spellbound together. 'I knew it that day of the storm,' he said, 'when you hurled that pretty hawking glove into the sea.'

How could he have known about that, I wondered. But then, he *was* a druid.

'I'm not doing anything,' I said, which was true.

'But you want to,' he said.

'She was mine before she was his,' I said.

'Don't be simple,' he said. 'You were children. As hare-brained as Arthur and Morgana.' He frowned, scratching his cheek. 'Although I don't recall them ever murdering a man and feeding his corpse to the crabs, but still, that's not the point.' He tilted his staff towards me and there was more than a touch of threat in the gesture. 'Arthur needs you, Lancelot,' he said. 'He needs you.'

'Arthur is my friend,' I said. I felt then as though I had betrayed Arthur, yet I had done nothing other than try to avoid Guinevere since she came to Camelot. 'He is my friend,' I said again. 'I would do anything for him.'

Merlin smiled and nodded. 'Yes. I believe you would,' he said. 'But women can make such fools of us.'

'We can make fools of ourselves,' I said, remembering how I had burned for Guinevere to look at me up on the hill when Arthur and Mordred were getting reacquainted. And how, years before, I used to run up the Mount to catch a glimpse of her leaving the Lady's keep to gather herbs before sunrise.

'That is probably the wisest thing I've ever heard you say,' Merlin said. Then his right eyebrow arched like a drawn bow. 'You will do nothing stupid?'

'She barely acknowledges me,' I said.

'You will do nothing stupid,' he repeated, this time more a statement than a question.

'They are married,' I said. 'What she and I had together is gone.'

The druid nodded and pointed his staff into the forest, muttering something about needing to lay eyes on two magpies on his right-hand side to nullify the ill omen of the owl pellet. But we never saw any magpies that day. And as for me doing anything stupid as far as Guinevere was concerned, I never got the chance.

It was winter. Folk collected wood or cut turves and peat to stack and dry for the fire. They cut reeds and sedges to dry for thatching and gathered bracken to use as bedding for cattle. On those days when it was too wet to work outside, there was still threshing and winnowing to be done. It was the time when we made preparations for the hardships of the cold, dark months when men did little but busy themselves with handicrafts and sit by the hearth drinking ale, or mead if they could get it. When women spun thread and made trews and cloaks and tunics, or cooked warming broths. When dung was collected from the barns and stored to be mixed with marl and spread on the fields.

It was a time when the earth slept and men did not venture far from their own roofs, and when their swords hung in their scabbards on pegs gathering cobwebs.

And yet that winter, when we did not expect it, war came to Dumnonia.

Arthur's great hall was complete and so too were many other buildings which crowned Camelot's plateau. Dwellings, storerooms, armouries, workshops, granaries, stables and a smithy which rang almost day and night with the sound of the hammer striking the anvil, so busy were Arthur's smiths making spear blades and swords, helmets, shield bosses and arrowheads and the iron shoes which Arthur's horses wore to protect their hooves on the stone-paved Roman roads which still criss-crossed Britain.

'The time to prepare for war is when there is peace,' Arthur had told me. And none of us had expected to have to fight before the spring. Yet I welcomed the news, when it came from Caer Gwinntguic to the east, that a war band of Saxons led by a king called Aella had landed at Selsey. Aella had beaten off a force of Britons from Rhegin who had tried to oppose their landing and now the enemy marched west, their ranks swollen with Saxons who had been born in Britain, their fore-fathers those whom King Vortigern invited here by the boatload to guard the eastern shore in return for land and silver.

'They are flocking to this King Aella because he promises every spearman a share of the spoils,' the messenger from the fort of Venta Belgarum told Arthur. 'The main army is camped outside our western wall to prevent Dumnonia's spearmen from joining with us,' the man said, sweeping an arm out wide, 'but their raiding bands are on the move. Burning. Stealing cattle. Murdering. Raping.'

Men shook their heads and touched the iron of their blades or growled promises of vengeance. Easy words when you are still safe behind ramparts and palisades.

We were gathered in the new hall, whose beams and thatch were sweet-smelling and bright, not ingrained with the smoke from ten thousand hearth fires. Arthur's war leaders Gawain, Bedwyr and Cai were there, as well as many of his more experienced horse warriors and spearmen. Guinevere was there, too, standing at Arthur's shoul-der. Watching him. She had not yet met my eye, but I had not sought it, for Merlin was in the hall and after our conversation in the woods I felt self-conscious.

'The Saxons of Caer Gwinntguic have been waiting for someone to lead them ever since Uther killed King Beorn,' Gawain said. He was dressed for war and mud-spattered, having ridden to make sure that no Saxons had yet strayed into Dumnonia's eastern borderlands. It seemed they had not, but it was surely a matter of when, not if. 'They want more land,' he said. 'Always more.'

I had looked at Arthur then and known that he too wanted to fight, no matter that some of the older warriors warned him that we were not yet ready for war, that we must wait until we were stronger. Until we were joined by at least some of the kings of Britain. King Cynfelyn ap Arthwys of Cynwidion perhaps. Or Lord Farasan who led the spearmen of Caer Celemion to the north of Caer Gwinntguic.

'Let King Deroch and your cousin blunt their spears on the whoresons,' one of Arthur's scarred-faced horse warriors suggested. His name was Parcefal and someone had cut him from below his right eye, down his cheek, through his lips and down his chin, so that a stark white line ran through his dark beard. He was a frightening-looking warrior and yet he was as kind a man as I have known and a favourite with the younger spearmen for his humour and willingness to help them with any task, from putting the keenest edge on their blades, to adjusting their saddle girths to get the best from their horses. Parcefal smiled his unnerving lip-splitting smile. 'If the Saxons kill Lord Constantine it will save you the trouble, Arthur.'

'Are you afraid to fight them?' Mordred challenged Parcefal.

The hall fell silent. Arthur shook his head at Mordred and raised a placating hand at Parcefal, but the scarred warrior just grinned at Mordred. 'Careful, boy,' he said, 'I don't want to tan your arse in front of everyone.'

Mordred glowered but had the sense to hold his tongue, and Arthur half smiled to himself.

'We could wait for them here,' an older warrior named Ector said. He had been one of Uther's men but had left Britain with Arthur those years ago and had fought beside him ever since. 'We could make Aella think we're weak or too afraid to fight him. Let him come here to us.' He gestured up at the golden thatch. 'He might imagine himself living in this hall. Let him imagine it and we'll be ready. I say let the dogs die in our ditches. Come Beltane their skulls will look good on the palisade.'

But Arthur shook his head at the idea. 'This King Aella won't waste men attacking us here. He would try to trap us in Camelot and raid Dumnonia around us. But if we help Caer Gwinntguic now, King Deroch will be in our debt and the other kings of Britain will see that I am a man of my word.' There were murmurs of disagreement but Arthur cut them off with a raised hand. 'And they will see how good we are at war,' he said. And that, of course, was his intention. Arthur would use King Aella's incursions to show what his famed horsemen on their armoured mounts could do to packs of spearmen who had strayed too far from their own camp.

'I agree,' Gawain said. 'Hit them hard and fast. They will expect us to wait for better weather. They think they can roam all winter unchecked.' He grimaced. 'Like wolves out for sheep that have strayed from the flock.'

'Strike them now,' Bedwyr said, thumping a fist into the cup of his empty hand. 'Aella is stretching his hand out towards the fire,' he added, doing the same thing himself because the flames in Arthur's new hearth were tall and reaching, casting us all in their copper glare. 'Let us burn it for him,' he said. Only, we were the fire in Bedwyr's analogy, and the men around me nodded and hoomed. Teeth shone in the fire glow.

The men in that hall were experienced fighters, warriors who had fought in Gaul against the Franks and in Armorica too, and even here in Britain against Arthur's cousin Lord Constantine. They were not farmers who snatched up their spears to march with their lord every other summer. They were well trained and well armed. And they had Arthur.

'We'll do more than burn it, Bedwyr,' Arthur said, looking at me. There was a fire in his eyes and there was a quickening in my blood. I nodded and Arthur nodded back, and I knew we were going to war.

We followed the old Roman Portway that ran between Old Sarum and Calleva Atrebatum, then took the road which I have heard men call the Devil's Highway because only a god or some supreme spirit could have laid such a structure across the green land and through thick forest. But I had seen the walls of Hadrian and Antoninus with my own eyes and I knew what the Romans had been capable of. Yet many of Arthur's spearmen, especially the younger ones who had not campaigned with him before, were awestruck. Some were even too afraid to set foot on the raised stone way and preferred making their slow progress through the trees either side.

We sent no word to King Deroch that we rode east into Caer Gwinntguic, because we did not want the Saxons to get wind of our coming. Nor did Arthur want his cousin Lord Constantine to know it, for we could not be sure that Constantine would not try to betray Arthur again, even if it meant allying himself with the Saxons.

Really, Arthur wanted to create a spectacle with his horses. He wanted to roll across Caer Gwinntguic like thunder. He wanted to come upon the Saxons like a squall and wreck them. And any survivors from his slaughter would carry word of it back to their people, who would not have known such an enemy for more than a hundred years and the time of Maximus. Thus would terror spread amongst the Saxons like a plague and the name of Lord Arthur, son of the Pendragon, would haunt men's dreams.

That is perhaps how a cheap bard might sing it. In reality it did not happen as we'd hoped.

It started well. We rode in column two abreast, sixty men on armoured horses and I mounted on Tormaigh my dun stallion, who tossed his head as though he were as eager to fight as the rest of us. He so reminded me of Malo, that horse, and if those two had ever met there would have been teeth, flying hooves and blood. I wondered what had become of my father's stallion and though it was a small thing I hoped my uncle the traitor had suffered the worst of Malo's black temper through the years.

Behind us marched just short of a hundred spearmen. It was an impressive force and in truth Arthur had left only old men and beard-less boys to man Camelot's walls, not that our enemies would know that. And not that our enemies would be foolish enough to attack up Camelot's steep banks and ditches. So Arthur had assured those who came to his hall with creased brows at the prospect of their protector, their lord, leading his warriors out of Camelot.

'And yet the Roman soldiers did,' Guinevere said, drawing eyes. As if there were not already eyes on her. 'When the legions came to Brit-ain they took this hill and butchered every man, woman and child who lived here. Merlin will tell you.'

'Where is Merlin?' Bedwyr asked, but no one could answer him, not even Arthur.

'Just like him to be gone when it might be useful to know the auguries,' Cai said with a wry grin. The druid would disappear, some-times for weeks at a time, then his voice would announce him in some dark corner and you would wonder if he had in fact been there all along.

Guinevere's dark eyes shone like flint shards. 'I was a little girl but I remember my father telling me that this hill ran with blood,' she said, unafraid to speak her mind in a room full of battle-scarred men.

The hall fell silent when she spoke. Her words *were* ominous, and I sensed folk's macabre thrill as they imagined our hill running with blood. But Guinevere could have been talking about the best willow woods near Camelot for harvesting withies and even the mice in the floor reeds would have ceased their scrabbling.

What wife wants her husband to ride to war? But Arthur had already made up his mind, for all that his brow darkened at Guinevere's tale.

Perhaps he wondered why Lord Leodegan had told such a story to a little girl.

'Saxons want booty and ale,' Gawain announced, his gruff voice like rusty shears cutting the invisible threads by which Guinevere held those gathered in her husband's hall. Her hall, too.

'And they want women,' he added, then glanced at Guinevere, though if a blush of red came to his cheeks, Guinevere's remained pale as marble. 'The Roman general who sent his men up this hill wanted more,' he said, and I saw men and women flinch under his gaze. 'He craved a power that would make the Pendragon's dominion in Britain look like a game between children. He wanted immortality, and to achieve this he made sure that his men were more afraid of him than they were of our forebears who waited for them up here on this hill.'

'We don't have the spears to man two walls, let alone four,' a man with long white moustaches said. Old as he was, he looked gnarly and experienced. A man who could still cause mischief with a spear.

'The banks are higher now. The ditches deeper, the walls stronger. You or I wouldn't lead men up this hill, Tudual,' Ector said. Arthur had given Ector command of Camelot in his absence. It had occurred to Arthur, or perhaps Gawain or one of his other men had whispered in his ear, that Ector was getting too stiff of limb, too short of breath, to be sleeping beneath the winter stars and riding spearmen down next day.

Arthur turned to Ector now. 'Any trouble, you light the fires,' Arthur said.

Ector nodded. 'You're the one who'll be causing the trouble, Arthur,' he said. 'I just wish I was coming with you.'

'I need you here, Ector,' Arthur said, and Ector made a convincing show of looking disappointed, though both men knew the game they played. Ector's reward for his long and faithful service was for Arthur to publicly command him to stay behind and defend Camelot from the comfort of his own chair by the hearth.

But we had felt like lords of war riding out, our bear shields freshly painted, our spear blades gleaming dully in the grey day and our horses' boiled leather shaffrons and breastplates cleaned and rubbed with beeswax so that they looked like polished oak.

Tormaigh had not cared for the armour, which I had made him wear as I got to know him, riding up and down the practice yard at the foot of the northern slope, impaling and hacking straw targets with spear and sword. He did not seem to mind the hide and ringmail coat which protected his flanks, but the head protection he could not abide and would toss his head and try to bite at the leather. He would even rub the shaffron against the wall of his stall when I left it on to get him used to it. And yet when we rode out through the south-west gate to the muffled sobbing of women and the excited chatter of children who strode beside us, as if they too were off to war, Tormaigh was rightly proud of his accoutrements.

'He is Achilles in horse form,' Arthur had told me when he gave me Tormaigh. 'A fighter like you, Lancelot. And young like you.' His smile had been as broad as I had ever seen it, for he was pleased with his gift, though surely not as pleased as I was. Most of Arthur's men rode mares or geldings because they are less given to ill temperament and more governable than stallions. Nor would it be sensible to have an equal number of mares and stallions in his stables for the chaos that would ensue when the mares were on heat. But Arthur had liked Tormaigh, given to him as a colt by Lord Leodegan as part of Guinevere's dowry, and thought the horse and I were a good match.

If I'd known that before he gave me the horse, about the dowry, I might have hated the stallion, or even contrived some reason to refuse the gift. But it was too late now. I had fallen in love with Tormaigh and the stallion tolerated me.

'It takes most of them a summer to get used to the noise and the armour, the iron shoes and the chaos of the melee,' Arthur said, patting Tormaigh's muscled neck where the bulging veins were beginning to get lost beneath his winter coat. 'But war is in this one's blood.'

On the fourth day out of Camelot, when Bors called out to draw our eyes to black smoke in the grey sky, I knew we would find out if Arthur was right about Tormaigh.

We could not see the source of the fire, for it lay beyond the swell of a hill to the east, but no one thought it was hearth smoke leaking through roof thatch. It had that sickly yellow tinge you see when the thatch itself is burning. When old wattle and mud walls and wool and other things that should not be on fire *are* on fire.

Following Arthur's lead, we sped to a trot, leaving the spearmen behind under the command of a huge warrior called Geraint, whom I had never seen sit a horse, perhaps because no horse would willingly endure such a burden. And when we came over the hill's crest we saw our first Saxons. There were forty-six of them and they were on foot, though they had some draught animals with them, including a pair of oxen hauling a cart which swayed, creaking beneath the weight of plunder piled on it.

The round they left behind was a slaughter yard. A section of palisade had been torn down and that was where most of the unmoving bodies were. From the high ground we could see, even through the smoke from the two buildings which the Saxons had torched, the dead lying where they had fallen. Mutilated and despoiled. Still and pale against the mud, like wind-scattered leaves.

Those dead were not our countrymen. We were deep into Caer Gwinntguic and so those slaughtered folk had bent their knee to King Deroch. But to look at Arthur anyone would have thought he was gazing at the corpses of men and women he had known, folk with whom he had eaten and drunk and danced. And now the sight of them, and of the fire and destruction wrought by Saxon hands, fanned the forge that was Arthur's great heart into flames.

'Kill them!' he roared. 'Send them lame and sightless and screaming to their gods!' he commanded, and we roared our fury from that hill as we kicked our heels and flicked the reins and rode.

The Saxons did not know how to fight us. It seemed some of them didn't want to fight us at all, a group of fifteen or so turning and haring back to the round. Or else they intended to mount a defence in the gap they had torn in the palisade. Whatever, we flew down that slope and thundered across the winter meadow, Arthur's silken dragon wind banner streaming from Cai's spear blade which pointed at the leaden sky.

'We'd never have done this had we stayed on Karrek,' Bors beside me yelled, his eyes wide and wild and his mare already slathering at the bit.

If my cousin looked at me, all he would have seen was a wild grin between the cheek guards of Benesek's helmet. And then the knot of Saxons who had stayed to face us, perhaps rooted by fear, broke apart bit by bit, like a child's sand tower besieged by the incoming tide. They discarded shields and ran for their lives and most of them died never seeing the savage joy in our faces.

I took a Saxon square between his shoulder blades, pulling my spear free of his flesh before his dead weight could wrench it from my grip. I saw Arthur ride a man down and spear another Saxon in his open mouth as the man turned to face his doom. Beside him Mordred, dressed in scale armour like his father, turned this way and that, looking for his kill but not finding it. Arthur had ordered Mordred to stay close to him, but the enemy fled from Arthur like rabbits from a swooping hawk and Mordred was enraged, so eager was the young man to prove himself in front of his father.

I saw Bors miss the man he had gone for but bring his spear across to his left and with incredible strength swing it to slash open the neck of a Saxon who stood with a battle axe, roaring defiance. Bors rode on and I left my spear in a Saxon's belly and drew Boar's Tusk, which was really too short for such work. Not that there was much work left to do. All around me Saxons shrieked and tried to flee and died.

I hauled Tormaigh round, looking for a man to kill. I saw Gawain hack his big sword down and lop off an arm, the stump spurting crimson. I saw Bedwyr spear two men and trample a third, and I saw Cai cleave a Saxon's shield with his sword, then split the man's skull, all the while holding Arthur's silken wind banner aloft on his spear.

Arthur had told us to send these Saxons shrieking to their gods, but our enemies must have thought *we* were gods, riding strange, leather-skinned beasts.

In reality they had little time to think. For a moment it had seemed they would stand, some of them at least, and show us their shields and spear points. But the sight of sixty armoured fiends thundering towards them out of the grey day had stripped them of resolve. The vision of Arthur in his bronze scale armour, his red cloak and plume trailing behind him, his face enclosed in iron and silver and gold, had shredded their courage and cast it away like the mud clods flung from our horses' hooves.

They died badly, those men from across the Morimaru, and I daresay they went to the afterlife as pathetic and wailing as Arthur had intended, yet even he could take little joy in their slaughter.

It was just too easy.

I killed one more man before Arthur called a halt to the day's butchery. He looked my age, though unlike me he had managed to grow a beard. A thin beard it was, but he was proud enough of it to have a square-headed little iron hammer amulet tied into the end, a dedication to the Saxon thunder god Thunor, who bore more similarities than just his name to our own Taranis.

This young Saxon had been one of those men who made it into the round while we massacred their brethren. These fifteen men formed a shieldwall across the breach they had torn in the enclosure earlier that day before they had made their own slaughter of its people. And we had dismounted because we knew our horses would see that unmoving shieldwall and think it was a part of the palisade and so would not be compelled to charge it.

'Prisoners, Arthur?' Parcefal asked.

Arthur was still the war god in bronze, silver, gold and iron, and he roared at Parcefal that there would be no prisoners.

'Why should these men live when they ran, leaving their brothers to die?' Arthur asked. 'Do cowards deserve to live?'

Men agreed that they did not, though who was to say these fifteen men had not made a tactical decision to run back to the settlement? That they had not always intended to make a proper fight of it from a more advantageous position than their companions, who had frozen in fear then broken in panic?

Not that Arthur was in the mood to consider this possibility. Not with those poor folk of Caer Gwinntguic lying ripped in the mud. And not with his own blood still running hot in his veins.

Arthur told his older, more experienced men to hold the horses, then turned to the rest of us. 'Shieldwall!' he yelled and only needed to give the command once. We moved with well-practised efficiency until thirty-six of us stood shoulder to shoulder in two rows, our shields overlapping so that we each had the added protection of our neighbour's shield. We in the first row had swords or long knives in our right hands. Our task, to hold our rampart of shields steady and strong and stab at shoulders or bellies, or, if we could, lean into our shields from the crouch and thrust our blades up into men's groins or thighs.

The men behind us gripped spears, ready to thrust them between us into enemy faces. They would do most of the killing and maiming while we shoved and strained and sweated.

'We push them back from the palisade and they'll die fast,' Bors said, and I knew he was right. It had taken all of the Saxons to fill the gap, so that their shieldwall was just one man deep, whilst ours was two deep and could be four or five if Arthur gave the command. But he would not need to, for we would push the Saxons back and once inside the round we would overwhelm them and it would be soon over.

'Make way,' a creaking voice said. 'Make way at the front,' and Mordred shouldered his way into the shieldwall. Arthur must have given his permission, not wanting Mordred to feel the shame of ending this day with his blades still bright and clean. He came into position on my left and I told him to keep the rim of his shield kissing my shield boss and to keep his chin down. His eyes were round and his knuckles bone-white on his sword grip but he did not seem afraid, and I admired him for choosing to stand in the first row and he but sixteen years old. Never say that Mordred ap Arthur lacked courage.

The few grim-faced Saxons in the breach were thumping their sword hilts against their shields in a resigned rhythm that might as well have been their hearts marking out their last beats.

I looked over my shoulder and locked eyes with Arthur. He gave an almost imperceptible nod and I knew what he wanted from me and so I turned back to face those men who had thought to maraud through Caer Gwinntguic and perhaps even Dumnonia after that.

Those doomed men.

'Forward!' I yelled, pointing Boar's Tusk at the Saxon shieldwall. I had never been in a shieldwall fight, though we had practised them often, and nor would this be the kind that bards sing of, but Arthur wanted me to lead his men and so I would.

'Heads down, shields tight,' I told the young men around me. Bors was on my right, Mordred on my left, and we all moved forward as one.

Five paces.

'For Dumnonia!' someone in our line shouted.

Three paces.

'For Arthur!' I shouted.

Two paces. The blood in my veins simmering. Then grunts and wood thumping wood and iron shield bosses thudding together and more screams as the spearmen in our second line found unprotected faces and necks, their thirsty spear blades drinking Saxon blood. The man whose shield I slammed my own into was broad and thick-limbed and for a moment he held his ground, growling and frothing at the mouth with effort, fear and hatred. But a spear blade flashed and the man beside him reeled away howling, his face streaming blood, and in that moment I got Boar's Tusk under my shield and under my opponent's shield and thrust it. The big Saxon bellowed and brought his shield down on my arm.

'Take him,' I yelled at Mordred, who drove his own blade into the man's throat, snarling like some beast, his soul gripped by blood lust. And the Saxons broke for the second time that day. Some were already dead and these fell the moment the men either side stepped backwards. Others threw themselves at us and died well, defying us, cursing us in their tongue as the life left their bodies. The rest, some nine men, retreated back into the settlement and I told our men to hold, wanting Arthur to confirm that he did not want any prisoners. Neither did I want one of the Saxons landing a killing blow on one of our men when all we had to do was take our time and surround them three or four to a man and make sure the job was done properly.

But Mordred had other ideas. Ignoring my command, he strode forward and one of the Saxons must have thought he would kill at least one more Briton before he came to the afterlife, for he stepped up to meet Mordred, spitting onto the mud and thumping his sword against the inside of his shield in readiness to fight.

'Mordred!' I yelled. 'Back. Get back.'

'Let him be, Lancelot,' Arthur called, urging Llamrei to walk across the threshold into the round. Arthur's face was ashen. His son had so recently returned to him but now there was every chance he would die beneath this dangerous-looking Saxon's sword. And yet Arthur could not, or rather would not, embarrass Mordred in front of the men by forbidding him to fight.

The other Saxons did not need to speak our language to know what was happening and they stepped back to give the two men room, muttering encouragement to their spear-brother, who might give them one last good memory to take with them to the hereafter.

The Saxon facing Mordred thrust his sword into the mud – he knew he would never have to clean or repair it again – then lifted the iron hammer which was plaited into the end of his fair beard and touched the amulet to his lips, whispering words I could not hear.

Shining in the bronze scale armour which had been a gift from Arthur, Mordred looked over his shoulder as though he sought encouragement. Arthur said nothing but Gawain growled at him to gut the Saxon son of a sow. Mordred nodded, managed a grin, then turned and stalked towards the Saxon, who had pulled his sword from the earth and waited. Perhaps he had been dedicating his own inevitable death to his gods, or perhaps he had beseeched his ancestors to fill a horn of mead for him in Woden's hall, for such was his people's belief: that the afterlife was one never-ending feast.

Mordred attacked first and by the gods he was fast. Strong too, given that he yet had some growing to do, and he hammered his sword down onto the Saxon's shield, forehand and backhand, blow after savage blow. But the Saxon took those hammer blows, always moving, using his knees to pivot his body away from Mordred and thus lessening the impact of the blows whilst saving the strength in his shield arm.

'He's wild,' Bors beside me said of Mordred.

'But the Saxon is clever,' I said, because while Mordred was trying to batter the man into the next life, the Saxon was learning his opponent's strengths and weaknesses. Weaknesses such as Mordred's tendency to drop his shield wide to the left when making a downward cut; poor form which Mordred might correct, or at least learn to hide, given more experience. If he lived through this.

The Saxon caught another blow on his shield and deflected it wide, then made a cut at Mordred's legs and I winced but the greave on Mordred's right shin took the blow. Yet it was obvious why the Saxon had tried that cut, for another of Mordred's bad habits was to drop his shield to protect his legs, rather than lifting his leading leg up behind his shield. Mordred had struck a score of blows but landed not one of them, while his enemy had made just three half-hearted attacks. And yet the Saxon now knew how to win. I knew how he would win, too, and so did Arthur, who I noticed was touching the iron ring of Llamrei's brow band for luck.

'Keep that shield up, lad,' Bedwyr called to Mordred, whose face was streaming sweat now, which was not surprising given the weight of all that scale armour. On horseback that armour made you feel like a god, but on foot it sapped your strength terribly.

'Lad's got courage,' Cai on my left said, the long wind banner hanging limply from his spear, the dragon's eye watching Mordred fight.

'Courage isn't enough,' Bedwyr said under his breath.

Mordred launched a flurry of blows and took a piece off the Saxon's shield, but the bulk of it held and Mordred paced backwards, dragging his sword arm across his sweat-glossed head and panting for breath. Now the Saxon, who had ignored his countrymen's shouts to attack, saw that his moment had come. He moved fast, flying at Mordred and taking Arthur's son by surprise with his sudden vigour. In desperation Mordred parried twice with his sword and once with his shield and then scythed his sword at the Saxon's face, but the Saxon bent back like a linden sapling, then dropped to make a low cut. Down came Mordred's shield but the cut was a feint, and as the Saxon's legs straightened he swept his sword backhanded at Mordred's face and there was no shield to stop it.

Mordred turned his head and the blow struck his helmet's left cheek guard, cutting it in two and sending Mordred spinning to land in the mud. The Saxons cheered as the young man with the Thunor's hammer knotted in his beard ran forward to finish Mordred where he lay dazed.

'Mordred!' Arthur yelled.

The red snake banner flew through the grey day and the spear it clung to took the Saxon mid run through the neck, so that he staggered wide of Mordred and fell on his side, the spear shaft pointing at the leaden sky.

'Balor's breath, Lancelot,' Cai said, his arm still outstretched as though waiting for someone to return the wind-banner spear to his hand.

'Kill them!' Arthur roared, kicking Llamrei forward and swinging his sword. Thus did the Saxons die in a welter of blood.

It was over before the young Saxon with the iron hammer in his beard finished choking to death in the mud. But when it was over, Mordred flew at me.

'Peace, Mordred,' Bors said, stepping between us, but Mordred tried to get around him and it took Bedwyr to help Bors keep him off me.

'What did you do?' Mordred spat, wild eyes accusing me. Blood ran down his left cheek, dripping from his chin. 'What did you do, Lancelot?'

'You'd had the wits knocked out of your skull, lad,' Bedwyr said. 'You'd be dead now if not for Lancelot.'

'You lie,' Mordred accused Bedwyr. 'Get your hands off me.'

Bors and Bedwyr kept hold of him.

'You're clumsy, Mordred,' I said. 'The Saxon played you.'

'Lies!' Mordred spat again. 'I would have beaten him. You had no right. You cheated me of my kill. You cheated me.'

And perhaps I had. Only the gods can say. But I had thought that Saxon would stave in Mordred's skull. That Arthur would watch his boy be butchered in the mud. And so I had snatched Cai's spear and cast it and the Saxon had died. But now Mordred was furious.

'Peace, Mordred,' Arthur said, striding over, gesturing at Bors and Bedwyr to release the young man. 'Peace, my son,' he said. 'Lancelot acted nobly. On my word. Come now, let us see to that wound.'

Mordred glowered at me, blood dripping still, then let Arthur send him off with a man named Gofan who was skilled in the treatment of cuts.

'So, no prisoners?' Geraint said, having led the remainder of Arthur's spearmen into the round to see the extent of our massacre for themselves.

'No prisoners,' Gawain admitted, using a swath of wool ripped from a dead Saxon to clean the gore off his sword.

We looked around. The victory was complete but we had left no Saxons alive to carry word of Arthur and his horses back to sow fear among their people. Still, we had made a great slaughter and lost just one man, killed by a Saxon spear after his mare had thrown him, though several others and two of the horses had taken wounds.

And yet we had been too late to save the people of that settlement, and it was a chilling thought that Saxon war bands were free to kill and burn this far west with King Deroch unable to stop them. No doubt we would learn more when we rode to the king's fort of Venta Belgarum.

I had cut the little iron hammer amulet from the young Saxon's beard and was examining it when Bors came over to get a closer look. I had not wanted the Saxon's war gear, which was mine by right. Not because I thought Mordred wanted it, or because he might resent me even more for taking it, but because I had not fought the Saxon. I had killed him but I had not fought him. Perhaps I had acted dishonourably by interfering in a fight that was none of my business. But I liked that little iron hammer and decided to keep it, and now I handed it to Bors, who held it up between finger and thumb.

'Benesek could not have made that throw,' he said.

'He could have made it with his eyes closed,' I said, watching Cai pull his spear free of the dead Saxon. There was blood on the dragon banner but it would not show against the red silk when it dried.

Seeing Arthur walking towards me, Bors gave the little hammer back and slapped my shoulder before walking off to join the others looting the enemy corpses. Even without the helmet enclosing his face, to look at Arthur I could not guess if he was angry or pleased.

'He fought well,' I said and meant it. I had seen enough of Mordred to know that the heads which he'd brought to Camelot tied to his saddle had been taken from men killed by his own hand.

'He's reckless,' Arthur said, 'and gives himself away. He lacks experience.' Then he gave a half-smile. 'But he does not lack courage.'

'He does not,' I agreed.

Arthur turned his face and let his gaze linger on the Saxon who had so nearly killed his son. The young man had been stripped and left half naked. Soon the crows would come. Wolves too.

'If my cousin still lives, we cannot afford to lose men fighting him,' Arthur said.

This took me aback. 'You would make peace with Lord Constantine?' I asked.

Arthur looked back to me. 'Look how close the Saxons are to Dumnonia, Lancelot,' he said. He was right, of course. The men we had killed were just one band of raiders. There were doubtless more such bands and Arthur knew that he did not have enough men to be in several places at once. 'We will need Constantine,' he said. 'If he lives. And if he will accept my leadership.'

I frowned, reluctant to accept the truth he spoke.

Then Arthur took hold of my shoulders and when he looked into my eyes Arthur the Prince of Dumnonia and lord of war was gone. In his place was Arthur the man. The father who had been complicit in the attempted murder of his son and who had lived with that guilt ever since.

'Thank you, my friend,' he said.

I did not know what to say and so mumbled something about us having to teach Mordred to lift his leading leg behind his shield. Arthur nodded, still holding my eye.

'Thank you,' he said.

Then he went to help Gofan treat our wounded.

21

A Storm of Blades

THE WEATHER WAS FOUL when we came to Venta Belgarum. Freezing rain flayed Caer Gwinntguic and a thin wind, thin as a blade, cut through wet clothes into our raw flesh and the bones beneath. We rode round-shouldered, heads pulled in, rain spilling from helmet rims and dripping from sodden cloaks, our hands on the reins blue and numb from cold.

Worse than this, when the walls of the old Roman town came into view, we saw no sign of Aella's main army, which we had been told was encamped to the west of Venta Belgarum.

Above the town, smoke from hearth fires shredded on the wind. We could just make out the figures of spearmen on the ramparts peering westward through the foul day. But between them and us, where we had expected to see a great swathe of tents and Saxons and smouldering fires hissing sullenly against the rain, we saw nothing.

'Aella has withdrawn,' Bedwyr said, spitting from the saddle in disgust. Rain sheeted from his helmet and dripped from his beard.

'No, Bedwyr,' Arthur said, his keen eyes taking in the great ruins of Roman buildings and those parts of the outer wall which had fallen long ago or been robbed for its stone and replaced since with wooden stakes. 'He's taken it,' he said, meaning that Aella had taken Venta Belgarum.

'How do you know?' Gawain asked.

'Because if you were King Deroch, would you have let us venture this close without sending riders?' Arthur said, sweeping an arm behind him towards the mass of spearmen who had formed on a ridge of high ground, their bear shields announcing that Arthur had come.

'No,' Gawain admitted. 'I'd be scolding you for bringing an army into my kingdom without my invitation. Then I'd make you pay your respects, you being a mere prince, and after all that I'd be thanking you for coming to save my royal arse.' Gawain winked at me.

'So, if Aella has taken Venta Belgarum, then where in Balor's ball-bag is King Deroch?' Bedwyr asked, still looking aggrieved at being cheated of a fight.

'And where is Lord Constantine?' Parcefal asked.

But not even Arthur could answer that.

'What do we do now?' I asked Arthur. I was clenching and unclenching my hands to get some life back into them. It was just as well we weren't going to fight that day, for I couldn't have been sure my numb fingers would be able to grip sword hilt or spear.

Arthur was still looking at the old Roman town, perhaps admiring the workmanship of the buildings which yet stood, as much as he was wondering what had happened to the king of Caer Gwinntguic.

'We take it back,' he said.

Arthur's magnificent horses would be of no use in the fight to retake Venta Belgarum and Arthur blamed King Deroch for giving up his fort. That was, until the day after we arrived before the walls and the Saxons hauled a man onto the ramparts, barking at us until they had Arthur's attention.

'Don't give them the pleasure,' Gawain said, but Arthur watched anyway as they hauled the prisoner's head back, cut his throat and pushed the body over the wall to land in the mud. We had no intention of putting ourselves in range of arrows and spears just to get a closer look at the corpse, but we did not need to. A tall oaken chair followed the dead man over the wall, landing on its back in the filth beside the man who had used to sit in it when passing judgements on his people. It was King Deroch's high seat and the sight of it lying there in the filth, outside the fort, was as poignant as it was ominous.

I heard Arthur whisper an apology to the corpse lying there, throat cut and paling, or perhaps to the man's ghost, for the King of Caer Gwinntguic had not given the place up as we had thought. He had fought for it and lost and now he was carrion, so it was up to us to take Venta Belgarum back, war horses or no, or else invite yet more Saxons to stalk Dumnonia's eastern border like wolves edging the herd.

'We'll do it at night,' Arthur said, 'before the new moon.' His face in that enclosed helmet was grim in the dusk and I knew he burned to avenge the Saxons' ill treatment of a king of Britain.

'The Saxons are in a foreign land,' Merlin added. The druid had reappeared the night before we rode out of Camelot and now took his accustomed place among Arthur's war council. 'A land of unknown gods.'

We had gathered around the great stump of an ancient oak which must have been an awe-inspiring sight for hundreds of years, until age or storm or man had laid it low. Merlin had etched a triskele on the stump, like the one on his hand, the triple spiral lit now by a lamp horn which cast its glow on the faces of Arthur's most trusted. Men such as Gawain and Bedwyr, Cai, Parcefal, Gofan and Mordred.

'Our enemies find themselves in a land stalked by unfamiliar spirits. By terrors that come in the night,' the druid said, his eyes shining by the lamplight.

'And by men who know how to kill Saxons,' Parcefal said, grinning as others agreed with that.

That night, the moon was waning crescent, its glow seeping through breeze-swayed boughs, so we would not have to wait long, though a day or two was all to the good, because Merlin needed some time to make his own preparations. And three nights later, when the sky was black and the air was cold and so still that the smoke from our fires just hung amongst us in veils, we attacked Venta Belgarum.

We did not try to surprise the enemy. On the contrary, we told them we were coming. We did not tell them in their own language or even in ours, but we told them.

When Merlin had a score of Arthur's horsemen ride out to the nearest rounds which had not yet fallen prey to Saxon war bands, and bring women back to our camp, there were whispers of some dark blood ritual. Some said the druid intended to sacrifice the women to win the favour of Balor, god of death. But the fifty or so women came willingly enough, it seemed to me. Besides which, I knew Arthur would not agree to any such sacrifice of innocents, not even to win over a god.

Now, as I stood in my war finery preparing to lead men through the darkness, I understood why Merlin had brought women to Venta Belgarum. The druid positioned them in a loose ring facing the palisade but beyond spear range. I could not see them, and neither could the Saxons, but we could all hear them, wailing and moaning in the darkness. It was an eerie sound, like that of seals keening on some offshore spit of rock, or even like the lament of so many tortured souls.

With this strange moaning rising in the night like a wind which could not be felt on the skin, Arthur gave the order for forty men on heavy, armoured horses to ride up and down along the palisade. These men were taking a risk, being so close, but the darkness was itself armour and I did not hear of any being struck by arrows or spears. Back and forth they galloped, the noise of the hooves like thunder rising from the earth. Added to this, sixty of our spearmen stood scattered around the fort in knots of five, all singing the Slaughter Song of Taranis, master of war, and thumping their spears against their shields in time with each other.

Arthur and Merlin's aim was to put terror in Saxon bellies and I daresay they did just that. Even Bors beside me was tight-jawed and heavy-browed, and though part of that must have been pre-battle nerves, I knew the weird cacophony chilled his blood as it did my own.

Yet even with so many trying to sow dread and doubt in Saxon hearts and make them fear the darkness of the land they coveted, there were some fifty of us who were as quiet as King Deroch's corpse, which still lay beside his high seat in the mud.

Thirty, including Mordred, Gawain and Bedwyr, waited with Arthur in the shadows by the main southern gate. Twenty, including myself, Bors and Gofan, waited under Parcefal's command beyond the eastern palisade on the fortress's far side. We waited for Cai, who was with a small group of spearmen by the western wall, to blow his blast horn, at which moment we would turn the black night red.

We stood with our cloaks wrapped round us, even though there was no moonlight and it was too cloudy for glint from blades, strapends or helmets. In that silence, each of us was alone with our own thoughts. And so I ached for Cai to give the signal.

When it came, Bors and I looked at each other unsure, and I saw the whites of other eyes around me as men strained their ears. With the women's wailing, the galloping horses, the spearmen singing and the drumming of spear shafts on limewood shields, I could not be certain that the sound I'd heard was Cai's horn.

'Listen,' Parcefal said, his head cocked towards the west, and there might have been another drone amongst the eerie chaos, but it did not matter because the next thing we knew there was fire in the night. We saw it as a glow above the town walls in the west and I knew that Cai's men were hurling faggots of burning wood across the ditch to land against the wooden enclosure. We heard the Saxons yelling, heard their own war horns bellowing as their spearmen rushed to deal with the threat of fire and spears. And so we ran, hunched and bent, spears held low, towards the section of stone wall on the east.

For Merlin's women and Arthur's horses were not only sowing chaos to grow fear in our enemies' hearts. They were soaking the night with noise and strangeness so that in the confusion the Saxons would not know from where our attack came. They saw our spearmen flinging bundles of sticks soaked in pitch at the western palisade and they saw Arthur's warriors gathering at the south gate, shields raised, teeth bared, blades and eyes glinting by flamelight. And perhaps the western palisade would burn and our men would kick aside the flame-eaten timbers and there would be a great slaughter in that gap. Or perhaps Arthur would somehow breach the main gate. But we twenty were the real threat.

The Saxons were no fools. They might have suspected that the fire was a diversion, and no doubt they kept warriors at the ramparts all around the town; men peering into the dark, hands tight as knots on spear shafts, some of them perhaps beginning to wish they had never left their homelands across the grey sea.

Even so, it was only natural that they would be more protective of the wooden stake sections of wall than those of Roman stone that still stood. They would fear axes hacking through the palisade. Fear ropes hauling the stakes down into the ditch.

Which was why we were running up ladders set against a section of that Roman wall which Arthur so admired.

Parcefal went up first, disappearing over the top of the wall without a cry of alarm sounding on our section. I was next and I waited four rungs from the summit, my spear in one hand, my shield slung across my back.

I heard a grunt followed by the *crump* of a body hitting the stone and three long heartbeats later I saw Parcefal's horribly scarred face leering down at me. Up I went, Bors behind me, and we were down the earthen bank and deep into the town before the first Saxons saw us.

'Keep going,' Parcefal roared in reply to the harsh cries which told us there was no need for stealth now, and we ran for the southern gate beyond which Arthur waited with thirty men. Two Saxons appeared in front of us, wide-eyed and doomed. Parcefal swept his spear across, ripping out the first Saxon's throat, and I leapt, thrusting my spear over the other man's shield through mail and leather into his chest.

A spear streaked out of the dark and I batted it aside with my shield without breaking stride. I heard an arrow *tonk* off a shield boss and Bors laughed and we ran through the shadows like wraiths on Samhain.

Even with more Saxons hurrying towards the fire glow at the western wall there were still two dozen Saxons guarding the south gate. But when they saw us running towards them these men must have been struck by the terrifying prospect that we had already taken the town, for some of them turned and scrambled up the earthen ramparts, instinct driving them to higher ground. The remaining men were too late to lock shields and we were amongst them, stabbing and cutting with savage efficiency. We knew that we had only moments to kill them and open the gates. Because if our enemy rallied, we would die in the flame-gilded darkness and the Saxons would hold Venta Belgarum.

Parcefal was a great fighter, strong and fierce, while Gofan was fast and precise, but both were deadly. As for myself, the Saxons seemed slow and cumbersome against my spear. They fell for my feints and they swung wildly and they died and went to their ancestors one after another.

I was killing while Bors and three others were lifting the thick beam out of the brackets, trusting the rest of us to keep the Saxons off them. A man beside me staggered backwards, clutching the spear in his chest which had been thrown by a Saxon above us on the bank.

'Get it open!' Parcefal roared, taking an axe on his shield before thrusting his sword into a bearded face. The Saxon dropped. 'Get it open now!'

A loud creaking announced the opening of those big gates and the first face I saw was Arthur's, his wolf grin lit by flamelight. He and his thirty men poured through the gap, some of them helping us to kill the remaining defenders while others formed a shieldwall facing into the town.

'Up there,' I said to Arthur, pointing my spear at those Saxons atop the ramparts who were still a threat, lobbing stones and spears down at us.

'Leave it to me,' Bedwyr said, and led a knot of men up the bank to claim the high ground and secure the gate so that more of our spearmen could come through unopposed.

'Here they come,' Gawain called to us over his shoulder. He stood in the middle of the growing shieldwall beyond which the Saxons swarmed in the dark, coming from all parts of the town now they knew that the battle was here, at the south gate.

There was another fight going on, at the western palisade where the fire had caught and our men had pulled down enough stakes to make a breach. But most of Arthur's army was here.

'If they make a decent wall we won't be able to hold them,' a man beside me said. 'Not if Aella has all his people here.'

'We're not going to hold them,' Arthur said, 'we're going to kill them.' He turned to me, the scales of his armour shining red, the red plume trailing from his helmet just as the white one hung from my own. 'Lancelot, see there by the smithy,' he said, pointing Excalibur to the left of the growing Saxon horde. I saw a huge man swathed in furs, his beard braided into a rope thick enough to use as an ox halter. He carried a long axe whose massive crescent head silently promised mutilation and death. 'That must be King Aella,' Arthur said.

I nodded. Even in the darkness I could see that the best-armed Saxons, the ones in mail and helmets and carrying swords, were gathered around that giant of a man, whose arms bore warrior rings and whose face was broad and craggy as a cliff face.

'Can we get to him, Lancelot?' Arthur asked. I knew what Arthur was thinking. If we could kill Aella quickly, before the Saxons built their enormous shieldwall, we might break their resolve and win. For a king is a gift-giver, a bestower of silver, but only if he is alive. If a warrior is not going to earn silver because his lord is dead, he is more likely to seek the next best thing: survival.

I held my own lord's eye and nodded, even so feeling the worm of doubt squirm in my stomach. I did not care for silver. Maybe there were plenty of men like me, who revelled not in riches and rewards but in war itself. Men who would fight over Aella's body until they won or were themselves cut down.

Only one way to know.

'Kill Aella!' Arthur said.

'Kill Aella!' Mordred echoed, shining in scales like his father, his sword dark with gore.

I ran at the Saxon king. Others ran with me. I could sense them at my back, one of them almost on my shoulder, yet even had they stood rooted to the earth like oaks I would have gone for Aella.

The Saxons had not expected us to attack. They were still building their shieldwall, preparing for that hot, stinking, shoving match in which blades come at you unseen; the scramasax beneath the shield into the groin. The spear blade in the eye as a man risks a glance over his shield rim. Now a knot of them tried to close round their king, raising shields to me and coming forward as one.

Boar's Tusk in my right hand, I spun the spear shaft in my left and thrust the butt end against the bottom half of a man's shield, tilting the whole thing so that suddenly the man's face was there before me, eyes bulging with horror as Boar's Tusk filled his mouth, bursting from his neck.

A Saxon to my left fell back with a grunt and a spray of blood, his sword falling to the mud, and I knew it could not have been Bors who killed him, for Bors could not have kept up with me across that ground. I spun my spear and thrust the blade into a neck while sweeping a spear point aside with Boar's Tusk. And I moved like wind on that still day. I moved without thought, without fear; muscle, sinew and bone so alive in the midst of death as I performed the strikes and parries which over the years had become as natural as breathing.

I stabbed and slashed, spun and dropped low to cut the hamstrings of a young Saxon who screeched in shock. Then I was up and driving towards Aella, who I could see through the press was waiting for me with his huge axe and a grin.

Not yet. Too many men and shields between us. I felt a blade cut the air by my right cheek and I drove my spear down into a warrior's foot, then punched Boar's Tusk into another man's belly, twisting the blade to free it from the sucking flesh, just as Pelleas had taught me so many years ago. A half-breath later it was in another man's throat and blood struck my face, hot and salty, sweet and cloying.

I was strong and fast. The fight around me was the tune but I was the harp and the Saxons' blades could not touch me.

Yet I was not the only one sending those men from across the sea to feast with their grandfathers in Woden's hall. The man who had hit the Saxon line a heartbeat after me was killing and maiming as easily as fire. I snatched glimpses of him, of his iron helmet and his breast-plate of hardened leather, as he drove into the enemy, carving through them, like me, fighting with spear and shield. Like me, cutting a path towards the Saxon king.

There were others with us too now, Bors and Gawain and even Mordred, who fought beside Arthur, the two of them gripped by the battle lust. But this broad-shouldered killer with me was weaving a song for the bards. He was inexorable and relentless. Somehow he had pushed ahead of me, so that as I put a grey-bearded Saxon down, leaving my spear in his belly, I saw that this unknown warrior was now face to face with Aella.

The Saxon king was looping his great axe through the air, that wicked sharp blade sighing its own battle song. I saw the unknown warrior hurl his spear. Saw the Saxon's luck as that spear blade glanced off the axe's long haft and flew harmlessly wide. Then the king stepped forward and, roaring, swung the axe at chest height, and the unknown warrior, having no shield, threw himself at the king to avoid that crescent blade. Yet the haft itself struck him, sending him flying past the king to land in the mud.

I was there. I ducked the king's back swing, reversing my grip and twisting at the waist to bring Boar's Tusk up into the man's wrist, severing his hand, though that hand still gripped the haft which dropped to the ground by the king's feet.

The king bellowed in fury, hoisting the spurting stump to take a closer look at it, as I drove up with my legs and buried Boar's Tusk into the underside of his bearded chin, my momentum pushing the blade up until it lifted the helmet off his head. I let go the sword then, for I knew it would take some work to free it, and the huge warrior's legs gave way and he fell as I pulled my knife, turning to face the men who were surely rushing to avenge their king.

But I knew those men around me. They were my sword-brothers. Each of them sworn to Arthur and now driving on with shields and blades, on like a flood tide, swamping the enemy, calling Arthur's name as they killed.

The Saxons fought on for a while, but word of their leader's death spread like a bloodstain amongst them. Warriors will always look for omens. Even in the midst of battle they look for them, they seek portents that will give them a glimpse of their own likely fate. Seeing their axe-wielding lord cut down before they could make the shield-wall was the blackest of omens and I sensed it clawing at their resolve.

They broke. Not straight away, but soon enough. They died or they ran, and many of those who fled into the darkness lived, but many more were cut down by Arthur's horse warriors who slaughtered them by the light of the flames which had taken hold of the palisade and some of the dwellings inside the town.

When it was over and Venta Belgarum was ours, I sought out the warrior who had fought so well, laying Saxons low with sword and spear work which was as a mirror to my own. I found him with Arthur, who was commending the warrior for his skill and courage, the two of them standing over the Saxon king's body because Arthur would not have it further mutilated by his eager young spearmen.

'Lancelot,' Arthur called to me as I stepped over corpses to reach them, 'this man says he knows you and I believe him, having seen him fight. By the gods, he's another you!'

He didn't kill Aella though, I thought, keeping that petulance to myself. Then the warrior removed his helmet and turned to me and I heard the curse escape my lips, though it was drowned by the roar of nearby flames.

'Lancelot, I would have killed that big lump of dung had you not slunk in to steal my glory.'

'It seemed to me you were telling the worms that I was preparing a feast for them,' I said, at which he managed a sour grin.

We did not shake hands, though if Arthur thought that strange he said nothing, turning to speak with Gawain who had brought him word of some Saxons who had made a stand in woods east of the town.

I should have known when I saw the way he fought. I had faced him myself times beyond counting, but the helmet's cheek pieces had hidden his face and there was neither moon nor starlight, and besides, I had not expected to see him.

But I saw him now and even with my blood still thrumming hot in my veins from the fight, there was a cold undercurrent as I looked at him.

Melwas.

The victory feast celebration shook the timbers of Arthur's hall. The sound of our revelry must have carried from Camelot's summit far and wide into the cold, damp night. Owl, fox, badger and deer must have shuddered at the sound, wide eyes turned towards that great hill looming over forest and field.

Likewise, folk in nearby rounds would have heard the singing and the chanting and the thumping of hands on the boards when men recounted their deeds and triumphs, or when someone lifted his cup towards our lord and evoked booming acclamations of *'Arthur, Arthur, Arthur.'*

And perhaps those folk of Dumnonia raised their own cups towards Camelot and spoke Arthur's name in awe and reverence, because they need not fear the Saxons the way the flock fears the wolf.

We had won back Venta Belgarum and made a great slaughter. While the kings of Britain sat by their hearths and talked of fighting the Saxons come the spring, Arthur had led his winter army and all but driven the enemy from Caer Gwinntguic. For in the days after the butchery within that old Roman town, we had ridden through the land to scour it of Saxon war bands. Some fought us, most surrendered. Those who ran, we killed. Those who surrendered, we disarmed and sent east, though not before taking their right hands so that they could never again wield a blade against us.

'Why not just kill them?' Mordred asked Arthur. He was after more Saxon heads for his collection. Merlin had already begun work on a great fence along Dumnonia's eastern border with Caer Gwinntguic, upon whose stakes he set dozens and dozens of heads taken from the Saxons we had killed. But Mordred wanted more. I could not say which of Merlin or Mordred had the greatest fondness for collecting heads.

'Because dead men cannot spread word of our victory here,' Arthur said patiently.

And it *was* a rare victory. Though the man I had killed was not King Aella. We learnt from the surviving Britons of Venta Belgarum, whose enslavement had not outlasted one moon, that the big, axe-swinging warrior had been King Aella's younger brother, Aebbe.

'They say Aella is bigger,' Bors told me, smiling.

'For his sake I hope he's better with a long axe,' I said.

Yet Aella, who it turned out was in Rhegin settling a dispute between two lesser warlords, must have reeled from the news of what had befallen his brother and so many of his warriors. The Saxon king sued for peace and Arthur, who did not have the spearmen to take the war to Rhegin, which was now firmly in Saxon hands, accepted.

'In the spring we will march again and kings will march with us, Lancelot,' Arthur said, throwing his arm around my shoulder that night when the victory fires blazed and harps and flutes and lusty voices filled the hall from floor reeds to thatch. 'King Masgwid and the men of Elmet,' Arthur said, 'King Cyngen and his men of Powys and the spearmen of Caer Gwinntguic, who crave vengeance for poor Deroch. And perhaps we can even tempt King Meirchion Gul to bring an army from Rheged, and together we will drive Aella back to his ships.'

'And then will you take your rightful place on Dumnonia's high seat?' I asked him.

'We'll see, Lancelot,' he said, drinking of his best red wine, which was all the sweeter for our victory. 'We'll win some more fights and we'll see.' Yet, sweet as the wine was, I lost my taste for it later that night.

Arthur's closest friends and brothers-in-arms thronged his hall for that feast, and Guinevere was there too, looking a queen in all but name, her dark hair tamed, combed straight and imprisoned by a criss-crossing arrangement of delicate gold chains and brightly coloured glass beads. She sat on her husband's left and when Arthur was deep in conversation with Merlin, I saw her watching the young harpist and I wondered if she was remembering herself in the girl's wistful eyes and nimble fingers.

And I wondered if she remembered other things too, or if her past was nothing more than a deep breath taken of a rose then exhaled and lost. Or water running beneath a bridge; once passed, gone for ever.

To my surprise, Melwas was there too. Impressed with his courage and skill, and perhaps thinking that Melwas and I were friends, Arthur had invited him to take his place amongst us. It was a great honour and Melwas revelled in it, feigning embarrassment when Arthur, staggered with drink, re-enacted Melwas's charge for the benefit of those who had not seen it. He all but danced through the throng, cutting down imaginary foes with cup and fleshy bone, eliciting cheers and gestures which saw the rushes soaked with wine and ale.

'I served the Lady Nimue of Karrek Loos yn Koos, my lords,' Melwas explained to Gawain, Bedwyr, Parcefal and the rest, 'but when word reached us that you were taking the war to the Saxons, I had to come. Taranis spoke Lord Arthur's name to me in a thunder clap and I knew I must come.'

Merlin's eyebrow hitched at that. 'And Lady Nimue did not mind your leaving?' the druid asked him. 'I am sure it is a loss to the Guardians of the Mount. A fighter of your skill.'

Melwas turned to Arthur. 'I came with the Lady's blessing, lord,' he said, 'and she sends you her compliments.'

Lies. Melwas had absconded. I knew it. Bors knew it. Having lost myself and Bors to Arthur, the Lady would never have allowed Melwas to leave too. With Benesek injured, Melwas would be invaluable, as a Guardian in his own right and as the leader of the younger men, who would still look to him as they always had.

'What need has Lady Nimue of young warriors?' old Ector asked us all, dismissing the very idea with a flap of his hand.

'Well, we are glad to have you, Melwas,' Arthur said. 'And I am sure you, Lancelot and Bors must have much to talk about.'

The three of us nodded at each other across the table. In truth, our ancient quarrels seemed petty things there in that golden hall, after the butchery of Venta Belgarum and in the face of Arthur's dream to remake Britain.

'Pelleas taught you all well, I'll say that for him,' Ector said. 'He was a rare fighter himself. We could have used him in Gaul.'

'He was the best swordsman I have ever seen,' I said, and Gawain and Bedwyr nodded solemnly, perhaps indulging me, perhaps not.

'It is a pleasure to be with my brothers again,' Melwas said, then turned to Guinevere and raised his cup towards her, 'but it is an honour to see you again, my lady.' He gave his best smile, the one that had ever accompanied his triumphs on Karrek. Broad enough to reach his ears. 'I always knew you would have a golden future.' He moved his eyes to Arthur. 'My lord,' he said, 'Lady Guinevere and Lancelot must have shared with you many stories about their time on the island.'

I looked at Guinevere and she looked at me. The oil lamps might have guttered for the movement of heads in Arthur's direction.

'We were but children,' Bors said, punching my shoulder to wake me from my stupor. 'Those days feel like another life, hey, cousin?'

I nodded.

'Lancelot was a wild little thing when I first met him,' Melwas said. 'He had a hawk, my lord. A vicious, screeching thing she was. You remember, my lady?' he asked.

'Enough of this idle musing, Melwas,' Merlin said, filling his own cup from a wine jug. 'Do you think we wish to hear about your childhood? About every sword stroke you and Lancelot made against some splintered post? Perhaps I should regale this hall with tales of how I went about learning the stories of Britain by heart? Of the twenty years spent mastering the art of divination, of how I can read a man's future in a pile of innards or precisely when mistletoe must be cut if it is to be used to cure barrenness?' He shook his head and drank.

'I'd rather fight a score of Saxons here and now,' Parcefal told Merlin, which had men grunting and murmuring agreement. The druid dipped his head at Melwas as if Parcefal and the others proved his point. But Arthur's eyes lingered on me as he smoothed his neat beard with fingers and thumb. It was just a moment. Three heartbeats, no more, yet long enough.

Bors banged his cup against mine, spilling wine across the boards. 'Drink up, cousin. If my skull is going to ache like it's been split with an axe come the morning, I don't see why yours shouldn't too.'

I smiled at Bors, draining my cup, and when I looked back across the table Guinevere was talking to old Ector while Arthur was laughing about something with Cai and Gawain. The hall flooded with noise once again and slaves moved through the smoky fug bearing more platters of roasted meats and jugs of rich red wine. Melwas took hold of a pretty slave girl's wrist and pulled her down onto his lap, and no one seemed to think he was presuming too much for one sitting at Arthur's table for the first time. I did not mind, either. Better that Melwas played the young Achilles and revelled in the strength of his sword arm than stirred things with his flapping tongue.

The drink flowed and men boasted, the bluster of warriors

crowding my ears, shifting hearth smoke around the new pale beams above. I watched Arthur laughing and I saw him place his hand on Guinevere's. Saw her curl a thumb over his knuckles, her face still turned to Ector, and told myself that no harm had been done. And perhaps I owed Merlin for that.

But when I ran my eyes over the rest of the room and the faces of those whom Arthur held closest and dearest, I saw that Mordred was watching me.

22

A Gift

BORS GOT HIS WISH and next morning I could have been fooled
into thinking that Aebbe, brother of Aella, had struck my skull a
blow with that great axe of his after all. So blurry was the cold, grey
world to my eyes and so sour my belly that all I could think about
when a boy roused me from sleep was how Arthur managed to spring
up each morning before cock's crow, his eyes bright even if his beard
and hair were wild and in need of water and a comb, no matter how
much wine or ale he had seen off the night before.

'Lord Arthur wants to see you,' the boy said, his eyes round as coins.
I knew my reputation had spread on the wings of our victory at Venta
Belgarum. I'd even heard that bards sang of my killing of Aebbe, their
accounts doubtless embroidered like a rich lady's kirtle. No doubt Aebbe
was eight feet tall in their songs and I had slain a score of men to reach
him. Still, I had killed my share and the young messenger sent to drag
me from my bed regarded me as one might a wolf with a bloody snout.

'He is with Llamrei,' the boy said. I swear he had not taken a breath
since coming to the foot of my bed.

I was halfway across the plateau, drinking the cold air like clean
water, by the time I remembered what Melwas had said to Arthur the
previous night and my stomach sank with the recollection. I recalled
the way Arthur had looked at me. Had he seen Guinevere and me look
at each other when Melwas revealed our shared past? Clearly Arthur
had not known, meaning Guinevere must not have told him of her time
on Karrek. Why had she kept it from him? But of course I knew why.

I pulled my cloak tight round my neck against a sudden thin wind
which stabbed from the north and I winced, feeling water seep
through my leather boots. It had rained in the night and the puddles
on Camelot's heights had not yet drained.

And I thought of Mordred, who had been staring at me when all the others had fallen back to the feast. Had he spoken to Melwas?

A horse whinnied and I blinked watery eyes. There were only a few souls up and about their business in the chill dawn. One of them was Arthur, whom I saw when I rounded the corner of his stables, his cheek against Llamrei's as he gently wiped around her eyes with a soft cloth. The mare nickered, enjoying the attention, and Arthur took up a brush and proceeded to work it through Llamrei's tail.

'Sleep well?' he asked, without looking up from his work. Llamrei gleamed even on that dull day, so that I knew Arthur had been a while grooming her.

'Well enough, until I was woken,' I said, rubbing at a crick in my neck. I sensed something and looked round, and to my horror saw that Guinevere was there too.

'Good morning, Lancelot,' she said, looking from me to Arthur, her eyes as full of questions as I had been on the walk from my hut to my lord and lady's hall. She was swathed in a long ermine cloak as white as her skin, and her hair tumbled in all its raven glory and my heart ached in my chest at the sight of her.

'Good morning, my lady,' I managed.

'You want to ride, Lancelot?' Arthur said. I saw his spear leaning against the stable wall. 'The three of us,' he said, then looked up at the sullen clouds which scudded southward. 'I don't think it will rain again.'

'You want to hunt now?' I asked, though I knew that he liked to ride out early, before others were awake. It had saved his life that dawn at Tintagel when his cousin Constantine had tried to carve himself a kingdom with treachery and steel.

'Why not?' Arthur said, giving Llamrei's hip a gentle pat. 'There's a bite in the air but the thrill of spying some worthy prey will warm the blood.' His spear had a crosspiece below the blade to stop an enraged boar driving its pierced body further down the shaft to attack its killer before dying. 'It's the best practice for killing Saxons,' he said. 'Or we could ride east to Merlin's fence. See if Aella's men have dared to pull it down, or if they've had their own wizards counter Merlin's magic in some way.' He looked up at Guinevere as he pulled Llamrei's long tail hairs from the brush. 'Guinevere doesn't mind the cold, do you, dear? Though I wonder if Merlin's rotting heads might be a bit much so early in the day.'

Guinevere pulled the ermine cloak a little tighter round her shoulders and lifted her eyes to me as Arthur began brushing Llamrei's mane.

'Perhaps you know better than I, Lancelot?' Arthur suggested.

'Know what?' I asked, looking from Guinevere to Arthur. I knew what he was getting at, even with my head pounding and my belly sour with last night's wine.

'You must know Guinevere well. If memory serves, the island of Karrek Loos yn Koos is not much bigger than this hill.' He pulled the stiff bristles through a knot and Llamrei tossed her head in complaint. 'Shhh, there, girl. Nearly done,' he soothed.

'The boys and girls were kept apart for the most,' I said, not looking at Guinevere in case Arthur could see my heart through my eyes. Though for all I knew, Guinevere had confessed to Arthur in the night and now I was being tested. 'We spent the days learning our weapons,' I said. I looked at Guinevere then, needing her to deny our friendship or admit it, needing her to say something at least, so that I would know down which path we rode.

'We were friends once, Lancelot and I,' she said. 'When my father's ship brought me to the island, it struck the rocks and broke apart.'

The brush went still in Arthur's hand and he frowned at Guinevere, as if he could not understand why she had never told him this before.

'My nurse drowned along with everyone aboard. I would have drowned too but Lancelot swam out.' Her eyes were on mine now and I wanted to look away, for Arthur's sake, yet I could not. 'I still remember how calm it was below the surface. Away from the storm. But Lancelot found me. He was just a boy.'

'I did what anyone would do, lord,' I said. 'I happened to be on the cliff and saw the ship go down.' The memory of that day was still sharp in my mind.

'So, we both owe you our lives,' Arthur said, and in that moment he seemed to be both grateful and resentful of the fact. He swept the brush through the white mane though it was already smooth as silk. 'I understand why you did not wish to tell me that Lord Leodegan sent you to live on Karrek,' he told Guinevere. 'My mother told me long ago why some girls are sent to Lady Nimue. To learn the herb lore and other . . . secret arts. Though I am surprised Leodegan encouraged you in that regard. He is a Christian now, is he not?'

Guinevere nodded. 'You know that he is,' she said. 'He showed you the temple ruins by the stream where he planned to build a church. He tried to give you one of his priests as part of my dowry.'

Arthur saw my surprise at that and smiled.

'I told Leodegan that we have enough gods already without needing another, but that if his priest could beat Gawain in single combat then I would consider his god worth having on my side,' he said, putting a plain quilted cloth on Llamrei's back and smoothing out the creases. 'The priest and Leodegan both declined the challenge.'

'My father's hall draws Christians like a dog draws fleas,' Guinevere said. 'I was an embarrassment to him. That is why he sent me to the Lady.'

'No, Guinevere,' Arthur said. His face was stern again. He put the brush down on the table which stood by the stable wall and hefted up his saddle, throwing it over his mare's back. 'He gave you to the Lady's keeping because he knew that otherwise some fat old king would come courting with his silver and gold and take you away from him for ever.'

A smile touched Guinevere's lips then. 'So, he was saving me for you?' she asked Arthur. 'Not a king but a prince. A prince who spends all his silver and gold on big horses and soldiers.' She reached out and ran a finger over the crosspiece on Arthur's big boar spear. 'Who is more fond of iron than silver and gold,' she said. 'A man who spends more time at war than in his hall with his new wife?'

'At least I am not fat,' Arthur said. 'And not too old. Not yet,' he added, glancing at me as though he had expected me to challenge his point. He was, after all, more than ten years older than I. Not that he looked it then.

We stood there in silence, Guinevere and I watching Arthur adjust the girth strap. Nearby, a moorhen waded in a puddle, stabbing down now and then, its red beak showing like a drop of blood against its black plumage in the bleak dawn light.

I knew that Arthur wanted me to put his mind at ease. I was his friend, closer to him perhaps even than Gawain, and all he wanted was for me to make a good explanation so that we could enjoy a dawn ride together while Camelot dreamed still.

And yet what could I say? To talk would be to lie, for I could not tell Arthur all of it. For Guinevere's sake and Arthur's sake and my own sake too, I could not.

'What I cannot grasp is why neither of you told me that you knew the other,' Arthur said, securing the breast and breaching straps to keep the saddle firmly in place. 'Mordred has it from your friend Melwas that you were . . . close.'

I might have known Mordred would see a potential ally in Melwas, and that Melwas, the dust of the journey still on his cloak, would waste no time in causing trouble for me.

'And you, Lancelot,' Arthur went on, 'that day we dug the eastern ramparts. I told you of Guinevere. I spoke of Lord Leodegan if I recall. You must have known then but you said nothing. Why?' He stopped his work now and faced me, a look of confusion weighing on his handsome face.

I had to tell him. Otherwise it might stay like a blade in the flesh and go bad. He was my friend.

'When I left, I made Lancelot promise never to tell anyone that I had lived on the island,' Guinevere said before I could speak.

Arthur swung round to her. 'Why?' he asked.

'I have the gift, husband,' Guinevere said. 'I can make my soul leave my body. Sometimes.'

Arthur glanced at me, his eyes questioning if I had known that, too. He knew the answer and looked back to Guinevere.

'The ability is gods-given,' Guinevere said. 'So Merlin says. And Lady Nimue.' She tilted her head slightly and touched her neck and when she took her hand away there were red lines on the white skin. 'I think my father knew that too, for all his new god. And rather than let the Christians beat the talent out of me, for they think it a curse, he sent me to the Lady, knowing that she would help me. She would teach me.'

Above the hill to the south a murder of rooks jostled above their roosts, in the distance looking like so many specks of wind-blown ash. Now and then their raucous cries carried to us on a chill gust and for a while Arthur watched those birds, though really he was considering all that he had heard.

Guinevere had lied. Not about the reasons for Lord Leodegan sending her to live on the island – I knew that to be true – but about her having made me swear to tell no one. I remembered the night she left Karrek as if it were days ago, not years. Edern and Benesek had rowed her to The Edge to meet her father, and I had railed so that

Madern and Melwas had to hold me to stop me doing something stupid. In the end and to my shame, I had watched on my knees that currach bear Guinevere across the flame-glossed water, tears in my eyes as the darkness swallowed her.

She had lied to Arthur. Yet I did not gainsay her. Perhaps there was no reason to. The past is water running in a stream. It is already long gone and you can never bring it back.

'You feared I would think the worst,' Arthur said, looking from Guinevere to me. He reached out and took Guinevere's hands in his own. 'That I would see visions of sweet young love and grow jealous,' he said, a childlike smile breaking his golden beard.

'Husband, you are the light and sword of Britain and can be jealous of no man,' she said.

I wondered if that crossbar on Arthur's spear would stop me running myself through with it.

'Go for your ride,' Guinevere said, nodding at us both. 'Go and spear some poor creature or admire a few hundred rotting heads or whatever it is that will soothe your wine-addled heads. I have work to do here.' With that she stood on her toes and kissed Arthur, and when she pulled away he looked embarrassed but happy.

'I'll fetch Tormaigh,' I said, turning away from them.

And with the low clouds threatening rain on that bleak winter dawn, Arthur and I rode to see Merlin's fence.

Three days after Arthur and I rode out to Merlin's fence of the dead, I saw Guinevere again. It was a bright winter day of blue sky and crisp air and traders from all over Dumnonia and beyond had come to Camelot. They set up their stalls outside the gatehouse at the fort's south-western corner, folk selling jewellery and leather goods: belts, horse tack, purses, scabbards, shoes. There were skins spread upon the ground covered in wooden cups and platters, pottery tableware, beeswax candles, jars of honey and joints of smoked meat. There were baskets of spun wool dyed red or yellow, coils of rope, racks of fleeces and whetstones and good ash shafts for spears and axes and planed limewood boards to make shields.

It was uncommon to see so many traders set up thus in the heart of winter, but news of our victory over Aella's Saxons had spread through all of Britain, let alone Dumnonia, so perhaps it was not surprising that people saw an opportunity. They knew that the spearmen of Camelot were rich in silver and coin, amber and iron, and all the war booty they had taken in the fight for Caer Gwinntguic, and there were a thousand souls living in and around Camelot by then.

I'd heard that a hunter had brought a cartload of pelts and so Bors and I had gone down to buy something to keep us warm when the snows came. We each bought a bear skin, paying more than we should have, but it was worth it for the laughter.

'You look like a Saxon,' I told my cousin, who was a hulking brute in that thick fur, looking like a bear himself. I was not as broad, yet I still felt barbarous with that heavy black pelt round my shoulders. I had given Aebbe's fur as a gift to Arthur, though it would have drowned him and I could not imagine him wearing it. Still, his own symbol, the one on his banners and our shields, being a bear, he had appreciated the gift.

'We smell like Saxons too,' Bors said, grinning as we walked along the stalls, getting wary looks, for it was not really cold enough that day for so much fur. At least the heads had been removed, and I thought I should be warm enough even were I to venture once more past the Wall of Antoninus, only next time on some white winter day when the air scalds the lungs with every breath.

We had stopped and I thought Bors was admiring a polished horn cup amongst an array of blowing horns, drinking horns and bone flutes, when I realized he was actually admiring the big-eyed young woman whose goods they were.

That was when I saw Guinevere.

She stood with a purveyor of herbs, her cupped hands full of some dried flowers which she held up to her nose, eyes closed as she breathed in the aroma. When she opened her eyes again she saw me.

'I'll give you a moment,' I told Bors, though he didn't seem to hear me, busy as he was persuading the girl with the big brown eyes to stroke him, or rather his new bear skin.

'Woundwort?' I said, nodding at the dried flower heads, which Guinevere poured back into a linen bag.

She nodded. 'That's the Saxons' name for it.'

'Yarrow flower then,' I said.

She looked at me askance. 'So you *were* listening sometimes,' she said.

I shrugged. 'We all know it. Some call it soldier's herb. I have seen men make a poultice with it and spread it on a wound. I've seen them chew the leaves to help a toothache.'

She lifted one of her dark eyebrows at me. 'You could have just said you remembered some of what I taught you,' she said. She was right, of course. But it irked me still that she had kissed Arthur so tenderly in front of me. 'I am his wife, Lancelot,' she said.

That came like a blow. I wondered if she was using her craft to read my thoughts. 'It's on your face,' she said, and I knew it was.

'Why did you go?' I said. It was a childish question to ask after all those years, yet she did not chide me.

'I had to go,' she said. 'I could not refuse my father. No more than could the Lady.'

I knew she was right, but no words, no simple explanation could throw off the shroud I had borne, far heavier than the thick bear skin around my shoulders, ever since I had watched her go to The Edge.

'You will be queen,' I said. It was a simple statement. Though of course what I meant was she would be Arthur's queen.

'Perhaps,' she said.

She could stand there, two feet away, the spearmen and traders and women of Camelot flowing around us, and she could pretend that we were nothing more than old friends. Yet our eyes were in each other. Entangled. Entwined with memories and intimacies. And I ached for what might have been.

'Does Arthur have a bad tooth?' I asked, nodding at the bag in her hand.

'He wouldn't tell me if he did,' she said.

'I once saw him dance like a fiend even with a sword wound that had been sewn up that very morning,' I said, touching my left hip at the point where Odgar, champion of Ebrauc, had cut Arthur. 'He laughed and leapt like a salmon. Broke the stitches of course.' The thought made me smile. I chose not to mention the dark-eyed girls with whom Arthur had been leaping and cavorting.

'He is too careless of himself,' Guinevere said, a frown betraying her fears for him. She looked down at the linen bag. 'I shall sew some of these flowers into his clothes. In the hem of his tunic and at the neck of his cloak. It will protect him from disease.' She smiled. 'In the summer I feared he was starting a fever and so added the juice from

twelve foxglove leaves to his beer. It is supposed to only work for children,' she said, bringing the bag of yarrow up to her nose once more,
'but the next day he woke without a sweat and hale as ever.' She swung
her eyes back up to mine. 'Don't tell him,' she said. 'He would not
approve.'

We have worse secrets than that, I thought, but nodded anyway. It
was not that Arthur did not believe in magic and charms – he kept
Merlin around, after all – but he ever believed himself to be the forger
of his own fate.

The gods help the man who helps himself, he had told me once. I had
not been able to disagree. Yet clearly he had not known of Guinevere's
talents, her ability to journey even as far as a druid, and now he might
associate her craft with her time on Karrek. Her time with me.

'Are you happy?' I asked. The words were out before I could stop
them. Never before had I asked someone a question to which I wanted
them to answer both yes and no.

'I *am* happy,' she said.

I nodded, having no words to that.

'You look like a beast in that fur,' she said. She was in the ermine
cloak, white as new snow but for the hem, which had taken up some
mud. I could not see where the little skins had been joined. It must
have cost five times the price Bors and I had paid between us for our
bear skins.

'Bors says we smell like Saxons in them,' I said.

'An improvement, I'm sure,' Guinevere said, her lips pursing to
restrain a smile.

I looked back to see that Bors was still making friends with the
young woman who sold the horns and polished cups. She was showing him a drinking horn and it seemed his interest was genuine. Then
for some reason I looked up at the hill to the south, above which the
rooks clamoured as they always did when they were not off foraging.
There was a man up there on that hill, sitting a white horse. Just sitting, still as a rock, a spear in his hand and looking down at the
market which thronged outside the grand gatehouse. The gatehouse
which he himself had planned in the Roman style and upon which
he had laboured, hefting timbers on his shoulder and placing the
stone rubble between the framework with his own hands. I knew
the horse and I knew the man sitting it, still and watchful against the

blue sky and the rooks and jackdaws bickering above the skeletons of elm and ash.

It was Arthur.

The snows came. They lay thick upon thatch and on the ramparts and filled the ditches, so that Camelot's formidable aspect was lost and our hill-fort looked little more than a white hump in the landscape, but for the smoke which it belched into the sky. For the cold kept folk inside and our hearth fires burned day and night.

Merlin remarked one day that from the flat land to the north, Camelot resembled a great dragon sleeping under the snow-veiled earth, its foul, smoky breath rising to the wintry sky as proof that it was alive and well and just waiting.

It was an evocative image, made even more poignant for High King Uther having been the Pendragon of Britain, the warrior who had made it his life's work to stem the Saxon tide. Now we had Arthur to continue that work. Perhaps even to finish it.

'The Saxons will find this dragon roused soon enough,' Arthur had replied to Merlin, though Arthur himself and those of us who were never far from his side had not been idle, even with snow thick on the ground. Every other day we took the horses out, visiting Dumnonia's rounds and being sure to be seen, our war gear glinting on sunny days, our helmet plumes brightening darker ones. We had to keep the horses fit, of course, but Arthur knew that come the spring he would need to call spearmen from all over Dumnonia, and so it was important that he was seen to be doing his part, out there protecting them, his hands numbing on the reins while they warmed theirs by the fire.

We rode east, too, past Merlin's fence, upon whose stakes the heads would still have been recognized by those who knew the men in life. The crows had taken most of the eyes and shredded their lips, but the cold had slowed the rot. Neither had the Saxons dared tear down the fence, which told us that they feared Merlin's magic. This pleased the druid enormously.

For three weeks snow lay on Dumnonia. They were quiet days. Even the land was quiet, sound muffled as if by a great fur, creatures hiding in their dens but for fox and hare, whose tracks made stitches in the white mantle.

And then iron-grey clouds from the west brought a great downpour which washed it all away and turned the ground to mud. That mud froze solid soon after and we did not take the horses out then in case they cut their feet on the hard ruts and peaks. We would need every one of those big horses soon enough when Arthur took the war to King Aella in Rhegin, and could not afford for any to go lame.

The hard ground delayed ploughing but there was plenty of other work that could begin again now the worst of winter was behind us. None worked as tirelessly as Tinas the blacksmith and his apprentices. Arthur had brought Tinas from Tintagel, promising the smith nothing but hard work and fair pay, but even to Arthur's surprise Tinas had come with his wife and children and set up a new forge on the northeast edge of the plateau, set apart from the dwellings to spare folk the worst of the constant hammering and thick, pungent smoke.

One afternoon, Arthur invited me to visit Tinas with him. He had found me by the copse a short walk from the east gate, where I often went to practise my weapons. Bors sometimes came with me, but he had taken up with the pretty horn trader with the big eyes, whose name was Emblyn, and I had not seen much of him since. I assumed they were snugged up somewhere warm like hibernating bears. I could not envy my cousin, only admire his talent for happiness.

'I'd wager you could take a sparrow on the wing, Lancelot,' Arthur said. I had known he was there, one foot up on a coppiced alder stool and leaning over that leg, quiet so as not to put me off my throw. His hunting hound, Caval, sat patiently at his heel.

'A plump pigeon perhaps, but not a sparrow,' I said, turning to greet him, meeting smile with smile. Caval barked and wagged his tail as I greeted him too, scratching behind his ears as he liked.

My spear had pierced the middle of the matted reed target which I had wedged between an elm's diverging trunk forty feet away. Not dead centre – in truth Arthur being there *had* put me off – but it was a decent cast all the same.

'Do you think of nothing but war, my friend?' he asked. We shook hands, though he did not throw his arm round my shoulder as he usually did.

'Do you?' I asked, and he cocked an eyebrow in acknowledgement of a riposte well made, then smiled again.

'Come to the forge with me, Lancelot,' he said. 'Tinas has been working on something I want you to see.'

'A new sword?' I said, teasing him. Excalibur was at his hip even then on that late winter day with no enemies within fifty miles. Because folk wanted to see that long sword at Arthur's hip. They expected to see it. But I had seen Arthur fight with another sword for fear of Excalibur's ancient blade breaking in the midst of battle. That would be a bad omen, hard to ignore, so that I had once suggested he ask Tinas to make him another sword which resembled Excalibur, even matching the dark wood of the spherical pommel which was smooth and shiny with age and wear.

'She has a few more good years in her yet, Lancelot,' Arthur said, his left hand closing around Excalibur's ivory grip. 'No, there's something else I want to show you.'

So we had walked up between the ramparts which he and I had dug together, and through the gate, where the guards stood straighter as Arthur passed. And I knew there was something weighing on Arthur's mind, if only by the number of sticks which he gathered up to hurl for Caval to bring back to us, his tail making a breeze. It was easy to forget what a fierce beast that dog could be when there was the scent of fox or boar, badger or deer on the air.

As ever, Tinas was hard at work and did not even stop to greet his lord, but kept on hammering a small piece of iron which already looked flat to my eyes. We waited and watched and only when Tinas was satisfied with his work did he stop and look up at us, arming sweat from his greasy forehead despite the chill of the day.

'What do you reckon, lord?' he asked Arthur, holding up the piece after having plunged it in the quenching trough. I saw then that it was the cheek piece from a helmet of the kind Arthur and I both wore. The edge of it had been bent but no longer.

'I can see nothing wrong with it,' Arthur said, 'though I would say that anyway, if only to have you making spear heads instead. We shall need more spears than fine helmets.'

Tinas lifted his bearded chin and showed his teeth. 'You want to tell Bedwyr that I'm too busy making spear heads to fix his helmet?'

Arthur laughed and raised a placating hand. 'I'd rather not,' he said.

'They're ready, lord,' Tinas said. 'I assume that's what you've come for.'

Arthur nodded. He seemed nervous. We watched Tinas go over to the bench behind him where lay all the tools of his trade, and he picked up a bundle, just over a foot in length and wrapped in soft leather, and brought it over to us. He leant over his anvil and looked down at my legs, then nodded with a grunt that seemed to convey satisfaction. I looked at Arthur but his eyes were fixed on the package which Tinas was unwrapping with reverence, despite being himself the creator of whatever was within.

'I could not have done better,' Tinas said, examining the work in his hands with an expression which could have been pride, or shame. It was impossible to say. 'No,' he said, picking up a cloth and giving the thing a last polish, 'I could not have done better, Arthur,' he said.

'Then no man could,' Arthur said, not minding the blacksmith's familiarity. A man who could, by fire, water and skill, make bright strong metal or blades from rough ore, deserved respect even from his lord. Even from kings.

His eyes still on Arthur, Tinas nodded towards me. Arthur dipped his head, consenting, and the smith handed me the worked metal the way a mother might hand her newborn to another.

It was a pair of greaves, each shaped to protect a man's leg from foot to knee. Somehow, though, Tinas had crafted the iron to show the muscles of the lower leg, similar to the old Roman breastplates that I had seen which depict the muscles of a fit man's stomach and chest. Even more impressive than the muscle definition was the decoration over the knee. It was a hawk, all beak and glaring eye and bristled feathers.

'Tinas impresses the iron from behind to form the raised image,' Arthur said. 'I saw it done.'

'Bronze, mind,' Tinas said, 'so they won't stop a Saxon axe from taking your leg off. But they're light. You'll still be able to dance in them,' he said, as though he had heard about my fighting style and did not altogether approve.

'I have seen ancient greaves with lions on the knee,' Arthur said, 'but I thought a hawk was fitting.'

I was running my fingers over the hawk's curved beak and down the lines of the calf muscles, speechless with admiration at Tinas's workmanship. Speechless too at the generosity of Arthur's gift.

'Do you like them?' Arthur asked me. I looked up to see that he was grinning. He knew that I did.

'They are beautiful,' I said, pressing fingers deep into the felt and leather padding inside.

'They are,' Arthur agreed. 'Achilles himself would have been proud to wear them as he fought beneath the walls of Troy.'

'My wife stitched the liners,' Tinas said, seeming prouder of that work than of the shaped bronze and the hawk's head, which must have taken so many hours of gentle hammering to bring out the detail.

I saw then the tiny holes in the bronze through which fine gut thread secured the felt liners top and bottom.

'Sulgwenn still has the eyesight of a girl,' the smith said, jerking his beard up to the sky. 'Swears she can see folk moving about on the moon sometimes. Says she can see them dancing, on a clear night,' he said, talking over his embarrassment for his skill, which those bright greaves embodied. And perhaps to avoid being drawn into this weighty moment between friends.

'I don't deserve such a gift,' I told Arthur.

He frowned. 'The man who won Venta Belgarum?' he said. 'Who killed Aebbe and broke the Saxons? You deserve much more, Lancelot.'

'If you'll excuse me, Arthur, Lancelot,' Tinas muttered, 'I've proper work to do.'

'Spear blades, Tinas,' Arthur said. 'Arrowheads, too. As many as there are stars in the night sky.'

'Bring me iron, Arthur, from bog or mine, and I'll make your spear heads,' the blacksmith said, tossing handfuls of charcoal into the forge's bright heart.

Arthur nodded, commended Tinas once more for his work and turned away from the smithy, suggesting that I might want to join him inspecting Camelot's defences, and so I thanked Tinas, who nodded without looking up from his work, and followed Arthur.

It was cold enough that our breath fogged and Caval steamed like hot broth from his exertions, having scattered several hordes of foraging crows from the slope beyond the palisade. Arthur and I stood looking east towards Caer Gwinntguic, beyond which King Aella still held Rhegin.

'Cai has seen scouts but nothing that has him concerned. Not yet,' Arthur said.

He had left Cai in charge of Venta Belgarum with a garrison of fifty spearmen to bolster the town's defences until the people of Caer Gwinntguic could choose a new king to sit on King Deroch's high seat.

'And you and I will be at Aella's throat before he's ready to march west again,' I said.

Arthur nodded but said nothing to that. Caval had gone bounding down the ramparts after a hare and Arthur cursed the hound, fearing it might break a leg in its foolishness, for its prey was long gone.

'I won't clear the ditches out again,' he said. 'It was a mistake. Better to let them fill with gorse and bramble. Harder for the enemy to pass but won't protect them from our spears,' he said. He was right. The outer ditches were fairly shallow, minor obstacles to a determined attacker, but filled with thorn, briar and nettle they would hamper the enemy. They would slow any attack, giving our men more time to kill them with Tinas's spear blades.

Caval looked up at us and barked, as if asking us where that hare had gone.

'There is something I need you to do, Lancelot,' Arthur said.

I had known something was coming and here it was at last. I looked down at the greaves in my hand, breath-stealing, wondrous and polished so that they looked like gold, and I thought of the deerskin hawking glove which the lady had given me after I won the foot race on Karrek. Stitched by a craftsman in Cambria, supple as thought and gleaming with oils.

'Anything, Arthur,' I said. 'Did I not swear an oath?'

'To serve the next king of Dumnonia,' he said, 'and I am not yet king.'

'You will be,' I said.

He nodded. 'Perhaps. But I ask you this as a friend, Lancelot, not as your lord or would-be king.'

A creeping dread stalked me for I knew that Arthur's gift of the greaves was his attempt to sweeten the coming draught. I nodded, showing I was ready for whatever he needed of me.

'You know I was myself sworn to King Syagrius in Gaul?' he said.

'I know you fought for him,' I said. 'Gawain told me Syagrius treated you like a son. That he trusted no one more. I did not know you were oath-tied to him,' I said, that new knowledge already weighing on me, because an oath is a heavy thing.

Arthur nodded. 'When I left Dumnonia for Gaul, old Syagrius took me in. Though he wasn't old then. Just seemed so to me.' He smiled. 'I was younger than you are now,' he said. 'His sons, the princes, were as my brothers. King Syagrius was kind to me.' His lips tightened. 'More generous than I had a right to expect,' he said, his guilt rising again for having been complicit in Uther's plan to sink the infant Mordred down to the seabed.

'And you swore allegiance to him,' I said.

He nodded. 'So long as he remained a friend to Dumnonia,' he said. 'Syagrius taught me war. The Roman art of war. It was he who showed me what big, well-trained, armoured horses could do to a disorganized enemy.' He smiled, brimming with memory. 'I found my talent for war in his service, Lancelot. Ten years of fighting to keep the Franks at bay. And now this,' he said, jutting a chin in the direction of a different enemy who would engulf him if they could.

'Did King Syagrius release you from the oath?' I asked, though I knew the answer now.

'No, Lancelot,' Arthur said, 'and he only let me bring men to Britain on my word that I would return were I not affirmed king after Uther's death.' He shrugged. 'I am no king,' he said.

'But you cannot leave,' I said. 'Without you here, Caer Gwinntguic will fall. Dumnonia after that. Then Cornubia. And they will just be the first. In the north, Elmet will fall to the Saxons of Lindisware and after that—'

Arthur raised a hand to stop me naming all the kingdoms that would fall like apples in an autumn gale were he not leading his armoured horsemen and Dumnonia's spearmen against the Saxons.

'I cannot leave Britain again,' he said, watching his far-away hound rooting and sniffing at a badger's sett in the outermost rampart, which we had cleared of lime and birch the previous summer. 'If I did, the kings would never welcome me back again.' He shook his head. 'No, I cannot leave. But you can.'

I turned to him, though he kept his eyes fastened on Caval.

'I need you to fulfil my obligations in Soissons, Lancelot. I need you to take my place and fight for King Syagrius.' He looked up, his eyes following a heron's flight into the east, the grey bird's long neck retracted like a wary snake, its wingbeats slow but strong. 'I hear he has secured his borders in the north as far as Cambrai and to the Meuse in the east,' he said.

'Then why does he need you? Or me?' I asked.

'He is in the south now, fighting the Alaric Goths. A Saxon people,

The very people who sacked Rome itself in my grandfather's time,' he said. 'Syagrius is fighting Alaric's brother, King Euric.' The heron was far away now, but still Arthur watched it. 'Help Syagrius win his peace, Lancelot, and he will let you bring my remaining men back to Britain. I will have the king's blessing and you shall have my gratitude. More important still, I will have my men and my horses.' He turned to face me now and I saw the strain in his face. 'I need those men,' he said. 'Honour my oath, Lancelot, and help Syagrius win. Then bring my soldiers back to Camelot and together we shall drive the Saxons into the sea.'

My head swam as though I had been drinking Arthur's wine, and yet my stomach was heavy with a sense of trepidation.

'We have barely begun here,' I said, gesturing eastward. 'The young spearmen are not ready. I would fight at your shoulder in the spring.'

'You are the only one I can send,' he said. 'Syagrius must have my best.' He looked into my eyes and must have seen the disappointment in them. 'You are my best, Lancelot. The king will see that, for he knows fighting men. He will trust you to lead my men. Give them some victories and they will trust you too. Enough to follow you back across the sea once you've dealt with this Euric.'

'Can Gawain not go?' I asked. 'Or Bedwyr?'

Arthur shook his head. 'Gawain left a girl in Soissons. Not just any girl. Syagrius's daughter, Aemiliana.' He half smiled. 'I fear my nephew would not be welcome at the king's table. As for Bedwyr, I need him here to lead my cataphracts.'

That made sense, for though I could ride and fight well enough from the saddle, I preferred to fight on my own two feet. Certainly, I lacked Bedwyr's long experience of leading Arthur's cavalry.

But the real truth was that neither Gawain nor Bedwyr were in love with Arthur's wife. That was why it had to be me. Arthur would not say it but I knew it to be so.

'I'll go, Arthur,' I heard myself say.

Arthur sighed, as though releasing a breath that had been trapped inside him all the day. 'Thank you, Lancelot,' he said.

'When?' I asked.

'The sooner you go, the sooner I'll have you back,' he said.

I nodded. What else could I do? I had sworn to serve Arthur. He needed me to make good his oath so that we would have more warriors in the coming war against the enemy. But more than this, he was my friend.

And so I would go to Gaul.

I rode out of Camelot three days later. Bors and five good men on big horses rode with me. We would not impress King Syagrius with our numbers, but Arthur could ill afford to lose seven men, let alone more. Yet we made a splendid sight in our polished mail and plumed helmets as we passed through the main gate on a crisp late winter morning, the sun pulling free of the eastern horizon to bathe Camelot in crimson. Three ponies followed with our provisions and war gear, including all the leather armour for our mounts as well as our own shields and spears.

I had told Bors he should stay. He and Emblyn planned to marry in the spring and I saw no reason why my cousin should leave his love behind and cross the Dividing Sea for a land he did not know, to fight for a king he was not sworn to, against men who had done him no harm.

'You think I'd let you ride off and claim all the glory for yourself?' he asked, his big eyes looking incredulous. 'No, I think I'll have one more adventure before I settle down beside the hearth to bounce squawking babes on my knee.' He looked at me from beneath an arched brow. 'Besides which, Lord Arthur told me I'd be going with you.'

He did not need to say more about how Arthur's affection for him had cooled since learning of Bors's and my shared past with Guinevere on Karrek, and nor did I try to persuade my cousin to stay. I believed that in truth Bors feared being married more than he feared battle itself, and for my part, I was glad to have him beside me that dawn as we rode through sunlit clouds of our own breath.

Arthur and I had said our goodbyes the previous night over the last summer's mead. Even Mordred had wished me luck, though I could not believe he meant it, or that his smile was for any other reason than because he was glad to see the back of me. He and Melwas were already great friends, so I heard, and I shuddered to think of that.

'Melwas will try to make himself Arthur's champion,' I had said to Bors, like a jealous lover.

'And being not as good as he thinks he is, he'll likely lose his balls to a Saxon spear,' Bors replied with a wicked grin.

There was no feast to mark our leaving, no harp song, no bards telling tales of long-dead warriors and worthy quests. We simply rode out and took the south road towards the coast, where Arthur's silver would buy us passage to a tidal island called Mont Tombe, named for the old Roman tombs which it resembled in shape. From that island, which I had heard bore a great resemblance to Karrek Loos yn Koos, we would ride south to Adecavus and King Syagrius's stronghold on the banks of the Liger.

'What have we here?' Bors said, sitting tall in the saddle, his chin lifted towards the road ahead. We had passed the coppice but were not yet an arrow-shot into the ancient oak wood beyond it, and someone was waiting for us amongst the trees.

'Merlin?' Bors suggested, for the stranger was cowled and cloaked in shadow.

'Not Merlin,' I said, my stomach rolling over itself.

'Ah,' Bors said, understanding. 'You'll catch us up, then,' he said, and he led the others on past the figure, which stood head bowed until they had gone.

Tormaigh snorted and tossed his head, frustrated that we had stopped while the others rode on.

'You shouldn't be out here alone,' I said. There were plenty of landless, lordless men roaming the forests and hills of Dumnonia and while I held no fear of such men, my blood thrummed in my veins now. The muscles in my legs quivered as they did before a battle.

'I am not unarmed,' Guinevere said, pushing back her hood.

I filled my eyes with her.

'What will your husband say?' I asked. I had not spoken Arthur's name. It did not feel right to, given what I felt looking at Guinevere then.

'He thinks I am taking dried raspberry leaves to Ector's daughter. She's with child.' She tilted her head on one side and narrowed her green eyes at me. 'You would have left without saying goodbye,' she said. Not a question, seeing as I was already on the road with Camelot at my back. 'Am I so easy to leave, Lancelot? Is this your revenge?'

I almost kicked my heels into Tormaigh's flanks then. Part of me wanted to canter off along that shady track and not look back. Another part of me wanted to dismount and pull Guinevere to me and let a hundred men try to part us.

'I thought it best,' I said. 'We cannot be friends. Not now.' I meant it, though the words sounded like they came from someone else's mouth.

'I know,' she said, like a blade in my chest.

Tormaigh neighed and I growled to quiet him, letting my eyes explore every part of Guinevere's face. I don't think either of us had blinked since she pushed back her cowl.

'I gave him my oath,' I said.

'As did I,' she said, meaning the marriage oath of a wife to her husband.

'I don't know when I shall return,' I said.

She nodded and it seemed her eyes were saying everything that her mouth could not. She bit her bottom lip and took a small step back. 'Be safe, Lancelot.'

Tears then. In her eyes and mine.

I reached into the neck of my tunic, took hold of the rings I wore around my neck and pulled hard, breaking the leather thong.

For a moment I sat there, just looking at her, thinking how unfair it all was. Had I not been the one who found her in the beginning? Had we not found each other? Long before any of this.

'Here,' I said, leaning from the saddle to give her the smaller of the rings. It had been hers once. It would be hers again. 'I cannot keep it,' I said, unable to swallow.

I thought she might insist that I did keep that silver ring. Perhaps I hoped that she would, but she nodded and came forward, closing a pale fist around the ring, feeling the warmth of my body on it.

'Look after him,' I said, and I kicked my heels but now Tormaigh refused to move. I flicked the reins and clicked my tongue and at last to my relief, and to my anguish, he walked on along that woodland path.

I did not look back.

23

Lord of War

I BARREL THROUGH UNDERBRUSH, *through bramble and mire, feeling neither thorn nor insect bite. I feel my own strength, though, savage and raw and unstoppable. I am a bristling mass of muscle and fury, forcing my head like a plough amongst the forest litter, upturning soil and stones and whatever is in my way. I root up bulbs and plants, scavenge nuts, berries and seeds. Feast on worms and insects, rats, snakes and carrion. Nothing can stop me. All the world is a bounty for me to feast upon. It passes beneath my feet in a blur, yet I smell everything, taste everything, my own scent sharp in the air through which I move.*

Only Man can harm me, yet I do not fear him. I have gored a man with these tusks. Ripped into his reeking bowels and charged on into the woods, leaving him shrieking.

When I possess some creature of the sky, then I am truly free. But when I journey with the boar, all bulk and rage, I fly across the earth, fleet and fearless, insatiable and rampant, the sound of snapping undergrowth announcing my passing.

Almost too wild, this creature, so that I can barely govern him. Barely command so much bulk or bring his great head up from the rich earth through which he delves.

I smell the taint of Man on the air, long before I see signs of him with these small, deep-set eyes. I smell fresh blood, too, and I haul this head up then. Swinging it this way and that. I sniff the air and grunt. I want to turn away. There is nothing for me that way, not even the sweet blood and open flesh. Not until the men have gone. But some other, stronger need compels me on, nosing towards the pungent scent.

I push through thick furze, across marsh and ancient, gleaming bones, and come to the place. It takes all my will to root these hooves to the ground. To stand stiff-legged, head up, my nose tasting the air. To watch.

He has changed. He is older, of course. He wears the years on him, heavy as that coat of bronze scales. He could almost be Arthur in that war finery, that silver-chased helmet hiding his face, all of it shining dully in the unnatural twilight of thick forest. For the way others look at him. The awe in their eyes. Their desire to prove themselves to him.

He bellows orders and men hurry from him, gory blades in their hands. Towards the clamour of iron and killing.

Blood sweet in my nose. I taste it and stand my ground.

Another man shouts and the lord of war looks up as a wild, half-naked figure flies at him, shrieking and flashing with steel. The lord of battle moves fast as thought, takes the shrieker by the neck, slams him against a pine trunk and thrusts a long blade through his neck, pinning him there.

The general turns back to the others, leaving his enemy to gurgle and hammer his heels against the spruce; the last thumping heartbeats of his life. I hear them.

Yes, older now. Fiercer. And yet it is not hard to see the boy he once was in the man he has become.

He points sharp steel into the dimness, towards the blood stench and noise. Others run that way. I feel their footfalls through the earth, up into my own stiff forelegs. I only have to turn my nose towards them to smell their fear, yet they run towards death. For him.

I smell no fear on the battle lord.

He turns and looks through the forest. He sees me and I see him, his eyes bright within that white-tailed helm. White and red. Bone and blood.

I have known him always.

A spearman had ridden ahead from Mont Tombe to tell me that she was coming. I sent my own man back with word that she must wait for me on the island. That I would come when I could.

She did not wait.

There was a summer storm on the day I saw her again. The forest canopy was as good as thatch for keeping the rain off, but it was dark enough amongst the trees that it felt like dusk though it was the middle of the day.

I had not thought to see her again, not in this life. How long had it been? Seven years? Eight? Years of bloodshed in a foreign land, in deep forests of pine and beech which smelled like my childhood. Years of war, at first for Arthur, paying his debts to King Syagrius, but then for myself. Revelling in my gods-given talent, as a hawk revels in the currents of the sky.

Trying to forget.

She came at the head of a column of spearmen. Not in their midst, but at their head, like a general herself, though armed only with her terrible beauty. And when she dismounted in that gloom, the rain hissing in the boughs above us, my heart hammered faster than a thousand screaming tribesmen had ever caused it to.

'You have changed, Lancelot,' she said.

'You have not, lady,' I said, my loins flooding with warmth as I stared, hoping my scowl hid my desire for her.

I had not expected to see her, yet she said nothing of the blood, of the filth and the stench which I had grown used to. Neither did she show any unease at the way my men looked at her, yet she must have felt their eyes like maggots on her skin. They were wild, those men. Made savage by war. I trusted them and they followed me, but I could no more command their eyes or tame their hunger for what the long years had denied them than could I tell myself that I did not want to take Guinevere to my bed there and then.

'It is not safe here.' I nodded to a part of the forest that had been thinned of trees to feed our fires and build our palisades. 'Our camp is nearby. I will have a tent cleared for you.'

She nodded and we walked together through the unnatural gloaming, through the rain's sibilance in the heavy boughs and the murmurs of spearmen, Guinevere's charm being two-fold: for her own beguiling beauty, and for being Lord Arthur's wife, that prince's fame having flown far and wide in those years. Arthur, the curse of the Saxons. Arthur, the Bear of Britannia. Arthur, the king that shall be. And here was his woman. His Guinevere. The wife to whom he comes bloody and broken from the battle. The wife who knows his ambitions and his fears. The ointment for his flesh, the balm for his soul.

Guinevere and Bors embraced, as she and I had not, and jealousy stirred in my belly like a serpent waking after sleep. And yet I was not the man she had known. Not any more.

My tent was little more than a great canvas stretched between the trees. Large enough for my warlords to gather within on freezing winter days, but lacking any comforts beyond those which a warrior needs.

'Why have you come?' I asked her, when Bors had excused himself in order to show Arthur's men where to pitch their own tents.

Not the words she had expected to hear once we were alone. Her eyes told me that. They did not seem to recognize me.

'There was no one else,' she said. 'No one else whom Arthur trusted.'

I had offered her a seat, yet she stood, watching me as I removed my war gear, putting my helmet on the bed in case she did want the stool, and hanging my sword belt on the stub of a pine branch.

She filled two cups with wine which she had brought with her from Mont Tombe. It had been a long time since I had drunk anything so good.

'I heard about your uncle,' she said. She was searching my eyes, as if she alone knew that Balsant's death had not pleased me, as others had thought it must.

'A hunting accident,' I said. 'He took a wound from a boar. A small cut, so they said, but it turned bad.' Just talking about my uncle brought the shame seeping back into me like pus into a bandage. I had sworn vengeance on him times beyond counting. As a boy I had looked south across the Dividing Sea and promised him such terrors, and Guinevere had been witness to my pledge. But in the event some nothing wound, or perhaps it was the gods, had made me false. Had proved me an oath-breaker, for my uncle the traitor had died in his bed.

I had not avenged my father, nor my mother nor Hector. And in the years since, I had often felt their disappointment, their condemnation, even through the veil which separates our world from Annwn.

King Syagrius's enemies had suffered for my shame.

'At least he is dead,' Guinevere said, still holding my eyes. I nodded, trying to rebury Balsant in the past and turning my thoughts back to Arthur.

'Why has he sent you here?' I asked.

'He needs you, Lancelot,' she said, offering me a cup.

I drank. 'He still remembers me, then?' I asked.

She frowned. 'Of course he does,' she said.

'It's not safe for you here,' I said. 'The enemy is close.'

'But you are winning,' she said.

I nodded. 'And Arthur?'

Guinevere considered how to answer that, looking back out into the camp. The rain was lighter now but the forest was still dark. Water dripped on the canvas above our heads where trapped insects mustered.

'He needs you,' she said again. 'The Picts have come south and King Einion of Ebrauc demands Arthur's help in return for the spearmen from northern Britain who marched for High King Uther. The Saxons of Lindisware are raiding west into Elmet and south into Caer Lerion. Cerdic, the Saxon king in the north, is even more ambitious than Aella. King Meirchion Gul of Rheged is dead and the new king is no friend to Arthur. Spearmen from Rheged have moved on Powys, so that King Cyngen, who has been a strong ally these last years, must now look to his northern borders as well as west and to the Irish.'

'And Constantine?' I asked. 'Where is he these days?'

Guinevere pressed a hand into the small of her back, easing some ache from the long ride. 'He has bent the knee to Arthur,' she said, 'and Arthur has sent him to defend Venta Belgarum.'

I had gathered scraps of news from Britain, from traders and King Syagrius himself, who sometimes received emissaries from Armorica, but I had not known how bad things were. All that Arthur had fought for, all that he had dreamed of for Britain, was crumbling.

'You still hold Camelot?' I asked, fearing that Arthur might have retreated back to Tintagel, having no choice but to cede the heart of Britain to the enemy.

'Camelot is as you left it,' Guinevere said. *Nothing else is the same*, her face said.

'But Aella lives?'

She nodded. There was a golden torc at her neck. Enough gold to buy a hundred or more Frankish mercenaries. And she not a queen. But appearances were important to Arthur. I knew he could not show weakness, and yet he must be weak to have sent Guinevere across the sea.

'Could he not have sent Gawain? Or Parcefal?' I asked.

'Would you have preferred that?' she asked. I saw the challenge in her eyes.

'No,' I said, knowing I was behaving like a pigheaded fool, yet unable to stop myself.

She sipped her wine. 'It's his way of saying sorry,' she said. 'For sending you away.'

'You say it as if he banished me,' I said. 'I came to make good his oaths.'

'And it has taken you eight years?' she asked. 'Surely you have given this Roman king enough? He cannot ask more of you. Or of Arthur.'

'Arthur owes him nothing now. I have given Syagrius a dozen victories.'

'And still you did not come home,' she said. That was an accusation and I could not ignore it.

'What would you have me do?' I asked her. 'Should I have watched you together, day after day, year after year? Should I have honoured Arthur as my lord and friend, and honoured you as my lady, and found a wife for myself? Should I have pretended that I did not love you?'

She jerked her head back as though I had struck her, then shook her head, whether in disappointment or denial I could not know. Yet she had opened the old wound. Opened it just by being there in my tent in a dark forest in Gaul, where she was not supposed to be. I had left her far away. And years away. Now, I could smell her hair and skin, and yet if I had any courage at all, it was not enough to reach out my hand and touch her.

'What do you want from me, Guinevere?' I asked. 'What have you ever wanted?'

She took the wine cup in both hands as though to draw comfort from it. Hands which I saw were trembling a little. Just a quiver, like that in a butterfly's wings as it warms itself on a tree trunk.

'He needs you,' she said.

'But you do not,' I said.

'He is my husband,' she said.

I nodded. 'He is.' I drained my cup, then went to the table and filled it again.

'Why did he send you?' I asked.

'There are few that he trusts now,' she said. 'He has changed, Lancelot.'

'Why did he send you?' I asked again.

Her eyes widened. 'Because of all I have just told you,' she said, then pressed her lips together and nodded. 'And because he knew that if I asked you, you would come.'

I felt that like a spear butt to the stomach. How could Arthur know that of me? How had he known what lay in the shadow of my heart?

I drank, holding the draught in my mouth, tasting the long summer days in the grape. Gathering myself. 'He is well?' I asked, watching her face closely for sign of the half-truth.

I was a general then. A man whose reputation was worth fifty men on armoured horses. One hundred and fifty spearmen. I was a lord of war, not some lovesick youth. Yet, I missed my friend still. The times I had breathed in the pine-scented air and thought of Arthur, imagined him sharpening his young claws for Syagrius. Making his own reputation. I missed him. The years had not blunted it.

'He is tired,' she said at last. 'He has borne such a burden these long years. So much war. So many treaties made and broken and made anew.' She shook her head. 'We all ask too much of him. Britain expects too much of him.' A line etched itself into her forehead. 'He does not know whom to trust,' she said.

'Merlin lives?' I asked, for Arthur had always sought the druid's advice and I believed for his part Merlin loved Arthur.

Guinevere nodded. 'He lives,' she said, 'but we do not see him these days. He has his own matters to attend, and so Arthur listens more and more to Mordred, but I do not trust him.'

'I would not trust him, either,' I said.

'Arthur needs you, Lancelot,' she said.

'He could have sent for me.'

'Would you have come back?'

I thought about that. 'Perhaps,' I said.

'But you will come now?' Guinevere asked. 'He misses you.'

'I am tired of this war,' I said.

Guinevere nodded.

We had driven King Syagrius's enemies back year on year, but at a terrible cost. Next summer, or the one after that, the Goths would push back. And in the north, Syagrius was hard pressed against the Franks. Soissons would fall. It was only a matter of time. But my loyalty was to Arthur. I had sworn an oath before High King Uther, to serve and protect Arthur. It mattered not that he was no king. Arthur needed me now, and so I would return to Britain.

That night, I slept outside Guinevere's tent, as I had slept outside her door when we were children, and the very next day I rode north, having sought neither King Syagrius's permission nor his blessing.

Arthur had asked that I bring the last of his men, those spearmen who were still loyal to him, who had pledged their swords to him at the beginning, but after the years and the fighting and the plagues that always ravage an army on campaign, there were just twelve men left and only seven who remembered their oaths and were willing to cross the Dividing Sea with us.

'I was thinking we would never see Britain again,' Bors said as we neared the coast, watching the gulls wheeling in the summer sky, the tang of sea air in our noses and making the horses skittish with nerves. The three of us rode together at the head of the column, Guinevere between Bors and me. 'How is Emblyn?' Bors asked Guinevere. 'Well, I hope? With children tripping her up and a man who is good to her?' There was a wistful smile on his lips but his sentiment was sincere. He had not expected Emblyn to wait for him. And yet, perhaps there was still some sliver of vain hope.

'She married a spearman,' Guinevere said. 'There is a boy.'

Bors nodded. 'Good,' he said. 'That's good.'

Then it struck me that I did not know if Guinevere had children. It was surely likely, not only because she and Arthur had been married for years, but because Arthur needed a son with her. He might already rule in Dumnonia but one day he would be king and a king needed a legitimate heir, one whom no one would refute, as they might Mordred.

'And you, my lady?' Bors asked, knowing that I wanted to but could not. 'Do you and Lord Arthur have children?'

I looked straight ahead and rubbed Tormaigh on his poll.

'The gods have not blessed us with children,' Guinevere said.

'The gods are cruel,' Bors said.

I followed Guinevere's eyes and saw a kestrel against the blue sky, its wingtips extended and its tail fanned as it hovered in the sea breeze, looking for prey amongst the grass. 'Perhaps when the war is won,' Guinevere said, watching that bird.

But the war would never be won. Having fought King Euric's hordes, I knew that now. Like them, the Saxons would keep coming. Every season, more boats would cross the Morimaru, the dead sea, and come to Britain's eastern shores. We would fight them as our ancestors had. And after us, our children would fight them, but eventually men like Aella and Cerdic would take Britain. I knew it. Perhaps Arthur knew it too, but knowing it was not the same as accepting it, and so Arthur and I would bleed the enemy. We would make them pay in blood for every meadow, hill and wood which they may one day call their own. Arthur would fight for Britain. I would fight for Arthur. And Guinevere would always own my soul.

The gods are cruel.

Arthur's eagle-owl was called Hades and she was magnificent. She was even larger than my father's gyrfalcon had been, and to my child's eye that gyrfalcon had been the king of all birds. Yet this bird boasted talons which could crush the skull of a fox or sheep.

'She is fearless,' Arthur said, 'and will go for anything, whether it flies, runs or swims. I have seen her take a roe deer,' he said, glancing across at me as we walked, to see if I was impressed. How could I not be? I had never heard of anyone hunting with an eagle-owl as one might with a hawk, but was eager to see if it could be done.

That bird glared at me with bright, reddish eyes, as though it could see into my heart. As though it were weighing me in the scales; my sins in one dish, my honour in the other, and would whisper in Arthur's ear its findings.

Yet I knew owls were in truth stupid birds and I took comfort in the knowledge. Old Hoel had taught me that. A lifetime ago, it seemed.

'Men think that because they look so solemn and keep their own counsel, owls are wise and canny,' the old falconer had said, then sighed. 'Men always judge with their eye. Looks doesn't mean a thing, boy. Size neither,' he said, for he knew how the white gyrfalcon captivated me. Had seen me staring at her often enough. 'I've seen a falcon lose an eye to a rook,' he said, touching the scarred flesh around his own dead, white eye. 'Seen a goshawk lose a talon to a crow.'

Perhaps that was another reason why he gave me the sparhawk that night when fire lit the darkness and blood melted the snow. Another lesson. The last one he would ever teach me.

'She'll outfly a pheasant and take a duck on the rise in the dark,' Arthur said, hauling my mind from the past. 'Though I cannot take the credit for her.'

I gave him a knowing look. 'If I'd thought you were manning birds and hunting every other day, while I was up to my neck in tribesmen who had been taught how to fight by Romans . . .' I raised an eyebrow at him. 'I'd have come back sooner,' I said.

'I wish you had,' he said, looking at me with tired eyes. The years lay heavy on him. His beard had been the gold of ripe wheat when I left his hall that morning eight years before. Now it was hearth-ash grey, as was the hair at his temples. He was leaner too, his face almost gaunt, which made his eyes even more arresting.

'I'm here now,' I said. He nodded.

We walked on up the ridge, which was fragrant with the tramped grass and yellow rock rose and purple betony, which Guinevere had once told me could stop dreams coming if hung about the neck. Insects thrummed round our knees and butterflies tumbled here and there like wind-blown blossom, and in that moment we might have forgotten we were at war.

It had been Arthur's idea to go hunting with the eagle-owl and I had not questioned it even though I saw that some of the others, including Gawain and Bors, thought us mad. A Saxon war band had been sighted in the south of Caer Gwinntguic and tomorrow I would lead one hundred spearmen out to face them, while Arthur prepared to march north to fight alongside Einion of Ebrauc against the Picts. But first Arthur and I would hunt together no matter what anyone thought about it.

We moved with care now across the dry, crisp forest floor, avoiding the dappled sunlight filtering down through the shimmering beech canopy. The warm rising air was shrill with the songs of chaffinch and robin.

'Syagrius must be sorry you've gone,' Arthur said. 'I have heard bards singing of your victories in Gaul.' As we walked, he stroked his forefinger down Hades's collar and back, as the bird turned her head this way and that, searching for prey amongst the trees.

'Leading men does not come easily to me,' I said, swinging my spear forward to plant its butt end in the litter with every other step.

'Yet they fight for you. They win for you,' he said. 'Did you know, folk all across Britain talk of Lancelot's courage, Lancelot's skill?'

'I know the people of Britain have more important things to talk about,' I said.

Arthur made a *hoom* in the back of his throat. After I left for Gaul, Arthur had taken the war to the Saxons and the kings of Britain had played their part. But that four years of victories was long in the past now and it seemed that Arthur's dream of Britain was unravelling before his eyes. The kings looked only to their own borders. Britons fought Britons and the Saxons were strong again.

'Still, you were the most famed warrior in Gaul,' Arthur said, unwilling to let me off the hook. 'A man can grow to have a taste for fame. He can thirst for it as one might thirst for wine. It is a craving that can be upon him from the moment he wakes until the moment he falls asleep.'

I looked at him but he kept his own eyes busy searching ahead for prey, though I did not think he would release the bird in these woods. Safer to wait for open ground.

'What are you saying?' I asked him.

Above us, a nuthatch called in alarm at seeing Hades, or it might have been because of the squirrel I heard scrabbling amongst the foliage overhead.

'Mordred questions why you came back,' Arthur said.

'I came because you sent for me,' I said, sensing the cold undercurrent to the conversation and not liking it. 'What does Mordred believe?' I asked. From the corner of my eye I saw the squirrel race along a branch. A little streak of fire, then it was gone.

'He thinks you want Dumnonia,' Arthur said. 'That you would sit on Uther's old high seat.'

This was not what I had expected to hear and it came like a blow.

'Do you see a war host at my back, Arthur? Spearmen flying my banner?' I said, not caring now if I chased away every creature within a mile so that Hades never stretched those great wings and we returned empty-handed to Camelot.

'It was proposed that you and King Syagrius have an arrangement,' Arthur said. 'Why else would the king let you, his general, his champion, leave Gaul?' He shrugged. 'But if he loses Soissons, as he surely must sooner or later, then perhaps he sees a future here.'

'What future? He is as old as Uther was,' I said.

'He has sons,' Arthur said. 'They are his future.'

I stopped and stood glaring at him as he took two more steps then turned to face me, the bird on his arm preening her scapular feathers.

'I left all of it, the day after Guinevere came,' I said, appalled at what I was hearing. 'I did not even seek the king's blessing. I just walked away. From my responsibilities. From my men. Why? Because you need me.'

'You knew Guinevere was coming,' he said. 'You sent word telling her to wait for you on Mont Tombe.' He lifted an eyebrow. 'Which she ignored, of course. But you could have written to Syagrius. He could have promised you spearmen in return for Caer Gwinntguic. Or even Dumnonia, with you as his warlord. Why else would you leave those men who looked to you for leadership? Why abandon men with whom you have fought and bled?'

'For you,' I said. I held my spear wide and turned my empty hand palm uppermost, showing that I had nothing to hide, nor anything else to give, other than myself. 'For you, Arthur,' I said again, glaring my challenge at him.

Perhaps I was more stupid even than that bird on Arthur's glove. Perhaps I had been a fool to come back. I looked at Arthur and wondered if the years had changed him so much that I could no longer read his face as I had used to. Then to my relief he gave a slight nod and I saw in that gesture the old Arthur and I knew that he did not believe his own words. That those words had tasted foul to him, for all that he had not been able to leave them unsaid. And now he was glad to be rid of them.

Poison must be drawn, I heard Merlin say in my mind.

'You don't believe any of this,' I told him, relief flooding my body like the warm glow of spiced wine.

He shook his head and let out a long breath. 'I don't,' he said.

The eagle-owl must have been heavy on his arm, easily as heavy as a sword, yet he kept that leather-sheathed arm as still as the leaf-laden boughs above us. 'I don't think Mordred does, either. Not really.' His brow furrowed. 'He doesn't like you, Lancelot. Ever since that day we ran into those Saxons in Caer Gwinntguic and you spoiled his fight.'

Spoiled his fight? That was one way of putting it. As I remembered it the fight was over and Mordred had been about to die in the mud, when my spear took the young Saxon's life and gave Mordred a future.

In the years I had been gone, Mordred had become a renowned warrior in his own right and one of Arthur's ablest warlords. And yet he still hated me for saving his life.

'He does not forgive easily,' Arthur said, alluding to the sixteen or so years that Mordred had spent hating him, until at last he had come to Camelot to forgive his father and pledge his sword to Arthur's service. 'I fear you and Mordred will never be friends,' Arthur said.

I did not answer that. Arthur was stroking Hades. The bird bobbed its head, those long ear tufts giving it an indignant look which somehow reminded me of Merlin, who had not been seen for years, so that some folk believed that the druid was dead.

Arthur lifted his chin, his eyes boring into mine. 'But we are friends, are we not?' he said.

I had the absurd idea then that he was going to throw his arm and send that barrel-shaped bird streaking towards me in a flurry of beak, feather and talon.

'Of course we are friends,' I said.

He nodded. 'Come,' he said.

We made our way amongst the trees again, heading east through shafts of golden summer sunlight which speared through the canopy, towards the wood's edge and the meadow beyond.

'Then as my friend, tell me how you felt when you saw Guinevere again,' Arthur said, stepping over deadfall without breaking stride.

My mouth tasted sour. I would rather have fought off the eagle-owl than have that question hurled at me, and as I planted my spear I caught a glimpse of my own eyes reflected in the blade.

'I would have the truth, whatever it is,' Arthur said, as though he knew I was asking questions of myself.

We walked on, the bird song, the buzz of flies and the snap of dry sticks beneath our feet seeming to grow louder, like waves rolling up the shingle.

'I was happy to see her,' I said at last.

Arthur considered that for a long moment. 'Just happy?' he said.

So this was why we were alone in the woods with that bird who, for all her magnificence, would surely rather have been snugged up in her roost waiting for nightfall. As it was, King Einion of Ebrauc would have to wait a day longer. So too the people of southern Caer Gwinntguic who saw Saxon spear blades and helmets glinting in the sun. All of Britain would wait, because Arthur must know if I was in love with his wife.

But how could I be in love with Guinevere? Until seven days ago I had not laid eyes on her for eight years. Before that, she and I had barely spoken since she came to Camelot. Whatever Guinevere and I had once shared, it lay in the far-flung past. It was the heady days of early spring only barely recalled in the long winter dark. It was a half-remembered melody. An old feeling given fleeting life by a smell or a song.

How could Arthur imagine that my heart would still clench in my chest at the thought of Guinevere? That my blood would beat like a drum in my ears at the sight of her gathering herbs from Camelot's ramparts or tying the worm's knot to cure a restive cow, or shearing wool from a black sheep to cure a child's earache.

How had he known that I had ever loved her?

Because he knew Guinevere, that's how. Because he loved her too, and he knew me as well as I knew him. And because he was no fool.

Above us, the crack of squirrels breaking hazelnuts. To my right, a rustling in the litter, then silence as the unseen creature waited for us to pass.

'I do not know your Guinevere, Arthur,' I said.

It was the truth, yet I could see that Arthur did not know how to take it for the implicit admission that she had once been mine. Or at least, I had been hers and fool enough to believe she was mine.

'I want her to be happy,' I said.

An easier truth for him, that. I saw his teeth pulling at his lip, but whatever he was thinking of saying remained unsaid as we broke from the trees and came onto open land again.

We turned north-west, keeping the warm breeze on our faces so as to be downwind of any prey.

'I am sorry I cannot give you more than a score of horse,' Arthur said. He was taking sixty horsemen north to Ebrauc to fight the Picts, leaving me with just twenty.

'A score will be enough,' I said. We had learnt that just the sight of those big men on their armoured mounts was often enough to sow fear into the Saxons. And men in fear's grip fight only for themselves, not for their spear-brothers, and that was when shieldwalls broke and death poured in.

'No prisoners, Lancelot,' he said.

'No prisoners,' I said.

We had already agreed our strategies. He would help King Einion drive the Picts back into the north, then ride east to fight with King Masgwid the Lame of Elmet against King Cerdic's Saxons. Gawain and Bedwyr would go with him, as would Mordred and Melwas, who was Mordred's man these days. My task was to kill those Saxons who had come west into Caer Gwinntguic and then take the fight to Rhegin and the Saxons' settlements there. I was to bleed the enemy in the south so that they would not be strong enough to venture north for at least two seasons. By showing that his sword still reached all across Britain, and by helping these kings in their own wars, Arthur would be proving himself High King in all but name. Next spring, he would sit on the Pendragon's high seat whether he was acclaimed or not. He would rule and even if we could not throw the Saxons back into the sea, maybe they would be content to farm the land they had in Rhegin and Lindisware and Britain would know peace. And maybe the clouds themselves would take the shape of the bears which adorned our shields and war banners, and every stream would chime with songs of our victories, and the flames in folks' hearths would whisper the name of Arthur.

'There,' I said under my breath, reaching out to stop Arthur mid-stride.

'She's seen it,' he said, moving only his eyes down to the eagle-owl on his arm.

Sixty paces away, partly shaded by the spreading canopy of a beech whose leaves flickered with the breeze, was a hare, its grizzled yellow-brown fur a smudge amongst long green grass.

I watched Hades fasten her eyes on her prey, as my little sparhawk had used to do long ago. Saw her body tense on the glove and the feathers around her face lift slightly with anticipation. I held my breath and with graceful fluidity Arthur lifted his arm and Hades flew, her huge wings, their span as long as I was tall, skimming the grass as she beat upwind.

I saw the hare lift its head, sensing the danger, then it dashed away across the meadow, fast as an arrow off the string but not fast enough. Spreading those great wings to stop herself, Hades struck the hare, which squealed in terror and pain. I heard the crunch of bone as the bird sank her wicked talons deep.

'The hardest part is getting her to give it over,' Arthur said as we hurried across the field, both of us thrumming with the excitement of the kill. Both thankful for the distraction from that which the day had really been about.

It was funny in the end, the two of us standing there over that bird who refused to relinquish her kill, with Arthur holding up a mouse by its tail as a trade, having brought it with him for this very reason.

'Well, don't ask *me* to try to steal the thing away from her,' I said, when Arthur swore under his breath and looked up at me, shaking his head with frustration. We were the protectors of Britain. We were leaders of men and lords of war. And yet we could not take a dead hare from a bird.

Hades glared at us as if daring us to steal what she alone had won. But we did not dare and so we laughed, the sound of it rising on the warm breeze of that summer morning.

And the next day, we went to war.

24

Black Bryony and Bittersweet

I SPLIT MY ARMY into three parts and sent Bors ahead with fifty spearmen, telling him not to fight the enemy. Telling him to avoid a fight even if it meant showing the Saxons his back and running away. Unsurprisingly he had not liked that, but he understood what I needed of him.

Our scouts had spotted a Saxon war band camped between the Tarant River and the old Roman town of Noviomagus. Two hundred of King Aella's wolves, sent to prowl east along Caer Gwinntguic's southern borderlands and try Arthur's strength. Aella knew of Arthur's obligations, of the treaties he had made with the other kings of Britain. The Saxon king knew that Arthur was being pulled east and north. He knew that Arthur would be drawn into King Masgwid of Elmet's war against King Cerdic, too, and so he was testing our spears. Bors's job was to make Aella think he had found us wanting.

'Find them, and let them get a good look at you,' I told Bors. 'Make it seem that you will fight. But do not fight.'

'What if we run into their skirmishers? If we outnumber them, yet do not fight?' Agga said.

Bors and I had been amazed to see Agga again. Like Melwas before him, he had left Karrek and the Lady to come and fight for Arthur, the promise of war being a lure too bright for a young man who has given his life to the practice of weapon craft to ignore.

'Then they will think we cannot risk losses, Agga,' I said. 'They will think us weaker than we are and that will make their chieftain even more eager to kill you. But you will not fight him.' I had turned back to Bors, to impress upon Agga that Bors was in charge, hoping to soothe my cousin's wounded pride, for it turned out that Agga was the spearman of whom Guinevere had spoken. He had married Bors's one-time sweetheart Emblyn, and though Bors did not blame Agga, it was no easy draught to swallow.

'You will find good ground,' I told Bors. 'High ground. Set yourself up on some hill, raise your banner and wait for me.'

That's what Bors had done, and it was a good hill, too. Steep and boulder-strewn on three sides, but one side sloping onto wide, rolling pasture. A gentle enough slope not to deter a war host from climbing it, even in formation with shield rims kissing. Gentle enough for the leader of that host not to even consider splitting his force and sending some men up the steep and difficult sides. No, he would take his two hundred spearmen straight up that slope, confident that he could strike the Britons off the summit of that hill, as his god Thunor might knock apples off a tree with his smith's hammer.

But the Saxons would never reach the top of that hill.

The night before the battle I dreamt of my father. He was dressed in his war gear, his helmet and mail, as though he would fight at my side the following day. He did not speak in my dream. I too was dressed for battle and I had thought my father would be surprised to see me older and possessing the accoutrements of a warlord, yet he did not speak. And I stood before him, then held him in my arms in such an embrace as I hoped would hold him to this world. And I wept like a child, so that I woke unbalanced and weary and as heavy as if a druid had laid a curse upon me. For in my dream my father had been so real. So immense and strong, and I had touched him. But when I woke he was nothing but the void of his absence, the empty air through which he had once moved.

Yet I took some small heart from having seen him again, ready to fight at my side, so that I almost pitied the enemies that I would face that day. And later that morning, as I waited with my fifty warriors at the foot of the hill's northern side, hidden from Bors and the enemy ranged below him on the eastern slope, I saw another omen.

I was strapping on the greaves which Arthur had given me, when Agga touched my shoulder and pointed into the northern sky, where a distant clamour of rooks stood out like a black cloud against the deep blue of cornflowers. We did not say anything but just watched those birds, both of us aware of the ill portent should those carrion-feeders fly over the hill's summit and Bors's men who waited up there, or over those of us at the foot of the hill. Then, for reasons only the gods know, those raucous birds turned before they reached the hill and swept eastward, so that the Saxons must have felt their cool shadow wash over them and felt the bad omen in that.

Agga grinned at me, looking like the freckle-faced, copper-haired boy I had known on Karrek, and I nodded and bent to finish strapping on the greaves. We had never been true friends on the island but I had always liked Agga better than Melwas and I was glad to have him with me then, even if he and I had never fought in a proper battle together.

Then, before our savage eagerness for the fray could become tainted by the doubt and fears that seep into men made to wait too long for a fight, Bors's man up on the hill sounded his war horn. Still we waited, because I knew that Cai and Parcefal and their twenty armoured cataphracts would be skirting the hill's southern side at the canter, making their way up to the pasture so as to get behind the Saxons.

That horn blast meant that the Saxons had started to advance uphill. Bors had let them see him and then retreated in search of a good place to make a stand. Now our foes had taken the bait and those men from some land across the grey Morimaru must have thought they would make a slaughter to have their long-dead ancestors thumping their fists on the mead benches of their god Woden. They looked up at that rise and saw not Arthur's bear but Uther's dragon, vivid and blood-red against cloth which had once been white but now was grey. I had sent Agga to fetch that banner from the old hall at Tintagel and we had fixed it between two new long boar spears so that the cloth would stretch and that dragon could stand in all its sharp-clawed and winged glory, even on a windless day.

Seeing Uther's dragon would confuse the Saxons. Perhaps they would think we Britons hoped to invoke the old warlord's spirit. Or they might presume that Arthur's son Mordred had taken up his grandfather's symbol as his own and that it must be he who now waited to die on that hill. Certainly they would think that Arthur had taken his war horses north, which he had. But he had not taken all of them.

The horn sounded again, like the lowing of some great bull, and that meant that Cai and Parcefal were killing. Their men arrayed in an arrowhead formation, they had thundered across that summer meadow, spears couched, and struck the Saxon rear, and so now it was our turn.

'Let them hear you,' I told my men as we set off at a fast walk, striding up the northern slope, beating our spear shafts against the inside of our shields, singing the death hymn of Balor, that mournful tune rising on the warm breeze. And when we crested the rise we saw the carnage which our armoured men and horses had wrought. We saw the terror which they sowed.

The Saxon shieldwall had been three men deep and facing uphill, and the last thing those men had expected to see was Lord Arthur's famed horse warriors bearing down on them. They had barely the time to turn in that tight press and get their shields up before this wedge of horseflesh, muscle, iron and blade had ploughed into them. The riders' long spears punching through shields and leather and mail and the frail bodies beneath. The horses themselves smashing bones and throwing men to the ground. Iron-shod hooves trampling them, pummelling flesh and cracking skulls.

Having left a chaos of shrieking, dying, bloody men in their wake, those horsemen had re-formed on the uphill slope, Parcefal glinting in scales at the point and Cai on his right shoulder, Arthur's dragon-headed wind banner, which whistled and keened when the wind blew through its open mouth, raised up, the silk streaming from it like blood. Now they brought their bloodied spear points down, kicked their heels and charged again, and like sheep seeking the safety of the flock, the Saxons sought desperately to mass together as best they could, given the mess of bodies and shields littering the ground.

We sang for Balor, god of death, promising slaughter in his honour. I looked up the hill and saw Bors thrust his spear into the air. Saw him yelling the order to attack, though could not hear his voice above my men's singing and the battle clamour ahead of us now that Parcefal and his twenty war horses had struck the Saxons again. Though this time they did not punch through the Saxons but rather stayed amongst them, stabbing down with their spears, wheeling their mounts and running men down – but holding their ground, because what they had done was split the enemy into two parts.

'Now!' I roared, and I ran to join the fray, and my spearmen ran with me. No song raised in honour of our gods. Just screams, raw and wild and given to the terrible joy of battle.

The Saxons had not expected to face armoured horse. Now those of them who were not fighting for their lives looked up and saw Britons flying down the slope at them, spear blades and shield bosses flashing in the sun. Some of those Saxons looked north and saw yet more Britons charging towards them, led by a god of war in gleaming bronze scales and a silver-chased helm, its white plume streaming.

'Kill them all!' Agga cried, and threw his spear at the run. I saw it streak across the distance and plunge into a man's chest as he turned to face this new threat, the violence of Agga's cast throwing the Saxon back as a rain-filled gale might flatten barley.

Then we were amongst them.

I held on to my own spear, using it to turn a Saxon spear blade before scything it back to savage his eyes.

They still outnumbered us, and had it been a fight between two shieldwalls we would likely have lost. But there were no shieldwalls now. There was just a maelstrom of bodies and blades, and the Saxons, skilled and fierce as they were, were reeling with shock and terror. For they must have known that we had trapped them. They saw enemies on all sides and they saw big, armoured horses amongst them and they must have thought that Arthur himself, the warlord of Britain, had come to kill them.

Agga killed the man I had blinded, while I buried my spear in the soft place under a Saxon's arm as he thrust his spear overhead at the man on my right. Then I drew Boar's Tusk and started killing.

I lopped off a man's sword arm then opened his bowels to the air. I spun, taking an axe blow on my shield, and slashed through a bearded neck. I was fast and strong, honed by years of battle and blessed by the gods of war, and my enemies could not touch me with their blades. Agga, too, was deadly. He moved with fluid grace, striking and cutting with prowess earned from boyhood. From a life dedicated to the craft. And somewhere on the other side of our horse warriors who stabbed and thrust about them, Bors too was reaping lives. We three were Pelleas and Benesek, Edern and Madern. We were the amalgam of their skill and experience, and where we fought the Saxons died.

A horse squealed and I saw it go down, its rider hauled from the saddle and butchered with spears and long knives before his companions could kick their own mounts close enough to help him.

'Agga,' I called, pointing Boar's Tusk at a Saxon who wore a long mail coat and a gilded iron helmet which had a face mask comprising eye-sockets, eyebrows, moustache, mouth and a nose made from tinned bronze.

Agga nodded. Men instinctively flanked Agga, just as they flanked me, and we both worked our way towards that magnificent helmet, like converging streams, and the Saxons before us either gave way or died.

Yet neither I nor Agga killed that Saxon warlord. Before we could get close enough to fight his bodyguards, Parcefal on his enormous mare forced his way through the press, laying about him with a long and gore-slathered sword. For he too had seen that helmet shining in the sun. Whoever that Saxon was, he saw death coming for him through the eye-holes of that mask, and even though I never saw his face, I was certain there was no fear in it. He eyed Agga and me, waiting for us to reach him, his scarred shield across his chest and his spear blade pointed at the sky.

Parcefal's sword took off his head. For the Saxons around him, the sight of that lustrous helmet, head and all, tumbling down into the shadowed crush of feet and filth, was as bad an omen as if the sun had suddenly gone from the summer sky. A shudder ran through the Saxon throng and perhaps many of them would have thrown down their weapons and begged for their lives had they not known we would kill them even if they did so.

And so many more Britons died before the end. When that end came, it was sudden, swift and bloody. A knot of Saxons on the downhill slope dropped their shields and ran. Seeing this, those of their spear-brothers who were not fighting for their lives broke and fled, so that those remaining were outnumbered and easily cut down.

'Fools,' Bors snarled, panting beside me as we watched the last of the Saxons break and hare down the hill. 'They'd have been better off running up the damn hill,' he said. Blood-spattered, streaming with sweat and round-eyed with the savage thrill of butchery, my cousin made a fearsome sight.

'The end would be the same,' I said, as Parcefal and Cai and the sixteen men and horses still able to fight kicked back their heels, lowered their long spears and galloped after the enemy. 'Did you see the rooks fly over them,' I said, 'when you were up on the hill?'

Bors knuckled sweat from his eyes. 'I saw them,' he said.

Merlin, wherever he was, would have said that that omen was a message from the gods and perhaps it was. What he would have said about my dream before the battle, in which my father and I clung to each other as we had never done while he was alive, I could not guess. But what did it matter now? We had lured the enemy into our trap and slaughtered them. I stood there on that gentle slope, aware of the blood coursing through my veins and my heart thumping beneath my breastbone and the leather and scale armour. I thought the gods were with me. I thought myself invincible. And we had won.

That summer we marched east and took the war to Rhegin. Spearmen from Caer Gwinntguic joined us, wanting revenge for King Deroch whom the Saxons had murdered and thrown off the ramparts of Venta Belgarum along with his high seat. Furthermore, hearing of the great slaughter we had made, one hundred and twenty warriors led by Lord Farasan marched south from Caer Celemion to swell our numbers. Lord Farasan was a good fighter and a useful ally, having for years held his southern border, and these days his northern territories, too, against the Saxons advancing along the Tamesis valley.

I would have given much for thirty, even twenty more of Arthur's horse soldiers, but those long-experienced warriors were in the north with their lord and I had to make do with the seventeen that I had. Still, there were times when I strapped on Tormaigh's boiled leather armour and rode him into battle alongside Cai and Parcefal, revelling in the stallion's strength and quickness. Loving the freedom of it. Thrilling in the charge like a hawk folding its wings and stooping to the quarry.

We fought the Saxons whenever we found them outside their forts or beyond the frontier which they had long ago agreed with Ambrosius Aurelius, but which King Aella refused to recognize.

It was a summer of blood, and by the time the first cold dewy mornings came, and the days turned still and heavy with the air smelling of damp earth, we had killed and maimed, mutilated and butchered more Saxons than we knew had ever come to our shores. And still there seemed no end to them. The spears on their ramparts were forests. The clamour of their war songs was thunder on the air and we knew that come next spring there would be more boats crunching the shingle of Rhegin's southern shore. More ambitious young men hungry for land and plunder and glory.

We had seen over two hundred of our own warriors killed and

many more wounded so that they might never again carry a spear in defence of their homes and kin. Just eight war horses were left now and only six men experienced enough to ride them. Our blades were dull from killing, our shields were splintered and our bodies were weary. And even if we had not won, in as much as we had not even come close to driving the invaders back into the sea, we had not lost. Not one battle.

I had led our brave men into the fray time and again. Whether mounted on Tormaigh or fighting on foot I was the first to blood the enemy and the last to sheathe my sword. The Saxons had learnt to fear me. They saw my scale armour and my white-plumed helmet, which had once been Benesek's, and they knew death was coming.

It was a summer of blood, and at that summer's end, when the low sun threw long shadows across the land, we had done enough to check the enemy's advances and send Aella to ground like a fox before the hounds.

I had done what Arthur asked of me. But then came news far worse than any omen. Worse even than the certainty of more ships and more Saxons coming in the spring.

I was tired from war and sick of the stench of death, but I was feared and respected. I was Arthur ap Uther's right hand. I was a lord of war. And yet when this news came from the north, I cried like a child.

Word came from the north like an ill wind. Riders carried it first to Camelot and from there a man rode east to find me camped in a valley a half-day's ride south of Venta Belgarum. Despite having had several days to practise their delivery of the news, the messengers were rigid and tight-faced as they dismounted sweat-lathered horses and walked towards me across mud glistening in the light of a watery, corn-coloured sun.

'My lord Lancelot,' the older of them said, white hands balled at his sides, his eyes flicking from me to Bors to Parcefal, who had come from his tent to hear what they had to say. 'Lords,' he said, including the others. 'It is my duty to—' He stopped and cleared his throat, then scratched awkwardly at his bearded neck.

'Out with it, man,' Bors said.

The messenger nodded. 'Lord Arthur is dead,' he said.

I looked at Bors, then at Parcefal, who had known Arthur for many years, stupidly thinking that Parcefal would tell the messenger that it was not so, that he had made some mistake.

'How?' Parcefal asked, blunt as an old knife, before I could find my tongue.

'Slain in a battle north of Galwyddel,' the man said, deliberately emphasizing the name of that place, as if to make a point of how far away it was. 'Our lord and future king is slain helping the King of the North,' he said, the words escaping tight lips. Clearly he did not think his lord should have been fighting another man's war, though he stopped short of saying so.

'And King Einion?' I asked. If he was dead too, Britain must surely face ruin.

'Alive,' the messenger said.

'And Mordred?' Parcefal asked, for Arthur might not be king but he was the protector of Britain, and as such, Mordred was his heir.

'Alive,' the man said, nodding at Parcefal, who nodded back, taking some small comfort in that fact at least.

'Mordred has . . . the body?' I asked. I did not know why I asked that then. Perhaps I simply needed to know where my friend was beneath the sky. Even if his soul had flown the flesh.

The messenger glanced at his younger companion, who it was clear did not want to play any further part other than having ridden all this way.

'Lord Arthur's body was lost,' the other man said.

Bors shook his head and cursed. I looked at Parcefal, whose scarred face now looked as fierce as it had ever done in battle.

I turned my glare back on the Dumnonian. 'Lost how?' I asked.

He frowned. 'In the melee, lord,' he said.

'Then perhaps he is alive,' I said, seeing a glimmer of hope in his grim account.

But the man shook his head. 'Mordred saw him fall. He tried to reach Arthur but there were too many of the enemy. He was forced to ride clear or else be cut down beside his father.'

Parcefal grunted, as if to suggest that would have been the thing to do under the circumstances.

'And Gawain?' Bors asked.

'He and Bedwyr are alive. They withdrew at Mordred's command,' the man said. 'They are riding south to Camelot with what's left of the army.'

It was barely autumn but that news made my blood run cold. My thoughts struggled in their own melee and I found it difficult to draw an even breath. Arthur dead? It did not seem possible.

'Was the battle won?' I asked.

'Neither won nor lost,' the messenger said.

'Yet Mordred is riding back to Camelot.'

'With Arthur dead, Lord Mordred believes any obligations to the King of the North are void.'

'I agree with him on that,' Parcefal said. 'Why waste more men fighting the Picts when we have enough enemies of our own at the gates?'

Still, I felt more contempt than ever for Mordred then, knowing he had left Arthur's body to the enemy. I shuddered to think how the Picts would treat such a trophy. I shuddered even more to think how Guinevere would take the news. Her husband, the Lord of Dumnonia, the hope of Britain . . . and my best friend, was dead.

Facing Guinevere was harder than killing Saxons. Much harder. She had known before me, of course, but when I saw her, after a meeting of Arthur's warlords, it was as if she had seen Arthur cut down. She was pale and glassy-eyed with grief, the way some men are after their first battle, or after taking a blow to the head. And yet even in her anguish she shone in that dark hall. Brighter than the beeswax candles and the polished bosses of the bear shields which hung on the walls.

'I should have been with him,' I said, not knowing what else to say. I had waited until the hall was empty but for two or three slaves who scurried about gathering cups and plates and scraping food leavings into a bucket for the pigs. Guinevere did not meet my eye but watched a young Saxon boy scattering clean reeds upon those made dirty by so many warriors' boots.

'You cannot protect us all, Lancelot,' she said.

Our eyes had met earlier, while Mordred talked of how he had tried and tried again to reach Arthur before the Picts could unhorse him and deal the death blow. And in that look I had told her that we must speak, for all that I detested the idea of seeing her pain up close, her agony at losing the man we both loved. But now she would not look at me.

'What will you do?' I asked.

'What will any of us do?' she said. Hers was the better question, for without Arthur to unite the kingdoms, Britain was doomed. There was no one else. No lord or king who looked beyond his own borders to see what Britain could be if only we stood together against our enemies.

She looked over to Arthur's chair, carved in oak as Uther's had been, but incised with a bear's face high on the splat and paws on its arms, their claws already wearing smooth from Arthur's touch.

Mordred's chair now, I thought. Perhaps that's what Guinevere was thinking too. For Mordred had just declared his right to rule in his father's place. More than this, he had claimed it was his duty to assume the mantle of Lord of Dumnonia and protect the kingdom as his father had. He had not gone as far as to suggest that he be proclaimed king, as Uther had been and as Arthur intended to be. But he would, in time. I knew it.

'Why did you not speak against him?' Guinevere asked me. She turned and looked at me and I saw that she had not been sleeping.

'Why should I speak against Mordred?' I asked, then lifted my chin towards Arthur's high seat. 'I do not want it,' I said. 'Neither does Gawain. Nor Bedwyr. Nor Parcefal. Arthur was the only one—' I stopped. Saying his name put a lump in my throat. 'He was the only one who believed Britain can be whole again, as it was when Maximus reigned.'

'Mordred wants it,' she said, looking back at that bear-carved chair.

I shrugged. 'Perhaps he is the best man to sit there. At least he wants it. And he is Arthur's son. Uther's grandson.'

'He hates you,' she said.

'He does,' I said. 'But he cannot harm me.'

Mordred had changed much in the years I had been in Gaul. No brooding boy now, he was a full-grown man and a warrior of reputation. He commanded his own loyal spearmen and was as brave as any man in battle. Perhaps he *was* the only man in Dumnonia who could lead. But no matter how much he hated me, I did not fear him.

'I'm sorry,' I said.

'You didn't kill him,' she said. There were no tears in her tired eyes. Perhaps she had done all her crying already. She pursed her lips and released a long breath whilst pressing the heel of her hand against her chest. As though staunching the blood from a wound.

'You are still the Lady of this hall,' I said.

'Mordred does not want me here. He'll bring Morgana to Camelot now Arthur is gone.'

'He won't dare move against you,' I said. But she did not seem to care.

'Why did you give me back the ring?' she asked. I thought I saw a glistening of her eyes then, by the light of the nearby candle.

I considered her question for a moment. 'Because the ring was a promise,' I said. 'A promise you could not keep.'

'I was just a girl,' she said.

'A promise neither of us could keep,' I corrected. I remembered that day when I had ridden away from Camelot, having pulled that silver ring from my neck and given it back to her. 'You had a different life. A new life.'

She worked a thumb into the palm of her other hand. 'And what do I have now?'

I wanted to take those pale hands in my own and put them to my lips. I wanted to breathe warm breath into them.

'You have me,' I said.

She closed her eyes and shook her head as if I had spoken disrespectfully. And perhaps I should have regretted those words. Perhaps I was without honour. And yet, it was the truth. She *did* have me then, in that sorrow-filled hall, with Arthur's high seat standing empty as though waiting for him. Just as she had always had me, since that day when we were both children and I had cheated the sea god Manannán mac Lir of his rich haul.

'Lancelot, I see you have come sniffing like a hound after scraps.' We turned to see Mordred standing in the doorway. 'Or have you been eyeing my father's seat?' He leant against the thick doorpost, lifted his chin and scratched his fair beard. So much like his father then. 'Or perhaps you covet both? My father's wife *and* Dumnonia?'

'Careful, Mordred,' I said as he grinned and came deeper into the hall. As always, Melwas was with him, close as a shadow, and he leered when he saw Guinevere and me together in the shadows near the bear-carved chair.

'Now, now, Lancelot,' Melwas said, jutting his chin at me. 'You should show respect to the Lord of Dumnonia.' He snatched a wine jug and two cups off a passing slave.

'And you should have protected Arthur,' I said, to Melwas and Mordred both.

Melwas slammed the cups and wine down and dropped a hand to his sword's hilt, but Mordred's raised hand stopped him drawing the weapon. More of Mordred's men were coming blathering and laughing into the hall and he did not want to begin his reign by spilling blood there. How could he unite the Britons if he could not keep peace in his own hall? Besides which, he knew I was not afraid to fight him or Melwas or anyone else in all of Britain. I had been Arthur's champion. Mordred knew I was the best. I knew it too.

'Get out, Lancelot,' Mordred said. 'Both of you,' he added, turning hate-filled eyes on Guinevere. 'Out of my hall. You dishonour my father by being here together.'

I squared my shoulders to him, ignoring the hands that were on weapons and the murmurs on lips. 'Talk to my Lady like that again and I'll kill you,' I said. I did not need to touch Boar's Tusk to give weight to that threat, and every man in the hall fell silent then, their eyes round in the flamelight.

'Go, Lancelot,' Guinevere said, loud enough for all to hear.

I did not move from that spot on the dirty rushes.

'You see, even she grows tired of you,' Mordred said.

I looked at Guinevere.

'Don't worry about me,' she said. 'I'll not be chased out of my own hall.' She gave me a sad smile. 'Go.'

I looked at Mordred, hating him. I looked at Melwas and could almost feel how he hungered to fight me. The other men in that hall simply looked on, scenting blood and doubtless hoping to see some.

'Go,' Guinevere said again. 'I'm safe here. Just go.'

And so I went.

There was a crust of old snow on the ground the night they came for me. Camelot was a frozen mound in a black land. A silent, smoke-wreathed bastion rising from the coastal plain and wetlands of eastern Dumnonia like a statement of defiance. Hope in the darkness.

It was a cold night, cold enough for extra bed skins. Cold enough to see your own breath fogging, even indoors if you neglected to keep the hearth well fed. Summer was a distant memory, of bright wheat fields and heavy air thick with buzzing insects. Of golden dawns clamorous with bird song, and green pastures and the sweet breezes after rain. Of war too. Corpses littering hillsides like pale stones.

Wolves prowling in the wake of our army, like gulls flocking behind a fishing skiff. Of crows and ravens sidling and hopping amongst the wreckage, all black wings and bickering and greed-glossed eyes as they feasted upon the dead.

The land slept, swathed in ice and muted. Watched over by the distant glimmering stars and perhaps by the gods, too. Such a night that even our foes the Saxons must have been snugged up in thick furs, perhaps remembering winters in their old northern homelands across the cold sea. But the Saxons were not my enemies that night.

I should have known they would come. I knew Mordred hated me and had done since the day we met, when he had ridden into Camelot with four severed heads tied to his saddle horns. In the autumn he had brought his mother, Morgana, to Camelot, just as Guinevere said he would. For years Mordred had sought Arthur's permission to bring Morgana to court but always Arthur refused.

'I don't want her here, Lancelot,' he had told me once. 'No good can come of it, and Mordred needs to understand that.' It was no surprise that Arthur did not want his half-sister around, not after the shame of begetting a child with her. 'Anyway, Morgana despises me,' he said. 'Not that I blame her. I did nothing to stop Uther's plan to have the infant killed.'

'You were young,' I had said, trying to soothe his tortured conscience. 'And your father was the High King. What could you do?'

Arthur's lip had curled. 'Still, I earned Morgana's hate. Mordred's too.'

Despite Arthur's joy at having Mordred at his side, he had never relented in this matter. Now, though, Mordred was free to do as he liked, and so Morgana, who had hissed at me the day Uther died, lived in Arthur's hall. And Morgana despised Guinevere. Not that Guinevere had let her and Mordred drive her from the place. She lived at one end of the hall while Mordred and his mother lived at the other, and I imagined that the air itself in that hall must have been cold as frost, no matter how high the flames in the hearth.

Yet for all the hate that hung over Camelot, its whispers unmuffled by the snow that smothered rooftops and softened the points of palisades, I had not thought Mordred would act on it. I was still young enough and arrogant enough to think that he would not dare.

I was wrong.

I woke at the sound of booted feet tramping across the brittle snow and was upright in my bed, long knife in hand, even before someone hammered my door with the pommel of a sword.

Pulling Boar's Tusk from its sheath so that I was as well armed as I could be having just blinked awake, I walked past the hearth and opened the door to see Gawain looming in the night, his breath fogging around his big beard. I saw three spearmen behind him. Good men with whom I had fought many times, though now they were grim-faced and threatening.

'Mordred wants your head, Lancelot,' Gawain said.

'Then tell him to come and take it,' I said.

He grinned. 'I did. But he insisted I do it. Some sort of test, I suppose.'

I looked at him. Felt the cold air on my bare chest. Felt the familiar comfort of the knife hilt in my left hand and Boar's Tusk's hilt in my right.

'So, have you come to kill me, Gawain?' I asked him. He was my friend. We had shared campfires and wine, bloodshed and sorrow. We had both shared Arthur's dream and a love for the man himself.

'No,' he said, pressing a finger against his broken nose to close one nostril, then turning away to blow a wad of snot into the snow. His sword was sheathed, though I saw that his hand was on the hilt. 'I've come to tell you that you'd best leave. Tonight.'

'I thought you said Mordred wants my head,' I said.

'He does,' Gawain said. 'So you're lucky he asked me to pluck it for him.'

'And them?' I said, jerking my head to indicate the fur- and mail-clad warriors waiting in the starlit gloom behind him.

'They do what I say,' he said. He sighed and I smelled wine on his breath. 'I'll talk to Mordred,' he said. 'I'll tell him that we need you. Come the spring, with Saxon ships scraping up the shingle, he'll beg you to come back. But spring is a way off. For now, you'd better go. I'll say you weren't here. That you must have known somehow. He'll believe me.'

'And if he doesn't?' I asked.

He shrugged. 'I don't care. He needs me and he knows it. He'll seek to make amends with you soon enough, but it'll be best for all of us if you're not here in Camelot for a while.'

'What about Guinevere?' I asked.

'She's safe. He won't hurt her. The men still love Arthur too much. Mordred knows it. Even Morgana won't risk their anger.'

'And Bors?' I asked. I knew that Bors was loyal to me. Mordred knew it too, which meant that if I was in danger, so was my cousin.

'Bors is snoring in his bed. I've got men watching his place to make sure he stays out of this. We don't want blood spilt. Bors is safe, you have my word. I'll tell him what happened.' He raised an eyebrow. 'When you're gone,' he said, stressing those last words.

I wanted to put on my war gear and tramp through the snow to Arthur's hall and challenge Mordred there and then. He had always been jealous of me and now he wanted me dead, so let us fight man against man. Let the gods and men watch. But I knew that Gawain could not allow me to challenge the new ruler of Dumnonia, let alone kill him. And Gawain was my friend, and so I would go.

'I'll talk to him,' Gawain assured me when I had packed my gear, my scale armour and weapons, my furs and blankets, cloaks and food, and thrown my saddle upon Tormaigh, who snorted with derision at being brought out of his warm stable into the frigid night.

'Don't waste your breath, my friend,' I said. 'I will not come back. Not even if Mordred begs.' I looked around at the buildings upon Camelot's summit, most of them exhaling smoke to add murk to the darkness. It was not the same place without Arthur. As for Guinevere, my being there put her in danger, which I should have realized before then. I was sick of war. Tired of it. Wearied by years of fighting enemies I knew I could never beat, not in five lifetimes. And besides, I was not the first to turn my back on Dumnonia, on Britain herself. The gods had done that already.

'You're a good man, Lancelot,' Gawain said. 'I'm proud to call you my friend.'

'And I you, Gawain,' I said. 'But do not ask me to fight for Dumnonia again, for I will not.'

He seemed about to say something, but then his lips tightened and he nodded. I mounted Tormaigh and took up the reins. 'And look after Guinevere,' I said. 'For Arthur's sake,' I added.

He nodded again. Then, the fire still burning back in my hearth, I turned Tormaigh round and walked him away across the icy ground towards the south-west gate.

No one challenged me. It was likely that no one saw me, that Tormaigh and I moved through the freezing, smoke-haunted dark like shades stalking the night on Samhain. But then, when I was almost at the gate, above which two sentries stood huddled in furs beside a flaming brazier, I heard hooves breaking the old snow behind me. My hand fell to one of the spears which I had tied to my saddle and I turned Tormaigh to face whoever was following me. Mordred perhaps. He had learnt what Gawain had done and he had come to kill me himself. I hoped it was Mordred, and the battle thrill fluttered in my chest and in the muscles of my thighs.

Then the rider came within the glow of the sentries' fires which reflected off the snow and I saw that it was not Mordred. Neither was it Gawain come to make sure that I left. Nor Bors, having ridden to say goodbye or intending to come with me perhaps.

Mounted on Eilwen, her white mare, Guinevere was swathed in wolf pelts and ermine, her face hidden but for a sliver of pale skin and her eyes, dark pools amongst the pelts. If not for Eilwen, no one would take her for the Lady of Camelot. But then I hardly looked like the champion of Dumnonia. My old bear skin was well-worn but still thick, and with Tormaigh's winter coat shaggy at his breast and neck, in the dark it would be hard to see where I ended and the horse began. We must have appeared like some huge, hairy beast.

'What in Arawn's name are you doing?' I said.

She walked Eilwen closer, her gaze fixed on me as she pulled the skins down to uncover her mouth. Her breath plumed on the night air and for a long moment it seemed we were the only living souls on that Dumnonian hill. 'Gawain said you are not coming back.'

Strands of dark hair had fallen across her left eye and in that moment I remembered the girl she had been on Karrek Loos yn Koos. Inscrutable and knowing and yet somehow wild.

'There's nothing for me here,' I said.

She considered that. 'And Dumnonia?' she said.

'I fought for Arthur, nothing else,' I said.

'Because you swore an oath to King Uther?' she said.

I shook my head. 'The oath had nothing to do with it.'

She almost smiled at that. 'And now?'

'Mordred is not Arthur,' I said. 'I owe him nothing.'

'Where will you go?' she asked.

I shrugged.

'I have something for you,' she said and reached towards me. I put out my own hand and she put something in it, and in that moment as our skin touched, my blood coursed with elation and guilt, desire and shame.

I opened my palm and looked at the silver ring sitting in it. The same ring which Guinevere had given me in the doorway of the Lady's keep those years ago. The ring which I had returned to her when I rode out of Camelot to war in Gaul, I the one leaving, yet letting her go.

'I'm not in the mood for games,' I said, though I closed my fist around the ring, feeling its warmth in my hand.

'No games, Lancelot,' Guinevere said.

'Announce yourself,' a spearman called down from the gatehouse.

'Lancelot,' I said without turning.

'You're going out now, my lord?' the man asked.

'Open the gate,' I said. I was still looking at Guinevere, though I noticed the leather knapsacks tied to Eilwen's saddle horns and suddenly I knew.

'You're coming with me,' I said.

'Why would I stay?' she asked me.

'You are the Lady of Dumnonia,' I said.

'I am Arthur's wife,' she said. 'But Arthur is gone.'

Even then it seemed unreal. How could Arthur not be drawing the same cold air into his lungs? How could Arthur be just a memory?

'You would give up all of this?' I asked her, glancing left and right towards the dark buildings which sat squat and leaking smoke into the night.

The hint of a smile touched her lips. 'If I stay I'll only end up putting wolfsbane in Morgana's wine,' she said.

I smiled at that. Morgana hated Guinevere as much as Mordred hated me, and ever since she had come to Camelot Mordred's mother had tainted the very air, for all that she wanted men to revere her, for her beauty and her new status as the mother of the future king.

Behind me, the creak of the gate announced its opening. A rush of cold night air licked the back of my neck and I heard a vixen screech somewhere in the south.

'I'm never coming back,' I said again, needing her to know that.

Needing her to be sure. Hardly daring to believe why she had saddled Eilwen and followed me in the cold dark.

'I know,' she said. 'Where will we go?'

'Caer Gloui,' I suggested. In truth I did not know where I would go, only that I would leave Camelot before I killed Mordred or he killed me.

Guinevere looked over her shoulder. Camelot slept and there were no signs that she or I had been followed. But that did not mean Mordred would not send men after us once he knew that I had ridden out of the south-west gate unharmed. I wondered if Gawain would draw his sword against me if it came to it. I wished I had said goodbye to Bors, but I knew it was better this way.

'We should go,' Guinevere said. 'We need to be far away come dawn. And even then we must make sure that they cannot follow our tracks.'

I knew spearmen who would baulk at the thought of riding out into such a night as that, with no promise of a fire or a roof to sleep under. With night spirits stalking and cut-throats lingering in woodland beside the roads. Not Guinevere. I nodded, my heart swelling to know that the years had not tamed her. She was still the girl who would scale ledges and crags for a gull's egg. Who would dive through high waves and climb to the tops of slender trees to rob them of mistletoe. She was the girl whom a sea god had wanted but could not have. Whom I had wanted, but could not have.

But now I turned Tormaigh towards the gate and Guinevere urged Eilwen forward, so that we rode out through the snow-crusted ramparts together, the gate creaking behind us and the bleak, bitter night before us.

Thus did I turn my back on Camelot and Dumnonia, and on Britain herself. Let armies tear each other apart. Let the gods sow chaos and reap souls. I did not care.

I move between worlds. Brisk and nimble through the forest litter. Skittering up trunks, scampering out along gnarly branches. Sharp claws finding purchase, strong hind legs impelling me up and up. Leaping from tree to tree as fast as fire running through dry thatch. I know all the paths and the nooks and all the secret places. I remember all my hoards, too, buried when the air turned thin and cold, scavenged long since.

I run and jump, deft and brave, bounding below the sky yet above the ground, a frenzy of theft and movement. Always looking out for shifts and changes and dangers and opportunities.

A sound in the forest stills me. A predator? From the corner of my eye I watch. Wait. A fawn, foraging amongst the forest flowers. No enemy of mine. I am all quickness again, darting from bough to bough, seeking like a breeze amongst the green canopy.

Vigilance. Fleetness. Agility. These are mine.

Another sound. I stiffen. There. I see them. A woman and a man walk- ing together. Smiling. Laughing. They come to a glade where the bracken is thick and lush. A green bed. No threat to me, these two, yet I hold to the spot, feeling the breeze-fluttered leaves through the slender branch beneath my feet.

Truly a restless spirit, this creature. It takes all my talent to hold him. But I do hold him to that branch and I watch.

The man treads the bracken down and she watches him, and when it is done she takes the cloak from his back. Lays it down. They undress each other. They stand white and dappled gold by the warm dusk sun. Their eyes on each other like predators and like prey. They lower each other to the cloak.

It takes an age. But I watch.

She lies, looking up at the sky through flickering leaves. Her hair on his cloak like a raven's wing spread in flight. Then she looks at him and smiles, her lips red as rowan berries, as his own dark hair falls to hide her face.

I watch, seeing neither now, and yet both. Grappling and grasping, entwined like black bryony or bittersweet on the sun-stippled forest floor.

25

Red in the South

W E WERE TRULY HAPPY that summer. Perhaps as happy as we had been on the island, when the world was still new to us and the summers seemed to stretch on for ever. We lived in an old woodsman's hut in the beech woods on the borderlands between northern Dumnonia and Caer Gloui. Long abandoned, the hut had all but been swallowed by the forest, though with sweat and resolve we reclaimed it and made it our own. Other than that simple dwelling and our horses, and those few belongings which we had carried that night we turned our backs on Camelot, we had nothing. And yet we had everything.

In our own ways we mourned Arthur, and for a while his absence was as an invisible rampart between us. But one night, when we had finished laying the thatch of reeds across the old roof beams and a summer rain hissed down to test our labours, we became in body what we had only been in mind. Whether we made a silent pact to let Arthur go, or whether we were simply too tired to maintain the pretence of propriety, only the gods can say. But under that new thatch, at the edge of a creek hidden amongst the reed beds, we gave in to ourselves and each other.

It was a golden time. Like the island home which we had used to roam, free as the hawk and the hare, the woods were our sanctuary, a haven far from war and people, and from time itself, or so it seemed. But we were no longer children and the summer, as glorious and yet simple as it was, could not last.

It was dawn. Samhain was approaching, when the veil between our world and the world beyond is at its thinnest. I had been out to fetch more wood, my breath fogging in the damp, earthy air and droplets of dew falling from the sodden leaves above, when I took a moment to watch the first light creep through the forest. A small brown shape caught my eye, some creature bounding through the beech mast. A weasel, I realized, then watched with growing unease as it did not veer away but capered towards me, the white fur of its belly and chin flashing as it leapt. I spat towards the creature to avert the evil which his behaviour presaged and he stopped, stood upright, glaring at me, then hopped away amongst the trees, leaving me to ponder that ill portent. And yet it was forgotten the moment I went back inside, set the logs down by the hearth and turned to see Guinevere stretching upon the bed skins. How she could steal my breath even then.

'It's red in the south,' I said.

Guinevere's beauty was timeless. Gods-given, I believed, and perhaps that's why Arawn had coveted her and schemed with Manannán mac Lir to drown her that storm-flayed day when she had been but a child.

'Then we shall have rain and cold,' she said, sitting up, thinking nothing of her nakedness and sweeping her hair back from her face. It was as though she did not know her own power, nor how it could affect me still, like a horse kick to the chest.

'Then I'll take the bow and get a duck before it rains,' I said.

'I'll come,' she said, glancing at the hunting bow which leant unstrung against the wall. Next to it on a peg hung a quiver of arrows which we had fletched with goose and swan feathers in the summer. 'I have the better eye,' she said, those green eyes full of challenge, 'and you don't know how to stay quiet. You always scare them away before you get close enough,' she said, the corner of her lips curled in a wry smile.

'Do I, now?' I said, folding my arms. Feigning offence.

'Yes, Lancelot, you do,' she said, climbing from the bed to make use of the fuel I had fetched.

I stepped into her path and she stopped and shot me a defiant look, her head tilted to the side so that her hair fell away from her face.

'But it will turn cold?' I said.

'If it was red in the south,' she said, her eyes narrowing with suspicion.

'Then we should work some warmth into our flesh before we go out,' I said.

'Should we?' she asked, trying not to smile.

I nodded and swept her up into my arms and she laughed because she was a full-grown woman, not some slip of a girl, but I carried her back to the bed.

And I was happy, but it could not last for ever.

Guinevere heard them first. Her hand tightened on my arm and she held her breath and I was looking into her eyes when the door thumped open, sending a pair of spears clattering to the floor and some roosting bird flapping and squawking up from the reed thatch roof.

I rolled over on the bed skins, snatched my long knife from its hook on the wall and sat upright, the blade raised. And to my horror I saw who had come.

He stood there in the doorway, Excalibur in his hand, his face ashen, his mouth hanging open.

'It can't be,' I said. 'How can it be? Arthur?'

I thought it must be Samhain already. That this must be Arthur's shade returned to haunt me.

His eyes were wide, bulging in his grey face, as they filled themselves with the sight. Torturing him.

He bellowed and flew across the small space, Excalibur raised as though to strike, and he swung his gaze from Guinevere to me and back to Guinevere, as if he could not decide which of us to kill first. Which of us most deserved to die.

'Arthur! We thought you were dead,' I said, having thrown my arm and the long knife wide, rather than threaten my lord and friend with it. And yet I held on to that knife.

Arthur screamed a curse at me, spittle flying from his mouth and catching in his beard, then he turned and swung Excalibur, sinking the blade into a roof post, and I used that moment to put myself between him and Guinevere, whose face was all incredulous horror as she watched Arthur wrench his sword free of the wood.

'She's my wife!' he roared, swinging his baleful glare back to me.

Mordred was in the doorway behind him, looking more like his father than he had ever done. Melwas was there, too, though his eyes were in Guinevere like hooks.

'My wife,' Arthur said again, his unblinking gaze still fixed on me. Though this time the words were small. Almost lost things. Fragile as the last autumn leaf. There were tears in his eyes.

'Arthur,' I said, holding my arms wide to show I meant him no harm as I moved to the edge of the bed and stood, feeling his hot breath on the bare skin of my chest. 'They said you were dead.' I dropped my chin and slowly placed my long knife on the bed by Guinevere's bare feet. She had pulled the bed skins up to cover herself, not that it stopped Melwas staring. I had my trews on, though nothing more. 'Mordred said he saw you killed,' I said.

Arthur was breathing fast. His flesh trembled, as if a hateful spirit inside him fought to break out of his skin and drown the dawn in blood.

'How could I know the Picts had taken him prisoner?' Mordred said from the doorway. 'All I have done is protect Dumnonia. But you, Lancelot? Look what you have done.'

Arthur lifted Excalibur towards me until the point rested above my chest, in the hollow of my throat. One thrust and it would be over. Part of me wanted him to do it. I think he saw that in my eyes, and perhaps that's why he did not. But his eyes burned into mine, his teeth clenched in a snarl. A grimace of unbearable pain.

'Husband,' Guinevere said, the word unsure, as though she were testing it. As though it tasted different now on her tongue. 'We didn't know.'

He turned on her, though kept Excalibur pressed against my throat, cold iron against hot flesh. 'You have bewitched him,' he snarled at Guinevere. 'I can smell it.' He spat towards her. 'You have done this.' Tears dripped from his beard, once golden but now greying. 'You have . . . broken it,' he said.

In that bitter moment, as much as I pitied my friend for what we had done to him, I hated him for the agony I saw in Guinevere's face. We had thought Arthur dead, yet here he was, not his restless spirit come back to our realm, but flesh and blood and tears. Arthur had returned and found only betrayal.

I saw his eyes flick down to the bed and linger there a while. What tortures his mind must have summoned. Then those tear-brimmed eyes came back to me and his brows lifted, giving him such an aspect of sadness as could have darkened the dawn.

'Never before here. In this place,' I said, answering what he could not ask. 'Only since we thought you dead. I swear it.' I needed him to know that. For what it was worth.

He lowered Excalibur, looking at me as though I were a familiar stranger whose likeness he was trying to place. 'And before?' he said. 'When you lived on Lady Nimue's island?'

I blinked slowly, wanting more than anything to spare him that wound, yet knowing I could not lie to him.

'Yes,' I said. 'There, yes.'

Arthur nodded. Took a breath. 'Mordred, take her,' he said.

'No,' I told Mordred, who approached with that leech Melwas at his side, their swords raised.

'It's all right, Lancelot,' Guinevere said, gesturing at Mordred to pass her the long overdress which lay on the rush-strewn floor. Mordred did, offering the dress on the end of his sword. No sooner had she put it on than he took hold of her arm and pulled her towards the door.

'Take your hands off her, Mordred,' I snarled.

'You presume to order my son?' Arthur rasped at me.

'I'll kill you, Mordred,' I said.

Mordred grinned, thrusting Guinevere to the threshold, where she stopped and looked back at me.

'Do nothing, Lancelot,' she said, and for a brief moment we saw the end of everything in each other's eyes.

Outside, a horse whinnied and I knew that Mordred had made Guinevere mount Eilwen, her mare.

'You did this,' Arthur told me, then he turned away as though he could no longer bear to look at me. 'You did this,' he said, walking back to the doorway through which the first spits of rain were gusting on a thin breeze.

Melwas stood there still, in a warlord's scale armour, his sword raised towards me.

'Arthur,' I called, but Arthur was gone and a few moments later I heard the three of them gallop off into the beech wood.

'Just you and me now, Lancelot,' Melwas said, not quite smiling. 'I've waited a long time for this.'

'I'm better than you, Melwas,' I said.

'You have always thought so,' he said, then pointed his sword at Boar's Tusk which hung in its scabbard from a peg by the open door. 'I'll be waiting outside.'

And he was.

He came at me fast and hard, his sword a grey blur in the grey dawn, but I was unencumbered by armour and quick, almost as agile as I had ever been, and I knew better than anyone alive how Melwas fought. He lunged and jabbed, scythed and swung, but his blade could not cut me. He feinted high and swept low, tried the wrath blow, swinging from above and diagonally, aiming for my ear, and the low blow, seeking my arms, but I saw every cut before it came. I knew his next move even before he had finished the last, knew his patterns as a spider knows its own web. And as he tried to kill me, I moved like smoke weaving through a crowded hall.

Still, he was good. Better even than I remembered. Perhaps his hate lent him speed. Perhaps the years of enmity had honed him more than years of war had, for he parried and twisted, thrust and cut beyond anything I'd seen, so that thrice he forced me back and I felt the close passing of his sword on my bare skin. He was good, was Melwas. So very good.

But I was better. I had always been better. And even if Melwas had never admitted it to himself, he knew it then because he had given everything he had, tried every cut, every dance, every trick, yet I was unharmed. Not once had his sword found the bare flesh of my arms, chest or back, and now he was sweat-sheened and panting and his eyes said that he knew.

I spun Boar's Tusk forward, as I had done so often when we had fought each other as boys, and I grinned at Melwas. Even in the midst of that appalling dawn and the misery it had wrought, my blood thrummed, flowing hot and urgent as it always did when I beat an enemy.

I killed Melwas with a cut to his neck. I gave him a quick death, for no other reason than because we had grown to manhood together under the same sky, but as he died I thought of my sparhawk, that angry, yellow-eyed bird. I whispered to her that she had been avenged. After all the years.

Then, leaving Melwas where he lay, I went inside and took my scale armour, my greaves and my helmet with its long white plume from the chest where I had stored them in oiled skins. Much of the bronze was covered in a green crust, but I had a jar of apple vinegar and would clean the war gear until it shone like the summer which had gone for ever. I would comb the horse-tail crest and polish Tormaigh's boiled leather armour. I would hone Boar's Tusk until it was sharp enough to cut bonds of blood and memory.

They had taken her from me again. And so I would go back despite having sworn that I never would. I was Lancelot, son of Ban and lord of battle. They had taken her from me.

And I was going to war.

26

Trial by Fire

I RIDE TOWARDS THE FIRE. Towards chaos. Tormaigh encased in leather armour, his shaffron and breastplate gleaming like chestnuts, his mouth flecking at the bit as I drive him on. The stallion lives for the charge and knows he carries a lord of war, though he does not know what I must ask of him now.

We weave amongst the trees, Tormaigh's breath as loud as forge bellows, his black mane bouncing and shattering. His iron-shod hooves pummelling the ground like a drum beating to war. In my right hand I grip a long spear, in my left the reins, though all the stallion needs is the touch of leather against his neck to veer the opposite way, so that we thread the forest as neatly as a goshawk. In truth I need only look in the direction I want him to go, and we break from the tree line and I let out the reins and lean forward, pressing my heels, and now we really are flying, flinging mud into the past, Tormaigh's black mane given to the wind like a silken war banner.

That wind is in my face, cold and sweet with woodsmoke, yet still Tormaigh's hoofbeats carry to the crowd up on the rise which shifts like a current through the sea, faces turning to the coming thunder. They see a war horse, one of the legendary beasts which their enemies have learnt to fear, charging towards them in leather and mail. On its back a lord of battle in bronze scales burnished to shine like the sun. In polished iron helmet, his face enclosed in silver-chased cheek pieces, its white plume streaming behind, white like the cloak on his back. They see the steel glint of his spear blade and the bronze greaves on his lower legs, a gift as famous in Dumnonia as the friendship which had them forged.

They know me. Know why I have come. And they stare with wide eyes, touching iron for luck, pushing against strangers to clear a path.

Tormaigh does not slow. If anything, we ascend the slope even faster now, the stallion's great heart beating us up like wings lifting a hawk into the sky, and I feel the cold air on my teeth as we crest the ridge, the crowd ebbing from us, and I see the flame leaping from the brand in Arthur's hand. I see a billow of black smoke behind him, and a golden bloom amongst the dry stalks of last summer's barley.

Spearmen run to face me, shields and shafts raised, but Tormaigh doesn't slow and my spear blade opens a man's throat and we are through, and now I see her, bound to the stake by an iron chain, her dark hair blowing around her pale face. A Christian priest harangues the flame, spitting at it.

'Burn the witch!' he cries, his thin voice sharp enough to pierce the murmur and shouts of the crowd, as Arthur turns, his own scale armour full of the fire he carries, and sees that I have come.

If they had thought I would come at all, they had not thought I would come from the trees, and now I see warriors with bear shields pushing west through the congregation, skirting the little hill of timbers and the sacrifice at its heart, reckless in their eagerness to get to me and to protect their lord.

A spear flies from the throng but misses me. Another blade streaks through the smoke and I duck and it sails above my head, then I pull Tormaigh up and dismount in one movement and I am striding towards Guinevere.

A spearman blocks my path so I cut him down.

'No, Lancelot!' someone cries. It is Agga, with whom I learnt blade craft, and now he raises his shield and spear and sets himself before me, but the fire is growing, questing towards Guinevere, and I feint high and sweep low, taking Agga in his shin. He drops to one knee and I leap high, thrusting down over his raised shield into his side and he is dead as my feet hit the ground once more and I stride on.

More are coming. Perhaps this was a trap. Perhaps he lit the fire because he knew I would come. Would he put out the flames if his men cut me down? Would he scramble onto that pile of timber and cut Guinevere free, if I lay dead in the grass?

'Hold, Lancelot!' Bedwyr, horse lord, pushes through the crowd on his black mare, flanked by two more men who had been my brothers once. 'Hold!' Bedwyr bellows, but I cannot, and my spear flies. Such a throw as would have made Benesek proud. It impales Bedwyr through his chest before he can even lift his shield. A moan rises from Dumnonian throats to see their hero, Bedwyr slayer of Saxons, slumped dead in his saddle.

I pull Boar's Tusk from its scabbard as the other two drive their mounts towards me, but they are hampered by the moving swell of folk who have come to watch Arthur punish us who betrayed him.

I see Arthur's eyes now within his helmet. We had thought him killed in the north, gone for ever, yet now he looks at *me* as one might glare at a long-dead friend on Samhain night, and I hold his gaze, as Gawain, coming up beside him, roars at the spearmen of Dumnonia.

'Kill him!' Gawain yells. Gawain, my old friend. 'Kill the traitor!' he shouts.

Two more spearmen try and both die for it.

Though he yet holds that fire brand, Arthur has not drawn Excalibur and so I walk past him and climb onto the pyre and he just watches as I hammer Boar's Tusk against the iron chain, not taking my eyes from Guinevere's.

'Kill them all,' she says, wild and full of hate.

The heat is ferocious, a loud inexorable breath on my skin, accompanied by the crack and spit of the dry fuel. The flames are around our feet now, licking up through the gaps. Hungry. Flapping like little war pennants in the wind.

The chain breaks and a spear embeds in the stake where Guinevere was a heartbeat before. She and I clamber down into the maw of the congregation, men and women shrieking at us as we run hand in hand back to Tormaigh, and more spearmen burst from the crowd.

'Go,' I tell Guinevere, pointing my sword at the stallion, who has savaged a spearman who tried to take his reins. But Guinevere will not go without me and I cut a man down and send another reeling.

Then I lock eyes with a third and see that it is Bors. He lifts his chin to the two horsemen, who are free of the crowd now and waiting for me, their spears levelled.

They spur their mounts forward and a shaft cuts through the smoke and takes one of them in his neck, knocking him backwards off his horse.

'Go, cousin,' Bors says, running to meet the last rider, who is not quick enough. Bors twists away from his spear and rotates, driving up with his legs and thrusting his sword into the man's belly, and I mount, pulling Guinevere up behind me. I turn Tormaigh in tight circles, the stallion shrieking from the blood and fire, the noise and the acrid smoke, and I see Arthur still standing there, watching me, the torch still in his hand, its fire reflected in his scale armour, making him look like a golden king.

Bors is mounted now too, looming in the saddle which he'd emptied with a throw better than any I had ever made, and we kick our heels and ride, seeking a way through the spearmen who swarm around us now, thrusting and lunging but wary of the beasts which have been trained to trample their enemies. One of them is Mordred, his face twisted with hate as he jabs his spear up at me, calling me traitor.

A spear blade slides off my right greave and Tormaigh rears, squealing, mane flying, his forelegs striking men's shields and heads and throwing them back, and Guinevere somehow holds on and then the stallion's ironshod hooves thump onto the ground and we plough through the throng. Through the drifting grey haze, back towards the trees from whence we came.

'Bors,' Guinevere says. I feel her go rigid and I haul on the reins and turn back towards the chaos and the pyre which is all flame now, roaring with fury at being cheated of its offering. But Bors is not with us. There is just the horse, walking riderless down the slope in our wake. Its eyes wide. Its flanks red.

And so I turn Tormaigh back towards the woods and kick my heels and the ground flies beneath us.

We hold each other against the cold and the night. Against the very air itself, as though it would harm us if it could.

'I love you, Lancelot,' she says, her first words since. I tell her that I love her, too. That I have always loved her, even from that first day of storm and drowning, when I should have been too young to know. Her tears are for Bors. I feel them pressed between our cheeks, warm and wet, and do not wipe them away. 'He said I bewitched you.'

'You did,' I say, moving just enough to kiss her lips, which taste of salt.

She thinks about that. 'My father sent him a priest, to free him from the spells I had used to bind him, just as I bound you. The fire would do the rest.'

I tell her that I cannot believe that Arthur would have let her burn. That I do not want to believe it.

Her eyes hold mine with a beseeching force. 'We betrayed him,' she says.

I say, 'You were mine before you were his,' but she does not answer that and I hear how petulant it sounds. How wrong, too. Guinevere had never belonged to me, nor to Arthur, nor even to her father, who had sent her to live in the shadow of the Mount. Some creatures must always be free.

She unties a ribbon of green silk from her wrist and ties back her hair. 'What will we do?' she asks.

A sound in the woods beyond our lean-to shelter. The whites of Guinevere's eyes as we hold our breath, peering between the upright branches and green yew boughs. Nothing moving in the dark woods. Just fat drops falling from sodden branches. I wonder if the pyre still burns, or if the rain has made it a seething, smoking hill. I wonder if Arthur stands beside it still. Staring west after us.

'We will live,' I say.

'And Arthur? Dumnonia?' she asks.

I breathe in the earthy, woody scent that fills that dark den. Dying leaves and damp air. Death and decay.

'Arthur is nothing to me now.' I remember him standing by the pyre. Watching me. Why hadn't he drawn Excalibur and fought me? Had he wanted me to free Guinevere? 'I fought for Arthur, not Dumnonia,' I say. 'All of it is gone now.' I hold her and kiss her forehead. I bury my face in her hair and breathe her in, smelling the woodsmoke from what would have been her balefire. I tell her that none of it matters. Not my reputation, nor the wars nor Dumnonia. I tell her that she is all I need.

'Poor Bors,' she says. 'He loved you, Lancelot.'

'And I him,' I say, my throat tightening like a knot. I do not want to think of my cousin and how he died helping us escape, yet I keep seeing in my mind that riderless, blood-drenched horse, and I wonder if I shall see it all the days of my life.

'You will be with him again,' Guinevere assures me, her breath warm on my neck. And perhaps I will. But for now he is gone, my cousin and my friend. My good, brave Bors. And all I can do is hold Guinevere tighter, my own tears falling in the dark.

Next day, we ride south all the hours of light and bed down in a shepherd's hut, flames flickering in the hearth while a keening wind tears at the world. We lie together as though for the first time, or the last, and after, as I rest in her arms and she in mine, I think I would not fight if death came for me.

When we come to the sea we turn west and ride on, and if not for Tormaigh, the fishermen and simple folk along the coast might think us no more than a man and wife out to find a new life, perhaps fleeing some round in Caer Gwinntguic plagued by Saxons.

'You will have to sell him,' Guinevere says. 'As it is, they will come after us. You cannot hide a horse like Tormaigh.'

She is right. Last night was last night. Now, on this new day, I would fight one hundred men. I would live through disease and defy the gods. Anything to stay with Guinevere. I imagine Mordred out looking for us, asking men if they have seen the traitors who turned on their lord. And men would answer that they had seen a man and a woman on a big dun war horse and point off in the direction we had ridden.

But I cannot part with Tormaigh and we ride west into Cornubia. I tell Guinevere that I do not care if I never see Dumnonia again.

'I have you,' I say. 'I want nothing more.' She smiles and asks me where has the warlord gone? Where is the grim warrior whom she found prowling through the dark forests of Gaul?

'Sometimes I can still see you as the boy you were, Lancelot,' she says.

Sometimes I feel I am still the boy who took the sparhawk from the old smokehouse. I am still the boy who wished he had taken the gyrfalcon instead, so that his father would have been proud. I think all this but say nothing, and we ride on, the low sun at our backs throwing long misshapen shadows on the old Roman road.

We sleep in the ruins of a Roman temple which has been used as a winter byre for cattle, though there are still patches of white plaster on the walls and the faint remains of long-dead people painted by a skilled hand. Guinevere did not want to sleep in a place once inhabited by foreign gods and said she would rather make another shelter in the woods. But the weather has turned cold and dismal. Grey clouds drift down from the sky while a frigid mist rises from the earth, so that we ride through a damp miasma that chills the blood. And we are both so tired.

'Just one night,' I had said, and she nodded, too weary to argue.

I think of asking her to use her talent, to let her spirit wander free of the flesh and journey in search of Arthur and Mordred, to learn if they are coming after us. But I know the journeying takes a heavy toll on her and she is already so tired. Besides, I have not seen her use the talent since that night long ago, when she and Merlin had flown far together, until I broke the spell by attacking the druid. Had I done that because I could not bear to see Guinevere used in that way? Or was it because I had not liked that which I could not understand? Or perhaps it had been jealousy, because Guinevere had given herself to the enchantment and left me behind. Whatever the reason, I had thrown Merlin against the wall and brought them both back to their bodies, and even now I do not think I can bring myself to ask Guinevere to give herself to the craft.

The night is long and dark in that place, with the ghosts of those who once prayed there for company, but at last I fall into a dreamless sleep.

I'm woken not by dawn, which has come and gone, but by a wind-driven rain spitting through a hole in the roof. I sit up in the skins and furs and it is as though an invisible fist, like the unseen hand of some Roman god, has struck me in the stomach, driving the air from my body. The green ribbon, with which she had tied back her hair, lies amongst the furs. I snatch it up and call out, but get no reply other than the rain gusting against the roof tiles. I run outside and find Tormaigh alone, cropping the wet grass, and I call out again, my voice raspy from sleep and smoke. But I know it is in vain.

I know that Guinevere is gone.

I am rat. I move in the shadows, in the corners and cracks, scurrying across the straw and reeds unlit by hearth flame and lamplight. I am hunted and hated, yet nothing stops me scavenging and feasting on the prizes which they leave behind and which their hounds have not gobbled up.

I feel this creature's loyalty to its tribe, the need to nurture its young. Its readiness to fight if necessary. I sense its mastery of our surroundings, of this hall in which it was born and has given birth. And yet I know that at the first whiff of danger, of smoke in the thatch or a bitch at her nest, she would pick up her litter and flee, venturing into the unknown without once looking back.

Up the table leg now, sinking my claws into the soft wood, climbing as deftly as a squirrel up an oak's rugged trunk. Onto the boards, where trenchers of flesh and plates of cheese and cups of berry-smelling liquid sit abandoned. As well that my belly is full, else I could not prevent this creature gorging on such a feast.

But there! The golden man, glinting in scales by the candlelight, reeking of the blood of other men. He who sent the rest of them scurrying from his hall, his wrath like the storms which sometimes shake the stout door in its frame or lift thatch from the roof.

I feel his misery. It comes off him like dampness. Like the pungent scent of fruit beginning to rot. He drinks long and deeply and when he bangs the cup down upon the board it rattles my limbs.

Now the other man stalks back to the table, he too stinking of horses and blood and hate. His eyes the same eyes. His body covered in the same burnished scales.

I scamper through spilled liquid, past an overturned cup, and cower against a loaf which radiates heat from deep inside. I sniff the air, my ears reaching forward, then stand on my hind legs and slowly move my head from side to side, trying to see better with these poor eyes.

Their voices are as the rumbles of sullen grey skies. The golden man turns his gaunt face up, stares at the roof beams where some bird has its nest. He holds on to the table's edge as if he fears being swept away by a great torrent of water. He closes his eyes and bows his head, and I feel my tail flick this way and that. This creature trying to shake me off. Knowing it is a dangerous game we play. That one of them may see her and kill her. Kill us both, perhaps.

The younger man pours red liquid into a cup, filling it to the brim. Gives it to the golden man, who bares his teeth at the offering but takes the cup to his lips. When the cup thumps down the other man fills it again. Then looks up and sees me and I squeal in fear.

Down onto all fours, I turn but he is upon me with the jug, smashing it down so that I feel the baneful snap of bones and the hot, wet ruin of my innards. Down it comes again and I shriek, desperately calling my spirit back lest it be trapped in this dying creature and snuffed out like a candle.

The taste of blood and terror and the creature's last gasp.

I fly.

27

Death of a Dream

FOR TWO DAYS I retrace our steps, like a man retreading his own footprints in the snow. Like a hunter trailing a deer. My fear, that she means to go back to Arthur. To make things right between them. Between us all.

I do not care who sees me or who they might tell. I ask anyone I find if they have seen her: women braving the day to gather firewood and men cutting peat. A bent old crone gathering bracken. A man and his son driving a cart full of reeds and sedge for thatching. I even ask the creatures I come across. An oystercatcher stabbing at worms in the mud. A hare gnawing the bark of a birch tree. But no one has seen her and I have already ridden further than she could have walked, and so I turn back and go west again, avoiding the old Roman temple this time and sleeping beneath the sky, lest that place and the ghosts of old gods had brought me bad luck.

Sometimes men recognize me, if they have carried a spear against the Saxons. Even with my helmet hanging from a saddle horn and my scale armour rolled up in leather behind me, they know who I am and they call Taranis's blessings upon me and ask Cernunnos to protect me, that I may in turn protect them against their enemies. I wonder, would they do the same if they knew my crimes? If they knew that my spear had killed Bedwyr, the master of Lord Arthur's famed horses. What will the bards say of me when I am gone? Will I be remembered as the man who broke his oath to Arthur?

Lancelot the betrayer.

Let them scorn my name for a thousand years. I care not, so long as I am with her.

But she is gone, and so I ride west in search of her, like a man chasing the sun that has already fallen beyond the far horizon. West into

the land of the people of the horn, named for the Cornubian peninsula which juts into the Dividing Sea.

I cannot lose her again. I will not.

The fisherman was one of King Menadoc's Sun Shields once. He
knows me and says he was there that day long years ago at Tintagel,
when High King Uther died.

'I wasn't in the hall, of course, being a nobody,' he says, though his
old warrior's pride lights his tired eyes. 'But we heard about you. How
Merlin brought you to the Pendragon's bedside and old Uther had you
swear an oath to protect the next king. And you just a beardless lad
and all.' He grins at the memory of that distant summer. 'We saw you
after and knew you must be something special. You helped Arthur
find the sword, didn't you? Is he king in Dumnonia now?'

'They have never acclaimed him,' I say.

'And where would we be without him?' he asks, touching the iron
of his fishing knife at the thought of Britain without Arthur.

He agrees to take me across the water on the rising tide and swears
that his grandson will look after Tormaigh. I offer him coin but he
will not hear of it, saying that it is an honour to serve Lord Arthur's
champion and friend. Cringing inside my skin, I nod and thank him
and push the skiff into the surf, the hem of my white cloak billowing
in the cold water before I jump aboard, almost numbed by the sight
before me.

'Don't see folk coming and going these days,' he says, insisting on
rowing us himself. Still proud, though his only armour these days is
the fish scales glittering on his tunic and trews and in the little boat's
bilge.

I say nothing, too full of memory now to speak.

It looks the same as the first day I saw it. A great tree-swathed hill
rising from the grey sea. Granite and gorse and a tower on its crown,
looming against the sky in which gulls tumble and shriek.

'You know the Lady?' he says.

'Yes,' I say, feeling as though I am coming home. I see myself swimming through time and tide. I see the boys training with spear and
shield on the eastern slope. I hear Guinevere laughing as we run
together across the rocks, jumping pools, our bare feet slipping on
bladderwrack and slick weed. Nothing but memories now.

I tell the fisherman to meet me in the little bay at dawn two days hence and he says he hopes I find who I am looking for. Not what, but who, and I wonder how he knows.

And yet as soon as I step ashore, I know that Guinevere is not there. Perhaps I have arrived here first, as when we were children, though I had not known that I was waiting for her then. Yet the air itself changed the day she came. As unmistakable as the scent of green leaves opening after summer rain.

Now Karrek is as it had been before her. I feel her absence even as I see the toll which the years have taken on this place. The hut in which I had lived with Pelleas is a ruin, its roof fallen in. A memory flashes in my mind, like an eel rolling in the pail, of fever and tears. Of Pelleas kneeling and telling me I was his friend. Of steeling myself to put Boar's Tusk to the hollow between his neck and collarbone. Of pushing the blade down.

Some of the huts still stand and while weather-beaten and neglected might yet keep the rain off, but ghosts care nothing for rain.

I feel like a ghost myself. A soul lingering long after the body has been given to flame or earth. Seeking all that it has lost. A spirit full of envy for things that never were but which might have been. I think of Benoic and my family and I try to picture my brother with a man's face and bearing. I think of my mother, loving her and hating her too, for choosing my uncle over her own husband. And I think of him, my father the king, and I wish I could meet him as a man, without fear, and know him properly.

'Lancelot, is that you?'

I turn to see a man come from one of the huts and for a long moment I just stare at him, hardly daring to believe my eyes.

'Benesek,' I say, and a moment later we are locked in an embrace, holding each other fiercely because neither of us has the words.

Eventually we both pull away and he looks me in the eye and asks me where Bors is.

'He is dead,' I tell him, hoping that he does not ask more, seeing the hurt I have done him with that news. Though his eyes tell me this is just the newest pain, like fresh snow falling on layers of old ice. 'Where is everyone?' I ask.

He frowns, pulling at one fork of his long moustache, which is white now. He is smaller than I remember him, not bent with age nor wasted to bone. Just smaller somehow.

'All gone,' he says. 'Nearly all. Left to fight in Arthur's wars. Or just left.' He shrugs. 'Or died.' He waves a hand towards the bay, in the direction of the place on the far shore which we used to call The Edge. 'The girls went home or to husbands,' he says. 'No new ones came.'

I think of little Geldrin, always the weakest of us, and of long, lean Jowan, whose arm Melwas had broken the first time I ran in the annual foot race. I wonder what became of pretty Erwana, and Alana who had kept Guinevere's and my secret and helped us to cover our tracks more times than I could remember.

'Guinevere is not here?' I ask, though I do not need to.

The old warrior eyes me with suspicion. 'Why would she be?'

I say nothing and he asks what I am doing there. He says that if I've come looking for more spearmen then I have had a wasted journey, but then he grunts, as though understanding. 'Arthur needs Merlin,' he says, watching my eyes for confirmation.

'Merlin is here?' I say.

'Of course he's here.' He cocks his head back towards the Mount rising behind him and I look up, half expecting to see the druid watching us from the top of the keep. 'They were lovers once,' he says. 'Long time ago. Long before your time here.'

That raises goose flesh on my arms. Although, in a way, haven't I always known there was something deep and old running between those two? It made sense of why Pelleas and Benesek had never liked the druid. Why they had always been so protective of the Lady.

'He came when he found out,' Benesek says. 'I don't know how he knew, and I didn't ask. But he knew.' It is as if a shadow falls across his face then, even though there is no sun visible in the pallid sky. 'She's dying, Lancelot,' he says. 'I don't know what of. Neither does Merlin, but it won't be long now. That's why he came.'

A sudden coldness moves inside me, somewhere deep down, and Benesek looks away for a long moment, giving me time alone with that revelation. In my mind the Lady is as she was the day she stood on the shore and watched Benesek, Bors and me board the *Swan* bound for Tintagel; not young but not old. Golden and ethereal and so far beyond the ravages of years and disease as to seem protected by the gods.

Benesek tilts his head and examines me as a man might study a horse before making the trader an offer. He says, 'She will be glad to see you again. She's missed you, Lancelot. You more than any of them.'

'And I have missed her,' I say. 'You too, my old friend.' I reach out and grip Benesek's shoulder, wondering where the years have gone. Wondering if the Lady's sickness is one of the heart because we have all abandoned her. Not all, I reflect, looking at the old warrior and thinking that here is a man who knows how to hold to an oath. A better man than I.

I turn and see that the fisherman in his little boat is more than halfway across the bay and I hope he keeps his word and does not betray me. He could buy a ship with the money he could get for Tormaigh and my war gear.

'You still have my helmet?' Benesek asks. I tell him I do and he seems happy about that. 'Well, I suppose you may as well keep it now,' he says, and we both smile in spite of everything. Then he lifts his chin and says, 'It's quite a reputation you've earned. They say you're the best in all Britain. There are songs about you and Arthur,' he says, hitching a lip to reveal his last few teeth, 'and not one of them mentions how you lost my sword.' He lifts an eyebrow. 'I must have taught you well.'

'You could teach me even now,' I say.

He likes that. Then he shakes his head. 'A vicious little brawl that was. That day at Tintagel. Had a damned limp ever since.' He pats himself above the left hip. 'I can still throw a spear, mind.'

'I don't doubt it,' I say and mean it, though he must be at least fifty-five years old.

He looks at me, the sea breathing at my back, gulls crying above us. 'You ready then?' he asks, turning an eye up towards the keep, as uneasy as I am about the prospect of going up there.

I nod, fingering the iron pommel of the long knife at my waist, and we start up the well-worn hill and I am flooded with memories.

'Don't expect her to be like she was,' Benesek says, already breathing hard, though he does not let the old wound frustrate his efforts. 'She barely eats. A brisk wind could carry her off like a dry leaf.' He stops and turns to me, pointing a finger in warning. 'Just don't expect her to be as she was.'

I fix his eyes with mine. 'I know, Benesek,' I say, and he nods, grunts and continues along the path, and I see myself running up that hill. I hear Agga's footfalls behind me and his ragged breath. I see Melwas ahead, his shorn scalp glistening with sweat, and I feel my chest tighten, hear the blood gushing in my ears. Pounding, like an echo of my younger heart. A thousand memories fill me, blending like one of the Lady's herbal draughts.

I see myself running up this path to meet Guinevere. Even the trees either side of the path, the birch, hazel and yew, seem to whisper to me in remembrance, as does the smell of wet earth and rock, bark and leaves. The gusting tang of the sea and the weed on the strand, and the years recede like the tide, so that I ascend that hill now like the shadow cast by my younger self. I follow the boy I once was. I feel his hopes and fears. His sorrows and all his loss and his resolve to outrun them. To be first. To win.

Then we are at the top and I turn and look out across the sea, filling myself with breath and looking back towards the mainland.

'Where are you?' I whisper into the wind.

'Memories, eh?' Benesek says. 'Like a knife in the guts. Come on then. I daresay she knows you're here.'

But I stand there a little longer, watching two crows above the red, brown and copper woods, riding the gusts perhaps for no other reason than the joy of it. Then I turn and walk across the age- and wind-worn rock, following my old friend into the keep.

'Lancelot,' she says and she smiles. 'I have missed your face.' I sit on the stool beside her bed and take her hand, enclosing it in both of mine because it feels so cold, though there are logs burning in the hearth.

'I am sorry I did not come sooner,' I say, hoping she cannot see the horror in my eyes. Knowing that she must. She is Nimue, Lady of Karrek. Yet she looks like a living skeleton.

'Lancelot has been too busy breaking Britain,' Merlin says from where he stands by the small window slit through which I glimpse gulls wheeling in the white sky. 'Busy rutting like a beast. Busy killing like a fox in the hen coop. Busy forsaking oaths and that sort of thing.'

I have not seen Merlin for years and this is the first time he has acknowledged me since Benesek brought me into the Lady's chamber. There had been rumours that the druid was dead, or else gone from Britain for ever, yet here he is, acting as though no more than a day or two has passed since our last meeting.

'What do you know of Britain these days, Merlin?' I ask him. 'You have not been seen in years.' I did not want to make trouble, not in front of the Lady, but neither would I meekly bear his insults.

'More than I could tell you in your remaining years, Lancelot,' he says. 'That's what I know of Britain. Britain then, Britain now. Even the Britain that is to come.' He curls a lip and I see that, unlike Benesek, the druid seems to have all his teeth. 'But none of that matters,' he says. Then he lifts an accusing eyebrow. 'I know something else too. That I did not betray Arthur.'

'Enough,' Benesek says. 'Show some respect or get out.' He fixes us both with fierce eyes then brings another fur from a chest at the foot of the bed and lays it over the Lady.

She thanks him with a look. 'We are to blame,' the Lady tells Merlin. 'Not Lancelot.'

The druid concedes this with a flash of his palm. 'I know,' he says. 'I know.'

'To blame for what?' I ask, looking from the Lady to the druid.

Merlin moves to the table and pours wine into a cup. 'Benesek is right,' he says. 'Now is not the time.'

'If not now, when?' the Lady says. Her voice is a dry rasp. 'What is left unsaid here will be ashes on the wind soon enough.'

'Rest, my Lady,' I tell her, squeezing her hand in mine. Her hair is thin and grey. I can see her scalp through it. Her eyes are sunken and her lips are dry and thin as twine. I tell her she owes me nothing and I remember that night in the Beggar King's hall, when my father was betrayed and my family put to the sword. If not for the Lady I would have died that night. Before I had even lived. I owed her my life but I had repaid her by leaving and only returning now, when it was all too late.

'You were meant to go, Lancelot,' she says, and I flinch, wondering if I had spoken my thoughts aloud. 'You were ready. It was meant to be.' She looks over at Merlin, who in his black robes seems little more than a shadow in the dark room. 'We both dreamt it, Merlin and I. Many years ago.'

I glance up at Benesek but he shrugs. *Don't look at me*, he says without speaking.

'After the dreams, I came to find you, Lancelot,' the Lady says.

I smell the staleness of her breath. The sickness in the room, despite the little bags of lavender here and there and the woodsmoke.

'I was nearly too late,' she says.

That night flashes in my mind like lightning in the dark. I see my brother, brave Hector, hacking down a man who would have killed me. I do not want to summon the next part. The gods know I don't. But memories are unbiddable and in the eye of my mind I see my brother with a man's spear in him. I have heard his cry countless times across the years, in a vixen's scream. In a white owl's cry around Samhain.

The Lady reaches across and puts her other hand upon mine. 'You were so small, Lancelot, but even then I knew you were the one. Knew it that day you came into my tent.'

'Foxes don't like being chased,' Merlin says, accusing me with his cup. I wonder what became of Flame, the fox which had befriended the boy I was back in Benoic. So long as he had a better life than the sparhawk, I think.

Benesek brings a cup over to the Lady and holds it to her lips so that she and I do not have to let go each other's hands. 'You never told us why we had to bring the boy,' he says to her, his own mind reaching back through the years to that night in Armorica. He had been a warrior in his prime then. He and Pelleas both. 'We never asked. Just did as we were told. Good men died,' he says.

The Lady turns her eyes on me and they still have that piercing, knowing quality which I have only ever seen in one other person. 'You were the child of war, Lancelot. We knew that Britain would need you. That's why we brought you here. To keep you safe. To make you ready.' She closes her eyes for a long moment. Just talking seems to take all the strength she has. But when she opens her eyes they seem a little brighter, as though she has asked some higher power for a moment's respite and been granted it. 'Your gift is from the gods, Lancelot, but we did what we could.'

'Not that any of it matters now,' Merlin says, turning his back on us to look out of the window. Darkening the chamber by blocking the daylight. 'Britain is lost.'

'Lost?' Benesek folds his arms over his chest. 'You know Arthur. He'll move against Aella in the spring. The kings will send spearmen.'

'Arthur is a broken man,' Merlin says, still looking at the world beyond the keep. 'He has turned his back on the old gods and so they slip even further away into the darkness. Britain will descend into chaos.' He turns back to the room and eyes Benesek. 'Did you know he keeps a Christian priest at Camelot?'

Benesek touches the hilt of the sword at his hip. 'Lord Arthur knows how to win,' he says. 'That's all I know. He and his big horses are the reason why all of Britain isn't crawling with Saxons.' He lifts his white-bearded chin to me. 'Arthur and his horses and Lancelot here. If not for them, Aella and Cerdic would carve Britain up between them.'

'Oh yes, Benesek, Lancelot has played his part,' Merlin says, casting his gaze on me. A hawk's spiteful scrutiny. 'And now Arthur is lost and Britain with him.'

'What's he talking about?' Benesek asks me.

I feel the Lady's heartbeat in her thin wrist, thumping weakly against the bone. Refusing to be stilled. 'It doesn't matter now,' I say, looking into the Lady's eyes. She knows. I can see it. She knows how Guinevere and I broke Arthur's heart. And how Arthur told all of Britain that Guinevere had bewitched me. How he told himself that, rather than believe his best friend had wilfully betrayed him. Or perhaps he does believe that Guinevere ensnared me with secret enchantments. That she bound me to her and I was led to ruin as an ox to slaughter. But the Lady knows. About the fire and the crowd and the blood on my hands. Even so, she does not hate me for it. I see only love in her eyes, and pity, and that is enough to make the breath catch in my throat.

'None of it matters now,' I say to myself.

'We have all failed,' Merlin says. 'The Saxons will drive us away as we have scattered our own gods to the winds. We tried but we failed.'

'Where will you go, Lancelot?' the Lady asks.

'I don't know,' I say. 'I will look for her.'

'You're a fool, Lancelot,' Merlin says.

'You will not find her,' the Lady says. A tear escapes her eye and rolls into the hollow of her cheek.

I shrug. 'Then it does not matter,' I say.

The Lady lifts my hands to her mouth and I feel her dry lips on my skin. After that kiss, she smiles and for a brief moment I see the golden woman again. 'Thank you, Lancelot. You protected them both,' she says. 'The rest was too much to ask.'

I say nothing. I have no words.

28

The Boy

THE DOOR IS FLUNG open and the boy comes in, the unstrung bow in one hand, and in the other a brace of dead hares tied by their hind legs.

'I saw the big stag, Father,' he says, the hut flooded now with the last golden blush of the day. 'Near the mud wallow.' He grins, his cheeks ruddy from the late autumn air and his nose glistening with a dew drop. 'He's strutting around looking for a fight. Did you hear him roaring?'

'No,' I say, smiling because he is smiling.

I have been stitching a leather bracer for him now he is strong enough to draw the bow and good enough with it to see us well fed. The skin of his left forearm is red from the string's lash, but I have nearly finished the bracer.

'He is not as big as he was though,' he says, hanging the hares on a peg. 'He looks thinner.'

'That's because he is the king,' I say, 'and must see off every rival or else lose his hinds. He has no time to eat.'

He wipes his nose on the back of his hand and sniffs. 'Worth being hungry if you can be the king,' he says.

'Perhaps,' I say, then I show him the bracer. 'It will be ready tomorrow.'

He comes over and takes the leather arm guard, wrapping it around his forearm. My needle work is poor and the leather is unadorned but for a small sun which I have incised in it, the rays streaking out all around, yet the boy stares at the bracer as if it is crafted from Cornubian silver. Though it does shine, from the beeswax which I have rubbed into it.

'Can we fight with the spears, Father?' he asks. He feels like a warrior with that hardened leather against his skin. His hair, as fair as his mother's, sticks up like a hedgehog's spines.

'It will be dark soon. Maybe tomorrow,' I say, and see the disappointment in his face. That scowl which is so deep that even in the pitch black of night you would know of its arrival, for there is almost heat in it. A day is a long time to wait when you are nine years old, and yet the scowl is gone in a heartbeat. He smiles and it fills his blue eyes as his mother's smile used to fill hers. Though his eyes, I know, are mine.

'If I land a hit, can we go to the Samhain fire at Castle Dore?' he asks, handing the bracer back to me. 'Please, Father.'

It is my turn to frown now, for it is rare that we leave the woods, rarer still that we go to the hill-fort where King Cyn-March has his hall. But he is just a boy and one day he will live his own life amongst people, not as we live now, hiding from the world. And anyway, the Samhain fire will be on the hill beyond the fort's eastern gate, and it will be dark. No one will take any note of a boy and his father watching the flames leaping and questing into the night sky.

'If you land a hit,' I say, holding up a finger, 'we'll go to see the fire. If not, you can help me cut reeds.'

'Because you're getting too old to bend and swing the scythe,' he says, grinning with mischief. I growl and call him a toad and grab him and he wriggles like a fish but I hold him tight, not letting him get away. And he doesn't want to get away.

I have taught him to hunt and in the use of the spear and shield. We have practised with the wooden swords like Roman gladiators in our woodland arena, and soon he will be strong enough to use an iron sword. He is already fast and agile. We will work on his stamina until he can run to Thunder Hill and back again without stopping.

But I cannot give him a mother's love. Her gentle hands when he has a cut or scrape that needs cleaning. Her protective arms and her voice in his ear when he wakes from a bad dream, his eyes wide with night-time terrors.

I know he misses her, though he does not say so, perhaps for my sake. We shed our tears when the fever took hold of her and bore her to Annwn on a river of raving misery. I have not seen the boy cry for a year.

I sometimes wonder, will I see Helaine again in the next life? Or will it be Guinevere I find in the sun-warmed meadows where the flowers never fade and wither? Will our souls seek each other, drawn together as horizon to sky? As sea to shore, so that in Arawn's realm we will make up for all that we have missed in this life. The emptiness made full. All that was forbidden allowed to grow under the sky.

Guinevere. An ache even now.

Perhaps such thoughts are unworthy beneath this roof. But I love the boy. I love the boy for myself and I love him for the mother who cannot. I love him for everyone and everything I have lost.

'Have you fed Tormaigh?' I ask.

'I'll do it now,' he says. My old stallion is a sullen beast but he loves the boy too.

The boy carries a pail to the grain sack and it takes all his strength to lift the sack and steady it so as to pour out a measure, but he does not ask for help.

And I pick up the leather bracer and the needle and thread.

I hear Tormaigh snort and nicker in greeting and I go to the hearth and ladle hot spiced wine into a cup, thinking the boy will need a warm drink inside him after being out all morning. I sent him to find valerian root, for I have been sleeping fitfully and I remember something from a long time ago, about how that root, dried and taken in a tincture, will bring on a deep sleep. But the voice I hear softly greeting the old stallion is not the boy's, and I set the ladle on the hearth stone and straighten, staring at the door, unable to move. Waiting.

No one knocks. No one calls in greeting.

I cannot breathe. It is Samhain eve. The gods torment me, I think. No, the gods forgot me long ago, and Tormaigh would not have greeted a shade thus, so I go to the door. I reach out, for a heartbeat watching the quiver in my hand on the latch. Then I lift it and open the door and it is as though I am looking at a memory made flesh. As though I have conjured it just by wanting it to be so.

Living apart from others, with just the boy and Tormaigh for company, I have little use for words. Now I cannot find any and so I just stare.

'You look well,' she says, her eyes shining from within the shadow of her cowl. She wears black robes, like a druid, drawn in at her waist by a rope.

I stare at her and she stares at me and I see the quiver in her lips, faint as the tremble in a moth's wing, but I see it.

'May I come in?' she asks. Spoken as though she is not confident of my answer, but after a long moment I nod and stand back from the door. She glances back to the dun palfrey, which seems content cropping the grass, then swings her gaze back to me. Breathes deeply. Steels herself, then steps forward but stops on the threshold a moment, hands holding the door frame, eyes settling on the interior. She walks in and I watch her like a hawk, half expecting her to change form, like the Morrigán, her black robes to become a flock of crows and tumble back out into the day to taunt me for a fool. A fool who has not slept a full night since I can remember. Whose mind is dazed as if by wine.

I watch her and I smell the cold air and the dampness of the forest on her.

'Take off the hood,' I say. She does, slowly as though she is not used to being free of it, and then I let go the breath that had been caught inside me. She is still so beautiful, my heart, my Guinevere.

'I have a son,' I say. The words come unbidden.

'I know,' she says. She smiles and I remember a hundred such smiles. I remember those lips on my lips and her breath in my mouth, hot and needful.

'I looked for you,' I say. 'For so long.'

She nods as though she had known it.

'Why?' I ask her.

'Does it matter now, Lancelot? After all the years?'

'It matters,' I say. I give her the cup of hot spiced wine and she wraps her hands around it, clinging to it.

'Do you really think we could have been happy?' she asks.

'Yes,' I say, and she shakes her head and I feel like a child who knows nothing of the world.

'He would have found us,' she says. 'They would have killed you.'

I tell her that I would have killed them, but I hear how foolish it sounds. What is to be gained from saying such things now, so many years too late?

She says, 'He would never have allowed us to live together, as husband and wife. It would have been too much for his honour. Too much for his heart.' She lifts the cup to her mouth and sips the wine, watching me through the steam rising from it.

'We could have left Britain,' I say. 'We could have gone to Armorica. Anywhere.' I might as well be plunging a blade into my own chest, and yet I must give voice to the quiet torments of the years. 'I would have protected you,' I say.

She frowns, my words hurting her as they hurt me. 'Manannán mac Lir was supposed to take me, that day of the storm,' she says. 'He had promised me to Arawn. But you saved me. You cheated Manannán.' Her teeth pull at her bottom lip as her eyes explore my face and the years in it. 'That is what Merlin says. He told me when I was just a girl. He said the reason you saved me was so that I could be Arthur's. So that I could help Arthur save Britain.' She falls silent then, though she need not say the rest. By loving each other and by betraying Arthur, we had brought ruin to these isles.

Since the day Arthur had found us together, chaos had reigned. The Saxons had not been brought to battle for years. Each spring brought new boatloads of warriors to swell Aella and Cerdic's armies, so that the dream we once had, of driving the Saxons back into the sea, was like long-vanished smoke from Uther Pendragon's balefire. In the years since our last victories, famine and plague had come to the land. The kings, who for a time united under Arthur, now mistrusted each other and fought like dogs, for land and revenge and for silver to buy peace with the Saxons.

But I had turned my back on all of it.

'I would have fought Arthur and the gods themselves if you had let me,' I say.

'I know, Lancelot,' she says in a tired voice, closing her eyes for a moment. 'But it is too late now.'

I want to tell her she is wrong. That it is not too late. And I look at her black robes and wonder if she is a druid now, like Merlin, or if she has given herself to the Christians' god and has been living a life of prayer and silence somewhere no one, not even Arthur, could find her.

She opens her mouth to speak but the working of the door latch stops her.

It is the boy. He comes in, his eyes fastening on Guinevere with undisguised suspicion.

'Hello,' she says. 'I'm Guinevere.'

He frowns, his cheeks red and his eyes watery from the cold.

Guinevere says, 'What is your name?'

He looks at me and I nod.

'Galahad,' he says.

She dips her head. 'I am happy to meet you, Galahad. I am an old friend of your father.'

'I've never heard of you,' the boy says. As if he doesn't believe her. But she smiles anyway, and I cannot take my eyes off her face, and that smile is so true, as if she remembers the boy, as if she and he were friends once.

And yet there is such a sadness in her face too, and it is almost too much for me to bear.

'Well, Galahad,' she says, 'will you look after your father for me?'

The boy does not know what to make of this request. He looks at me and then back to Guinevere. But he nods and I think how precious he is and how lucky I am to have him. My son.

'Thank you,' she says. Then she says, 'I had best go.'

'You won't stay the night?' I ask.

'No,' she says.

I tell the boy that he is dropping soil all over the floor and to take the valerian to the stream and wash off the roots. He lingers a moment, watching Guinevere, then he is gone.

'Why did you come?' I ask her.

She puts the cup on the table and shakes her head. She says, 'You have a life now. You have a beautiful boy. I am happy for you, Lancelot.'

'Why now?' I ask. 'Why did you come now?'

She shakes her head again and walks towards the door but I get there first and put myself in her way. 'Tell me,' I say, horrified that she is slipping away again, like a good dream which you are not ready to let go. I ask her again why she is here. She has opened the old wound. Not that it had ever really healed. I tell her I must know why.

She presses her palms together in front of pursed lips, looking over to where Galahad's short spear leans up against the wall beside my own. Then she brings her eyes back to me and closes them.

When she opens them again there are tears.

'It is Arthur,' she says.

'You came here for him?' Anger flares in my chest but she shakes her head.

'He does not know I am here, but he did come to me,' she says. 'It is the only time I have seen him since that day.'

'What did he want?' I ask.

Her eyes widen. 'Forgiveness,' she says.

I think about that for a long moment. 'And did you forgive him?' I ask.

'I forgave Arthur long ago,' she says. 'I told him I do not hate him for what he did. He is not the man he was. He is old, Lancelot. We hurt him so very deeply. But he *is* sorry.'

'Why does he need your forgiveness now?' I ask.

She sighs. 'He has gone to war,' she says. 'The Saxons have marched. King Aella means to crush Arthur once and for all and take Dumnonia.'

'But the kings won't fight beside Arthur,' I say.

'King Cyngen will,' she says. 'And King Cyn-March has sent spearmen.'

'It is not enough,' I say.

'No, it is not,' she admits. 'And Arthur knows it, but he must fight. What else can he do? He must try or else Britain is lost.'

'Britain is already lost,' I say, thinking of what Merlin and the Lady had told me those years before at Karrek. They had been right. Without Arthur there could be no Britain. And Arthur could not win this fight.

'You came here to tell me that Arthur is going to war?' I say.

'I should go,' she says.

I reach out and take her hands in mine and a shiver runs through her body into my own flesh. 'Why did you come? Tell me, Guinevere.'

She lets out a halting breath. 'I came to ask you to help him,' she says. 'He needs you, Lancelot. He always has. I thought that perhaps if you could be friends again, that he would be the Arthur he once was. That if I could bring you and Arthur together again, that you could win. And perhaps the gods will forgive us.' She shakes her head, her dark hair still untamed as it ever was. 'But now I don't want you to go to him.'

Her blue-green eyes implore me. 'I want you to stay here and watch your boy grow to be a man. I want you to live, Lancelot.'

She lets go my hands and reaches up, placing her own hands either side of my face, then she kisses my mouth, her lips tasting of the spiced wine and of the past. When she pulls away she says, 'You have lost so much, Lancelot. I want you to live and find happiness again. I want Galahad to know who his father is.'

'I care nothing for the gods' forgiveness,' I say. 'And I renounced my oath to Arthur the day he took you from me.'

She blinks slowly and nods, accepting that.

'Please be happy,' she says, pulling her cowl back over her head.

I cannot speak. I just stand aside and she opens the door and walks out. And when she has mounted the palfrey she looks back at me one last time, and I know she is replacing her memories of the young man she once knew with the timeworn man who stands before her now, letting her go.

I want to tell her that I love her. That I have always loved her. But I cannot speak. I just watch her turn the palfrey and ride away, knowing that I will not see her again in this life.

Even after so long, the padded leather tunic and scale armour coat feel familiar. They are a little tighter than they once were perhaps, but they fit me still, though the armour is heavy, dragging me down until I strap on my belt to take some of the weight onto my hips. It will feel as nothing when I am on Tormaigh's back, and just putting the war gear on again stirs memories of long-ago battles, so that even as I stand here in the forest clearing, the ground mist knee-high and the trees dripping, I can almost hear the clash of arms and the shouts of men and the shrieks of Arthur's war horses.

The boy helped me scrub the little bronze plates until we could see our faces in them and now he kneels on the wet grass behind me, strapping on my greaves. He treats my war gear with reverence and awe and I tell him that the greaves were a gift from Lord Arthur himself, though I suspect he thinks I am teasing, and when he is finished with the straps he fetches my helmet, whose long plume he has washed and combed so that it streams like white water.

'See, Father,' the boy says, and I look up at a pair of swans beating southward through the grey dawn, trumpeting as they go. The boy looks at me, waiting for me to infer some omen from the birds, but I just ask him to fetch my spear and he runs off while I strap on Boar's Tusk, gripping its silver-wire-bound hilt and checking that it slides easily from the scabbard.

Then together the boy and I array Tormaigh for war, laying mail upon a woollen blanket across his back, then strapping on the hardened leather breastplate upon which is incised a larger version of the sun that adorns the boy's arm bracer. After that, we put on the boiled leather shaffron which covers the top and sides of Tormaigh's head and face and goes down to his nostrils, the armour having been made specially for him so that the eyeholes are in just the right place.

When it is done I mount and pull the boy up behind me and we ride east through the rising mist which hangs over the land like a shroud.

Later, with the wintry sun still low in a pallid sky and Tormaigh's nostrils flaring, catching scents on the air, the boy tightens his grip around my waist. He has never heard the clamour of battle before and it frightens him, though he does not say as much, and we crest a rise overlooking the struggle. Having lived alone in the clean air of the forest, we three smell the armies below. The stench of sweat and leather and dirty flesh. The sharp tang of blood and the fetor of human dung.

'Who is winning, Father?' the boy asks.

I dismount and lift the boy down, then drop to my knees so that I can look into his eyes. 'You will stay here,' I say. 'I love you, Galahad. You know that, don't you?' He nods, catching sight of something, and I turn to see a brown hare standing tall on its hind legs in the long grass. Ears raised, it watches us with golden eyes. Unafraid.

'Stay here and I will find you after.' I pull the boy to me, barely feeling his small body against mine because of the scale armour and thick tunic. 'I am proud of you. My son.'

Then I stand and mount Tormaigh again and lean forward in the saddle so that my mouth is near his ear. 'Just one more time, my old friend,' I tell the stallion, and he nickers softly and nods his head. He is old and tired. His muzzle is grey and there are grey flecks in his coat too, hidden now by his armour.

The boy watches me and when he sees that I am ready, he hands me my big spear and I smile at him, resting the spear across Tormaigh's neck. Below us butchery is being done. I see the Britons arrayed in three shieldwalls, two sweeping back from the main one like wings. The central and largest body of men is comprised of Dumnonians. The left wing, King Cyngen's men of Powys, their stag antler banner stretched out between two boar spears behind them. The right wing is made up of spearmen from Cornubia, sent by King Cyn-March, who is duty bound to fight for Dumnonia. On the far right, behind the Cornubians, are Mordred's warriors, placed as a reserve and to bolster Cyn-March's men if need be. And it won't be long, for the Saxons are winning.

Arrayed in the shape of a great boar's snout, hundreds of Saxons have driven into the Dumnonians' centre, bowing the line. Seeking to carve a way through to Arthur's own bear standard, where forty horsemen wait. I see Arthur amongst them, tall in the saddle, watching his lines and waiting for his moment. He looks magnificent on his white mare, his armour glinting in the day, his red cloak and red helmet plume bright as blood. But there are too many of the enemy.

I look round at the boy one last time and nod to him. He nods back and I flick the reins and kick with my heels and Tormaigh walks forward down the gentle slope.

29

A Hawk Still

CANTERING NOW, TORMAIGH'S iron shoes drumming a three-beat gait upon the ground. My heartbeat in my ears, deafening inside the padded leather liner and helmet with its closed cheek guards. On the right, the Cornubians are breaking under the Saxon onslaught. Mordred must take his men to help King Cyn-March drive the enemy back before it is too late.

The spear's shaft is warm in my hand, the ash intimate and reassuring. Tied below the wicked sharp blade, a green silken ribbon flies, having long ago bound hair as black as a raven's wing and as red as fire.

Some of the Britons in the rearmost ranks are twisting their necks to see who is coming so late to the fight. They see a lord of war, resplendent in burnished bronze, iron and steel, on a great stallion sheathed in shining leather. They know me but they think it cannot be, and it takes one of them shouting my name to make the others believe it.

'Lancelot!' the man is yelling. I hear that even above the clamour of battle, the drumming of hooves and the pulsing in my ears. 'Lancelot!' the spearman yells, and now others shout it too. 'Lancelot! Lancelot has come!'

And my blood gushes in spate through my limbs.

'Lancelot!'

Those men in the rear ranks hoist their spears skyward in time with the chorus, which rises to the grey sky now in a rhythm like the heartbeat of Taranis, god of war.

'Lancelot! Lancelot! Lancelot!'

The armoured men on the armoured horses are twisting in their saddles, even pulling their mounts around to see for themselves if it can be true. That is when Arthur sees me, though I cannot tell what is in his mind as I ride towards him. Enclosed within his silver and gold-chased helmet, his face is battle grim. His eyes are cold and iron-grey. Around him are faces I know, though older now, scarred and etched by years of war, beards grey that once were fair or dark. Parcefal and Gofan. Cai and Geraint and Arthur's nephew Gawain, who looks as formidable as ever he did. They nod to me in greeting, these warriors of Britain, these chosen of Arthur, as though this is just another fight. Not the end of a dream.

Arthur's grey eyes flash and he bares his teeth in a grin as savage as a sword cut in flesh. Then he hauls his reins, pulling his mare back around to face the enemy and yelling at Cai to sound his war horn.

The note is long and piercing and hangs on the air still when a great cheer goes up from the British lines. Then before us the Dumnonian shieldwall is moving, dividing in its centre, the ranks of spearmen parting to create a channel so that I see the Saxon front ranks now, their shields raised before them and their helmets turning this way and that. They do not know what is coming but they should fear it.

I walk Tormaigh forward until I am beside Arthur on his right. He turns and our eyes meet and I nod and he nods back. Then Gawain hoists his spear high. 'For Arthur! For Arthur!'

'For Arthur!' more than two thousand voices cry.

Arthur points his own spear at the enemy who wait at the other end of that cleared path, then we kick our heels and our horses whinny and shriek. And we charge.

We hit the Saxons like a storm of steel, driving through them, splintering shields and bone, piercing flesh, disembowelling men where they stand and trampling them to bloody ruin. They scream and try to escape us but cannot because of the press, and we thrust our spears down and urge our mounts on and kill.

Arthur is wild, his spear lost now but scything Excalibur at men's heads, driving his horse on, deeper into the thronging mass of the enemy.

Gawain swings an axe left and right, splitting skulls and shields and stealing lives. And I urge Tormaigh on, the stallion swinging his leather-sheathed head at the enemy, eyes rolling, teeth bared, white spittle flying from his mouth. My spear is like a living creature in my hands, thirsting blood as it used to. Craving it. And I am death.

And yet the enemy are too numerous. Their warriors fall only for others to take their place and I see Gofan gored by a spear and pulled from his horse. I see Parcefal's mare stumble and fall and then I lose sight of him.

Thrust, pull back, thrust again. I kill and kill but there are too many.

Tormaigh shrieks and I feel the pain resonate through his flesh. My spear blade splits a shield but snags in the wood and I cast it aside and draw Boar's Tusk, laying about me, having to lean out of the saddle because it is not a long blade.

The Dumnonian spearmen had charged with us and are amongst us now, but they too are being enveloped. I see Geraint, the huge warrior who led Arthur's spearmen whenever Arthur was mounted. He sees me and shouts that we are betrayed! That Mordred has turned against us and has led his men into Arthur's allies the Cornubians. Mordred, his ambition laid bare at last, has made an agreement with King Aella and now sows carnage in Arthur's right wing. I feel it. A shudder running through the Britons' line. A knife in Arthur's heart.

I take a man's head from his shoulders and turn just in time to see the big Saxon driving his spear into Tormaigh's throat latch. The stallion screams and swings his head at the Saxon, blood spraying from the wound, and he stumbles on, carrying me forward still, towards Arthur. He and Gawain loom above the swarming enemy, hacking and thrusting, unable to turn their mounts now for the press, the two of them shining above the sea of grey like a sunset on the edge of the western sea.

I drive Tormaigh on, scything my sword backward and feeling it bite, carving a way through the enemy, and I see Gawain's horse go down, but Geraint is there, shielding Gawain, driving men back with his spear and his great strength. And I scream at Tormaigh to keep going, asking more of him than I have a right to, but my old friend pushes on under a deluge of blades, his pride and courage defying them all, and I am just a spear-throw from Arthur when I see a Saxon bring a long axe down poll first onto his mare's shaffron. A killing blow. Arthur is still swinging Excalibur as he falls – but I see nothing more. Because Tormaigh's forelegs buckle and the ground seems to rise up, and once I might have leapt clear but the scale armour drives me onto the earth, knocking the wind from me.

I climb to my feet, drawing my long knife, blocking spear thrusts with the knife and lunging with Boar's Tusk. Twisting and cleaving. Cutting and stabbing and striding on.

I am Lancelot. There is no one better.

'Arthur!' I bellow, turning a sword aside and cutting a throat. 'Arthur!'

A knot of warriors to my right splits and Mordred is there, bloody and fierce-eyed. He takes Geraint's spear on his shield, ducks and swings his sword, taking off Geraint's left leg below the knee, and the big warrior lows like a bull as Mordred's men plunge their spears down. Then Gawain carves into them with his axe, scattering them like a swirl of autumn leaves.

'Lancelot!' Arthur cries, his eyes blazing within his red-plumed helmet, our grins like vicious reflections in gleaming bronze. Then he throws himself at Mordred and their blades ring as if to summon gods.

I look west and see Parcefal, mounted again, at the head of a dozen horse warriors, hewing a path through the Saxons to reach us. To save his lord.

I think of the boy watching from the hill and I put a man down but another takes his place. They know me, these Saxons. Know my reputation and covet my war gear, and they die for their ambitions, but I see Mordred pull his sword from Arthur's shoulder. I see the bright blood on the blade. I see Arthur deflect Mordred's next strike. See him thrust Excalibur into Mordred's chest, forcing the sword deeper until the two of them are bound in a mortal embrace, and in that moment the air itself is changed. A shiver runs through Briton and Saxon, like wind seeking through a forest canopy, leaves whispering to leaves that the season has turned, and perhaps the gods themselves hold their breath then.

Gawain still fights, cursing his enemies, his helmet long gone, his lank hair flinging sweat. Parcefal and his horse warriors are closer, parting the Saxons as the sea turns before a ship's bow. But our enemies are too many. They are all around us. I twist and strike. I crack shields and break spear staves. Blades strike me, perhaps biting, perhaps not. Bronze scales fly from me, glittering in the grey day.

There are too many.

A blow staggers me. I cut low, taking a man in the thigh. A blade scrapes off my helmet and I turn, driving my sword into an open mouth.

Too many.

Gawain is sheeted in blood but fighting still. Cursing still.

Arthur is behind me, barely upright and glimmered with blood yet reaping lives with Excalibur.

We will not yield. We are the swords of Britain. The lords of battle.

Another blow puts me down on one knee and I parry a spear with my knife and lunge with Boar's Tusk. I cannot breathe. There is no air. They are all around us, darkening the world like an unnatural dusk. I think of her and I stand again, spinning, sweeping my blades around to throw men back. Gasping for breath.

Lancelot. I am here.

I thrust and withdraw. I sweep a sword wide and hack into flesh.

I am with you, Lancelot.

She has come. She is inside me as she has always been.

Do not fear, my heart. I am with you now.

There are too many. But I am Lancelot.

I love you. I love you. I love you.

I cannot find a breath.

I am with you.

I fall and I rise.

And I rise.

Author's Note

THE ROOTS OF THIS novel go all the way back to 1995. I had dropped out of uni and into the music business, and I read Bernard Cornwell's *The Winter King*, the first in his *Warlord Chronicles* trilogy about King Arthur. I was mesmerized, so much so that during that time I was either floating through the cheesy world of pop or else wading through the mud and gore of a fifth-century Britain ruled by a reluctant warlord. Cornwell's retelling of this island's greatest myth struck a resonating chord inside me. I saw in vivid detail this world which he had re-created. I felt it, heard it, smelled it. And it's fair to say these books crystallized in me what had up until then been a somewhat vague, if enduring, ambition to become a writer. Before *The Winter King*, I knew I wanted to write, to explore language creatively and express myself through writing. After that book, I realized that I needed to feel completely immersed in such tales of the past again. And that the best and most indulgent way to do that would be to write them myself. I've been trying to immerse myself neck-deep ever since.

Fast forward, then, to 2012. *The Bleeding Land* was published and I was head down in the fray writing the sequel, *Brothers' Fury*, continuing the story of a family ripped apart by that most brutal conflict the English (or British) Civil Wars. Even in the midst of the conflict (and by conflict I mean the actual day-to-day writing, which for me, at least, is a struggle), I was peering with one beady eye through the cannon and musket smoke to the next story. And whilst hoping to seize upon a big name to inspire an idea, it struck me. Yes, the story of Arthur has been told and retold in hundreds of ways over hundreds of years, from Geoffrey of Monmouth's *History of the Kings of Britain* (c. 1138), the works of late-twelfth-century French poet Chrétien de

Troyes, and Sir Thomas Malory's *Le Morte d'Arthur*, to T. H. White's *The Once and Future King*, Rosemary Sutcliff's *Sword at Sunset*, and Bernard Cornwell's *Warlord Chronicles*. The screen, too, has burned brightly with Arthuriana, from the 1963 movie *The Sword in the Stone*, to John Boorman's 1981 fantasy film *Excalibur*, and Guy Ritchie's 2017 movie *King Arthur: Legend of the Sword*. And of course one can't not mention *Monty Python and the Holy Grail*. And yet throughout all the adaptations of the myth, we've seen little of Arthur's greatest knight and closest friend, the man whose tragic love affair with Arthur's wife Guinevere presaged the downfall of a kingdom. We've all *heard* of Lancelot, and of that most celebrated love-triangle in European literature, but many of us don't know much more than that. In literary terms, we might call Lancelot an under-developed, even flat character. The editorial note might say: 'This character could do with another scene or two. Could benefit from some fleshing out.'

I thought, wouldn't it be something to find out who Lancelot is, to get inside his skin and rewrite his story for today? Not that I sat down and started writing it back then. I still had Civil War to wage and Viking ships to row. Indeed, I would write *The Rise of Sigurd* trilogy and co-author a book with Wilbur Smith before I got there, but I knew that in *Lancelot* I had a great title. Well, you've got to start somewhere.

Eventually (you're not ready till you're ready), it was this story's time and I wondered which of the numerous versions of the myth I would use as my running thread. But being me: lazy, impatient, far more eager to get creating than I am to wade through research and reference material, I decided to figure it out as I went. This, then, is my warning, my disclaimer to the reader who may stumble across this note before buying or borrowing the book. (If you've already read the book, too late!) It's my way of saying, don't waste your time holding my story up against Tennyson and de Troyes, searching for the touchstones in this tale, trying to draw forth the old motifs and classic influences like so many swords from the Arthurian stone. I'm no academic. No Arthurian expert. I'm just a storyteller. I'm the kind of person who's as likely to be inspired by the Disney cartoon as by some literary masterpiece.

As for Cornwell's tour de force, though I loved it deeply, I didn't fancy having my one-volume story being compared with his three-book masterwork, and so I did what I tend to do. I went my own way. I started writing and almost immediately I felt that, for better or worse, this would be unlike any book I've written before. But then, just as I was finding my feet with the tale, my father fell suddenly ill. After several brutal weeks, and unimaginably, given his energy, determination and personal charisma, he died just two days before his seventieth birthday. He was gone. My world fractured and in the black shadow of shock and grief, I questioned everything. How trivial, even frivolous, to sit here making up stories in the midst of death and loss. How could I think that what I was doing was worthwhile? How did it make sense to be sitting here at my desk making stuff up while my heart was breaking?

And yet, some other part of me asked, in a guilty whisper, why do we write and read stories, if not to escape the mundane realities and torments of our lives? For a while I did not hear this small voice, and the writing was hard. During that time, the last place I wanted to be physically was stuck in a room on my own. Mentally, the last place I wanted to be was hanging out inside my own head, writing what is in essence a tragedy. Moreover, I wondered what was the point in writing books at all if my father wasn't around to be proud of me for it. It was a precarious time for me.

But writing is my job, and my publisher had signed up *Lancelot*, and, well, what else was I going to do? And so, I set my mind to doing the best I could. My father would never get the chance to read this book, but I did get to tell him, in the hospital, that he would be *in* it. Not as a character but as an inspiration, because of the courage he showed in those dark days. And because I knew I would give this book my best shot, if only for him. And so, whatever story I had originally set out to tell, it transmuted into . . . something else. It became less a story of events, of heroic deeds and familiar Arthurian tropes, and more a tale of love and loss, of all that might have been, and of a sense of time and place which stays with a person, so that even though time has moved on, and you are a man, and everything has changed, you are still the boy you were, and in many ways nothing has changed at all.

Lancelot is, then, in every sense a reimagining. For me it was a journey of spirit and memory, of imagination and of the senses. I hope that for you it is at least a passable story, though I sincerely hope you forgive me if it perhaps wasn't quite the Arthurian tale you expected. I did my best. Promise.

*

Stephen King said no one writes a long novel alone. Well, this is a fairly long novel and I would like to take this opportunity to thank some of the people who have played a part in it.

Both Bill Hamilton and Simon Taylor championed *Lancelot* from the beginning and first mention of the title. Taking on an Arthurian book is somewhat intimidating, yet with those two gentlemen in my corner I knew I was in safe hands. They gave me the confidence to believe I had more than just an idea, and when the story was written, Simon's editorial wisdom was, as always, so gratefully received. To Jennifer Custer, who has the task of trying to convince foreign publishers that they should take this book, but who has by now left A. M. Heath to pursue new goals, I'll always be grateful. It never stops being a thrill seeing my tales in Nynorsk or Hungarian or Cyrillic script, even if sometimes when some foreign edition turns up I don't know which of my books it is or what language it's in! All the best for the future, Jennifer, and if right now you're on a 3500 km hike through the Appalachian Trail, I hope you've remembered your bear spray.

Here's to my friends in the Historical Writers Association. I can't tell you how cathartic it is to listen to others enthusing and bitching in equal measure about the business of writing and the state of publishing. This is a weird, unhealthy, isolating addiction that we have. Whilst drowning in silence and bathed in the screen's glow, it's comforting to know that one is not alone. A particular shout out goes to Manda Scott for helping me learn from the dreams and give myself fully to the words. Integrity in one's creative writing is as important as the words themselves. Thank you, Manda, for inspiring me to strive for it. To Katy Gulliver, for being willing to read an early draft with all its many faults, and for your first impressions, thank you! And to Anthony Hewson, who read the manuscript, gave of his expertise and told me when I'd gone a metaphor too far or when the prose was turning just a shade too purple. Anthony, you are the bee's knees and I'm glad to know you. My band of brothers with whom I raided Lindisfarne Priory and shared a saga-worthy experience, thank you. Drew, Phil and Pietro, I can't think of better companions with whom to get stranded on St Cuthbert's Island in the dangerous dark as the tide floods in. It was an amazing distraction from the writing and I'm sure it did me the world of good, and whilst it may have been the mead, I swear I heard the ghost of St Cuthbert laughing at us.

To my creative partner in crime Philip Stevens (who when he's not busy being a film director or lecturing also happens to be the voice of my audiobooks) thank you seems short change. Phil has lived and breathed this story from beginning to end. He's had to put up with me on the other end of the phone trying to write myself out of troubled waters and tight corners. With his uncanny storytelling instinct, Phil would often respond to my ramblings with: 'If I were shooting this as a movie . . .' This sometimes led us on wild and wonderful diversions, but ultimately those eight words from Phil would have my fingers tapping away again in no time at all. Phil, I hope the end result lives up to all our excited expectations.

My dear children, Freyja and Aksel, I'm sorry that your pappa wasn't always fully present during the writing of this book. This story was constantly gnawing away in my skull, like a grub in an apple. I'm certain that over the last year and a half people have said of me, observing my dazed expression, 'The lights are on but no one's home.' It's good to be back though, and whilst I would never wish the years away, I do look forward to the time when you kids can read *Lancelot* and at least find out where I was during that time. Freyja, my little bookworm, I'm so proud that you are the reader I never was at your age. So many stories and adventures are yours for the taking. Go for it! Aksel, before you ask, I'm not sure who are the goodies and who are the baddies in this tale, but I promise you there are plenty of swords.

Thank you, Lynne and Andrew, for all your help, for being brilliant grandparents and for giving Sally and me a much-needed break now and again. It's conducive to the whole sanity thing, believe me. To my wife Sally, what can I say? You have saved me more than once. Without you I wouldn't have got any further than the title. I mean it. Do you remember the beginning and my all-consuming dream to be an author? All those rejection letters and you saying it's their loss, keep going. Who'd have thought we'd get to this point, our tenth published novel? Though I wonder if I'll ever stop feeling like an imposter.

To James and Jackie, in your own ways you both support me unfailingly and are the very best advocates for the books. Thank you! I hope you enjoy this one. If nothing else the size of it surely provides a decent excuse to book a holiday and some peaceful reading time. Sibling obligations must be met, right? To my mother, your strength staggers me. Your love humbles me. Your dedication to your family inspires me. Look, Mum, not a Viking in sight! And I tried not to be too gruesome in this one. I hope I succeeded.

And to my father. I can't say whether you would have enjoyed this book, but I know you would have read every page. Every word. I hope you would have been proud of me for seeing it through. I'm so glad that I did.

Giles Kristian
8 January 2018

Dramatis Personae

Lancelot – The narrator of the story. Son of King Ban of Benoic
Arthur – A warlord and son of Uther Pendragon, High King of Britain
Guinevere – Daughter of Lord Leodegan
The Lady Nimue – Mistress of Karrek Loos yn Koos (The Mount)
Merlin – Druid and adviser to King Uther
Oswine – Merlin's Saxon slave
King Uther Pendragon – King of Dumnonia and High King of Britain
Queen Igraine – Wife of Uther Pendragon
Mordred – Son of Arthur and Morgana
Morgana – Daughter of Gorlois and Igraine. Arthur's half-sister
Lord Constantine – A warlord of Dumnonia. Nephew of King Uther and son of Ambrosius

King Claudas – A king of Armorica (Brittany)
King Ban – King of Benoic and Lancelot's father
Queen Elaine – Wife of King Ban
Balsant – King Ban's brother and uncle to Lancelot
Hector – Son of King Ban. Brother of Lancelot
Govran – King Ban's groom

Benesek – A Guardian of the Mount
Pelleas – A Guardian of the Mount
Edern – A Guardian of the Mount
Madern – A Guardian of the Mount

Bors – Son of King Bors of Gannes. Lancelot's cousin
Melwas – A warrior of the Mount
Agga – A warrior of the Mount

Gawain – One of Arthur's warriors
Bedwyr – One of Arthur's warriors
Cai – One of Arthur's warriors
Parcefal – One of Arthur's warriors
Ector – One of Arthur's warriors
Gofan – One of Arthur's warriors
Geraint – One of Arthur's warriors

Lord Leodegan – A lord of Dumnonia. Guinevere's father
King Menadoc – King of Cornubia
King Cyngen Glodrydd – King of Powys
King Einion ap Mor – King of Ebrauc (King of Northern Britain)
King Gruffyd ap Gwrgan – King of Glywyssing
King Cynfelyn ap Arthwys – King of Cynwidion
King Deroch – King of Caer Gwinntguic
King Meirchion Gul – King of Rheged
King Masgwid the Lame – King of Elmet
King Cyn-March – King of Cornubia
King Aella – Saxon warlord
Uradech – Pictish chieftain
King Syagrius – A king of northern Gaul

ABOUT THE AUTHOR

Family history (he is half Norwegian) and a passion for the fiction of Bernard Cornwell inspired **Giles Kristian** to write. Set in the Viking world, his bestselling trilogies 'Raven' and 'The Rise of Sigurd' have been acclaimed by his peers, reviewers and readers alike. The novels *The Bleeding Land* and *Brothers' Fury* tell the story of a family torn apart by the English Civil War and he co-wrote Wilbur Smith's No.1 bestseller, *Golden Lion*. In his new novel, *Lancelot*, Giles plunges into the rich and swirling waters of our greatest island 'history': the Arthurian legend.

Giles Kristian lives in Leicestershire.